BUFFALO PALACE

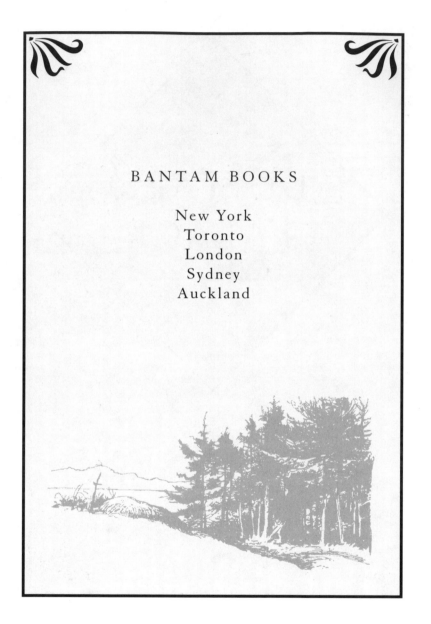

BANTAM BOOKS

New York
Toronto
London
Sydney
Auckland

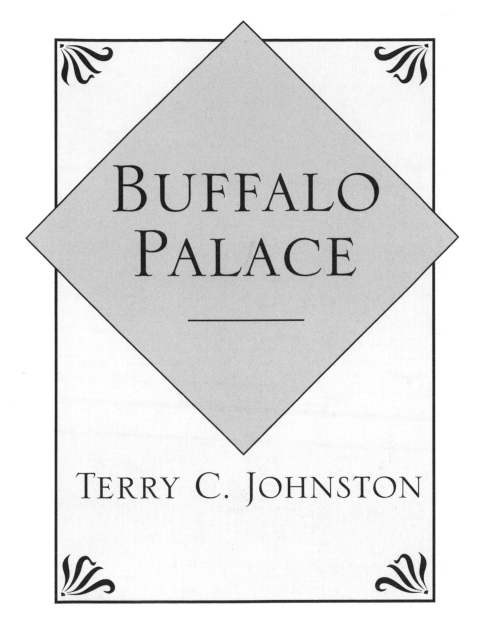

BUFFALO PALACE

TERRY C. JOHNSTON

BUFFALO PALACE

A Bantam Book/November 1996

All rights reserved.

Copyright © 1996 by Terry C. Johnston.

Cover art copyright © 1996 by Lou Glanzman.

Map design by Jeffrey Ward.

For information address: Bantam Books.

Library of Congress Cataloging-in-Publication Data

Johnston, Terry C., 1947–
Buffalo Palace : a novel / by Terry C. Johnston
p.   cm.
ISBN 0-553-09074-7
I. Title.
PS3560.O392B84   1996
813'.54—dc20   96-7099
CIP

Published simultaneously in the United States and Canada

Bantam Books are published by Bantam Books, a division of Bantam Doubleday Dell
Publishing Group, Inc. Its trademark, consisting of the words "Bantam Books" and the
portrayal of a rooster, is Registered in U.S. Patent and Trademark Office and in other
countries. Marca Registrada, Bantam Books, 1540 Broadway, New York, New York
10036.

PRINTED IN THE UNITED STATES OF AMERICA

BVG   10   9   8   7   6   5   4   3   2   1

for all the faith he had in me
and my vision of the old west
right from the very first,
I dedicate this novel of the time Titus Bass
reaches his beloved Shining Mountains
to
BILL GOLLIHER,
with my deepest appreciation for putting
Ol' Scratch and *Carry the Wind*
in all those stores
up and down the Colorado Rockies ten long years ago.

The history of any land begins with nature, and all histories must end with nature.

—J. Frank Dobie

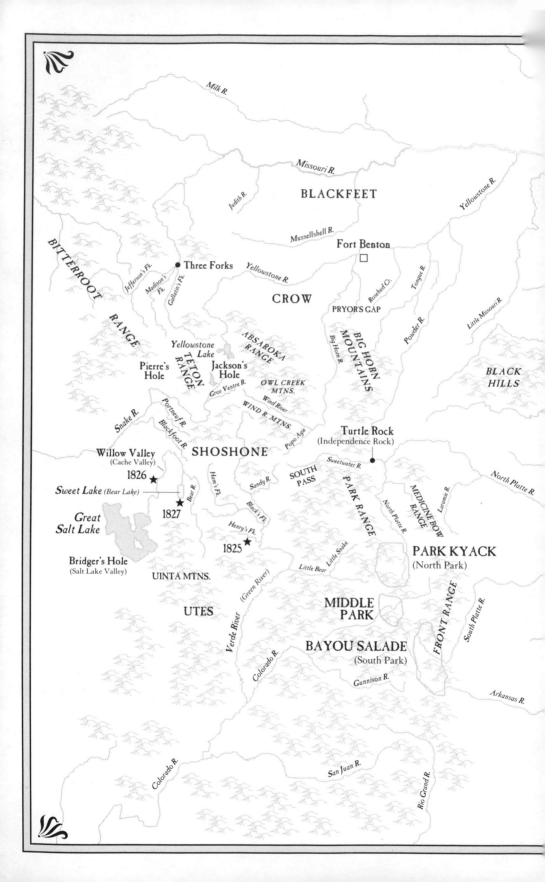

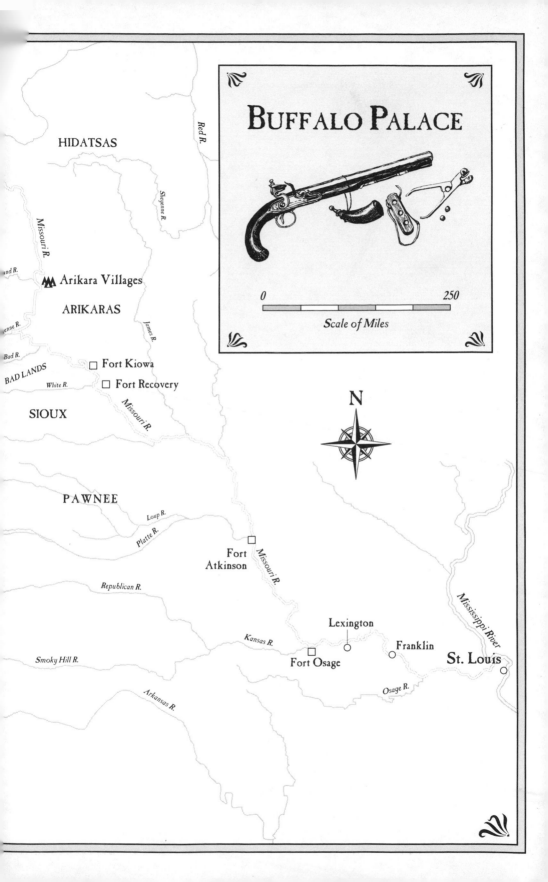

ONE

Reining away from Troost's Livery, Titus Bass gave the jug-headed Indian pony urgent taps of his heels, pointing it down the muddy, rutted ruin of Second Street.

Puddles of rain glittered as the sun continued its leisurely rise, the surface of each tiny pool left behind by last night's rain reflecting rose light like broken panes of glass scattered here and there among the heaps of wheel-cut ruts and piles of dung gone cold. Shadows still cloaked nearly all of St. Louis, save for the tallest rooftops gently steaming as they warmed.

Instead of heading directly north, he hurried south out of town, downriver some four miles until he reached the shady glen far from the clutter of settlement and folk. Far from the clatter of man's comings and goings. Someplace far from being underfoot. After all this time Titus was again gratified at the utter peace he sensed there as he halted, dismounted, and tied the two animals off to one of the trees ringing the glade. Plodding quietly in his thick-soled boots across the grassy carpet grown lush already this early spring, he had no trouble locating the mound. Stopping a few feet away, he took it in, finding many of the wildflowers he had transplanted nearly a year before budding once again with renewed life here above the old trapper's resting place.

Down in this grove the shadows lingered long of a morning. And the damp mist clung in among the trees, wispy among the climbing ivy and grape. Eventually, Titus inched forward, stopping at the foot of the grave.

"Isaac. It's me: Titus," he said barely above a whisper, the way a man might first address someone he found sleeping. "I come . . . come here to tell you my fare-thees, Isaac. I'm bound away—for where the two of us was counting on going together. Out yondering to them prerras and far mountains you told me of again and again."

Then he realized and suddenly snatched the floppy felt hat from his head, dropping his eyes as if in apology for his discourteous oversight.

"Wish you was going along," Bass continued. "Probably asking yourself why I ain't gone already, ain'cha? So let me tell you that you being here—dead and buried—that's the onliest reason I ain't gone afore now. There I was, planning all the time on tagging 'long with you . . . then you go and get yourself kill't. That was—hell, it felt just like one of them old brood mares I was shoeing for Troost gone and kicked me right in the gut."

He dropped the hat onto the foot of the grave there among the profusion of newly emerging wildflowers and slowly went to his knees. Placing one palm flat on the grave, Titus continued.

"Took me some time to get over your dying, Isaac Washburn. Pained me like few other things ever pained me afore in my life. I was counting on something so hard—then you go and act the idjit and you're gone . . . gone along with my dreams of ever getting to them Shining Mountains you seen with your own eyes."

He felt that first sting of tears burn, and swiped at his eyes with a single cold finger as a ray of sun burst through the canopy overhead, the first to streak into the glade.

"Took me a long time to get over the loss of you and my dreams both, Isaac. Didn't get over it till I up and figgered out I could damn well go on my own. I didn't need you like I figured I did. Got me a fine gun of my own now. The rest of our plunder and truck tied up in them bundles over yonder on them horses. And I'm riding your pony my own self. Taking it back to the prerra where I figure it belongs."

Slowly he dragged a sleeve of his blanket coat beneath his dribbling nose and sighed.

"At first I hated what you done to both of us, Isaac. For killing yourself and killing my dream of going to them far mountains by way of the Platte with you. Nursed on that hate for too damn long—so long that I didn't ever come back here to speak at you . . . not since I buried you in this pretty place. I'm glad to see you ain't kill't the flowers I planted over you, you sour-assed son of a bitch."

Then he gradually rose to his feet, sweeping up his hat and snugging it down upon his thick, curly brown hair, glancing at the single shaft of sunlight streaming into the glade, slowly marching across the nodding grass toward the grave.

"Best be going now, Gut. Wanted to come to tell you I was on my way out yonder. Don't know if I'd ever get back this way. And . . . and I come to tell you I owe you more'n I'd ever be able to pay you. So"—and he swallowed hard, tasting the ball of sentiment at the back of his throat—"so I figure the only way I'll ever come close to repaying you for what good you done me . . . is to go on out yonder and live the way your kind was meant to live. The way I callate I was meant to live out my days too."

Swiping the palm of his hand across his whole face, smearing tears and his blubbering nose, Titus bent quickly and patted the top of the grave mound with a hand, then straightened.

"I'll fare well, Isaac Washburn," he whispered, barely above a harsh croak. "Thanks to you, I'll fare well."

Hurrying back to the horses, he untied them quickly and vaulted onto the pony's back, glanced once at the shaft of sunlight just then touching the old trapper's resting place, the wildflowers grown luminescent with that first blush of dawn's light.

Tapping the pony's ribs, he moved out once more. North this time. Back four miles to St. Louis. By the time he reached town and Second Street once more, the day was birthing to the east across the mighty river.

Titus Bass hadn't felt this new in more years than he cared to remember.

While he owned far less than his pap had owned at thirty-one, far less than his grandpap before him, at this moment Titus now possessed more than he had ever claimed before in his life. Not much in the way of prize stock: not this hand-me-down Indian pony he was riding, nor Hysham Troost's gift of an old dun mare to use as a packhorse. And there sure as hell wasn't all that much strapped in two modest blanket-wrapped bundles lashed on the back of the mare as he was taking his leave of this place. Yet in that moment as the sun rose at his shoulder, Titus Bass realized he was a wealthy man nonetheless.

Most men would simply never be this free.

Second Street ended at the far edge of town where the muddy, rutted road northwest to St. Charles began. The sun had climbed above the tops of the leafing trees by the time he left the last huts and shanties behind. No more did the air reek of offal and refuse pitched carelessly into the streets. No more did his nose discern the tang of woodsmoke on the damp dew of the morning. It lay behind him now. So much lay behind him now.

While the rest of his ever-living life was spreading itself before him.

Turning in the saddle to watch the last of the hovels disappear behind him, Titus gazed at the smoke columns rising from hundreds of chimneys and stacks above the thick green canopy. Then he took a deep breath. And a second, his eyes half closing as it sank into his lungs. No morning had ever tasted sweeter.

That early spring morn, in the year of 1825, Titus Bass was barely thirty-one. Not a youngster by any means. He'd been broke to harness more than once. Time and again in his life he had come to know the value of hard work. And, too, Titus realized he was near twice the age of a few of those fellows who had been hiring out to the fur companies pushing their keels up the muddy Missouri River lo these past four-odd years. While he might be green at what he'd set his course to do, he sure as the devil wasn't wet behind the ears.

By damn, those years under his belt ought to count for something besides mere seasoning. Why, a hiring man would be hard-pressed to find any new hand more eager to pit himself against those prairies and plains, those high and terrible places that now lay before Titus Bass.

Where the well-traveled road twisted itself up the long, gradual slope and emerged from the oak and elm, Bass reined up and turned about to gaze back at the riverside town. Stone estates hid behind high walls where the French protected themselves from the lower classes. Those long rows of warehouses along Wharf Street, tiny shops of all descriptions pressed elbow to elbow along Main. And on the outskirts lay the smoke-blackened shanties where the whiskey and rum was poured, where the women of all hue and size plied their ancient trade.

In many a way it felt as if he had only lived there but a brief time. In other ways, it seemed as if he had been there nearly all his life.

"That's right, girls—gonna take myself a last look," he spoke quietly to the animals. "Don't have much a notion I'll ever see St. Lou again. Leastways, not for a long, long time to come."

He watched as the sun tore itself fully from the edge of the earth across the great, brown, meandering swath of the Mississippi, then nudged the horses into motion and put the place behind him. Turning his back on the scars and the women too. Those years of pain as he did his damnedest to waste away to nothing at the bottom of one mug after another of metheglin, sweet rum, or apple beer. Not that he didn't figure he would ever escape that good, clean hunger for a woman, or suppress that honest thirst for something heady and raw washing down his gullet from time to time. Just that Titus realized that out where he was heading, such hungers and thirsts might not trouble a man the way they did with so many folks living damn well on top of one another, breathing the same air.

Out where away he was bound, there would surely be other lures.

He drank in another long draft of morning cold as he pointed his nose toward St. Charles and the Missouri. Yessiree. A whole new batch of temptations waited out there to dangle themselves before a man.

By the time he felt the sun strike his back, warming the long, unkempt curls that spilled across his shoulders, Titus suddenly thought of Eli Gamble. A tall, lanky backwoodsman who had been traveling down the Ohio on his journey to St. Louis and beyond some fifteen summers before. Those long, warm days of the Longhunter Fair when the hill folk gathered to celebrate another planting season, peruse the cart vendors' and drummers' wares, drink and dance, and compete in tests of skill.

"Wonder if you'd beat me if we had us a shooting match today?" Titus asked out loud, surprised at the sound of his voice after so many miles of virtual silence put behind him.

That summer of 1810 he had been a green sixteen-year-old youth shooting in competition with the menfolk for the first time, pitted in that final relay of the fair against a frontiersman bound away to St. Lou for to join up with the Spaniard Manuel Lisa, trading and trapping for furs on the Upper Missouri. While Titus went on to ply the great waters of the Ohio and Mississippi aboard a Kentucky flatboat, Eli Gamble disappeared into the west, determined to go where Lisa was luring frontiersmen eager to see for themselves the tall peaks and open country.

Bass wondered if Eli ever made it.

And now he regretted never asking Isaac Washburn if he'd ever heard tell of a man called Eli Gamble. Chances were they had to know of one another—what with both of them attached to Manuel Lisa's outfits. But then . . . maybe Eli never made it upriver with Andrew Henry that season of 1810–11—the same Andrew Henry who a decade later led Ashley's brigade overland to the northern rivers.

"The Bighorn." Titus repeated that magical name as he had so many times across this past year . . . after Washburn had shown up at Troost's Livery to kindle that flame of yondering. One after another the names of other rivers came rolling out like mystical, even mythical, places, so far from everything Bass had ever known.

"The Powder," he sighed this morning. "And Tongue. Yallerstone too."

Yet first he had to reach the Platte. And that's when he remembered Hugh Glass. How Washburn and Glass had crossed the Platte River country after they were put afoot by Pawnee, the pair eventually stumbling into Fort Lookout on the Missouri. Glass went one way—back to the mountain country to pit himself against fate once more—and Isaac Washburn turned south to St. Louis to have himself a well-deserved spree.

If Gamble weren't up there still, was Glass? Nigh onto fifteen years now for Eli, but not anywhere near that long since Hugh Glass turned back to the Rockies—alone.

The French and American settlers in St. Charles paid Bass little mind as he entered their village of squat huts and tiny stone houses, many thatched with hay in the old French style, others roofed with cedar shakes split when the sap was down to be sure they did not curl. Smoke whispered up from every chimney here as the day began to age. Smells assaulted his nostrils in this muddy lane leading through town to the Missouri River itself. And the sounds of folk and farm animals grew loud upon his ears.

How might total silence feel about him?

Even in those forests where he had grown into a man, especially on the mighty rivers, there was always some noise. Wings flapped and birds called out. The wind soughed through the trees. Water lapped against the yellow poplar side of Ebenezer Zane's broadhorn Kentucky flatboat as it floated down the great eastern rivers.

So naturally he wondered how would it be to find himself out where Washburn claimed the land went on for days and days beneath an endless blue dome of sky, a distance so immense that it seemed to swallow all sound itself—a piece of country so quiet that a man could hear his own thoughts rattle noisily about inside his head.

"I damn well don't believe it!" Titus had protested to the cantankerous fur trapper one night as they sat over their brown bottles of sugared rum freighted upriver from New Orleans, brought there on high-masted ships from the islands of the far Indies.

"You don't gotta believe me just how quiet it be," Gut Washburn said matter-of-factly. "Hell, coon—you're gonna find out for yerself one day soon."

Here he was, for God's sake! On his way to find out for certain. Had it not been for Washburn showing up at Troost's Livery that rainy night a year back, Titus himself might well be dead by now and laying in a pauper's grave. As it turned out, Bass had been the one to lay Isaac to his eternal rest.

Now he was heading west . . . alone.

At St. Charles he had turned southwest with the Missouri. At times the road lay wide in spots, other times it narrowed. Barely enough room through the trees and brush for a single wagon to pass, slashing its iron rims down into the rich black loam. This was plainly a farmer's land, Titus thought to himself. Good land, this—for a man such as his father, Thaddeus.

So it was he thought on his mother, back across these many years. Fifteen winters already since last he had seen those gray sprigs in her hair; heard her voice soothing one child or another; felt the sure touch of her hand upon his shoulder, warm at the back of his neck whenever he felt unsteady of himself. After all this time he thought now on those biscuits she had baked that last night and left out for him. And the new shirt just finished for Thaddeus, lying there on the rough-hewn plank table. As certain today as he was that autumn morn as he slipped off from hearth and home—that she had left the shirt out for him to take in his leaving.

Little settlements, each one, he rode through as the Missouri River Road led him past St. Albans, then Labadie, and after more than a week he put Gasconade behind him. Two days later he passed Bonnots Mill. Eventually the river meandered back to the northwest. By the time he reached the tiny settlement of Rocheport, Titus found himself growing more comfortable with the long stretches of country wherein he did not lay eyes on another human. Each day becoming content with the Indian pony and the dun mare, with the company of nothing more than the sounds of the hardwood forests where he arose every morning and hurriedly ate what was left of the meat he had cooked for last night's supper. Finding himself content with those nightsounds in the timber—calls of owls and all the tiny animals that hid from those wide-winged predators as the sun went down and the stars winked into view overhead through the leafy branches where the smoke from his fire rose and dispersed.

Never did he go hungry—in fact, his belly had never been so full with the rich, fat meat of the field. Here in this country of thick timber he encountered more game than he thought possible. Better hunting was it here than it had ever been for him back in Kentucky.

Then he sorted through to the reason for that: surely there were far fewer people here to stir up the critters, to drive them this way and that, to harry them and deplete their numbers. Clearly this was country where a man could provide for his family, live off the land without ever slashing a plowshare through the earth's crust. Yet as good as that might be for some, Titus pushed on west.

For three cents he was ferried across the river to the settlement of Franklin, which sat on the north bank.

"Right here you're standing where the Santa Fe Trail begins," explained the stocky, pockmarked storekeeper. "Takes a man a little south of west, eventual to the land of them greasers."

"Greasers?"

"Mex," came the reply. "Some of the fellers travel the trail last few trading seasons call 'em sun-grinners. Damn, but from the sounds of what I been told, they're a people ain't worth a shit but for their handsome women."

Titus swallowed, his Adam's apple bobbing as he thought back on those hungers he had been pushing down, like an aggravating tickle. "W-women."

"Dark-skinned they be—so I'm told by them what pass through here bound for Santa Fe." The man scratched at a two-day growth of patchy whiskers sprouting on his cheeks, eying the slight stranger who stood just shy of six feet on that rough-plank floor. "Greaser women what wear they's skirts up to the knees, and their shirts clear down to here: so they all but hang right out for a man to see near ever'thing."

"This trail you're talking about," Titus asked, hopeful, "it go west by way of the Platte?"

The fat jowls waddled as the man shook his head, eyes squinting as they took measure of the newcomer. Dirt and smoke stained every one of the storekeeper's deep pockmarks and the crow's-feet wrinkling both corners of his bloodshot eyes. "That be too far north of here, mister—the Platte would. Like I tol't you, Santa Fe Trail takes a man off southwest from here."

"Sounds to me that this be the place a man makes up his mind, don't it?"

The jowly storekeeper nodded. "Head south to the land of the greasers. Or push on upriver."

"And the Platte?"

"Still upriver a goodly piece."

"Was hoping to run onto it afore now," Titus said with disappointment. "Seems like I been riding forever already."

"Something on the order of two hunnert thirty miles."

"What's two hundred thirty miles?"

The man scratched at his chin absently and replied, "That's how far you come from the mouth of the Missouri."

"Happen to know how long I got to go to reach the Platte?"

"Hmmm," the man considered. "That's a handsome piece."

"Farther'n I come already?"

"Dare say, mister. Yep, a good bit farther'n you come already."

That depressing news sank within him like a stone tossed into the swimming pond back in Rabbit Hash, Boone County, Kentucky. For a moment he wondered on another option. "How's the country lay on that trail to Mexico?"

With a sudden, broad smile the storekeeper said, "Now, that's something to show you've got a good head about you. I can outfit you for such a trip right handily."

"The country. Tell me 'bout the country."

"Halfway there, I'm told—you'll run onto a desert that lasts near the rest of your journey."

"A d-desert?"

"Sand and lizards and sun, mister. All it's fit for, so they say."

"Why would any man wanna go there—if'n that's all he's bound to come across?"

"I told you awready." The wide-shouldered shopkeeper grinned with teeth the color of hickory shavings. "They set their eye on that greaser country for the womens. Most trade for mules, and bring back the greasers' gold."

"Say a man don't want none of that. How's the land lay up in that Platte country?"

With a shrug the man answered, "Ain't worth a spit for building—you ask me. Not much timber like we got here." He pointed. "A feller runs out of trees a bit west of here."

Watching the man chew at a fingernail, Titus asked, "Then?"

"Then you find yourself in nothing but grass. Taller'n your horse's belly it grows. Miles and miles, and it goes on for longer'n I care to know. Country ain't fit for a decent man to settle his family in—what with no wood and the Injuns all about."

"Pawnee."

That caused the shopkeeper to raise an eyebrow. "You heard of 'em?"

"I heard," Bass answered.

"Leave that godforsaken country to the likes of them, I say," the man snarled sourly. "Ain't fit for nothing but what Injuns and buffalo out there—all that can live in them parts—"

"Buffalo?" he interrupted almost too quietly. "B-buffalo, you said."

For a moment the storekeeper studied Bass's face with the first real interest he had shown all afternoon. "You're looking for to find them buffalo, is it?"

His head bobbed every bit as eagerly as a young boy's. "Yes. I aim to see me them herds of buffalo I heard tell was out there on the Platte."

"They're there all right, mister. Them, and the thieving, murdering Injuns too. If I was to do it—I'd lay my sights on greaser country."

"Looks to be I'm pushing on north."

With a snort of derision the shopkeeper said, "To see them buffalo and have your ha'r lifted by the Pawnee?"

"I figure a fella can watch hisself and stay out of harm's way."

With a sudden, low blat of laughter that reminded Titus of a peal of some faraway thunder, the storekeeper erupted, slapping a flat hand down on the counter so as to rattle a nearby display of tin cups. "If that ain't some now! Why, from the way you was talking—I'd wager you and your outfit ain't ever been out in that country off yonder."

"Ain't," Bass admitted.

"So how you fellas figure you're gonna keep from getting sideways with the Pawnee, seeing how you'll need be crossing so much of it to get to that far country? Best pray there's a whole bunch of sharp-eyed sonsabitches with y'—"

"J-just me," Titus bristled, annoyed at the storekeeper's amused smirk and downright nosiness. "Ain't no one else along. Ain't no *outfit* of us."

Like the passing of a cloud, the pockmarked face went grave as the storekeeper leaned forward on the plank counter, suddenly inches from Bass's nose. Something of great import rang in the tone of voice as he said, "Tell me how you're fixed for lead and powder?"

"Got me all I figure a man ought'n carry on a packhorse."

Leaning back with a smug smile, the man suggested, "Might well think about packing you all you *can*. Where you're headed, it won't be no desert trail what'll kill you with thirst or p'isenous lizards. No, sir—it jest might be them god-blame-ed Pawnee!"

As the last few words tumbled dramatically out of his mouth, of a sudden the storekeeper went silent, his eyes snapping to the narrow doorway, where Titus watched a middle-aged woman and a brood of children appear out of the sun, shuffling into the cooler shadows of the shanty store.

"You keep your hands to yourselves, hear me now?" she instructed the young ones as they came to a halt on either side of her, like a brood of chicks clustered around their hen. "Don't make me scold you again like last time we was here."

Titus studied her in that instant: the way she turned aside to one batch of children, then to the others as she instructed them all in a sure tone of voice. Her well-seamed face, tanned to the color of a native pecan even at this early season of the year, showed more than the simple ravage of time. That sallow countenance registered the toll of many live, and a few still, births, reflected the slash of ceaseless wind and the scouring of a life suffered beneath the unrepentant sun—all those countless days spent at her man's shoulder . . . the two of them pleading with the ground, the sky, and ultimately to their God again and again to grant them enough of a crop to feed themselves and thereby survive one more year.

Then, as she finished instructing her flock in those quietly stern directives, the woman looked up at last: her bright, fiery, optimistic eyes seeming to come directly to Titus, dawdling just enough as they halted there to cause him to swallow hard. As a child or man, he'd never been what anyone could dare call handsome—fact was, Bass considered himself firmly on the homely side—so when her eyes appeared to take their measure of him, Bass felt his cheeks redden. He was relieved when the woman's gaze turned aside to land on the storekeeper.

"Bailey," she began in a loud, sure voice she flung across the shabby, low-roofed store, "what's cornmeal these days?"

"This time of year it's twenty-five dollar the hundredweight, Mrs. Grigsby."

She drew her lips into a wrinkled purse, licked them quickly in grave thought, then replied, "Gimme ten pounds. Got coffee?"

"Some come in just last week."

The woman asked, "You tried it your own self?"

"The missus made some for us just this morning."

"And?" she prodded, nudging her head to the side, out of the way of some ironmongery hanging from the rafters as she took two steps forward, her brood shuttling hurriedly to stay at the hem of her dress.

"As fine a cup as I've ever had on either side of the river, ma'am."

Drawing her shoulders back, Mrs. Grigsby declared, "Should have known *you'd* claim it was nigh onto being the nectar of the gods, Bailey Henline. How much you want for this grand coffee of your'n?" Then, almost in afterthought, she wagged her head and commented, " 'Tis a curse when a woman cain't seem to wean a man from his coffee."

With a smile the storekeeper answered, "Land, but I know he's a one to drink it morning, noon, and evening too—was it that you had it always brewed for him. Tell you the honest, for this last shipment, I gotta have fifty cents the pound."

"Lord bless and preserve me!" she exclaimed, suddenly snagging the wrist of one of the younger children and taking from the hand something the offending youngster had been closely inspecting behind her mother's back. She replaced the waxed parcel back among the display on the rough plank shelving and turned back to Henline. "Will you see fit to give us five pounds of your coffee on account?"

He sighed. "I can add it to the books for you, Mrs. Grigsby. You're good folks—and I'll stand by honest stock like you and the mister."

"No one can say you ain't stood by us these last two troublesome seasons, Bailey," she declared with the sort of undisguised gratitude that was hard for a proud woman to let show. "You know we're good for it. And . . . if it's all right, I'd like to get each of the young'uns a little treat out of your jars over here. We don't get in here much as I'd like—"

"Go right ahead, ma'am. Let 'em each pick what they want. Ain't no trouble to just put their treats on the books too."

With a meaningful nod she said, "Thank you, Bailey."

Bass watched her turn away with her children as she bent her head and murmured to them softly. One by one they began to approach the shelf where rested the immense, odd-colored jars and small wicker baskets filled with rock candy and other sugared delights. Taking a step back toward the counter, Titus grew thoughtful as he cupped the small skin pouch inside the worn blanket satchel slung over his shoulder—fingering what he had left in the way of hard coin.

Titus cleared his throat, drawing Henline's attention and said, "Best have me some of that cornmeal and your coffee too my own self."

"Good thinking, mister," the storekeeper replied, rubbing the palms of both hands down the front of his sweat-stained shirt that had likely been the better part of a month without a scrubbing. " 'Cepting for the army sutler upriver, this here be the last place you'll run onto such victuals. What'll it be of the cornmeal?"

"Fifty pound," Bass said, swallowing down the sudden flush of apprehension he felt at spending the last of his money.

Turning aside to move off, Henline asked, "And your coffee?"

"Maybe best I have us count what I got left after you get that cornmeal," Bass replied. "We'll see how much coffee I can do with."

"You have American?" Bailey asked, eying him up and down.

"Yes. I have American."

With an approving nod the storekeeper continued about his chore of scooping cornmeal from a large oaken hogshead into linen sacking.

It was money, Titus reminded himself as he fretted. Only money. Never had he been captive of it, because his whole life had either been feast or famine: Titus at times had earned all the money he wanted at Troost's Livery and had survived nicely; while at other times he had none to speak of in his empty pocket, and had survived just as well. Maybe money was just like whiskey and women. All three were the same: when a man had 'em—he best drink up while the drinking was good . . . lay while the women were spreading their legs for him . . . or spend that money before it wore a hole in his britches. Many were the times he'd gotten by without the whiskey, or the whores, and more often than not he had survived without coins jangling in his purse.

Besides, he suddenly decided. Like the storekeeper said—west of here there wasn't but one more goddamned place to spend one's money anyhow. Why would a man want to carry anything west when it weren't going to do him any good out there?

Then and there a candle's flicker of impulse made him suddenly decide to empty his purse. This would be the last in the way of hard currency he figured he would see for many a season to come. While some men buried their money away against some greatly feared lean time like squirrels hoarding their store of nuts for the coming winter, Titus no longer saw any need to have the feel of it stitched up in his waistband the way he and the rest of Kingsbury's boatmen had carted their gold specie north from New Orleans on up the Natchez Trace. And he was surely not the sort who had ever needed the reassuring jangle of coins at his side, the feel of specie caressing his palm.

Money was to be used, he had come to believe with certainty. Not something to be hoarded. And where he was going, money sure as hell was something a man could not use. This was, he realized of that moment, the very edge of the world as he had known it: the border between all that he had been, and all that he wanted his life to be. Money, like so many other things, was clearly a part of the world he was leaving behind. Best to leave here what little money he had left. Leave it behind with all the rest of his old life he would no longer need take with him.

They settled up on what Titus owed for the cornmeal and coffee, the three bags sitting there on the dusty counter, in their midst the stack of coin, which now belonged to the storekeeper. The few that remained with Titus he turned over and over in his palm.

"Something more I can do for you, mister?" Henline asked expectantly, an eyebrow raising.

He licked his lips, gazing down at the few coins left him. "What you got in the way of tobaccy?"

The fleshy eyes studied the whipcord-lean wayfarer again, as one might regard a person of questionable sanity. "Don't wan'cha no powder, or lead? Don't need you no axes or knives?"

Shaking his head, Titus declared, "That tobaccy there," and he pointed to the large cedar crate on the plank counter, the top of which had been pried off to expose the dark carrot twists of dried tobacco leaf. "How much is the asking?"

"You a chewing man, are you?"

"I am, a'times. What's the toll for a plug?"

"Ten for a dollar."

"That's steep."

"It's American—and it's come a fur distance, mister. Kentucky, I'm told. Freighted down the Ohio, then up the Missouri." Henline scratched at a fleshy jowl again as he eyed the coins Titus set one by one down on the meal-dusted counter. "Tell you what I'll do: with what you got left there . . . I can make you a good trade—fifteen for the dollar."

"How much 'baccy that gimme?" he asked suspiciously.

With his beefy hands Henline began to pull out the carrots, counting out loud as two of the woman's children inched close, intently studying the process, their eyes just above counter level. When he was done, the storekeeper again rubbed his hands down the front of his dirty pullover shirt and said, "Sixty of them twists—makes for four dollars' worth. So that should just about use up the last of what you got left there."

Instead of agreeing immediately, Titus regarded the immense pile of dark twists of fragrant burly. Taking one from the stack, he brought it to his nose and sniffed in appraisal. "Kentucky, you said?"

"So I'm told. Fine smoking. Even finer a chew—if I do say so my own self."

"And this here sixty twists will finish me off?"

"Less'n you got more money hid on you," Henline replied, a fat paw beginning to sweep the last of Bass's coins toward his side of the counter, "there ain't no more you can spend."

Firmly, yet without a hint of malice, Titus quickly clamped his hand down on the storekeeper's wrist, looking Bailey Henline in the eyes. "That what you got under this hand pays for the tobaccy—"

"I done said that," Henline interrupted with irritation that mottled his cheeks in anger.

"And," Bass continued, ". . . pays off all the candy for them young'uns there." Titus nodded once toward the far end of the counter where the woman and the children stood watching like a gaggle of wide-eyed geese, frozen for the moment beside the colored jars of sugared treats.

Immediately shaking his head, Henline uttered the first sounds of protest— but they were squeezed off as Titus clenched the wrist all the harder.

"Listen, mister: you're making a fine profit on me this day," Bass said with quiet assurance. "Enough a profit you can give these here young'uns their treat 'thout it weighing down this woman's account."

For a long moment the shopkeeper looked down at the hand holding his wrist prisoner, then glanced over at the woman. Reluctantly, he nodded. "Awright. The treats is on you, mister."

Taking his hand off the storekeeper, Titus glanced quickly to the side, not sure if he read gratitude in the woman's eyes, or scorn because she wanted none of his pity.

"This here's American all right," Henline declared as he finished sweeping up all the coins together and shoving them deep within the side pocket on his drop-front button britches. "Cain't ever be too sure out here in this country— what's good money and what's not. Guineas, pistoles—"

"My money was always good, Mr. Henline. Worked hard for it, and I was always one to give a man my sweat for a day's pay."

"Franklin's damn well the last place on the road you chose to take," the shopkeeper emphasized with a roll of his eyes in that direction. "On west of here is Fort Osage. Only other place yonder'n that is Fort Atkinson. At Osage the river changes course, runs north from there up to Atkinson, you see."

The name pricked him. Titus leaned in a little to ask, "Ain't that the place, the fort you just said—the one they built at the mouth of the Platte?"

"That's right, mister. You figure to ride through Pawnee land, by the time you reach Atkinson—a man turns himself left and heads due west as the sun goes."

With a shake of his head Bass replied, "I ain't got me any plans to be riding nowhere close to Atkinson."

"Maybe for the best," Henline declared as he stuffed the last of the tobacco twists into a fourth and fifth linen sack and began to tie off the tops with length of twine cordage. "Up and down this part of the river, word is that the army don't want no one in that yonder country out there . . . no man but soldiers and them fur companies."

"I heard such, yes."

With a smile creasing the fleshy jowls, Henline ventured, "Hell, maybe it's better you spend some time behind the bars in that army pokey up at Fort Atkinson than you lose your hair to them bugger Pawnee."

Sweeping the first of the satchels from the storekeeper's counter, Bass replied, "I don't plan on spending no time with the army or leaving my hair with the Pawnee. Thank you just the same for the meal, coffee, and tobaccy." He hefted the last of his goods across both laden arms and turned toward that doorway patch of bright sun splaying a fan of its bright saffron into the shop's cool shadows.

Just as Titus reached the door, he stopped to step aside for a pair of mud-caked men who eyed the newcomer before striding dutifully over to the row of wooden dowels driven into one wall where stood several tall, two-man saws.

"Thank you, mister," the woman said suddenly, blurting it out as if honor bound to express her gratitude, but then her eyes softened as she tugged a child to her hip beneath each arm. "Tell the man thankee, children."

They all shyly muttered their appreciation—every bit as prideful as their mother—eyes watching the stranger shuffle his feet self-consciously, his arms sagging beneath the weight of the last worldly goods he would buy for hard cash money.

"I was . . . I'm glad to do it," Titus replied, glancing over the faces of the children as they licked and sucked on their treats. How they reminded him of Amy's brothers and sisters back in Rabbit Hash.

Then Henline intruded. "Stranger—since you're of a mind to go out yonder to that saint-forsaken land on your lonesome—you mind my asking one more thing?"

"What's that?" Titus responded, turning his head from the young eyes to look at the storekeeper. At that very moment Bass became aware the two men had ceased their talk and their noisy handling of the saws behind him.

Scratching at the side of his pockmarked nose, Henline inquired, "Mind telling me if . . . well, if you're a praying man?"

For but a moment Titus glanced at the mud-plastered pair who interrupted their appraisal of the saws so they could study him critically. Plain enough to see they were settlers. Farmers. Had the same look to them that Thaddeus Bass had himself.

When Titus brought his eyes back to the storekeeper, finding himself suddenly irritated at the way Henline's jaw hung open smugly, Bass almost wished one of the big bottle-green flies buzzing about the low-roofed shanty would flit its way right into that gaping hole in Bailey Henline's face.

Titus repeated the question. "A praying man? Well, now. I s'pose any fella what takes off where I'm heading all on my lonesome better be a praying man, mister. That—or he's plain crazy."

TWO

"That trader man was wrong, mister."

With the sudden sound of the child's voice, Titus turned where he stood at the edge of the muddy, rutted path that passed for a main street here in Franklin. It was the oldest girl among that woman's brood wanting hard candy back in the mercantile. Bass continued stuffing the first of the cornmeal sacks into the bundles lashed on either side of the mare's back.

"Oh?" he asked absently. "What was he so wrong about?"

"This'r ain't the last place you run onto."

"It ain't."

"No, mister. It ain't."

Jabbing the second sack down into the bundle on the far side of the mare's packs, Titus figured he was being goaded into asking. He sighed with a little exasperation, then glanced again at the gangly girl who appeared about to enter her adolescence—and the impatience drained from him. She so reminded him of his oldest sister. Every day slowly rounded out those hard angles on her body now that she was ready to flower into womanhood.

"All right," he said. "S'pose you tell me what you come to tell me."

"See: this'r ain't the last place there's white folks."

"Just what the devil that mean to me?" He growled it more

than he had wanted it to come out, turning away because he was angry at himself—in that moment remembering how he had marveled at the way another young girl's bony form rounded itself into a woman's body back in Rabbit Hash.

"Means there's white folks on yonder," the girl declared, then pointed, turning away with a gesture to the north. "Mama said for me to come tell you that."

His fingers stopped their tying of the canvas lashes. "Your mama in there . . . she told you come tell me that?"

With a nod the girl replied, "Our place is up to Boone's Lick. I figger she's due for a vis'tor. Ever since't my da took sick and died sudden-like late last summer—we ain't had all that much in the way of company. Mama ain't much of a talker, but I knows she tires of us'ns—"

"Your . . . father died?"

She nodded again. "Mama took it real hard."

"You mean she's caring for you young'uns on your place all by herself?"

"No. We got my uncle and his wife with us. But Mama works out to the fields like Da used to, and my auntie cares to us chirrun and the meals."

He stared off to the north. "Just up to Boone's Lick, you say?"

"Yes, mister."

"That a town?"

"Not likely, it ain't. Just a bunch of folks settled nearby to one 'nother and give the place a name years back."

"After Dan'l Boone, I'll wager."

"Truth be, I dunno."

"Likely they done so, girl," he replied as he yanked on the last knot. "Same Boone what they named the county for where at I was born and raised up."

"Where's that?"

"Kentucky," he finally said, the word hard to come out at first, fraught the way it was with so many memories both good and bad—like more strands of a sticky spider's web than he could ever free himself from.

"So, mister—you come see us?"

He looked back at the girl again, mystified by the invitation . . . although he understood. Many were the folks who lived their lives set apart from others, only to gather at Sunday services, for funerals and weddings and baptisms—along with the annual Longhunter Fair. Theirs was the lone and hardy stock who took great pleasure in the infrequent passerby who carried news of distant people and places.

Titus asked, "That what your mama told you come ask me?"

Openmouthed, she nodded. "Said you got our welcome to come by on your way upriver."

Glancing over the girl's shoulder, for the first time he noticed two of the younger children standing in the store's open doorway, watching the stranger and their sister. "You're on your way back to home now?"

"Mama said to tell you be ahead on your way and we'd come along shortly."

"You riding?"

The girl giggled quickly behind her hand, her eyes twinkling as she answered, "Hell no." Then her faced flushed in embarrassment. "Y-you won't tell Mama I cursed, w-will you?"

With a smile and a wag of his head, Titus loosened the packmare's halter, then reached for the rein to the Indian pony. He bent his head down to whisper, "That's our secret. I swear it."

"Just that . . . all we got left us is that one ol' mule," and she pointed across the rutted path at the animal. "Does all our plowing, and we bring it to town with us for to carry home all what we take out on barter from Mr. Henline in there."

His heart felt a tug at that moment, staring at the old mule, the way it hung its head and kept weight off one of its legs. Clearly, the hock was swollen with spavin. Easy enough to see that it wouldn't be long before the mule came up lame on them. "You sure your mama wants me to stop by?"

"She said so for me to tell you."

"I can't be stopping off every place I go by now," he grumbled, suddenly perturbed at the intrusion on his journey. Bass jabbed his left foot in the stirrup of the worn saddle.

"Mama said to tell you she figured you look like'n you needed a home-cooked meal." The girl prodded, taking a step forward as Titus rose onto the back of the pony. "Likely you ain't had none such in quite a time."

He opened his mouth to snap back at her about no longer needing no home-cooked meals . . . then decided better. Why, it did sound good. But, just the same, he had some new victuals of his own—so he wasn't all that bad off. Best to keep pushing on.

"I got me a long, long way to go, girl. You tell your mama—"

"Last place a body gets to talk with civil white folks," she blurted in.

Impatient to be on his way, Titus was on the verge of tapping heels into the pony's ribs when he stopped and brooded on that. "No other place on yonder from you? Now, I can't believe that."

"There's the forts upriver," and she flung an arm in that general direction. "Soldiers, traders. Men come down from upriver. But there ain't no more plain white working folk after us. Mama thought you'd like to have yourself a hot meal and maybe some man talk with my uncle."

Slowly he turned to gaze at the doorway once again. A third small face had poked itself around the jamb—watching expectantly.

"All right," he answered, not all that sure of his resolve. "You go tell your mama I'm most grateful for her kindness . . . and tell her I'll feel better riding along home with your bunch. Now, be off with you and have your mama finish up inside so we can get on our way. Gonna be getting dark soon enough as it is."

Twilight was just beginning to squeeze the last light of the day from the sky when the girl and her oldest brother led the lot of them up a wide path into the yard surrounding four squat buildings and a half-dozen rickety pole lean-tos. After introductions the flush-faced aunt announced that supper was simmering over the fire and ready soon as everyone washed up and sat themselves down.

"Your belly ready for that home-cooked meal I promised you?" the widow asked Titus, her dark-gray eyes finally meeting his again for the first time since they began their walk north from Franklin.

The eyes softened as he gazed back at them . . . and the voice was nice enough too. "I'm always ready, yes, ma'am."

Night came down easily, and the breeze had kicked up by the time Bass shoved himself away from the long, crude table and rose from his half-log bench, its legs scraping across the puncheon floor. The woman's brother-in-law got to his feet along with Titus, turning to retrieve a pipe and tobacco pouch from the stone mantel above the fireplace, which provided the only light for the low-roofed room besides a dozen or more candles and Betty lamps filled with oil he figured could only have been rendered from a bear.

"Let's us use my tobaccy," Bass suggested. "Find some way to pay you back for that meal."

"No paying back necessary," the widow replied from across the table as she rose, her hands filled with wooden trenchers. "You already done that at Bailey Henline's shop."

Plainly needled, the man kept his eyes on Titus as he asked his sister-in-law, "What you go and get yourself in debt with Bailey for now?"

"She don't owe nobody nothing," Bass quickly intervened, putting his hand up as the widow was about to protest. "I had me a little something extra after trading with the man. And them young'uns was just having 'em a gander at the hard candy. I paid for 'em to have a sweet treat. Didn't amount to nothing."

"An' you have y' some of Henline's tobaccy?"

Bass nodded. "Mine now. I'll be off to fetch it."

The two of them settled out front beneath the narrow porch awning on half-log stools, leaning back against the rough-log wall chinked with Missouri clay, and slowly sucked down more than one bowlful apiece that evening. While the settler dragged out as much news as he could about what all was happening downriver in St. Louis and beyond, Titus pried out as much information as he could on what lay upriver.

"Fort Osage be a fella's next stop," the man declared. "South bank. But— you cain't count on soldiers and folks allays being there."

"They closed the fort down?"

"Not all the time."

"How far?" Bass inquired.

With a shrug he answered, "Only been up that way once afore. Can't really say. It's a piece."

"How many days you figure?"

"You ain't got no ragtag along and can keep your horses on the scat—I'd figure a little better'n a week."

"That long?" And he watched the settler nod, drawing on his pipe, then dropped his eyes to peer into the bowl the way the man did after nearly every puff.

"Fine tobaccy, this," the man offered after a moment of silence between them.

"You know anything of what's north of Osage?"

"Next place be Atkinson's post. If, like you said, you're hankering to foller the Platte west, I hear that's where you pick up the river what'll take you all the way to them far mountains."

The sound of that distant country made his mouth dry then and there. It seemed like he'd journeyed so damned far already. Fifteen winters it was—as far back as 1810 . . . as far east as Kentucky in the great bend country of the Ohio River. And lately it seemed everyone he ran onto was telling him he'd only begun his journey. From what he'd seen, maybeso those folks were right.

Back east on the Ohio and the great Mississippi, in those forests and along the trails and traces—things weren't really all that spread out and far apart. Even in traveling the wilderness along the Natchez Trace, a man knew he would come across a stand—a wayside inn—with some frequency. But from what he had seen out here already . . . not only was a man running out of folks and settlements, it was as if the land itself damn well seemed to be growing all the bigger on him the farther west he set his feet down.

While the sky domed overhead, endlessly stretching to the western horizon, the country itself he was crossing appeared to swell with every mile he put behind him. And more than once he had come near scaring himself to the marrow: just to think that by some underhanded jigger-pokey magic the land puffed itself up beneath him like a blister, making it so those far mountains arose farther and farther away the faster he rode to find them, the harder he yearned to have that first glimpse of them.

"Yes," Titus finally answered the settler, and stared down into the bowl of his pipe. His tobacco had gone out, and it had grown quieter inside the main house behind them as well as the children's quarters nearby, connected to the squat cabin by a roofed dogtrot.

With a sigh the settler rocked forward and knocked his pipe against the side of his nankeen britches slick and shiny with age and wear. A small black dollop dropped from his clay pipe bowl. Then he peered squarely at the visitor. "I don't s'pose there's any use of a feller to try talkin' you into staying put right here, is there?"

He looked at the plea in the man's eyes for a polite moment before he answered. "No. I'm sorry. Was a time I figgered there'd be nothing for me but to stay on my own place back to Kentucky. But—I found out I ain't the kind to stay on."

With sad resignation the man nodded and said, "Coulda used a hand. You look to be a likely sort for work."

Titus watched the settler twist and turn the small clay pipe in his big hands, the dirt scored into every wrinkle and crevice the way indigo ink would highlight a seafarer's tattoo. "I'm sure the woman's trying to give all she can."

"It was hard enough at times afore my brother passed on," he admitted. "Yes—I know Edna's trying. Just that . . . this is a man's work and she ain't got no business . . ." Then his voice faded off as he looked up at Bass's eyes and saw no softening there. "God knows it ain't a woman's lot to do what that woman does on this place."

"She don't seem the sort to shy at hefting her share of the load."

With a doleful wag the settler explained, "Edna ain't never shied away from her share of the work."

"I figure she does what she has to for her young'uns," Titus replied, whacking his pipe bowl against the sole of his worn boot.

"Time and again I tried to send her and them all back to her family."

After waiting while the settler paused, he asked, "And?"

"And she wouldn't have nothing of it. Said this was where my brother counted on setting down roots and making his stand. Said that's why she was staying. Said she would stay close by where he was planted—right out yonder we laid him . . . and she wanted to be planted right next to him come her time to pass on to the great by and by."

"How long's it been?"

"Last summer," he answered quietly. Then he wagged his head and stared at the tiny pipe in his big, rough hands. "She stayed with him all those days till the end while my woman saw to the young'uns. Then of a early morning when Heber died, just afore sunup, Edna cleaned him, put some fresh clothes on him while I dug his grave—and we buried him that very day. But what got to me was the way she shuffled the kids off to the house here when we was walking back from the grave. Told 'em to go with their auntie and mind her. Said she had work to be doing out with me."

"That when she went to work with you in the fields yonder?"

"The very afternoon we buried my brother. She went in and put on a old pair of his britches, cinched 'em up with some twine, and told me we had us work to be doing out to the fields. And . . . she ain't grieved a bit since then, what I know of."

"She ain't cried none?"

"Not since she walked away from Heber's grave."

"That's a strong woman," Titus ventured, not sure if it were strength or not that kept a body from grieving.

"Thought so my own self at first," the man replied eventually. "But now . . . I just wonder if she ain't in trouble."

"What you mean—trouble?"

Rocking forward on his half-log stool again, the settler rose to his feet and kneaded the back of one thigh before he spoke. "A body's gotta grieve the loss of a love, Mr. Bass. Edna ain't yet grieved proper. She holds it all in—no telling how it'll eat away at her."

At last Titus quietly offered, "A strong woman like that—one what helps you to the fields and pulls her own weight, never asking for any slack in the rope—she'll come through her grieving in her own way. And she'll be fine."

He looked at Bass a moment, then replied, "I ain't got no choice but to trust in just that, mister. Hope is that Edna will grieve in her own way, and not keep it all tied up inside her like a bag full of knots."

Titus watched the man turn and move off, stopping at the doorway.

The settler asked, "You'll make do over there at the lean-to you picked out for yourself?"

"I'll be fine. Thankee much."

"I'm up afore light, Mr. Bass. So I'll see we have coffee together afore you pull out."

"I'll look forward to it."

For several minutes Titus waited there on the porch, listening to the soft sounds of people moving quietly about inside the main cabin, thinking he might have himself another bowl of that tobacco—then the place got quiet and he decided to be off to quiet himself. He slowly rocked himself up off the stool and stood to regard the stars dusting the sky above him, just beyond the edge of the slightly sagging porch roof.

The last Titus remembered was that he had crossed the rutted, hoof-pocked yard and squatted in the dim starlight below the slant of his log and brush lean-to, yanked off his boots, then kicked the blankets over himself and laid his head atop his coat he had folded over his old saddle. Closing his eyes, he faded off to sleep thinking about that far land where the mountains scraped the sky and the buffalo blackened the earth.

"Shhh," the voice whispered to him in his dream. "Lemme in there with you. It's cold out here."

Beyond the lip of the shelter, the sky still hung inky black as he blinked his eyes open, sensing the hands lifting the blankets, fluffing them back over them both as the press of a body came against his. His hand tightened on the pistol between his knees as he came more awake. Rigid and wary.

"Lay still," the woman's voice husked against his ear. "We both stay warmer that way."

Swallowing hard, Bass lay as still as a stalk of grass on a windless day, while he felt her screwge herself against his back, draping an arm over him. Her gasps of breath teased the long hair curled at the collar of his linen shirt, warming him.

"Ed-Edna?"

As quickly as he uttered her name, the woman brought her hand up and laid two fingers on his mouth.

"It's me. Now shush an' lay quiet aside me."

He was afraid he already knew the answer to his question before he asked it. "What you doing here?"

"I'll swear. Back to Bailey Henline's place in Franklin you didn't strike me as a man so thick in the head not to know what I'm here for."

"I s'pose I ain't so thick I can't figger things out in the middle of the night," he whispered, starting to roll on his side toward her. But the woman clamped her arm around Titus, stopping him. He lay perfectly still for a moment, then said quietly, "Long as I can remember, you womenfolk been the biggest of mystery to me. I don't mind owning up to this here being a mystery to me too."

For a long time she did not speak. Then, "It's been a long, long time since't I laid with a man."

That sweet tang of prickly anxiety rose in him like an awakening. He even felt the stir in his flesh as her fingers came away from his lips and traced their way down his chest to his belly, where she pulled and jerked at the tail of his shirt to free it from his button-front leather britches. As her fingers lightly brushed across the skin of his bared belly, Bass sensed himself growing. Enjoying it. Yet afraid of what was to come.

"We ought'n not t-to . . . ," he started with a bit of a stammer as her fingers no longer stroked his skin lightly but began to knead the flesh and muscle at the waistband of his britches. "I c-can't."

"Why?" she whispered huskily in his ear. "Ain'cha been with a woman?"

"I have—"

"You ain't no boy," she interrupted, pulling her hand away suddenly. "Could tell that right off there in Bailey Henline's store. You had a look about you. I knowed you was the kind what'd had you many a woman. Likely a lot of whores too."

He felt her shuffling the blankets behind him, tugging more at his shirt until she had the back tail out and yanked up nearly to his shoulders.

"Ain't gonna deny none of that," he answered at last.

"But I never took you for the kind what didn't know the difference twixt a whore . . . and a woman in need."

"In . . . in need?"

"Bad in need of you," Edna answered. "Been a long time, Mr. Bass. And though the thought's crossed my mind a time or two, I ain't about to go to my own husband's brother with my . . . need."

As she said it, the woman came against him once more with her body heat. And this time he was sure he sensed more of that warmth, now that she had raised his shirt—now that she had her breasts pressed against his bare back.

"Someone gonna hear us," he whispered, suddenly aware of how quiet the night had become around them. "Your young'uns. Maybe your brother—"

"No one gonna hear us," she breathed at his ear, reaching around him again and taking one of his hands in hers. "Less'n you're one what likes to scream when he climbs atop a woman."

"I ain't . . . no, never did I scream."

"Just shush then and feel what I'm giving you this dark, cold night."

Her hand tightened on his, guiding it over his hip to hers. Surprised, he froze the briefest of moments, finding her hip bare. Leading his hand up and down her thigh, then sweeping it back over her buttock, Edna began to groan, low and feral. Her hand left his as Titus continued to explore on his own.

"You didn't wear nothing at all?" he asked.

Huskily, she replied, "Just a ol' coat I shimmied out of."

By now he felt himself become fully erect as she grabbed hold of his hand again and led it directly between her thighs, locking it where she was the warmest. He sensed a shudder shoot through the woman as his fingers explored, finding her moist.

"Y-you're a widow woman—"

"That don't mean nothing."

Starting to roll toward him, Edna immediately had her fingers at the buttons of his britches, sitting up slightly so she could get both hands working to yank at the front of his pants. The blankets slid off her shoulder. In the dim starshine he got his first good look at her bare neck, a shoulder where the coat had slipped down her arm, and then her breasts.

Her hand hungrily grabbed his rigid flesh as the front of his britches opened. Up and down she toyed with him, first squeezing about as hard as she could, then lightly brushing a single finger up, then down. "You're ready for me, ain'cha, Mr. Bass?"

"Get out of your coat," he ordered hungrily, his eyes flicking a last time across the starlit yard toward the small buildings. There were no second thoughts now.

"Just soon's I get you outta your shucks," she said, yanking, pulling, tearing at his canvas pants.

At the same time, he was tearing his shirt the rest of the way over his head and off his arms, flinging his clothing to the side in a careless heap.

As she leaned back to slip off the coat that lay open, he leaned forward, taking one of her breasts into his mouth and began to kiss, fondle, suck. A tremor shot through her body and she moaned once more, hurriedly shaking the coat from her arms. The instant it was off, she had a hand encircling his rigid flesh once more while at the same time collapsing to her back beside him there.

He found himself between her legs as he brought the blankets over them, the cold night wind sharp as freshly stoned knife against their flesh. Impatiently, Edna guided him with the one hand, her other insistent, pressing at the small of his back, urging him forward. After several moments of lunging against her in vain, Edna's warmth eventually wrapped itself around him as he drove himself up to the hilt.

Now as one they began to rock there beneath the stars on that moonless night as the earth spun toward dawn. The closer he got to spending himself within her, it seemed the larger his penis grew. And the more Edna whimpered. Low and sporadic at first, now she tangled her fingers in his long hair, pulling him down, holding him there so that she could press her lips against his ear as he continued to thrust himself against her with a growing urgency.

Then a high-pitched, staccato, and almost silent screech escaped her throat as she shook volcanically beneath him in those seconds Titus finished inside her. Her scream quickly became a whimper, then a raspy, breathless whisper at his ear as he collapsed fully atop her. Spent, as weak as a newborn calf.

"You sleep for 'while now, Mr. Bass." Her words brushed his flesh as she nestled her head against his neck. "Then I'll be rousing you well afore first light another time. That way I can be back with the young'uns and no one's the wiser come morning."

She was true to her word, Edna was.

It seemed like no time at all until he was nudged awake. Bass found her kissing on his neck and down his chest, her hands busy as ever stroking him, her small breasts brushing and tantalizing against his shoulder, his arm, his belly as she shifted beside him.

Then, just as she had promised, after that second feral coupling the woman rolled herself away from him, peeled her coat from the jumble of his blankets, and wrapped herself within it before she leaned over him.

"Mr. Bass," she whispered, her lips almost against his, her eyes staring right into him. "I ain't no young woman no more. And I ain't got a damn prospect one way out here where Heber brought us for to find his dream. So I'm telling you to take what I give you of Edna Mae Grigsby and ride off come morning. I damn well know you're gonna 'member the smell of me when you're out there fighting off them Pawnee or any them other nasty Injuns. An' then maybeso you'll wanna come riding back here to me, to what you had you a taste of this night."

The guilt rose in him like an underground spring. "I . . . I don't want you getting the wrong idea—"

"Don't have me no idea a'tall, Mr. Bass," she interrupted. "Fact is, you'll likely not ever be back. But if you've got yourself a hankering for a good woman to spend out your days with—just remember I'm here."

"Edna." He said it in such a way that she already knew.

Apologetically.

And the woman put her fingers on his lips to silence any more rejection of her. Edna drew her face back from his as he fought to find the words to explain.

"Then go, Mr. Bass," she whispered. "I figger we both got what we wanted here tonight. You're on your way out there for something. And I got what I been needing—needing for the better part of a year since my Heber gone and left me with young'uns to raise and fields to plow."

"But you ain't never cried," he said. "That's what—"

"No I ain't," she admitted, her lip stiffening. "But likely I will one of these days soon, Mr. Bass. At first, I only got dead inside when Heber died. It hurt so bad him going that I made myself go all dead inside, like a dried-up autumn leaf. Then I tol't myself another man be coming along and want the pleasure I could give him for the rest of his days. Didn't know if'n it'd be you . . ." She wagged her head as she leaned back. "So be it."

The look on her face, the sag in her shoulders—it caused him such pain inside. "I didn't tend to hurt no one, Edna."

"Hush now. Ain't you caused me the hurt," she said, brushing her fingers down the side of his face, her eyes pooling, shiny in the inky starlight. "I figger leastways now I can go on and shed myself of these tears."

Feeling the first of them spill hot upon his chest, Titus pulled the woman against him, nestling her head in the crook of his neck as she began to sob. He cradled her there as Edna cried after all those months, her body shaking harder than it had when she twice rocked beneath him. Then her sobbing grew quieter, and it seemed she drifted off to sleep there within his embrace.

Out east on the horizon the sky was graying when he came awake himself, one of his arms gone to sleep, tingling beneath the woman.

Suddenly he smelled the woodsmoke, rising slightly to gaze across the yard at the cabin where he realized a fire had been lit and coffee set to boil.

"Edna!" he whispered down at her sharply.

She came awake immediately, rubbing at her eyes and realizing. "I best go," she said in a small voice, throwing back the covers, slipping out, then carefully tucking them back against his naked body.

Titus asked, "You . . . things gonna be all right with you?"

With a sad smile she leaned close to him again. "I'll make out just fine."

"You'll make some man a handsome wife again one day real soon."

"Thank you, Mr. Bass. Thank you." She bent over his face, kissed him lightly, then rose to her knee, pulling the long flaps of the wool coat about her bare legs. "You don't find what you're looking for out there, you come riding on back here and look for me."

He couldn't help but grin. "That's a awful tempting offer, Edna Mae."

"It's a offer only a *crazy* man like you'd turn down, ain't it?"

Remembering what he had told the Franklin shopkeeper, Titus leaned forward, kissed her forehead. "I am a bit crazy. But—a man never knows what the future holds for him."

"Ever' now and then . . . you remember me, won'cha?"

"Said I was *crazy*," he replied with a wide grin. "Not no idjit what can't remember the feel of a good woman. And you are a good woman."

Reluctantly she got to her feet. "Good-bye, Mr. Bass."

"Good-bye, Edna Mae."

He watched her turn and quickly sprint across the grassy yard, her feet slicked with dew until she was lost in the dark shadows of the dogtrot, where she would slip back into her cabin, to wait out the minutes until sunrise with her children.

In the sudden cold vacuum that she left, he felt sorry for leaving her and this place. Then he felt an even deeper remorse for having decided to stop over. But as he yanked on his clothes, Titus decided what was done was done. Some unseen hand had guided him here, perhaps. And there was no denying that he might well have needed her as much as she had needed him.

Edna Mae was putting an end to something.

What with Titus Bass standing at the precipice of the adventure of his lifetime.

Maybeso they had both been fated to cross paths just when they needed each other the most.

By the time he had the blankets rolled up and ready to lash onto the mare, he heard the scrape of the door across its jamb. Turning, he found the settler emerging from the cabin, a steaming china cup in each hand as he stepped off the narrow porch and onto the dewy grass.

"Promised you coffee, Titus," he said as he presented the cup to Bass.

Self-consciously, he took it from the man. "Smells damned good." Nervously twisting inside as he took that first steaming sip, Titus figured the settler couldn't help but know.

Eyes not touching, they drank in silence for some time, savoring the quiet of the morning as the gray turned to bluish-purple off in the distance—back to the east where both of them had left a life behind them.

"You're ready to be off . . . it appears to me," the man said to break that stillness of time.

"Dallied long enough," he replied, then hated himself for saying it. Making it sound the way he did, what with the man knowing about Edna Mae creeping off to the lean-to.

The farmer asked, "You a breakfast man?"

"A'times, I am."

"Maybe you'll stay on while I rustle us up some—"

"I-I feel the pull to be on my way," Titus interrupted, feeling the embarrassment bordering on shame all the way down to the soles of his feet.

"I could have the missus wrap up some of the leavin's from supper—"

"I thankee for your kindness and all," Bass broke in again. "But—I'll do just fine."

Taking a step closer to Titus, the settler looked Bass squarely in the eye, and with an even voice he said, "She needed you . . . so there ain't no reason to feel ashamed for it."

"Damn," he sighed with disgust at having his fears confirmed. "I shouldn't have got myself—"

"Listen here, Mr. Bass," the man interrupted this time with a doleful wag of his head. "Edna Mae is her own woman. Allays has been. I figure she knows her own mind too, and I don't hold you on account for that. She's a widow now. Been one too damned long for my way of thinking. True enough, she may've been my brother's wife, but likely you done her what she needed."

"Look here—I swear I didn't come out here for none of that to happen."

He held his empty hand up as if to silence Bass and pursed his lips a moment before he said, "Like I said, chances are you done her what she needed. And . . . for that, I can thank you." He switched the coffee cup to his left hand and held out the right. "I wish you God's speed, Mr. Bass."

Eagerly he accepted the man's big, muscular, dirt-imprinted hand, and they shook. "I thankee for all you done."

As he accepted the empty cup from Titus, the settler asked, "You'll be careful out yonder now?"

Taking up the rein to the Indian pony, Bass turned and stuffed a foot into the stirrup. "Didn't get near this old 'thout watching out for my own hide." He rose to saddle, settled, and said, "Time was I didn't figger I'd see my thirtieth year. But"—and he leaned back with a sigh—"look at me now. Here I've put that thirtieth year ahind me, and I'm on my way to the Rocky Mountains."

"Likely so it's the right time for you."

"Believe it is," Titus responded, then nodded toward the cabin, where he was sure he saw at least two small faces pressed against the smudged isinglass panes on that solitary window. "You'll tell Edna Mae I took leave of here wishing her all the best fortune to come her way."

"I will do that."

"You tell her again I ain't got a fear one she ain't gonna find a good man to care for her and the young'uns."

"I'll tell her." And he took a step back, flinging the coffee from his own cup, then looping both cup handles over the fingers of one hand as he shoved some unruly hair back from his eyes.

"You're the kind to take care of all of them, ain't you?"

The man gazed up at Bass. "If that's what the Lord calls upon me to do."

With a smile Titus replied, "Then you're just the sort like my own kin . . . my own pap. I'm glad all of them here got you to depend on."

And before the settler could utter another word, Bass tapped his heels into the pony's ribs and yanked sharply on the mare's lead rope.

Moving off in a hurry, with the newborn sun rising at his back.

He didn't see a human or smell firesmoke for something close to another two hundred river miles.

Then of a sudden, on the warming midday breeze, he drew up, catching that first whiff of burning wood. As much as he strained his eyes to see beyond the thick timber clustered along the hillside, Titus could not make out a puff, much less a column, of smoke. The thick, stinging gorge rose in his throat—remembering so many years before having been caught flat-footed along the Mississippi by a Chickasaw hunting party.

It would not happen again, he swore under his breath.

Quickly he urged the animals toward a thick copse of leafy green and hurled himself out of the saddle, landing as quietly as he could upon the thick carpet of spring grass. Lashing the horses to a low-hanging limb, Titus retrieved his rifle and crept toward the side of a low hill a quarter of a mile ahead of him. Hugging the shadows offered by the thick hardwood timber that bordered this southern bank of the Missouri, Bass carefully picked his way around the brow of the knoll. For all he knew, he had made it to Pawnee country and had blundered smack-dab into them—just about the way he had bumped into those Chickasaw warriors while out hunting for Ebenezer Zane's boat crew.

Dropping to his knees as the wind came full into his face, rank with the sharp tang of woodsmoke grown strong in his nostrils, Titus crept forward, parting the brush with the muzzle of the fullstock flintlock rifle. Yard by yard he pressed until he stopped: hearing the familiar call of birds in the distance, followed by the roll of at least one woodpecker thundering its echo within a nearby glen. Were it an Indian camp, he figured, there sure as hell wouldn't be such routine noise from the forest creatures.

Swallowing down the dry lump clogging his throat, Bass again parted the branches of the brush and pushed his way forward until he sat at the edge of the clearing. Ahead of him bobbed waves of tall grass that seemed to stretch all the way to the sharp-cut north bank of the Missouri. He dared to raise his head a little higher, catching a glimpse of the river at the foot of that north bank—still not all that certain he wouldn't see a cluster of Indian wickiups.

Across the river to the south the spring sky was sullied with but a single thin trail of smoke rising from a solitary stone chimney that protruded over the top of a stockade wall. The double gate stood open just wide enough to easily admit a wagon, almost as if expecting visitors.

Quickly glancing left down the south bank, then north, Bass thought it curious he did not lay eyes on any humans. Then he spotted a pair of draft horses picketed just outside the stockade wall, contentedly grazing on the spring grass. He craned his neck to see more of that western side of the stockade. Beyond the pair grazed three more horses.

After all these days without sign of another human—just possibly there was life here.

At first the open gate and no sight of folks had unnerved him—causing him to fear the place had been attacked, its inhabitants killed, and the fort left empty. But it just didn't figure that Injuns would leave good horseflesh behind.

A voice called out from the woods beyond the fort, surprising him. Bass craned his neck to the east to watch a figure emerge from the line of trees, an ax over one shoulder and his shirt carelessly draped over the other. Again he called back to the timber, and almost immediately two other men burst from the woods to join the first. The heaviest of them, also naked to the waist, tugged at leather braces, slipping them over both arms, then adjusting the belt line of his drop-front britches below his more-than-ample belly. That one mopped his face with a bright-yellow bandanna, then stuffed it into the back of his pants.

As he tried to study the trio, Titus could hear their talk, three distinct voices—but could not make out any words at this distance across the muddy, runoff swollen river. As the three turned the northeast corner of the stockade, Bass realized they all wore the same pants and ankle-high, square-toed boots.

"Soldiers." Both dust and sweat stained the light-blue wool of those britches as the men turned through the open gate and disappeared from view. Almost as quickly the fat man reappeared, dragging behind him a small two-wheeled cart with a long double-tree attached to the front. It bounced and rumbled across the rutted, pocked ground as he turned the corner of the stockade, headed back toward the timber where the trio had emerged just minutes before.

For some time Titus sat there thinking on it, wondering if these three might well try to keep him from pushing on west to the mountains. At least that's what Isaac Washburn had proclaimed last year when each night they had laid their plans for their journey to the Rockies. From the Missouri River country on west across the plains, Gut had explained, a man must either be a dragoon stationed at one of the riverside posts, or he had to belong to a licensed fur brigade sent upriver by one of the big companies being outfitted and setting off every spring from St. Louis these past few years.

For the longest time the trade in western furs had all but died off—what with the trouble the British raised among the upriver tribes during the years they waged war on the young country of America; not to mention the losses of men Manuel Lisa suffered at the hand of the Blackfeet high in the northern Rockies. Wary at best, the St. Louis merchants had pulled in their horns, licked their wounds, and confined themselves to doing what trading they could with the Sauk, Fox, Omaha, and the other more peaceable tribes along the lower river.

Then three years ago the Americans recruited by Ashley and Henry again flung themselves at the upper river, against the distant and hostile tribes, against that fabled land so rich in thick, prime fur.

But Titus Bass wasn't about to join the army—not going to cut wood or dig slip-trench latrines at one of these river posts—hell, no, he wouldn't do that and be forced to gaze out longingly at all that expanse of open wilderness he would never get to see as long as he was a soldier.

And he sure as hell wasn't the sort to be a joiner either. Not about to sign on with one of those brigades that promised each man a rifle, traps, and two meals a day . . . and in return each dumb brute must promise the muscles of his back, his arms and legs, for the grueling labor of warping and cordelling laden keelboats against the fickle Missouri's mighty current. No, sir. All that talk he overheard in the St. Louis watering holes and knocking shops sure didn't sound like much of a life to him: taking commands from some smooth-faced army officer, or from a slick-tongued fur trader bound to grow rich off the labors of others.

Perhaps if he rested right here in the brush and tall grass—watching the small post across the river for a while longer, he might learn for sure if more than those three were quartered at the fort. After all, there were five horses grazing outside the stockade walls. And then he chuckled, imagining the sight of that big-bellied one bouncing along at an ungainly gallop upon one of those horses.

A moment more and Bass slapped his knee, wagging his head for his short-sighted stupidity. As well as he knew horses, Titus chided himself for not seeing it earlier. Those sure as hell weren't dragoon animals meant to be ridden. They were wagon stock: thick-hipped and high-backed. Which meant this place was peopled with foot soldiers.

It wasn't long before the thin trail of smoke from that lone chimney became a thick column. One of those soldiers had punched life back into their fire.

That's when Titus noticed the angle of the shadows and looked into the west to measure the descent of the sun. Those soldiers were done with their fatigue for the day and were preparing their supper. Just thinking of it made his stomach grumble. More than a week and a half ago he had left Boone's Lick and Arrow Rock behind. He remembered now the last meal cooked by the hand of a woman. She had warmed his belly that evening and, in the darkness of that same night, come to warm his blankets. How he wished Edna Mae well in her search for a husband: a man for her bed, and a father for her children.

Then he gazed at the river, studying the far landing constructed of thick poplar and oak pilings buried into the bank, where river travelers would tie up their craft. To one of the pilings were lashed three crude pirogues carved out of thick-trunked trees, each of them bobbing against the wharf and each other with a rhythmic, dull clunk as the Missouri pushed on past. On the grassy bank itself lay two canoes, upside down, their bellies pointing at the cloudless afternoon sky.

He could well slip on around the post himself, unseen by those soldiers. But sooner or later, Titus realized, he would have to cross the Missouri. Once she pointed her way north—he would have to make his way over to the yonder bank anyway. For more minutes as the sun slipped closer to the far edge of the earth, he brooded on it—whether or not to chance these soldiers and this post. Or to pass them on by.

He racked his memory of all those sober or whiskey-sodden nights spent with Isaac Washburn. Besides Fort Kiowa, where old Hugh Glass had crawled after being mauled by the she-grizz, the only fort his recollections came up with was the one Gut spoke of near the mouth of the Platte—the one called Atkinson. For the life of him, Titus couldn't remember the old fur trapper warning him of any others. Atkinson was the one Gut vowed they would give wide berth as they made their way west.

But this stockade—what the hell was this post sitting here of a sudden on the south bank of the Missouri?

As the shadows stretched long and the afternoon breeze cooled against his shaggy cheek, Titus wrestled with it the way he had manhandled a piece of strap iron at Hysham Troost's forge: all fire and muscle. And as the day grew old and evening beckoned out of the east, Bass owned up to what he'd been hankering to do almost from the moment he first set eyes on that stockade across the river.

THREE

"Sergeant!"

At that cry from the south shore Bass's head bobbed out of the muddy water, his eyes blinking, immediately landing on the open gates, where one of the soldiers stood turned half-around to hurl his voice into the stockade.

"Pull, girl!" he called out to the mare dragging him against the Missouri's strong current. He gripped her tail as firmly as he had ever held on to a woman at that moment of blissful union. "That's it—pull!"

As he did his best to hold the rifle high overhead and out of the water, the mare fought the strong current, pulling them slowly toward that south bank where a second soldier appeared, joining the first. Eventually the big-bellied one hurried up to complete the trio about the time the Indian pony's hooves touched bottom beside the mare. Together both animals struggled to find their footing on the slick river bottom, stumbled and shifted, both nearly going down as they continued to fight for a foothold. As the river surged against them, the mare managed to keep her head fully above water while all he saw of the pony in that instant was its nostrils. Then the pony was back up, eyes as big as tea saucers, ears slicked back in both fear and the effort she was giving her swim across the frothy current as the bottom of the sun's orb sank onto the far western prairie with an audible sigh.

At the moment the mare nearly jerked him free of her tail, Bass's bare feet scraped across the muddy, brush-choked bottom some fifty yards below the wharf where the pirogues continued to clunk together. All three soldiers moved down together to stand some twenty yards up the grassy bank, just past the two upside-down canoes as Titus finally got his legs under him, slapping the rump of both animals as they clawed their way out of the Missouri, clattering onto dry land.

He stood gasping, eyeing the trio as both horses shimmied beneath their loads, then turned their big eyes to regard the naked, white-skinned human with something bordering on a warning never to repeat such a crossing, if not outright contempt. Glancing at the big soldier who held a Harpers Ferry musket pointed his way, Titus clambered a little farther up the slope and collapsed to his knees on the grass.

"Just who the hell are you?"

Rubbing some of the river's grit from his eyes, he felt his breathing slow, then replied, "Name's Bass. Up from St. Louis."

The thinnest one of the three took a step forward, a large-bored pistol hanging at the end of his arm, which he quickly waved at the two horses audibly tearing off shoots of the new grass. "There any more of you coming across?"

He wagged his head, slinging water from his shoulder-length hair. The breeze prickled his naked skin, and he grew chilled as he glanced back at the north bank. "Nary a soul. Just me."

When Bass turned to step toward the mare, the thin one snapped, "Stand your ground, stranger!"

For that silent moment his teeth chattered, his eyes flashing over the three of them and the muzzles of those two pistols that had joined the fat man's musket in staring back at him.

"J-just getting m-my shucks." He gestured to the top of the mare's packs, where he had stuffed his clothing beneath the ropes.

"Your shucks?" asked the third man, clearly the oldest of the lot.

"My clothes," Titus replied, wrapping his arms around himself, shuddering with the breeze that seemed to pick up speed and muscle as the sun continued to sink in the west. "Wasn't about to get 'em wet in making that crossing, you see. Now, if you fellas'll just let me get back in my warm clothes."

"Yes," replied the thin one. "By all means. None of us particular like watching a naked man shake and shrivel up afore our eyes."

With a grateful nod Bass turned to the mare, patted her on the neck, and retrieved his shirt, britches, and boots from beneath the ropes lashing the bundles to the horse's back.

As Titus began to hop one-legged into his leather britches, the thin man out front asked him, "What the devil are you doing up here from St. Louis?"

"Headed west."

"West?" the fat man demanded in a gush. "West, from here?"

"What you aim to do going west?" the thin one demanded. "Off to Santa Fe all by yourself?"

Stuffing the wooden buttons through their holes in the britches, Bass shook his head. "Ain't going south to Santy Fee. Pointing my nose out yonder to them mountains."

"You don't say?" the third one replied with a bit of wonder. For the most part, he had been all but silent.

Bass dragged his yoke-shouldered linen shirt over his sopping wet head and asked, "You got room to put a man up for the night?"

"Do we, Sergeant?" the fat one asked. He let the Harpers Ferry musket droop until it pointed at the ground.

"I don't know about putting you up here at the post," the thin one began.

"Then I'll just set myself up right out here," Titus responded.

"Aw, c'mon, Sergeant," the big-bellied man pleaded. "We ain't none of us had no one new to talk with inside of weeks."

"That's right," the third one agreed. "Maybe he's got some news from downriver what ain't gone rotted with time."

Jabbing his big horse pistol into the waistband of his military breeches, the thin man inquired, "You ain't a scout from one of them fur outfits, are you? Rest of 'em coming 'long behind you?"

On the ground where he plopped to pull on his boots, Bass declared, "Like I said, I'm on my lonesome."

"And you know exactly where the hell you're going?"

Titus pointed quickly in the general direction. "West. Out yonder."

The younger, thin man with the beaklike nose chuckled, then said, "So do you know where you are?"

"I'm on the Missouri River," Bass replied, flinging a thumb over his shoulder at the frothy, muddy, runoff swollen water. "Still east of the big bend."

"Ain't that far to the bend now!" the third man cheered.

"How far?" Titus replied eagerly, standing, stomping his heels down into the old boots.

With a shrug the older man said, "Not far. I never was one to measure things out exact."

"He's right," the sergeant injected. "So you reach the big bend, what's that mean to you?"

"Means the Missouri heads north," Bass replied. "And me with it."

With a bob of his head the big soldier said, "Sounds like he's got him a notion of where he's off to, Sergeant."

"Could be, Culpepper," the thin one replied, jabbing his thumb over his shoulder at the stockade for emphasis. "But—still don't sound like he knows where he's landed."

Titus tugged the broad-brimmed hat firmly down on his head. "You mean this here post on the Missouri?"

The sergeant swelled out his chest proudly, swinging an arm expansively, proudly, over all his regal holdings. "Osage, it's called," he offered. "Fort Osage."*

It was a sometimes proposition, this Fort Osage was.

During the early 1820s it had become the jumping-off point for those traders headed down the Santa Fe Trail.

"But there's been a post here back to O-eight," the thin man called Lancaster explained as they sat with Titus at the stone fireplace in what served as the fort's mess hall.

From the size of the stockade down to the tiny barracks, it was plain for any visitor to see that a large force had never manned Fort Osage.

"That's back when General Clark chose this here place for a government trading house," Sergeant Clayton explained. "I s'pose that's why to some folks this place'll always be known as Fort Clark."

In fact, to those on the Lewis and Clark expedition marching west to the Pacific Ocean, this location was first noted as a favorable site for a post and ever after became known as Fort Point on June 23, 1804—perhaps because of the low bluff on which the post would be eventually situated. The red-haired William Clark again passed by the site early in the fall of 1808 with a troop of dragoon cavalry on his way to make a treaty with the Osage. On November 13 of that year, upon his return trip downriver, General Clark christened the post that would be abandoned less than five years later during the war scare—the government, army, and civilians alike believing the British in Canada were goading the tribes along the upper river to rise en masse and descend the Missouri, slaughtering all Americans in their path. The army did not garrison Fort Osage again, nor operate the post as a government trading house with the Indians west of the Missouri, until 1816.

Bass nodded, kneeling to take a twig from the fire, lighting his pipe. "So like you told me—there ain't soldiers here all the time?"

Clayton said, "No there ain't. Nowadays just when some fur trader gets some business going with the tribes upriver. Maybeso they station us here in the spring and the fall, what with the Santa Fe trade going and coming those times of year."

"Last bunch of soldiers stationed here," Culpepper said, jumping into the conversation enthusiastically, his eyes dancing, "three of 'em deserted."

"Deserted?"

"Yep. Run off with all the lead and shot they could carry—"

Clayton interrupted, " 'Cepting the sergeant. He damn well didn't desert his station."

"Yup." Culpepper's head bobbed as he declared, "Three soldiers tied that poor bastard up to the fur press out there in the compound afore they took off for parts unknown."

"Must've been days later when some fellas finally showed up—coming

---

* Reconstructed near present-day Sibley, in Jackson County, Missouri

downriver in a canoe what they tied up yonder," Lancaster joined in. "They come up to find the gates open, and the sergeant sitting right out there—all trussed up like a Christmas hog."

"He was still alive after all that time?" Bass inquired.

"Barely," Clayton answered. "Poor son of a bitch's wrists was flayed and bloody trying his best to break outta them ropes."

"An' he could barely utter a word," Culpepper added. "Hoarse as a sour-mouthed bullfrog. Been screaming and cussing for all he was worth since the day them three run off."

Lancaster wagged his head, saying, "No one to hear him anyway. Don't know why he didn't just shut his yap and wait till someone showed up."

"Would you?" Culpepper demanded, turning on the older soldier. "Just sit there?"

"Still say it didn't do him a bit of good," Lancaster replied sourly.

"What ever become of him?" Titus asked.

"I heard the poor soul's still mending down to St. Louis," Sergeant Clayton explained.

Bass puffed on his pipe. "Army decided to send up some more men, even after them others run off?"

"These are good men," Clayton replied, nodding at the others. "Both of 'em hard workers, and they're loyal too."

"Not like them last three," Culpepper spouted.

Nearby, Fire Prairie Creek meandered out of the timber toward the bluff where the stockade stood and eventually spilled into the Missouri. Many years before William Clark had ever chosen the site, Fire Prairie had acquired its name among the local tribes when four Osage warriors were killed by a large band of attacking Pawnee, who surrounded their enemies, then burned them alive, setting fire to the dry grass in a nearby meadow. To the peaceful bands situated in that big-bend country of the Missouri River, the army's post and government factory had long been commonly known as Fire Prairie Fort.

"We had to drive off four sonsabitches when we got here," Culpepper boasted.

"Interlopers," Sergeant Clayton explained. "Civilian interlopers—likely taking squatters' rights here to conduct some illegal whiskey trade with the peaceable bands in the country hereabouts."

"They sure didn't put up much of a argument," Culpepper added. "Likely they figured we was just the advance of a hull big outfit."

"So they skedaddled."

Titus asked, "Where they go?"

Clayton shrugged. "Who knows? Last we saw of 'em they was heading west toward the bend. Ain't none of my concern now."

Bass gazed around the small, low-roofed room again, then asked, "They take anything you know of?"

"Not the way they was packing up in a hurry under our eyes," Lancaster said. "For sure they was a snakey-looking lot—the sort what'd trade whiskey with the Injuns and be slick-handed at it too."

As the first drops of rain hit the plank and sod roof overhead, Bass looked at the sergeant, asking, "You hear tell of anyone trading whiskey with them Pawnee up on the Platte?"

Shaking his head, Clayton said, "Not lately. Them soldiers quartered up at Atkinson see to it none of that slips by 'em."

"Whiskey makes an Injun mean," Culpepper instructed as if he were spouting gospel.

"You seen Injuns before, ain't you?" the sergeant asked of Bass.

"I seen my share of Chickasaw . . . years ago now."

"No," Lancaster joined in. "Did you ever see any of these Injuns here abouts?"

"River Injuns," Culpepper commented with self-satisfaction. "The ones what're still wild."

"I seen a few come through St. Lou," Bass admitted. "But I s'pose I ain't seen a real *wild* Injun in many a year."

The wind gusted, rain battering against the small mullioned panes of glass on the two windows that looked out on the compound, where a torch sputtered in the sudden downpour. Titus got to his feet and left the warm corona near the fireplace to go to the door. He opened it and stared out at the heavy rain drowning the countryside as the torch outside flickered, then hissed—snuffed out and throwing the stockade's compound into utter blackness. It sent a chill down his spine like a drop of January ice water.

"Close that son of a bitch," Culpepper ordered. "Damn, but you let in all that cold so to make my bones ache."

Slowly shoving the iron-hinged door back into its jamb, Bass returned to the half-log benches, where he rejoined the others.

After a long period of silence as the sergeant continued to stare at the flames, Clayton finally asked, "What you figure to see out yonder to the west what's so all-fired important?"

"First off—I want to see me some buffalo."

"Buffalo?" Culpepper exclaimed.

"That's right. I been hankering on seeing them big beasts for about as long as I can remember."

The sergeant prodded for more. " 'Sides the buffalo, what else?"

"Them mountains," Bass added. "I've heard me stories—"

"Me too," Culpepper interrupted enthusiastically. "The way some fellas talk about them mountains being so this and so that, why—I figure what with all that unlordly talk, them fellers is full of shit right up to the bung!"

"I knowed me one what ought to know," Titus explained. "He was a fur trapper in that upcountry—on the likes of the Bighorn and the Yallerstone."

"Bighorn," Clayton repeated wistfully. "Yallerstone too?"

"So what'd he have to say for hisself?" Culpepper demanded.

"Yeah," Lancaster joined in, "what'd he tell you 'bout that country?"

"I figure them mountains gonna be something for a man to see."

Lancaster leaned forward now, elbows on his knees. "Ain't you seen mountains before, Bass?"

"If what Washburn tol't me was the true: then all the mountains I've seen till now back east be nothing but foothills to them what lay out yonder."

"Where you're dead set on going," Clayton observed solemnly.

Titus finally owned up, "I don't figure I can rest till I do."

A doubtful Lancaster prodded, "Once you do, what then?"

"If'n I like 'em—I plan to stay on."

"Doin' what?" Culpepper asked.

"Trapping beaver."

"So you're for sure a fur man, are you?" Clayton inquired. "We hear most of them fur men what go upriver don't ever come back down, leastwise with their hair still on. Them I hear what does come back got 'em lots of ghosty stories to tell of that country and the Injuns running things out there."

Rising to his feet again, Titus bristled at the challenge. He boasted, "I ain't scared of them mountains, not the Injuns neither. And I damn well don't believe in no man's ghosty stories. I've heard my share of windbags and Sunday-blowers to know what to lay stock in and what not. Can't think of a damned thing gonna turn me aside from what I've been fixing on doing for a long time now."

"Where you headed?" Clayton inquired as the civilian turned away from the trio.

Grumpily he said, "Off to my blankets."

"But the night's still early, Bass!" Culpepper cheered.

Titus stopped and turned to explain, "Not when I've got more miles to put under me tomorrow. If it's all the same to you fellas, I'll make me my bed right over here where I dropped my truck."

"Anywhere you lay your head be fine by me," Clayton declared. "Just as long as you don't settle down on the spot there in the corner where you see I laid me my tick and blankets."

No matter that there were only four of them in that whole fort—Titus Bass still felt cramped.

By the time the sky grayed, he was already wide-eyed and awake, anxious to be gone from this place. To go at last where he would be troubled by no man, rubbed against, and questioned. Maybeso to leave white folks behind wouldn't be all that bad for a while.

Then Bass worked hard to think back on the last time he had been truly on his own. More than a decade it had been since the Mississippi flatboat crew had set him afoot on the west bank of the river, where he had taken off north to St. Louis—alone until he came across Able Guthrie's barn and that warm, inviting hay where he lay his weary self down. Even longer still since he had run off from home and spent those first nights in the woods on his own. Alone and growing all the hungrier until he presented himself at Ebenezer Zane's night fire, joining the pilot's Kentucky boatmen.

Two of the soldiers snored close by in the thinning darkness. Each of them grumbling, gurgling, snorting at times. This fort room smelled damp with the seepage from last night's rain. The timbers grown sodden and dank. How well he knew places like this took on a rank smell after man had been there too long.

Titus sat up quietly and pulled aside his blankets. After dragging on his old boots he slipped from the door, leaving it partially open rather than make more noise in closing it. From side to side he dodged the patchwork of puddles in the open compound left by last night's rain, then passed by the tall, forlorn fur-press when he saw the Indian pony turn at the sound of his approach. The mare raised her head and stomped a hoof expectantly as well.

Aswirl with moisture, the air felt heavy to breathe here in the moments just before dawn. Light drops fell to prick the surface of each puddle and rut as he untied both horses from their hitching rings and moved off toward the gate. There he dragged aside the heavy wooden hasp and heaved back on one side of the gate until it swung open wide enough to let him slip out with the animals.

The goatsuckers were still out in the graying light, winging this way and that over the tall grass that stretched endlessly toward the timber on three sides of the stockade: several different species of birds that fed on moths and gnats—whippoorwills and nighthawks mostly, all swooping, diving, and feeding here in the cold, damp dawn.

Following a well-worn footpath, Titus led the two horses away from the walls toward the timber south of the fort. After two hundred yards he found the spring Lancaster had described. He released the animals and went to his knees, rocking forward over the surface of the water, where he could lap its cold with his tongue. Renewed, and anxious to be done with his leaving, Titus stood and waited for the horses to finish.

Sergeant Clayton had Lancaster working corn mush into cakes by the time Bass returned. Culpepper sat by the fireplace, feeding the flames and heating a skillet in which he was melting bear lard to fry their breakfast.

"You wasn't about to run off without something in your belly, was you?" Lancaster asked, dragging his fingers down into a wooden bowl and emerging with more of the soggy cornmeal he began to pat between his palms.

"What's for breakfast?"

The sergeant looked at Bass with astonishment, saying, "Here I thought you told us you wasn't a breakfast man."

Drinking in the fragrances with a deep breath for a moment, he found the three of them looking expectantly at him. "S'pose I'll take time this morning,"

Titus replied. "Seeing how this be the last morning I figger to be eating with white folks for some time to come."

"A apple tart with hot buttered rum sauce," Culpepper spoke right out of the blue.

"What the hell you talking about?" Lancaster grumbled at the rounder man.

With a shrug, the big-bellied soldier said, "Just sitting here thinking of what I'd like to have me a taste of."

Clayton set the piggin of water on the plank table with a clatter. The small pail was made with stave wood: that hardwood used to make thin-shaped strips set edge to edge to form a small bucket or barrel. He asked, "A apple tart, is it?"

"Back to home in Nashville—that's what was my favored thing to sink my teeth into."

"Your mama made it?" Lancaster asked.

Nodding, Culpepper continued, "She made the best tarts—and always used some of my da's rum to pour on 'em just before we sunk our teeth into 'em." He smacked his lips noisily, then peered down at the skillet to find his lard had melted. "Hey, ol' soldier—you best get them cakes over here in a shuffle-quick. I'm ready to cook!"

Lancaster legged back the bench he had been sitting on and rose with the pewter platter he had piled high with mush cakes. "You're gonna stay long 'nough to eat, ain'cha, Bass?"

Drawing in another deep breath of that room no longer rank with the smell of rain and men living too close to one another—but now filled with the strong, corn-tinged fragrance of memories, Titus said, "Yes. Them pone cakes do sound good this morning."

"Pone?" Clayton repeated. "You from somewhere south, mister?"

"Kentucky. Hard by the Ohio."

At the fire Lancaster slipped a fourth cake into the heated oil in the skillet. "Ain't heard these'r called pone in a spell."

"My . . ." And he struggled to get the rest out without his voice cracking in remembrance. "My mam most times made all us young'uns pone cakes of a cold autumn morning."

"I growed up calling 'em hoecakes," Culpepper declared as he jabbed at the frying mush with a long iron fork.

"Maybeso they're nothing more'n johnnycakes," Clayton said, turning away from Bass as if he appeared to recognize something familiar in the look on the older man's face.

Titus was grateful the young sergeant had turned away as his eyes began to mist up and he troubled his Adam's apple up and down repeatedly, trying to swallow the sour gob of sentiment that threatened to choke him.

His damp leather britches and wool coat began to steam there in the heat of the mess hall—arousing a long-ago memory all of its own. The smells of frying oil, the crackling of the wood beneath the heady fragrance of the crisping corn. He remembered those long years gone by: how his grandmother always used conte in baking some sweet treats—that spice made from powdered China briar she would mix into her corn fritters fried in bear's oil, then sweetened with honey.

At the side of the fire the steaming coffeepot began to boil, and as quickly Sergeant Clayton tossed in two handfuls of the coarse coffee grounds, then tugged on the bail to move the pot off the dancing flames and onto the coals at the stone hearth.

Blinking his eyes with those tears of remembrance, Titus savored the earthy perfume of that frying pan bread. Corn. His father's crop. What his grandpap before him had grown in that rich bottomland of the canebrakes they cleared of every stone and tree, season after season slowly enlarging their fields. Corn. It not only fed Thaddeus Bass's family, but the stalks and tops of the harvested crop fed their horses and milch cows. Corn had fattened their hogs—which meant lard for their lamps during those long winter nights there near the frozen Ohio in Boone County. And what corn was left over after the family and the stock were properly cared for, after some had been sold and shipped south to New Orleans on the flatboats, then Thaddeus, like his father before him, would boil down into whiskey mash for proper occasions like birthing, marrying, or funerals: time when a man was planted back in that very ground where he had spent his life in toil.

"Don't ever let me catch you spitting in my fireplace again!" his mam had scolded him that first time Titus so proudly attempted to show off his new skill at the ripe old age of five and a half.

"Your mama uses them ashes," his pap had explained, sharply yanking the youngster to his knee. *"Uses 'em to make her prized hominy, Titus. So don't ever let either of us catch you spitting in the fireplace. G'won outside with that sort of thing."*

How he fondly recalled her frumenty, their wooden bowls heaped with boiled grains of wheat served with a topping of hot milk and sugar. Not at all like the rye mush a working man had to settle for in the tippling houses along the banks of the Ohio, back there in St. Louis. Nothing more than meal, salt, and water brought to a boil before it was set before him—nothing more than animal fodder to fill his belly until a midday meal.

And, oh: his mam's crackling bread. How his mouth began to water with the remembrance as he settled on a half-log bench across from Lancaster, right beside the fireplace where Culpepper tended to the hoecakes. Crackling bread: made tasty with a crisp crust, flavored with generous handfuls of leaf-hard hog cracklings turned into the batter just before baking in the Dutch oven.

On his tongue this cold, wet morning rested the remembered taste of those meals he had not recalled in far too many years since leaving home that autumn of 1810. Only sixteen back then, but certain sure he was man enough to make out on his own. And so he had for nearly fifteen years now. Yet the memories came all the more into focus on mornings like this when he missed most the johnnycakes smeared with butter and dripping with his mam's preserves. Or all those evenings spent remembering how as a skinny child he had climbed up to sit astraddle the

top rail of the snakeline fence his pap had thrown up around their fields—
patiently watching the western fall of the sun and wondering on those yonder
places his grandpap spoke so dearly of, munching on the crackling, earthy taste of
parched corn there at the end of the day. How the coming quiet of each evening
allowed him to listen to familiar sounds of the forest softly roll across the dark,
plowed ground to reach his ears: the mournful toodle of the whippoorwill calling
out to its sweetheart, often interrupted by the abusive cry of a strident catbird.

Homespun memories were all he was left with now—especially now that he
had chosen a'purpose to be without a home of his own.

"The Missouri makes her bend to the north little more'n ten leagues upriver
from here," Sergeant Clayton reminded him later when the time had come.

He had shaken hands with Culpepper and Lancaster there that drizzly
morning as the rain became more insistent, and now Titus grasped the young
sergeant's. "You've made me welcome . . . and for that I am in your debt."

"Think nothing by it," Clayton said. "Those tales you spun of your whoring
back to St. Louis, and them wild windies that ol' feller Washburn told you of the
far wilderness—why, they made your layover with us a genuine pleasure, Mr.
Bass."

"Next time you hap to come by—maybe on your way back to St. Louie,"
Lancaster added, "I'll wager you'll have some wild windies of your own to tell us."

Turning away, Titus rose to the saddle and tugged on the mare's lead rope.
"Thanks all the same for the invite, soldiers—but I don't plan to be back this way
a'tall. Have to be something damned important—nothing less'n life and death
. . . to bring me back to St. Lou."

As the river meandered, Titus had to cross more than thirty more miles before he
reached the big bend of the Missouri, its roiling surface seeming to grow muddier
with every hour he put behind him that first long day after leaving Fort Osage.
Before the sun had climbed all that high that following morning, Titus realized
the river had changed directions for good and no longer flowed out of the west.
Now he would follow the Missouri north. Mile after mile he watched how it was
becoming even more the color of unsweetened chocolate, frothing and bobbing
with snags and clutter, tumbling with drift and refuse carried down from far
upriver.

A river become the color of the quadroon's skin. That warm-fleshed whore
who abandoned her tiny crib down on Wharf Street where she had to belong for
an hour at a time to any man with a guinea or pistole in his pocket, choosing to
have herself put up in a fancy house where she would belong thereafter to only one
wealthy Frenchman who could afford to provide himself the sweet delights his
frigid wife would no longer pleasure him with.

That color of unsweetened chocolate she was, all over. How the turbulent,
brown Missouri reminded him now of their tempestuous coupling.

As the pony picked its way along, several yards out from the brushy river-bank, and they pointed their noses north to the mouth of the Platte, Bass dug into the blanket pouch he wore slung over his shoulder. Dragging out the blue scarf the coffee-skinned quadroon gave him not all that long ago, he drank deeply of its fragrance. Disappointed to find that her scent no longer filled the cloth. Her smell was as gone as she herself was. Crumpling the scarf in his hand, angry to learn that some memories were far too fragile to last out the miles and the years, he stuffed it back into the pouch—no more did he want to think upon her and the joy she brought to his body.

Still, far easier was the chocolate-skinned whore to remember than was . . . Marissa.

There beneath the breaking clouds Titus squeezed down hard to expel the sudden appearance of Able Guthrie's daughter at the horizon of his memories. The soft, sweaty, sticky feel of her heated flesh against his as they lay that summer in her father's barn. The dusty fragrance of hay and the pungent scent of the animals rising from the stalls below them. Oh, for so long, how he had done his best to hold her image at bay, to prevent it from nibbling away at the edges of his certainty that he had done the right thing by leaving.

Opening his eyes to the spring sun, Bass scratched at the back of his neck, there beneath the brown curls at the collar of the warm shirt he had put on that morning at Fort Osage: square-armholed, drop-shouldered, sewn from flax and wool . . . hoping he had not taken on tiny varmints during his brief layover among the soldiers. He should have known better, he scolded himself—such places had the reputation of sharing lice, mites, and fleas with all visitors. All it took was but one man to bring them in.

As it had been on Ebenezer Zane's Kentucky flatboat. By the time Hames Kingsbury got the dead pilot's load of hemp, ironmongery, flour, and tobacco down to New Orleans, even Titus found himself cursed with what the boatmen affectionately called the "Scotch-Irish itch." Few, if any, of those men who made the rivers their life ever bathed in the waters of the Ohio or the Mississippi. Much less did they patronize the public baths in New Orleans's "Swamp" at journey's end. Simply put, most Kentucky boatmen of the era shunned anything that re-motely resembled soap and water.

Pretty sure of it he was, what with the way such vermin bit and burrowed, that he might well have himself a case of them already. At least one tormentor back there, and maybe as many as a handful. With a fingertip he tried to find one there at his collar, remembering how many a boatman would remove his colorful crimson bandanna to expose his neck made raw and red itself from a row of lice all lined up on the irritated flesh like a string of pearlish beads.

He brought his hand up before his eyes, staring at the louse he had captured between thumb and forefinger—then crushed it between his nails and flung it aside as the recognizable border of trees came in sight. Reining up among the brush on the bank minutes later, Bass peered across the river flowing in from the west, dumping its clear flow into the muddy Missouri.

"What the hell you figure that be?" he asked almost in a whisper as he patted the Indian pony on the side of the neck.

Bass straightened, peering to the north and west, stretching some saddle kinks out of his back. Eventually he admitted to the two horses, "I s'pose it don't matter. This here's the Missouri—and to follow it, a man's gotta cross this'un. Giddap."

With his heels he urged the pony into motion, moving along the brush, tugging on the lead rope to the mare. In no more than a half mile Bass found what he figured was a suitable place to make his crossing. Down the grassy bank and into the sparkling water, loosening up on the reins to give the pony its head— allowing it to find its own footing as it slowly took its rider deeper, step by step toward the middle of the river. Cold wicked up his boots, flowed over the top to bite at his calves, then billowed over his knees. Spring runoff soaked his thighs, saddle, and blanket by the time the pony began swimming at midstream. With every yard the horse carried him, Titus was compelled to raise his rifle all the higher until he held it high overhead.

Just as Bass began to heave himself off the back of the saddle onto the pony's haunches, ready to swim alongside the animal, the pony instead recovered its footing with a sudden start that almost jerked him free of his hold on a thick strip of latigo woven into the back of the saddle pad.

Titus came out of the water, sputtering, his right arm still held aloft with the rifle—cursing the river and the pony, cursing the soft-bottomed crossing.

On the north side the pony and mare lurched up the muddy, grassy bank as he slid off the wet saddle—ultimately cursing himself for not yanking off his shucks before plunging into the river. He slogged over to the brush, water sluicing from his clothes as he stood tying off the two horses. Their flesh quivered as Titus quickly collapsed to the grass, yanking at the waterlogged boots. Standing again to tug at the wet leather britches, he struggled to pull them off one leg at a time, and finally yanking free of the wool and flax shirt.

For those first moments he was cold, chilled to his marrow as he suffered the breeze left in the wake of last night's thunderstorm. But it wasn't long before the climbing sun began to work its eternal magic, caressing his goose-pimpled skin with its warmth. Every bead of water dippling his arms or clustered at the base of each tiny hair on his chest, across the top of his bare thighs—all of them shimmered like tiny, iridescent rainbows as the sun began to dry every one.

Raising his face toward the sky, eyes closed, "Thank you," he said quietly.

Surprised that he had. Not knowing what had come over him of that moment, causing him to offer his gratitude right out loud. Out of the corner of one eye, Titus glanced quickly at the sky, self-consciously regarding that great tumble of white-and-gray clouds dabbed against the pale-blue dome. With the rustle of the wind through newly leafed brush, he suddenly felt the presence of something greater than himself, something so immense here across the wide Missouri that it was almost impossible to comprehend.

At that moment he looked around him, certain that he was standing shamelessly naked within the sight of someone. But try as he might, he could not see, nor did he hear, another being, save for the two horses gently tearing off the green shoots at their feet as they dripped and dried in the sun, now spearing bright shafts through the breaking clouds.

This was as good a place as any, he decided. A fine spot, indeed. So from his shooting pouch he retrieved a small tin the size of his palm, then laid it among some stones where he figured he would build his fire. Titus began to scrounge among the brush for dry kindling. After the showers of the last two days, it was not all that easy to find dry wood, but eventually he had all in readiness.

From the German silver tin he removed the firesteel curved in a large and elegant *C* big enough to fit over the four fingers of his right hand. In his left he gathered some charred cloth, a bit of dried cotton boll, and the large gray chunk of flint. Striking downward on the sharp-edged stone with the firesteel, he began creating sparks, a few of which soon caught hold on the cloth, smoldering there within the boll's loose fibers. Very softly he blew on the reddish coal he had created until it burned bright enough for him to slip the char beneath the tiny cone of kindling he had stacked up right at his knees.

One by one he set bigger and bigger twigs, then broke thicker branches to lay upon the flames until he had no fear of the fire sputtering out. Quickly rubbing his hands together over the rising heat, and at long last beginning to sense the fledgling fire's warmth radiating on his chest and belly, Bass stepped over to the mare and threw back the dirty oiled Russian sheeting lashed on the off side of her packs, removing the blackened coffeepot. With the pot half-filled from the river he had just crossed, Titus set the water to boil while he went in search of some coffee among the supplies purchased back in Franklin.

With it and one of his dented cups set near his cheery fire, Bass finally draped his britches and shirt over clumps of nearby brush so the sun's rays would strike them as he waited for the water to come to a boil. Then he stretched out on the grass, flat on his back, lacing his fingers behind his head to stare up at the spring sky, savoring the crackle of the fire close by, relishing the way the gentle warmth washed down from the sky to caress his skin.

As he closed his eyes, he remembered how good it had been to slip off into the forests of Boone County, Kentucky—his grandpap's old fullstock flinter at the end of his arm, with the family's old hound, Tink, loping ahead through the dapple of sunlight and shadow as Titus sought out rabbit or squirrel, turkey, or even some venison.

Like most boys growing up there at the edge of the frontier that stretched to the west a little farther with every new year, Titus spent every moment his pap allowed him immersing himself in the woods. School and church and work behind the plow: those were the had-to's. But for most young fellas like Titus, time was never sweeter than when it was spent hunting or setting snares and deadfall traps, learning the herbs and fruits and nuts one could gather from the forest's bounty.

Most children learned early what it took to read game trails or the moss on the trees, the whorl of certain flowering plants or the caliber of the wind—all those things they must remember so they would never become lost or put themselves in danger of being hurt, alone and far from the family ground. When he and the other boys his age gathered at one farm or another, there would of course always be a tall tree to shinny up, there to lie along its wide branches and gaze down on the world below. Or the boys plunged deep into that band of thick timber and limestone bordering the Ohio River itself, where they explored sinkholes, caves, and rockhouses—imagining themselves to be river pirates or the flatboatmen who would repel any such bloody and vicious attack.

Of course, there was always the swimming hole. He smiled, remembering how he and the others had knotted an old rope to a high limb so they could swing out over the surface of the water shaded by that same tree, flinging themselves naked out through the summer air crackling with the buzz and drone of flies and mosquitoes, letting go of that rope at just the right moment so they could sail for those deliciously brief seconds totally free before they hurled downward into the cold green swimming hole.

Come a time in a young man's life—it was only the boys who went to the pool they had dammed up for swimming. As a girl's body began to change and bloom, she would no longer join her brothers and their friends.

Through his reverie Titus could hear the faint tumble of the water's first turn to a boil. And likewise felt the tingle of his own flesh stir with the memory of Amy Whistler.

How fully had she bloomed in those weeks and months before they had consummated their young passion there on a summer night beside the moonlit swimming pond. So full and soft were the curves of her, the roundness to the feel of her gliding up to him in the water . . . there beneath him where he laid her back on the grass beside the great boulders. But with that aching physical memory of the exquisite pleasure Amy brought him came also a flash point of anger at the coquette in her that had attempted to possess and corral him before he was ready to have his wings clipped, ready to be put in the wire cage the way a woman had done to his grandpap . . . the way his very own mother had imprisoned his pap.

Amy. Or Marissa. Oh, the wiles women used to snare men from the beginning of time. Roping them down with pleasures of the flesh, then later with the coming of children, and finally snaring them to stay on the land—plowed land. Land where a man walked behind an ox or mule, lashed and laboring as surely as did his beasts.

The boiling water hissed and tumbled, calling him from his reverie.

From the small pouch of pounded coffee beans Titus took a handful and flung the grounds into the pot, then carefully hooked a finger within the wire bail and dragged the pot from the edge of his fire. As the water continued to turn, Bass stood and moved off to test his wet clothing.

Dry enough they were. Into the still-damp britches he stuffed his legs, then slipped his arms into the warmth of his shirt. Around his waist he finally drew the wide belt and tightened it before kneeling at the fire, pouring himself a cup, then rocking back on his haunches to first draw in the savory fragrance of the coffee. Only then did he sip at the steaming brew.

Because the wool shirt itched when it became damp, he thought he might change back to the linen shirt. He smiled, recalling how riverboatmen like Hames Kingsbury and the rest were really no different from other men on the razor's edge of the frontier: they would wear one set of clothes until it fairly rotted off, then they promptly rooted around for something new to wear out completely in its time.

Not so very different was that from his own childhood, he mused as he sipped on the coffee there in the sun's spring light. Most young'uns had no more than one change of clothing: their everyday wear, along with those clothes saved for Sunday-morning meeting as well as those rare special celebrations of life. The marryings, birthings, and the funerals of friends and family . . . those cords of remembrance he felt still binding him to that past and that place had begun to grow thin and weak—very much like spider's silk stretched to the breaking.

It struck Titus there by the rivers' junction, now that he was here on the yonder side of the wide Missouri: he had been gone from home for almost as long as he had spent growing up in the house of his father. Considering, too, how Thaddeus Bass himself had known little else but the place where his father had set down roots before him. Yet, unlike Titus, never had Thaddeus desired to reach out, to explore, to search beyond what lay there in that small section of Boone County he plowed and planted. And that failure was something Thaddeus's son could not fathom.

Staring down at the surface of the coffee in his cup, Titus wondered now about his family. How his pap had aged. How the intervening years might have marked his mam with gray and lines. His brothers and sister—they all were grown and would surely have families of their own now. Children carrying on the family cycle on the land.

And all he had to his name were these two hand-me-down horses, his guns, and the clothes on his back, along with what little else was packed on that mare.

A shadow flitted past him across the ground, startling him. He looked up in time to catch the crimson flutter of the cardinal as it disappeared among the timber north of his fire. So he smiled.

He might not own all that much, Titus decided as he stood and gazed into the west. For certain he sure as hell didn't own much by most men's standards.

But right now—he sensed he had all of that out yonder to call his very own.

FOUR

The sheer size of the abandoned Indian camp was the first thing that struck him as he cautiously ventured in on foot, wary and watchful . . . having hidden the horses back downriver when he came across the first flurry of tracks.

But he found the village empty, deserted.

Now Bass could swallow down the lump of fear at last. His lungs felt as if he were taking his first breath in more than an hour. Titus forced his heart back down and finally emerged from the brush at the river's edge to stare across the Platte at what some band of Pawnee had left behind. Then quickly he decided he'd best backtrack and fetch up the animals. No sense swimming the river on his own.

An hour later, dripping naked in the sun after another crossing, he dismounted on the north bank among the small rings of river stone he discovered near the center of each elliptical circle of pounded grass and hardened ground. For the most part the entire camp formed a great horseshoe, the horns of its crescent opening back to the east whence he had come.

Finding a good patch of grass near the trees along the bank, Bass ground-hobbled the horses and turned back to explore this wondrous, frightening place.

More than fifty circles and all that foot-pounded earth plainly showed where this band of Indians had camped for some time this spring. At the western extent of the site Titus came across the wide trail of tracks and pole scrapings that led off to the west. They were wandering upriver.

"Maybeso they move off come the spring," he said quietly in the silence of that big country as he turned about and stepped back into the camp crescent itself.

Here the land lay painfully silent. As quiet as anything he had ever experienced in those eastern forests growing as thick as quills on a porcupine's back, as those forests he had come to know flatboating down the great waters of the Ohio and Mississippi, or walking north along the Natchez Trace.

More than two weeks had passed now since he had given wide berth to the dragoons and their Fort Atkinson. The day before he came in sight of the distant stockade, Bass had run across more and more signs of man's passing: shod hoofprints, the heel stamp of soldiers' boots, the crude cut of a wagon's iron tires slashing down into the fragile earth. Trail and scent and sign that warned he was drawing close enough to that cluster of white mankind.

Turning abruptly, Titus had pointed his nose to the west—intending to ride two, maybe three days at the most in a roundabout to give himself plenty of room around the soldier post. But late that second day after cautiously leaving the Missouri behind and striking out overland, he was surprised when his westward path brought him right into a great, wide loop in the Platte River itself before it eventually gentled him back to the north. Surprised was he to discover as well that so shallow a river could enjoy such a formidable reputation among those frontiersmen who returned to St. Louis—men like Isaac Washburn.

Had the old trapper been yanking on his leg with all his bawdy tales of everything being bigger, or faster, or just plain wilder out here in the great beyond? Or dare he consider that he had not yet reached the Platte, that this was some minor river? Yet something innate within him told Titus he could not be mistaken on it—fact was that the big dragoon's post did lay at the mouth of the Platte.

Shallow indeed, yet every bit as wide here as Washburn had claimed. So for the first time that afternoon, Titus had looked off to the west, gazing toward the river's far source. Away yonder among the distant, yet unseen mountains that gave birth to these waters. On the south bank he had knelt in the mud and grass beside the river, cupped his hands, and pulled forth a little of that mountain water. Bass looked down into it with something bordering on reverence, then brought it prayerfully to his lips.

As silt laden as it was, how much sweeter did it taste knowing he was that much closer to those high mountain snows giving birth to these waters! He drank his fill that day before turning west along the south bank of the river he knew would one day deliver him to the buffalo country, the great course of the Platte that allowed a man to pierce the kingdom of black, shaggy beasts Washburn guaranteed him ruled a great, rolling wilderness out there. How good its taste lay upon his tongue, this water from the Platte that was really all the more than a river: a magical road that would lead him to and through the buffalo ground, then ultimately deliver him to the high and terrible places few if any had ever seen.

Following the south bank another few days, Bass found the river led him back in a huge, sweeping curve to the south of west. Damn! but these western rivers could confuse and exasperate a man, he brooded. Every bit as disconcerting as a fickle woman who could turn back on herself just as soon as a man began to think he had her figured out!

First he had followed its bank into the west. Then the Platte led him north. And now it was wandering off to the south. And after all this meandering, just where in hell were those mountains that gave birth to this river, after all? A part of him prayed again that Washburn wasn't as crazed as Hysham Troost had warned Titus the aging fur trapper would prove himself to be.

Oh, the many times he had yearned to strike out due west, leaving the Platte behind—resenting himself for having to depend on the river, forced to rely on a dead man's guarantee. Now that he had come to stand beside this fabled Platte himself, he had no reason not to believe he shouldn't catch his first glimpse of the mountains rising just beyond the next stand of hills. If not them, perhaps those hills just beyond.

Indeed, Titus had left the hardwood forests behind some days back, emerging almost of a sudden onto a plain where he reined up, then slowly dropped from the saddle to stand in utter awe at the rolling immensity of what lay before him. From that point on it was clear the trees no longer grew in great mats of thick, meandering forest blanketing hillside and valley alike. Instead, the green lay in clusters dotting the great tableland, confined to pockets and ravines wrinkling the countryside, the emerald-green vegetation for the most part tracing the path of streams and creeks and what narrow, gurgling rivers fed the flat, shallow expanse of the Platte itself.

At that night's fire Titus had sensed he had just crossed an even more indelible border than was the barrier of the Missouri River itself. Oh, with his own sixteen-year-old eyes he had marveled as the great eastern forests had given way to rolling delta while the riverboat crew steered their craft past the Walnut Hills and old Fort McHenry, floating down the lower reaches of the Mississippi. Yet, for the most part, the immense trees and timbered forests still predominated those riverbanks and the high bluffs where great-winged birds took flight from wide, stately branches bedecked with long gray beards of Spanish moss.

But out here the trees no longer grew as tall, no more were their trunks as big around. No more did he recognize the familiar leaf of the elm, the maple, the varieties of oak. Almost as if this harsh and difficult land stunted what was allowed to grow upon its own breast.

"Water," he had decided.

It was all because of water. Or more so the want of it. Back east vegetation grew in abundance—a green, leafy, shady profusion. But out here the brush and trees struggled for want of water, sending roots deep to penetrate the sands for what moisture the land had captured during the passing of spring thunderstorms.

So as he had stood there at that margin of immense hardwood forest thinning itself to become the borderland that would take him on west into his yondering quest, Titus found himself liking this land best. Far better than that to the east and south was it. Back there he found it hard to see long distances, so thick did the vegetation grow. But here—yes, from here on out—a man could gaze so far that he just might see halfway into tomorrow itself.

Beneath the floppy brim of his old beaver-felt hat, Titus had stared across the distance, determining that to survive in such a land he would have to train his eyes to take in more. A man back east, why—he didn't have to concern himself with more than a few rods of open ground . . . the distance across a glen or meadow, before he plunged back into the tangle of thick and verdant forest.

But out here a man had to accustom his eyes to measuring the heft of great distance. He must teach himself to read all manner of things from far off. The course of rivers and streams recognized only by their dim green outline disappearing at the distant horizon. Too, a man had to better read the game he would pursue across great distances—startling the whitetail out of the brush and across the open ground, the turkey and quail that roosted where they found shade and protection along the water courses. And he reminded himself he must make certain his eyes always moved from one point of the compass to the next. Constantly—for there were other men who traveled this wild, open country too, seeking game, horses, plunder, and scalps.

Readily did he see that in a land such as this, a man must be vigilant in assuring that he did not stand out against the horizon, against the country itself.

Then it had struck him. How did he ever come to know such a startling fact of life and death?

That core of him that had been honed, ground to a fine edge in the eastern forests of his youth—then all but ignored, lying fallow and forgotten there in St. Louis beside the Mississippi all those years—he sensed that core of him had been pricked, aroused, enlivened anew in his arrival at the edge of such a vast wilderness. Again, something within him gave thanks to that same force that traced out the course of rivers, the comings and goings of the wild animals with each season, the force that strummed some nerve with a responsive chord, awakening something buried within him after so long a time of mute deafness.

In looking about him then, as if to weigh the presence of that force far greater than mere man would ever be, Titus squinted—studying distance. Hefting the sheer meaninglessness of time out here in all that abundance of space. Realizing that he feared. Knowing that his fear was the selfsame as that of the wild things.

Indeed, his instincts told him this was a far more dangerous place than that eastern land of the Shawnee, Mingo, and Chickasaw. For here there might be no place for a man to hide.

At the root of him, a tiny part of Titus had yearned for the protection of those thick forests, those great bulking shoulders of gray limestone jutting from the red earth where one might take cover, there to lie in wait for game or man. And he remembered the smell of that country. Damp enough that a woodsman could come to know the scent of saltpeter caves—homing in on them with nothing more than his nose, there to gather some of that mineral for making his own gunpowder.

Bass had trembled slightly, staring out at this vastness he did not know, a space and wilderness that he did not understand. Back there, in those eastern forests, he had grown up learning what it took to live well. He knew which was the chestnut oak a man gathered for its tanbark: that wood containing the yellowish tannin he could use in curing the hides of the creatures he shot and skinned. A man likewise knew to look for white oak, harvested for barrel staves.

A child spent his youth back there among the hemlocks dotting the ripplewalled sandstone quarries lying among the canebrakes. On the high ridges of the pine forests, cedar jutted from the pale limestone walls. A world of many colors that was made for a child: yellowing poplars reaching for the sky among the opalescent yellow of hickory and chestnut and beech, the red and gold of maple and sweet gum, the deep bloody crimson of black gum and dogwood. Even the leafy oaks, his favorite, often lingered until spring, their color gradually changing from autumnal red, to bronze, and then to the brown of decay as they clung to their branches.

But out here an endless plain of green lay stretched beneath that forever blue of the sky. Across it—the scar that marked the Pawnees' route west.

All around him in this abandoned camp stood the remnants of their meat-drying racks and the litter of slender shreds of hides crusted with hair. He knew what they had been doing here: scraping the skins of animals to remove all the excess fat and flesh as close as they could to the edge of each hide, that narrow border left raw, then trimmed away and discarded. Small animals—deer and antelope. Now that winter had released this land, the people living upon it would no longer have to survive on the small creatures.

Now they would hunt the shaggy beasts.

For some distance around the camp Bass could see how the ground was trampled, the grassy swales cropped by a herd of ponies he figured were filling their own bellies on the new green shoots after a long, long winter. Then he turned to look at the two animals delivering him there. While the mare ate and ate every bit as much as did the Indian pony, she did not appear to flourish on her diet of spring grass. Not that she had noticeably weakened, but beneath the packsaddle his fingertips had begun to discern the emerging ridge of backbone, the faint corduroy of the old girl's ribs.

And in staring out at the wide scar of trampled ground that disappeared over the rolling hills to the west, Titus wondered how smart he would be in following that Indian trail carved beside the Platte. What with the grass eaten down, perhaps not so wise a choice for feeding his hungry animals.

Yet something primal told him to follow their trail . . . for these Pawnee most surely were gone in search of the same shaggy beasts they had hunted ever since a time long forgotten.

That afternoon, not long after leaving the abandoned village, good sense convinced Bass to recross to the south side of the river, where he pushed on ever more cautiously, his eyes searching the ground that lay before him, hoping to find a knoll tall enough that would allow him to locate the Indian village on the march somewhere out before him. How far ahead of him were they? How long had it really been since they had passed through this piece of country?

Growing frustrated, he admitted he did not know. Then cursed himself for not knowing how to know. Surely there must be some means by which a man would tell from the age of the hoofprints on that wide trail, from the dryness of the limbs used to build their meat-drying racks, from the depth and age and texture of the ashes in those half-a-hundred fire pits lying at the center of those rings of trampled ground.

There must be some way to learn—there had to be . . . before a man was forced to learn his lessons all too late. The way he had learned about Chickasaw warriors all too well back in his sixteenth summer. Learning all he had ever wanted to know.

But he was nearly twice as old now. And that angered him: what had he learned in those intervening years that was of any good to him now? How to get a Kentucky flatboat and its crew of randy, hardy men down the great Mississippi with its cargo, which could be sold for a rich man's ransom in the bustling, multihued seaport of New Orleans? How to love a woman who warned him not to—a woman who one day left without warning, without a word of explanation? How to build a barn, from cutting down the trees for lumber to seating the pegs a man used instead of iron nails on the frontier? All that and a little something of the black art of fire and iron, of sweat and muscle? Perhaps that most of all: from Able Guthrie and Hysham Troost, he had come to know how to bend metal to his will, fashion it to the task at hand.

Yet in the end Titus had learned best just how deeply satisfied a man could become in a job done well. For its own sake. Not for the faint, fleeting praise of others. But the true value of his toil, his effort, his devotion to the task.

Out here, he realized, there were no others to judge him. As well, there were no others to depend upon. Very simply, if he was to make it, it was up to him alone to feed, clothe, and protect himself from the elements . . . from the savage men who roamed this savage wilderness.

With his realization Bass sensed his own personal power grow as he put mile after mile behind him, as the east and everything of it fell farther and farther at his back. But in this great test of solitude and oneness with himself, he knew he had to come to terms with and control the loneliness. There were, after all, times in his life when he could recall wanting company so badly that . . . that it hurt more than he cared to remember.

Just as he was fleeing all the hold the east had on him, so was Titus attempting to escape that need in him to depend upon others, that loneliness so keen it often caused him great pain. So it was he realized he needed to keep his mind out of those dark places that made him long for any of what had been abandoned back there, to yearn for any of those left behind.

Those days seeped one into the next like the spring storms that he watched approaching out of the west, clouds tumbling one over the other as they drew nigh—clouds gone white to gray and gray to black. Yet despite the storms, each new day the air warmed that much more, and the land gently rose beneath him.

One morning birthed so clear, so quiet, the entire prairie seemed a bell jar of silence—no other living thing in sight but him and the two horses, no birds above nor four-legged critters bounding off through the tall, waving grass, no stir of life down among the water courses that lay in the land-wrinkles lying against the sides of every hill.

For the life of him, it appeared the country was changing, evolving again. Not near as abruptly as the land had converted itself from thick forest to open plain where the trees clustered here and there only . . . but as he turned to gaze back, he was all the more sure the land now became something unto itself. Land only now, denied of forests and thick stands of timber. Forgotten by all but the hardiest of narrow streams and shallow rivers. Cast here essentially alone beneath the great pale-blue dome of sky, the land came to exist of and for itself. Beyond him the hills rolled up in the distance to abruptly become striated bluffs topped with the waving feathers of the tall grass. He felt himself shrinking in all that vastness—this sudden compression suffered here beneath the endlessness of the sky as it and the land stretched on and on, and on.

Like nothing he had ever seen before back there. Like nothing he could have prepared himself for.

The infinite quality of it permeated him all the more because his pace seemed so agonizingly slow when measured against the vastness of the landscape. There were days when it felt as if he had barely moved from morning get-up, coffee and breakfast, until he chose a campsite that night where he curled up in blankets as the stars winked into view overhead. For more than two weeks now he put at least twenty-five, sometimes more than thirty, miles behind him in a day. Yet in country such as this, that sort of travel often left a man to turn around and look back upon reaching his evening's camp—able to see some feature of the land that showed where he had crawled from his bed that very morning.

So open and without borders was this kingdom. So utterly vast that few landmarks really existed. Little was there beyond the Platte and the endless river bluffs to excite his attention, to prick his interest. Then the land became monotonous enough to lull him to sleep in the saddle as the pony gentled him west, always keeping the south bank of the muddy, meandering Platte in sight. From time to time he would open his eyes into slits, staring off this way and that to assure that he was the only thing moving in all that vastness, then let his eyelids droop once more as he continued to rock in that old saddle he had repaired for Isaac Washburn.

The afternoon was aging a handful of days later—the sun fallen enough that it had just slipped beneath the brim of his hat to where it scoured his face as it continued its descent into the west. He had been dozing lightly, off and on mostly, as the pony's gait kept him nestled in sleep.

Yet now he awoke, aware of the dryness in his mouth, and tried to swallow. And found his tongue so parched, he could barely force any spit down his throat.

Water was all that consumed his thoughts.

Titus kicked his right leg over the saddle horn, landing on the left side of the pony even before it stopped—both of them having reached the banks of the Platte at the same time. As he collapsed to his knees and dunked his head under the murky water, Bass could not remember ever being any thirstier. When he brought his head out, gasping for air, the packmare stood up to her fetlocks in the river on his left, lapping at the water. The pony drank at his right shoulder.

Stuffing his face back into the Platte, Titus drank until his belly ached, then plopped back on his rump there in the water, surveying what lay around him. A horse on either side, the animals lapped their fill, stirring the murky bottom. As he squinted into the late-afternoon sun, he spotted it.

For a moment Titus just stared at the bleached skeleton lying akimbo on the nearby riverbank, upstream. Stared at the way the sun slanted through the huge prison bars of its rib cage, the sheer bulk of its massive backbone. What had to have been a monstrous creature of immense weight.

Finally he convinced himself to move from that spot, almost afraid the skeleton would prove to be nothing more than some heat mirage that would disappear should he attempt to move in its direction. Slowly rising from the cool water of the Platte, Bass stood and slogged upstream more than ten yards—his eyes locked hypnotically on the skeleton. The closer he got, the more he could see of the length of it. Surely, the creature had fallen here a long, long time ago—so white, so sun bleached were its bones. Its final resting place lay far enough up the sharp bank of the river that the Platte had not been able to claim that fallen creature, nor its skeleton, even with the capricious spring floods.

So here it had lain just inches above the river's surface, now only an arm's length away as he came to a stop. As the Platte continued to lap around his knees, Bass reached out a hand, his breathing became shallow, his heart hammering as he took in the sheer size of the skull, the immense span between the horn tips. Oh, he had seen oxen before that might well have a wider spread of horn from tip to tip—but never had Titus laid eyes on a skull so large. Great, gaping eye sockets, one of which stared blankly back at him from its riverbank grave.

From the back of that skull his eyes marveled at the vast sweep of the backbone, then slowly traced the immense amalgamation of vertebrae that began to diminish in size over the rear flanks and finally into the tail root. It was then he discovered his mouth had gone dry again, and he found himself trembling.

At the bank he squatted beside the bones—touching, running his fingers over the huge plates of skull, tracing the horn core, down the snout, then back over the rise and fall of its massive backbone. Could this . . . could this be?

And he looked up at the far bank, finally staring off in the direction both he and the sun were headed that afternoon. Were they out there, somewhere close at hand?

Titus looked back at the skeleton, positioned so that its head pointed down toward the water, lying on its right side. The massive legs stilled in death. How he wanted to believe. Enough to reach out and hold the one horn core, gripping it in fear of his hope's disappearing like a desert mirage.

Nothing else could it be. What other monstrous, four-legged creature was there? Even this bare skeleton was more impressive than his dreams of it had ever been.

Buffalo.

At one time they had been right here, Titus told himself. Right where he sat, stilled to utter wonder.

Perhaps he would find they had been driven farther west now by the creeping advance of white settlement. Oh, how he cursed those in places like Franklin—it was just as he had always feared: to lay eyes on the buffalo would mean a man had to travel far toward the setting sun.

But at least they had been here of a time past.

He sat there in the grass and mud long enough that the Indian pony and mare slogged up to stand near him as the Platte continued its relentless march past them all. Past the skeleton of a creature and time long gone by. Eventually he stood—reluctantly. And touched the bleaching skeleton one last time before sweeping up the rein, stuffing his soaked boot into the stirrup, and mounting.

It was a long time before he grew aware of his leather britches, how they began to chafe as they dried. So long had he been riding, thinking—dwelling on that skeleton and nothing else as the pony carried him west while the sun disappeared and the air grew cool, the mosquitoes rising like vapors along the riverbank where he eventually decided to stop for the night.

That evening, when he finally closed his eyes beside his small fire and pulled the blankets up over his shoulders, Titus could not remember for sure if he had eaten an evening meal, or what had consumed his time that night—only that his thoughts were on the unshakable beyond that lay just past the next hill, on the far side of the next bend in the great Platte River, on yonder through that country he had to endure until he ultimately discovered where the buffalo would be found.

More than myth. More than mere skeleton. Where they were flesh and bone, hide and horn.

How many more days, how many more weeks of riding would it take until he had put the last vestiges of white man's forts and settlements and civilization far enough behind him . . . all the distance it would take before he discovered his first living, breathing buffalo? How well had he come to understand that the forts and outlying settlements, the white man himself, all were the greatest enemies to the wild creature he sought.

But it had been so long now, he ruminated as he eventually drifted off to sleep that night—so many weeks and countless miles since he had left the Missouri and the last bastions of white civilization all behind.

When would he ever possess the answers to those questions he had carried inside him for more than half his lifetime?

When would his mortal prayers finally be answered?

Late of the morning two days later he sensed the breeze come up, relishing its cooling touch across his cheek as it swept beneath the wide brim of the low-crowned hat that for the most part protected his face from the unforgiving sun in this open country. Hell, it was about all the shade to be found out here: for the past two days there hadn't been trees big enough for a man to squat under and get out of the sun. What shade there was, the three of them were making for themselves: right below the horses' bellies, and right below his hat's floppy brim.

The pony snorted, jostling him awake with a start. Jehoshaphat—hadn't it been a good dream too! His nose nestled down between the quadroon's breasts where the sweat pooled and he could taste the salty earthiness of her coffee-skinned body as he crawled atop the woman in that ramshackle Wharf Street house of pleasure built crib upon tiny crib.

Immediately his hand tightened reflexively around the rifle laid upon his thighs, his eyes blinking as they came open in the late-morning light. Turning his head to the south, he quickly scanned the distant horizon, then turned to the right, studying the abrupt, low bluffs that bordered the river near at hand.

"What the hell you wake me for?" he demanded of the Indian pony as he loosened his white-knuckle grip on the rifle's stock, slipped the reins into his right hand along with the weapon, then patted the horse along the neck. "I s'pose you caught yourself falling asleep too—that it, girl?"

She seemed to roll her eyes back at him.

"Yeah, I know. Hot as hell, ain't it? And the way I figger it—this country gonna get hotter afore we get higher and cooler."

As he said it, Titus cocked his head, peering up from beneath the wide brim of his dark-brown hat to find the offending yellow orb warming him to sleep at the same time it made him more thirsty than he had ever been in his life. Licking his dry, cracked lips, he mentally cursed the sun and its incessant heat, then blinked again and turned away from it, praying for more of that cooling wisp of breeze.

It was then that he saw them. Far off in the distance. Black specks swirling across the blue sky, off to the north and west of him. As the ponies plodded on, he watched, becoming almost hypnotized by the way the flock swooped and dived, then wheeled about and rose in the sky once more. Black specks diverging for but a moment, scattering like water striders on the surface of a Kentucky pond—then suddenly congealing in an ever-darker mass as they came down in a loud fluttering of wings, all of them disappearing from view.

His throat went even drier. That was the first great flock of birds he had seen like that. They must be tiny, for they had no real form at this distance. One of them would have been all but invisible, he decided as he reined the pony gently to the north, toward the river. Maybe even a few of them would still have trouble making themselves visible. But the innumerable masses of them flocking together in that one black cloud across the spring blue was enough to capture any man's attention.

As he reached the water's edge and halted the animals, Bass saw the faint puffing of dust rise beyond the bluff, a dirty smudging of the blue horizon far beyond his line of sight.

"Shit," he grumbled.

Angry at himself, Titus sat there a moment in the saddle, watching those birds rise again, swoop to the north, climb ever higher to the cloudless sky, then sweep back to the south before settling once more behind the bluff.

What stirred that dust? What caused those birds to take to flight like they did—spooked perhaps, then descending to roost once again?

Heart thumping, afraid he had made the last mistake of his life . . . yes, Bass was angry with himself for all but bumping into the rear of the Indian village after so many days, weeks now, of taking such pains to avoid the Pawnee. So damned many miles during which he had been so very careful that if he had a fire, he built it beneath one of the rare leafy trees where the branches would disperse the smoke, or beneath an overhanging shelf of a ravine where he could again hide himself, the glow of his fire, and his camp for another night. Just enough fire dug down in a hole to boil some coffee.

Still, there had been those nights when something in his gut told him he'd best make it a cold camp: lying up with the horses close enough that he could swing atop the pony and make a run for it if fate dictated that he would be discovered there in the dark beneath the prairie stars. Suspicious enough, even afraid enough too there at times, that he only traveled at night for more than eight days—back there along the Platte after first running across the village site.

Those tepee rings and meat racks and the size of that trail had been enough to scare him. Hell, just such a sight was enough to pucker any thinking man's bunghole.

He'd seen for himself how the Chickasaw stole in to work over their enemies—night creatures that they were, sneaking on board that flatboat as Ebenezer Zane's men lay tied up on the far side of the Mississippi. Yes, Titus had seen with his own eyes just how bloody ruthless Indians could be . . . and from Isaac Washburn's accounts of his own cross-country trek with Hugh Glass last year, these river Pawnee might well be all the worse than those Mississippi Chickasaw.

There was simply no taking chances. A younger man might, and lose his hair in the bargain. Hell, who was he kidding anyway? If he was dumb enough to pull a stunt like heading out to the far mountains on his own, then he just might be stupid enough to get himself in some big trouble.

"Damn," he muttered in exasperation, slamming a palm down on the saddle horn as he stared at that rising, swirling dust cloud.

That's what had happened, he decided. No doubt about it, he had run right up on the rear of that village moseying upriver on the north bank as the season warmed, likely searching for new hunting grounds. And here he was, traipsing right along behind that village until he'd run right smack into them.

Was it run, or turn back?

Turning to look left, then right, he decided this south bank of the shallow river was not the place to hide out the rest of the day. Over there, across the Platte, the bluffs rose, cut by sharp-sided ravines where he might find a place for himself and the animals until nightfall. Only then would he chance recrossing to the south bank and hurrying wide around them. Get in front of those Pawnee where he would not have to worry about bumping into them again.

It sounded as good as any idea he'd ever had as he got down from the saddle, threw up the stirrup fender, and slipped his fingers beneath the cinch. Tugging, he figured it was tight enough still. Likewise he checked the cinch and straps on the mare's packsaddle. When he had stripped off his clothes and stuffed them under the packsaddle's ropes, Titus figured he had them all ready for another crossing and remounted.

Nudging the pony upstream, Bass soon found a wide, sandy slope pocked with hundreds of huge prints. It was there he stopped, the horses' hooves just barely in the water, as he studied the route across the river to the far bluffs more than two hundred yards beyond. Again he looked down at the damp hoofprints embedded in the moist sand. Then again out to the river, studying that brush emerging from sandbars and islands in the middle of the Platte, brush that barely poked its head above the turbulent flow at this season of mountain runoff far to the west.

"Awright," he said quietly to them. "Let's go."

Just get across before anyone spotted them there among the brush and stunted trees on the bank.

They hadn't gone but a third of the way across when the pony suddenly volved its head around and tried to peer back at its rider, eyes wide as clay mug-bottoms. On all sides around the three of them, the water seemed to boil, alive with silt and stinging sand. Then the pony stumbled on the shifting bottom, going down. It reemerged from the water with its rider, both of them snorting water, muddy silt gushing from its muzzle. Bass coughed, spitting sand, his eyes gritty.

Then the horse got its footing with a jerk and fought hard at the reins to whirl about in that moment, straining to head back to the south bank rather than to push on any farther, any deeper.

"Goddammit!" he growled, yanking to snub up the rein, sawing on it with all his might as the pony fought against him, twisting nose around into the current.

Water immediately swept over the pony's head once more. In the next heartbeat it felt as if the bottom came out from under them as the animal lost its footing on the roiling river bottom, legs clawing desperately at nothing but murky water, head bobbing frantically into the muddy current that rushed into its eyes and nostrils, streaming over Titus with a persistent tug that threatened to shove him loose, to unhorse him in the middle of that great river.

As he continued to cuss and grumble, spit and spew—one hand on the rein and the other on the rifle held over his head—Bass's gut tightened on reflex. He was frightened—not knowing what to do about all that was going on beneath him, around him . . . unable to do a damned thing for the animal he rode as it fought the bit and refused his commands.

Now it became all he could do to hang on to the pony as the water swept him backward, off the cantle of the saddle. As the animal lunged forward into the murky water, the rifle went under as he clung desperately, that solitary arm straining against the muscular neck as the pony thrashed its head from side to side, fighting to free itself from the watery prison, from this strong eddy that forced the animal ever farther into the muddy current as they sidestepped deeper and deeper into the heart of the river . . . all while the wild-eyed mare whinnied and neighed behind them—her head bobbing barely above the froth as the Platte's force heaved against her two great packs, tugging her farther and farther downstream from him.

Sideways in the stream he clung to the Indian pony with one arm around its neck, the long, thick lead rope to the packmare burning that bare hand as the current tugged and hurtled the mare away from him. Stretched across the surface of the mighty Platte, he felt himself swallow more and more of the gritty water, drowning his cries of terror.

God—how he hated deep water!

He had to let go of one or the other . . . then the decision was made for him as the river's force pulled his desperate grip from the Indian pony's mane. He let go the mare's lead rope next, sensing the relief in his rope-burned hand, his strength failing as he desperately hugged the rifle to his chest, locked within both arms. His head just above water, Titus spun around slowly in the current, capturing one last glimpse of the pack animal as she bobbed out of the brown, frothy current, then went down again as she was wheeled in a tight circle beneath her heavy packs.

"Damn you, now!" he twisted his head to shout at the Indian pony behind him as it clawed for a moment at the air with its two forelegs.

He just might make it to the pony if he could stroke with one arm, try swimming toward the horse—get hold of the animal's neck. Then he was spun about again. Felt something beneath one foot that must surely be the bottom . . . but as quickly it fell away again, and he slid under the water with the heavy rifle still gripped in his hand like life itself.

Another man's words he remembered now as the water took him and the rifle, closing in over him—grit forcing him to clench his eyes tight as he tried again to yell out in numbing terror. Finding he could only sputter with a mouthful of murky, silt-laden water. Washburn had told him about this shifting bottom. Warned him about the quicksands that could spell danger to any man crossing the Platte.

"Try, goddammit!"

The words echoed in his memory, recalling how his pap had hollered to him as a small, skinny youngster that summer afternoon Titus had jumped into a riverside pool too deep for him. Remembering how he caught fleeting glimpses of his father and the others on the Ohio riverbank as Titus bobbed up and down, arms flailing as he fought for air, struggled to stay on the surface.

"You gotta try, goddammit!"

He was crying now—the burn of memory hot in his eyes. Knowing his pap was not there to dive in and drag him out of the Platte as he had been that fateful spring day so many, many years before. The last glimpse Titus had of his pap—watching his father yanking off his big boots and jerking down the galluses from his shoulders as he shucked out of his heavy canvas britches before leaping in after his eldest son.

"Do it your own self, Titus!"

With the one arm he began to stroke, wanting to open his eyes, daring not as the swirling sand slapped and scratched his face.

"I'm coming, boy! I'm coming for you!"

Bass felt something huge and powerful brush against him in the raging current, hurtling him aside—and knocking out what little air he had left in his lungs. Titus rolled over in the water, there just below the surface . . . but he kept on swinging with that one free arm, feeling his tired muscles grown so damned heavy. Weighing him down, dragging at him from that shifting, sandy, murky bottom where the darkness gathered and the mud conspired to bury him.

With that solitary arm he fought like he had never fought before. And suddenly burst back to the surface for a fleeting moment in time—blinking his stinging eyes against the sand and the foam, feeling the warm wind brush his cheek.

"I'm here, boy!"

Oh, how he had clung to his pap then as Thaddeus had dragged him to the shore. "I'm right here now, son. Just hold on to me and ever'thin' be awright."

One yard at a time Titus dragged the arm through the thickening water, back under the surface as the river rolled him over onto his side . . . praying to feel the air at his cheeks once more—beginning suddenly to catch glimpses of that big, shady clearing back in Boone County, scenes so frighteningly clear and vivid behind the eyelids he clamped shut so fiercely that he knew he was dying. Quick little vignettes of his old hound, Tink . . . the copper-muzzled mule his pap used to pull stumps . . . those elusive gray squirrels he hunted whenever he dared run away . . . the dark, deep grave where they laid his grandpap to the old man's final rest. Remembering suddenly how that had been the very first time he ever remembered thinking on this thing called death. So afraid of it then as a youngster.

So terrified that it finally had him now.

Then he burst into the wind. Spewing dirty, murky water in a gush from his lungs that screamed out—sucking in air as he bobbed back down into the current, blinking his eyes . . . and catching a glimpse of the far bank.

There was no one there. Not his pap. Not his mam. Not none of the others that day so long, long ago. It was not the Ohio. This was the bank of the Platte— bare, but beckoning. Urging him on.

Clumsily switching the rifle to his left hand below the surface, Titus began to stroke with the right arm—by far his stronger—pulling himself yard by yard toward the north bank, shoved relentlessly downriver, until he felt the sandy bottom drag beneath his toes.

With that first attempt to stand on the slowly shifting bottom, he slipped and nearly went under again. But on his second try he managed to lunge up on his hands and knees, suddenly heaving forward—vomiting dirty water.

Again and again . . . then at last he emptied his belly, coughed painfully with that gritty sting at his throat, and struggled to his feet, something beyond him compelling Titus to slog the rest of the way out of the churning Platte all crouched over, his stomach in spasms, chest gasping still, coughing up even more of the river's grit.

At the edge of the water Titus collapsed, clutching the rifle against him as he slowly regained his breath. As he rolled over on his side his stomach brought up a last heave of the bile and sand. Dragging a hand across his messy bearded chin, Titus caught sight of the packmare's head far downstream as she fought her way within the grasp of the river, bobbing now and then in the roiling current.

Pushing himself up from the sandy, grassy bank, his elbow slipped as he struggled to rise, spilling down on his knees again. Bass grumbled a curse as he hauled himself back up, coughing and spitting as he used the rifle as a crutch to stand. His legs felt so weary, they almost did not respond to his commands as he swung his bare arms, hacking away at the brush, fighting his way through the tangle of undergrowth to struggle up the side of the bank, where he immediately turned to hobble downstream.

Desperation pulled him onward when his muscles threatened to fail. From time to time he caught a brief glimpse of the mare through the maze of leafy brush as the current drew her closer and closer to the north bank, swimming with all her might against the river that pushed downstream faster than she was making any headway toward the north bank.

For only a moment did he stop, parting the brush with a hand and the long fullstock rifle, peering upstream and down for some glimpse of the Indian pony. Squinting against the harsh sunlight glittering from the frothy, muddy surface, Bass could not find a clue to what happened to the horse . . . then he heard the distant whinny. His attention snapped back to the packmare far, far downstream now.

Through the brush that clawed at his face and the backs of his hands, raking his bare white flesh . . . in and out of the thick, soggy mud that relentlessly pulled at each one of his feet, dragging each foot out with a sucking sound as he struggled on, Titus hurried despite the straining wheeze in his chest, the terrible, fiery pain in his weakening legs. He heard the packmare cry out again.

No more could he see her, desperately fearing she had whinnied that one last time before the river had conquered her final shred of strength and pulled her under. All that weight in those packs. And she already so old.

But perhaps he could . . . dare he hope? Trusting to nothing but luck? Maybe he would find her carcass snagged on some river debris downstream and from the packs take what he needed to somehow survive in this open, endless, unforgiving land. He pushed on through the brush that clawed bloody welts along every inch of his flesh—downriver, downriver . . .

When at last he spotted her, the mare lay with her rump still in the river. One side of her packs had torn loose, the ropes floating on the Platte's surface like leafless grapevine. Sensing the coming of even greater despair, Titus told himself that at least he had some of his plunder. No animals, but he wouldn't be entirely naked, completely destitute here in the wilderness. It was cheering enough to help him lunge through the brush onto the sandy bank. To get his hands on what he had left—now things would not be all so bad—

She lifted her head wearily and stared at him with one big eye a moment, causing him to jerk to a sudden halt there on the sand. As he watched, the mare struggled to drag her rear legs beneath her and strained forward, then back, grueling work to rise on her forelegs. In utter shock he stood frozen, staring down the sharp-cut bank at the horse, unable to speak as the tears welled up in his eyes and streaked the mud on his cheeks as they tumbled into his sand-caked beard and mustache.

How she had survived . . . hell—how he had survived! Erupting into action, he heaved himself off the grassy bank to the muddy sand where she fought to stand on the uneven, soggy ground. Titus snatched hold of the lead rope, tugging on it, calling out to her, offering what encouragement he could—then he burst back along her side to heave against the last of the two packs that had to be weighing her down.

Wearily she got the hind legs under her and stood, shuddered in sheer fatigue, then obediently plodded up the bank, leaving Bass behind to stand in wonder at her.

To that moment he had considered her nothing more than an aging plodder—a good and gentle horse for children to ride, perhaps for nothing more strenuous than a slow carriage through the countryside surrounding St. Louis. But now he marveled at her strength and resolve, how she turned slowly at the top of the bank to look back at him there with the Platte River lapping at his ankles, mud splattered from his toes to his armpits.

There she shuddered again and tossed her head from side to side, flinging muddy phlegm from her nostrils and shaking gritty water from her coat and the one pack clinging to her back that made her stand off balance.

As soon as he joined the mare on the sunny bank, Bass looped an arm over her neck, patting the great, graceful animal he had given up for lost beneath her burden as the river seized them all.

"You s'pose we lost the Injun pony?" he whispered near the mare's ear.

Then he sighed and turned away slightly, the pain of it all threatening to overwhelm him. "Maybeso we ought'n go have ourselves a look to be certain."

Wearily he shifted the one pack so that it sat more squarely atop her broad back, then took up the lead rope as she turned about to plod back downstream behind Bass.

After something on the order of two miles he found the carcass. The Indian pony lay snagged in a quiet pool the Platte had formed near its northern bank after the spring runoff had laid up a tangled dam of drift timber and snags. After tying off the mare, Titus plunged into the shallow water, coming to a halt by the pony's head—still hopeful that the pony would somehow be alive, just as he had found the mare. Slowly he dragged the head around so he could look into its eyes. And lost all hope when he found them already glazing in death.

Crying out with a low sob now that the horse's death was real, vivid, and immediate, Bass carefully slid from beneath the pony's muzzle and dragged his muddy legs under him. At the animal's side he struggled with the twisted, mud-caked cinch in frustration until he finally freed the strap. After several attempts Titus finally succeeded in tugging the saddle from the dead horse's back. Followed by the heavy, soggy blanket, he dragged both up the bank and flung down in utter exhaustion.

As if she somehow understood the fate of the pony, the mare tossed her head, then inched closer to lower her nose, sniffing at the saddle. She snorted and turned away, returning to browse among the leafy brush.

Again he heaved the wet saddle and blanket, dropping them farther up the bank near his rifle, then collapsed himself to the damp grass in the bright midday light. He sat there for a long time, barely able to move until he realized his skin was beginning to burn.

With agonizing slowness he went to the mare and found only his shirt had survived the tug and pull of the river. No leather britches nor his boots. In exasperation he yanked loose the ropes and let the last heavy pack drop to the ground, where he fell upon it—tearing it apart until he found his old pair of wool britches and three pair of Isaac Washburn's moccasins.

Then he remembered—the dust. The Pawnee close at hand. Scrambling through the packs, he found the tin of powder kept dry in the river crossing. In another pouch he found Washburn's pair of old pistols. Tearing rags from his patching material, Bass hurriedly began pulling the loads in his heavy weapons: dragging out the heavy lead balls with sheer muscle and a rifleman's screw he set in the end of his ramrod, replacing powder, too, after carefully drying the pans and reoiling the barrels.

He was surprised to find that little effort sapped a lot of what he had left for strength. So he sat there a long time with the rifle and pistols at hand, listening for sounds of approaching enemy, staring at the muddy river that had stolen so much from him—yet in the end that river had spat out both him and the packmare. Was he to be angry . . . or grateful?

Remembering those memories of drowning. Sensing the same tug of warring feelings for the man who had fathered him, pulled him from the Ohio. Resentful of both Thaddeus and the Platte. Yet finding himself so grateful that in the end both had spat him free to carry on as he alone chose to carry on.

It was sometime later as the sun slipped out of midsky when he became aware of the swooping, noisy flock of birds once more. Perhaps they had always been there at the corner of his vision and he just did not pay heed and notice them. Was it their distant squawking cries, or the great ripples they made upon the aching blue overhead, or even the shadows they made of themselves winging back and forth across the land beyond those first hills?

Whatever it was, he watched now—aware that time had slipped past him as he sat regarding the river like time itself: there, then suddenly here at hand right before him, but gone immediately.

"C'mere, girl," he called out as he wearily rose to his feet.

Dragging up the saddle blanket, he wrung it out best he could, kneeling to knead what water he could from it before flinging it atop the mare's packsaddle. With a lot of effort he redistributed what he had left into two small packs and lashed them to the horse's back. Finally Bass nestled the old saddle down into the vee between the packs and untied the long lead rope from the willow.

"Let's go."

Through the tall grass he led the mare, their hooves and moccasins dragging against the thick, sturdy stalks. Heading upstream once more. This time on the north bank, angling a bit into the first line of hills—from time to time adjusting his course as he kept himself between the Platte and a line where he would intersect those flocks of tiny black birds.

The sun had nearly dried his clothes, and no longer did they chafe him that late afternoon as he trudged through the low hills, beginning to think on making camp in some ravine out of sight of any wandering Pawnee . . . beginning to dwell too much on his empty belly and curling up for the night in what must still be damp blankets lashed back there on the packmare. The slope was long as he ascended the sandy hillside, casting a long shadow behind him, hoping from the top he would spot some likely campsite, perhaps in the brush beside a narrow creek that fed the mighty Platte. There he could hide, and sleep.

With just a matter of another two steps to the top of the rise, he prepared to catch his breath and blow, the same way horses blew after an exhausting climb. He blinked into the falling sun—missing his hat even more already. And waited those few seconds for the mare to come up behind him. With the sun's bright glare he blinked some more as the ground in the middistance seemed to undulate, quiver— just the way ol' Tink's skin would ripple when you gave her a particularly good scratching.

For a moment more he stared, not sure . . . not taking a breath. Not even daring to.

The great flocks of tiny black birds swept from right to left, then south back to north—all but directly overhead now. He became suddenly aware of their incessant racket, those tiny throats and flapping wings, whereas it had seemed so deathly silent for so, so long. Then heard the snorting and bellowing, the lowing of huge animals.

Slowly, Titus Bass became aware of the great hump-backed beasts that blackened the endless miles of what rolling prairie lay before him.

FIVE

Titus hadn't moved for the longest time the rest of that afternoon—watching the knotted herd of buffalo below him as the packmare contentedly cropped at the grassy hillside nearby.

For what must have been hours he did nothing more than sit and watch how the great beasts moseyed this way, then that, before ambling off in a different direction just as slow as you'd please, flowing together like coagulate, then gradually splitting apart as individuals and small bunches went their own way in grazing the hillsides and prairie floor. He was content to do nothing more than watch the great, hump-backed creatures . . . all the while trying to control the hammering of his heart, trying desperately to remember to breathe in his excitement.

As the sun began to fall into the western hills, Bass got to his feet and gathered up the long lead rope, taking the packmare from the crest of the knoll where he had remained mesmerized for so long. Angling to the south, he kept to the far fringes of the herd until he found a suitable ravine deep enough for him to make camp for the night. By the time he had pulled the mare into the upper reaches of the ravine, the sky had begun to dim and shadows had grown as long as they would ever be.

After freeing the two smaller packs and dropping them into the tall grass one at a time, Bass slapped the mare on the rump and sent her off to have herself a roll. Next came the task of spreading the still-damp blankets over the nearby brush to finish drying while he gathered up what dead limbs he could find. Making tufts of some dead grass after he had scraped out a small hole at the bottom of the ravine, Titus struck his evening fire, then took up the bail to his coffeepot and headed over to the nearby creek. At the top of the ravine, which put him level with the rest of the prairie, he turned round to gaze back at the campsite—anxious that no wandering eye should spot the smoke from that small fire.

After a trip that led him back toward the Platte, Titus found a clear-running stream, where he dipped both the blackened pot and his wooden canteen. Quickly yanking off his clothes, Bass swabbed as much of the mud as he could wash off— then, shivering, jumped back into the wool shirt and britches. After tying his moccasins, he sat there at the creek a few minutes, drinking his fill once more, realizing just how this arid country dried him out, made him more thirsty than he thought possible. How good the water tasted to his parched tongue.

As he neared the landmark brow of the hill he used to locate his ravine, Bass overheard muted snorts that grew in volume the closer he neared his camp. Instantly concerned for the mare, Titus set off at an ungainly trot with the canteen swinging at the end of one arm, the pot sloshing from the other. Reaching the top of the ravine, he skidded to a halt, staring down to find the mare grazing content-edly at the mouth of the ravine . . . no more than fifteen yards away from where one of the dark-skinned beasts rooted about in a circle, slowly hobbling round and round, clearly in some sort of distress.

From time to time the animal jerked its head around toward its hindquar-ters, tongue flicking out in vain as if to lap at the source of its discomfort. From his vantage point Bass glanced at the other buffalo grazing nearby, none of which paid any attention to the commotion—instead, some went on grazing, while at this time of the day most had already found themselves a suitable patch of ground, where they collapsed to their bellies and began to chew their cud with great self-satisfaction.

"Just like Pap's damned cows," he muttered, then remembered how he never got all that good at coaxing milk from an udder. "N-never was my cows anyhow," he said as he settled to the grass to watch the scene at the mouth of the ravine.

The short-horned beast continued to paw at the ground, nostrils snorting in short bursts, then lolled its tongue in a pant, interspersed with rapid-fire bellows as it nosed round and round on all fours . . . then without any ceremony or warn-ing the creature stopped dead in its tracks and let out a long, guttural cry as it shuddered the entire length of its body. And as Bass watched in dumbfounded amazement, the animal humped up its back just as a bluish membrane began to emerge from its rear quarters, the glistening mass expanding longer and thicker as the beast snorted, bellowing in pain.

"Jumpin' Jehoshaphat! That there's a buffler cow," he exclaimed, licking his lips in anticipation of watching the event. "And she's 'bout to shed herself of a calf."

Pretty durn close to watching one of the family's cows drop a calf, he thought.

The newborn buffalo had dropped close to halfway out when the cow's quivering hindquarters weakened and she collapsed, sprawling on the ground there at the mouth of Bass's ravine, fully in the seizure of labor.

It was characteristic of the buffalo cow to seek out a site all her own when she was due to give birth—forsaking all companionship with other cows, much less the bulls. The entire birth process usually took close to two hours after the onset of the first contraction.

Here at this late stage Bass watched the cow squirming on her side, at times raising her uppermost hind leg in an attempt to ease the birth process as she jerked her neck backward in spasms of pain. From time to time she thrashed that hind leg as more of the grayish-blue sack continued to slither onto the grassy prairie.

From the end of that fetal sack Titus watched a tiny hoof thrash, suddenly poking its way free, tearing the membrane near its own hindquarters. Then the leg lay completely still. Fearing that the calf was stillborn, Bass rocked up on his knees, expectant. After the cow huffed through those final moments of her exertion, she began to roll onto her legs, pulling herself away from the fetal sack that lay still upon the grass, slowly clambering to her feet before she turned about to sniff at what had just issued from her.

After inspecting the sack from top to bottom, the cow began to chew at the several holes torn in the membrane, appearing to rip at the sack, enlarging the holes through which Bass caught glimpses of the shiny, dark hide of the newborn calf tucked inside. Slowly, mouthful by mouthful—and beginning not at the head but at that hind hoof that protruded from the glistening membrane—the cow went about steadily devouring that slimy sack crusted with grass and dirt at the mouth of the ravine.

Cautiously the packmare began to advance, her nose on the wind as she picked up more of the birthing scent. But she did not approach all that close before the cow caught sight of the horse and whirled on the mare—snorting, bellowing her warning with a long-tongued bawl. It was evident the mare understood that most primitive of warnings, turning away with a whinny of her own. Likely she had given birth to colts her own self, Titus brooded. In her own primal way she would understand just how protective the cow would choose to be at just such a moment.

Returning to her calf, the cow continued tearing at the membrane, devouring every shred of it from the newborn's shiny, slick body, eventually eating the last of it plastered around the calf's head. Barely breathing himself, Titus waited, anxious as the cow licked up and down the length of the calf's muzzle, its nostrils—stimulating her baby. Finally the young animal squirmed at long last, moving on its own.

Strange behavior, this—especially for an animal not in the least considered a carnivore. Yet something innate and intrinsic compelled the cow to continue to lovingly lick at the newborn calf's coat until she had expelled the afterbirth, then devoured it as well.

The sun had fallen fully beyond the hills by the time some other cows moseyed over to the mouth of the ravine to give this newcomer a cursory sniff, perhaps to help the mother lick its coat—all of them tolerated by the cow with the exception of one yearling bull she swiped at with a horn and drove off with a warning bawl.

As the cow stood protectively over it in the coming twilight, the calf now made its first attempt to stand—here something on the order of half an hour following birth. It caused Titus to remember how the family's newborn calves and even colts attempted to pull themselves up on their spindly legs, wobbling ungainly before spilling to the ground once more. But here the buffalo calf was, tottering about on its quaking legs sooner than either of those domestic animals Bass had come to know. Again and again the calf heaved this way, then that, before it collapsed in a heap, but was quick to rise again.

Each time the calf managed to stay up longer, long enough to careen about in a crazy circle and finally locate its mother nearby—tottering over to jab its wet nose beneath the cow's front legs, where it probed with its pink tongue and very little luck. When the cow shifted herself, so did the calf, this time nuzzling along its mother's belly until it found a teat and latched on. As the calf greedily pulled at the nipple, it was plain to see it had been rewarded with warm milk.

"From now on, li'l one," Titus said quietly from the side of the ravine, "you'll know where to go first off, you wanna get fed."

His own stomach growled of a sudden, reminding him he hadn't fed it either. Glancing into the west, he got to his feet, sweeping up the bail to the pot and the leather strap nailed to the canteen, saying, "Be dark soon, won't it, Titus? Ain't got your supper started. Hell, you ain't even got yourself a fire to hunker over come full dark."

Of a sudden he remembered he would be bedding down tonight one horse shy of how he had taken his leave of St. Louis. It might be enough to take the starch out of any man—to cause lesser men to turn back. But Bass vowed he would press on.

Reaching the end of the ravine, he squatted next to the burned-out remnants of his fire and dragged his pouch over, pulling flint and steel from it once more.

"Leastwise that pack animal swum out like I done," he muttered, trying hard to cheer himself as he blew on the red coal until he could set it beneath another knotted twist of dried grass. "Leastwise I got some of what fixin's I come out with," he convinced himself.

But, damn, did he ever hate to walk. Never took too much to that in his life, Titus decided. Even when Kingsbury and the rest of the boatmen were faced with walking back north to Kentucky's Ohio River country along the Natchez Trace, they had bartered themselves a ride on wagons from New Orleans to the river port of Natchez itself, then walked only until they reached the Muscle Shoals, where the slavers jumped them.

For the rest of that journey north there had been the slavers' horses for them to ride, keeping a constant and wary eye over their shoulders, ever watchful for that pair of white cutthroats who had escaped the fate of the other slavers there near the Tennessee River when those land pirates had come for Hezekiah Christmas.

A tall, shiny-skinned, bald-headed beauty of a Negro. Not no more'n ten years older than Titus himself. A man Bass soon give his freedom to, set free to go west from Owensboro on his own—a freedman with the whole of a wide-open wilderness to explore.

"Where you now, Hezekiah?" he asked quietly as the limbs caught hold of the flames and Titus finally set the coffeepot to boil.

Tonight he would eat the last strips of his dried venison and go off to shoot his first buffalo come morning.

"You et your first buffalo yet, Hezekiah?" he asked the hills about him. "How 'bout you, Eli Gamble? You find them beaver big as blankets in that upcountry you was yearning to see?"

He shuddered with the coming darkness, feeling smaller as the night came down than he had ever felt before—come here to a monstrous land ruled by these huge beasts. Never had he felt so small. Nor so alone.

Gazing at the stars just peeking into view overhead, Titus asked, "Are you alone, Eli? Like me?"

Then Titus stared at the fire as the nightsounds of the nearby herd drifted in to him. "Naw, I don't suppose a man like you would ever be alone, Eli Gamble. Not nowhere near as lonely as men like Hezekiah Christmas. Sure as hell not nowhere like Titus Bass his own self right now."

Plopped down here in the middle of everything he had ever wanted . . . but without another single living soul to share in the glory of it.

Although he had been awake long before the sun rose, Titus wasn't ready to go in search of a buffalo to kill until sometime after first light.

For most of the night he had tossed in his blankets. From time to time he either went out to gather more kindling for his tiny fire, or he walked off toward the north bank of the Platte, where he sat for a long time, brooding at the murky river, its rolling surface a glimmering ribbon beneath the dim moonshine. He had remained there until at last he saw the sky had grayed enough to venture out—first to the west, then he walked a wide swing to the north across the night prairie.

He had searched for Indian sign. A village of rings, fire pits, and meat racks as he had discovered before. Perhaps to find a herd of their ponies.

Instead, all he found was the bedding grounds of the far-ranging buffalo herd he had run across yesterday afternoon, stretching from horizon to horizon. Assured that the roar of his rifle would pose no danger, perhaps now he could take the chance of hunting his first buffalo. How his heart pounded against his ribs as he dwelt on that one thought all that walk back to his camp, where the packmare awaited him just before sunrise.

The little red-skinned calves were up already by the time he walked along the side of the hills bordering the great, grassy plain near the Platte itself. While the youngest of them still hugged their mothers' sides, the others, perhaps days and weeks old, scampered about. Some of the oldest calves even butted heads in mock battle.

The sun had fully torn itself from the horizon when Bass sank to the ground, gone weak in the knees again just to stare at all of the countless thousands as the grassland slowly warmed that new day. With gold light the orb painted all the far surrounding hillsides in patches of sandy ocher where the tall green stems refused to grow. A breeze came up as the air warmed, carrying on it the muted sounds of the thousands as they arose from their bellies and ambled off in all directions to graze.

For a long while he studied the biggest ones: monstrous shaggy heads from which protruded a pair of resplendent black horns; those dark chin whiskers that gave the bulls their unique mark; and finally that great hump rising from their shoulders nearly as huge as their massive heads.

Easiest for him to pick out were the smaller cows—not near so large a head and horns, with nowhere near the great hump. Besides, most of the cows either were already mothers that late spring morning, or would be in a matter of hours or days, destined to drop more of the small, playful, impish red calves.

So that left only the fourth group of buffalo he watched in growing excitement to drop one himself at long, long last. They, the yearling bulls. Perhaps nearly as big as some of the older cows, yet distinguished by shortened horns and that straggly beard, not to mention the growing hump. Maybeso a yearling bull or an older cow, he mused, deciding it should be one or the other he would shoot this morning.

Not the calves nor their suckling cows—let the young ones frolic or their mothers breed for seasons to come. Nor should it be one of those old rangy bulls, he brooded. If nothing else, a bull would simply be too big. Far too much meat for him to take with him, he decided, realizing he would feel ashamed to leave so much behind for what predators were sure to feast on such a kill. His grandpap had given Titus that much a legacy: even in times of plenty a man must not be wasteful, for there will surely come times of want.

Was this ever a time of plenty!

It would have been an easy thing for him to seethe in anger at the river once again—to grow saddened as well that Washburn's Indian pony was gone, for she and the packmare could have carried far more of the buffalo meat he would butcher this morning than the mare could all on her own. But face the truth he did—realizing he sat here in the middle of this foreign land inhabited by strange peoples and stranger animals . . . knowing he had only the mare to carry everything he called his own, and what meat he would pack along taking his leave of this place.

Then he figured a yearling it would be!

His heart beat all the more fiercely, his mouth gone dry as sand, as he carefully ran his eyes over those buffalo grazing nearby. Praying he would not be disappointed with the meat of so big a creature, Titus swallowed hard, his tongue parched, as he chose the one. Yes—that one would be his first buffalo.

Slowly he rose from his knees and stood, testing the breeze there on the long, lazy slope of the sandy hill. It was good, for the wind came from that portion of the herd dotting the endless valley all the way to the far horizon. He had the breeze in his face, out of the northwest here at sunrise.

Growing all the more cautious when he was some one hundred yards out from the fringe of the herd where the yearling stood cropping the grass with other youngsters, Bass dragged the hammer back to half-cock and flipped the frizzen off the pan. His right hand shook nervously as he sprinkled a few more of the fine grains of black powder into the concave surface of the pan. With the priming horn once more suspended from his pouch strap, Titus gently tapped the lock of the rifle to assure that a portion of the pan's grains slipped through the touchhole where they would ignite the coarser powder packed behind the .54-caliber lead ball.

Should he stand or sit or lie for this first shot he would make at the bull grazing contentedly down the slope? And as quickly he decided he would sit, knees bent, elbows locked within his legs to steady the long-barreled, heavy, iron-mounted rifle.

Now he pulled the graceful curve of the hammer all the way back to full-cock. Bass quickly licked the pad of his right thumb before running the thumb across the sharp, knapped edge of the huge gray flint that lay imprisoned within the screw jaws of the hammer. He brought the thumb away and inspected it, finding a thin, telltale black line of powder flash he had just wiped off the flint. Better that this be no misfire because of powder residue built up on the knapped surface.

Then, as he nestled the full curvature of the butt plate into the crook of his shoulder, Bass let out a sigh.

"Easy now, Titus," he whispered barely under his breath, aware that he was growing all the more anxious with every pounding beat of his heart.

He hadn't felt this way but few times before—and they all came with being close to a warm and scented woman. Even his first back in Boone County. Amy Whistler had been a woman in all respects, he recalled fondly. Not taking herself a husband as early as most girls did on the frontier, she had instead waited for young Titus Bass, pressing him to complete his schooling before he took up the plow to work that portion of the family lands that Titus's father would turn over to his firstborn son. But she was like Marissa Guthrie, who came to trouble his life a few years later, quickly becoming the one woman he felt he could truly love with all his heart—in the end both women had sought to tie him to the soil when what he wanted most was to wander.

If either had shown any interest in his way of life rather than their fathers', he likely would have asked one or the other to join him in venturing west. But with both Titus knew better. Neither young woman would have taken to this dangerous, challenging existence the way he had. Truth was, neither woman was daring enough, nor was either of them the sort to take that grave risk this frontier required of all who ventured beyond the pale. Simply put, he had long ago realized that both Amy and Marissa were not the sort to leap into the unknown as he had.

Taking on a woman was pure foolishness, he had determined some time back. To do so was to lash oneself to a single place, to imprison oneself with the land and young'uns and all the shoulds it would take to near suffocate a man. Better that he was alone, he reminded himself now, angrily. Far, far better was it to be here without some woman's whining cant constantly at his ear.

Slowly he brought the brass front blade down onto the back of the yearling's front shoulder—suddenly realizing he had no idea where to aim on such an animal. Then quickly Titus convinced himself he would aim as he would at any four-legged: the heart and lights were in there, close behind the leg, after all.

With the front blade held near the midline of the young bull, Bass brought that brass blade down into the crescent of the buckhorn rear sight. Then raised his sight picture even higher on the animal since he was shooting downslope. With the pad of his index finger he gently pulled on the rear trigger, setting the front trigger to something less than a hair's response. Then he began squeezing while he held his breath—

The rifle shoved itself back into his shoulder, surprising him as the muzzle spat fire. In that fraction of a moment before the pan and muzzle smoke obscured his view, Bass saw the small puff of dust erupt from the blackish hide—meaning the lead ball had struck the yearling high on the rib cage, above midline.

Quickly he rolled onto his knees, yanking the rifle's muzzle to his lips to blow down the long barrel as he watched the animal sidestep and thrash its head a few times . . . then it went back to eating after it had attempted to lick at its side, that long pink tongue darting out against the backdrop of that dark, shaggy coat. It lazily cropped a few more mouthfuls of the tall grass while Titus poured down a measured charge of powder, then sank the ball home within its nest of a greased patch with the long hickory ramrod. Quickly he flipped back the graceful goosenecked hammer, popping forward the frizzen before he sprinkled in more of the priming powder.

Down came the frizzen over the pan, his thumb continuing on back to pull the hammer to full-cock as he brought the rifle up to his shoulder, settling back on his rump.

"By damn, I'll hold this lady lower on you this time," he muttered, laying the brass blade down into the notch filed in the bottom of the buckhorn rear sight.

Just at the bull's midline the second bullet struck the young buffalo—causing him to sidestep again with a grunt, twisting his massive, furry head to the side to inspect his hide where that second ball had made another dusty eruption.

"Shit," he grumbled as he rocked to his knees and began the reloading process once more, angry with himself for muffing that second shot. It had been too long for him to remember the last time he had needed two shots to drop some game, much less three.

Maybe it was the angle of his shot, he decided as he held once more on the dark creature still standing below him at the base of the slope, grazing as if those half-inch lead balls had been no more than tormenting mosquitoes slapping him.

This time Titus determined he would hold low, down on the brisket behind the front leg, and squeezed the trigger.

With a shudder the yearling sidled a bit, then collapsed of a sudden, his legs gone out from under him as if all four of them had been cut at the same moment.

"Damn you anyway," Titus mumbled as he rocked back onto his knees, reloading quickly, keeping his eyes on the fallen beast while he did so.

Other buffalo grazing nearby now meandered up to give their fallen comrade a sniff or two, and a few even licked at the bloody hide before they moseyed on off to resume their feeding. While some raised their shiny black noses into the air to measure the wind for some scent of danger, most took little notice of the two-legged creature inching his way down the grassy slope until he was within fifty yards. The first beast to notice the hunter turned his body so that he appeared ready to confront the intruder, raising his muzzle into the air to determine just what sort of creature this was approaching the edge of the herd.

With a snort and a bellow, the old bull wheeled about and set off at an ungainly lope, his warning cry enough to drive a hundred or more before him. In moments the nearby prairie lay empty except for the fallen yearling. Then, as suddenly as they had bolted into action, the rest of the thousands rolled to a halt half a mile away and resumed their grazing, their numbers darkening the rounded hills in places, blanketing the prairie with solid black in others.

The air was growing hotter when Bass reached the carcass, cautiously approaching it, his rifle leveled at the yearling, expecting it just might leap up any moment. Then he caught a glimpse of his own shadow cast upon the grass as he crept stealthily around the carcass and stopped, laughing out loud at just how silly that shadow appeared.

When he quit laughing at himself, Titus inched forward carefully and jabbed at the buffalo with the muzzle of the rifle.

"Sure 'nough dead, ain'cha."

On its dark, curly coat, Bass recognized the shiny patches of blood where the first two shots had struck.

"Can't aim high," he muttered as he measured where that first shot had connected. "And that'un in the middle didn't bring you down neither, did it?"

Only the one low on the brisket, there behind the front leg. Bass rubbed the spot with the muzzle of the flintlock as if to embed its location within his mind. Lucky, he thought now, that the creatures didn't tear off once they heard the boom of the big gun. Maybe buffalo didn't hear all that good. And the way that huge bull momentarily stood in challenge to him, long, shaggy fur dangling over its eyes—perhaps these creatures were half-blind as well as being near deaf.

Easy enough for a man to creep up near them, Titus thought. They ain't a wary, watchful critter when it comes to danger. No wonder they got themselves killed off back east.

Stepping around to venture inside the sprawl of the four legs, he knelt on one knee.

"Now, how you s'pose a body's to go about dressing such a big critter?"

Laying his rifle in the crook of the bull's neck, Titus removed the big skinning knife from the scabbard hanging at the back of his belt. Checking one last time at the horizon to the west and north, Bass hefted the left front leg, locked it over his shoulder, and plunged the knife into the furry throat. Using a sawing motion, he dragged the sharp blade back a few inches at a time through the thick hide, down the breastbone and across the belly, until he was confronted with the huge ham of that hind leg, all but impossible to move by himself. Nothing else to do but try his hand at some skinning.

"So be it," Bass decided, now putting his knife to work slowly inching the curly hide back from the long incision.

Jerking his bloody hands back suddenly, he stared at the tiny insects swarming over his flesh all the way up to the elbows where he had rolled his shirtsleeves. Smearing more blood on himself, Titus brushed from each arm the tiny, hopping fleas along with several fat ticks so swollen they were about to burst. He caught one between his thumb and forefinger, squeezing it until it popped with a bloody ooze, then tossed it aside. Titus went back to work, gradually working the hide back from that first long cut.

It took some doing, but he had almost half of the furry coat laid on the far side of the animal by the time the sun was well into the second quarter of the sky. Standing back to catch his breath and wipe the sweat from his face with the back of a bloody hand, Bass regarded his work to that point, figuring he would have to decide on what portions to pack with him as he continued his journey west to the far mountains.

Laying a knee against the massive rib cage, Titus next butchered a few long steaks from between the hump ribs, tossing each portion onto the green flap of hide draped across the grass on the far side of the carcass. Then he peeled back more of the hide from the rear leg until he could cut himself out two large hams.

At last he stood, using the knife to scrape off the blood, gore, and tiny vermin from each forearm before stuffing the blade back into its scabbard. Taking up his rifle once more, Titus turned away from the carcass, hurrying back toward his camp.

Once there he quickly rearranged each of the two packs so that he could lay his meat in between them along the packmare's spine, then cover it with the saddle and finally the canvas shroud he would fling over it all. Leading the mare down the ravine and onto the prairie floor, he skirted along the side of the hill to reach the carcass.

"Damn you!" he growled when he got close enough to see the creatures clustered around the young bull.

Scurvy, thieving dogs they were.

"Get!" he bellowed.

Most raised their heads. A few growled at him menacingly. "G'won! Get, I told you!" he hollered louder still, dropping the mare's lead rope and darting toward the carcass, swinging his rifle from side to side.

Most slinked off a ways, but three dropped to a crouch, snarling, their bloody muzzles showing how they had worked up a blood hunger dining at the bull's innards. As Bass drew close enough, one of them sprang at him, snapping its jaws.

In a blur he brought the rifle butt up, connecting right beneath the creature's lower jaw with a resounding crack. Immediately the second of the predators lunged for him as Bass continued swinging, wading into their midst. By the time two of the creatures lay wounded nearby, the rest decided retreat would offer the best path.

Yet they did not retreat far. Some thirty yards off the dozen or so turned as if on cue and sat down among the prairie grass to stare back at him and their feast.

"This is mine, goddammit!" he howled at them, his voice loud in the stillness of those far hills. "Mine, you hear?" he said a bit more quietly, mustering all the bravado he could, and pounded his chest one time with his left fist to emphasize his claim.

Quickly he bent over each one of the mangy creatures in turn, then brought the rifle butt down to crush their skulls for good measure.

"See?" he turned and asked of the pack sitting a safe distance away. "If'n you ain't seen enough, I'll show you what's done to thieving sonsabitches like you!"

Suddenly he jerked up the rifle, dropped the blade on the center dog, set the back trigger, then pulled the front. As the roar and muzzle smoke disappeared, he watched the other dogs suddenly leap away in retreat—leaving one more of their dead among the tall grass.

"Don't you ever dare come slipping in on my kill no more, I tell you!" he grumbled as he began reloading.

Out on the prairie one of the predators slunk back in to sniff at its dead companion Bass had just shot. Then another, and a third. Pretty soon they were tearing at the dead one in a fury of hunger.

"Black-hearted sonsabitches. Damned dog-critters—just you go get!"

With the rifle reloaded and laid again in the curve of the yearling's neck, Titus dragged the canvas cover and saddle off the mare's back so he could lay in what meat he would take with him. At last he straightened the canvas over the two packs and began lashing it down in a diamond-hitch to protect everything from any rain they might encounter. He had lost all his cornmeal flour in that drenching they had suffered crossing the capricious Platte River—but the coffee beans and tobacco had dried out nicely, spread out on the canvas overnight. He would miss his johnny bread: the smell, the taste, the texture of corn dodgers in his mouth. Adding pinches of clean ash from the fire as he had stirred up a batch of corn biscuits, his mouth watered with the thought. But there would be no such bread from here on out.

Then he realized: oftentimes if a man really wanted to grab hold of something, he had to let go his grip of something else. Maybeso his bidding farewell to those pasty sacks of cornmeal back there by the muddy river just left a hand empty and open to grab on to something new that might well present itself on down the trail. Best just to forget all that he had left behind in the settlements, and that included those sacks of Franklin cornmeal.

Besides, Titus reminded himself again as he took up the lead rope, tonight for the first time in his life he would sup on buffalo.

Yes, he sighed as he stared at the horizon and charted his course toward the western hills for the rest of that morning—his fortunes just might be about to change out here in this wild land. True enough—he was about due for things to go his way . . . for the very first time in his life.

For the next few days he had found massive clumps of coarse buffalo fur clinging to the brush and bark of nearly every small tree near the riverbank. Each time he shot one of the shaggy creatures in the weeks to follow, he was constantly reminded how summer must surely be on its way to this land—if not there already—for the buffalo were shedding their heavy winter coats.

Every few days as he encountered another herd, Titus would shoot another yearling—far tastier and more flavorful than the beef and pork he had grown accustomed to back east, even better than the game meat he had grown up on in the forests of Kentucky. The savory fragrance of each loin steak or batch of hump ribs he set to sizzle over his fire each evening caused his mouth to water in anticipation. Bass had never eaten anything better than buffalo and doubted he would ever find any meat that could surpass it.

So he taught himself to cut free a large section of each green hide in which he would wrap those choice selections he had butchered from each kill, that satchel to be carried by his most obedient packmare. Each of those pieces of hide he found to be all but rubbed free of the last tufts of last winter's hair still clinging to the animal's midsection and hindquarters. Protected inside that green hide satchel, the meat would last the better part of three days or so before he would be forced to leave behind what had gone sour on him and compelled to hunt fresh game.

Those longest of days tumbled past in slow succession as high summer arrived and he reached the forks of the Platte.

"Damn if Isaac Washburn didn't tell me none of this," he grumbled in confusion bordering on exasperation the afternoon he reached that union of the north and south forks.

But as frustrated as he was, in the end Titus decided to stay with the northernmost. The way he saw things, it only made sense because that was where he should be headed after all: to the central if not the northern reaches of the Rocky Mountains. Washburn had mentioned nothing of those southern mountains, failing to say if there even were mountains down in that country. So if ol' Gut hadn't said nothing about it—why, then, Bass figured there wasn't much worth concerning himself about down south anyways.

Sure enough, the old trapper had been right on target with most everything he had told Titus before he got himself killed back there in St. Louis. Right about everything except that warning about the Pawnee who lived along the Platte. There had been plenty enough chance to bump right into them all along. Yet except for running across sign of that village migrating along the great river before its trail started moseying its way off to the north away from the Platte, Titus hadn't seen a feather or war pony either one.

"Nothing more'n pure, dumb luck," he had muttered to himself more than once in all those weeks since, thinking back how consumed with caution and cold camps he had been.

Dumb luck—which meant he walked straight on through Pawnee country without a single run-in. Far better luck than ol' Gut and Hugh Glass had themselves when they had headed east to St. Louis, deviled by the Pawnee near the whole way.

Days past those forks, the country started to evolve once more as he pushed ever westward, leading that packmare day after day, wearing down the soles of his first pair of Washburn's moccasins and starting on the second. As the ground beneath his feet was crusting into a flaky hardpan, Titus worried so much about walking himself out of his last two pairs of moccasins that he took to cutting pieces of green buffalo hide he could lash around the soles of his thinning footwear.

Now the hills became more sharply defined, and all the creeks and streams slashed their way down through the land to form sharp-sided bluffs and buttes, each one striated over centuries of constant erosion by water and wind. Here he found more timber, willow, and brush flourishing along each water course he came across. It was clear he had passed out of the rolling tableland, where the buffalo ruled as undisputed monarchs, entering a country where he no longer had the herds of those shaggy beasts constantly in sight as he plodded west on foot.

He found this to be a country populated by varieties of deer—some surprisingly larger than others. He hunted them down in the brushy bottoms where they spent their days, or waited for them near the creeks and streams where the creatures came to water early of every morning or late of the evenings before scampering off to their beds. Most of the males were already coming into velvet, their antlers covered with that thin, mosslike covering that at times hung in tatters all about their faces.

And there were other creatures he spotted from a distance: the sharp-snouted badger and wolverine, and those wild turkey, which roosted in the low branches of the trees very much the same as their cousins did back east, not to mention what he took to be tiny prairie gophers he encountered, animals that barked at him just like dogs in those huge colonies where they lived together for mutual protection against the great-winged birds who hunted with claw and beak, sweeping over the towns pocked with burrows. Most every day he had to pass through one such community, he and the mare assaulted by the yip-yipping of so many tiny, angry voices.

At times he even caught sight of a brown- or a reddish-coated bear—animals that whirled and loped away at the first sight of him and the horse. Not a day passed that Titus did not spot what he figured to be a variety of prong-horned deer on the nearby slopes—almost a sort of long-legged goat-shaped creature, he surmised—a bit smaller but even more fleet than its mule-eared or white-tailed cousins. And most every night he went to sleep serenaded with the distant crooning of those song-dogs crying out from the surrounding hillsides as if to announce his presence to others of their kind.

Lo, the birds! As big as he had known them to be back east along the Ohio and Mississippi, they proved to be all the bigger the farther west he progressed. Although he had seen many a hawk before, the immense wingspans on these western species came as no small wonder to Bass. Not to mention how big those eagles grew hunting the skies along his line of march. As well, he grew astounded at the size of the wrinkle-necked turkey and black vultures, which congregated at the remains of what carrion the wild dogs and rangy wolves had not consumed.

So it was that time and again he was struck that this was a harsh land devoid of all mankind—although he occasionally did come across some old Indian trail of pocked pony prints and the scraping of poles as those people went about their seasonal migrations. Not a day passed when he did not fear he would run onto a village, or that he would be discovered by a wandering hunting party.

Not to see the enemy proved to be far more frightening than knowing right where the brownskins were, or just how many he might have to confront.

Fact was, none of Bass's contacts with Indians had ever fostered in him a favorable view of brownskins. Especially that run for his life from the Chickasaw there along the Mississippi River when he was but sixteen years old and fleeing the constraints of his family. And what few Indians had wandered into or traveled through old St. Louis hadn't impressed him to feel much in the way of human charity as well: they either presented themselves as a haughty, distant, and foreign race characterized by arrogance, or they appeared to be nothing more than a race of flea-bitten beggars trampled over in a rush of settlers and slowly being whittled away by the white man's dominant culture.

One or the other, Titus had long ago decided, there wasn't much to admire in or desire to emulate any brownskin. They looked different, talked different, in fact—everything about them was entirely foreign as another life could be from how he himself had grown up and come to be a man. Struggle as he might, there was little he could think of that he would possibly want to talk over with one of those haughty, better-than-thou warrior chiefs or grease-stained, hand-held-out beggars.

No sense in a man trying his damndest to run onto any Injuns, he decided. Best to just stay as far from any brownskins as he possibly could . . . for at the worst such two-legged creatures might well spell danger for him, at the least an ignorant Indian was nothing but a pure-dee waste of effort for any white man venturing into an unknown wilderness.

Better that his own dumb luck hold so he could continue on his way for the mountains, untroubled and alone.

Alone was just how he was feeling that midafternoon as he plodded on beneath the baking sun, leading the packmare through the easy footing he found a quarter mile or so out from the Platte. He discovered he could almost doze as he trudged along, laying one foot in front of the other, his eyes barely open as he picked his way through the waist-high buffalo grass. Almost like sleeping: with the warmth on his back and the rhythmic sway to his gait, accompanied by that hypnotic clop of the packmare following behind.

For the last few hours his thinking had been consumed with wondering on how many more days and weeks it would take for him to reach those high and shining mountains described so eloquently by an unlettered Isaac Washburn in terms of undisguised awe that bordered on nothing short of reverence.

Arousing himself from his dull stupor, Titus licked his dry lips . . . then, squinting to be sure, he studied the distant horizon as it seemed to waver and strangely take shape far, far out there before him—heat shimmers all dark and purple and jumbled there at the edge of the earth. For a moment he glanced up at the sun, hung ahead him nearly at the three-quarters mark of its path across the sky . . . then quickly back to stare at that shifting, shimmering horizon.

"Damnation. Likely we got another of them windy storms boiling up out yonder," he muttered, turning to direct his comment to the mare as he lurched to a weary halt. "Mayhap we should find us a place to make camp afore that rain rolls over us like some of 'em have."

Quickly he scanned the southwest, then took himself a measure of the land off to the northwest, seeking something that might hold promise in the way of forting up against the bluster of a bullying storm replete with horrific wind, rain, and ofttimes hail. Already he had come to expect a brief thunderstorm most every afternoon out here along the upper reaches of the Platte—but, damn, did he hate the hail. Those icy shards hurt each time they came hurtling out of a particularly angry patch of blue-black clouds overhead. Hurt the mare so bad, she cried out in something close to humanlike pain as he scampered to take shelter under her belly and those packs she carried atop her ribby sides, the only cover there often was for miles around.

"We ain't gonna be caught this day, no, we're not, girl," he promised the mare. "There, yonder—I see some big trees not too far off. We'll skedaddle down there now till that storm blows on over."

Off to the side of the bluffs he hurried the horse, down from the ridgetop where he first spotted the dim outline of the storm's approach. Among an extensive grove of cottonwood Titus prepared for the bad weather by dropping the packs from the mare's back, tying her rope to one of the trees, where she should have adequate shelter against the pelting hail. Then he went over to settle down between the two small packs himself, dragging the canvas over the packs and his head too. Breathing a sigh of satisfaction that he was at last prepared for the impending onslaught, Titus listened expectantly for telltale sounds of the storm's approach.

Squatting there, he waited and listened. At times Bass caught himself dozing off. And waited some more. But through it all he did not hear the wind whipping itself into a fury, driving the rain and hail before it.

The longer he listened, the more he grew suspicious—thinking the storm had taken a different track to the north or south around them.

"Let's go have ourselves a look-see," he told the mare as he threw back his canvas shelter, stood, and untied her long rope.

He vaulted onto her bare back, saying, "Maybe that storm moved on by us— what say we go find out for my own self?"

Side to side he switchbacked the horse up the side of the bluff they had descended to take shelter, then brought the mare to a halt at the top to survey the heavens overhead. A blue expanse dotted with white, fluffy clouds—as beautiful as a man would want his sky to be. To the south, and north, and even to the west as far as he could see, the sky remained unthreatening—except that jagged line of purple-blue thunderhead still clinging to the far western horizon.

"Ain't like nothing I ever seen: just sitting out there 'thout coming this way a'tall," he muttered in confusion to the horse, more in disgust that he had been ready this time when no storm came crashing over them.

Yet as he continued to stare at the distant smoked-glass horizon—it slowly dawned on him. Perhaps . . . yes, there might be a reason this truly wasn't like any storm he had ever seen—especially now that he had himself a good, long gander at it . . . because maybe, just maybe, that wasn't a jagged, roiling, rumbling thunderstorm gathering on the far horizon after all.

"Do you think?" he asked himself aloud, leaning forward to speak into the mare's ear. "Could it be . . . them far, far mountains?"

To see them at long, long last for the first time, sitting atop that steady old horse there on that rocky bluff of pale ocher, the gentle summer breeze strong in his face, perhaps a wind bringing him the scent of those far-off and terrible places. No, not clouds at all hulking way off yonder at the end of his mortal sight . . . but the . . . the god-blamed Rocky Mountains!

"Jumpin' Jehoshaphat!" he shrieked in a sudden gust of realization at the same moment he began to hammer the mare's ribs with his heels.

She gamely shot away, obediently rolling into a trot.

"Whaaaa-hooooo!"

Into a lope she finally took herself, then eased up into a gallop as he hugged close to her neck, one hand double-wrapped with that lead rope, the other hand tangled in her mane as they raced west toward that thin purple-blue border of jagged landscape. Down the far end of the bluff they tore together, right onto the rolling, rugged valley—ever westward!

"By damn—we gonna make it to them Rocky Mountains, ol' girl!" he whooped in ecstasy, then bellowed again at the top of his lungs as the mare surged ahead with all the speed she could muster for her rider. "Whaaaa-hooooo!"

It had taken so many weeks, and months too, just to leave that hardwood country behind, then suddenly to find himself pitched into a monotonously bare and rolling tableland when through all his waiting Titus had figured the country would become increasingly more hilly the closer he got to those distant, shining mountains. But instead the world around him had only become flatter, ideal for the numberless buffalo that grazed on the land's rich bounty of grass.

"Glory! Glory! Glory!" he repeated in a wild screech as the hot breeze whipped tears from his eyes.

So long had he waited to see them with his own eyes, each night along the way remembering just how he had let his imagination paint such vivid pictures in his mind while Isaac Washburn had told him this and told him that about the far places of the west the old man had himself seen. Night after night of imagining and dreaming on them, it seemed those mountains had grown all the larger, loomed all the bigger until here he was at last—suddenly struck with disappointment that what lay before him was not as tall, nowhere near as grand, nor jagged, nor threatening, nor ultimately challenging as Washburn had made them out to be.

Nowhere near the majestic mountain ranges his very own rich and fertile and ready imagination had been making them out to be all these months.

So in no small measure of disappointment he began to pull back on the rope, slowing the mare out of her surging run to the west.

For well over a year Titus had been preparing for this moment—yet here he was, of a sudden trying to make sense of it, to reconcile Gut's description of the Rocky Mountains with what undramatic and uneven outline lay there against the far horizon.

At last he brought the horse to a halt. Bass slid to the ground but continued to stare until he kicked a toe at a clump of bunchgrass.

"Damn—if I ain't got a head filled with stupids!" he roared, feeling the fool of a sudden. "It ain't that them mountains is puny, girl . . . just that they be too damned far away for us to see 'em proper!"

He sat there some more soaking in that distant vista before slowly turning the mare about to retrace their path. And from time to time he glanced back over his shoulder at the far jagged line.

"Gonna take us a few days afore we get there," he consoled himself. "Least-ways, now we see where it is we been heading all this time. Out there—why, that be the end of our journey, girl!"

Like everything else in his life, he decided, this was to be only a matter of keeping one foot landing in front of the other—hard times or slick. He'd come this far by putting his head down and not giving up no matter if the water was bad or the game was scarce, no matter that there'd been cold camps for lack of firewood or the possibility of scalp hunters out and afoot. But no matter any of that, Titus Bass was here at the brink of the Rocky Mountains—where he could look out there and see them for the first time in all his born days.

And so it was that after he had repacked the mule and set forth once again, Bass vowed that he would never stray too far from those distant mountains ever again. Once he arrived, he promised never to leave them. Never to wander so far away that he could no longer see them at the edge of his sight, just as they were right then. They were to be his compass, his lodestone, the very anchor for his life from there on out. The way some men back east dared never to wander too far from the rivers where they plied their trade and lived out their lives . . . Titus swore these mountains would from that day forth be the marrow of his world, swore that on a mighty oath for what would be the rest of his natural days.

Late that afternoon after pushing farther west, Titus brought down one of those prong-horned goat creatures he found were almost too curious for their own good. He skinned back the tan-and-white hide, butchered off the steaks and two hams he wanted from the rear flanks, then moved on west to scare up a good camp for the night. Not until the sun had disappeared behind the jagged wall of peaks far beyond did Titus discover just what he wanted.

It was a shady nook at the side of a hill that offered good water from a stream coming in from the south, plenty of firewood, and enough trees that his smoke would be dispersed among the branches—in the event any brownskins were lurking about. But most of all, the campsite sat just so: positioned in a way where he could gaze into the west as the meat broiled on sticks hung over the fire and the coffee began to boil.

After stuffing himself, with great care he loaded his old briar pipe with tobacco as twilight sank around him. How he enjoyed the utter silence of the night as it came stealing over the land, broken only by an occasional call from the wild dogs populating the nearby hills.

Like a gentle nudge, something caused him to turn and look back to the east where it had already grown dark as pitch—the sky flecked with the first stars. Back yonder, to what he had left behind, to what he had chosen to abandon. Funny, he thought—but he could not see anything back there that reminded him of what was left behind. Nothing there to show him what he had abandoned . . . yet right here in this spot he could look upon his goal.

So Titus turned back to gaze into the west once more. The mountains were there—limned in indigo light by the long-ago falling of the sun. They were reachable and real. No longer something of legend and myth. Indeed, he told himself, after all these days and the many, many miles, he had come so far that he no longer could see what had been, could no longer see *who* he had been.

Yet on this evening, with the light rapidly draining from the summer sky, it was possible for him to catch a glimpse of what he was now to be . . . to fathom at long, long last the man he was to become.

The mountains were there, finally within reach. He had only to stay his course for the next few days, with that jagged line looming larger against the sky with every step he took.

After nigh onto a lifetime of waiting, Titus Bass had come to the Rocky Mountains. And in the deepening embrace of that twilight, he joyously welcomed the man he was to become.

SIX

Dry and wispy as old ash, the snowflakes struck his cheeks as he stepped out from the copse of aspen trees and stared up at the graying sky. Just a few flakes for now. But with that look of the horizon, this appeared to have the making of the first hard snow of the winter.

Hard to tell just what month of the year it was anymore up this high. Titus had been up here, wandering through these southern foothills and into the lower reaches of the mountains, since late summer and early autumn. Some time back he'd given up trying to sort things out like keeping track of months, deciding that none of it really mattered out here no more anyway. Long ago—back to late spring as he'd pushed west along the Platte River—he had decided that keeping track of days at this or days at that was a fool's errand, and though he might well be accused of being a fool on other counts, he vowed not to be a counting fool. All that folderol about numbers and ciphering their meaning was merely one thing more to be shet of and left behind back there where he had lived another life.

With that sort of thing at his back, Titus had moved through the summer not in the least worrying what month it must surely be. June wasn't all that hard to sort out—it had already been June before he'd first spotted his Rocky Mountains off in the distance. And July brought true warmth to the days he'd spent climbing with the mare into those first pine-shaded places south by west of the Platte River, where a narrowing stream led him into the high country. From there he could look all the farther to the west and the northwest, seeing for the first time how the snow lingered on those distant peaks. From his high vantage point it was plain to see that even at this late season the white still mantled some of those mountains nearly halfway down their dark sides.

"That's where I'm wagering we'll find the best beaver hides," he had confided to the mare, the only creature thereabouts to listen to him.

More and more of late he had taken to talking out loud to her, if for no other reason than to hear the sound of his own voice. Likely, it was the only human voice for hundreds of miles around, he told himself.

Bass had tried setting Washburn's traps in that cold stream leading him up through that first high ground,* at times in those feeder creeks that spilled into it, too. Each time he did just as Isaac had instructed him back in St. Louis: with the bait-stick and the trap-shelf and the float-stick too. But for all his effort, only a half-dozen scrawny muskrats had been curious enough to get themselves caught. Titus hadn't even thought enough of them to skin them. Why, compared to the beaver hides he had seen congregate in huge packs on the wharfs at St. Louis from the upriver country, those half-dozen puny skins weren't worth the trouble it would take to bloody his skinning knife.

"Weather's bound to be lot more the sort that makes a flat-tail critter put on a heavy hide up there," he commented to the mare as they moseyed on west toward the distant white-capped peaks. "Snow means cold, and cold means thick fur, seems to me, girl."

That sort of reasoning made sense to him, it did. Especially after he had managed to trap four unwary beaver in that small range of high mountains off to the southwest—just four, after all those days he went out to his labors among the streams and those aspen that quaked with the slightest breeze on the hillsides above him. And now that he had wandered down from those unproductive mountains in bitter resignation, striking out for the northwest—yearning to reach that range where the snow looked to lay all the heavier at those upper elevations, even as summer was lost to the first signs of autumn.

Into those foothills he had led the mare as the seasons began to turn and the days grew imperceptibly shorter—climbing ever higher, trying this stream, then that. A bit more luck had he, but not near as much as Bass had hoped when he'd moved into the southern reaches of this extensive mountain range. For some days now the quakies had begun to turn gold.

There had been two quick dustings of snow already, weeks ago. Both had melted by the following day, the air steaming in the shafts of golden light piercing the leafy branches of the trees. Then of late the weather turned downright warm

---

* The LaRamee, or Laramie, River

again as Indian summer set in. But up here among the high foothills, where it seemed he spent one fruitless day after another, the cycle of life was soon to change. After less than two weeks of sunny days and cool nights, it had smelled of snow this morning when he'd kicked his way out of his blankets.

After watering the bushes Titus took the mare out a distance from camp where she could graze on some good grass; then he returned to kindle his fire and set the remains of last night's coffee on to reboil. With a breakfast of venison steak washed down, it was time to bring the old mare in and pack her up for their daily routine: a trip out to set more traps. This morning, like so many that had gone before, he promised himself it would be different. His luck was bound to change today.

It had begun to snow those dry, ashen white flakes by the time he got himself moving out to fetch up the mare. Through the trees he saw her, some distance off, kicking a hind leg, then whipping her head around to nuzzle at her belly. At the edge of the clearing he stopped, watching, frightened at what he saw. When she began to stretch her neck out before bringing her head around again to nuzzle at her stomach, he was finally convinced.

"Damn, if you don't likely have the colic," he grumbled as he approached and untied the long lead rope from a tree. She was hard to lead at first, bobbing her head, pulling back from him, near yanking him off his feet when she did, then stopping suddenly to blindly kick one hind leg or the other.

"That's it, girl." He tried to soothe best he could, knowing how a horse with the colic sensed the growing pain in its belly, suffered the bloating swell and the unrelieved pressure, kicking their legs, stretching out their necks, nosing their own bellies in some frantic, dull-witted desire to release that pent-up pressure.

"Troost always walked the colic off," he told her as he tried to draw close to her head.

But she stretched out her neck again, then nearly knocked him to the ground as she suddenly whipped around to try nuzzling her belly once more.

"C'mon—we're gonna walk it off," he told her with a tug on the rope that got her moving slowly. "Always worked before."

And he hoped it would work again.

Hysham Troost had called it the sand colic: what a horse got when it ate a bunch of sand mixed in with its feed, so much sand that it collected in every one of those low bends and twists of the horse's gut until it was nearly impossible for any of the animal's feed to make it on through their system. That's when the real trouble with sand colic started—when the mare got bloated up with all that unrelieved pressure that would have to be eased or else.

Or else.

For more than an hour he led the mare around and around that small clearing, with the horse meandering more and more slowly each time they made the circle. Finally he admitted that with the way she was acting so poorly, they would not be venturing out that morning to set more traps. If nothing else, it was a relief just to get the mare back to camp, where he could water her and keep her close at hand while the colic worked itself out of her system.

Tossing some more limbs onto his fire, Bass slid the coffeepot over to the edge of the flames to rewarm what was left from two heatings. Then he turned to grab up one of the big, heavy woolen blankets he intended to wrap around himself as he sat by the fire . . . when he heard her go down.

As Titus wheeled around, a big part of him was already praying that he hadn't heard the animal collapse. Any horseman knew the chances were somewhere between slim and damn poor for a horse that went down. If you could keep them on their feet, you had yourself a chance. But once an animal went down . . .

He felt like swearing as he flung the blanket off his shoulders among the rest and lunged toward her as the big neck and head were the last to hit the forest floor covered with a thick carpet of pine needles. But swearing wouldn't help—as much as he wanted to curse someone, some thing . . . to keep from cursing his own self.

Down on his knees Titus slid the last few feet to slowly reach under her head, bringing it gently into his lap. Her eyes were wild, glazed with pain, her sides heaving as she thrashed that upper hind leg. Something noxious and foul gushed from her hind end . . . then she seemed to lie still, nostrils flaring, eyes still rolling. From time to time they even seemed to come to a rest looking at him—pleading, perhaps—then moved on.

"Maybe that means you got it on outta your system," he pleaded with the mare quietly, figuring the gush had been just that, the way a man might get himself the green-apple quickstep and with all that pressure built up inside him from the unripe fruit might well make himself feel right pert once he had himself a decent shit.

"Let's hope that'll fix you—"

Then she thrashed her head a little as he held her, vainly trying to raise it enough to reach back to nuzzle her belly, at the same time that top rear leg began to fling about again. And he knew she hadn't found any relief by ridding herself of whatever foul substance had gushed from her hind end.

He didn't know how long he stayed there cradling the mare's head that morning but realized the coffeepot boiled again—smelling it, downwind of the fire as he was. Over time his fire burned down to nothing but thin wisps of smoke, then slowly went out as he watched. And waited. And tried to think of what more Hysham Troost would be doing for a horse suffering the sand colic.

He didn't realize he'd fallen asleep right there with the mare's head in his lap the way it was until he came awake with something tapping on the sole of his boot and a voice booming in his ears.

"I'll be go to hell!" the deep voice cried. "It be a white nigger for sure!"

Bass jerked up, his eyes squinting, blinking, straining to see through the veil of trees and gently falling snow as the dark form moved back from him and brought up a rifle to point at his belly.

Bass sat frozen, his bowels run cold—come awake suddenly to stare up, then down the immense figure before him. The man was dressed in a blanket coat, hood pulled over his head, with a black beard that reached to midchest and a belt around his waist where several long black scalps hung near his knife scabbard. From the greasy, muddy bottom of his coat extended his legs, stuffed within two faded, red-wool blanket tubes, fringe gently swaying at their outer seam above thick winter moccasins.

How Titus wished now that he'd brought the rifle close. "What . . . just who the hell are you—"

"Injuns! By damn, we're Injuns!" a new voice shrieked from the timber, drawing Bass's attention as another figure leaped into the camp clearing—dressed completely as an Indian like the first, the fringe on his leather war shirt whirling round and round as he danced toward Titus: whooping and hollering, rhythmically clapping his hand over his mouth, *woo-woo*ing and stomping round and round in some ungainly imitation of a scalp dance.

Suddenly that figure whirled up beside the first man and stopped, asking, "What you figger him to be doin' just a'squatting there by that horse, Silas?"

Titus set his eyes again on the tall, dimly lit figure in the hooded coat standing over him in that gentle fall of early snow, his face hidden in shadow.

The tall figure said, "Shit—stupid son of a bitch appears to be rockin' that god-danged horse to sleep, don't he, Billy?"

Then a third voice laughed along with the two standing there in front of Bass. From the shadows that new voice shouted.

"Injuns!"

And a third long-haired Indian-look-alike came stomping and whirling and *woo-woo-woo-woo*ing into the clearing, shrill and sounding every bit like a savage warrior bent on taking a scalp.

Damn! Titus swallowed hard, watching the third hairy, bearded man dance up, watched how the second joined in the dance and chanting, watched with growing uneasiness the way the first figure continued to stare right down at him— his face hidden within the hood of his blanket coat.

No, Bass told himself—I don't wanna fear no man, red nor white.

"You're wolf bait now for sure, pilgrim!" cried the second man; then he let out a bloodcurdling scream, dragging his knife from its scabbard and shaking it in Bass's face.

Titus's eyes quickly shot to where his rifle stood against a tree, and where the pistol lay beyond it. These had to be white men, he told himself as he ran his tongue around the inside of his dry mouth, suddenly surprised that it had the texture of sand. After all, they spoke his tongue, didn't they?

Then it struck him: Why, he hadn't heard the sound of a human voice other than his in . . . in a damned long time. Damn, but why was these white fellas in Injun clothes?

"How—howdy, fellas . . . whyn't all of you g'won over there by my fire and have yourselves a sit," he called out in a croak, the words emerging squeaky from that dry throat.

The tall hooded one stretched out his arms, a gesture that immediately slowed the two wild dancers. With a booming voice he said, "By damn, boys—'pears we got us an invite to help that son of a bitch rock his horse to sleep!"

"You sure he ain't no dangerous Injun killer, Silas?" the third voice finally asked.

The second man's face lit up with mirth as he asked, "How the bejesus can this pilgrim be a Injun killer when he ain't got him no gun?"

Again Bass glanced at his weapons across the small clearing, there among his bedding. All he had here at hand was the belt knife.

"He won't do us no harm," the nearest one said inside the shadow of his hood.

Suddenly there was the face of the man who had spoken. Bass jerked his head up, watching the figure step closer, yanking back on the hood to his blanket coat then and there in the murky shadows as snow fell into the camp clearing. Damn near as tall as any man he'd ever seen, damn near as big as Hezekiah Christmas. And Hezekiah was the biggest man he'd ever laid his mortal eyes on.

"Don't figger we need to cover him no more, eh?" the second man said as he stepped out of the shadows no more than twenty feet away.

Then some needles snapped behind Titus. He twisted his head around to watch the third man advance into the camp clearing.

"He ain't got a gun on him," this third one said. "Don't figger he's about to kill none of us by axe-see-dent."

The big man in the center came a step closer. Titus studied the way he carried his rifle captured in the crook of his left arm and a pistol ready, there in his right hand. Now the tall one began to wave that pistol at the second man.

"Billy—punch that fire so I can warm my ass."

"Helluva way to go and wake a man up," Bass grumbled, angry at himself for feeling embarrassed at being caught flat-footed and unarmed.

The tall man watched his eyes flick over to the rifle again. "One thing y'll learn, son—y' best keep your guns at your side. No matter you're taking a shit"—and that made the second man guffaw with a great gust of laughter—"or y' be rolled up with nothing more'n your own dreams to keep y' warm at night."

"Just who . . . who the blue blazes are you?" Bass inquired.

Pounding the pistol barrel against his chest, the big man replied, "Me? Why, hell—my name's Silas Cooper."

"He's the big bull in this lick, he is—that Silas. Yessirreebob!" the second man said, his head nodding in emphasis.

Cooper came a bit closer, his eyes narrowing. "So who might be you?"

Bass's eyes went back to Cooper's. "Titus . . . Titus Bass."

"Where you come from?" the third man demanded as he came around to a spot where Bass could see him without turning his head. He looked a tarnal mess with his long, unkempt beard.

"St. L-louis," he answered with that croaky voice.

"This here's Bud Tuttle," Cooper introduced the third man, pointing at him with his pistol.

"Ain't my first name, but everyone calls me Bud."

" 'Cause he don't like Hyrum none!" the second man gushed with a wild giggle.

"That's right," Tuttle replied. "My name's Bud."

Just as Titus began to nod his head to the third man, ready to ask the last man his name, Cooper began to move off to the right, stuffing his pistol into the wide, colorful sash he had tied about his waist. The tall man asked, "How long y' been up here in these parts, Titus Bass?"

"Since end of summer."

"That long, eh?" Cooper asked as he neared the mare's rear flanks, sniffing, wrinkling his nose up at the strong stench.

"Ain't had you much luck trapping, have you?" the second man asked.

"Was going out this morning—when the horse here was took with sand colic," Bass explained.

"Damnation," Cooper said with a sigh as he settled some distance back from the horse's tail and studied the ground around the mare's hind end.

"What is it, Silas?" Tuttle asked.

"G'won now, Billy," and he looked up at the second man. "Y' get yourself introduced proper, then get that fire punched."

With an open-faced grin that second man snagged the fur cap off his head and bowed slightly from the waist, showing that he kept his long hair tied back in a long queue. He flashed a handsome, gap-toothed smile, announcing, "Name's Hooks, mister. Billy Hooks."

"So now y' know us all. Silas be my name," Cooper repeated as he looked up from the moist ground he had been inspecting near the horse's flank, "that's Billy y' just met, and him over there is Bud."

"Pleased," Bass replied, reaching up to scratch at the incessant itch there at his collar, "pleased to meet you all."

"Bet y' are," Cooper growled. "Better us'n some half-starved red niggers out for hair or coup."

"K-koo?"

The tall man slipped his wide-brimmed felt hat off the back of his head, grabbed a gob of his own long black hair in one hand, and pulled it straight up while his other hand whipped out his belt knife and dragged the back of the blade showily across his throat—while he made a scratchy, wheezing sound.

"Meaning the red bellies gonna slit your goddamned pilgrim, idjit, pork-eater throat, the sonsabitches would," Silas grumbled, stuffing the knife away and pulling the hat back over his head.

"I . . . I don't eat no pork," Titus explained sheep-faced. "Don't eat no more Ned."

"Then y' have the makings of a good man, Titus Bass," Cooper declared with a sudden smile. "There be enough god-blamed Frenchie pork-eaters in these here mountains awready!"

Billy gushed with that easy laughter of his as he came over from the fire to squat near Titus, grinning as if he'd just made himself a new friend for life.

"What you think, Silas?" Tuttle asked as he came up to stand behind Cooper, peering down at the horse's hind end.

"Black water—ain't no two ways about it," Silas clucked, then shook his head one time for emphasis.

"B-black water?" Titus repeated. "Nawww. She's just got her a li'l case of colic. Likely it be the sand colic—"

"I said it was black water, Titus Bass," Cooper snapped, rising to point down at the remains of the dark, murky liquid the mare had spewed on the ground behind her. "Come see here for your own self."

"Ah right. Black . . . black water," Titus repeated, not daring to move, not daring to show Cooper he doubted him. He felt cold in his belly of a sudden. Looking down into the mare's one eye staring wildly up at him. If it was black water, then there wasn't much a man could do. Not much time neither. "I was . . . hoping it was the colic."

"Bet y' walked her, didn't you?" Cooper asked.

How helpless he felt, maybe having a hand in killing his only horse. "Yes . . . well—I thought it was the colic!"

"It's awright, son," Silas said, suddenly sounding almost fatherly so soon after he had been downright snarly. "Most folks don't know how to tell the black water until it's too late."

"Too late?"

"Listen, Titus Bass," Cooper said as he came over to kneel beside Titus, "this critter's in some terrible pain. And when a body's in pain—it's allays best to put it right outta its misery, ain't it?"

Lord, he fought not to sob, especially when Cooper leaned over to put an arm around his shoulder, just the way his grandpap used to do. Bass could feel the tears sting as they started to well in his eyes.

"Y'll get along just fine—won't he, Bud?" Silas offered.

"That's right, Titus," Tuttle replied, pushing some of his long sandy-blond hair back out of his eyes. "Where's your other horses?"

"Other . . . other horses?" Bass asked dumbly.

Cooper asked, "Y' got mules?"

"I ain't got no other'ns."

Billy shrieked with sudden unrestrained belly laughter, clamping a hand over his mouth when Cooper shot him a stern, disapproving look.

Then Silas was tugging Titus up. "Bud, gimme a hand getting Titus up on his feet. Here, son—that's it, Titus . . . y' don't wanna go down like your only horse there, now—do you?"

As much as Titus tried to think of speaking, of what to say, of what the hell to do, his mouth just wagged wordlessly.

"Y' mean to bald-face tell me you come out here to the mountains with one horse only?" Cooper inquired.

"Started off with two from St. Louie."

Tuttle asked, "So what happed to the other'n?"

"Lost it—crossing the Platte."

"Spring flood?" Billy asked, that big grin brightening his face.

With a shake of his head Titus shrugged and replied, "Don't know—bottom just gone out from under us and we . . . this mare and me, we barely swum ourselves out."

"Y' ever find the other horse?"

He looked at Cooper and nodded. "Dragged the saddle off'n it. Was a Injun pony."

"Injun pony?" Tuttle asked, concern on his face. "What sort of Injun pony?"

"Don't rightly know. Just that it come down from Fort Kiowa with a friend of mine."

"Friend?" Billy asked.

"Isaac Washburn. The Injun pony was his."

"And this here mare's yours?" Silas said.

Bass looked down at the horse. She flailed that rear leg about again, only this time with a much more feeble movement. "She was give me by a man in St. Louis."

Cooper flung his long arm around Titus's shoulder, saying, "A good horse this was, Titus Bass, weren't it?"

"She got me here—all the way here."

Then he felt what Cooper suddenly pressed into his belly. Slowly he looked down and saw the pistol pushed against his blanket coat. Fear knotted cold in his gut.

"Take it, Titus Bass," Cooper demanded. "Finish off the god-blamed animal, y' idjit. Cain't y' see she's in some awful pain?"

"F-finish?"

"Shoot her!" Billy cried. "She's dying anyways—so, shoot her now!"

"I . . . ain't there nothing can be done?" he begged of Cooper, turning toward the tall man, trying to push away the pistol the tall man shoved into his belly.

"Not when a critter's gone and got black water," Cooper said quietly, his big, beautiful eyes gone sad and limpid. "Once a horse goes down with black water—that critter ain't never getting up on his legs again. Y' cain't be squamp-shus about it. Time for y' to do the decent thing, Titus Bass."

"I can't shoot her," he pleaded. "Don't have me no other horse. This here's the only one—"

"Gimme the goddamned pistol, y' weasel-stoned pup!" Cooper growled angrily as he yanked the weapon from Bass's hand and dragged back the hammer.

"*No!*" Titus bellowed, hurling himself at the man's long, powerful arm. "No—don't you see if it's to be done, I'm the one gotta do it?"

Cooper looked down at him with those long-lashed, limpid eyes of his that Bass was sure could hypnotize lesser men. "That's right, Titus Bass. Now you're showing a lick of good sense: see that you're the one what's gotta do it—if'n you're man enough."

"The nigger ain't man enough!" Billy cried, sidestepping a little jig in eager anticipation. "Ain't man enough!"

"Shuddup, Billy!" Tuttle ordered. "Leave 'im be."

With gratitude Bass glanced at Bud Tuttle and found there in the man's homely face something that said he understood Bass's reluctance—something that said he just plain understood.

"I'll do it . . . if'n there's no other way," Bass reluctantly said.

Cooper and the others backed away a few steps. Then Silas said, "She's been good to y'. Now's time for y' to return that good, Titus Bass. Take her outta her misery."

With two trembling hands he pulled the hammer back to full-cock, brought the muzzle down to aim at a spot behind her ear.

"Y' might miss there," Cooper advised. "Go up on her head," and he jabbed with one long finger at a spot midway between the eyes—up between the eyes and the ears. "Horse got it a little brain . . . y' don't put that ball into it just right, y' gonna cause the mare all the more pain, Titus Bass."

Still trembling, he moved the muzzle to that new target, trying to hold it on the spot Cooper described.

"Nawww—hold it again' her head," Silas instructed. "Now, y' want one of us to go and do—"

"No! I'll . . . I'll do it," he interrupted, forcing down the stinging bile that gathered at the back of his throat as he brought the muzzle squarely against the mare's forehead. Titus glanced one more time into that one wild, bloodshot, pain-crazed eye, then closed both of his and pulled back on the trigger.

The pistol leaped in his hand, and he sensed the immediate splatter of warm blood across his bare flesh as he keeled backward with instant regret—not wanting to look, not daring to open his eyes until he had turned away. Bass held the pistol out at the end of his arm, loosely in his grip—hoping one of them would take it.

Cooper swept the weapon out of the hand before it dropped, looping his other arm over Bass's shoulder. He almost cooed, saying, "Y' done good by her,

Titus Bass. I allays said a man's only as good as he is to his animals. And y' done right by your mare."

"Tough thing you did—but the right thing," Tuttle added.

"Weren't nothing to laugh at, Titus," Billy said. "Sorry I am I laughed at you."

"The world's a merry place to Billy Hooks," Silas replied. "Y' just gotta understand him is all, Titus Bass."

He peeled himself from under Cooper's arm and trudged over to his rekindled fire. There he squatted on his hands and knees, feeding the coals until he had more warmth from the flames.

"Whyn't you two go fetch up the animals?" Cooper instructed somewhere behind him.

"Sure, Silas," Tuttle replied. "C'mon, Billy. Let's go fetch up the horses."

Hooks came bounding up on foot to stop near Bass's shoulder as he asked, "Silas—ain'cha gonna give one of our Injun ponies to this here Titus Bass feller?"

"I s'pose it's the thing to do, don't y' figger?"

"Yessirreebob!" Billy replied. "I do figger so. He needs him a horse, and we got alla them what we took off them red niggers few days back."

"R-red niggers?" Titus repeated, looking up to the faces of the three standing over him.

"Injuns, Titus Bass," Tuttle replied. "C'mon, Billy."

"Dirty, thieving red sonsabitches what tried to steal our ponies, our plews, and our scalps too!" Cooper growled as the other two started off into the shadows. The snow gathered on the shoulders of his blanket coat, lying there so stark against the gleaming black of his long hair that spilled over his shoulders, tangled in with his long, dark beard.

"Where?" Titus asked, feeling his palms sweat.

"North o' here," Cooper replied, then squatted to help break off some more branches for the fire. "Likely they was Blackfeet, though they call themselves Blood Injuns. Part of the same sonsabitches anyways. Don't make me no never mind to kill any of 'em."

"F-far from here?"

"We been riding six days since," Silas answered. "Why, now—do I see me that y' got yourself skairt of Injuns?"

"Nawww," Bass said with feigned bravado. "Fought me Injuns afore."

"Where?"

"Mississippi," Bass replied. "Chickasaw, they was."

"Chickasaw."

"Yep."

Silas shook his head. "Them ain't real Injuns no more."

"They was real Injuns when I fought 'em," Titus explained. "My first Injun scrap. Fifteen winters ago. Took my flatboat pilot. A friend of mine."

"So y' was a riverman afore y' come to the mountains?"

"For a short time," he admitted, then knew he ought to admit it. "One trip, then I come up the Natchez Trace for that one and only walk back to the Ohio River country."

"That make y' a Kentucky man?"

Bass nodded. "Boone County."

"I hail out of what they're calling the Illinois now," Cooper explained. "Them other two: Billy's from down around the Cape on the Missouri—"

"Cape Girardeau?"

"Y' know of it?" Silas asked.

"Sure as hell do," Bass said with some of the cold departing his stomach as he rubbed his cold hands over the flames. "Spent me many years in St. Louis."

Cooper continued. "And, Bud there—he's a Pennsylvania man. Don't rightly know if he'll ever make a trapper howsomever. Them Pennsylvania folk are slow on the take-up—leastways every one of 'em I've run onto. Trapping don't seem to be Tuttle's calling."

"Why's he stay out here?"

"Hell," Cooper snorted, "he's like the rest of us what stayed on out here after those early days with Lisa—ain't got much left for us back—"

"Lisa?" Titus interrupted, his voice rising, turning suddenly to look at Cooper beside the fire. "Manuel Lisa?"

"Y' heard of that thieving Spanee-yard, have y'?"

"You mean you fellas worked for him?"

"Damn if he didn't make all of us bust our humps for him—and some of us died for it too!"

"Then you'll know . . . maybe you'll know a man—fella by the name of Eli, Eli Gamble?"

For a moment there was nothing more than a blank look on Cooper's face; then the eyes started to crinkle. "Ol' Eli. Yes, I remember Gamble, I do. A good man—"

"What become of him?"

"Y' be a friend of his?"

Titus shrugged, gazing back down at the fire again, rubbing his hands that refused to get warm as the snowflakes spat into the fire with a hiss. "Knowed him once. Of a time I shot against him in a rifle match. Just 'bout beat him too."

Squinting one eye in appraisal of Bass, Cooper commented, "Always heard Eli was some with a rifle. A man what could shoot straight and hit center, Gamble was. Y' say you just 'bout beat him?"

"I'd a'beat him," Titus grumped. "But I was young back then."

Silas looked Titus up and down with a widening grin. "I should say you was young then! That had to be many a summer ago!"

"I was sixteen," he said proudly. "And I beat every other man 'cept Eli Gamble." Then Titus had to snort with a grin, "Sly son of a bitch wasn't even from Boone County neither—not like the rest of us shooting that day!"

"Pushing west, weren't he?"

"Tol't me he was fixing to join up with Lisa's brigade," Titus explained. "Lisa been crossing all that country north of the Ohio for to get fellas to sign on—"

Nodding, Cooper interrupted, "We all of us signed on in just such a way."

"Then all of you know Gamble?"

"Might say we knowed of him, Titus," he answered, his eyes narrowing. "He was in that bunch went over to the Three Forks with Major Henry. We was sent off to work other country."

Bass itched for an answer. "W-what become of Gamble?"

Cooper shrugged a shoulder, then turned at the sound of the others' approach. "Don't rightly claim to know, Titus Bass." He stood slowly, turning his rump to the fire and rubbing warmth back into it. "There was too many a good man we never knowed what become of up there in that Blackfoot country."

"Blackfoot? Like that bunch you say you run onto a few days back?"

Billy Hooks burst into the camp clearing on horseback, Tuttle right behind, both of them leading a small herd of horses and mules.

As he dismounted, Hooks cried out, "Blackfoot be the baddest red niggers you'd ever wanna doe-see-doe with, Titus Bass!"

There were more than a dozen of the animals altogether. Some immediately winded the dead horse sprawled on the ground and shied away, others just got wide-eyed, snorting, and pawing.

"Best y' get them tied off down in that meadow yonder," Cooper ordered the other two.

"So is this here Titus Bass gonna pick him out a new horse and pack animal this morning, Silas?" Hooks asked as he started to step away, pulling on the lead ropes to a half dozen of the horses.

Cooper turned to look steadily at Bass, the black eyes again reflecting nothing more than good human charity. "S'pose he will for sure, Billy. But first he's gotta decide if'n he's gonna throw in with us."

Over the next few weeks the frequent snows succeeded in pushing the four of them down the mountainsides a little more with each camp as they trapped their way around the southern reaches of the Wind River range.

At their first camp after leaving the carcass of Bass's mare behind, the three experienced trappers had awakened Titus in the cold, frosty darkness the next morning.

"Rise and shine!" Billy exclaimed, then laughed merrily, his eyes dancing as he tapped at Bass's toes again.

"Jumpin' Jehoshaphat!" Titus grumbled, rubbing some fingers in a gritty eye as he sat upright in his blankets. "What the devil are you three doing? It's still dark!"

"Damn right it is, Titus Bass," Silas Cooper replied solemnly. "Time we kick off your l'arning."

"Learning?"

Billy snorted. "How to be a trapper, Titus."

"I'm already a trapper," he groused, more than a little nettled that some man might say he had a lot to learn about trapping—then hawked up some night gather in the back of his throat as he dug at the bothersome itch on the back of his neck.

Cooper said, "Only thing it 'pears y' catched was a few dumb beaver stupid enough to mosey on by your traps. Lucky is all y' are."

"Truth be: lucky we run onto you, yessirreebob," Hooks added.

"Damn good thing we found you afore any red niggers lifted your hair," Tuttle chimed in. "C'mon now, Silas gonna l'arn you how it's done."

Beneath one irritating armpit Bass dug with his fingernails as he kicked his blankets off his legs; then he dug at the other.

"Varmints," Billy declared to the others. "Son of a bitch is rotted with 'em, I'll wager."

"C'mon, Titus," Cooper said, starting to turn away into the darkness. "Man what wants to catch hisself some beaver better be up afore the beaver."

Bass wanted badly to say something about the fact that he had always risen early, as far back as he could remember on his father's farm, on through his days of work on the wharf at Owensboro and even in Troost's Livery . . . but as he started to open his mouth, the three of them turned their backs on him and started trudging out of the timber toward the nearby stream.

"Up before the beaver, my ass," Titus hissed under his breath as he stood and knew he had to pee in the worst way.

Quickly he unbuttoned the front of his worn and patched wool britches as he stumbled over to a far tree and drained himself with a sigh. The three had disappeared in the dark by the time Bass had on his coat, moccasins, and the wool cap he had fashioned from some blanketing cut from the bottom of his capote. Titus slung the leather trap sack over his shoulder and set off at a trot through the grass and elk cabbage that crackled with frost underfoot with every step. Eventually he caught up with them, following their muted whispers as the three of them stopped, turned about, and waited for the newcomer to join them.

"Thar's the stream, Titus Bass," Cooper declared. "What's to do?"

"Set my traps, natural as you please," he said, believing he gave the right answer.

"Just like that?" Billy asked.

Bass replied with a nod, "Just like that."

"Nigger—are you ever wrong!" Hooks guffawed.

"Hold your goddamned noise down!" Silas snapped. "I declare, Billy—y' go and run off the beaver with your mouth one more time, I'll cut out your goddamned tongue my own self!"

Hooks dropped his eyes, contrite and chastened as he pursed his lips into a narrow line of silence.

Bass felt sorry for him as he turned back to look at Cooper. "All right— s'pose you tell me what I do first."

"Now you're l'arning, Titus Bass," Silas said with a faint smile. "Y' do everything *I* tell you, the *way* I tell you, and *when* I tell you to do it—y'll be a master trapper in no time . . . and we'll get along fine."

At first he glanced to the quiet Tuttle, then back to Cooper. "Awright, so tell me."

The tall leader began to discourse on how a man first inspected a section of stream, looking for beaver slides, dams, or lodges built out in the middle of those ponds the efficient rodents had created in engineering their environment to suit themselves—mostly to protect their kind from four-legged, nonswimming predators. As Cooper had done yesterday afternoon before twilight while the others had established camp, he showed them how a man was to determine where best to set his traps. Silas led the other three into the leafless willow right to the streambank.

"There, Titus Bass," and he pointed. "Show me what to do now."

Bass yanked upon the sack's drawstring and pulled one of the square-jawed iron traps from the leather bag. Setting it upright on the ground, he squatted over it as Washburn had taught him, pushing down on the two jaws with his heels, allowing them to flap down so he could set the pan trigger within the notch filed in the pan arm.

"Whatcha gonna do with it now, Titus Bass?" Hooks asked in a harsh whisper.

"Set it in the water," Bass replied, hopeful he would get some of this right.

Billy wagged his head. "Not till you got your set made."

"Set?"

Tuttle explained, "Where you gonna lay it, Titus."

"How?"

Cooper nudged Hooks forward. "Billy, y' show him."

"C'mere, Titus Bass," Hooks instructed, tugging Bass's sleeve. "I be the one to show you first whack."

"First . . . first whack?" Titus asked.

"Right off. Means I show you right off." Hooks held out his hand. "Gimme one of your float-sticks. You got float-sticks, don'cha?"

"Here," and he slapped one down in Billy's open palm as Hooks pulled the second mitten from his hand by placing it beneath his armpit.

That reminded Bass how much he itched, so he dug fingernails again, not only at his neck and armpits, but also stuffing a hand in there between the folds of his blanket coat where he could get at his groin.

"You do got the varmits, don't you?" Tuttle replied.

Bass shrugged and said, "They ain't been troubling me long."

He didn't take his eyes off Hooks as Billy knelt on the bank, leaned over, whacked the stick against the thick rime of ice crusted at the surface of the water near the bank, and began digging and scraping beneath the surface with the end of the long float-stick. After a short time he shoved his coat sleeve up his arm, then stuck nearly the whole length of it under the surface.

When he brought the arm out and shook it, Billy stood, saying, "Put your damned hand down there, Titus Bass—and see what I made for your trap to sit itself on."

Kneeling right where Hooks had, Titus stuffed his arm into the shockingly cold water, a chill that felt all the worse because of the dark at this predawn hour. His fingertips walked down the side of the bank until he felt the underwater shelf Billy had crudely dug out of the bank.

"I feel it. So you gone and made a flat place for the trap under the water."

Cooper said, "Tell him what it's for, Tuttle."

"Put your trap down there, under the water, so the goddamned beaver don't see it, you idjit."

As he pulled his hand out of the freezing water, Bass turned to ask of Cooper, "What good does it do to hide your trap?"

"Beaver ain't too stupid a animal, Titus," Silas explained. "They smell your scent—where y've walked, where y' go and spit—they won't come anywhere near. Y' been a stupid pilgrim to leave your traps on top of the bank afore now?"

"Yeah, I done that."

Silas wagged his head. "Don't y' see that trap got your scent, maybeso that dead horse's smell on it from packing it out here from St. Louis," Cooper declared. "But under water—the beaver can't pick up no man-scent."

"And 'sides—you gotta have bait!" Billy added.

Tuttle asked, "Maybeso you didn't have no bait to set out, did you?"

"B-bait? Hell—I ain't fishin' . . . I'm trapping beaver!"

Hooks and the other two snorted laughter behind their hands to muffle as much of the shrill sound of it as they could—a sound that grated Titus like a coarse file drawn across rusted iron.

"You was a lucky nigger," Tuttle reminded him. "To catch a few old beaver 'thout no bait, and your traps sitting right on the bare ground, bold as can be."

"I found me a place where there was tracks," Titus protested. "And I caught me some beaver."

Billy cheered, "You gotta l'arn to be sneaky!"

"How'd y' like to learn yourself how to catch least *two* beaver to every *three* traps y' set out?" Cooper said.

"That's how good Silas here does—yessirreebob," Billy declared.

"T-two beaver for every three sets?"

"And sometimes Silas fills 'em all," Tuttle added. "Damn but he's so good, it puts me to shame."

"Maybe you an' me just ain't got the knack of it the way Silas do," Hooks cautioned.

Standing, Titus measured the tall, black-haired man before him. "You really mean sometimes you fill all your god-blamed traps?"

"These here partners of mine speak the truth. I tried to teach 'em the best I could," Cooper said. Then he leaned forward and said in a whisper, "Y' wanna learn how to be as good as me—y'll have to learn from me, Titus."

And learn he did.

From that morning on Bass hung on every one of Silas Cooper's words, soaking in all he could, asking questions of all three, and being sure he was the first to rise in the morning, the last to return to camp in the evenings after checking his sets. And right from that very first morning Titus got better and better at selecting where he should set the traps, deciding which side of the stream he would use for his set, and figuring how to leave his bait behind on the long willow limbs he jabbed into the frozen ground, the other end daubed in the "beaver milk" given him by the other three until he had caught enough animals to acquire some of the smelly bait for himself.

It did not take him long before he was able to surpass Bud Tuttle's catch at each camping site. Then for weeks he worked hard to equal the tally of Billy Hooks's beaver. And in the end, as winter set in hard and drove the group down out of the Wind River Mountains, south for the southern Rockies, Titus Bass knew he would never be content until he beat Silas Cooper.

Just the way he had come, oh, so close to beating Eli Gamble in that shooting match back to Boone County fifteen summers before.

"So how old a man are y' now, Titus Bass?" Cooper asked one blustery evening as the clouds parted enough to let the moon and some stars shine through not long after twilight.

He shivered, knowing it would be a cold one this night. "I turn thirty-two this coming Janee-ary."

"Won't none of us rightly know when that is!" Tuttle advised.

"Maybe we go and have us a li'l celebration anyways," Cooper said, shivering himself. "Time we get down to Park Kyack, we'll likely have to fort up for the winter—as far out of the wind as a man can get hisself."

Titus dug up behind an ear, his fingertip feeling for the tiny hard vermin about the size of a small grain of rice. "Park Kyack?"

"Where we plan on winterin'," Bud Tuttle said.

Hooks pointed at Bass, squealing, "Just throw that grayback in the damn fire!"

"Your goddamned nits better not come jumpin' over here on me," Tuttle grumbled.

"Titus Bass," Silas started, " 'bout time y' owned up that you're fixed with the nits."

"Rode on him alla way from the settlements, I'd imagine," Tuttle said.

"Whores got 'em. Ever' last whore I knowed," Billy said. "That and the pox too. Man takes his poison from a whore in small doses, but, damn, I hate the Irish itch the way you got it!"

Bass's scalp crawled all the more just for the speaking of it. Sheepishly he dug his fingers along the top of his scalp, searching, feeling more and more of the tiny varmints infesting him.

Cooper asked, "Whores, was it?"

Wagging his head, Bass replied, "Ain't been with a whore since early last spring."

"You itch right after?" Tuttle inquired.

"Not till I was out 'long the Platte."

Silas roared, "Say, boys—any Pawnee what had raised that varmit's skelp—they'd get the grayback nits for all their trouble!"

The three of them laughed heartily, generously, at Bass's incessant torment. It had gotten worse since meeting up with the trio—if only because one or the other would always comment about his all-but-nonstop itching. When Titus was alone, at least there hadn't been anyone around to remind him he played host to a troublesome infestation. But looking back at this moment, he decided it had to be that he took on those vermin from the damned soldiers at Fort Osage . . . that, or from the widow woman up north of Franklin.

"Chances were good it were soldiers," he declared, not wanting to mention Edna Grigsby as he dug at the back of his neck, pulling a louse free and pitching it into the coals, where it popped and hissed as it was quickly consumed.

"Soldiers?" Cooper demanded.

"Where abouts you run onto 'em out on the Platte?" Hooks asked.

"Wasn't there," Titus replied. "Back to Fort Osage."

"Oh," Tuttle said with relief crossing his face. "Good thing they didn't just make you a soldier with 'em. They do that, you know? They can press you into service if'n they take a mind to."

Bass defended, "These were good fellas—"

"Damn 'em all!" Hooks interrupted. "Soldiers is just like them graybacks. Serve for no good."

Cooper leaned over and slapped a big hand on Bass's knee to ask, "Y' been anywhere else't but that soldier post where you'd take on a herd of nits?"

A bit embarrassed at telling of his encounter with the widow, Bass looked down, away from the prying eyes, to stare at the fire. It was as good as admitting to it.

"Where, Titus?" Tuttle demanded.

"A woman."

"Tell us! Tell us now!" Billy roared, clapping his hands twice.

"Billy loves him stories of the womens, he surely does," Cooper declared. "So tell us your woman story, Bass. And make it a good'un. We all been without for too long, and likely be some weeks afore we winter up with some friendly Injun gals."

"Injun gals!" Hooks repeated with enthusiasm, rubbing his crotch and humping his hand. "Good poontang, them Injun gals for Billy Hooks."

"Best part of living in the mountains for the man," Silas said. "So, y' gonna tell us 'bout your woman?"

"A widow woman," Bass finally admitted. "Just a lonely . . . widow woman. Been 'thout a man for a long time."

"Them's the best kind!" Cooper exclaimed with a smile. "They know just how a man gets—going too long 'thout a wet woman wrapped around his stinger. Damned thankful too—no matter how a fella treats 'em."

"Yeah—them widder-women kind get the hunger bad as us," Tuttle added.

"So," Cooper announced in a loud voice suddenly, "before Titus Bass here spins his tale of the widder woman and how she give him the grayback nits . . . I believe it be time we give our new partner here a new name."

"N-new name?" Bass stammered.

Billy chimed right in, "Yes, yes! A new name!"

"You got something in mind?" Tuttle asked of Cooper.

Silas shrugged. "S'pose I do, Bud. Just look for yourself. Lookee what he's got hisself doing for days on end now."

"Itching," Tuttle replied as he stared at Bass. "He's scratching all over hisself. Damn but he's got him a passel of them nits, and bad!"

"Scratchin' is what he's doing," Silas said. "So—I say let's give him a new name what's fittin' for all them nits he's been digging at."

"We gonna call him nit?" Hooks asked with a silly grin.

"Nawww," Cooper growled as he stood and stepped over behind Bass with his warm tin cup of coffee in hand—which he slowly began to pour on Titus's head.

When Bass started to jerk aside to get away, Cooper's empty hand came down to clamp on one of his shoulders as he continued to pour the warm coffee on the newcomer's long brown hair. His head and shoulders steamed in the cold, frosty air, just like their coffee tins.

Then Cooper flung his cup aside and spread a hand over the crown of Bass's head, raising his eyes to the black of that winter night, his voice booming in declaration.

"Henceforth and for yonder time—let all men know this here pilgrim nigger no longer be called Titus Bass, greenhorn . . . but from now on he be the free trapper we gonna know as—*Scratch!*"

SEVEN

"There h'ain't no use to pushing on," Silas Cooper announced to the other three that late afternoon as the wind and snow battered them with such force that it nearly wore a man out. "We'll hunker down to camp here."

"Don't figger we can make it?" Bud Tuttle asked before he swung out of the saddle right behind Cooper in the deep, swirling snow they had been slogging their way through.

"Sun's falling," Silas explained, looking off to the west, then looked up ahead of them. "Clouds dropped on that pass up yonder. H'ain't no way we're gonna make it over an' back down to timber afore dark no way."

Titus watched them both anxiously. In the last few weeks he had come to trust their judgment on just about everything. And now the four of them had just passed timberline into the open, where the wind battered and bruised them without respite. The animals were beginning to bog down in ever-deeper snow. All around them the soft white flakes kept on falling, gusting, swirling in what was close to becoming a whiteout.

"We gonna get ourselves snowed in here, Silas!" Billy Hooks whined.

"What about game?" Titus asked, anxious, his belly growling. "Game?"

Bass continued, "How we gonna eat?"

"There'll be game, Scratch. Don't y' fret yourself 'bout that."

"And if there ain't, for balls' sake?" Tuttle demanded, slogging up through the snow that reached to their knees.

"Then we'll eat our damned horses," Cooper replied, glaring at Bud. "Beginning with yours!"

For a moment the two men stared at one another, shoulders loose, hands encased in those crude blanket mittens ready to snatch up a belt pistol or knife if the other jumped.

"C'mon, boys," Hooks finally cooed. "Let's g'won back down there some to that last big patch of trees where we can fort up."

Without taking his eyes off Tuttle, Cooper said, "Plumb center idee you got, Billy. Let's camp, boys."

Until Silas and Billy yanked their horses and mules around and started back down the slope on foot, followed a moment later by Bud Tuttle, Bass didn't realize he had been gripping the butt of the big pistol he carried stuffed in the wide belt at his waist.

There was something deadly about Silas Cooper—something always there right under the surface, something that he figured could strike with the quickness of a cottonmouth while the man was still smiling at you, talking to you . . . giving you no warning of the danger. In his thirty-one years Titus had learned that some men were easy to steer clear of because you had a clear sense of who they were and the danger they posed. And then there were a few like Cooper. They were the scariest of all.

The sort who could turn on you in the blink of an eye. When you had no idea it was coming.

Down the gentle slope the four men slid and skidded, plunging between the sparse, wind-tortured scrub cedar until they reached the copse of stunted pine Hooks had suggested. Here at least, Titus thought as they crowded into the cluster of trees, they would be out of most of that wind driving the snow into thick, wavering banners of ground blizzard, a wind that this high could cut through a man like a hot pewter knife would slide right through Marissa Guthrie's freshly churned butter.

"I-I . . . ," and Bass worked hard to keep his teeth from chattering in the cold. "I ain't n-never been this g-goddamned high afore."

Tuttle turned his head to regard the leaden sky, the clouds no more than fifty, maybe as much as a hundred, feet at the most over their heads. "You best watch your swearing, Scratch. We're up high enough on these mountains a man might just run hisself into a angel or two!"

Hooks laughed easily with that. "Long as them angels is womens—I don't mind running onto 'em at all! Yessirreebob! Been dreaming more an' more about soft breasties and a woman humping up and down on my stinger. I'd take me a angel right about now—right here in the snow!"

Tuttle wagged his head, looking at Bass to say, "Billy and his womens. Always got a passel of 'em on the brain."

"Been thinking on women my own self," Titus admitted.

Tuttle smiled. "Ain't hard to figger, Scratch. Not when a man's been doing so long without."

"Sounds like you think on the womens too, Bud."

Tuttle stopped his horse, turned toward it to throw up the stirrup and grab the cinch. "I'm a man—like any else, I s'pose."

"You think back on a special girl?" Titus inquired.

"Just remember women. First one of 'em to come into my head. I ain't never been particular when it comes to poking a woman center . . . so why should I be particular when it comes to thinking about 'em?"

"I remember this one gal back along the Ohio," Titus began to explain. "She weren't my first, but she was a whore—so she was the first what showed me how much fun poking could be with a woman."

"You 'member her name?" Bud asked as he dragged the saddle and blanket from his horse.

"Abigail—uh, Mincemeat was her given name."

"There been others, ain't there?"

"A few. Sweet farmer's daughter and a mess of dark-skinned backwater whores."

"And don't forget that widow woman what give you them passel of gray-back nits."

"Even thought on her a time or two, I have," Bass admitted. "All them lonely nights I camped along the Platte, even after I got out here to these mountains."

"Sometimes all the quiet out here can make a man's mind turn to such things as womenfolk, the women a man left him back there," Tuttle suggested as he turned away to gaze at the rest of their pack stock Cooper and Hooks were driving into the trees.

"Only natural, ain't it—"

The loud shriek of the mule interrupted the two of them. In the copse of stunted pine, there amid the jostling mass of pack animals and horses, Bass could see Cooper lunging about, swinging a long tree limb—and each time he connected with a sound audible over the crying wind, one of the mules bawled in a painful bray.

Titus began to step in Silas's direction. "What the devil do you think—"

But Tuttle leaped out, grabbing Bass's sleeve, snagging it and stopping Titus in his tracks. "For balls' sake—don't! It ain't none of your business, Scratch."

"Any man beating his animals, that is my business," he said as he whipped his arm free of Tuttle's grip.

As Titus moved this way, then that, to cut a path through the milling stock, which Cooper and Hooks were corralling within a roped-off area strung between that stand of trees, Titus watched Silas work himself into a fury, lashing out, lunging, swinging that long tree limb at the back of the mule mare that reared and scree-hawed in pain and fear, clumsy because only half her packs had been taken from her back. As Bass got closer, he saw the limb snap in half at the back of the mule's head. Dazed, the animal stumbled sideways, wild-eyed with fear, nostrils throbbing as it tried to swing its haunches around and kick out.

Cooper swung once more with the short half of the limb he clutched like a war club in both hands—but didn't make contact as the mule lunged aside. His rage boiling over, Silas hurled the limb down into the skiff of snow, where he fought a moment for footing, then dragged his big smoothbore horse pistol from the wide sash that held his blanket coat closed. As the weapon came up, Cooper was cursing above the bawl of the mule and the cry of the wind, dragging the hammer back two clicks to full-cock . . . then pointed the muzzle directly at the mule's head, little more than an arm's length from the frightened eyes that stared at the human, the beast not knowing its next breath would be its last.

Leaping and shoving his way through the anxious, milling, frightened animals, Titus landed next to Cooper, grabbing Silas's left wrist—and clamped down with all the strength he could muster. All he could remember was how the packmare's eye stared up at him as he pulled the trigger.

"You weasel-stoned son of a bitch!" Cooper growled as he jerked around to stare right into Bass's face. "Let go a'me!"

"Put it away!" Titus snapped, feeling the big man's arm tremble in fury.

"Gonna shoot you first!"

Struggling to keep the oak-thick arm down and the pistol pointed at the ground, Bass pleaded, "Don't shoot that mule—damn, please don't shoot it."

Cooper's eyes narrowed, and he immediately quit trying to thrash his arm loose of Bass's two-handed grip. "The mule? The mule, is it?"

"Don't kill 'er."

"That mare ain't been nothing but trouble since we took 'er on," Cooper said, his eyes still seething. "Time I got rid of what makes trouble for me. Now, y' just let go a'me and stand back. I got work to finish—"

"I ain't letting go," Bass said resolutely, watching how his words startled the bigger man. "You cain't go an kill her for no good reason."

"No good reason?" Cooper shrieked. "I got good reason, Titus Bass . . . and for nothing more'n the hell of it if'n I wanna."

Desperate not to watch another animal die with a lead ball in its brain, Titus blurted, "L-lemme have 'er."

Something came across Silas's face in that next moment as he stared down at Titus Bass, standing there toe to toe, only inches between them. "Y' . . . y' say y' want this cantankerous pile of mule shit for yourself?"

"Just lemme have 'er and you won't have to waste your time no more on the mule."

Silas wagged his head. "But I awready give y' a mule to use for packin' your truck and plews."

Titus nodded, sensing his arms growing weary as he continued to grip Cooper's wrist. "I'll trade you. That's what we'll do."

"A trade." Finally Silas nodded, then gazed at where Bass held his wrist. "Awright. We'll work us a fair trade. Now, y' best let go a'me, Titus."

He immediately released Cooper's arm. "You gimme that mule and I'll give you back the one you gimme that first day you run onto me."

Cooper rubbed the wrist Bass had held imprisoned for those long, terrifying moments. "Hold on there: it ain't so easy to trade pack stock. You're just a dumb pilgrim when it comes to tradin', ain'cha, Scratch? Y' see, y' made the mistake of letting the other man find out just how willing y' was to be trading—showed me plain just how much y' wanted what I got to trade."

"We're just swapping the mules, one for t'other," Bass said.

"That's only fair, Silas," Tuttle agreed, licking his cracked lips nervously.

"One for t'other. One for t'other," Billy Hooks repeated with that ready smile of his as he shifted back and forth from foot to foot.

"No," Cooper snapped. "If'n y' want this mule so bad, then we'll trade. But it's gonna cost y' more'n just that fly-bait mule I give y' when I first took you on. That'uns the wust in our hull bunch."

Bass swallowed. "What's it gonna cost me?"

Silas appeared to regard that for a long moment as he peered over at the mule carrying all that Bass owned in the world. "Y' been doing good at trappin', Scratch."

"I been catching on what you learned me, yeah."

"Got better'n Tuttle, y' have—right off."

Bud snorted. "That ain't hard for ary a man to do!"

"And you're damn near good as Billy Hooks right now."

Titus said, "I'd wager I *am* as good as Billy right now."

"Maybeso you're better'n me," Hooks injected, "but you'll never be good as Silas Cooper!"

"Maybe I will," Bass replied, watching those coal-black eyes come back to rest on him. "One day real soon."

Cooper asked quietly, "Y' want this here mule, Scratch?"

"You know I do, goddammit," he snapped, knowing full well it was going to cost him dearly.

"Then I'll trade y'," Cooper offered. "For your ol' fly-bait animal, and half what plews y'll catch this winter."

Tuttle gasped. "T-that mean from here on out, Silas?"

"No, that means half of everything Scratch trapped up till now, and half till we reach ronnyvoo come summer."

Titus seethed inside. "W-what's ronnyvoo?"

Silas explained, "Where I tol't you we was gonna barter in our beaver come next summer. Drink some whiskey and poke a squar or two . . . barter us plunder for next year. Ronnyvoo."

Bass swallowed hard, knowing he had nowhere to wiggle in the negotiations. "H-half of my hides this winter . . . till ronnyvoo—"

"You want the mule . . . or don'cha?"

"I want it," Bass said squarely.

"Then it's a deal," Cooper said, sticking out his bare right hand in that bitterly cold wind.

Bass yanked off his mitten, took the hand, and shook as he gazed up into those marblelike eyes of Cooper's. "It's a deal."

Then he felt Silas slowly start squeezing, bearing down harder, slowly harder as the muscles and bones of his hand cried out in sudden, hot pain. When he looked back up at Cooper's eyes, they were lit with cold, cold fire.

Behind that big grin of his, Silas said, "And . . . one more thing, Titus Bass."

That hand hurt like hell, so much it was hard to speak. "What's . . . what's that, Silas?"

"Don't y' ever, ever again lay a hand on me . . ."

He interrupted, "I don't figger I'll have cause to lay a hand on—"

But Cooper snarled, interrupting, "Or the next time y'll pull back a bloody stump."

That mule-for-beaver bargain had been nothing short of mountain thievery.

And for certain there had been times since that very first day when Titus Bass wished he'd let Silas Cooper go right on ahead and put a lead ball in that mule's head.

But for all the trouble she'd give him in those days and weeks that would come to pass—besides the pain of having to trade off that half of his beaver plews to boot—Scratch remained steadfastly hopeful that the sorrel mule would one day come around and behave like a decent, docile, and obedient animal . . . the sort that would prove herself to be a true partner to a man, just like those mules that had faithfully plowed the ground for his pap back in Boone County.

Why, Titus had even named the stubborn, stiff-backed mule—something new for him: Bass had never before named a horse or mule, ever—but feeling this time that to give her a name might not only make it seem she was just that much more special to him, but she might well come to know the sound of her own name, learn to recognize it, and might thereby figure she was pretty damned special to him.

"Hannah," he had told her aloud the third morning of that storm, after sitting and studying her for the longest time, watching the sorrel's big eyes study him in turn as she worked on a patch of ground he had cleared of snow. "I've always favored that name—for a wife of my own, thought maybeso for my daughter. So I'd like you to have it . . . Hannah."

As hard as he was to work in the weeks to come, hoping that the mule might just one day come around to his way of thinking and try a little to be his friend . . . well—trouble was, the two of them were still a long, long way off from that glorious day.

The early-winter storm on the pass had indeed continued another three days and nights, dumping an icy snow without stop. In their sheltering ring of trees the four men chopped what firewood they needed from the limbs and branches of that copse of stunted pine. A part of each morning they used their time to scrape and chisel down through the new snow to reach some bare ground for the horses and mules grown weary of digging for themselves with bloody hooves. Most afternoons two of the men ventured out to hunt in relay, going as far off as they would dare—every one of them aware how a man could easily get himself turned around in the endless white blur of a blizzard.

What they managed to bring in for all their effort was hardly enough to keep one man well fed, much less four hearty appetites in that subzero cold: a few snowshoe hares, a handful of blue grouse, and a fat marmot—one more than Titus ever wanted to see again in his life. Nevertheless, that poor fare along with the one bony Indian pony they sacrificed kept those men alive enough so that after five more days, when the weather cleared, they were strong enough to urge their animals on up past timberline, across the loose, shifting talus and shale of that treacherous saddle, then down the far side of the eastern slopes into the trees, where they would surely have more luck hunting what game had been driven down, ever down, to lower elevations by the winter storms.

"That back there be Buffalo Pass," Cooper announced near twilight of that ninth day as they reached a meadow where the snow had blown clear on the lee side.

"You been up there afore?" Titus asked.

"We have," Tuttle answered, flicking a glance at Cooper. "But we ain't ever come this way."

Turning to Cooper, Titus inquired, "How'd you know what the pass is called?"

"Only know cause I just named it," Silas admitted. "Look for yourself."

The three others turned to look up behind them as the gray clouds were beginning to drop, hurrying in to obscure the high granite formations that marked the very trail they had made across the saddle. Stark against the darkening clouds lowering on the pass was one formation in particular that from this side appeared to closely resemble a buffalo bull's head—horns, chin whiskers and all.

"Buffalo Pass, it be, Silas," Tuttle agreed as he clambered to the ground, stood a moment rubbing life back into his cold knees and thighs, then started to trudge back to the pack animals. "Scratch, you and Billy get some rope strung out in them trees for a corral, an' I'll bring in the cavvyyard."

"Cavvy . . . cavvyyard?" Bass repeated.

"The remuda," Billy said with that impish grin of his. "The horses . . . our herd, you idjit!"

"Cavvyyard," Titus repeated again, liking the feel of it on his tongue. "I ain't never heard it called such—and you called it something else?"

"A remuda."

"Yeah," he said. "A remuda."

"Billy's picked up all he could of that greaser talk," Cooper explained.

Hooks defended himself. "Some of them greaser words I really took a shine to, Silas."

Cooper sneered. "That's all them greasers good for, Billy—an' don't y' forget it."

Billy leaned close to Titus, saying, "Silas don't like him them greasers down south in the Mexican Territory. We run onto a few of 'em trapping with American boys outta the greaser settlements a time or two—so Silas come to hate them people more ever' time we bump into 'em."

As he walked past with a horse at the end of each arm trailing behind him, Tuttle said, "Maybeso that's why this is about as far south as we ever go nowadays, don't you figger, Billy?"

"Silas's medicine tells him we best stay in the country somewheres atween the Blackfoots and the greasers," Hooks continued as Titus tied off one end of a long rope to one of the trees, then began to play out the rope to another tree.

As he wrapped the weathered hemp rope around the tree once, then moved off for the next, Bass inquired, "What's up there in that north country make a man wanna get troubled by them Blackfoots anyway, Billy?"

"Beaver," Hooks replied.

"For balls' sake—big beaver!" Tuttle added as he finished tying off the second horse to the first section of their rope corral.

Cooper moved past with two horses and said, "The biggest beaver a man ever lay his eyes on."

"That's it?" Titus asked.

Stopping, Silas regarded Bass a moment, then added, "Beaver big enough— ever' last one of 'em seal fat an' sleek, so fine that a man might damn well risk his own hair just to lay down his traps in that country."

"Three Forks: my, my," Hooks commented with a cluck of his tongue.

"Fine country," Tuttle agreed.

"Country just crawling with Blackfoot niggers—yessirreebob," Hooks replied.

On his way past Titus to fetch another pair of the animals, Cooper slapped Bass on the back of the shoulders. "Maybeso that's where we'll take Scratch here come next winter."

"Blackfoot country?" Titus repeated. How the name of that land ignited images of a forbidden land.

"Beaver pelts nigh big as blankets," Tuttle said. "Just big enough to bury a man in when those red niggers lift his hair!"

"Bud's a might squampshus, you understand," Cooper declared. "He h'ain't much a trapper, so it don't seem worthwhile to go up to that country and stick his neck out for the prime beaver."

"Prime beaver," Billy repeated in a shrill voice. "Beaver just calling out, 'Yoohoo! Come an' get me Bud Tuttle!' Then 'nother beaver cross the stream hollers out, 'No, Bud Tuttle—come an' get *me*!' Pretty soon all them beavers is scrapping and fighting so hard to be the one what gets catched in Bud's trap that the poor nigger never does catch him very many!"

"Sometimes, Billy Hooks," Tuttle growled, his face flushing with anger, "you're nothing more'n lucky. A lucky son of a bitch for what little brains you got left, what little ain't already poured out your bunghole."

"I may not be smart as you, Bud—but I'm sure as hell a better trapper'n you're ever gonna be!"

"Right now all I want out o' the two of you is for all you boys go drag in some timber—since you finished stringing up our corral, Billy." Silas jumped into the argument as he brought up the last two horses. "Hush up your yammerin' and get us plenty of wood. It's fixin' to get dark on us real quick."

Tuttle strode up with the last of the mules in tow, asking, "How long you figger afore we'll make it down to Park Kyack, Silas?"

"The north park? Why, lookee down there, Bud—an' the rest of you. There it lay. Park Kyack."

Hook wheeled about on his heel, his smile broadening. "Kyack? Down yonder's where we'll winter up with the Yutas?"

Cooper nodded. "That's right, Billy. Y' know what that means, don'cha?"

Leaping into the air with a wild, whirling, primal dance, Hooks shook and trembled like an old dog whose master had just returned home from a long, long journey. "Means womens! Womens! And more womens!"

That night Titus tossed in his blankets, unable to warm himself enough to escape the deliciously tempting dreams that flitted about the broken pieces of what shattered sleep he could capture.

Everywhere he looked, it was black. Up, down, and in all directions—then he realized he was floating in the water as black as the sky, stretching far, far to the horizon, where it touched the black sky and they became one. Only when Titus moved his arms to keep himself afloat did the starshine ripple across the surface of the water . . . then she was there.

Amy slowly pushed her way toward him across the black starlit water rippling in front of her as she slowly flung her arms out to stroke. As she drew ever closer, he could even see her bare feet break the surface now and again as her long legs kicked and paddled. Her shoulders bare and glistening with the water. Her white neck so long, and her dark hair strung out behind her. Then he saw a hint of the flesh at the tops of her breasts as they broke the surface, side to side with each stroke as she came closer, closer.

Waiting for her, Titus could feel his flesh harden, stiffen, lengthen—knowing that she was coming to him here in their secret pond. Here where they met to satisfy their great hunger.

Anxious, he reached out his arms to Amy—ready to draw her to him, to lift her up, then urge her down on the throbbing flesh between his legs . . . but as he strained to reach for her, she took a breath and disappeared beneath the surface.

"Titus," a gentle voice called out to him over his shoulder, so close he could almost feel the woman's breath on his skin. "Titus Bass."

He turned from the ripples where Amy had disappeared to watch Marissa Guthrie drawing close, stopping there on the edge of the bank, stalks and flecks of hay cluttering her hair the way it always had when they had savagely coupled in the loft of her father's barn there south of St. Louis.

"Oh, Marissa—it is you!" he heard himself exclaim, heart hammering, beginning to paddle for her.

"Come to me, Titus! I'll give you children, and this land—give you everything a man could ever want—just come to me!"

How quickly she threw off her dress, naked beneath—then dived into the water. He felt almost ready to agree with anything Marissa asked as he reached her . . . her head coming out of the water right in front of him. Titus grabbed her naked shoulders in his two hands and lifted her hungrily out of the water to catch a glimpse of her breasts. How he had loved kissing them, sucking them, fondling them as it drove her wild with desire for him.

Bending, Titus nuzzled and sucked on them, lost in the pure heaven of the smell, the taste, the feel of her flesh. Then he brought his face up, planting his mouth over hers and opening her lips as he drew her breath into his lungs.

She tasted of cornmeal and hard cider, the tang of old smoke and that morning's hog sausage gone stale on her breath. Marissa had never smelled quite like that before.

Titus drew his head back in wonder to ask her why, now, did she smell so . . . when he found he was holding the widow. She smiled, her eyes filled as they tearfully uttered their thanks; then she pulled his head down between her breasts once more, pressing him close, close, so close he could not breathe anything but the scent of her ravenous sex as she reached out and took hold of his hardened flesh, beginning to stroke it rapidly, urgently, savagely.

How he wanted in her before he exploded. And oh, how he begged the woman to place him there, but just as he began to murmur to her, the first great waves of relief washed over him. How miraculous it felt to have her hand sliding up and down the length of him as he rocked against her, his face buried between her breasts as he groaned in sheer happiness.

Moments later, as he finished, Titus suddenly realized the water had disappeared, and with it the black sky overhead. Yet worst of all was the startling cold where his cheek lay. Instead of the widow woman's breasts, his face lay against the old, scarred, unforgiving leather of his saddle. And instead of her hand wrapped around his hardened flesh, Bass realized it was his own.

Just as it was his loneliness for a woman—any woman—that troubled him with these dreams most every night now. How he prayed each time he awoke that it was not Amy nor Marissa, not even the widow woman the dreams were telling him he should join himself to. Praying it was nothing more than the woman hunger Tuttle spoke of, the sort of appetite every man in the mountains must endure for long periods of drought before he can dance and revel in the land of plenty with brown-skinned squaws who are every bit as hungry to have a man between their legs as a man is ravenous in his appetites to have himself planted in their moist heat.

Lying there, Titus found the night so quiet that he could hear the flames lick along the length of some of the limbs in their fire. Raising his head, Titus looked round at the other three, all four of them radiating out from the fire like spokes of a wheel. He dragged his cracked, thin-soled moccasins back under the layer of thick blankets and covered his head once more. Warmer was it to breathe here in the dark, he thought.

And closing his eyes again, brooding on how his own stark white flesh might well look pressed against the dark thigh or gently rounded belly of an Injun woman, Bass put himself back to sleep. Behind his eyes the white and brown flesh rubbed together so fast and with such savage fury that he wasn't sure any longer if he really was master to his fate in coming here to this far, foreign, and frightening place . . . or in the end had he only discovered that he was nothing more than a slave to his hungers.

She smelled of smoke and grease.

Her clothing, which lay discarded at the far side of this tiny lodge, smelled strongly of her woman scent mixed in with the firesmoke and the spatter of cooking grease. Even her skin and hair—spread there beneath his nose and across his chest like black, glossy tendrils as she lay sleeping—all of it smelled of smoke and grease and the shocking cold of winter forest.

Tui-rua-ci.

Fawn, she was called.

Coals still glowed in the fire pit, and it was warm with her under the buffalo robes and heavy wool blankets. Morning would be a long time getting here in the heart of winter. Here, nestled in the marrow of the mountains. At long last now he could luxuriate in not having to rise before sunup to check a trapline.

Weary, Titus closed his eyes again, letting the blackness ooze over him once more. No longer did he worry about where the others were or what became of them. Silas, Bud, and Billy were all three likely out cold right about then— noisily sawing lumber the way they snored—having danced themselves silly in the ballet of that beast with two backs. Hooks was a hungry, voracious man with a sexual appetite that drove him to couple repeatedly with any woman, wife or daughter, young or middling, who either had her the slightest inclination to bed him or was graciously turned over to the white man as a gift from a good host.

And Bass figured Tuttle and Cooper weren't the sort to lag far behind Hooks in the hunger department.

Most days in winter camp the four white men gathered to do nothing more than did the Ute men in winter camp: sit, eat, smoke, and swap their stories of past battles or their exploits in killing a bear or capturing an eagle for its feathers. Over the past weeks Titus came to understand the rudiments of that talk Silas, Bud, and Billy had with the Ute, slowly learning that universal language of the fingers, hand, and arm moving in a graceful dance of silent expression.

Then each night, from the Ute widow who had taken Titus into her lodge, he learned a little more of the tribe's spoken tongue.

Not that she was all that much to feast your eyes on, but he could tell right off that second day after they reached the Ute's winter camp that she was good of heart. Besides, she knew just how to pleasure him in the blankets, and what she cooked over her lodge fires he could eat with relish. Although it had taken him some to get used to her boiling all them organs.

In fact, their first night together she had fed him elk heart—turned slimy and gelatinous simmering there in the kettle for what must surely have been the better part of the past three days.

"The ol' man here," Cooper had explained that first afternoon, telling Titus the results of a long exchange of sign language, some dutiful handshaking, and loud elocutions in both Ute and white tongues, "he's the gal's uncle."

"Whose uncle?" Bass had inquired, his eyes searching the crowd of women and children who had gathered behind their men in welcoming the white men into their midst when the four had burst out of the timber into the bottomland, whooping and hollering to beat the band, firing their rifles into the air to greet the young warriors who had hurried out to meet them—their dark, brazen frowns turned quickly to happy smiles all round. Indeed, Titus could readily see why Tuttle had repeatedly emphasized that the Ute were a good people to hunker down with for the winter.

"Why," Silas replied, "the woman who said she'd take y' in, Scratch."

"T-take me in?" he echoed, then immediately grew particular. "She be young or old?"

"Y' grown particular?" and Cooper flashed him a disapproving look. "It don't matter, do it?"

With a shrug Bass glanced over the female faces and said, "Long as it's a place to sleep, I s'pose it don't."

Cooper slapped a hand on Bass's shoulder. "Leastways, she's old enough to be a widder woman."

"A widder woman!" Billy shrieked. "Ah-hah! Scratch's gonna fork him a widder woman for winter!"

"Just like the widder woman what give him the nits!" Tuttle had gushed with laughter too.

Enough laughter that it made Bass's cheeks burn in embarrassment, and his stomach churn with a sudden angry seizure. Maybe he had no business expecting anything better, what with his being the greenest among them, but to be made the butt of their jokes once again—after all this time and after so many jokes played on him . . . now, that galled him all the more.

"A widow woman," Titus repeated, the words tasting sour. He swallowed hard, forcing down the bitter tang of them as he was of a sudden reminded of the Widow Grigsby. Then he jutted out his chin. "By damn, you niggers—at least that squaw'll be no stranger to gathering firewood!" He whirled on black-haired Billy to say right to the man's face, "And I'll wager she knows her way around a kettle pot too, Billy Hooks! Better'n I can say for you!"

Cooper banged Tuttle on the back, roaring with good-natured laughter, throwing his head back and letting his voice rise to the winter sky. "Why, if the greenhorn here ain't got him a bit of ha'r after all!"

Bass continued, "So if'n it's here we're to plop down for the winter, by Jehoshaphat, I figure to stay warm and keep my belly full at that widder woman's fire!"

Tuttle slapped a hand on Hooks's shoulder, the both of them sniggering uncontrollably. Bud said, "I'll . . . I'll bet that widder woman knows her way round under a buffler robe too, Titus Bass!"

Silas Cooper roared again at that, his Adam's apple bouncing up and down between the thick, muscular cords in his neck, then told his three companions, "Good for us it be that all this high-larity come at just the time when these here Ute bucks is all smiling and acting good-natured themselves."

"Wouldn't be for us to be laughing at that ol' chief's gift of his niece, would it, now?" Tuttle observed, winking at Bass.

"Boys, looks to be we got us as prime a place to hunker down for the next few weeks as there be in the mountains," Silas repeated later as the crowd began to disperse and the four chosen women remained behind in the bright afternoon light to take home their white lodge guests. "Empty your packs and keep your plunder at your side this first night. Be sartin y' picket your animals outside your door come sundown—so it be close at hand for the first few nights. Jest in case."

Tuttle asked, "You skeery of these here Yutas, Silas?"

"They seem to be a good sort and welcomed us all and one," Cooper replied. "But it don't ever pay to let down your guard with red niggers—now, do it?"

"When we get together again, Silas?" Tuttle inquired, some consternation crossing his face as the four women began to inch away to their own lodges, each one signaling for her guest to follow.

Cooper smiled within his dark beard, his eyes dancing like a bull elk about to rut. "I don't see me any reason to gather back up till morning, boys—when we're damn good and ready to roll out of the she-wimmens' warm blankets," he said, looping his long arm over the shoulder of the sharp-nosed woman who was taking Cooper in.

Titus gave the three other women a quick study and decided his must surely be the oldest among them. Yet she had the kindest face. In his book such an attribute went a long, long way to making him feel content enough to leave the company of the others and follow her home.

That first day he had looked back once, watching the others splitting up, leading their horses and pack animals away in four different directions. Then she had pulled on his elbow, motioning wordlessly, and pointed to a small smoke-blackened lodge off at the edge of the village circle near a copse of bare-limbed aspens.

For sure, he had decided right then and there: it was one thing to saddle up and push west all on one's own—totally alone. Such solitude was something Titus had no problem enduring; indeed, he had welcomed that longed-for aloneness. But that evening for those first few hours there in the Ute camp, he found himself feeling something altogether different. Sensing most a bit of despair and frustration at being brought here and handed off to stay among a foreign people, not knowing their language nor their customs . . . all that mingled with his own excitable male anxiety at again being set adrift with a woman—almost exactly the same feeling he had experienced when the riverboat pilot Ebenezer Zane had arranged it so that for an entire night a very young Titus Bass was to be alone and undisturbed with an Ohio River whore named Mincemeat.

Many things that first awkward night with the Ute widow made him fondly recall his nervousness and self-doubt with the skinny, chicken-winged whore. But, like Mincemeat, this squaw with the young child slung in a blanket at her back certainly did her best to make the white stranger feel welcome, at home, and very much wanted.

It came as no surprise when she openly nursed the child in front of him after she had rekindled the fire, brought in some water from the frozen creek nearby, then put on a kettle to continue boiling that elk heart. Once the child had fallen asleep at her breast, the woman had nested the young boy back among the buffalo robes at the side of the lodge, pulled back on her own hide coat, and ducked out the lodge door. In minutes she was back—but only to fetch up her crude, rusted camp ax. Again she left the lodge, but as soon as he heard her chopping at wood with the ax, Titus pulled on his blanket coat and went out to help her.

Inside once again with the woodpile replenished to the left of the door, they shed their coats and the woman took some dried greens from a round rawhide container, dropping them into the boiling water where the elk heart rolled and tumbled in its gelatinous juices, slowly cooking. She poured him a tin cup of water from a small skin she had hung from a rope that went from pole to pole, wrapped about each one, inside that small lodge. As he sipped slowly, Titus silently inspected how there was a separate section of hides suspended from that rope so that they formed an inner liner tied some five feet high from ground to rope. A portion of that liner was even lashed across the doorway so that it now formed a double inner barrier against winter's cold, holding within even more of the small fire's warmth.

That proved to be no problem: keeping enough of the fire's radiant heat. He soon discovered a small fire was quite enough to warm such an insulated lodge. Many were the early mornings when he routinely awoke in the gray, predawn cold, or those evenings as he drifted off to sleep with her already snoring softly beside him, or on each of those dark nights when he slowly came awake for no good reason he could fathom, listening to the nightsounds in the camp around him, staring up at the black scrap of sky between the two large flaps of buffalo hide that surrounded the smoke hole, helping direct and pull the fire's smoke from the lodge. It was up there where the poles came together in their unique spiral—the collection of poles rising slowly, gently, even beautifully, rising in a swirl as smoke itself would spiral slowly on its way to the heavens.

So warm had it been some of the past winter days that the woman would pull back the liner flap and push aside the door, leaving the entrance open, allowing a breeze to slip into the lodge and rise up through the smoke hole, creating a cool current of air that pleased him. If the day was a sunny one, and the others were not dragging him off to check on their traplines, the four white men would join the warriors old and young sitting in the sun. There the trappers each had a chance to practice more of their spoken Ute and the Indians practiced their English. Still, because most of their conversations could not be expressed aloud, there were many hours that winter for Titus to practice his sign language. For the longest time he continued to speak aloud the words his moving hands formed—and soon discovered that some of the warriors, like the widow, did their best to mimic his English for certain objects, actions, or feelings.

Like the routine he had learned on his father's farm, or that daily ritual he grew accustomed to on Ebenezer Zane's Kentucky flatboat as it floated downriver to New Orleans in the autumn of 1810, this easy rhythm of a trapper's winter life as a man went about the predawn setting of the traps and the twilight harvest of his beaver—this too was a satisfying existence of routine and regularity.

Somewhere in the darkness out beyond the nearby fringe of lodgepole pine, Bass heard a dog bark now. Easy enough to tell it was a camp dog, not one of those wild dogs Billy explained were called coyotes. No, this one barked in the gray light of dawn-coming, reminding him a bit of how old Tink had bayed back in Boone County . . . not with the yip-yipping howl of the coyotes that stayed back among the hills or warily crossed the prairielands.

The sun would still be some time before making an appearance this morning, yet there was enough gray light seeping down from the smoke hole above him for Titus to begin to make out the shapes of things in the lodge, where his rifle stood close at hand, the small mound of blankets and buffalo robes where the woman's child slept, the boy breathing softly. And he could even make out where he hung his buckskin shirt and the two tube leggings the woman had sewn for him.

That first night in the Ute camp she had wasted no time in attempting to explain that he needed to throw out the worn, grease-slickened wool clothing he was then wearing. By pinching her nose and pointing at his britches, jabbing a finger inside the folds of his blanket coat at his linsey-woolsey shirt, it became abundantly clear what she thought of his smelly, frayed, and worn apparel.

And the widow hadn't put up with her guest's poor hygiene for long at all either. It was only the second morning when he awoke to find her beating on his shirt spread out atop a large, flat stone, a small stone gripped in her hand as she repeatedly pounded his smoke- and sweat-blackened clothing.

"What the devil are you doing!" he shrieked at her, lunging out to wrench his shirt from her as he sat up, completely naked in the buffalo robe and blanket bed.

Just as promptly Fawn had grabbed the shirt back, holding it up before him to show the collar, pointing out the mashed bodies of the lice he had hosted for some time.

"I . . . I see," Titus had told her sheepishly, pantomiming for her to continue her killing of the varmints, hammering his fist down on the big rock. "Go 'head on, woman. Kill every last one of 'em for all I care!"

Again and again she pounded, until she leaned back in exasperation and gazed at him. No matter that he could not understand what words she chattered in disgust at the moment. But clearly there was resolve on her lined face as Fawn wrenched up his shirt and canvas breeches and quickly ducked from the lodge with them in hand.

"Where you going?" he demanded as the door flap slid back in place, a chilling gust of winter breeze tickling across his bare flesh.

With a shiver Titus pulled a smoke-scented blanket around his shoulders and scurried out the doorway in a crouch. Squinting in the new day's light reflected off the snow, he followed her as she stomped off toward a fire several other women were tending that early morning. Holding the shirt out as far as she could at the end of one arm, along with the breeches and his wool longhandles in the other hand, the widow instructed the others to stand back from their work at smoking a large elk hide draped over a tripod of saplings.

His bare feet began to complain with the cold of the trampled snow as he shrieked in frustration, "Said to you—where in hell you going with my clothes?"

Turning to look over her shoulder at him, Fawn muttered something in Ute to the others, then without further ceremony hurled the breeches beneath the kettle.

"Wait!" he hollered, lunging forward, not sure how he was going to rescue the pants from the flames that smoldered, sputtered, then suddenly began to catch hold of the greasy wool fabric.

"Damn you!" Titus said as he neared the woman.

But Fawn paid him no mind as she proceeded to fling the shirt atop the breeches—waited a few heartbeats until they began to smoke in kind—then hurled the filthy, faded red longhandles over the flames. Sighing with finality she stepped back, crossing her arms across her breasts, no small degree of self-satisfaction apparent on her face.

Skidding to a stop at the fire's side in a flurry of powdery snow, he grabbed a long stirring stick away from one of the other women. She immediately jerked it back from him so he had no choice but to whirl on the widow.

"What in . . . what'm I gonna do now?" he roared. "Woman—them's the only clothes I got me in the whole world! Damn if you women aren't the most consarned, exasperating creatures! Jehoshaphat—I s'pose you didn't figger I had to wear nothing more'n this goddamned blanket for the rest of the winter, did you?"

Behind their hands the women young and old sniggered at him. One of the oldest crones even pointed at his skinny white prairie-chicken legs protruding from the bottom of the pale-blue blanket and giggled, her wrinkled, old crow eyes merry. Titus looked down at his calves and ankles and feet, toes gone numb and turning blue as he stood there on the trammeled snow. Shivering, he realized he must look a sight. Maybe they laughed at just how silly a white man looked in nothing but a blanket, he decided—instead of how embarrassing it was for him that Fawn had thrown his old worn shucks in their morning fire.

He stood there blue-lipped and trembling inside his blanket with that bunch of women, all of them watching together as the flames consumed the last of his earthly clothing—until the widow turned, shot him a glance as she passed by, headed back to her lodge.

"Wait up!" he growled, wheeling barefoot in the snow, feeling club-footed with his unresponsive legs struggling to set themselves into motion.

From the corner of his eye he spotted Billy Hooks poking his head from a distant lodge, and nearby Tuttle came out to stand in the first shafts of winter sunlight, likely drawn by the early-morning commotion.

"Morning, Scratch!" Bud hollered out merrily, waving in genuine greeting. "How was your weddin' night?"

"Simply fine, goddammit!" he grumbled as he stumbled along stiff-legged. "Thanks for asking!"

Hooks laughed as he waved. "Better you put on some clothes, Scratch— afore you leave out to go calling on your neighbors!"

"Damn you too, Billy Hooks!" he spat, just about the time Fawn ducked her head and disappeared into the lodge.

Titus was right behind her.

Standing there inside the warmth of the lodge, he no longer shivered near as much, realizing just how cold he had been outside. And he tried to figure out what the hell to say to the widow—to tell her how angry he was—dismayed, really—that she had destroyed his clothing. But the more he watched her back as she knelt and started pulling at the laces on a rawhide container, the less he could think of what to say, and how to make Fawn understand just how she had poked a stick into his hornet's nest.

With the noise of their return, the child awoke and sat up, calling for its mother. She said something to the boy softly, and he lay back down, his wide, round, black eyes shifting from his mother to stare at the white man still standing near the door.

After a moment of rustling among the robes, Fawn turned to Bass and stood.

From her hands hung a large fringed buckskin shirt. She spoke to him, then shrugged, pantomiming that he was to take it. Bass held out one hand, still clutching the pale-blue blanket about him with the other.

"This for me?" he asked, then tapped his chest with a finger. "For me?"

With a nod the woman bent again and scooped up some more of the leather he now saw folded within a large, flat rawhide case. In each hand she held a legging as she stood. These too she held out for him to take.

"You," she said in poor imitation of his English. "You."

"Me?" and he allowed her to lay the two long tubes of buckskin over that arm of his clutching the shirt.

For a moment she stared at his crotch, then mimed a hand motion from waist to knee, up and down. And finally shrugged. Dropping to her knees again, she yanked her knife from her belt and pulled at a flap of the canvas he had draped over the piles of his possessions. The moment she jabbed the knife's point into the dirty cloth and began to cut a foot-wide strip from its edge, he howled in dismay.

"Wait!" and he went to his knees beside her, reaching to stop the knife.

Fawn pushed him back and frowned at him as he shrank back from her threat when she brought the knife up in front of his face. Bass whimpered as the woman went back to work over the canvas until she had a strip a good seven to eight feet long.

Standing, she stepped over to the liner rope and retrieved Bass's belt before returning to stop right in front of him.

"You," she repeated.

Glancing quickly at the boy child, Titus stood obediently. The woman tugged the blanket off one of his shoulders, then waited for him to complete the disrobing. Impatiently she tugged it off his other shoulder and started to pull the blanket from him.

Embarrassed, he stammered, "W-wait—I don't know what y-you're 'bout to—"

Tugging one last time, she managed to wrench the blanket out of his hands and rip it away from him. Now he stood before her totally naked, dropping his hands down to cover his manhood. Suspicious that this strange, frightening creature of a woman wanted him to poke her right there in front of the child.

But instead Fawn slipped her hands in behind his forearms and flung the leather belt around his waist, slipped the end through the buckle and latched it loosely over his bony hips. Then she retrieved the long strip of foot-wide canvas at her feet and stuffed one end up through the front of his belt, taking hold of the other end to jab it between his knees. Stunned into stone silence, Bass remained motionless as the widow went deftly about her work.

Looking over his shoulders, he watched as Fawn pulled the canvas up between his thighs, stuffed it up through the belt at the small of his back, then tugged it down until the end almost reached the back of his knees. Quickly she stepped in front of him and tugged on that end of the cloth until it too hung just at his knees. Only then did she step back and swiftly admire her work.

Fawn was soon back in motion. She took the buckskin shirt from where it hung over his arm and spread it over her hands so that she exposed the wide neck hole trimmed with red wool. Quietly she said, "You."

He nodded and quietly murmured, "Yeah, me."

Bass dipped his head forward for her to slip the shirt over his hair, then brought his two arms up to poke them into the long fringed sleeves. Pulling down on the long bottom of the garment, the widow smoothed the shirt out, stood back a moment, then went to his right arm. There she rolled up the long sleeve into a cuff to shorten it.

As she began to work the same alteration on the left arm, Titus said, "I s'pose your husband is a . . . *was* a bigger man than me."

That was plain to see from the way Bass swam in the sheer size of the shirt: the width of it draped across his bony shoulders, the length of the sleeves she had to cuff to shorten for him, and the immense girth of the shirt festooned with ermine skins and finished off with wide strips of colorful decoration.

As she bent to retrieve one of the leggings from the floor of the lodge, Titus tapped a finger against one of the strips of decoration.

"What's this?" he asked.

Instead of answering, the widow knelt before him, tugging at his foot until he grabbed hold of a lodgepole to steady himself and raised the cold foot. She shoved the legging up his leg, pulled his foot down, then pushed up the bottom of the shirt so that she could tie the two straps at the top of the legging in a loop over his belt. With the second legging knotted, the widow brought forth a few pair of moccasins. Again she knelt and pulled up one of his bare feet.

But as quickly she sat back on her haunches and shook her head. It was plain to see that the white man's feet were much too small for the moccasins. She flung them back onto the rawhide container, then appraised her work thoughtfully. With his old pair of moccasins and that canvas breechclout, the dead warrior's clothing would do him for now.

Then she turned from Titus, sat, and pulled the boy from his blankets as she tugged at the open side of her hide dress to expose a full breast.

Bass swallowed uncomfortably and sat, trying not to look at the breast. His heart hammered again in his chest as it had last night as he'd tossed and turned—thinking of the woman lying just a matter of feet away in the lodge, yet not knowing the ways of these people, how to approach an Indian woman with any suggestion of their coupling. So here she was, again exposing that soft round breast to him as she began softly humming to the child cradled across her lap in the rumpled blankets as she rocked him while he had his warm breakfast.

"Titus," he said finally, quietly—standing there above them.

She did not look up immediately when he spoke to her from the other side of the small lodge that he feared she hadn't heard.

"Titus."

When he repeated it, she raised her head and smiled.

Bass tapped his chest. "Titus."

"Ti-tuzz."

He nodded. "Me."

"Ti-tuzz you."

"Yepper. Titus. Me."

It grew quiet in the lodge once more as his cold, frozen feet warmed by the fire. Then he asked, "You?" and pointed at her.

"You. Ti-tuzz."

"No," he replied, and shook his head, then scooted a little closer to them, just near enough to lean forward and touch the top of her arm where the boy's head was cradled. "You."

Her eyes grew all the wider, round and black as berries thick on the hopvines back in Boone County, hard by the Ohio. With them she softly peered at the white man, looking into him; then the tip of her pink tongue licked at her lips before she spoke.

"Tui-rua-ci."

"Titus, me. You, Tui-rua-ci."

She nodded, smiling at him with more genuine happiness than he had seen on her face since coming to her lodge the day before yesterday. It was a smile that made him forgive her for burning his clothes, made him forgive the three trappers for bringing him here to such a foreign and frightening place, made him forgive himself for wanting another man's widow so badly.

"Tui-rua-ci," Fawn repeated, then her eyes dropped behind those lashes as she said his name softer than he could ever remember hearing it spoken: "Ti-tuzz."

EIGHT

Every few days during the heart of that winter when the weather tempered, the four of them left the village with some of the Ute warriors for a few days of hunting. Not only did they seek game to take back to the hungry mouths awaiting them in the winter camp, but the brownskins also surveyed the countryside for pony tracks, for firesmoke, for any sign of their enemies.

" 'Rapaho?" Titus repeated Tuttle's admonition as the white men came to a halt at the tree line bordering a clearing where the advance warriors had just come across some hoofprints.

"That's what these niggers say they was," Billy Hooks responded instead. " 'Rapaho. Good-sized war party of 'em too."

As the last of the group halted, most of the warriors dropped to the ground to inspect the tracks.

Silas Cooper agreed. "More red-bellies—out looking for ponies, h'ar, and coup!"

"How they so sure what band it were?" Titus asked, intrigued.

With a shrug Cooper explained, "Maybeso they figger to tell us they know the difference atween 'Rapaho and Shian—but I'll be damned if I can. C'mon over here with me, fellers—an' let's have us a look-see."

The three dismounted to join Cooper, dispersing among the

Ute, who were carefully moving up and down within the many foot- and hoof-prints, each blanket-coated warrior bent over, closely studying the enemy's spoor. The winter breeze tousled the feathers tied to loose, flowing hair or to those animal skins the warriors had pulled over their heads in the fashion of caps, each one tied with a rawhide string beneath a bare brown chin.

"That one," Cooper announced, pointing to one of the warriors, "he says that spot be where one of 'em got off his pony to look at a bad hoof." Silas bent over and studied the snowy, crusted ground himself. "Yep—I can see it plain my own self too. There be that nigger's pony prints . . . and there be where the nigger clumb down afoot."

Tuttle commented, "Then you're telling us these Yutas know what sort of red nigger made them tracks just from the mokerson prints?"

"That be the how of it," Cooper replied.

"Nawww—them could'a been Shian, Silas," Billy Hooks protested. "Them niggers are in this country alla time too. Kissin' cousins to them 'Rapaho, yessir-reebob!"

"Maybeso you're center, Billy boy," Cooper agreed, then looked over at Bass. "Them Shians do keep close company with the 'Rapaho anyways."

"Likely they'd all lift a Yuta scalp if'n any of 'em had their chance, Silas," Tuttle observed.

"Not this day," Cooper vowed with unmasked bravado as he straightened and patted one of the two pistols he carried at his belt. "Them stupid 'Rapaho out hunting ponies and skelps in our part o' the country . . . maybeso we ought'n get these here Yutas go with us to hunt down them 'Rapahos."

"Skelps and ponies!" Hooks repeated joyfully, clapping his blanket mittens together. "Yessirreebob! Skelps and ponies for us all!"

But as it turned out, the leader of the hunting party would not be dissuaded from his goal: securing meat for those left behind in the winter camp. He stead-fastly told Cooper and the other white men that their first rule was to provide for the village, and only when there was enough meat back in camp would a Ute warrior go traipsing off to follow an enemy trail in hopes of bringing home ponies, scalps, enemy weapons, and war honors.

Cooper and Hooks grumbled, threatening to pull out and turn back to the village on their own. But in the end they hung in with the meat hunters as the afternoon waned and the day began to grow old. As the horse rocked beneath him and the sun fell below the furry wrinkle of his old coyote-skin cap, Titus found his eyelids growing heavy. His mind drifted back to his first hunting trip out with the Ute warriors—the first time he had left Fawn and her son, White Horse, behind.

The new year itself had come and gone on that hunting trip—the first Titus could recollect not boisterously celebrating among white men. The fact that it might well be the first day of 1826 hadn't even made no never mind to the other three trappers. No man among them had a calendar anyway—so it didn't seem vital in the least to celebrate one day's importance over another. Not a Christmas neither.

"For balls' sakes, such doin's as that be the whatnot and befugglin' a man's gotta leave behin't when you come out here to these mountains," Tuttle had declared, explaining how the three of them felt about holidays.

"Only one time a year do a man got him any reason to celebrate, Scratch," Cooper went on to explain. "That be the summer: time when a man cain't trap, seein' how the plew h'ain't prime no more . . . an' seein' how that's when the trader says he'll be back to buy our furs and maybeso have some likker to sell us this time out."

"Trader?" Bass inquired, his mind fired. "Likker? You said a trader'd have some likker? Like rum or whiskey? Where in blue hell—"

"Right here in the mountains—yessirreebob!" Billy exclaimed, his eyes dancing as he licked his lips with the tip of a pink tongue.

Titus wagged his head in disbelief. "Traders come out here to the mountains? Had me no idea."

"First time we heerd about it our own selves was just last winter," Tuttle declared. "Fellas said a trader named Ashley been out to the mountains with his own company of trappers. Word was Ashley wanted the news spread all over that he was coming back the next summer with trade goods and likker—not just for them fellers what come west with him in the seasons afore, but for all niggers like us what could allays use more powder and G'lena lead, coffee and sugar, all such."

"I heard of Ashley, I have," Titus declared. "He was the high-pockets behind a feller named Henry years back when that Henry feller pushed upriver . . . the year Hugh Glass got hisself chawed on by a grizzly bear."

Tuttle asked, "Washburn tol't you 'bout Glass?"

"Yepper."

Cooper said, "We heard of this here Glass."

"Last summer was some doin's, weren't it, fellers?" Hooks said with that ready, contagious smile.

"We was up to those hills where we run onto you," Cooper explained. "Run onto a band of Ashley's boys what tol't us 'bout the plans to rendezvous come that summer."

Billy's face grew most expressive as he recalled, "Just like they told us to, we moseyed on over to a place called Horse Creek on the Green, where we pitched camp with more trappers'n I see'd in all my days."

"More'n a hunnert!" Tuttle claimed. "And some three dozen more added in."

Cooper jumped into the recollection. "Few days later some Hudson's Bay come rollin' in. There was a bunch of Injuns tagging along with 'em—women and young'uns too. But, damn, if Ashley wasn't one to keep his trade packs closed till all *his* men was in."

" 'Ceptin' tobaccy," Hooks complained. "That was all he traded for till the last of his own moseyed on in."

Silas nodded. "Still had us a merry time of it—didn't we, Billy?"

Hooks dragged the back of a blanket mitten across his dry lips, eyes dancing. "Eatin', spinnin' tales . . . and, oh—them womens!"

"Long as it lasted," Tuttle grumbled. "Ashley had the beaver out of our packs and into his inside of two days afore he was turning back for St. Louie! Two goddamned days!"

"After all that waiting," Billy chimed in, "we wasn't about to sleep through none of it, Scratch! A man stayed awake through it all!"

Titus asked, "So you got yourselves good and drunk?"

"Shit—Ashley didn't have him a drop of likker!" Hooks groaned.

Cooper slammed a fist down into his palm. "And that son of a honey-fugglin' booshway give the best dollar for beaver to his own boys!"

"Three dollar the pound he paid 'em!" Tuttle exclaimed.

Hooks bobbed his head, saying, "An' for us he give only two."

"Said we was free trappers," Silas added. "Like we was something what didn't belong out here. Tol't us our kind wasn't bound to no man . . . so he wasn't bound to give us no more'n what dollar he damn well felt like giving us!"

"You took two dollar the pound?" Titus asked.

"Hell if we did!" Cooper spouted, his chest puffing. "Our packs was filled with prime plew—seal fat an' sleek. When he saw what we had to trade, why— that trader's eyes bugged out to see what we brung us into that Horse Creek camp."

"Ashley give us four dollar on some!" Tuttle boasted. "An' on some o' Cooper's fur he give Silas five dollar the pound!"

"No shit?" Scratch gasped, going dry-mouthed to think of what his own winter's catch might bring. "F-five dollar the pound?"

"Damn bet he did," Tuttle said. "Then we traded for what powder and coffee and sugar we needed to winter up to make it round for next summer— 'stead of us having to head east to the Missouri to barter our provisions."

"Trader says he's bound to bring him some likker out this year," Billy announced. "Then this child will have it all—womens and some whiskey!"

"Now, y' reckon why summer be the only time a mountain trapper got him to celebrate, Scratch?" Cooper asked.

"Ronnyvoo do surely shine," Tuttle added wistfully himself. "Hope that trader be true at his word—comin' back this summer."

Cooper gazed off wistfully. "Ashley took his caravan off to the north. Headed down the Bighorn to the Yallerstone. On to Missouri to float home to St. Louie."

Tuttle spoke up. "Seems a likely way for a man to go what has him a lot of furs, Silas."

Cooper nodded, speaking softly, dramatically. "Might be at that, Bud. Makes all the sense in the world."

Titus remembered how he had sensed the leap of tiny wings within his stomach when he asked, "We going to ronnyvoo this summer?"

"Come green-up," Silas assured. "When the plews stop being prime and sleek . . . four of us take off for Willow Valley,* where Ashley promised he's to show up by the middle o' summer."

"You know how to find this Willow Valley?" Bass inquired.

"We'll find it," Cooper claimed.

"H-how we know when it gonna be the middle of summer?" Titus asked, anxious. "Ain't none of us keep no calendar stuffed away in his plunder!"

"Middle of the summer, Scratch," Tuttle declared with a shrug. "Simple as that for a man to sort out."

Nodding, Silas said, "Soon's the high country starts to warm up, it's getting on to be summer down below. I figger that be the time for us to mosey down outta this beaver land and sashay on over to that Bear River for ronnyvoo."

"Bear River?"

Tuttle turned to Bass. "Near where them Ashley boys say we'll run onto Willow Valley."

"With all our plews!" Billy exclaimed. "Buy us whiskey and womens!"

"But first we gonna trap out what streams there is hereabouts, ain't we, Silas?" Titus inquired.

"Y' damn right we will," Cooper replied. "The way you're getting the hang of things—why, we gonna pull into ronnyvoo with more plews in our packs than any of them other niggers!"

"Only trouble is," Tuttle advised sourly, "we hear us that Ashley has him plans to put higher prices on his trade goods, and he don't figger to be offerin' top dollar for our fur no more."

Hooks moaned, "No more five dollar for prime plew."

"Why such?" Titus asked.

Cooper nudged his horse up close to Bass. "Y' 'member that fella Henry we knowed of come upriver with Lisa years ago?"

"Yeah, like I said—hear him and Ashley is partners now."

"Not no more," Tuttle explained as Bass was the last to clamber aboard his horse and they all began to move off behind the Ute hunters. "Henry figgers he's had him enough of the mountains."

"That cain't be true," Bass replied. "T'ain't possible for a man to get him enough of these mountains out here."

Cooper said, "True it be: for Ashley's took him on a new partner. Jedediah Smith. While Ashley goes back to St. Louie to fetch up for trade goods for ronnyvoo, Jed Smith has charge of the hull mountains."

---

* Cache Valley, on the present-day Utah-Idaho border

"So what's that mean to us come summer when we go off to sell our plews at ronnyvoo?" Titus asked.

"Means ever' man of us got to make his own choice," Cooper said with a shrug. "Man's gotta figger out for his own self if'n he's better off sellin' plew at ronnyvoo to them high-pocket St. Louie traders . . . or he heads down the Big Horn, Yallerstone, and the Missouri on his own to sell what's his back direct to them other traders at posts along the river."

"I've a good mind to keep my furs for the river traders!" Billy exclaimed. "Damn Ashley and the rest of them thievin' niggers!"

"That makes two of us, Billy," Cooper agreed. Then his eyes bounced from Tuttle to Bass. "I'll just have to wait till summer green-up to see what Ashley's offerin' for plew. So come that time, the both of you two'll have to figure out where your stick floats: mountain trader, or river trader."

Tuttle glanced quickly at Bass and hurriedly replied, "I'm in with you, Silas. What works out best for your plews works out best for all our plews, I say."

"What about you, Scratch?" Cooper asked.

"Back there to that village is my first season's catch," he started. "Worked hard for it—but I reckon I wouldn't have near none of it less'n you three come along to show me proper. Titus Bass gonna hang on and ride the whole trail with you . . . to the river, or to Ashley's ronnyvoo."

"That shines, Scratch!" Cooper cheered, his big teeth showing in his black beard.

"But this here ronnyvoo," Bass replied, "sure wouldst like to see me one of them, one of these days."

"You will, Scratch," Hooks said confidently. "Maybe even this summer. Right, Silas?"

"That be the square of it, Titus Bass. Man don't rightly know in winter just where he'll be come summer—"

Scratch's reverie shattered as a shrill scream split the dry, cold air ahead on the narrow trail winding its way out of the trees and into an open glade ringed by steep side slopes, a tumble of boulders, and more lodgepole pine than there were bristles on a strop-hog's back.

The hair rose at the back of Bass's neck in that next instant as a pony snorted, other horses whinnied, and some of the Ute cried out. Voices shrill and loud answered, shouting from the trees as enemy warriors appeared from behind the snowcapped rocks all about them. As he watched, mesmerized and frozen, the enemy materialized in a great crescent before the Ute, yanking back the rawhide strings on their short bows, letting fly a first volley of arrows—more than Titus had seen since his first and only Indian fight with the Chickasaw.

Cooper was bellowing as he and Tuttle hit the ground in a leap, smacking their horses in the flanks.

"C'mon, Scratch!" Hooks hollered as he kicked his leg over the neck of his horse and plopped into the snow. The animal screeched, sidestepping, then yanked away from Billy, an arrow quivering high in the animal's withers.

"C'mon, Billy!" Tuttle hollered a few yards ahead where the shadows split the ground into bars of sun and shadow. "We got us a Injun fight!"

Hooks wheeled for one last look at Bass as Titus leaped from the saddle. "Skelps! Them's Injun skelps for this here child!"

As Billy whirled away into the shadows of the lodgepole toward the bright patch of sunlight and snow just beyond where the Ute were milling in disarray as the enemy advanced, an Indian pony suddenly clattered out of the melee toward Bass. Wild-eyed and snorting, its head bobbing as it threaded its way through trees, other animals, and in among the men rushing past it—Titus suddenly saw the Ute warrior still atop the animal, holding on only with the strength of his legs.

Both of the man's bloody hands were wrapped around the shaft of an arrow, tugging, yanking, pulling with all his might to free it from the back of his throat where it had flown directly into his mouth and buried itself in the base of his tongue.

Titus watched the man weave past atop that careening pony, hearing the warrior's death-gurgle as the Ute strangled on his own blood.

Bass went cold, shuddering involuntarily as a few arrows hissed into the stand of lodgepole beside him, and some even thwacked into the trees with the splintered crack of winter ice breaking up. Dropping to his knees, he peered ahead at the confusion of bodies darting this way and that among the shadows and brilliant sunlight.

A scream shattered the forest behind him.

Bass whirled, bringing up the rifle, remembering the fleet-footed warriors who had chased him through the Mississippi River woods, all the way back to the rivermen's Kentucky boat.

He had no time to think. Barely enough to jerk back the hammer to full-cock and pull hard on the set trigger before yanking back on the front trigger. He hadn't aimed. Everything done on feel, impulse—as the enemy, with the top half of his face painted in black, leaped through the shadows, across that last five yards, a huge club circling over his head, sunlight glinting off the three sharp knife blades swinging down from the sky toward Bass's head.

For a moment more the black face screamed, then went silent, contorting as the warrior fell, skidding to his knees. It was as if the lower strings of a marionette had been suddenly cut as the warrior crumpled—yet with that headlong motion his right arm continued to bring that war club forward, released at the end of his arm: whirling onward with a dull hum.

Glinting. Flashing in the sun.

On instinct Bass brought up his rifle at the last moment, ducking aside as the club tumbled into him. Its long handle struck the rifle with a wooden clunk, and the blades tumbled on past.

Slicing.

He grunted as he fell, rolling onto his shoulder—finding the fall hurt as he spilled onto his belly in the snow. Afraid, remembering that his rifle was empty, Bass rocked onto his knees. Allowing the rifle to fall out of his hands, he turned to find the warrior spilled facedown in the snow. Titus yanked the pistol from his sash, cocked and pointed it, trembling, at the fallen enemy.

"Scratch!"

Whirling about on his knees in the deep snow, Bass saw Hooks thirty yards away, ramming home a ball, seating it deep against the powder and breech of his rifle. Racing halfway between the two white men, a warrior came to a halt in a spray of snow, went to one knee, and brought the string back on his bow as it came up to his cheek in one smooth, swift, blurred arc of motion.

Instead of firing, Bass dropped onto his shoulder—his mind suddenly iced with hot nausea as he rolled, then came back up on his hip and brought the pistol up, aimed at the warrior moving in a blur to pull a second arrow from the same hand that clutched the bow.

Jerking back on the pistol's trigger, he felt the weapon jump in his hand. A great gray puff of smoke issued from the short muzzle as Bass swapped the pistol to his left hand and with his right pulled the last weapon he could use for his defense.

With the knife held out before him he leaped upon the bowman who clutched his upper arm—a red, glistening ooze seeped between his fingers as his face showed surprise the moment the white man collided with him.

Titus seized a hunk of the Indian's hair in his left hand, drew the skinning knife back at the end of his fully extended right arm, and slashed downward with all the fury he could muster. It hurt so to feel the warrior wrenching away from his left arm . . . then suddenly his right hand felt warm. Flecks of warmth spat against Bass's face as the blood gushed.

No longer able to hold the struggling warrior with his weakened left arm, Titus flung the Indian backward as the enemy quivered and thrashed—his throat slashed so completely that his head keeled to the side, nearly severed from his body.

"That's the way to shine, nigger!"

Bass jerked up with a feral growl, finding Silas Cooper scuttling toward him out of the shadows. Behind the tall man there were muffled shouts and the whinny of horses. Cooper went to his knees beside Titus.

"That red nigger's skelp is yours, Scratch!" he cried out in exultation, slapping Bass on the back.

Wincing in pain, Titus grunted as icy shards filled the base of his skull, sent shooting stars exploding behind his eyelids as he struggled to maintain consciousness.

"Damn nigger!" Cooper's voice called out above him. "Scratch's hurt. Billy!"

For some time Titus struggled to keep from losing his breakfast, then remembered they hadn't really stopped for a noonday meal. Only a little yellow bile spilled up as his empty stomach revolted and he retched on the snow.

"You'll be awright," Hooks was saying over him somewhere.

Then someone was wiping cold snow on his face. Bass's eyes fluttered half-open so that he could look up into Billy's face.

Of a sudden, there beside Hooks's hairy face, was Tuttle's, both of them staring down at Bass like masks suspended in the air above him.

"It's over, Scratch," Bud confided softly.

As much as he tried to listen to the silence of that rocky lodgepole clearing, Titus couldn't hear anything. Maybe the silence meant that it really was over.

"Looks to be the greenhorn got two his own self!" Cooper suddenly bawled in triumph, appearing behind the other two, who continued to stare down at Bass. "How's he gonna fare, Billy?"

"Get me his coat off and I can tell you better, Silas."

They yanked and jerked, pulling his belt and sash off, then parted the blanket coat so that they could drag it down the left arm enough to look at the shoulder wound.

"It's deep," Hooks said solemnly.

"But clean enough," Tuttle added. "She'll knit up in time."

Bass's eyes opened now and then, fluttering in pain as the others prodded and pulled; then a great pressure was added to the source of his pain. He closed his eyes and wished they would just cut the arm off—it hurt so damned much.

"Don't you go to sleep on us," Tuttle commanded about the time Titus felt more cold snow rubbed on his cheeks, across his forehead, some of it spilling against his eyelids.

He blinked the cold away, trying to say something—to tell them to leave him sleep—but no words came.

"Think he wants us get him his skelps, Silas!" Billy roared over his shoulder at the tall man.

"By damn—this here pilgrim's got his first Injun ha'r, this'un does!" Cooper bellowed lustily. Then he stuffed his face right in between Hooks's and Tuttle's, saying in a softer voice, "Don't y' worry none, Scratch. I'll go right off an' fetch up them two skelps of your'n my own self for y'."

"Silas," Tuttle spoke through that thick, suffocating blackness slipping down over him, "I don't think Scratch heard you none."

There were pieces of it that came to him from time to time, like the ragged, painful consciousness that brought him awake with startling suddenness, yelping in protest before he would pass out again.

Yet, thankfully, Bass was able to pass through most of the homebound journey suspended in that blessed blackness where pain will take a man when it becomes more than he can bear.

Three of the injured Ute were dragged back to the village in improvised travois, like Scratch. The rest of the wounded stoically rode their ponies back to Park Kyack's southern reaches.

Four of those warriors who had been at the very lead of the hunt that terrible day returned to their people slung over the backs of their ponies.

Once again the Ute had paid an awful price in their ages-old warfare with the Arapaho, who season after season continued to contest any trespass onto land they considered their own, on either side of the great tall mountains scraping the undergut of the winter-blue sky. None of the old Ute warriors were ready to give in and move off, leaving the Arapaho the freedom to roam that country. And with this loss of four young, healthy men, the entire village was now even more resolved to resist the violent encroachments of a people who had only recently begun to push up from the eastern plains into the fastness of the Rocky Mountains.

To the Ute way of thinking, the Arapaho were the interlopers, nothing more than unwanted trespassers, dangerous and deadly newcomers . . . at the same time what white men the Ute had run across had posed no danger—after all, the trappers were far too few, showing up infrequently at best, then moving on quickly enough without setting down roots. In short, the pale-skinned beaver hunters posed no real threat to Ute sovereignty of these high mountains, parks, and pine-ringed valleys.

But, like the Apache and Navajo to the south, like those Comanche raiding out of the southeast, now the Arapaho and the Cheyenne were threatening along the borders of Ute land from their traditional haunts on the eastern plains.

Within days it would be time for the Ute chiefs to deliberate and argue where best to move their winter camp to another site with better grazing for their ponies, more wood for their fires, a place where the winds did not carry so much of the stench of human offal and rotting carcasses of game brought in to feed the many hungry mouths.

But Bass knew none of this.

Titus slept fitfully that first night he was dragged through the doorway and deposited upon the widow's blankets. Here at last, he told himself, he could try sleeping through the sharp pain as the edges of his wounds rubbed one another with the manhandling, the crude travois jouncing over uneven ground. To lay in one spot and just sleep. But the male voices were no sooner gone than the woman herself was busy above him.

Unable to get his coat off, Fawn did only what she could do. For a few minutes there he was somewhat conscious of hearing the heavy blanket wool being cut, sliced, hacked away with her cooking knife. Then it felt as if she were slowly, delicately, slashing along the seam of the left arm, down the left side of the shirt she had made for him weeks earlier. Finally he felt her tugging where the smoked leather of the shirt crossed over his left shoulder.

By cutting the shirt half off the left side of his body, Fawn was able to pull it off the right side, for the first time fully exposing the three deep gashes, blue and purple and a deep brown against his startling white flesh. So swollen, so oozy, were the wounds that she gasped and began to sob.

It might have been only the cold still air or the sudden silence there within the lodge, or it might have been her stifled sobs—but something made Titus open his eyes at that moment, finding it hard to focus in the dim light, the fire's reflection flickering on the lodge skin behind her. Then his eyes found her crumpled over beside him, her head pressed down in her hands, her tiny shoulders shuddering as she did her best to stifle the sobs that racked her.

She nearly jumped when his right hand reached out and gently touched her arm.

"I . . . I ain't gonna die," he said in English—forgetting himself—his mouth as dry as it had ever been.

Bass watched her eyes pool as she brushed fingers down his hairy cheek. The moment he licked his dry, cracked lips, she understood. Quickly she dragged over a small kettle of cool water and from it pulled a buffalo horn fashioned into a large spoon, which she used to slowly pour rivulets of life past his parched lips, blessed drops washing across his dry tongue, spilling into his throat.

In the end he had strength enough to nudge the horn spoon aside and turn his face away, closing his eyes once more. How he wanted to do nothing but sleep that night, for a few moments thinking just how sweet it would be to wake up in the dim light of early dawn, finding her naked beside him in the quiet stillness before first light . . . to awaken and find that all of this was nothing more than a dream. So sweet was it to imagine the feel of that freedom from the pain of his body, so real was it to feel her steamy flesh against his—

Scratch nearly came off the buffalo-robe bed, his back arching in sudden, unexpected, excruciating pain.

"I'm sorry!" she cried out to him in Ute.

He looked at her in surprise, perhaps some disgust, then peered over at his shoulder. The deepest wound had begun to bleed freely again. When he looked back at her, Bass found in her hands the rough ball of moss-green lichen dripping water and some of his crusted blood in the narrow strip of pounded dirt there between the robe bed and the fire pit.

"Damn you, Fawn," he growled in English. "That hurt like hell!"

"I'm sorry," she repeated again in her tongue.

Then it suddenly hurt him that he had lashed out and hurt her. His foggy, pain-crazed mind cleared, like a wind blowing away wisps of thick mist. "You were cleaning me?" Bass inquired in Ute.

"Yes. I need to open the wound, to clean it well before I can put my plants in it."

"P-plants," he stammered. Just the thought of any more scrubbing on the deep, jagged gashes . . . the prospect of anyone probing down into that torn, ugly, purple muscle was enough to make his head ache and spin as it was.

"Plants," she repeated, dragging up a large soft-skinned bag to lay across her lap as she sat there beside him, her legs tucked to the side in that way of a woman. Holding back the large flap, Fawn pulled several smaller pouches tied at their tops with thongs, then retrieved two wooden vials, at the top of which were stuffed wooden stoppers.

"You put your plants in my wounds?"

She nodded, biting her lip between her crooked teeth as if she knew for certain herself what pain that announcement must cause him.

"Your husband—you used your plants for him?"

Her eyes immediately dropped to her hands in her lap, shuffling absently some of the pouches and wooden vials. "No. I did not have a chance to try healing my husband. He was dead when they returned his body to our village."

How he wished he could trade places with one of the others right now, even simpleminded Billy Hooks. Staring up at the spiral of poles laced within one another at the top of the lodge, Titus hurt of the flesh from his wounds, hurt of the heart for what pain this woman endured.

"As I told you before, I won't die," he repeated, this time in Ute.

"Your wounds, they are terrible."

As much as he did not want to look, Titus turned his head slightly and peered down at them. And quickly looked away. They were ghastly. Long ribbons of flesh torn asunder by the sharp, tumbling knives on that Arapaho war club. If nothing else was done for them, he was sure someone would have to attempt pulling the edges of the flesh together once more.

At least that is what his grandpap, even his own pap, had done for animals who suffered tragic accidents or falls. Stuffing some moist, chawed tobacco down into the edges of the wound before using a woman's sewing needle and thread to draw things shut. Perhaps even some spider's web at the edges of the laceration, if one could find such a thing back in the corners of the cabin or barn. His mam claimed it helped in drying out the edges of the wound, helped the flesh knit back together as it dried. Healing the most natural way possible. Something folks on the frontier took in stride and Bass had always taken for granted.

The way a Chickasaw arrow was cut from the meat of Ebenezer Zane's leg. Or the way Beulah had bound up Hames Kingsbury's ribs, then prayed over him till he was healed. Or the many times the blackened but steady hands of Hysham Troost had laid poultices on wounds Titus brought home from the Wharf Street watering holes, drawing out the poisons until it was time to pull the flaps of skin together with some of Mother Troost's sewing thread.

But never had he laid eyes on anything near as terrible as this.

"Leave it be, Fawn," he told her softly as his eyes closed. "Just cover me now and let me sleep."

He felt her drag a wool blanket over him, gently laying the corner over that bloody shoulder and upper arm. Then she pulled a buffalo robe over that. The weight of it felt reassuring there as he began to drift off again into that nether-world somewhere between healthy sleep and what fitful unconsciousness the mind conjures up in its attempt to escape the brutal trespass of pain.

The last he remembered was the coolness of her hand and the roughened touch of the damp lichen she held in her fingers, brushing back the long, un-kempt hair from his forehead and the sides of his face. Cool water, as she contin-ued attempting to put out the fire of that fever she was certain was already on its way.

Somewhere in the darkness he was certain they were jabbing hot pitchforks into his side. Scooping a huge shovel filled with smoldering coals into his ears, one after another, so that his head filled with smoke and steam and unbearable heat, searing the back of his eyes, choking him with the rising torture.

How he thrashed and shuddered, kicking violently at the blankets and the robe, flinging them from his body until the pain reminded him of the wounds and he came close to wakefulness—enough to recognize just where and how much he hurt—fully expecting as he opened his eyes into pain-weary slits that he would see the tiny demons who were Old Lucifer's cloven-hoofed minions gathered in a tight ring all about him, jabbing at him with their instruments of interminable death.

Oh, how he had listened in childlike rapture to the wandering pastors who had circled back and forth across the length of Boone County when he had been young. Their breath smelling of fire and brimstone, each one invariably continued to preach to the family who invited them back to their land after church service for a home-cooked meal and a warm place to sleep over the Sabbath night before the circuit rider moved on the next morning.

But Scratch did not find Lucifer there at hand. Nor his diminutive demons. Nonetheless, as he lay there in Fawn's lodge, he believed the old bastard himself had just taken his leave of the place—hot as Bass was. For the love of a cool dip in that pond back home right about now. Even to have someone rub some snow on his burning skin right now.

Where was she?

"Fa . . . Fawn?"

He barely heard his own voice croak her name. Then he called out again, this time trying to force it, make it louder. She was there almost immediately—the sound of her coming through the door flap, the shadow of her holding the bail of the kettle in one hand, setting it on the low flames with a sputter.

"Water," he demanded in English, rubbing his dry, cracked lips. "Water."

She understood the word, the gesture, and sank to her knees at his side with the horn spoon, scooping up his head within an arm, pulling him up gently and pressing the spoon against his lips.

"The fire," she declared quietly as most of the water dribbled from the corner of his mouth, "the fire burns you up from inside."

"Fire," he repeated in a tortured croak. "Put out the fire, Fawn."

He closed his eyes to the tears of pain, to the drops of sweat running off his brow, to the dancing shapes of hideous reality flickering on the lodge skins, and tried to think back to that first Rocky Mountain snow last autumn as the high country began to cool and the aspen quaked in the breeze that carried on it the prophecy of winter. So cold and dry were the flakes that he caught them on his sleeve, on a blanket mitten, then blew them off like a sprinkling of ash. Cold, white ash landing on his face, tangled in his eyelashes, melting on his tongue. Like no snowflakes he had ever tasted back east along the Missouri, farther still in Kentucky—

The moment something was pressed against his lips, Titus opened his eyes again into narrow slits. He could see the movement of the woman so near that he heard her tiny bursts of breath coming fast and shallow. Slowly she poured the liquid against his parting lips. Bitter, so bitter a taste that he coughed, sputtering, spewing it from his mouth as he turned his head.

"No," she said sharply, that word spoken just as tough as the way she had uttered it that day long ago when she had destroyed those infested white-man clothes of his.

She grabbed hold of a clump of long hair at the nape of his neck and wrenched his head around into a cradle of her forearm.

"Drink," the woman commanded.

"No, tastes like shit," he whimpered in English, nearly a sob as his eyes filled with more stinging salt dripping from his forehead.

"Drink," she repeated. "Cold—for the fire inside you. Put out the fire."

"Put out the fire," he echoed in Ute.

So he drank a sip, physically forcing the foul-tasting, bitter liquid back on his tongue, down his throat. Then pursed his lips to drink a bit more. Then more until she no longer pressed the spoon against his lips.

Like sudden freedom, he savored those moments after Fawn laid his head back upon the buffalo robe and withdrew her arm, like stolen, furtive heartbeats he was sure were quickly going to lead him back into the escape of sleep now.

But instead she brushed more of the cool water across his forehead and face, then murmured something to him about a willow stick.

Bass felt an object pressed against his lips. Figuring it to be more of the fire-eating liquid, he opened his mouth slightly, his eyes tearing open into slits. But this time instead of the spoon, the widow pressed between his teeth a thin wand of willow.

"Bite on this," she instructed quietly, "when you want to cry out."

Cry out? Cry out for what? Nothing could be worse than what she had already put him through. He had no need to cry out now, not now that she had finished pouring that bitter water down his throat. All he needed now was to sleep . . . so why in the devil would she say he might want to cry out—

His back arched, convulsing with the sudden, sharp stab of pain at his shoulder, radiating clear to the roof of his head and to the soles of his feet.

Sputtering, Bass finally got his tongue to shove the willow wand out from between his teeth and started to growl, spittle dripping from both corners of his mouth.

As suddenly he felt big hands on him, sensed the peeled willow wand shoved not so gently against his teeth this time—clearly without the kindness of the widow.

Through the tears and drops of sweat pooling in his eyes, Titus tried to make out who was there with Fawn. Who held him down as he struggled against the thunderous pain in his shoulder, the torment shooting down the entire length of his left arm? Bass could not recognize him. Blinking, he wanted to be certain who it was because Titus swore to kill the bastard once he was healed and strong enough to go searching for the one who had forced him to endure this pain.

He shrieked, crying out, then whimpered in his fevered torture, trying his best to thrash back and forth, to arch his back up, throw off the oppressive weight of his handler, to kick free of the one who seemed to sit squarely on top of him.

Then as suddenly he felt as weak as a newborn calf, his legs gone to butter. Oh, the pain was still there, so he had to save what strength he had left so that he would not die. No more did he have anything to use in fighting this strong one.

Maybe it was Cooper. Big enough, strong enough to be. Cooper would be the sort to enjoy this. Maybe even simpleminded Billy Hooks. No, he decided: they would be off whoring with their squaws right now. Days of hunting away from camp meant they would have one thing and one thing only on their minds. So they would be with their women, thrashing about in the robes instead of thrashing about with a fevered friend.

Maybeso it was Tuttle. Of the three, he believed he could count on Bud.

Tightly Bass clamped his eyes shut, trying to squeeze all the moisture from them so when he opened his eyes, he could see who had come to help the widow.

Into slits, then open wider still . . . until he peered up at the old, lined face. Skin darker than an old saddle. More seams and wrinkles in it than a cottonwood trunk. Eyes old and all-seeing, yet somehow possessed of a deep kindness as they gazed down at him in these last few of the white man's futile, fevered convulsions.

She spoke to the old one in hushed tones. He replied in same. Behind them both the small boy whimpered. Fawn touched Bass's forehead one last time with her cool hand, then turned away and went to the child.

Likely to feed the boy, he thought as he laid his cheek against a damp, cool spot on the buffalo robe beneath him where some of his sweat had collected. How long had it been since he'd had to pee? Titus wondered. He couldn't remember peeing since before they were jumped by the Arapaho. And he wondered if he had done the unthinkable—to go and wet himself. Still, he felt wet everywhere on his body, everywhere his fingers touched. Maybe Fawn and this old man would not notice he had wet himself, since he was damp all over.

Then he realized it might just be all right. He hadn't done the unthinkable. The fever—it had taken every drop of moisture in his body, soaked it up, and poured it out through his skin. There'd been nothing left for him to pee.

Funny how a man thought on such things like that when walking up the threshold to death's door.

The strong, leathery arm raised his head. Bass felt the hard, smooth texture of the horn spoon pressed against his lips.

Yes, he thought. Water. The more I drink, maybe I can live. More, his mind echoed, convincing himself. This was sweet and clear. Not the bitter water she gave him. More.

Bass drank his fill until he could drink no more, and slept.

"You have been gone a long, long time," the voice said out of the darkness as Bass's eyes fluttered open.

His mouth was dry again, his lips so parched, he could feel the oozy cracks in them . . . but his skin no longer felt as tight and drawn as it had when he had been burning up with the fire of that fever.

For a moment he struggled to focus, then gazed at the old man's face, watching it withdraw and the widow's replace it right above him. Staring down at him with a wide, crooked-tooth smile.

"You are back from wandering the dark paths," she said, her fingertips lightly touching his brow. "For some time now you have not been hot. It is good."

"Yes," he said in English, recognizing only the Ute word for "good." Too hard to try remembering the Ute words now, to say them or understand them. If he ever could remember them again. So sure was he that the fever had burned away a good portion of what little he had in the way of his mind, just as a farmer set his fires to burn away the stalks from last year's crop so that the next spring's planting had that much better a chance.

"Yes," she repeated in English. "Are you hungry?"

He thought a few moments—then understood—assessing the way he felt there on the robes, and finally answered, "No. Not right now. Maybe later." He had said it in English, but when he shook his head slightly, she seemed to show some understanding.

"The old one came to guide you through the land of darkness, Me-Ti-tuzz." He remembered that was what she called him as Fawn signaled to the man. The old one came close enough for Bass to see once more.

"You . . . ," and then Scratch struggled to remember the Ute words, how to put a few of them together. "Two . . . help . . . me . . . no more fire?"

"No more fire," the old man repeated in his native tongue. "No more walk on the dark path."

"No more fire," Bass echoed confidently, remembering only tattered fragments of the fevered convulsions, how hot and wet he had been, how he had thrashed about.

Slowly, painfully, he raised his head to look down at himself. Surprised, he found upon his bare chest the smeared and many colors of patches and stripes of earth paint. Mystical symbols. Potent signs. And farther south on his belly were smeared what appeared to be dry, flaky powders, crude lines raked across his flesh by fingertips in some simplistic pictograph.

"This?" he asked weakly.

"You are better now," the old man said, then turned to Fawn. "Wash off the paint, woman."

Using that same clump of moss, she dipped cool water onto his flesh and gently scrubbed off the dried earth paint.

As she finished, the old man asked, "Should we tell the others with him?"

"They are gone," Fawn replied.

"Gone where?" Titus asked as soon as the words registered, afraid the trio had abandoned him, leaving him behind when they rode off for parts unknown.

"To the streams," she explained. Then, setting the moss scrubber aside, Fawn slapped her two open palms together with a smacking sound to imitate the animal's own method of signaling a warning. "To catch the flat-tails."

"Beaver!" he said in English with relief. And let his head sink back onto the buffalo robe beneath him.

"They come back soon," she continued. "This is good?"

"Yes," he said in Ute. "This is very good that they come back. I go with them when we leave for the spring."

"Spring," she repeated the word, her eyes drifting away. "It comes soon. And you go."

"Yes." He cheered himself with the thought. Then because he could not think of the words in Ute, Bass tried hard to explain in English, "To catch beaver in its prime! To mosey easy-like on down to ronnyvoo where the trader will have him whiskey! An' there'll be women too!"

In that next moment he suddenly realized what he had said. "Women for all the men what ain't had a good woman to wrap up in the robes with 'em all winter, Fawn," he tried to apologize in English.

Clumsily he reached out and took hold of one of the woman's hands. Again he spoke in Ute, "You know I leave soon. Come spring."

"Leave Fawn. Yes. Me-Ti-tuzz only a winter guest. Come again maybe next winter."

"Yes," he said sadly. "Maybe next winter."

She pulled her hands from his and turned aside as the old man continued to stuff things away in his shoulder pouch. Bass glanced again at his wounds, finding each of them covered with moistened leaves held down with thin strips of cloth.

"You both help me," Bass declared to them, watching their faces turn so they could look at him. "I will not forget. I may leave come spring . . . but I won't ever forget you both."

NINE

Imperceptibly at first, the days began to lengthen.

It happened that Bass realized it was a little brighter in the lodge those mornings when he awoke. Instead of the gray wash to everything just beginning to announce the coming of the sun, the light was already there to greet him each time he opened his eyes beside her.

As well, night was held at abeyance for just a little longer. Twilight seemed to swell about them in that high mountain park, the end of each succeeding day celebrating itself with just a few more heartbeats of gentle glow as the sun eased out of sight. Why, a man would have to be nothing short of blind not to notice that spring was on its way.

It was clear to Titus that the other three realized it too as the snow grew mushy beneath his own thick, fur-lined winter moccasins of buffalo hide. From time to time, yes—snow would fall from those clouds gathered up there near Buffalo Pass, then only from those clouds collared around the peaks to the far north. Eventually, there were no more storms.

As the snow retreated into the shadowed places, so the game retreated farther up the mountainsides. The men traveled higher, stayed out longer, to supply the camp with meat. And the nearby streams were nearly trapped out. Over the last few days Silas Cooper had been forced to take his trappers farther and farther still to run onto a creek where they stood a chance of finding beaver what would come to bait.

Plain as paint, the time was coming to move on.

"Where you set us to go?" Tuttle asked Cooper of an evening just days ago as they had sat in the last rays of the sun, smoking the bark of the red willow mixed with the pale dogwood. Some time back they had finished off the last of Bass's tobacco.

Silas sighed. "Yonder to the west."

"Them mountains we come through to get here?" Hooks inquired, digging a fingernail around inside the bowl of his clay pipe. Just then he struck a hot coal, sure enough, and jerked the finger out to suck on it like a child with a precious sliver or some such injury worth nursing.

Cooper quickly glanced round at the other three, then stared off to the high peaks bordering the sundown side of Park Kyack. "That be the direction a man takes him to mosey off to ronnyvoo, ain't it?"

"Surely it is," Bud agreed.

Cooper's gaze landed on Bass. "What say y' then, Scratch?"

"Say me to what?"

"Where away would y' lead this bunch, if'n it was you callin' the tune?"

Pulling the cane pipestem from his mouth slowly, Titus wiped the back of his hand across his lips thoughtfully. "Near as I recollect, there was many a stream in that country where a man would be smart to lay down his traps. Yessir, Silas. No two ways to it—that's good country yonder for a beaver man."

Cooper smiled as big as he had ever smiled, here with his plans given such credence. "Damn straight, Scratch. By bloody damn, boys! This here greenhorn pilgrim we come across't last fall h'ain't so wet ahin't his ears no more now."

"But afore we go and tramp off to this here Ashley's ronnyvoo," Scratch replied, "it's plain to me we best be taking our time through that high country."

"Take . . . taking our time?" Cooper asked, all but incredulous.

"Damn, but there's a ronnyvoo ain't a one of us wanna miss!" Hooks whined, worry in his eyes.

Titus looked at Billy, then at Tuttle. "You're cutting a trail through beaver country to reach ronnyvoo, ain'cha?"

Bud nodded, but Billy glanced at the dark-faced Cooper.

Silas said, "So, Scratch—what fur y' got to rub with me?"

"We're up there anyways," Titus began, "so let's set us some traps. Catch us some beaver on the tramp."

Hooks grinned, then scratched at the side of his face when he asked, "What you think of that, Silas?"

Warily, the way an animal might react as it kept itself from being backed into a corner, Cooper said, "If'n there's time, ary a man'd be struck with the stupids what he didn't try to trap what beaver he could."

Tuttle picked at a scab on his nose while the light sank out of the sky. "For balls' sake—ronnyvoo's still a far piece off. Take our time getting."

Hooks nodded amiably, saying, "Maybeso we ought'n head there straight off."

"No," Tuttle corrected, "plenty of time till ronnyvoo, more weeks'n I care to count."

Billy's shoulders sagged in disappointment. "I was hankering for that trader's whiskey—just to talk of ronnyvoo!"

"Soon enough, Billy," Silas replied, then turned to Bass. "Just how full was y' fixin' to get your beaver packs?"

"Full as I can," Bass answered. "I go through a piece of country what looks to be crawlin' with them flat-tails . . . I say let's drag what critters we can outta the streams on our way."

"Boys"—Cooper brightened of a sudden as he called out in his booming voice—"looks to be we took us on a greenhorn last autumn, and now we got us a master trapper as our partner, don't it?"

"Har! Har!" Tuttle exclaimed. "Scratch is a damn sight better trapper'n me—"

"Wouldn't take much for that!" Hooks gushed, belly-laughing.

Bud frowned. "An' I'd care to lay a set that he's some better'n you, Billy Hooks!"

The wide smile was whisked from Billy's face as Hooks looked over at Cooper.

Silas said, "I daresay Bud might well be dead center, Billy. Scratch awready got better'n you."

"Awright," Hooks replied with a single nod of his head, "then you the only one he ain't a'bettering—right, Silas?"

Cooper regarded Bass a moment. "For now, Billy. For now I'm still the best in this here trappin' outfit."

Hooks inquired, "What haps when Scratch gets better'n you, Silas?"

His eyes narrowing, Cooper chewed over that a moment, then replied, "It don't mean a thing's gonna change, Billy. This here still be my outfit—no two ways about it. No man take it from me. Y' understand that, Bud?"

Tuttle's eyes hugged the ground. "I figger I know how your stick floats, Silas."

Cooper continued. "Good. Might'n be some man pull more beaver'n me outta the water . . . but that don't mean he's man 'nough to lead my outfit."

Hooks grinned all over again, like he had come up with it in the first place. "You ain't got balls enough to lead this outfit, Scratch! Not man enough to take it 'way from Silas!"

"Never said I was," Bass defended. "Silas asked me a question, and I tol' him I was fixin' to trap me a bunch more beaver on the way to ronnyvoo."

"Your packs is damn near the heaviest there is right now!" Tuttle exclaimed.

"Hush up, now!" Cooper ordered, slapping a hand down on Tuttle's forearm. "If'n we find we got more packs'n we can carry—then we just get us more animals to carry 'em."

"More animals from where?" Billy asked.

"These here Yutas," Cooper said with a grin. "Afore we pull out come morning, what say we buy us some more ponies?"

"Good idea, Silas," Tuttle said. "You always was the thinkin' man in this outfit."

"An' I allays will be, Bud. Don't you ever forget that." Cooper's eyes left their faces as he peered over their shoulders. "Now, what y' suppose these ol' fellers got on their minds?"

The three turned, finding more than a dozen of the tribal elders and revered warriors headed their way, each of the Ute wrapped in a painted buffalo robe or in a blanket to which wide strips and rosettes of porcupine quills had been added.

By the time the old men came to a stop before the trappers, more of the village was gathering behind them. A lone man's voice began to sing out, startling Bass. Other men quickly joined in the song, and women trilled their tongues.

"What's goin' on, Bud?" Scratch whispered to Tuttle.

"Dunno," he answered with a shrug.

"I'd lay we're big men to this here village," Silas boasted as the song was coming to an end. "Something big up a stick to them."

"Yessirreebob! Gonna have to come back one day soon to visit that li'l squaw again," Hooks added, rubbing his groin with a grubby hand. "Been a fine thing, dipping into that honey-pot!"

When the last note of the song had drifted off toward the aspen and lodgepole pine surrounding their camp, the leader of the hunting party stepped forward. He gestured, wanting the four white men to stand.

As all four got to their feet, the crowd inched in even more tightly. Looking about him curiously, Titus studied the faces until he found Fawn, her young son, White Horse, clinging to her back, his little arms clamped around her neck. She smiled. And that went a long way to easing his apprehension.

One man after another began to speak in excited tones, some waving their weapons, others rattling a shield; then the hunting-party leader waved forward the old man Titus remembered from his delirium.

"That one says he knows y'," Cooper said, translating some of what was being said as the wrinkled one began to speak haltingly.

"I recollect he does," Bass said. "Name is Crane. Him and Fawn got me through the fever of my wounds."

Cooper turned an ear toward the talk. "Y' recollect any of what he said to y' when you was took with fever?"

"Nary a thing," Titus admitted.

"Seems to me this bunch figgers you was the big bull in that scrap," Cooper explained.

"I heard some talk of it my own self," Bass said. "Understood part of it—but it don't make no sense to me."

The old man pointed at Titus, waving him forward.

"G'won, now, Scratch." Tuttle prodded him with a shove of his hand.

As the old one started to speak again, he carefully removed two scalps from the pouch he wore slung over his shoulder. With one held aloft in each hand, the pair tied together with one long whang of leather, he began to tell the story of the hunt for food to fill the hungry bellies in their village, a hunt where they discovered sign of enemy Arapaho once again come trespassing on Ute land.

"There was no time to prepare for battle," the old man known as Crane explained, telling the crowd what must surely have been a well-known story by then. "No time for paint. No time to smoke one's pipe, only enough time to sing a prayer—before the Arapaho came down upon us."

Wild shouts erupted from the full ring of onlookers. Men yelped and women keened until the old man shook the scalps again, ordering quiet.

"In the battle that took four of our friends, uncles and nephews to us all—one man among our hunting party displayed great bravery!"

Again they raised their voices in shouts of joy.

"Now at last the time has passed for mourning," the wrinkled one declared. "We can celebrate the courage of our friends who helped save our people. Their guns helped win the day for our people!"

As more cheers rolled over the trappers, men and women alike leaned forward to pound the four white men on the backs and shoulders in congratulation.

"Yet there is one among them who showed more bravery than all the rest in the face of those enemy when they attacked us from behind!"

Now the crowd grew strangely quiet as the old man turned slowly, slowly about, the scalps still held at the end of his outstretched arms.

"He is the only warrior that day to take *two* enemy scalps! *Two!*"

Suddenly Bass found the pair of scalps held before his face as the old man shook them violently.

"This is the hair of our enemy!" Crane cried out to the crowd in his quavery voice—answered by great shouts leaping from more than a hundred throats. "Two enemy warriors are naked of hair in the beyond land now!"

Wheeling, the old man dropped the leather thong over Bass's head so the two scalps hung around his neck, high on either side of his chest.

"The courage of this white man saw his feet through on his terrible journey into the dark country, so deep were his wounds. He returned to us, granted life by the life-giver of us all. We give our thanks that he was spared for us: a true friend of the Ute, and sworn enemy of the Arapaho!"

Now again the leader of that hunting party stepped forward and put his arms around a stunned Titus Bass, hugging him once before he turned to address the crowd.

"As we planned, this is to be a night of celebration. Women! Bring out the meat! Children! Open a path for the men of this camp! Come, everyone! Celebrate tonight, for our white friends depart in the morning!"

As some in the crowd surged close and began to nudge the trappers along toward the center of the village, Cooper leaned close to Titus. "Y' get all of that, Scratch?"

"Maybeso enough."

"You're some big coon to these here red niggers," Silas grumbled.

"A big, big shit!" Hooks echoed with that ready grin of his.

"Ain't done nothing special," Bass replied, trying to make less of this spontaneous celebration in his honor.

"Y' something big up a stick to them," Cooper argued. "But mind y'—don't ever go figgering you be as savvy as me, hear? Don't ever y' figger y' can outtrap, outfight, outsquaw Silas Cooper! Y' got that, 'Rapaho-killer? Y' got that?"

"I . . . I don't aim to take nothing away from you—"

"Tell me, Bass! Right here an' now," Cooper interrupted. "Don't y' ever try to stand head to head with me like y' done once."

"Silas always give a man one chance to show his stupids," Hooks proclaimed. "What Silas always says: give ever' man one chance to show he can be a dead fool."

"Billy's right, Scratch," Cooper reminded. "And y' done had your chance back up there near Buffalo Pass when y' laid your hand on me."

Bass flinched with another look into Cooper's cold black eyes. Almost a good head taller than Bass, and with some eleven or twelve years on him too. "I understood you, then, Silas. An' I don't fix on ever giving you cause to raise a hand to me. Not among friends."

"That's right, 'Rapaho-killer!" Cooper roared, flinging his long arm over Titus's shoulder so suddenly that it surprised Bass as they came to a halt at the center of camp with the others. "We're friends, ain't we? Friends allays take good, good care of each other!"

The tight ring about the trappers loosened as women and men alike began to throw down blankets and robes, seating themselves around the huge fire ring as women came forward bearing rawhide platters heaped with boiled meat and roasted marrow bones, sections of stuffed elk gut and minced slices of raw liver one could dip into tiny bladders filled with tangy yellow gall. Everywhere folks began to talk at once, laugh together, sing out in merriment and exultation.

"Well?" Cooper demanded, turning on Bass, seizing Titus's shoulders in his big hands and squeezing hard. "I asked y'. H'ain't we friends?"

"Yes, Silas," he said, trying not to wince with the pain the big man created in that left shoulder, a hot, deep pain where it had not yet fully healed. At the same time he was determined not to show Cooper, nor the others, just how much he hurt. "We're friends."

"Allays will be?"

Bass nodded. "Yes, always will be friends, Silas."

"Good man!" and Silas pounded Titus on the top of the shoulders. "What say we stuff our gullets full this night, fellas . . . then each dog-man of us rut ary a squaw dry till mornin' light when Silas Cooper's outfit pulls out for the high country!"

"Womens tonight!" Hooks cheered. "Aye—an' the high country tomorry!"

Full as a tick about to burst he was as he waddled back to Fawn's lodge that night long after moonrise. He cradled the boy in his arms on that walk, then laid the sleeping youngster among the blankets where the widow made a warm nest for the child. Titus stood looking down on them both as she tugged up the buffalo robe, then turned and stood before him.

There in the red-hued glow of the dying fire, Fawn freed the sash from her worn blanket coat and flung them both to the far side of the lodge, her eyes never leaving his. Then with her left hand she pulled at the ties on her right shoulder, doing the same at her left shoulder, loosening the top of her dress enough to slowly slide the skins down over her arms, tugging the garment on down over her breasts, then down her rounded belly and hips, finally to let it spill off her thighs to lay in a heap around her ankles like that last, old snow withdrawing in a ragged ring around the trunk of every aspen, lodgepole, and patch of sage in the surrounding hills.

He found his mouth bone dry as he watched what the dim flicker of the last limbs and glowing coals did to the dark hue of her brown flesh. His eyes savored the roundness to her, the full sway of her breasts as she stepped on out of her dress, the soft, full curve of her hips as they molded back to her full bottom.

Just before she moved into him, Bass gazed down at the dark triangle of hair there where her thighs blended into her rounded belly. Then she pressed herself against him, arms encircling his waist, cheek buried against his chest.

Pushing her away slightly, Titus hurried out of his coat with a shudder of excitement—then yanked his shirt over his head as she hastened to pull at the buckle, loosening his belt so that breechclout and leggings fell together. She knelt immediately, tugging at his moccasins, eagerly yanking at the leggings in a rush of motion, her eyes crawling up his legs to where his flesh began to throb and grow in anticipation of her.

Then she stretched up over him like a big cat, pushing him back upon their bed, finally arching herself out to full length atop him, her mouth finding his. The taste of her, wild with red meat simmered until tender with those dried leaves she harvested last summer—again his heart sang with happiness that he had taught her to kiss him back. Their mouths sucking, drawing, savoring one another's as his hands stroked down that concave valley at the small of her back, then rising onto the rounded knoll of her bottom. Fingertips played over the fleshy fullness of her hips only briefly before his hunger drove him to push her off to the side where he could lick and suck on her breasts, running a hand down to that warm delta where she already grew moist.

Ready for him on this, their one last night.

Titus rose above her slowly, then suddenly descended as an animal would pounce while Fawn, the woman, pulled him into her feverishly, fingernails digging like puma's claws, laying claim to the muscles of his back.

There in the red glow of the fire's dying, he wordlessly spoke his good-bye in the one language he was sure she understood—for it was, after all, the same language they had spoken all winter long and into the coming of spring to these high places.

That language of need. Unspoken words that acknowledged you were taking what you needed from another and in return giving back what you thought the other needed most from you. A ferocious hunger there in the dark as the fire slowly went out.

Having dozed fitfully beside her that last night, morning came slowly—in some ways not soon enough; in others too long in the coming. When he turned to lift the buffalo robe gently, he found her already awake. She pulled at his wrist, turning Bass toward her so one hand could reach up to touch his face, the other slipping down to encircle the flesh that hardened with the barest of her touch.

She deserves this, he told himself as he mounted her. She deserves so much, much more than I can give her. So it was that he took his pleasure as she took hers from him, one last time.

And even before his heartbeat had slowed, he rolled from her and slipped from beneath the buffalo robes. Reaching first for his tradewool breechclout, Titus next pulled on the leggings, then yanked the shirt down over his head. He was aware of how she watched his every move as he bent to tie on his moccasins.

"I will miss your shadow in my lodge, Me-Ti-tuzz."

"Come outside to say good-bye to me," he said, his back to her still, not brave enough to look at her yet, afraid he would too easily respond to the plaintive sound in her voice.

"I will dress and bring the boy."

After buckling the wide belt around his coat, Titus pushed back the antelope hide Fawn used for a door cover and blinked with the first light of the coming sunrise. From their rope corral he retrieved Hannah, along with his saddle horse and one more pack animal, taking them all to the lodge, where he tied the three to a nearby aspen beginning to show the first signs of budding. Back and forth between the lodge and the mule Bass hefted what he had left in the way of pack goods, then finally his season's catch: those stiffened round beaver hides lashed together in hundredweight bales.

It was plain as sun that his animals were anxious, restive, eager to go at last. Somehow they knew this was not to be just another hunting trip—no, not with all three of them going. No, the loads Bass secured to their backs were too heavy to these trail-wise animals. This departure would mean they would not be returning to this place.

"Howdy, Titus!"

Bass turned to find Tuttle walking up in his well-greased dark-brown buck-skins.

Bud pointed behind him at his animals picketed at a nearby lodge. "All loaded, I am." Some of his sandy-brown hair hung down over his eyes, poking from beneath the wolverine-hide cap he had fashioned for himself. "You ready to pull out?"

"Just 'bout," he replied. "Where the others?"

"They's loading up," Tuttle answered. "Light enough to ride, so Silas sent me to fetch you up."

Just then Bass heard the movement of the lodge door against the taut, frozen lodge skins and turned. Fawn emerged into the cold morning, holding the young boy on her hip. She set him down on the cold ground, where he stood unmoving, clutching her leg and watching the two white men, little puffs of frost at his lips.

"I'll catch up with you in just a bit," he said, his eyes coming back to look at Tuttle. "Gonna say my farewells."

Bud nodded. "Don't be long, Scratch. Less'n you're fixin' to pack that squaw along for your wife—best you just kiss her, pat her on her sweet ass, and tell her thankee for warming your robes last winter . . . then turn around, never look back, an' be done with it."

Bass grimaced with the sudden, cold feel those words gave his belly. Not that he hadn't been the sort to just run off and leave the first gal he'd ever poked. Not that he wouldn't have run away from the Ohio River whore neither—but Abigail had beat him to the door. And then there'd been Marissa . . . the hardest one to leave, because he had come to realize that if he didn't run when he did, he'd be there still.

No, by Jehoshaphat—Titus Bass was no innocent, white-winged angel when it came to running off and hurting folks' feelings bad. But—just to hear Tuttle put it all to words the way he had, why . . . it gave a man pause to look back at the thoughtless things he'd done in the past, the sort of things a real man wouldn't have done.

Bristling at Tuttle, angry with himself for more than he cared to admit right about then, Titus snapped, "Said I'd be along, Bud. I won't be no time a'tall."

"S'awright by me," Bud replied with a slight shrug. "Just bear it to mind Silas ain't one to be waiting on no man."

"If'n he's set on leaving 'thout me, he can go right ahead," Bass said. "I'll be on your backtrail shortly."

Bass watched Tuttle turn away without another word, heading back to midcamp, where more and more people gathered in a growing congregation around Cooper and Hooks as the sun's light continued to creep on down the side of the mountain toward the shadowy valley where the village sat.

Bass sighed, as if steeling himself before he turned round to look at her for the last time. When he did, Bass found Fawn staring at the ground. Only the boy gazed up at him. So much like Amy's younger brothers and sisters—they reminded him—the wee ones who watched older folk with wide, questioning eyes that bored right through to the core of a person.

As he came to her, Fawn raised her face to him, cheeks wet. For a moment he started to stammer; then, in frustration, Bass quickly looped his arms about her shoulders and clutched her tight. The feel of her tremble within his grasp was almost more than he could bear.

Why the hell hadn't he just saddled up and gone before she ever awoke? he asked himself. Like he'd done before? Damned sight easier that way.

She quivered against him as she said, "My husband rode away one morning. He never came back."

That made him angry—then immediately sorry that his back hairs had bristled. She had every right to speak her heart.

"Fawn, I am not your husband."

Finally she admitted, "You are right. You come here for the winter. Now spring winds blow you on down the trail."

"You knew when I came—"

"Yes, I knew," she interrupted, squeezing her arms about his waist. "I . . . I did not count on letting my heart grow so fond of you."

"It is because you are so lonely," Bass explained, gazing down at the child. White Horse looked up at the two of them in wonder.

Fawn pulled her head back to gaze at him herself. "You were not lonely?" When he did not answer right away, she said, "Tell me that you could spend the winter by yourself—those long nights."

"If a man had to, I could do—"

"How alone would you be with your terrible wounds? Tell me that."

With pursed lips he finally nodded. "Yes, Fawn. You are right. I would have been lonely without you for the winter."

She pressed into him again. "But you go now. Because you go, it hurts to remember back when my husband went away—and he never came back either."

He could feel her quake as she said it, and that almost made his eyes spill. How rotten it made him feel to tell her, "But I never promised you I would return. I came to your lodge for the winter."

"Will you ever . . . will I ever see you again?"

It was hard to speak the truth. "I don't know. Chances are, I won't ever see you or your people again . . . not for a long time."

"You will always be welcome in my lodge, Me-Ti-tuzz," she said, pulling back from him to arm's length. "And my robes will always be warm for you."

"No, Fawn—you will find a husband to warm you in those robes." Titus put a hand out on the boy's head, rubbing it gently. "Someone to help this one grow."

"He needs an uncle, one who can name him when he is ready to be a warrior."

"Yes, Fawn—this boy will deserve a man's name." He turned slightly to look over his shoulder as the noise grew.

The three others had mounted up and had begun to pull out of the village with their pack animals in tow. Men, women, and especially children reached out to touch the horses, the moccasins and legs of the white men taking their leave. Cooper, Hooks, and Tuttle vigorously waved one arm, then another, shouting back at the clamoring crowd surging along with the trappers' horses and mules.

Suddenly Bass turned back to Fawn, gripping her shoulders tightly in his hands. "You will give him a strong name, Fawn."

"Yes."

"Promise me."

"Yes, I promise."

"Be sure he remembers my name."

"Yes. He will remember you."

"One day we may meet again, him and me."

"And what of us?"

"Do not watch the horizon for me, Fawn. No one among all of us can say what tomorrow or that horizon will bring. So don't watch the horizon and wait on me."

Rising on her toes and lifting her chin, Fawn pulled on the collar to Bass's coat, pressing her mouth against his. She was long and lingering in that kiss.

"I am glad I taught you how to do that," Titus told her.

"I like to touch your mouth," she said as she stepped back from him a ways, parted the fold of the blanket she clutched about her, and pulled a thong over her neck. Quickly she raised herself on her toes again and dropped it over his head.

Looking down, he took the small pouch, some four inches long, in his hand. It was nearly empty. "What is this?"

"A gift.

"Among my people every young man must find his own special medicine that allows him to become a warrior. A woman of his clan usually makes him a pouch in which that young man can put those special things that give him his power."

"This . . . this is my medicine pouch?"

Fawn nodded. "Yes."

As his fingers rubbed it together gently, Bass could tell the pouch was all but empty. "What have you put in it for me?"

"Some ashes from our last fire together," she said, her eyes misting now. "A few petals from the flowers just beginning to bloom in the meadow. You . . . you will have to fill it the rest of the way, Me-Ti-tuzz."

Clutching the pouch in one hand, Bass looped the other arm around her and brought her into a fierce embrace. He kissed her one last time, then kissed the tears streaking her cheeks.

She backed from him another two steps, putting an arm around the boy to hold him tightly to her side. "I will remember the touch of your mouth always."

"I'll never forget how you and Crane saved my life this winter."

"The old man's medicine helped," Fawn admitted. "But he said it was your power that kept your spirit from flying off to the Star Road."

Nearly choking, Bass sobbed, "I will remember you, Fawn. Always."

Turning on his heel before he tarried any longer, Bass hurried over to untie the lead rope to Hannah and the packhorse, released the lash to the saddle horse, and leaped into the saddle without using the stirrup. In one swift motion he brought the horse around in a half circle, not daring to look at her again, then immediately gave the animal his heels.

Into the middle of that camp he plunged as quickly as he could—the bodies of men, women, and children surging past him and his pony, past the two pack animals like water rending itself around a boulder in midstream. Their wishes, and prayers, and their strong-heart songs rocked against his ears as he parted them, slowed to an agonizing walk as the farewell noise grew in volume.

At last he reached the outer ring of lodges, pushed on to the willow flats, where he could yank on Hannah's lead rope and jab his heels into the ribs of that saddle horse. Far up ahead on the sunny slope Bass sighted the others climbing off to the left at an easy angle, beginning their switchback climb out of this great inner-mountain valley, reaching ever toward the Buffalo Pass.

He would follow without hesitation, for he needed those three far, far more than they would ever need him.

And tonight, without her warmth beside him—Titus would need something, anything, even the company of those hard-edged, iron-forged three to hold back the aching loneliness until days, perhaps even weeks, from now he would no longer hurt so keenly as he did at this terrible moment.

Into the first patch of sunlight creeping down the western slopes he hurried that morning, wondering if saying farewell ever got any easier.

The wild iris, as deep a purple as the Rocky Mountain twilight itself, stood waving in clusters, bobbing beneath the spring breeze that followed Titus across the meadow. Over his shoulder he lugged the weight of that oiled-leather trap sack he himself had sewn up back in Troost's Livery.

Bass stopped, turned, and squinted behind him in the afternoon light. The three had chosen again to move downstream. At camp after camp on their journey a little west of north, Silas and the others always set their traps downstream while Titus deemed to take a different path. Up this creek, like the other streams before it, he pushed on through the saw grass and skirted the leafy willow, past wild blue hyacinth and the brilliant lavender of flowering horsemint, making sure not to step upon the delicate brick-red petals of prairie smoke or those tiny white whorls of redwool saxifrage.

Except for the distant, mocking shriek of the Steller's jay or the cheep of the bluethroats singing from the branches of the trees over his head, Scratch marveled at the long stretches of silence when the breeze died. Then it would finger its way back down this narrow valley as the day cooled, soughing through the heavy, tossing branches of blue spruce and hearty fir. Back among the shady places, where a soft bed of rotting pine needles covered the forest floor beneath every evergreen and aspen, poked the sun-yellow centers of the pale-blue pasqueflower crocus, straining their saffron faces toward the falling of the sun.

It was for these few minutes he had alone, both morning and afternoon, that Titus had come to live. The quiet so deep, he could almost hear his own blood surging through his veins. Then the robber jay flashed its gray wings in a low swoop overhead, crying out with its squawk of alarm at the two-legged creature below it. Other birds rustled into flight, called out the general fright, and all grew quiet once more.

Nearby, the stream murmured in its gravel bed, talking on and on day and night without stop as it started last winter's snowpack on a rushing tumble toward the distant sea. For a long moment he gazed downstream, studying the tiny riffles and widening vees formed behind every small boulder midstream, wondering if that water passing by him right then would eventually boil into the North Platte, joining all the rest of spring's melting runoff to swell the prairie rivers, finally to spill into the muddy Missouri before merging itself with the mighty Mississippi as it lolled its way past St. Louis . . . down, down to N'Orleans, where the quadroon and many-hued whores plied their trade, where ebony-skinned slaves stood shackled on auction blocks, and the great sheets of canvas strained against the wind on those mighty, three-masted, oceangoing vessels come there from far off beyond the very curve of the earth.

Hell, right here where he stood Titus figured he was damn well far beyond the curve of the earth from everything he had ever known before. Even as high as he stood in these mountains, last winter's snowpack barely yards above him, the timberline not all that far beyond that, Bass could not look back and see the mouth of the Platte, not that widow's cabin at Boone's Lick nor trader's store at Franklin, much less the barn he had helped raise on the Guthrie farm south of St. Lou. As high into the sky as he stood at that moment—why, Titus couldn't even see beyond the jagged tumble of gray granite and emerald-green that marked cleft upon cleft as the mountain ranges stood hulking one against the other without apparent end.

But he knew these high peaks had to end the farther west he pushed . . . there they would allow a man to gently ride back down their sunset-side slopes onto the prairie among the burnt orange of the paintbrush and the sego lilies and the upwind sage that always filled a man's nostrils. He had never been there yet, not in all his searching to the west last autumn. Nor had Isaac Washburn.

But Silas, Bud, and Billy had, by damned. And that's where they were headed in this easy tramp toward rendezvous. They'd seen the end of the mountains and the beginning of the great dry basin that most said was where rivers eventually sank into oblivion and the desert stretched toward the sunset until it finally ran smack up against even more mountains.

Beyond that was rumored to be the great salt ocean where Lewis and his friend Clark had dared take their men some twenty years before. And now here he stood, squarely in that land of fable and myth that had no end until it dropped off suddenly into that salt ocean. At N'Orleans, Titus had looked out with sixteen-year-old eyes and tried to imagine where all that water could carry those tall-masted ships.

No more did he wonder on all that white canvas thrown up against the wind, for here, among the gigantic heave of granite escarpment thrust against the very same sky . . . here he could cast his gaze upon tumbling boulder fields of talus and scree stretching wider than the Ohio River itself, why—Titus stood beneath the white umbrella of clouds he could almost reach up and touch. There, just inches beyond the reach of his fingers.

He looked back to the east again, perhaps to will his vision to penetrate through the haze and all that distance just whence he had come. The Ohio River borderlands of Boone County. Then Louisville and Owensboro. Natchez-Under-the-Hill and the dense forest road that took a man north through the Chickasaws' and Choctaws' wilderness and on back to home.

But he saw none of that from here. Home now lay beneath the soles of his moccasins. And there was no wilderness back there anywhere near as mighty as was this where he dropped his trap sack and suddenly went to his knees to rock forward and lean out over that murmuring stream—just to sip at what must surely be God's own holy water, so cold it set his back teeth on edge.

Beard dripping, Scratch rocked back on his haunches and looked up at those cold snowfields mantled around the high peaks just beyond their camp. And there and then he closed his eyes—praying as best he could remember having learned to pray at his mam's knee: her old, yellow-eared Bible flung open and draped over her lap like two great wings of some bird that she was certain one day would lift her up and carry her away to everlasting paradise.

Rising once again, he brought the trap sack up with him and set off, sweeping around a bend in the creek another two hundred yards until he reached the edge of the flooded meadow where the flat-tailed rodents had long been at work. Perhaps since the day after the beginning of time. How his heart beat that much faster, just to let his eyes rush over all the signs of their industry: tender saplings and young trees hawed off by those busy front teeth less than a foot from the ground, more than two dozen muddy slides marked the beavers' descent from grassy banks into that watery world of their own making, and at least a double handful of those crude, dome-topped lodges rising from the middle of their pond—lodges where the animals were safe from all but one predator.

Last fall as he began his new life as a beaver-man, Titus had taken a sharpened sapling and waded out to the closest lodge. There he had curiously jabbed and levered, chipping away at the chewed limbs and mud chinking until he had broken through, then peered inside at the dark inner world abandoned by the frightened animals who kept right on slapping their tails on the surface of that pond nearby. He saw the inner shelf where the beaver crawled up and out of the water to sleep, there to feed on the tender green shoots and new limbs they dragged down the banks, into the water, then under the surface and into their lodges.

They would have that hole repaired inside of three days, maybe only two, he had estimated from how hard he saw the animals work. And when he had found the hole covered with new limbs and fresh mud the very next day, Bass felt a newfound respect for this creature he stalked, trapped, skinned, and sometimes ate.

"You gone an' hit dead center this time, ol' coon," he breathed all but to himself as he stared now at the immensity of the beaver pond.

Then quickly glanced downstream where he feared the others might have followed him there.

For a moment more he listened. Only the racket of a chirking squirrel complaining overhead and the shadow-flash of a swooping flock of black rosy finches broke the stillness. Then came the rustle of branches and a handful of leaves spilling to the surface of the pond. In and out of the shadows on the far side he made out the familiar waddle of the fat rodents all about their business of chewing back the forest's edge a tree at a time.

Cautiously he set down the sack, then freed the knot at the top, stuffed the strand of half-inch rope beneath his belt and plunged a hand into the sack to pull forth the first trap. With it set beside him in the grass, hidden there behind the clumps of low, leafy brush, Scratch used his belt knife to saw free a narrow branch, then sharpened the widest end to a point.

Standing again, he quietly slipped off downstream to a place where he could enter the water far from the beavers' slides. The first step wasn't the hardest. It was the third or fourth as he inched deeper into the stream—his body past the first, startling shock of the cold, this water just descended from glacial melt. Now his calves began to ache and his toes disappeared from all feeling. Still he plodded on, each leaden foot feeling its way forward across the rocky bottom, pressing his way upstream, back toward the flooded meadow.

Slowly he moved, keeping to the afternoon shadows as best he could, his eyes and ears alert to those beaver that might discover him as they went about their business on the far side of the pond, and he went about his. At the ninth slide he figured he had come far enough, nearly halfway around the meadow. It wouldn't do to press his luck beyond here, Titus figured.

There he jabbed the bait-stick into the side of the bank so that it hung low over the slide. Titus kept it down to make it all the easier for an unsuspecting animal to get himself a real good sniff of the end of that bait stick where he smeared some castor—that pale, milky substance taken from a pair of glands in the beaver's groin. The animal used it to sleek and waterproof its thick hide. But to smell strange castor come to their pond—why, that would pique the curiosity of any of these flat-tails hereabouts.

Quietly reseating the stopper in the bait bottle that hung from his belt, Scratch crouched forward, bending at the knee, and with one hand began to dig away at the bank there a half foot below the pond's surface. With a proper shelf excavated, he next worked at squeezing closed both of the tough iron springs on the trap so that the jaws fell open. Only then could he slip the trigger into the notch on the round pan that lay in the center of the open jaws.

Carefully he moved the trap under the water, settling it upon the shelf, then adjusted the end of the bait-stick so that it hovered right above the hidden trap. It wouldn't be long before one of the flat-tails came down that slide, winded the scent of a strange beaver, and waddled over to investigate. When it did, chances were almost certain it would end up stepping right on the pan in trying to get itself a good sniff of the bait—when the trigger would release, snapping the smooth iron jaws shut on the beaver's leg.

And what the frightened animal did then would be crucial to Scratch having a pelt to scrape and stretch and eventually barter off to a trader . . . or it would mean losing a trap somewhere at the muddy, grassy bottom of this forest pond.

From the back of his belt he took a long branch he had selected from a nearby stand of lodgepole. Then he stretched out the trap chain to its full length, one end of which was looped around a trap spring. Slipping the branch through the large eye-ring at the other end, Bass drove a sharp end into the bottom of the pond.

Once the jaws had slapped shut around the unwary beaver's leg, the animal would instinctively dive for the safety of deep water, paddling frantically for the middle of the pond and its lodge. But on the way it would be caught at the end of the trap chain that it had unknowingly dragged down the length of the branch, where the trap-ring would be snagged beneath a large knot. Reaching deep water near the middle of the pond, the beaver would find it impossible to swim back again to the surface, and drown without any damage to its glossy pelt, which would one day be fashioned into a fine top hat for some eastern gentleman, mayhap even a winter muffler for some gussied-up city gal all aswirl in yards upon yards of starched crinoline, taffeta, and satin.

Slowly Scratch turned, careful to make as little noise in the water as he could, keeping to the shadows as the sun continued its descent, here where a man grew his coldest in this water just recently given birth by ice fields. But it was here, just below the dripping shelves of snowy cataracts, just beneath the overhang of melting glaciers, that beaver grew their thickest pelts and maintained those winter coats long into the spring.

Trap after trap he set that afternoon, returning to his trap sack each time on the same circuitous route through the water so that his scent would not become entangled with the brush or the ground near any one of his sets. Ten bait-sticks he cut late that afternoon, and ten shelves he carved away beneath the water's surface there at the bottom of ten slides.

Ten beaver would he collect come morning light.

Those last two traps at the bottom of the sack felt as heavy as a small anvil to his weary arms as Scratch finally slogged downstream, taking his leave of the flooded meadow only after the sun had disappeared behind the high peaks looming far overhead.

Those ten beaver would again put him ahead of Cooper's catch. Even farther ahead of Billy's. And poor Tuttle wasn't even in the running. Yet Bud made himself useful around camp, scraping hides, whipping together the willow hoops on which the others would stretch their beaver plews into the distinctively round "beaver dollars." As poor a trapper as Bud Tuttle was, to Scratch's way of thinking he was a damned good man to have along as a camp keeper and fire tender.

His feet heavy, and shuddering with the chill of evening coming, Titus plodded back toward that distant flicker of their campfire signaling like a beacon through the quaking aspens. Coffee and some elk loin would set well on his stomach this night.

He vowed to keep the meadow secret until he had pulled his beaver come morning.

By damn! This would be the last night Silas Cooper would have to gloat.

Now they'd all see just who in tarnation was the master trapper in these parts!

TEN

That white-headed trader's whiskey tasted good enough, by damn—nonetheless, Titus still had him a serious hankering for some good old Monongahela rum, generously sweetened with raw cane sugar, the likes of which they served in every watering hole, tippling house, and gunboat brothel on the great rivers back east.

Bass licked his lips, savoring the tang of raw tobacco and red pepper on his tongue, the faintest sweetening of strap molasses . . . then slowly awoke, still running his tongue over his bottom lip—hoping there was more to drink.

Rubbing the grit from his eyes, Scratch sat up, finding the others still dead to the world around the coals in their fire pit, none of them more than shapeless mounds buried beneath an inch-thick, wet snow. That cold white blanket covered most everything as he reluctantly came awake—feeling as if the cold spring fog had pierced him to his marrow. He peered through the trees, finding the horses still as statues in their rope corral, not bothering to paw at the ground this early.

Shuddering, Scratch thought how good it would feel to have Fawn next to him. Maybeso there really would be women down to the trader's rendezvous in a few weeks' time, just as Billy and Silas had been saying over and over again. A man might hold out that long, he considered, working up hope once more. Yes, indeed: a man could get himself through the spring and the autumn . . . just so he could have him a woman at the height of summer, as long as he had one with him too through the deep of winter.

He kicked back the blankets, stood, and tightened the wide belt around his blanket capote. Then he reached into his possibles pouch and pulled out the blue scarf. Holding two opposite corners, Scratch whipped it into a thin band he tied around his head to hold the long hair over his ears for warmth. Stuffing his coyote-hide hat down on his head, Titus bent over the remnants of last night's elk. He dug among the chunks of the meat they had boiled, then set to cool in a second kettle. What they hadn't eaten now had a dusting of snow upon it. He blew some of the icy crust off each piece as he stuffed it into a large piece of oiled nankeen cloth, then rolled up the square so it would slip down into the shooting pouch he slapped over his right shoulder.

With the fullstock rifle in his blanket mitten and still no sign of life from the others, who went right on snoring in their buffalo-robe cocoons, Bass crept away into the cold mists of that spring morning in the high country, eager to get the jump on the day, and the jump on Silas's boys.

He hadn't covered much ground before the calves of his leggings were soaked by the wet, melting snow that clung heavily to everything in his path— frosted to every blade of grass and thick-leafed swamp cabbage, crusted on every willow or aspen leaf. The swirling, thick fog was cold all by itself as it danced and whirled on the ground around his knees, yet it became thicker still the closer he got to the upstream meadow where he had been taking beaver hand over fist for the last six days without seeming to put a dent in the rodents' population.

And every last one of them was a prime fur. "Seal fat and sleek," was how Billy Hooks had described the first of the pelts Titus had brought back to their camp.

"Damn near the finest I ever see'd," Tuttle had commented as he began to help Titus scrape the excess flesh and fat off the back of each hide before they stretched it upon a willow hoop.

Damn pretty things they were too—near as satiny as any fur Titus had laid eyes on were those plews of his. And dark, much darker than their lowland cousins he had trapped before. By Jehoshaphat, spring trapping was the prime doin's in a mountain nigger's life, he recalled Silas exclaiming more than once since leaving the Ute winter camp. Sure and certain, he thought again now—there were no two ways about it. Spring trapping up this high was where a man was sure to make himself a small fortune in beaver. No better time of the year for a man to bust his ass: knowing he'd soon be swapping those furs in on one hell of a spree come the time to meet the trader at rendezvous.

It was a life Bass knew he was going to relish. Hell, there wasn't a thing he didn't already love about this life he had decided to wager everything on more than a year ago back in St. Louis. No man to boss him around up here, why—a man rose or fell by his own efforts and not those of others. As much affection as he had felt for Hysham Troost, Titus purely savored working on his own hook.

Standing the rifle in a crook of some willow near his first set, Scratch stepped sideways off the slippery bank and into the freezing water that steamed into the cold air. Above him the granite peaks and talus slides were brushed with a golden rose in the coming of the sun as the day's first light touched only the highest places.

Down here life was still nothing but shadow as Bass inched toward the float-stick, snagged it with his bare hand, and dragged it over to the bank. At the end of the chain hung the trap, and in its square jaws hung a heavy beaver—slick and dripping as he eased it out of the water. Onto the bank he heaved it, then clambered up after the carcass. Squatting on the two powerful springs, Titus freed the animal's leg, laid the trap aside, and pulled the skinning knife from its scabbard at the back of his belt.

Rolling the beaver over onto its back, Scratch started the slit at the anus and worked the knife carefully up in a straight cut toward the lower jaw. That done, he sliced around the legs near the body itself and prepared to remove the precious plew. Now with the unnecessary legs removed and a quick whirl with the knife to hack off the large, scaly tail, Titus laid his finger along the flat top of his skinning knife and began the slow, careful work of separating hide from body, a few inches of connective tissue and fat at a time. Almost like peeling back the robe off Widow Grigsby's shoulders: pulling and slicing, pulling and slicing a little more as the plew relinquished its hold on the carcass.

From the rump end he worked forward, finally peeling the hide from the head itself, right down to the animal's nose. Holding it up, Bass inspected it quickly, as he did with every one, looking first at the flesh side to see that he hadn't been too quick and eager, and thereby sloppy, causing his knife to slip and cut through the plew. Then he could admire the thick, damp, oily fur on the opposite side.

After resetting the trap and smearing more of the sticky bait on the tip of the willow limb poised over that much-used slide the beaver had carved themselves down the slippery bank, Titus poked a long whang of stiffened rawhide through one of the empty eye sockets and slung the heavy green plew over his shoulder. Snagging the beaver's scaly tail root, he flung the carcass as far as he could into the brush away from the pond. A few feet away he retrieved his rifle, threaded his way back through the willow, and slogged on to the second set.

One after another one he pulled up a beaver. It had been this way for days. Not a single empty trap. Fourteen more plews by midmorning when he finished resetting his traps and turned back for camp. Those fourteen would make for a full day of fleshing and stretching. As boring as the work was, it remained somewhat joyous work, nevertheless: knowing now just what each one of those hides should be worth come the middle of summer when they got on over to the Willow Valley by the Sweet Lake.

Through the thin vertical straps of lodgepole shadow and the patches of early sunlight, he saw the gray film of firesmoke and the slow, deliberate movements of the three as he drew close. Cooper was late turning them out this morning.

"Ho! The camp!" Bass called out.

Billy Hooks turned, his face quickly painted with that ready smile. "Ho! Scratch!" Then he peered more carefully at Bass as Titus lumbered up with half of his burden at the end of each arm. "Will you lookee at that, boys?"

Bass himself turned to find Cooper squatting over a pile of his own beaver hides. Silas rose and set his big hands down on his hips. "Pound some powder up my ass and strike fire to my pecker! Looks to me like this here green pilgrim got him a haul of prime plew awready today, boys!"

Titus was proud to boast, "Fourteen of 'em, Silas!"

"Fourteen?" Cooper repeated as he came around Scratch's shoulder to have himself a look at the two heavy bundle of green hides. "All these since yestiddy?"

"Skinned 'em this mornin'."

"An' don't they look like big'uns too," Cooper went on, admiringly.

Bass glowed with the praise, fairly crowing. "Nearly every one—bigger'n any I ever catched."

Slapping his hand down on Bass's shoulder, Silas nodded once and said, "Fellas, this here greenhorn nigger gonna have him the finest pack of plew come time to talk to the trader, don't y' think?"

"For balls' sake if he won't!" Bud agreed, and Billy bobbed his head eagerly.

Then Tuttle stepped up to heft both rawhide straps from Titus, flinging the green hides toward the area of camp where they fleshed the skins and lashed them inside willow hoops—where more than two dozen of those willow hoops stood propped against trees this morning, their skins drying, hide side up.

"C'mon, y' two. We got us a long way to go this morning," Cooper ordered, the slash of a grin on his face. "We ought'n go see if we can catch ourselves some of them prime plew like Scratch here done."

Joking good-naturedly among themselves as they always did, the three gathered up their trap sacks and float-sticks, bait and weapons, before easing off downstream where they had been trapping for the last six days with moderate success. But unlike Bass's good fortune, the three had been forced to move farther and farther downstream with each succeeding day.

Once he had some more limbs steepled on the fire, and the coffeepot set on the flames to boil, Titus turned back to the fourteen green hides. One at a time he slid them off the thick rawhide whang, laid each down, and rolled it up tightly, flesh side in so they would not air-dry prematurely. All but the last one he tied up with thin cords of fringe to prevent them from unrolling. On that last one he began work there beside his morning fire as the coffeepot began to spew a thin trail of vapor from its spout.

From his leather possibles pouch, where he carried everything a man might require to survive in the wilderness, Scratch took one of those large iron awls he had fashioned for Isaac Washburn and himself back in Troost's St. Louis livery. Stuffing one of its two sharpened ends into the hole drilled in a rounded knob of wood that fit his palm, Scratch began to carefully poke holes around the outer circumference of the first plew, grabbing an empty willow hoop from those stacked to lean against some deadfall. When he had selected a long loop of raw-hide cord from among those hanging on knots and broken limbs around their campsite, Titus began the process of lashing the hide to the hoop.

Leaving himself better than a foot of the rawhide cord free, Scratch shoved the pointed end of the cord through the first hole he punched at the extreme edge of the soft green hide, then looped the cord over the thick willow limb and repeated the process of poking the cord through the next hole, round and round and round, over the willow hoop and through the succeeding holes until he had the beaver plew completely circumscribed.

Now began the most time-consuming part of the job at hand: ever so slowly stretching the hide into a large round shape to fit the round hoop. Tugging on loop by rawhide loop, Scratch painstakingly moved around the hoop again, stretching the hide out another fraction of an inch. A little more on the next trip around. Then stretched it more, and more. Finally, after uncounted trips around that willow hoop, the beaver plew had been worked as taut as the head of an Indian war drum, fashioned into that crude shape the mountain man called his "beaver dollar."

The coffee had begun to hiss and spew, so he grabbed a short limb and used it to pull on the bail to ease the pot back off the flames. There on the bed of glowing coals it would remain warm for some time to come. Then . . .

Oh, how Titus hated what grueling work came next: fleshing.

Yet he figured he should make a start of it before Tuttle came back to finish up the hides—at least flesh this first one. So far this spring they had them an easy bargain worked out. Titus was far better at lashing the plews within their willow hoops, so he did that for Bud. And Tuttle didn't much mind the fleshing, a chore most beaver men considered "squaw's work." Funny thing was that here, as in most camps of fur trappers, there simply weren't any squaws to complete the back-bending, shoulder-sore labor of removing every last bit of flesh, fat, and connective tissue from the backside of the beaver plew once it had been stretched on its frame.

Near a stack of empty willow hoops, Scratch found one of the fleshing tools, its half-round wooden handle well darkened with oil from the hands of those who had labored with it. Screwed between the two long halves of the wooden handle was a rounded piece of thin iron, sharpened on its convex side, enough room left in the iron blade so that a man's fingers could slip through the slot and firmly grip the flesher.

Flipping the hoop so it laid fur side down, Titus squatted, sighed, then knelt over the plew to begin dragging the sharp edge of the flesher against the grain of the beaver's skin—gradually lifting that excess flesh, thick straps of fatty tissue, and thin strips of connective fascia. Time and again he peeled the sticky residue from his crude flesher and went back to work, until he eventually had the hide scraped to within a thumb's width of the edge of the plew where the rawhide loops secured it to the willow hoop.

Slowly volving his shoulders as he rocked back on his haunches, Scratch felt the pull and tightness in his back with the hunched-up work he truly felt was fit only for a squaw. Weary as the work made him, the rest could wait until Tuttle returned, he figured. Then together they could begin to work on the other thirteen, plus what others Bud would manage to bring back from his own traps that morning.

Titus crabbed forward and poured himself half a tin cup of the steaming coffee as more of the sun shot down through the trees in narrow shafts of misting light. He scooted his rump over to lean back against a large trunk of some deadfall, his feet to the fire, and sipped his coffee.

Here in the sun, its warm rays creeping up his legs, the heated coffee tin cradled between his hands, Scratch slowly closed his eyes. No doubt was there that the best beaver men moved out of camp before first light. But just as sure was it that a man might reward himself with the luxury of a little nap once he was back in camp with the prior day's catch. Titus sat the coffee tin beside him on the trampled ground, folded his arms, and let his chin whiskers fall to his chest.

Startled by the chirk of a squirrel in the branches high overhead, he awoke sometime later, aware he had indeed been dozing with no recollection of just how much time had passed. But picking up the cup and taking a sip of the cold coffee gave him some idea of just how long. He flung out the dregs and poured himself another half cup. That was the way he had learned not to waste valuable coffee: drinking only a half cup at a time so that it wouldn't cool prematurely.

After a few sips on the hot brew that invigorated him, Scratch got to his feet and moved off toward his side of the small camp to roll up his bedding he had abandoned before first light. There among his pack goods he stopped of a sudden—staring down at the four packs of beaver hides he had trapped in valley and high-country streams since first reaching the mountains last autumn. Three . . . damn if three of the packs didn't look smaller than he remembered.

Bass rubbed his smoke-reddened eyes, thinking perhaps it was only because he was still groggy from napping that the packs somehow appeared smaller. Then he tilted his head to one side, appraising them. And tilted his head to the other. None of it made things appear any better.

Dropping quickly to his knees on the thick turf of fallen pine needles, Scratch worked to loosen the knots at the first of those three short packs. As his fingers clawed feverishly, he realized his heart was hammering a little faster with apprehension. Confusion. Pure bewilderment. And a sickening lump was starting to rise in the back of his throat, making it hard to swallow.

As he flung back the four long strands of thick rawhide, Titus became all the more despairing—thinking back to that very morning at the meadow pond where he had labored to skin those fourteen beaver: when he had realized those fourteen plews would be enough to finish out his fourth pack and provide a good start on a fifth. But now as his hands quickly parted the hides, counting them silently as his lips moved, trembling and fearful—Bass knew with growing certainty that he no longer had four full packs.

He quickly tore at the rawhide lashes on a second stack and began counting.

Suddenly Bass was confronting the fact that what he had now was far from enough to make even three full packs, much less the four. And as quickly he was afraid of just what that meant.

His hands froze at the knots securing the rawhide lash on the third short pack. Instead of releasing the knot, he turned slowly, staring across camp to where the others cached their plunder, possibles, and plews.

Titus was choking on the sour taste of it as he rose shakily, his knees wobbly as the realization sank in . . . slowly stumbling around the fire pit toward the far side where the trio's packs sat beneath drapes of dirty canvas.

There he stopped and stared down, seeking to weigh things before committing the unpardonable transgression of prowling through another man's belongings. From the way things appeared, Bud Tuttle didn't have near enough packs among his things for Bass to be concerned.

Maybe Billy. By damn, maybeso it was him. That handy smile and happy-go-lucky naybobbin' way of his might well be just the proper cover-up that would allow a jealous Hooks to get away with the theft of another man's furs.

Thievery.

There it was. A word yet unspoken, but big and bold all the same.

Kneeling beside Billy's possessions, Bass hurled back the end of the canvas, pulled the first stack toward him, and tore at the knots. But as he was beginning to count that first stack of furs, his eyes eventually, reluctantly, crawled to Cooper's hides bundled nearby.

Lord, how he didn't want it to be so.

Rising from Billy's uncounted furs, Bass trudged over to Silas's belongings with the air of a man forced to walk those last thirteen steps up to a hangman's noose. Sinking to his knees, he drew back the canvas drape. There sat better than five whole packs.

Titus looked once more at Tuttle's piddling catch. At Billy's best efforts. Then back again to regard how Silas's catch outstripped the other two. It was plain to see that Cooper had a sizable lead on Titus.

His hands were shaking as he began to pull at the knots on that first pack, trembling so bad that Scratch finally pulled his knife and slashed at the rawhide ties. Setting the skinning knife aside, Titus pulled the first hide off the top. He swallowed hard as he turned it over, eyes skipping quickly over the flesh side.

It bore Cooper's mark.

As did the second, and the third. And even the fourth.

He swept the knife up and cut free the rawhide bands on the second pack, beginning to inspect the hides in that pack. The first half dozen or so were clearly branded with Cooper's mark. Likewise he slashed at the rawhide thongs on the third pack. Growing more desperate as he went along, Titus tore into the fourth stack of beaver pelts, wondering what was worse: thinking Cooper was the thief, or finding out that Cooper was not . . . which meant Titus still had a great, unsettling mystery to solve.

Then eight plews down in that fourth pack he saw it.

His mark on the backside of a large, shiny, glossy beaver pelt. His mark, sure enough—except that Cooper had attempted to scratch his own mark right over Bass's.

Bass yanked it out of the stack, then pulled the seventh and studied it. Damn but the job was good, the way Cooper had carefully scratched a knife tip over the *T B* on the rough, stiffened, fleshy side of the pelt, turning the *T* into a careless *S*, and thickening out the *B,* adding a crude curve to the letter, which served to scrawl the *C* for Cooper.

Lunging for one of the stacks he had just inspected, Titus found the same to be true farther down in each pack. He hadn't looked deep enough, nor well enough. The top six or eight hides were Cooper's in each pack, to be sure. But they laid upon plew after plew that Scratch had trapped, skinned, and fleshed with Tuttle's help. Bass realized he hadn't seen the crude forgery at first—how Cooper's scrawl obscured all Titus's hard work.

"What the hell are y' doing in my packs, you weasel-stoned nigger?"

Bass wheeled at the growl, his hair rising on the back of his neck, skin prickling in fear as he stared at Cooper some two rods away. Just behind Silas stood Tuttle and Hooks, looking on—but not in disbelief or shock that Bass would be among Cooper's belongings . . . instead, looking at the scene with masks of knowing horror. He realized they knew.

Suddenly the massive Cooper had crossed those last few ten yards, seizing Bass's coat in one big paw, and hurled him to the ground. "Y' fixing to steal from me, you tit-sucking son of a bitch?"

"S-steal from you?" Titus's voice crackled as he rolled onto his knees, then arose slowly. He couldn't believe he had been accused of theft by the thief himself.

"Looks to me what you're fixin' to do!" Cooper spat. His big jaw jutted there in the middle of his wide, sloping shoulders that gave him the look of a man without a neck. Silas flung out his arm, pointing across the fire to Bass's packs torn apart and in disarray.

Titus wagged his head in disbelief and stammered, "Y-you . . . you're the one what's been—"

"Lookee there, boys!" Cooper interrupted, his long black beard waving on the breeze as he whirled on the other two. "I caught this greenhorn sumbitch fixing to line his packs with *my* furs!"

Beginning to shake in utter disbelief, Bass glanced quickly at Tuttle. Bud dropped his eyes just as quickly. Then Titus took a deep breath and dared the words, "Silas—you're the thievin' son of a bitch!"

Cooper had him again in an instant, flinging the smaller man backward before Bass even realized Silas had snagged the front of his coat again. This time Titus collided with a tree, knocking the wind out of him as he slid down its trunk, the shooting pain in his back so immense that he could taste it. The next time he inhaled it hurt so much he gasped—fighting to catch his breath. Scratch swallowed down his galloping heart and tried to speak as he struggled back to his feet.

Bass's arm was shaking as he pointed. "F-found my furs in your goddamned packs, Cooper!"

Silas brought the rifle into his right hand, his monstrous thumb drawing back the hammer.

"Silas! *No!*" Tuttle screeched, lunging toward Cooper, then suddenly remembering that he must not interfere.

The other three watched the rifle shudder in Cooper's grasp, as if he were tormented to keep from pulling the trigger.

Bass stared down at the muzzle. Never before had he looked at a weapon's yawning black hole . . . so damned close.

There beneath the gray-black wolf hide he had sewn into a cap so the pelt spilled over his shoulders and the wolf's face was pulled down to his brow to shade his black eyes, suddenly came an ugly, taunting, vicious look to the giant's face as he asked, "What . . . what'd you say 'bout me, Titus Bass?"

"You g-got my hides in your . . . your p-packs."

Hooks took a step closer saying, "Silas ain't stealin' your beaver, Titus. He only—"

"Shuddup, Billy!" Cooper snapped, hulking there in that lumbering side-to-side shuffle of his.

Bass watched how Hooks immediately clamped his mouth closed, eyes every bit as wide as Tuttle's, and both pairs of eyes filled with fear, the two men's faces blanched as they studied Cooper, then Bass, then back to Cooper.

Quietly, Tuttle started, "Maybe Titus don't under—"

"You shut your yap too, Bud!" Silas growled as he flung an arm menacingly in Tuttle's direction. "This here's a'tween Scratch'n me. Ain't it . . . Titus?"

For an instant Bass let his eyes flick to Tuttle, then to Hooks, and finally back to Cooper with the full realization. "That's r-right, Silas. A'tween only you an' me."

Cooper grinned, that crooked, one-sided smile, big and broad. He looked down at the rifle in his hand, then slowly squeezed on the trigger, lowering the hammer. "Billy."

Hooks came up as Cooper held the rifle back at the end of his arm. Billy took it from him.

"Bud."

"Yeah, Silas." Tuttle stepped forward obediently too, receiving the shooting pouch Cooper pulled over his head without taking his eyes off Titus.

"Now, Scratch," Silas began, his voice gotten strangely quiet, his eyes narrowing as his iron-strap jaw set firmly in that black beard that reached the middle of his chest. "What y' gotta say to me, face-to-face? Man to man?"

"Found some of m-my furs in your packs," Titus repeated, watching Cooper take a step closer.

God, how the man seemed to tower over him. Cooper possessed shoulders wide enough to carry the span of a hickory-ax handle with room to spare.

"Them's my furs, Titus," he said, all but in a harsh whisper, taking another yard-long step closer to Bass.

Scratch wanted to back up that same distance. Maintain that much room between him and the big, chisel-faced man. "Had my mark on alla them."

"Un-uh. All of 'em got *my* letters on 'em, Titus. Or ain't y' ever l'arn't to read, son?"

"I can read good as most any man," he said, his throat gone parched as Cooper came another long step closer. Easing in like a cat ready to pounce on a mouse. Toying. Playing.

This time Cooper's voice had less of a mocking tone, more of an edge. "So what'd y' read, greenhorn?"

"Saw wh-where you scratched over my letters . . . put your own letters on my hides."

Suddenly Silas snapped his shoulders back, enjoying how that made Bass flinch. He grinned again. "But them ain't your hides, nigger."

"I catched 'em, Silas." Titus wanted one of the others to say something, sure they knew, certain they realized the theft.

"They're mine, Scratch."

Bass shook his head slowly, daring that brave gesture as he watched the black cloud cross the big man's face. His stomach growled with dread as he coughed loose the words, "Them's my plews, Cooper."

Although his eyes remained narrowed, his smile now became a wolf-slash of a grin on Silas's lips while he said, "You 'member when y' grabbed hol't of my arm last fall, Scratch?"

His head bobbed once, not sure what meaning Cooper's question had. "Yeah. I 'member. When you was fixing to kill yourself a mule."

The grin widened in the black beard as Silas licked his lower lip. "Do y' recollect what I tol't you back then 'bout ever laying a hand on me?"

"Never forgot that, Silas," he said, the furrow between his own eyes deepening in consternation at the confusing direction things were taking. "But I ain't never laid a hand on you—"

"Y' go an' put your hands on what *belongs* to Silas Cooper," he interrupted with a bellow like a buffalo bull in the rut, "y' might as well gone an' put your hands on Silas Cooper his own self!"

Without any more warning than that, Bass found himself shrunken in the big man's shadow, seized, and flung backward with both powerful arms—smashing against the wide trunk of another old pine.

The breath driven out of his lungs a second time, shaking his head free of the mind-numbing stars, Titus remained helpless as Cooper yanked him up, held him out at the end of his left arm, and drew back his right arm.

"Silas!"

Cooper turned at Tuttle's screech.

"Don't hurt 'im, Silas," Billy pleaded too. "He don't know no better. We can teach him. Swear we'll teach him—Bud an' me."

But Silas shook his head, looking back at his two partners. "You can teach him, sure y' can. I don't doubt that a bit. But only after I've teached him my own self—"

Hanging there in the giant's grip, Bass flung out a fist, connecting with Cooper's left temple. God, did that ever hurt his knuckles, he thought . . . watching Silas turn back to look at him now, his marblelike eyes blinking a few times in surprise. Then flecking over in reddening anger.

"Why—the hairless pup got him some sand after all, boys!"

And the stars burned a fiery path through Bass's mind as Cooper's fist connected with the side of his head. It felt like he'd been kicked by one of them big draft Morgans.

Somewhere off in the distance Scratch heard men shouting, watched shadows and colors blur and swim before his eyes as he was yanked back up from the ground. This time Cooper drove a fist savagely into the pit of his belly. He stopped breathing, it hurt so bad. Then a second time the fist collided with his belly, and a third before Silas let Bass collapse onto his knees.

Titus huddled there, heaving slightly, waiting for his coffee to come up. But there wasn't enough of that in his stomach. Only angry yellow bile spewed fiery torment at the back of his throat as he fought for breath. Struggling to breathe against the pain in his ribs, slowly he raised his face to look up at the fuzzy apparition stepping over him.

"Don't kill 'im, Silas!"

"Shit, Billy," Cooper cried back with genuine joy as he snagged hold of Titus again, started dragging him to his feet once more, "I ain't got no druthers to kill the man."

Then he brought a wide left jab rocketing in to crash against Bass's jaw. Like the head on a stuffed doll, Scratch's skull flopped to the side, then back loosely. He could feel the teeth loosen and sensed that thick syrup of blood on his tongue. How salty it tasted.

"Don't wanna kill him," Cooper said as he switched hold of Bass now, drawing back his right arm, cocking it like the hammer on a huge weapon. "Why, this feller be our best trapper, boys! Wouldn't do to kill him, would it?"

Titus felt his nose crumple as the fist smashed against his face, blurring his vision, sensing the hot blood oozing from it over his mustache and onto his lips as Cooper let go and he sank to his knees.

"Tell 'im, Silas!" Tuttle pleaded, daring to take two steps closer to the savage beating where Bass knelt, gobs of blood seeping from nose and mouth. "Goddammit—tell 'im!"

"Tell 'im, Bud?" Cooper asked with an innocent sound to it, then suddenly brought the toe of his moccasin up brutally beneath Scratch's bloody and bearded chin, snapping his head backward with such force that it all but drove his body off the ground in an arch as he sailed into Cooper's packs.

Tuttle continued, "C'mon, Silas. He didn't know."

Cooper wheeled on Bud, his knuckles red, scuffed from the beating he was giving Bass. "Sumbitch'll know now, won't he?"

"He'll know, Silas," Billy promised, trying that infectious gap-toothed smile of his. "B-but you don't let 'im be, he cain't catch no furs."

Cooper stood over Scratch in that next moment, his shadow crossing Bass's face. Titus blinked up, trying to focus, sensing that the blood was pooling at the back of his throat from both nose and jaw. Knowing too that if he didn't get off the ground, he might well choke. Then it suddenly didn't matter because Silas drove his foot right into Bass's belly.

Titus doubled up, drawing his legs up reflexively, lying on his side in a fetal lump and coughing up blood on the hard, sharp pine needles that dug into the bloody side of his face.

"Maybeso they're right, Scratch," Silas snarled after he knelt right over the bloodied man, putting his face down within inches of Bass's.

Vainly, courageously, Titus tried to raise an arm, if only to push the cruel face away. In such utter pain, he found he didn't have any strength and dropped the arm with an agonized gush of air from his puffy, battered lips. As bad as his bones and belly felt, it was his spirit, the very heart of him, that hurt all the worse: lying there, beaten so badly without giving a good account of himself. Not like it had been back in St. Louis. Oh, for sure he had usually been beaten in those days of wenching and brawling, and beaten real good upon many an occasion. But such thumpings had always come after he had given back just about as good as he was forced to take—able to acquit himself honorably in those wharfside tippling houses and knocking shops.

But this . . . Bass spit blood out with his swollen tongue, the needles plastered to the sticky side of his face, and his stomach wrenched with more burning bile . . . this beating he was taking at the hands of the man who had come along to teach him how to trap, how to winter up, the man who had shown up to teach him how to keep his hair in the far mountains, was something altogether different.

This hadn't been any test of bloody knuckles between two drunken sports full of liquefied bravado simply out to prove one another's mettle. Nor had this been the sort of senseless bloodletting, robbery, and mugging that naturally occurred in the darkened back alleys and narrow lanes of any river town back east.

No, indeed—that look on the big man's face, the sheer gleam of it in his eyes, why—the very way Silas had driven his maul-sized fists into the flesh of Titus Bass showed him just how much Cooper had enjoyed handing out that beating.

It made Scratch all the sicker as he lay there in the dirt and that bed of decaying pine needles, unable to pick himself up, dust himself off, unable even to crawl back to his own damned blankets, all the sicker to have seen the deep vein of passion ignited in Silas.

Titus had just been on the receiving end of something very cruel, very brutal—and ultimately very, very personal.

How glad he was when the blurry face and the man's hot breath finally pulled back and Titus no longer had to stare up through his puffy eyelids at the taunting vision with its pitiless, crooked slash of a smile.

But just as Bass was celebrating that tiny flicker of momentary victory, Cooper grabbed a handful of Titus's hair, slowly dragging his head back so that he was again forced to look up at his tormentor. The face loomed close again, so Bass strained to stare instead across the camp as well as he could, unable to focus with the blood seeping in his eyes—yet able at least to see the two standing there, watching Cooper hunker over his fallen victim like a wide-shouldered, predatory vulture.

Even Billy Hooks, the man for whom life was one episode of fun after another, even he who found humor in most every event in his day—even he stood there, white-faced and stock-still, his jaw dropped in utter shock. Behind Bud's dirty-blond, tobacco-stained beard, his face was ashen, the baggy eyes standing out all the more in the homely, hound dog of a face. Perhaps it wasn't often enough that Cooper's fury exploded for them to grow accustomed to it. Rare enough, perhaps, that such eruptions shocked them . . . but furious and extreme enough was his rage that both had somehow learned to stay back out of the way when Silas flailed and pummeled and punished with such bloody effectiveness.

"Lookit me, dammit!" Cooper spat into Bass's face.

Painfully, slowly, Titus brought his eyes around, then twisted his head slightly beneath the clawlike grip on his hair—just enough so he could do as Cooper ordered him: look into the son of a bitch's face. Bass felt more blood at the back of his throat, tried to spit it out past his swollen bottom lip with his tongue, sensed it dribble down his chin into his whiskers instead.

"That's better," Silas said then, the edge to his voice surprisingly gone. "When I say y' lookit me—y' best lookit me. Lemme tell y', this here beatin's been a long time comin', Scratch. Way I see things, y' likely was needin' that for a long, long time. Hope this whuppin' takes, I do. Hope y' got outta this beatin' what I wan'cha to l'arn."

Still gripping Bass's hair, Cooper turned slightly to look at the others. "Y' figure he's l'arn't what he needs, boys?"

Hooks answered first. "Figure so, Silas."

"How 'bout you, Bud?"

After a moment Tuttle responded, "Y-yeah. He's the sort what l'arns fast, Silas."

Cooper looked back down at Scratch, smiling. "By damn if y' ain't right about that, Bud. Titus Bass do l'arn fast. Be it beaver . . . or be it beatin's. He l'arns fast. But what say I see for my own self if'n he's got him his lessons done for the day."

"Y-you ain't gonna hit him no more, are you, Silas?" Hooks pleaded suddenly as Cooper shifted over Bass.

"No, Billy. Not if'n he's got the answers to his lessons this day." Cooper leaned close again.

Titus tried to turn away, but Silas brutally yanked his head back, just like a man would grab a dog by the scruff of the neck and shake him—Cooper shook Bass's head so much there, once, twice, that Titus saw those stars again, felt the teeth rattle in his busted jaw.

"Don't turn 'way from me, son! I'm tellin' y' now," Cooper warned, then waited while Bass finally fought to focus, to bring his eyes back to bear on his tormentor.

"That's better. Now, then—s'pose y' tell me just who them pelts belong to what're over yonder in my packs. Whose pelts is they?"

Scratch blinked slowly, how it hurt the bruised eyelids swelling with blood, seeping with tears and coagulate. He swallowed a little more of the hot, thick crimson coating his tongue. "Y-yours," Titus whispered, able to speak no louder.

God, how it hurt to say those words, to speak anything less than the truth . . . but it hurt a damned sight less than did the beating he knew would come if he didn't say just that right then and there.

"That's right, Scratch," Cooper declared, victory clearly in his voice. Then he flung his words over his shoulder, louder still. "Y' hear that, boys? Bass knows his lessons for the day. Say it again, Scratch. All them pelts in my packs—ever' last one of the sumbitches—who they belong to?"

"You."

"Say it for me again, Scratch. A little louder so the other boys sure to hear. Tell me the name of the man what owns them pelts."

"Silas . . . Silas Cooper." Heartsick, he wanted to throw up, spewing it then and there.

"And y' know why, Scratch?"

"Y-you beat me and took 'em—"

Bass didn't get any more out as the huge fist was driven into the side of his jaw again. How he struggled to hold the warm, wet blackness at bay. He felt the crown of his head hurt where Cooper shook his scalp, his hand tangled in Titus's long hair.

"They're mine because y' owe me, Scratch. So say it!"

"I . . . I owe you."

"Y' owe me them pelts."

"Yes. Owe you."

"Very good, son. I damn well coulda kill't y' that first day an' took ever'thing y' owned, Titus Bass. You know that?"

"Kill't me. Yeah."

"But instead—my good nature tol't me to take y' on, like I took on these here others. Was my own good heart tol't me to show y' the ways of the mountains. If'n I hadn't, likely some red nigger been wearin' your hair on his belt by now, Titus Bass. If'n I hadn't come along, likely your bones be bleaching white under the sun long time ago—like all stupid niggers what come to the mountains and get theyselves kill't by grizz, or winter snows. Y' owe me, Bass."

"I . . . I owe you, Silas." Maybe he did, his hobbled head thought. Maybe it made good sense. Perhaps it would make even more perfect sense once he quit hurting. Once he stopped wanting to lay his head down and die right there in the bloody pine needles.

"Yes," Silas hissed with that smile. "Y' owe me for savin' your worthless hide. For not killin' y' my own self . . . for turnin' y' into the master trapper you become, Scratch. So them pelts y' been pullin' from your traps, why—one in ever' three is mine."

"One . . ."

"That's right. In ever' three," Cooper continued. "An' y' be damned glad it ain't more. Like I might well take me half. Right, Tuttle?"

"Yeah, Silas. Half."

"But the older I get, Bud—the kinder grows my nature. Scratch here only owes me one in three," Cooper explained. "You understan't all this, Titus Bass?"

With a growing fog clouding his brain, Scratch replied, "I . . . owe . . . you."

"Y' owe me your goddamned life, Scratch. Ever' day now y' live—when a red nigger or a grizz likely kill't y'—y' owe me your life ever' day from now on."

"Yeah. I owe."

Eventually Cooper took his fingers out of Bass's hair, watching Titus slowly keel to the side in exhaustion, his eyes blinking up in the bright sun to try gazing at Silas, as some feral animal, trapped, treed, and cornered would watch the predator closing in.

"Y' l'arnt good, Scratch. So I s'pect y' to be at your traps in the morning. You're good, son. Likely y' awready got beaver out there on your line. An' if y' got beaver, means I got beaver." And then Cooper sighed. "Best y' bring 'em all in, for us both. I got my share, don't y' see? Y' owe me my share for helping you *survive* out here in all these mountains, Titus Bass!"

"Owe you. Yes."

Then Silas stood, his great bulk throwing a shadow over Scratch's face at last. He turned to Tuttle. "From the looks of things, Bud—seems to be that Titus here brought in a passel of furs this morning, early on. Best y' be to getting 'em stretched and grained."

"I'll do that, straightaway, Silas."

"Good man, Tuttle." Then Cooper looked down at the fallen form at his feet. "Bud's a damned good man to help y' out, Scratch. He ain't never been all that good a trapper—but I keep him alive, and he keeps care of things round camp, don't he?"

Titus didn't answer.

"Billy, how 'bout y' puttin' coffee on to boil, then havin' yourself a start in on them pelts we brung in for ourselves?"

When the other two had turned away and moved off to busy themselves with their tasks, Cooper knelt over the bloodied man again. He laid a hand on Scratch's arm.

"I don't wanna kill y', Titus Bass. But if y' ain't l'arn't today, then your bound to l'arn soon enough—out here in this land each man is a law to hisself. An' what that means to me is that y' do and take for only yourself . . . and the others get what tit's left over when you're done. If there's 'nother man big enough, good enough to kill y' for what y' have—then so be it. But for now, I'm big bull in this lick. Y' remember that, an' I'll teach y' to keep your hair. Y' don't l'arn—an' y'll be dead as a three-week-ol' plew."

As weak as that newborn buffalo calf, Bass whispered, "T-teach me, Silas."

" 'At's a good lad now, Titus Bass," Cooper said, patting the arm again and rising once more. "I'll wager y'll go far in these here high and terrible places. Y' just remember who it is teaching y' to stay alive . . . and y'll go far in these here mountains."

ELEVEN

Spring was done for by the time they had trapped themselves out of the last of the high country and slowly worked their way down through the foothills. From time to time they set traps along any promising stretch of creek or stream cutting its course through the high benchland that stretched north away to the far mountains where the three first ran across Titus last autumn. This broken, rugged, parched, and high benchland appeared to extend all the way west to the distant, hazy horizon where the roll of the earth still hid the lure of Willow Valley.

There, in the yonder land of Sweet Lake, lay rendezvous.

It was the hive that, in these lengthening days of slow warming of the land, would draw the drones from all points on the compass— just as surely as the queen bee compelled her loyal subjects back with the fruits of their own far-flung labors.

West of north they moved now, beneath the sun sliding off midsky, following the yellowed orb in its western march these days until they reached the branches of a river Cooper said a few others called the Verde. Said it was greaser talk for "green." Word was that there they might just find more lowland beaver to catch. But no matter if they didn't end up seeing a single flat-tail . . . once in that country on the west side of the great continental spine, rendezvous wasn't but a few more days' ride on to the west.

This high-prairie country proved to be so different from the foothills, more different still than the mountains the four of them had just abandoned. Every day now they trampled unshod hooves through a warming land where lay carpets of the blue dicks in small flowering trumpets, or past the six open-faced purple blooms of the grass widow.

For the longest time Titus Bass cared little for, nor did he notice anything of, the beauty in that high, rolling wilderness. He was a long time healing. Scratch had hurt for days after that beating. Yet it was a hurt he swallowed down and let no man know.

If there was one small piece of Thaddeus Bass his son had carried away with him from Boone County, it was that a man did not complain of what ills he had brought on himself. No matter that a man might bemoan the unfathomable fates of weather, crop disease, or even the fickle nature of his breeding stock—what suffering a man brought to his own door must always be endured in silence.

For the rest of that horrible morning Titus lay where he had fallen, finding it hard to breathe deep for the sharp pain it caused him in his side and back. Most any change of position brought its instant reminder of the beating Cooper had just given him. It was not until late afternoon when Bass finally decided he was parched enough that he could no longer put off finding himself a drink of water.

Slowly and shakily rising onto his knees and one hand, Titus held the other arm splinted tight against the ribs that made it so hard to breathe, then crabbed inches at a time toward his side of camp, where water beckoned in a kettle—where his blankets lay.

From the corner of his eye he watched the three study him as he dragged himself along less than a foot at a time.

"Lemme help him, Silas," Hook begged.

"You stay put, Billy," Cooper warned. "Cain't y' see he's doin' fine on his own. Both y' g'won back 'bout your business an' don't worry 'bout that'un. He'll make it where he's headed."

No matter how badly his head hurt, the crushing pain in his face and jaw, too—Bass remembered those exact words for days to come. Yes, he thought to give himself the strength needed first to sit, later to stand and then walk, and finally what steel he needed in his backbone to stuff a foot in a stirrup and ride the morning Cooper's bunch was moving camp. He kept those words in his heart and on his lips in those first days.

He'll make it where he's headed.

By damn, I will, Scratch vowed.

There in his blankets, having lapped some water from the kettle into his cupped palm and brushed the sweet wetness against his swollen, bloodied lips, Titus collapsed for the rest of the afternoon. He awoke just after sundown, rubbing a crusty eye where blood had dried it shut, then peered across camp at the other three. While Silas cleaned and oiled weapons there by the fire, Hooks and

Tuttle finished the last of their day's catch—stretching and graining the big blanket beaver.

His eyes found the sun's last light, his groggy mind determining that evening was now at hand. If he was going to have enough strength to make it to his sets come morning, he needed two things most of all: sleep and a little food in his belly.

The first was not a concern; he knew he would easily fall into a cozy stupor once more. But the food—why, just the thought of it twisted his empty belly, caused it to rumble in protest. He had no appetite and doubted he ever would again, but realized that if he was to demand something of his body, then it would soon demand something of him.

When next he awoke, the night was dark and silent—all but for the snores of the others curled up in their blankets upon pine-bough beds and buffalo robes. Stirring painfully, Scratch pushed himself up on an elbow, clutching that set of busted ribs with the other arm, then inched himself over to the water in the kettle once more. He repeatedly dunked his hand into the kettle, licking all he could from his palm and fingers until thirst was no longer his greatest need. Then he thought of Hames Kingsbury's broken ribs—remembering how Beulah had wrapped them securely and seen the flatboat pilot through his healing.

There beside the kettle lay the fixings left over from his supper more than a day before. Bass pulled a chunk of meat from the pot, blew the dust off it, and brought it to his mouth. Slowly parting his swollen, crusted lips, opening his jaw to slivers of icy pain below each ear, he tore at small threads of the cooked meat, swallowing a little at a time, not sure just how his stomach would accept it.

Shred by shred of that old, crusted meat he forced down, licking water from the palm he dipped into the kettle, sitting there in the midst of those mountains, listening to the nightsounds of men sleeping, the rustle of the breeze whispering through the quakies and the soughing of the pine. When the wind died, he could hear the faint murmur of the nearby creek trickling along its bed.

Above him stood the dark, jagged outline of the high peaks thrust up against the paler, starlit sky—huge, ragged hunks of that sky obliterated by the mountaintops punching holes in the nighttime canopy.

Nowhere else you gonna see anything like that, Titus Bass, he told himself as he chewed slowly against the pain in his jaw and neck. Then remembered a song long ago sung to the tune of "Yankee Doodle," not come to his recollection in many, many a year:

> *We are a hardy, freeborn race,*
> *Each man to fear a stranger;*
> *Whate'er the game, we join the chase,*
> *Despising toil and danger.*

And if a hearty foe annoys,
No matter what his force is,
We'll show him that Kentucky boys
Are alligator horses!

Him, a Kentucky boy. Just like Ebenezer Zane and Hames Kingsbury. Such as them was alligator horses. No, not Titus Bass—for he hurt too damn much.

His thoughts pulled his eyes to the rifle standing against a nearby tree. Within easy enough reach. And yonder lay the pistol with his shooting bag and possibles pouch. Then he looked at the sleeping forms. There in the middle lay the biggest, clearly the one who had pummeled and kicked him like no better than a bad dog. And then he looked back at the rifle, studied the pistol again. Two bullets. If he did it then and there, which one of those three should get the second lead ball?

When he pulled the trigger on Cooper, the rifle's blast would bring the other two out of their blankets like the rising of the dead come Judgment Day. So which would it be? One would live—to be freed along with Bass from Cooper's grip. And then the choice became clear.

His mouth went dry just thinking about it. Murder is what they called it back there, down out of these here mountains and back east. Murder was to take another man's life while that man lay sleeping in his blankets.

Licking his cracked lips, Titus began to drag himself over toward the tree, wincing with the sharp pain in his ribs. It was good, he thought, biting his bottom lip to keep from groaning as he inched toward his weapons. Such pain reminded him why he would take the life of a sleeping man.

His fingers locked around the rifle at its wrist, there behind the hammer, then climbed to that part of the forestock repaired with rawhide after the battle with the Arapaho raiding party. Bringing it down to his lap, Titus thumbed back the hammer—finding the pan filled. No man would want to chance a misfire when he set out to murder someone the likes of Silas Cooper.

Snagging hold of the pistol, Scratch moved his other hand as far up the rifle barrel as he could. Arm outstretched, he planted the rifle at his side, then slowly began to rise on shaky legs, pulling himself up an inch at a time on the makeshift crutch that in moments would take another man's life. A wave of nausea swept over him as he stood, rocking against the long barrel—he was so light-headed that his temples throbbed. Yet Scratch swallowed down that faint misgiving and stuffed the pistol in his belt.

The second would be Billy Hooks.

Of the two, only Tuttle might have enough misgivings about shooting Bass. Hooks would have to die.

He pursed his lips together forcefully, hoping to muffle his grunts of pain as he began to hobble toward the fire pit. Scattered on the far side lay the three of them. In a few moments there would be only one left . . . and he prayed Tuttle would realize that now he was free—

"Don't do it, Scratch."

That sharp whisper made him freeze, rocking there atop his rifle like a peg-legged crutch. Titus wasn't sure in those seconds when he didn't breathe, his eyes peering over the three forms, just which one had called out to him.

Then Tuttle slowly sat up. "I figger I know what you're about to do, Scratch. But—killin' him ain't right."

"You saw. He . . . he almost kill't me."

For a long time Tuttle just stared at Bass in that crimson-tinged darkness, his face grave in the low flames and shimmering coals of their fire, his eyes deadly serious. Then he finally spoke. "Them was his furs—his fair share, Scratch. The man could've kill't you long time back. 'Stead, he took you on. You learned to trap, to live up here, and you kept your hair. You owe him."

"The way you see it: I owe him."

"That's right," Tuttle emphasized.

"Bet you owe him too."

"I do—an' that's the devil's gospel. For balls' sake, Cooper's saved my hash more'n I care to count. You owe him, same as me."

"You got a gun on me, eh?"

After a long silence Tuttle quietly said, "I have."

"I could kill him afore you took me, Bud."

"But you won't, Titus. I know you can't. I know you see what he's saying. You owe him your goddamned life. You won't kill him 'cause you can't take the life what give you back your own."

Titus sighed long and deep, and, oh, how it hurt to fill his lungs like that. He tore his eyes off Tuttle and stared at the other sleeping form beneath its blankets.

"He right 'bout me goin' under, Tuttle?"

"He saw to it you made yourself a trapper, Titus. Don't figger you was a nigger what was gonna keep hisself alive out here when we found you."

It was like lancing a festering, fevered boil . . . sensing that poison ooze out of him. Suddenly he felt as weak as a wobbly-legged, newborn calf.

Starting to turn away, pivoting on his rifle, Bass stopped and whispered, "You can put your gun down, Tuttle. The killin' fever's gone."

"I'll be here to mornin' for you, Titus," Bud replied. "Goin' with you out to your sets like Cooper told me."

He choked hard on the pain. "Don' know if I can."

"I'll be with you ever' step of the way."

Titus sighed wearily, completing his turn, and began to hobble off to his blankets, sleepier than he could remember being in a long, long time.

"Get your rest, Titus Bass."

That voice froze Scratch where he stood.

"Y'll need your strength come sunup," it said.

Slowly he turned his head, peering over his shoulder—finding Silas Cooper pulling the sawed-off, shortened smoothbore trade gun from beneath his blankets now, laying it in plain view atop his belly. It was one of the trophies he had claimed off the dead Arapaho warriors.

"You just learn't me something more, didn't you, Silas?"

"Mayhaps I did, Scratch. G'won now—get in your blankets."

He did just that, painfully settling back atop that single buffalo robe Fawn had given him, a robe he had laid over some pine boughs in making his bed at this campsite. After pulling the blankets up to his chin, he stared across the fire at the chertlike eyes gleaming back at him in the glow of the red coals. Then Cooper closed them.

And all that glimmered was the dull-brown sheen of the barrel on that stubby trade gun filled with lead shot that likely would have cut him in half had things come down to it.

That's twice now he could've damn well killed me, Titus thought as he rolled painfully to attempt finding a position comfortable enough to sleep.

He seen me coming for him, thinking him asleep—could've had me dead to rights.

. . . Mayhaps I do owe him.

Yet that hurt most of all. Owing your life not once, but twice . . . twice to the bastard you've wanted to kill more than any other man alive.

From the Sierra Madre range rising west of the Medicine Bows, they continued north over the western rim of the Great Divide Basin, north still until they dropped into the southern tableland of the Red Desert Basin, where they struck out due west with the setting sun as their guiding lodestone.

Picking their way day by day between the jutting escarpments and low, solitary peaks of that parched, striated desert, the four always kept in view those mountains far to the north where the Wind River was given its birth. After striking the Verde River,* Cooper led them angling northwest along its meandering course until they reached the mouth of the Sandy. It was there they crossed to the west bank and finally left the Verde behind, making for the low range of mountains that lay almost due west.

"We get beyond them hills," Silas explained one evening in camp, "I was told we'd likely see Sweet Lake from a ways off."

"Yup—that's what we was told," Hooks agreed, dragging the back of his dust-crusted hand across his parched mouth.

Titus figured Billy had him the whiskey hunger bad. That, or he needed a woman soon in the worst way. Then Bass looked over at Tuttle, and Cooper too. And finally peered down at himself. If they all didn't look the sight!

---

* Present-day Green River

Hats, faces, hands, and damned near every exposed inch of clothing, even their horses and pack animals, from nostrils to tail root—all of it layered with a thin coating of superfine dust. Beneath the high summer sun the pale talc seemed to cling tenaciously to the horses and the men because of the sweat that poured out of them from sunup to well past sundown every one of those lengthening days.

At what those early trappers called Sweet Lake,* to distinguish it from the bitter-tasting and immense inland lake they called the Salt Sea, lying not all that far to the southwest, Silas Cooper had been told by Ashley's trappers that a man would have to decide upon one or the other of two courses from there on in to the rendezvous site. The southern route would lead them around the lakeshore until they were able to strike out due west toward the last range of mountains they would have to cross before dropping into the Willow Valley.

Cooper chose to take them on the longer route, but one that was bound to be much easier on man and horse alike. At the north end of Sweet Lake they picked up the Bear River, named years before by a brigade of British Hudson's Bay men, which they followed even farther north before it angled west, then quickly swept back again to the south, looping itself through some austere country dominated by lava beds, eventually flowing on around the far end of that tall range of mountains they might otherwise have had to cross.

"Damn easier going on these here animals," Titus declared as they made camp that first evening after they had pointed their noses south along the course of the Bear River. Nearby was a soda spring from which bubbled bitter water.

"Don't mind taking our time at it my own self," Tuttle said as they unloaded the weighty packs, dropped them to the ground.

Next came the task of picketing the animals out to graze in the tall blue grama, where most of the horses chose to plop down and give themselves a good roll and dusting before beginning to fill their bellies on the plentiful salt-rich grasses. From night to night Tuttle and Bass rotated these tasks with Cooper and Hooks, who this evening were gathering wood, starting the cookfire, and bringing in water for their coffee.

"Lookee there, Bud," Titus said, the hair standing on his arms as he slapped Tuttle on the back to get his attention. He pointed, his alarm growing. "You s'pose them to be Injuns?"

Tuttle squinted into the distance stretching far away to the north of them. "Don't figger so. Lookee there—you can see them niggers is riding with saddles. Legs bent up the way they is. Only red-bellies I ever knowed of rode barebacked: legs and feet hanging low on their ponies."

"Yeah, maybeso you're right," Titus agreed, peering into the shimmering distance as the sun secreted itself beyond the western hills. "Looks to be they got pack animals with 'em."

Tuttle asked, "How many you make it?"

---

*Present-day Bear Lake

Bass counted them off silently, his lips moving as he did. "Least ten. Ten of 'em for sure."

"We best us go tell Cooper and Billy we got folks coming in."

Silas was a cautious one on occasions such as this, Scratch thought. But, then—it made sense that Cooper would be. After all, why shouldn't a man who, without guilt or remorse, would take from another white man be suspicious that other white men might just ride on in and steal from him?

"Get your guns out and ready," Cooper ordered the other three. "Leave 'em handy. Leave 'em for them niggers to see in plain sight if'n there's to be trouble."

Tuttle tried to tell him, "I'd care to set they only some of Ashley's men goin' to ronnyvoo—same as us, Silas."

"Don't matter none to their kind to leave the bones of us'ns to be picked clean by the buzzards right here . . . an' take all our plews on in to ronnyvoo for themselves. Y' think about that, Bud Tuttle—and then y' tell me y' don't figger we ought'n be ready to keep what's ours."

So they stood spread out, the four did, as the ten approached at a walk. Then suddenly Cooper tore the wolf-hide cap off his head and waved it, whooping at the top of his lungs. It surprised Bass so much, he was scared for a moment—especially the next instant when Billy and Bud joined in, wheeling about to seize up their weapons as they cheered and hurrawed to the skies.

With the first whoop Titus lunged for his rifle, diving to crouch behind a pack of pelts where he would have some protection and a good rest for the weapon when the shooting started. He had no sooner taken cover than the ten riders began to screech and holler, pounding flat hands against their open mouths with a "woo-woo-woo," and raised their rifles in the air.

The first of those long weapons boomed with a great puff of gray smoke. Cooper squawked like a raven in reply, pointing his own rifle into the sky, firing it just before a second rider shot his off.

"What the blue hell?" Bass hollered into the noisy tumult.

Billy turned slightly, raising his rifle over his head, aiming for the puffy clouds. "It's a good sign, Scratch! Good medicine! They's emptying their guns!"

"That there be a likely bunch of good coons, boys!" Silas hollered. "I see me a couple faces I could lay to being at last summer's doin's."

In the end all but Bass had fired their rifles by the time the ten came close enough to plainly see the dust caked into the creases on the men's faces. A double handful of bearded, dirty, sweat-soaked, hard-bitten men who brought their animals to a halt there among the four and peered down from the saddle with widening grins.

"Been follerin' your sign for last three days, we have," the first man spoke.

He had twinkling eyes and a good smile, Bass decided. Then Titus looked over to fix his study on the second rider: not all that old, really—but it seemed that he, like the first rider, also spoke for the others. Still, he had given the older man at his side the first say.

"Welcome, boys! Get down an' camp if you're of a mind to," Cooper offered them all with a grand, sweeping gesture.

"Be much obliged," that young second rider replied.

Immediately a third said, "Figger you fellas be hurryin' on to ronnyvoos like us." He had a round face, that sort of easygoing countenance that naturally put most men at ease. "Bound for the Willow Valley?"

"Ain't no two ways of it!" Hooks cheered just before he turned back toward the fire and pushed the coffeepot closer to the flames. "Likker an' women it's gonna be for this here child!"

The second rider slowly eased out of the saddle, his damp flesh squeaking across the wet leather as he slid free. "We hear the general's bringing him likker out this year."

"Bound to be some shinin' times," the first rider agreed as he dropped to the ground.

Bass watched the older one take off his hat and slap it against his legs, stirring up a cloud of fine dust. He ain't much older'n me, Titus thought. His hair hung long and brown, some of it fair, well-bleached by the sun. For sure the wrinkles were worn there around the eyes, and his skin had long ago turned a shade of oak-tanned saddle leather like all the rest. But there were no creases at the sides of his mouth—he couldn't be a day over thirty, Titus figured.

Silas stepped up to the man, asking, "So your bunch making tracks to ronnyvoo now?"

The man nodded, then motioned off to the north. "The general sent out riders to pass the word that he was getting close."

"Close?" Hooks repeated, his voice rising a full octave in excitement.

That first rider nodded. "We figure him to be no more'n a few days out of Willow Valley." Then he held out his hand to the tall, slab-shouldered Cooper. "I'm the general's leader for this band. Name's Fitzpatrick. Tom Fitzpatrick."

That's when the second rider stepped up to Tuttle, holding out his hand. "An' my name be Jim Bridger. Outta Missouri."

Now, that youngster couldn't be a day over twenty, Titus thought as Bridger and Tuttle shook.

At that the last four riders sank to the ground, and the rest of the ten strode up among the rest, shaking hands all round with Cooper's bunch.

"Jumpin' Jehoshaphat!" Titus exclaimed, bent slightly at the waist to peer closely at the other man, his chin cocked in wonder, his hand suddenly frozen, stopped in midair between them. "You're . . . you ain't a negra, are you?"

"My pa was a Virginia landowner," the man said without a hint of shame, glancing at his empty hand before dropping it to his side. "Fortune had it that my mother happed to be one of his slaves. I was borned out to the slave quarters . . . but my pa brung us both into the house after his first wife died."

"Didn't mean you no offense by nothing I said," Scratch apologized, shame-faced and offering his hand out firmly before him. "Here. My name's Titus Bass."

The tall mulatto with Caucasian features and coffee-colored skin grinned warmly. "No offense taken. Name's Beckwith. After my pa. You can call me Jim . . . Jim Beckwith, of Richmond County, Virginia. But I was brung up in the woods near St. Charles. You know where that is on the Missouri River?"

"St. Charles? Same village lays north of St. Louie?"

The tall mulatto nodded, sweeping both his hands down his dust-coated but colorful buckskins in that manner of a genteel horseman settling his clothing upon dismounting. Bass had him figured for a man who liked to cut a dashing figure here among the greasy, rough-shorn, ramshackle hellions he rode in with.

"My pa figgered to move west, so he brung Ma an' me there back to O-nine."

"Hell, I was still a Kentucky boy back then my own self."

Beckwith stood at least six feet tall, perhaps a little more. He grinned, his kind eyes smiling. "Out there in that Lou'siana wilderness, I soon had me twelve brothers an' sisters."

Scratching at his beard, Bass replied, "Don't sound like you're no freedman neither."

"No, I ain't. Never needed freeing from my pa."

"Knowed me a Negra once't," Titus said, remembering. "He was a freedman. But I never knowed what become of him."

Beckwith explained, "No need bein' a freedman: my pa and ma was rightfully married. Means I ain't never been a slave."

"Your pap was well-off, I take it."

Shaking his head, Beckwith replied, "Nawww—we wasn't wealthy, by no means . . . but my pa had him a good heart, an' he made sure there was no question that his children was no slaves. Went himself off to a judge at court to declare my emancipation."

Confused, Titus tried to repeat the word, "E- . . . e-man-see—"

"Means his pa told the world Jim here was a free man," explained the thickset third rider as he came up and handed Beckwith the reins to a horse. "C'mon, Beckwith. We got us these critters to keer for—then we kin palaver all we want with these boys."

The two weren't a matching pair, by any means, it was plain to see. Whereas the one named Daniel Potts was short and beefy, trail dirty, besides being mud-homely to boot, the mulatto cut quite a figure compared to the rest, what with his colorful buckskins. He was tall too—the tallest there with the exception of Cooper himself—standing an inch or two over Bass and most of the others there on the prairie floor among Fitzpatrick's brigade. And Beckwith affected a bit of the dandy: wearing his long black hair in a profusion of tight, well-kept braids that hung past his shoulders. As the mulatto started to turn aside with Potts, Titus decided he might just try one of those braids in his own long hair—as handsome as they were on Beckwith.

With a booming voice Fitzpatrick offered, "Say, Cooper—we have us two elk quarters along we'd offer to lay up by the fire for us all if'n that makes you fellas no mind."

"Never make it a habit to turn down good meat," Silas said. "Bring it on— we'll likely chaw everything down to the bone this night!"

Most of the riders dropped their saddles, blankets, and packs onto the prairie near the quartet's fire, then turned back to see to their horses. After rubbing down their saddle mounts with thick tufts of prairie grass, Potts strode up with his arm around Beckwith's shoulder. Together they peered at Bass.

The stubby Potts asked, "Tell me something, mister—we look anywhar' as dirty an' bad off as the four of you scurvy niggers?"

Titus grinned, glancing down at his dusty, greasy, sweat-stained clothing. "I s'pose we do at that, Potts. Mayhaps even worse off."

"Call me by my Christian name, will you? It be Daniel."

"Sure—an' my given name's Titus."

Tuttle broke in, slapping Bass on the back and saying, "But he'd sooner answer to his real handle."

"What's that?" Beckwith asked.

"Scratch," Titus answered as Bud was getting his mouth open. "They give me the name Scratch some time back."

The mulatto asked, "Was it skeeters?"

Titus shook his head. "Fleas."

"Big'un's too," Tuttle said before he turned back to the fire, chuckling.

"Well, now—Scratch," Potts said, looking wistfully over at the translucent blue of the Bear River nearby, its border of tall emerald willow in full-leafed glory. He slapped Beckwith on the back and declared, "Me an' Jim here was cogitating that we'uns go find us a pool in that river yonder. Have us two a sit and a soak afore supper."

The idea struck Scratch like a fine one indeed. Impulsively he asked, "You mind company?"

Potts grinned readily. "Why—no. Allays good for a man to have a new face and new ears once't while. We both got stories Fitz, Frapp, and the other'n's is tired of hearin' . . . an' I'll wager you got a few tales to tell your own self."

"Yeah!" Beckwith agreed. "Damn right we'll all go have our own selves a sit in that cold river—either till we cain't stand the cold no more, or we turn the water to mud!"

"Likely that Negra boy gonna turn the water to mud, Scratch!" Billy Hooks was suddenly nearby, laughing and wagging his head with cruel sarcasm. "But that brown-assed Negra still gonna be a Negra when he comes out'n that river— no matter how hard the black son of a bitch scrubs hisself!"

Beckwith was turning on his heel to start for Hooks when the strong and stocky Potts locked his friend's arm and held the mulatto in place—at just the moment Bass stepped between the mulatto and Billy, staring Hooks in the eye.

"This man ain't done nothing to deserve the talk you're throwing at 'im, Billy."

Hysterically laughing, Hooks said, "Just look at him, Scratch! Why, I cain't hardly believe my own eyes. It's a Negra—out in these here mountains!"

Potts growled, struggling to hold Beckwith, "He's as good a man as any."

"If Beckwith here ain't the kind to walk away from the fight we had us with Blackfoot not long back," Bridger interrupted them all as he hurried up purposefully, Cooper and Fitzpatrick both scrambling to stay with him, "then he sure as hell ain't the kind to back off from no fight with you."

"Fight?" Cooper repeated as he stepped between the two, grinning from ear to ear, raking his long beard with his fingers, and taking a measure of those standing with the mulatto. "There ain't gonna be no fight here . . . will there, now, Billy?"

"No fight, Silas," Hooks agreed quickly, then giggled some more like a man willing to rub salt into another's wounds.

"Damn ride der' h'ain't be no fide here," declared a swarthy, dark-eyed, much older man as he eased up on the far side of Fitzpatrick, his fists clenched and ready.

It was plain the trapper had something on the order of twenty years on Bass, maybe as much as a decade older than Cooper. More than a life outdoors had aged his face: many a year on the frontier had clearly left their mark on the man. His accent was thick, throaty, yet something that sang of its own rhythm, an accent Titus could not remember hearing since those youthful days along the Lower Mississippi: maybe Natchez, more likely all the way down to New Orleans, where the Spanish, French, and Creole tongues mingled freely with the upriver frontier dialects.

"Easy there, Henry," Fitzpatrick coaxed the German-born Henry Fraeb. "Frapp here gets his blood up pretty quick, but there ain't no need for cross words, is there, fellas?"

"We're all friends here," Cooper readily agreed. "Right, Billy?"

Hooks giggled behind his hand, his eyes gleaming with childlike innocence again. "I ain't never see'd no Negra out here—"

"Beckwith is the name, not Negra," the mulatto repeated firmly. It was plain his pride had been wounded. He looked at Hooks steadily and said, "Beckwith. Maybeso you'll remember it one day."

"Why, you gonna be something big up on a stick?" Billy mocked, then suffered himself another fit of laughter.

"G'won and help them others with their plunder," Silas ordered sternly, slapping Hooks across the upper arm, plainly made uneasy by the readiness of the others to back the mulatto.

Cooper waited while Hooks moved off wagging his head, still giggling to himself. "Pay him no mind, fellas," he advised good-naturedly. He tapped a finger to the side of his head, explaining, "Billy's just . . . just a bit slow a'times. Why, he finds him some simple joy in most ever'thin'."

His eyes angry, Bridger argued, "Being soft-brained don't give a man no right—"

"You're right," Silas interrupted, nodding at the much younger man. "C'mon now, fellas. What say we forget this trouble . . . let's camp!"

"Man's right," Fitzpatrick said grudgingly, eyeing Bridger, Fraeb, and Beckwith with a look that told them all that he expected them to smooth their ruffled feathers and put the matter to rest. "Sun's down and this bunch ain't et since morning. 'Sides—we move on to shining times tomorrow."

Cooper shouldered in between Fitzpatrick and Bridger as the group moved toward the fire, asking, "You boys figger the general spoke the truth when he tol't us he'd pack likker this summer?"

Fitzpatrick said, "Ashley's a man allays done what he said he'd do. If he says there'll be likker to ronnyvoo—there'll be likker there, by God."

Bass watched the rest gradually settle near the fire with Cooper. But instead of joining them, Potts and Beckwith hung back with Titus.

"So, fellas," Scratch finally asked in that uneasy silence, "we still going to have us our soak?"

The mulatto shrugged dolefully. "S'pose I could use some water."

"Damn right you could use some water!" Potts exclaimed suddenly, joyfully, flailing an arm exuberantly at Beckwith. "You're coming to the river, or you're dang well stayin' downwind o' me from here on out!"

As cold as the water was, nonetheless Scratch plopped himself down in a little pool of it near the sandy bank, just as Potts and Beckwith readily did as twilight put a twinkle to the summer sky. They sat up to their armpits in a little backwater the Bear had long ago cut out of the side of the bank.

In the last of the real light Titus noticed the dull glimmer of something hung round the mulatto's neck on a narrow thong. "What's that you got yourself?"

Beckwith held it up, gazed down at it again a moment. "A guinea. First pay I ever got. Stamped with the year I was born." He held it up for Bass to see.

Leaning over, Titus stared in the fading light at the large round coin, a tiny hole drilled near its top right through the king's head. There below the nobleman's neck was emblazoned the date 1800. "You was born six years after me."

Potts suggested, "Tell him where you got your coin, Jim."

"We never was the best-off folks in Portage des Sioux outside of St. Charles," he explained. "So my pa set me to work with a blacksmith, learn me a trade."

"You don't say," Titus replied with happy recognition. "I worked for many a year in Hysham Troost's place."

"There in St. Lou? I heard of it, often," the mulatto replied. "Casner's was the blacksmith shop where I apprenticed for some five years."

"Then you come out here to the mountains?" Bass inquired.

"Nawww. Not when I left Casner's," Beckwith said. "First I fought Injuns with Colonel Johnson's expedition up to Fever River when I was released from Casner's indenture . . . only nineteen, I was by then. Short time later I figured to take me a ride on down to N'Awlins . . . where I got yellow fever for my trouble. Barely made it back home alive to my folks at Portage des Sioux, and there I stayed put, healing up, till I learned General Ashley was outfitting him a new brigade for the mountains."

"I first knowed of Ashley some time back—had him outfits going upriver for the last few years," Bass observed. "When was it you first come out with him?"

"Back to twenty-four," Jim answered, his eyes growing wide with excitement, "and that was the first year the general wasn't headed upriver with them keelboats to get on by the Ree villages. This time he was bound to ride overland for the mountains."

"Say, boys—my belly's beginning to holler for fodder," Potts declared, leaning over to scoop up a handful of sand from the bottom of the pool. "Telling me it's time to eat my fill of that elk we shot this morning."

For a few moments Titus watched with interest as Potts, then Beckwith, scooped up one handful after another and used it to scrub their skin.

"What're you two doing?"

Potts replied, "Givin' ourselves a good washing."

"Just sittin' there in the river isn't going to help a man much," the mulatto advised.

"When was the last time you sat your ass down in some water?" Potts asked.

With a shrug Titus said, "Been a long time. 'Cept for times I swum rivers with my critters and stood freezing in mountain streams—I ain't been near no washing water for more'n a year."

"Once a year," Potts instructed. "A man ought'n wash up proper . . . as good a cleaning as he can."

Bass said, "I never figgered I'd be one to carry me lye soap."

"We ain't the sort to carry no soap neither," Beckwith explained. "But a good hard scrubbin' with sand does a toler'ble job, Scratch."

"Awright," Titus answered them, scooping up a double handful of sand, which he smeared over his chest.

"Rub it hard, now," Potts said. "Gotta get shet of all that stink afore ronnyvoos."

"If you watch, you'll see your horses and mules does about the same thing when they have themselves a roll in the dirt," Beckwith said as he pulled one leg out of the water and began sanding it.

Next to his, Bass's leg was starkly white. In fact, Scratch was so pale, his legs reminded him of the skinny white legs on the pullets the family raised back on the place in Boone County. Only his hands from wrist down were deeply tanned, along with that wide vee extending from his neck onto his chest, as well as his darkened face. Except for those river crossings when he briefly stripped off his clothing, every other part of his pale hide had been protected from much exposure to the sun's light as far back as he could remember.

At first it was an odd sensation, rubbing the river bottom grit from chin to toe, but soon enough it became a right pleasant feeling. In fact, his skin began to tingle and glow the more he scrubbed.

"That 'bout does it for me," Beckwith announced as he rose out of the water, turned, and long-legged it onto the riverbank to stand dripping among the foxsedge.

"I'm done too," Potts agreed as he stood with a splash.

Bass watched in amusement as the two trembled and quaked, shaking what they could of the water from their flesh just like a hound. Then, as the evening breezes cooled, they quickly stepped into their clothing, despite still being a little damp. Potts pulled on leather britches and a ragged, dirty calico shirt. Beneath his linen shirt Beckwith wore a pair of leggings and a breechclout, same as Bass.

As Titus emerged from the water, shivering in the gentle movement of a cool wind, the other two plopped to the ground and began pulling on their moccasins.

"Dang if it ain't time to fill up my meatbag," Potts declared. "Been a long stretch since breakfast."

"C'mon, now—don't dally," Beckwith urged Bass. "Unless you hurry, there won't be a thing left for us to eat."

"He's right." Potts smacked with relish. "Them others can eat a horse by themselves—and all we got us is half a elk!"

Titus leaped into his clothes, suddenly discovering he was himself immensely hungry after the long day's ride, followed by that invigorating bath. As the trio neared the fire lighting the ring of deeply tanned faces, Fitzpatrick stood, wiping his greasy fingers in his hair as he called out.

"That you, Potts?"

They strode into the corona of firelight as Daniel announced, "It's me."

"You got Beckwith?"

"I'm here," the mulatto replied, coming into the light.

All three stopped near the fire ring. Potts was the first to yank his knife from his belt and bend down over one of the two roasting elk quarters. He sliced himself a long, narrow slab of the pink meat still dripping juice and blood into the flames below—each drop landing with a merry hiss.

"Just wanted to tell you what I reminded the rest here," Fitzpatrick declared. "When you roll out in the morning, see to it you trim off that beard of your'n."

Potts eyed the brigade leader. "All of it?"

Fitzpatrick nodded. "You too, Beckwith."

Scratching at the side of his face, the mulatto said, "A shame, Fitz. I been growing real particular to it since winter."

Sporting his own brown beard, Fitzpatrick replied, "If you don't wanna stay working for Ashley long, then a man can keep his beard, boys. Otherwise—you know the general's rule. He don't 'llow no beards on his men."

Titus asked, "Why's Ashley so all-fired against beards?"

"He's a trader, mind you," Fitzpatrick explained, stepping close. "And traders allays deal with them Injuns, don't they?"

"Yep," Billy Hooks answered, leaping into the conversation.

With a cursory glance at the mat of facial hair on Hooks, Fitzpatrick went on. "General's come to know Injuns don't like beards. They don't much favor any kind of hair on a man's face."

"That's why they pluck ever' damn hair out," Bridger added with a mock shudder. "Even the eyebrows too."

Fitzpatrick continued. "Few years back Ashley learned him that some Injun bands won't have nothing to do with a man wearing a beard. They say it hides a feller's face. And the Injuns is big on reading a man's face to see that he's talking straight."

"Man kin grow him a beard," Potts declared, "but he dare'st not let the general ever see it."

"All that fuss over a man's beard?" Tuttle inquired.

"You free trappers don't have to worry none over that," Fitzpatrick explained.

Potts stepped back with a second slice of elk hanging from his knife "But you free trappers best 'member the general takes care of his own fellas first."

"An' if Ashley's got anythin' left after he outfits his own for the next year," a new man spoke up with an accent that reminded Bass of the Spanish and French tongues heard at the mouth of the Mississippi, "then you free trappers might get to pick over the leavin's."

Bass studied that speaker for a moment as the older man bit down on one end of a long strip of meat, pulled the strip out from his lips with one hand, then used the knife he clutched in his other hand to slice off a good mouthful. He had long black hair prematurely sprinkled with gray where it hung loosely on either side of his well-wrinkled face, and his beard was starting to show a dusting of iron too, although the man was clearly younger than Titus.

Potts explained, "Louis here don't cotton much to you free trappers joining in on our ronnyvoos."

Around a mouthful of the meat, Louis Vasquez spoke up for himself, his dark Spanish eyes glaring at Daniel Potts. "This here's the general's doin's— ronnyvoo is. Them don't work for the general has no business barterin' plews for Ashley's trade goods."

" 'Sides powder and lead, coffee and sugar," Fitzpatrick said, "the rest of it's all foofaraw anyway, Vaskiss."

"Their kind wanna work for Ashley, eh?" Vasquez growled. "Let 'em sign on wit' Ashley."

Silas snorted. "An' fight Blackfeet up there in the devil's own country like you boys done? No thankee. I'll trap where I wanna trap an' stay aways from making trouble for myself."

Then Hooks chimed in, "That means us keeping our noses far from Blackfoot country!"

"Weren't all that far north of here," Bridger declared. "Was a good li'l scrap of it. Show 'em what I mean, fellas."

Five of the others brandished scalps they had hanging from their belts.

"That's five Blackfoot what ain't ever gonna raise my hair!" Bridger exclaimed.

" 'Nother'n was shot up bad—but the rest rode off with his carcass," Fitzpatrick said. "Couldn't raise his scalp."

"Makes six Blackfeet what won't devil none of us no more," Fraeb emphasized.

"Much trouble as them niggers are, the trapping's some up in them parts," Fitzpatrick said.

Titus asked, "Some?"

Potts turned to look at Bass. "Means it's just 'bout the best there is, child."

"Blanket beaver," Bridger added with an approving cluck. "And the rivers is so thick with 'em, all a man has to do is walk down to the water and club 'em over the head."

"Sounds like some crock of bald-faced to me!" Cooper spouted, a disbelieving grin creasing his dark beard.

The dour Fraeb scratched at his nose with the black crescent of a dirty fingernail. "Haps you free trappers ought just go on up there to that Blackfoot country and see for yourselves."

"No thankee," Cooper replied, eyes dancing with mirth as he winked at Hooks. "I favor my skelp to stay locked right where it is!"

Billy tore the fur cap from his head and grabbed a handful of his own long, greasy hair. "Ain't the red nigger born what can take this from me, Silas!"

Then Tuttle observed, "For balls' sake—only way you Ashley boys can poke your noses up there in that Blackfoot country at all is to travel in a hull bunch like you done."

"Yessirreebob!" Hooks added, spreading his arms wide. "And there ain't but four of us!"

Potts leaned close to Bass and asked under his breath, "You still so sartin sure you don't wanna throw in with us come ronnyvoos?"

For a few moments Titus looked over Fitzpatrick's bunch, then eyed what the ten had themselves in the way of fur. As much as there was, man for man, the Ashley trappers didn't have a thing on Cooper's bunch—despite having trapped that spring in the beaver-rich country haunted by the bloodthirsty Blackfoot.

Then Bass glanced at Tuttle, Hooks, and even the bruising hulk of Silas Cooper himself before he turned aside to Potts and said, "Thankee anyway, Daniel. You offer a handsome prospect, mind you. But the way I see it—I'd rather work for my friends than be working for some trader what brings his goods out to the mountains come once a year."

"Fitzpatrick's a good man to foller," Potts explained, "an' Bridger's gonna make him a fine booshway one day his own self."

"Booshway?"

"Man what leads a brigade hisself."

"Yeah," Scratch replied. "Plain as sun to see Bridger's older'n his years."

The jovial Potts tugged on Bass's elbow, whispering low. "Come join us, Scratch. You're a good man to have around for a smile or two."

As much as he might take pleasure in the honor of those words, Titus weighed matters a mite different from most, perhaps. Here he was offered the chance to cut the losses in beaver he'd already suffered and get out from under the ominous shadow of Silas Cooper . . . or he could stay on with the men who had come along to give him the companionship of an open hand—no matter that the same hand had closed itself into a brutal fist of a time. No, Titus saw himself as a loyal, steadfast man, the sort of man another could easily put his faith and trust in without question.

He wasn't the sort to let down those who had very likely saved his hide.

Bass slapped a hand on Daniel's shoulder, saying, "Thanks anyway, Potts— you're a good man, and this appears to be a likely bunch but . . . I got my own place where I already been took in."

TWELVE

"Ever you see anything like this before?" Tuttle asked.

All Bass could do was shake his head.

In his youth he had floated down two of America's greatest rivers, shoulder to shoulder with a crew of hard-bitten, double-dyed Kentucky boatmen. He had even reveled in the rum-sodden fleshpots of Natchez-Under-the-Hill and "The Swamp" farther down in the port of New Orleans. But none of that had prepared him for the sheer joy of camaraderie expressed by those men gathered on the grassy, willow-veined floor of what would one day very soon come to be known among the mountain trappers as Cache Valley.*

True enough, he had seen the hustle and bustle of those Ohio River port cities: Cincinnati and Louisville. And he had soaked in the heady, noisy air of raucous New Orleans, where more than a dozen languages were spoken around him. But never had Titus expected he would find anything quite like this out here in the middle of all this wilderness.

They had rolled in that afternoon with Fitzpatrick's brigade, Cooper's outfit joining all the rest whooping and bellering back at those who were screeching and shouting to welcome every group of new arrivals.

On the Cub River near present-day Cove, Utah

More than a hundred of them had already gathered in Willow Valley, at least half the faces pretty near scraped clean of whiskers. Out they came from beneath blanket and brush bowers to fire their rifles into the air, whoop like wild, red-eyed warriors, and greet these last to pull in. Lunging through the dottings of the large creamy flowers that towered along the tall stalks of the Spanish bayonet, they jumped and cavorted—slapping and jabbing at the horsemen they knew, offering their hands to those they did not. Horse hooves and moccasins trampled the bold sunflower-yellow of the arrowleaf balsamroot as every last one of these men celebrated this midsummer homecoming of old friends and new, drawn here from distant parts.

In addition to all those trappers Ashley was responsible for bringing to the mountains in the past few seasons, Etienne Provost led his own band of partisans, who had worked their way north out of Mexican territory far to the southeast, down below the international boundary of the Arkansas River. This redoubtable figure had first grown concerned, eventually desperate, in recent weeks when his own partner, Francois Leclerc, had failed to show up with supplies from Santa Fe at the appointed place and time for their own rendezvous. No telling what had happened—but the unspoken belief was there among Provost's men that Leclerc's outfit could well have been wiped out on its way north toward the Wasatch and Uintah country.

Along the banks of a stream stood more than a dozen small wickiups belonging to the wives of some twenty-five Iroquois trappers who, until a year ago, had been employed by the Hudson's Bay Company working out of English posts far to the north and west on the Columbia River. But in the summer of 1825 the Iroquois had encountered the shrewd William Ashley, who sweet-talked them into turning their backs on the English and trading their furs to him instead. That Ashley-instigated betrayal would be the beginning of some bad blood between the HBC's Snake-country outfits operating under the hard-bitten Scotsman John Work and those upstart and most undisciplined Americans probing ever deeper into the beaver country of the inner basin. A land the English had had all to themselves . . . until now.

Besides the lion's share in attendance—those who owed some sort of allegiance to one company or another—here gathered a generous sprinkling of free trappers already making their presence known in these fledgling years, plying the waters of the great continental spine on their own hook. Men who, like Provost, had originally plunged into the mountains from the north along the Upper Missouri River drainage, besides those many and more who had first come overland to the tiny villages of Taos and Santa Fe at the far northern reaches of Mexican Territory.

This summer at least two dozen such men were in attendance—men who, like Silas Cooper's bunch, owed allegiance to no man.

Yet one thing was as clear as those streams flowing down from the Bear River Range this midsummer of 1826: if a man didn't hanker to march all the way south to Taos country, or east over yonder to the posts on the Lower Missouri, then General William H. Ashley was offering them the only game in these parts. If a trapper wanted to deal himself in for the coming year, he damn well had to sit down at the general's table and be willing to play with the general's deck.

Not that Ashley hadn't had a tough time of it getting there himself. The overland journey, hauling his supplies and twenty-six men up the Platte to the Sweetwater then down to Ham's Fork, had turned out to be such a test of endurance that nearly half of his men had eventually deserted the general. But there on Ham's Fork that warm day back in late May, Ashley had been greeted with nearly sixty-five of his own trappers brought in by his partner, Jedediah Strong Smith, and the iron-legged Moses Harris. Their reunion was not to last long, for Ashley pushed the whole brigade on west to the Bear River, where they followed its meandering bend to the south, ultimately reaching the site he had designated last summer for this rendezvous—Willow Valley.

Near the site where the competitors under Danish sea captain John Weber and the mountain veteran Johnson Gardner had passed the previous winter, that late June day Ashley must surely have gazed about at plenty of tall, ripening grass gently waving in the breezes to fill the bellies of their stock, the many streams gurgling down from the circuit of sheltering hills, the thick vegetation choking every creekbank, branches and vines heavy with ripening fruit, as well as the beauty of the nearby peaks still mantled with snow at this early season . . . and decided it was good.

Here they would hold their second mountain rendezvous—now at the very dawn of that most glorious era of western exploration. Lewis and Clark had cracked open the portal, laying out the lure and the bait. Manuel Lisa and Alexander Henry had together been the first to throw their shoulders against the sturdy door to that imposing wilderness. And now it was these very men gathered in Willow Valley that hot summer of 1826—those trappers bound to Ashley as well as those bound to no other—who would in the seasons to come shove wide-open the gate, thrusting themselves against a barrier that would never, could never, be closed again.

Let there be no doubt, even in those earliest days of the mountain fur trade, these hardy hundred were ready for a celebration after all they had accomplished in the last season.

When the Ashley men had broken up into brigades for their spring hunt, Fitzpatrick's band had marched north to trap the Portneuf River all the way to the Snake—where they dodged Blackfoot war parties more times than they'd care to recount. A second brigade moved far afield that spring, pushing past the Great Salt Lake not only in search of beaver but in search of that wondrous new country off somewhere in the interior basin. Still another band pushed all the way north to Flathead country, plunging into the mountains that would soon become known as the Bitterroots, where they found sign of and bumped up against their competitors trapping for John Bull's Hudson's Bay Company.

Ashley's men had worked hard and repeatedly put their lives on the line to earn this rendezvous. A good thing it was Ashley had thought to bring liquor along for the first time this trip out. Even better that a large band of the western Shoshone had been curious enough at this growing gathering of the white men to wander in and join the celebration. Trouble was—no one knew at first if those horse-mounted warriors who suddenly appeared in the distance were friend or foe.

"Dammit all anyway," Bud Tuttle grumbled that second day after reaching the rendezvous site, "just when I was getting my dry gullet ready for some of Ashley's whiskey—those damned red niggers go an' show up and wanna fight!"

Every man had turned out that late morning as the alarm spread and weapons were taken up. The men were grumbling, for it was to have been that day Ashley tapped his kegs of raw, clear corn liquor . . . and now, by bloody damn, a few hundred Injuns showed up on the nearby hills to make trouble. But Bridger, Fraeb, and two others quickly mounted up bareback and started off loaded for bear—counting on determining if these strangers be the friendly sort, or a fighting breed.

"Where the blue blazes you think you're bound?" Cooper demanded the moment he realized Bass was pulling his horse free of its picket pin.

"Going with them yonder to have a look-see at the Injuns."

Silas snorted, wagging his head with a grin. "If'n that don't take the circle, boys! We got us a greenhorn what goes riding off to make hisself trouble with red niggers . . . like them red-bellies ain't trouble enough all by themselves!"

"This h'aint none of your 'ffair," the old German-born Fraeb grumbled as Bass joined the quartet loping toward the low hills.

"My skelp too—so I figgered to see for my own self," Titus replied as he reined his horse in alongside the others strung out in a broad front—their smooth faces bright in the summer sunshine of that morning, their long hair fluttering like battle flags behind these rough-edged knights-errant.

Bridger's eyes quickly dashed over the newcomer's outfit, spotting the pair of pistols stuffed down in his belt and the long, heavy, and serviceable mountain rifle clutched atop Bass's thighs. "Might'n be some of the same goddamned Blackfoots we fit not far north of here," he declared by way of warning to the older man riding on his left. "Maybeso they follered our sign, figgering to have themselves another go at us."

Fraeb asked, "Ever you fit Injuns?"

"Last spring it were," Titus answered as they watched the horsemen on the crest of the hill begin to spread themselves out in a wide front. " 'Rapahos, they was."

"That ain't a good bunch neither, 'Rapahos ain't," Bridger said to Fraeb with no small measure of approval.

"Wagh! 'Rapaho h'ain't never be no Blackfoot," the old German howled disparagingly. Then his eyes mocked Bass as he said, "An' one fide don' make you no fider."

"Leave 'im be, ol' man," Bridger scolded. "Sounds to me like this feller's got him a few wrinkles on his horns already."

As Fraeb glared at Bass a moment longer but ventured not one word more, it became immediately apparent to Titus how Fitzpatrick's men had come to respect that youngster from Missouri—no matter his age or theirs.

"Lookee thar!" hollered the man on the off side of Fraeb.

Scalplocks and feathers fluttered in the breeze as the warriors arrayed themselves on the crest of the hill in a battle front.

"How many you make it, Frapp?" Bridger demanded as they slowed their lope to a walk.

Just then a half-dozen of the brown-skinned horsemen punched ahead of the others from the center of that phalanx arrayed on the hill.

"Coot be more'n a hunnert," the old man roared. "H'ain't allays good at ciphers come times like dis!"

"We gonna have our hands full," commented one of the others. "Be no doubt of that."

"Gloree!" Bass cried. "Bridger! Don't count on a fight this day. Look yonder!"

The young partisan and the rest looked off where Bass was pointing, to the near side of the hill, where just then appeared more than a hundred women, children, and old ones among their packhorses and travois. Just to their rear one could begin to make out the beginnings of their pony herd.

"Believe this feller's right, Frapp!" Bridger hollered into the dry, hot wind. "Man don't bring him his squaws an' pups along when he's out for skelps and coup."

The old German snorted, his eyes flicking at Bass with something bordering contempt. "Mebbe we just run up again' a bunch on the move, Jim. Blackfoots move camp ever' now and den."

"These here ain't Blackfoot," Bridger declared as the six horsemen came to a halt at a point halfway between the broad front of warriors and the five white men.

"Why, them's Snakes!" one of the others stated.

"Damn right they are," Bridger agreed, getting close enough to recognize faces.

"Same bunch wintered up with us?" one of the others asked.

Bridger whooped, "By God, if they ain't!"

Following the young man's lead, the rest again urged their horses into a lope, reining up only when they came nose to nose with the Shoshone ponies.

"By damn, these are a handsome people, ain't they?" Bridger asked, turning aside to Bass. Then his hands grew busy, dropping rein and resting the rifle across his thighs as he commenced talking sign.

In the quiet of that brief conversation, disturbed only by the snorting and blowing of the horses and the shrill cry of a golden eagle that circled overhead, Bass watched the far slope as the ground behind the cordon of warriors filled with those the horsemen had been ready to defend: the old men, women, children, all those on foot and urging along the pack animals, travois, and pony herd.

One of those handsome, smiling warriors who had been using his flying hands to talk with Bridger now turned atop the bare back of his pony and signaled with the long feathered lance he held aloft and waved, scalps and birds' wings fluttering on the summer wind along the shaft.

Instantly a universal cry went up from the far hillside as the mounted warriors bellowed their happy approval and burst into motion—their ponies moving this way and that along the side of the hill, everyone waving, singing, shouting at those behind to hurry on into the valley.

"This feller's name is Washakie," Bridger explained, putting the emphasis on the last syllable. "One of the leaders of this here bunch what wintered up near one of our other brigades in these parts. Down yonder in that very valley."

"You don't say," Fraeb grumbled with disgust.

Bridger would not let the old German's sourness nettle him a bit. With a wry grin Jim said, "Washakie says he remembers him a feller named *Sobett*—"

"Don't he mean Sublette?" one of the others interrupted.

"One and the same," Bridger replied, his eyes twinkling. "An' he recalls a man what's so tanned by the sun Washakie says he has the face of a feller been burned with powder!"

"Only one coon like that," Fraeb roared. "Black Harris!"

By that time the front of the Shoshone procession had all but enveloped them. Titus reached out and grabbed young Bridger's arm. "This feller, Harris— he a Negra like Beckwith?"

Flopping his head back and laughing, Bridger ended up slapping a knee as he answered, "Not near as none of us know! Oh, he might have him some Negra blood back on one side of his family or t'other . . . but his skin ain't brown like no Negra's skin. No, his hide is like nothing I ain't never see'd afore—Washakie got it right: just like Harris gone and got his face burned with powder. There be a blue-blackish sheen to it, see? Ain't the color of his hands—not his skin nowhere else on him. Just on the man's face."

As the procession swept up to them, the Shoshone leaders nudged their ponies into motion. Reining their horses about in the midst of the Shoshone, the four white men began that short ride back to Ashley's camp, leading the noisy Shoshone cavalcade in grand order. As they drew closer to the streamside bowers and shelters the trappers had erected at the edge of a large meadow, brown-skinned singers suddenly began to raise their voices in half a hundred different songs of welcome, homecoming, or in the spirit of good hunting. At least that many or more beat on small handheld drums or shook rattles made of gourd, some constructed of dried animal bladders or animal scrotums filled with stream-washed pebbles, then tied to short peeled sticks. Children chattered, their high voices tremulous above all the others, and women occasionally shrieked at unruly ponies, flailing switches at those yapping, playful dogs darting in and out among the legs of people and ponies alike.

"What you think, Bass?"

Titus turned, finding the young Bridger had reined his horse into a walk beside him just before they entered the top of the trappers' camp. "About what?"

"Don't you figger these Snake women to be just about the purtiest a man can find him in these here mountains?"

"S-snake women?"

"Snake, Shoshone," Bridger repeated. "I s'pose they's called Snakes on account for the way they sign their tribe." Shifting his rifle to his rein hand, Jim raised the other and made a wriggling motion, in the manner a reptile would slither along the ground. "Snake."

Bass nodded, turning now to steal himself a look at some of the black-eyed women who were threading their way in among the warriors as the men of Ashley and Provost formed a long corridor for the Shoshone to pass through on their way to selecting a campsite farther south in Willow Valley. While he figured he would wait until he had himself a chance at a right-close inspection to offer his judgment on the pouting-lipped beauty of the squaws, he nonetheless could readily see that they were, by and large, a lighter-skinned people than the Ute he had come to know over the past winter.

Down, down through a wide gauntlet of grinning, gaping, brown-toothed white men the Shoshone paraded like royalty come to visit. While the trappers occasionally fired off a rifle into the air, perhaps a smoothbore musket or their belt pistols, the Snakes waved and sang, shouted and shrieked, pounding their drums and shaking their rattles even louder. A few warriors held eight-inch lengths of wing bone in their lips, small and delicate fluffs tied at the end of these whistles to dance on the wind while the men blew that eerie, high-pitched screech of a golden or bald-headed eagle. How easily its call rose above the noisy clamor of all the rest.

Bridger slapped Titus on the arm and motioned Bass to follow him away from the hubbub grown so noisy it was useless trying to talk. They joined Fraeb and the other two trappers angling off to the side of the procession, where they reined up to watch the parade pass them on by. The Shoshone streamed right on through the trappers' camp, down the valley a good half mile where their pony herd would not have a chance to mingle with the white man's horses and mules grazing across the creek on the benches farther up the valley.

More than a dozen men jogged up to stop among the five horsemen.

"Them's your Snakes, ain't they, Bridger?"

"They are that, Jedediah," Jim replied with a filial pride. "Prettiest people in these mountains, to my way of thinking."

"Appears Bridger's gone and got himself partial already," Harrison Rogers commented.

As brigade clerk, Rogers was never far from the side of the taller, square-jawed man who stood as erect as a hickory ramrod at the center of that group of men on foot. A devoutly Christian man, a New Englander who had carried his Bible into what many back east considered to be a godless heathens' wilderness, one of the handful who refrained from the burn of whiskey on his tongue or the heat of a naked squaw wrapped up with him in a blanket—this fire-eyed partisan was no less than Jedediah Strong Smith himself.

"If any of you men are going to partake in the sins of the flesh before we set off," Smith began, hurling his booming, fire-and-brimstone voice over those who had followed in his wake, "the next few days might well be your last for a long, long time to come."

One of the eleven called out, "You mean you're 'llowing us to have a spree with them Injun womens, Jed?"

Smith turned to John Reubasco. "Until I tell you it's time to pack up and move out, what sinning you do will be between you and your God."

"But I don't have me no God, Jed," cried Abraham LaPlant, another of Jed's brigade and one of Smith's closest friends, a man who could get away with joshing their devout leader.

Smith wagged his head, his grin widening. "Then all I can do is to warn you and your kind, Abe: best see that none of you go swilling down Ashley's liquor like it was baptismal water!"

They all laughed heartily at that, then Rogers inquired, "How long you figger till we're packing off to the southwest, Jed?"

In turn, Smith looked up at Bridger. "You got any news on the general's plans, Jim?"

Bridger shrugged. "I figger ronnyvoo's over when he gets him all the fur bought up."

Smith added, "Sure to snatch up what furs Provost and the others brung in too."

"Likely the general will light out for St. Louie soon as he has all of his packs filled with them geegaw goods traded out," Bridger continued. "Then there ain't no more reason for ary a man to hang on here at ronnyvoo, an' Ashley will pack up to move out."

"Talk is he's give up on the mountains," Fraeb announced, dour as ever, looking at Smith, Ashley's partner. His words appeared to stun all the rest into silence.

"That's likely just talk," Rogers declared testily as he turned to Jedediah for confirmation.

With a wag of his head Smith announced, "Maybe not, Harrison."

Bridger replied, "The general's made him his fortune awready in just more'n four years, ain't he?"

"And I hear tell he's got a purty gal back in St. Lou ready to marry 'im," Jed explained. "No man could blame Ashley for cashing in his plews and kicking up his boots now."

"What I heerd this morning is that we're due to be working for new booshways right soon," John Gaither, one of the horsemen beside Fraeb, suddenly disclosed.

"Who you figger's gonna booshway this new outfit?" Bridger demanded, eyes widening with interest.

"Could be that I'll stay on when the general quits the trade," Smith answered calmly.

Close to twenty sets of eyes immediately turned on him in surprise at the revelation.

"You h'ain't the only one to run these here mountains," Fraeb declared, making it sound as if he weren't sure it wasn't a joke.

But as surprising as was the news that Ashley was giving up the fur trade, it really came as no shock that Jedediah Strong Smith would be staying on. He was as driven, directed, and no-nonsense as they came out here in the far west. Some might even say he was, in his own Puritan way, consumed by his quest.

"So this here palaver ain't no bald-face, is it, Jed?" Bridger asked.

Smith shook his head. "Ashley come to me this morning," he explained, looking from face to face as he spoke to that breathless crowd. "But—it ain't just me gonna lead the new company, fellas. Understand that. General said he wanted to talk things over with a few of us."

"A few," Fraeb grumbled as if his belly was soured on green apples. "Who be the other'ns gonna talk things over?"

"Two of 'em," Smith answered. "Billy Sublette—"

Bridger interrupted, youthfully assertive, "Billy's a good man."

". . . and the third be Davy Jackson," Jed concluded.

"J-jackson!" Fraeb sputtered. "Why, that no-account sprout ain't got the right—"

"Davy's a damned workhorse, Frapp," Bridger interrupted before Smith got his mouth open. "He's allays worked harder'n any man I knows of out here."

Now Jed spoke up, "And that's why I'll partner with the man any season, Frapp. Ain't a trapper here what don't already know that Davy's brigades always brings in their furs. From only God knows where! But Jackson brings in the plews for to make the general a handsome profit."

"Hrrrumph," Fraeb snorted. "So it's to be Sublette, Smit', und Jackson, is it, now?"

With a shrug Jedediah Smith replied, "Don't know for sure, till we talk with the general: hear what he's got to offer about selling out. Don't know any of the rest, fellas—but I've already told my outfit that no matter me being booshway of a new company or not, we're setting out for a long ride to explore us that country to the southwest."

Daniel Potts came up to stop beside Bass, asking of Bridger, "Jim—if Smith's outfit heads off south, where you figger we'll be bound?"

With a smile young Bridger replied, "Fitz told me we're going back north."

"To Blackfeet country?" hollered a man from the crowd.

"Where the furs are sleek and the plews are prime, boys," Bridger replied.

Potts slapped an arm on Bass's shoulder. "You sure you don't wanna come north with Fitzpatrick's bunch?"

"What?" Titus responded in mock horror. "And leave my skelp to hang in some red nigger's lodge up there in Blackfeet country?"

"So, better that you leave it off to some mangy, flea-bit 'Rapaho buck, eh?" Beckwith prodded with a wide, toothy grin, coming up to the group as Smith and Bridger were dispersing the gathering.

"I sure as hell know my hair ain't near as purty as yours be, Jim Beckwith," Titus replied with a grin. "But I figger if'n I stay outta Blackfeet country, I'll stand a damn good chance of keeping my hair locked on right where it is!"

Back and forth for the better part of an hour a pair of Etienne Provost's free trappers gambled with the two older Shoshone warriors, all four of them squatting on the dusty buffalo robe so well used it had places where the hair had been rubbed off right down to the smooth hide.

Titus had watched men gamble with painted pasteboards before, sometimes throwing down their wagers on the strength of a particular hand, or no more than the fate held in a single card. From up the Ohio clear on down the Mississippi, he himself had watched the fever take hold of those who put their lives and fortunes into their varied games of chance. At times he had witnessed the sly work of those who dared not leave things to chance, but instead preferred offering sham games of skill and sleight of hand.

As much as he had tried, not once in all those years had Bass been able to guess which shell the pea was hiding under. And those games of bones proved no better a tempt of Dame Fortune for Titus. He had no earthly clue to the mysteries of how those dice rolled this combination or that—and why some men came out winners while most walked away with pockets much, much emptier than when they had stepped forward to take their chance at bucking the tiger.

But this here game was like nothing he had ever seen before.

The white men sat across from their brown-skinned counterparts, about two feet of bare buffalo fur between them where they tossed the short pieces of carved bone. Each one of the half-dozen bones was different in shape, marked with altogether different drawings, slashes, lightning bolts, and the like, each of the symbols first carved into the bone's surface, then filled with some dark, inky substance so that the scratchings stood out in bold relief against the yellowed surface of the old bone. Over the years of use each of the half-dozen had taken on a rich patina from much handling.

First one side, then the other was awarded possession of the bones. When the two Shoshone held three bones apiece, it was up to the trappers to place their wager on the blanket between them. It might be as little as a few glass beads, or a single flint big enough for a man to clamp in the huge lock on his tradegun or even in starting a fire with a good steel. But as the hour wore on, the betting grew richer—as it ofttimes does when the gambler no longer plays with his head, but begins to wager what lays dear to his heart.

Down came the skinning knife, its wood handle well oiled to a deeply burnished glow by the hand of the trapper now offering it.

All around Bass white men and Shoshone alike muttered their comments that no longer was this to be a game of beads and powder, vermilion and shiny girlews. Now, with the wager of that knife, it had become a game of some worth.

The two Shoshone looked at one another a long moment; then one shrugged and removed a strand of buffalo bones from around his neck. He laid it atop the knife and gazed at the white men to await their approval. Both nodded, accepting the wager, and the first warrior rubbed and clacked the magical bones within the hollow of his two hands, closing his eyes, raising his face to the sunny sky overhead, and chanting. His partner, the one who had offered his necklace, also chanted, but a different and discordant, off-key dirge that grew louder and louder until both Indians were nearly shouting their disparate songs.

All the time the two trappers kept their eyes locked on the jumping, flashing, clacking hands with such intensity, trying their best to shut out the disquieting noise of the two gamesters.

Then suddenly the hands flew open over the buffalo robe and the singing abruptly stopped as the bones tumbled across the fur. And four heads bent low to study the markings.

"God*dammit!*" cried one of the trappers in great disgust.

The other just wagged his head dolefully in silence.

The gleeful warrior picked up the knife and the necklace, glanced quickly at his companion, then flung the necklace back onto the buffalo robe.

Asked one of the trappers, "Jamus, you got anything what you can lay down?"

Into his shooting pouch Jamus stuffed his hand and came out with a long strip of blood-red trade ribbon, a woven cotton strip about an inch wide used to selvage the edge of garments to keep them from unraveling. This much-favored item of trade in the Indian country brought approving nods from the warriors, grunts from others gathered behind the players, and a squeal from at least one of the older women gathered nearby.

"Well, goddammit?" the first trapper demanded caustically of his opponents. "What you boys gonna lay down for that?"

Acting as if he did not know what to do about such a wager, one of the warriors turned to look over his shoulder at a woman nearby. Something unspoken passed between them. He turned back to look at his partner, then bent his head and pulled his shirt off, laying it neatly atop the pile.

"Awright," Jamus replied. "Now we got us a real game!"

The second Shoshone began to rub and clack his three bones, singing the furthest thing from harmony with his partner as they shook and rubbed, clacked and waved the bones around and around until a man was driven nearly insane with the waiting.

When they spilled onto the buffalo robe, four heads again dipped to inspect them. The silence of that breathless crowd was punctuated only by the firing of weapons nearby as men shot at a mark with their rifles—winning swallows of whiskey as the afternoon wore on.

"By damn! We won, Jamus!" he hollered, slapping his partner on the back as they swept their winnings back toward their knees.

"What you wanna bet now?"

He didn't have a ready answer for Jamus, not one near quick enough for the two warriors either.

The older of the two Shoshone immediately snatched his tomahawk from his belt and laid it upon the bare hide between the players. Most of the crowd were stunned: many of the Shoshone clamped hands over their mouths while white trappers muttered their approval of such a fine wager. There the tomahawk lay for a long, breathless moment, its fancy oiled wood gleaming in the sun, the forged iron head inlaid with pewter rings, a pair of deer dewclaws suspended from a latigo strip knotted at the bottom of the handle.

The anxious Shoshone grew impatient and soon made it plain the white men must wager or leave the game to others.

"Jamus?"

"I ain't got nothing near that fine, Spivey."

Then the Shoshone shut off their conversation and pointed.

"He wants our whiskey," Spivey declared.

"You figger he wants all of it?" Jamus demanded in a whisper, as if the Shoshone might understand their English.

"Dip your cup in our kettle there and see if that'll do for a wager."

Jamus did as was suggested, dipping his pint tin cup into the small kettle of throat-burning alcohol Ashley had brought to rendezvous, as promised the year before. Setting the dripping cup on the robe, they looked up to see the smiles crawl across the faces of the two Shoshone and knew they had themselves a wager.

"Let's play, boys!" Spivey whooped, scooping up three of the carved bones from the hide, beginning to rub and click them together inside his hands.

The white men won that go-round, then sat there taking the time to swill that cup of whiskey in front of their opponents as if to rub in the spoils of victory. The shirtless Shoshone flung down another tomahawk. And this time he won.

The pair of warriors savored the liquor from the cup, passing it back and forth as each man took small sips until the potent brew had disappeared and both had themselves a go at licking the inside of the tin.

Again that second tomahawk was wagered, and again another cup of whiskey. More clacking, singing, chanting, and cursing to disconcert the other side before the bones were hurled down. One side always groaned in dismay, the other side celebrated by toasting to their success. On it went as the sun began to sink until suddenly the tides turned against the warriors and it seemed the Shoshone could not win a single play. Repeatedly the white men scooped up shirts and leggings, belts and moccasins, until there was little left but breechclouts for the warriors to wager.

While the two trappers laughed at their own good fortune, the two Shoshone became more and more sullen, forced to listen to the muttered oaths from their kinsmen standing behind them as another cup of whiskey was set between the gamblers and the white trappers began to jostle and shake, weaving from side to side, laughing lustily in the face of the dour-eyed warriors with a new wager.

Like a blur one of the warriors leaped up, lunging for his knife that now lay beside the trappers. It flashed in the afternoon light as the Shoshone pressed the blade suddenly against Spivey's neck. All sound was sucked from the clamoring crowd, as if shut off by some magic.

Eyes like saucers, Spivey peered cross-eyed down at the hand clutching the knife, squeaking, "J-jamus! Do something!"

"An' get your goddamned throat cut?"

While he held the knife against the white man's throat with one hand, the warrior peeled open Spivey's fingers with the other, yanking from it the three bones. The other Shoshone retrieved the other bones from Jamus—then he reached down and took up the tin cup, bringing it to his lips to drink long and noisily—emptying the cup of every last drop.

The warrior handed it to Jamus, motioning that he wanted more.

"G-get it for him, goddammit!" Spivey squeaked. "Somebody, d-do something!"

"Red son of a bitch'll open your throat up," another trapper said with resignation. "Ain't a thing we can do for you then."

That second full cup of liquor was passed over to the warrior holding the knife on Spivey. While he pressed the blade into the taut, tanned flesh, he drank slow, his eyes widening as the burn began to turn his throat to fire. Just as he was finished, a loud voice bellowed.

"What the hell's going on here?"

They all turned, trapper and Shoshone, to find Fitzpatrick and Bridger lurching to a stop.

The warrior's eyes went down to his cup, then to the knife, and back to his cup. He upended the cup at his lips, quickly licking at what he knew would be those last few drops.

"You boys gambling, are you?" Bridger demanded of the pair.

"Things got real ugly, Fitz," someone called out from the crowd.

"I can see that plain as sun," Fitzpatrick replied as he knelt near Spivey's shoulder. "Jim—how 'bout you telling these here bucks to pull in their horns."

"I'll give it a push, Fitz," Bridger replied, then went on to speak what he could of the Shoshone tongue.

But the warriors interrupted him, growing excited, and most of their spectators with them, chattering all at once until Bridger waved both arms and quieted them.

Jim said, "These here bucks tell me you boys ain't been all the fair with 'em—"

"We're gambling, for God's sake, Bridger!" Jamus squawked.

"There's gambling," Bridger said, scratching his chin, "and then there's stealin'."

"We wasn't stealing!" Spivey roared, red-faced, his eyes looking down at the knife held against his windpipe.

"You so proud you wanna keep your liquor," Bridger replied, "or you don't mind getting your throat cut?"

"J-just give 'im the liquor, Bridger," Spivey whined. "The likker . . . none of it's wuth it."

Jim knelt at the shoulder of one of the Shoshone. "So what you two gonna do for these bucks you cheated?"

Jamus's eyes flashed up at young Bridger's. "I'll give 'em what's left of my likker."

"And?"

Now Jamus's face turned red. "Ain't given 'em nothing else!"

"Give 'em what they want, Jamus!" Spivey said, his eyes cross on the twitching hand that held the knife.

"All of it, goddammit," Jamus said grudgingly, his eyes filling with hate for Bridger as well as the Shoshone. "They can have all of it—that what you want, Spivey?"

"Right! Just give it all to 'em and get this red nigger off me!"

Rocking up on his knees slowly, Jamus shoved the Shoshone shirts and leggings, moccasins and tomahawks, knives and necklaces, back across the buffalo hide to the warriors.

As he did, Bridger said something understood only by the Shoshone gathered in a hush at the buffalo robe. With a sigh the warrior with the knife leaned back, taking his weapon from the trapper's neck. After stuffing his tomahawk back into his belt and rising, the warrior suddenly held out the knife, handle first, to Spivey, who continued to rub his throat, then check his fingers for sign of blood.

"What the hell's this for?" the trapper asked, his eyes going to Bridger's face.

"Says he's giving you his knife," Jim replied. "He figgers at least you won that fair and square."

Spivey wrenched it from the warrior before the two Shoshone gathered up their clothing from the buffalo robe and looked longingly at the small kettle of amber liquor—then turned away into the crowd of their own people.

"Maybe next time you fellas won't be so all-fired ready to get no Injuns drunk," Bridger snorted as he stood, then with Fitzpatrick started away from the crowd.

"C'mon," Potts said to Bass.

"Where'd you come from?" Titus asked of the man coming up to his elbow out of the milling group.

"Been looking high and low for you," Daniel explained. "Wan'cha have dinner over at our fire since't we'll be pulling away day after tomorrow."

"Ronnyvoo over?" They started away through the grove of cottonwood.

"Ashley's got him all the fur from his brigades, 'long with what he traded from Provost's bunch."

"He's got near all ours too," Titus replied.

"Best you get your outfit to be trading off any furs what you got left by tomorry morning, or the general likely won't have no more goods for you. Then what will them plews be wuth?"

Bass nodded. "Not much—when there ain't no one else out here what wants beaver fur in trade."

"Ever you et painter, Scratch?"

"P-painter?" Titus asked as they neared the fire where Fitzpatrick and Bridger's brigade had been bedding down.

"Sure. *Painter*," Potts repeated. "Mountain cat. Some calls it a lion. But most of the fellas I know calls that mountain cat a painter."

"And you eat that lion?"

Potts smacked his lips. "Some fine eatin'. C'mon—we'll get some on the fire. One of the boys shot a pair this morning up torst the hills yonder."

That mountain lion was a treat to the pallet and a tongue grown used to elk and venison. Bass eagerly went back for more, eventually slicing himself a third helping of the roast and loin steaks. Later on Bud Tuttle showed up in time to squeeze himself down by Bass and Potts as one of Fitzpatrick's men brought out his small concertina to the cheers and claps of all those Ashley men gathered at the fire.

Pulling two short leather latches from the tiny pegs that held the instrument closed, the player was then able to slip his hands into leather straps on either side and began to wheeze some air in and out of the squeezebox until he suddenly began to stomp one leg lustily, his foot pounding the ground as he whirled round and round, wailing out the words to the rollicking song accompanied by his concertina's wild strains.

Many of the others noisily clapped in rhythm as a few leaped to their feet, bowed low to one another, then began to circle round this way and round that, arms locked and head thrown back, wailing and caterwauling worse than any wharfside alley filled with tomcats.

"Man could grow used to this ever' night, couldn't he, Scratch?" Tuttle asked, jabbing an elbow into Bass's ribs. "Music, likker, and the womens!"

Scratch had almost forgotten about such seductive lures, doing his best to stay as far away as he could from the temptations of those young women and their flint-eyed menfolk downstream in the Shoshone village.

Titus looked off in the direction of the quartet's camp. "Cooper and Hooks didn't come with you?"

Tuttle grinned as he clapped along with the wheezing squeezebox. "They daubin' their stingers again."

"Hell, I should'a knowed," Titus replied. "Likely them two'll be daubin' their stingers when Gabriel blows his goddamned horn!"

"Maybe that, or Gabriel can find 'em laid out under a trader's likker kegs!"

A cloud quickly passed over Scratch's face as the firelight flickered on the dancers all. "Silas didn't go and drink up all our earnin's, did he?"

Tuttle bravely tried to maintain the smile, then admitted, "Ah, shit—Scratch. Him and Hooks been having themselves such a spree, they ain't give a damn thought one to seeing that we're outfitted for the coming winter."

"Where's the plews?"

Tuttle hemmed and hawed a moment, then answered.

Bass demanded, "How many packs you figger we got left?"

"Not near enough—"

"All gone in likker?" he squeaked in disbelief.

Dropping his head to look at his hands suddenly stilled even though the music, laughter, and merriment continued around them, Tuttle replied, "An' foofaraw for the squaws."

"Damn him," Bass muttered between clenched teeth. "Son of a bitch beat me near to death an' said I owed him my hides . . . so now he don't even use them hides he stole from me to trade for what it is we really need!"

"Trouble?" Jim Beckwith asked, curious when Bass's voice grew louder in the midst of the revelry.

Finally shaking his head, Titus answered, "No. No trouble, Jim."

As Beckwith turned back to clapping and stomping with the music, Titus grabbed Tuttle by his shirt. "Listen, Bud—we gotta be sure no more of them hides go to pay for geegaws and girlews so them two sonsabitches can stick some Injun gals with their peckers."

Tuttle's head bobbed, almost in time with his Adam's apple.

"You figger we can hide them plews somewhere's till morning?" Titus inquired. "When we can get 'em traded off to Ashley?"

"I s'pose—"

"Ain't no s'posin' about it, Bud," Titus interrupted. "We gotta do it first thing come morning—or Ashley ain't gonna have him no more powder and lead, no coffee and blankets left to trade."

"And we need flints bad."

"See? Just like I told you. Now, I want you get back to camp while them two is off knocking the dew off their lilies and drag the last of them packs off into the bushes somewhere outta camp where they can't find 'em—drunk or sober."

"M-me? Ain't you—"

"Awright, I'll damn well come and help you."

Tuttle seemed much relieved to have an accomplice in their crime.

"Hell, don't worry none, Bud," Titus explained. "If them two ever come back to camp tonight, I don't figger they'll be thinking none about plews till long after sunup anyways."

Bud chuckled. "I do believe you're likely right, Scratch. They'll have daubin' on their minds."

"C'mon."

By the time they had dragged what they had left in the way of those heavy packs out of their camp, away from their blanket and canvas bowers and into the nearby bushes, the half-moon was on its rise. It, along with the glittery stars overhead, was enough to cast some faint shadows as Bass and Tuttle made their way back through the raucous camp toward Fitzpatrick's fire, where the concertina player was taking himself a rest and many of the others were settling back, their cups filled with Ashley's liquor, jawing and swapping exaggerated tales of their experiences and exploits.

"How 'bout them two, Bridger?" someone called out as Tuttle and Bass came into the fire's light. "They hear your tale of the Salt Sea?"

As some of the bunch chuckled and jabbed elbows into one another's ribs, the young Bridger turned to gaze over his shoulder at the two free trappers. "Don't believe they have."

"Then tell 'em!"

Nonplussed, Jim turned around on his stump and asked the returning pair, "Since we run onto your outfit north of here, I ever tell you fellas about the time I floated down to the Great Salt Sea?"

"Y-you been all the way out there to the west?" Tuttle asked, turning slowly in disbelief to look at Bass.

Bud's question brought howls of laughter from a few of that bunch gathered round the fire.

"Don't pay these dunderheads no mind," Bridger confided.

"What they laughing at us for?" Titus asked, feeling sheepish—as if some joke were about to be played on them.

Bridger offered up a cup of liquor, handing it to Bass as he said, "Don't fret none, now: some of these here coons ain't got the brains God give a buffler gnat."

One of the scoffers cried out, "Just 'cause we don't believe you floated where you said you floated, don't mean we got us gnat-brains!"

"Sit yourselves down, fellas," young Bridger said, "an' I'll tell you 'bout that leetle trip I had me through hell's canyon in a bull boat—"

"All the way to the Salt Sea!" bellowed one of the doubters, accompanied by roars of laughter from the rest.

Wagging his head as if he was used to the good-natured ribbing, Jim exclaimed with mock seriousness, "I'll swear. There be times a mountain man is a most consarned critter, boys. Now, you go take a look at them niggers laughin' their bellies sore over there on their logs, and you'll see just what I mean. Some of these here beaver trappers are the most uncertainest fellers ever—cuz they'll argeefie about near anything. And that even includes argeein' about argeein'!"

THIRTEEN

"There t'weren't a bit of blamed sense in argeein' about it," Bridger declared, back to being solemn-faced now that he was warming to his tale. "But these here other yahoos good for that."

Many of the rest pounded their knees and backslapped one another in unbridled mirth, guffawing lustily as the liquor and the camaraderie warmed them all that summer night as stars shown like diamonds and the moon hung like a slice of translucent mother-of-pearl right over their heads.

"What they don't got in good sense," Fitzpatrick declared, "these fellers make up for with big grins!"

"Last year it were!" one of the laughers roared out, anxious to get on with the tale. "G'won, Jim—tell 'em!"

"I will," Bridger snorted, and turned back to Bass and Tuttle with a wink, "just as soon as you yabberin' yahoos shut your fly-traps!"

"Shut up! Shut up!" commanded one of the laughers, who stood, weaving a bit in his drunkenness, waving his arms at the others for quiet. When they all fell silent behind hands, he declared, "Go right on ahead, young Jim. We's a'waiting on your windy story."

Just then another unruly trapper cried out, "Best tell us only the true of it, boy!"

That sent the entire bunch into fits of laughter that did not end until Bridger had gone to the kettle with his tin cup, dipped some of the heady grain liquor from it, and resettled back on the trunk of a downed cottonwood. Casually he took himself a swig and looked round at those gathered there as things quieted once again.

He asked them, "You 'bout done with your pokin' fun at me?"

"G'won head, Jim," Fitzpatrick said gravely as he bent forward to select a stout cottonwood limb from the stack of wood near the fire. "I'll damn well thrash the next son of a bitch what interrupts young Bridger's story with his silly gaping!"

"Thankee, Fitz," Bridger replied, and took himself another sip of the liquor before he set the cup on the ground between his worn moccasins. "Like that bignosed yahoo over there told you, it were some two winters back."

"A year and a half ago?" Tuttle asked.

Nodding his head, Bridger replied, "Near 'bouts. Late fall it were."

"Hell, it could've been early winter too, Jim," declared Fitzpatrick. "Nobody was keeping track nohow."

"Leastwise—the first snows had come to this here country," Bridger continued. "Most of us was settling in for the winter not far on down this here same valley, it were." He pointed south with a wag of his arm. "Seemed that not all the trapping outfits was in yet—but most was already here."

Ashley's men were settling in real good, too, Jim explained. They had cut down strong saplings and lashed them together into eastern-style wickiups over which they interlaced branches to turn the dry snows of that high prairieland. Here in what they had come to call Willow Valley the previous year, the trappers had a good source of water, plenty of grass to last their animals for the winter, and plenty of protection from the harshest of the season's winds. Firewood lay within easy reach along the creeks and streams that tumbled out of the surrounding hills. Day by day they shot buffalo, laying in more and more of the hides they fleshed and draped over the wickiups for insulation, slicing and drying thin strips of the lean red meat over smoky fires . . . knowing the hard days of bitter cold and deep snows were not long in coming.

Just beyond that range of hills to the west of them lay the valley of the Bear—a river that would soon become the irritating source of contention between the Ashley men.

Earlier that July of 1824 more than fifty of them had followed Jedediah Smith and John Weber across the deceivingly low South Pass and on to the country of the Green River. By late August that year they had reached the crest of an unexplored mountain range and peered off to the west, down into the valley of a new river they would soon find had already been visited and named by the John Bull trappers for the Hudson's Bay Company.

From the heights Smith's men could see how the Bear flowed north out of a lake they would come to name for the sweet taste of its water. But upon following this new river the trappers discovered the river precipitously reversed itself in some forbidding lava beds. Steadfastly following the Bear upstream, the trappers continued their march south. Eventually that autumn they reached the Willow Valley, and there they decided to winter. Just to the southwest of their encampment the trappers could climb to high bluffs and stare down at the Bear River as it appeared to twist back to the north in the distance once more—but this time it flowed through a narrow canyon filled with thunderous white water.

Just as it is the way with any men who find too much time on their hands, the trappers turned their discussions of that unpredictable Bear River into an argument—with nearly every soul taking a side—and then that argument boiled into a matter of wagers: did that river continue north, or curl itself back south still another time? Hell, just what did happen to that fitful, fickle river after it disappeared in that high-walled gorge?

"Until Fitz here reminded ever' last nigger of us there weren't no way to know who'd win them wagers," Jim continued his story in the hush of that starry night, "because no man knowed for sure where that river went."

Fitzpatrick said, "Hell—I didn't figger there'd be a man among 'em what'd go to find out for his own self!"

"Didn't count on young Jim here!" Daniel Potts cried out.

"He's a struttin' cock if ever there was one!" another man shouted as others added their admiration.

"Wasn't like I jumped at the chance," Bridger admitted. "But some of these here yahoos come to me with such straight, no-account faces and told me I was the coon they could trust to take on that there canyon—which'd put their argeement to rest, once't and for all."

One of the group crowed, "We figgered you was the only one we could talk into it!"

"See what I mean, fellers?" Bridger asked Tuttle and Bass. "Well, now—I didn't know no better than to be proud they asked me."

"Shit, it made sense!" someone called out. "You was the youngest, boy!"

"So we figgered you was the best'un to try that hellhole river run," another added.

A new voice bellowed, "If'n you didn't come back—weren't no sad loss, you being the sprout of the brigade!"

With a shrug at all the abuse he was taking, Bridger continued, "Don't make me no never-mind now that I didn't know they figgered it to be a damn lark they was putting me up to . . . that trip sounded like it'd be just the chance to pull the tiger's tail."

One of the older, grizzle-bearded trappers declared, "Young'uns like Bridger allays wanna be first to pull on a tiger's tail!"

"Better'n sitting in winter camp all day, ever' day," Jim continued. "So I told 'em I'd settle their li'l argeement."

"Not one of these here gaping fools figgered Jim were serious," Fitzpatrick added. "Till next morning when they rolled outta their bed-shucks and found Bridger building hisself a boat."

"A b-boat?" Tuttle asked in surprise.

"T'weren't no big shakes—nothing more'n some stout willow branches I chopped down, just the way I'd watched the Injun squaws do it."

An apt and eager student, Bridger had relished this opportunity to try his own hand at building a bullboat. Driving the butt-ends of the willow into the ground around a four-to-five-foot circle, he bent the limbs over and tied all their narrow ends together to form something on the order of an upside-down basket.

"I tried to talk the fool out of it," Fitzpatrick explained.

"And some of the rest of us too," another claimed, "when we saw he'd got hisself serious 'bout going into that devil's canyon."

"You get that, boys? That morning while'st I was working on my boat, a handful of the ones what talked me into going come up to try talking me into *not* going," Bridger explained. " 'What, you're crazy as a March hare, young'un!' said one of 'em to me. 'Why, you don't even know if'n you can find your way back here to us!' said 'nother. 'How 'bout waterfalls—likely you'll drown like a rat!' Then 'nother of 'em warned me, 'How 'bout the Injuns? By God, you don't know a damned thing about what Injuns is in that country!' "

Fitzpatrick added, "And I told Jim it didn't matter a twit about which way the river goes anyhow."

"Didn't make me no never-mind," Bridger said. "I kept my hands busy. Far better, I figgered, to be going somewhere. Not like the rest of them what were having their fun with me—all they was doing was sitting on their arses in camp."

As the others laughed in agreement, Jim continued his story, telling how he had woven smaller willow limbs among the thicker ones, lashing each loop to make the framework as strong as he possibly could before he took a green buffalo hide and laid it over his small dome—hide to the inside. Then the detailed work began: sewing the buffalo skin to that willow framework, binding it all around the edge of that circular opening.

"By that next night I was ready to make her seaworthy," Jim boasted proudly.

At a cookfire he heated up a large kettle of tallow rendered from a bear recently shot while he built himself a small fire over which he set the upside-down boat. When the hide grew hot to the touch, Bridger took a small wooden spoon and began to smear the melted tallow over every seam and stitch and hole in that buffalo hide. That done, it was time to let his craftsmanship cool and harden.

"At sunup the following morning, I cut me as long a pole as I could find," Jim told the group. "Something to push along again' the bottom with, or shove me away from the rocks in the canyon, if that need be."

"I give him one last chance to stay back," Fitzpatrick stated with a shrug. "But he was bound to go, no matter what. I figgered I'd seen the last of the lad."

Bridger continued, "Got my rifle an' pouch, strapped on tomahawk and knife, then throwed in a big sack of some dried buffler meat—an I pulled that boat on over to the river."

Potts shook his head, saying, "We all thought we was seein' the last of Jim Bridger."

Finally in the river, he slipped away slowly at first. Jim waved to the men on the bank and settled into his boat, gripping his pole, pushing his way into the main current. The men on the bank waved and shouted their farewells, many taking off their hats and raising them into the air in salute to his courage. Then all too soon Bridger couldn't see them any longer. And beyond the second bend in the narrowing canyon, the river seemed to crash in upon itself, the current picking up speed.

Breathlessly, Bridger told the silent group, "It were like nothing I ever done afore."

The Bear picked up that tiny bullboat with its lone passenger and hurtled them along faster and faster between the rising walls of the river's canyon as the serene water transformed into a frothing, crashing, boiling cauldron that whirled Bridger round and round, bouncing the boat first against one wall, then against the rocks on the other side of the narrow chute. Eventually the sound of water crashing against rock began to thunder about him, pounding on his ears so brutally that it drowned out his own thoughts.

"I been drunk an' wild-headed afore," Jim explained. "But my head ain't never been that twisted round and round!"

It was a cold ride too. He had begun to shake—not just out of fear—but there in the early winter the river spray soaked him, the canyon wind chilled him . . . and before long he was shaking uncontrollably, frozen to the marrow. Yet somehow he maintained his death-grip on that long pole, struggling to push his boat this way, then that, doing his best to pitch through the center of the narrow gorge. And through it all he kept his rifle locked between his knees in the event he was pitched out by one of the many dizzying whirlpools, or by the series of frothy rapids he was flung over like driftwood, or hurled up against the boulders raising their heads in the middle of the channel—threatening to smash him and his tiny bullboat to splinters.

Then, despite his dulled reactions, Bridger realized the immense cold he was feeling was actually water. Looking down, he found his boat slowly filling with the dark, icy river. But try as he might in the next frantic minutes, Jim realized he wasn't going to shove the boat to either shore: there simply was no bank—only canyon walls. On and on he hurtled, slowly taking on more water with every mile.

"I figgered I was damn well going under," Bridger exclaimed calmly as he raised his face to the sky dramatically. "Began to think back to my time as a young'un in Missoura—I'd heard me many a story of the ol' salts who talked about rivers out here what disappear right underground on a man."

"Under . . . underground?" Titus asked with a gulp. Just like the rest of them, he was caught up in the young man's story now.

"Yup—that's what some of them ol' fellers tol't me. Them rivers go right down a hole in the ground. So I figgered it was just 'bout any time I'd be sucked right into some hole with that mighty river—an' I'd never see daylight, or the Rocky Mountains, or my friends ever again."

It was no wonder Bridger felt such dire fate awaited him.

By that time the late-autumn sky was beginning to cloud over and the sun was all but blotted out as he careened on down the canyon, its walls growing steadily steeper—the sky became nothing but a narrow and darkening strip far overhead. Now there were times when his bullboat was suddenly thrust against an outcropping of rocks, where it was suddenly wedged—with the full force of the water thundering against it—until Jim could free himself, using every last reserve in his young body . . . only to shove his boat back into the swirling madness of the gorge.

By then the boat was taking on more and more water, losing its natural buoyancy in the process as it slowly sank lower and lower in the freezing river. Then the strain of holding so much liquid began to tell on the bullboat's crude, handcrafted framework. Creaking and groaning, the limbs began to shift with the weight of the water, and then some of Bridger's sinew stitching began to unravel and loosen—the long strands of animal tendon becoming soaked to their limit.

"I figgered I was a goner an' if I didn't get sucked down under the ground with that river—then that river was bound to thrash me against the rocks," Bridger told the group grown quiet as they were drawn further and further into the desperate story.

"Only thing for me to do was try to save myself," Jim said. "So I reached down and felt in the water at the bottom of my boat to find my sack of meat. I stuffed it down inside my coat an' made ready to jump out and try for some rocks where I could least get outta the water. Maybeso I could get my strength back and climb up the side, get back to the prerra—anything before that river sucked me right under the ground with it."

But by some miraculous hand, right as he was preparing to cast his fate upon the water, the bullboat twisted around ungainly and Bridger caught a glimpse of what lay downriver.

"I'll be damned if it didn't look like smooth water!" Jim told the hushed crowd, many of whom had heard his story time and again—but found themselves caught up in its drama nonetheless.

Something told him to hang on, told him not to jump—giving him faint hope of riding it out a few moments longer. But he was sinking all the faster now, the river's surface inching closer and closer to the top of his unwieldy craft. Then as he listened and shook uncontrollably with cold, Bridger realized the thundering roar of the rapids had begun to fade behind him. After so many terrifying minutes that had seemed more like endless days—Jim finally thought he could hear the pounding of his own blood at his temples.

"I don't know how I done it, but I got that boatful of water poled over to the first stretch of sandy bank I come across. Just in time, too—for my boat was 'bout ready to go under for good."

Slogging out of the widening river, Bridger set his rifle and pouch in the limbs of a nearby tree, then returned to the bank, where he struggled to tip the bullboat over, completely filled with water as it was. Finally he was able to drag the heavy boat with its green waterlogged buffalo hide a few feet up the bank, where he turned it upside down to drain. Then he shivered as the cold wind came up, and decided he'd best build himself a fire.

"Later that afternoon when my buckskins was dried and I had pulled the wet load in my rifle, I figgered it was time to climb on up the rocks and see for myself just where that devil of a river did go off to."

High in those rocks as the late-autumn light started to fade, Bridger finally discovered just how the wagers would be won or lost. He could see that the river continued south. Meandering though it was, it seemed to continue angling off to a little west of due south.

"But that wasn't the pure marvel of it," he admitted now, just as he had told the tale many times before.

As he stared off into the distance, his eyes following the river toward the far horizon, "Of a sudden—way out yonder—I happed to see more water'n I ever see'd since the day I was born."

For a moment he turned and gazed back to the north, thinking about his original plans to return overland once he had determined just where the river flowed. But now, as he stared off into the distance, he felt again that unmistakable itch to search and discover, an itch that he knew he could not deny.

"Come sunup the next morning I put that bullboat back in the water and I was on my way. It weren't long afore the world around me went so quiet, it was like everything was dead. By the time I come to where the river opened up into a peaceful stretch of water, I dipped my hand over the side and brung it to my lips. Salt! Sweat of the Almighty—that's what I tasted, fellas. Salt! Good Lord, I thought—had that river floated me all the way to the far salt ocean?"

In actuality Bridger had drifted on out of the mouth of the Bear into a great bay some twenty miles wide,* where he could barely see land far off to the right and left of him—but where the bay opened up to the south, there was nothing but water . . . for as far as he could see.

"I ain't ashamed to tell you I was scairt," Bridger confided. "Figgering I'd made the ocean, I wasn't a stupid pilgrim about to go floating off to the other side of the world in that leaky ol' bullboat. So this child poled hisself over to the shore quick as he could. Stepped my mokersons out on a layer of salt that crunched under my feet, and I pulled that boat out behind me."

With the sun rising toward midsky, young Jim set out on foot instead,

---

* *Bear River Bay on the Great Salt Lake*

moving south along the shoreline. He had put miles behind him before he finally made out the first sign of distant land. The farther south he walked, the more it became clear what he was seeing was a huge island* rising far out in that lifeless, salty expanse of endless water. Far, far to the southeast, it appeared the shore he was walking went on forever.

"And I never did see the other side of it neither!" Jim exclaimed, handing his cup to one of his compatriots for refilling. "Still scairt pretty bad, I took off on the backtrack. Made it back to my bullboat just afore dark. Gathered in some wood, started me a fire, and rocked that boat up on its side to hold off the cold winter wind. Next morning I started walking north, back the way I come."

As he came up to those gathered around the fire and stopped, Jedediah Smith asked, "You know what Jim told us when he showed back up a few days later?"

Potts called out, "Bridger said, 'Hell, boys! I been clear to the Pay-cific Sea!'"

"Would've been nice, fellas," Smith said, gazing wistfully down at the fire, "if what Bridger did find two winters back was in fact a big bay of the Pacific Ocean."

"You figger some way Jim run onto the Buenaventura, Jed?" Harrison Rogers asked.

"It would be by the hand of God, if it were," Smith answered reverently, gazing off toward the west, where the legend of that fabled river dictated its waters would carry a man all the way from the spine of the Rockies clear down to the Pacific.

Fitzpatrick said, "Why, if it were the Buenaventury, Jed—we'd have only to pack our plews down to the shore, where the big ships would tie up and take on our beaver."

Rogers added, "Then and there they'd off-load our supplies and likker, fellas!"

Smith grinned in the yellow sheen of that fire. "Just think of it, men: Jim Bridger here could well be the feller what found it for us."

"That's what we're heading off tomorrow to find out, ain't we, Jed?" Rogers prodded.

With a nod Smith replied, "That's why we're marching south by west. Yes—to find out just where the Pacific is. To discover just how close . . . or how far we are, from the sea."

"I'll be damned," Tuttle exclaimed with a gush. He slapped a hand on Bass's knee. "Ain't that something, Scratch? Think on it, man! Just out there, maybeso not all that far off—the great salt ocean lays waiting for us to go see it!"

"That is something," Titus agreed quietly, the immensity of the thought almost overwhelming him.

Down at New Orleans he had looked out on that harbor and tried to fathom

---

* Present-day Antelope Island

the immensity of those great rolling oceans where tall triple-masted schooners rocked atop frothy waves as tall as houses, moving to and from faraway ports where folks of many colors spoke all those foreign tongues he had heard fall upon his ears on that youthful trip to New Orleans with Hames Kingsbury's boatmen. How so many of the sounds and sights and smells of the world were brought into that one place rolled up beside the ocean.

And now another such ocean might not be all that far away to the west, after all.

"Let's drink to young Jim Bridger!" Beckwith roared suddenly, standing with his cup held high. "And to Bridger's Hole!"*

Immediately they all shot to their feet. But Bridger was the last, looking young and sheepish among their lined faces scraped clean of beard these past few days. The fire danced in their eyes, flickered on the dull sheen of their tin cups, as together they roared, celebrating one of their own.

"Hear, hear! To young Jim Bridger!" Bass shouted with the others.

Taken altogether, those men gathered in Willow Valley that night were a pitifully small lot indeed.

"Hear, hear! To the far salt ocean!"

But few in numbers though they be, each man of them stood tall, head and shoulders above any who had chosen to stay behind, those who cowered east of the Missouri . . . this breed here and forever after to stand taller still than any of those who would come in their wake.

"To the beaver, by God!"

Here they were of a breed just newly born, yet already beginning to die . . . so short was their glorious era.

"To the Rocky Mountains, by damn!"

"Hear, hear!" Scratch shouted with them, tears coming to his eyes, so emotional was it to stand among these men strong enough to match those high and terrible places.

"To the very heart of the world!"

"To the Rocky Mountains!"

"Jumping Jehoshaphat!" Titus cried as he bolted to his feet with the first shots up the valley. "What you make of that?"

Cooper barely budged, his eyes fluttering open slightly. He squatted with his back resting against a pile of their bedding: buffalo robes and blankets. "Target shooting. Feller wins, he get hisself a drink of likker."

But those shots were coming too close together, Bass thought. And they damn well came from the wrong direction. From the Shoshone camp!

"What you think, Billy?" Bass inquired, nervously scratching at his bearded cheek.

---

* What some of the early Ashley men called the valley of the Great Salt Lake

Hooks kept on whittling the bark off another short section of willow. He had a pile of pale sticks on one side of him, and a rumpled pile of curled slivers of bark on the ground between his legs. "I figger them red niggers' business is their own business. Leave it be."

"But—the shootin'!"

"Ain't no one shootin' at us," Cooper snapped. "Just let it be and lemme sleep."

Then Bass whirled on Tuttle, "You think we ought'n go see what's the ruckus, Bud?" He watched Tuttle glance at Cooper, as if asking permission.

"Nawww," Bud finally answered, "like Silas said: ain't none of our affair—"

Hooves pounded up on the valley floor—three horses skidding to a halt as their riders leaned over to throw their news at the quartet of free trappers.

"A bunch of bad Injuns just jumped the Shoshone camp, boys!" a rider announced, pointing. "Come riding down off the hills. Cutting up the Snakes' camp something fierce. I s'pose they didn't know we was here—or didn't care."

Cooper stirred only enough to push his hat back from his face and ask, "What tribe?"

"Blackfeets."

"Blackfeet," Titus repeated almost at a whisper, his heart beginning to slam in his chest so hard, he thought it would squeeze right out between his ribs.

"That's right," a second horseman said. "Bug's Boys!"

"Grab your gun and c'mon!" the third Ashley man ordered as more hooves pounded close.

A half-dozen riders shot by, whooping and yelping, knees like pistons in the stirrups as the wind whipped back the brims on their hats, fluttered their long hair out behind them just the way it did the horses' manes and tails. In their wake came a rider who peeled himself off and brought his mount crow-hopping to a jarring halt before Titus and Tuttle as the other trio of riders kicked their horses into motion and tore out after the six.

"You comin', Scratch?" Jim Beckwith asked breathlessly.

"Fight them Blackfeets?"

He nodded, swallowing. "Ain't none of us ever gonna have a better chance to get in our licks."

Cooper snorted in derision, then said, "Sounds like pretty big words comin' from a black-assed Negra."

Beckwith glared for a moment at the giant, then snarled, "I sure as hell don't see you grabbin' up your gun to show us all just how brave you are."

"You come down off'n that horse, Negra-boy . . . I'll show you who's brave an' who I can pound into mule-squat!"

Beckwith turned from Cooper as if to ignore him the best he could. "I'm going, Scratch. You can come with me . . . or you can stay with these here."

"He'll stay with us," Silas snapped, " 'cause he knows better. That ain't his fight."

Hooks echoed, "Yup—not your fight, Scratch."

Then Titus watched another dozen or so riders race past in a flurry of hooves and hair, weapons, whooping, and dust a'flying.

"Maybeso it oughtta stay atween just them Shoshone against the Blackfoot," Tuttle apologized for his reluctance.

Wagging his head, Bass replied, "Looks to be it ain't just the Snakes' business. No, I gotta go."

As he whirled about to race over to unlash his horse from its picket pin, Cooper bellowed, "You go get yourself hurt in this foolishness—don't y' come whimperin' to me."

"I won't," Bass promised, his heart rising to his throat as he yanked his horse back toward the spot where his blankets lay.

Silas continued, "We got us plans for the fall hunt. If y' go off an' get yourself hurt—don't figger on trapping with us none. I ain't dragging along no bunged-up, strapped-down whimper boy!"

"Awright," Bass agreed as he swept up his rifle and dropped his pouch over one shoulder, "that's a bargain: I get myself hurt by them Blackfoots, you three just go on off to hunt 'thout me this year."

Cooper was beginning to rise, his face growing more crimson as he found his warnings were going unheeded. "You 'member that scuffle we had us with the Arapaho, don't y'?"

"I do," Titus replied, leaping atop the horse, bareback.

"You was cut up good, y' dumb nigger," Silas reminded. "You was damned lucky it were winter time so we had us the time to wait on y' to heal up—or we'd damn well left y' to rot on your lonesome right there with them Utes!"

"C'mon, Beckwith," Bass said bravely as he reined around, turning his back on Cooper. "There's Blackfeet to fight."

He gave the horse his heels in its ribs and flanks, setting the animal into a run. Although Bass could not make out the loud, angry words Silas flung at his back, he hoped Cooper's anger would cool by the time he returned. It just might be an even wager: fighting the worst Indians in the northern Rockies, or suffering another one of Silas Cooper's beatings.

After no more than a quarter of a mile's run they spotted the first of the buffalo-hide lodges in the distance. And gathered just this side of them were a swirling knot of trappers dismounting and handing off their horses to others on foot. At their center stood three men: Fitzpatrick, Fraeb, and one man Bass did not know.

Leaping to the ground near the group, Titus asked Beckwith, "Who's that younger fella with Fitz and Ol' Man Frapp?"

"Sublette."

Scratch joined Beckwith at the fringe of the group, whispering to the mulatto, "Billy Sublette?"

Beckwith nodded as a small party of Shoshone raced up through the village on horseback. The trappers backed away slightly as the warrior leader sought out the chief of the trappers.

"Cut Face!" the Shoshone called in English when he recognized Sublette.

"I am Cut Face, yes!" the partisan replied, stepping forward.

In troubled English the chief explained to Sublette, "Three of my warriors and two of our women—out gathering roots on the other side of camp—they are killed by the Blackfeet!"

"I know," Sublette hurried to say above the crackle of gunfire on the far side of the village. "We are here to help you fight those Blackfeet!"

For a moment the Shoshone leader's eyes roamed over the crowd. "You say that your warriors can fight, Cut Face? You say that they are great braves?"

"They are brave fighters."

"Now let me see them fight—so that I may know your words are true."

Clutching his rifle to his breast with one hand, Sublette swept the other arm in a wide arc to indicate the white trappers. "You shall see them fight, and then you will know that they are all brave men."

"They are ready to die today?"

Nodding, Sublette answered for them all, "I have no cowards among my men. Yes, we are ready to die for our Snake friends!"

The chief turned briefly as the gunfire seemed to rumble all the closer, accompanied by the yells of men in battle. "Then bring your warriors to join mine."

Sublette turned from the war chief and shouted above the battle's din to the trappers, "Now, men—I want every brave man to go and fight these Blackfeet. We must whip them—so the Snakes can see that we can fight. By damn, we'll do our best in front of the Snakes and the Blackfeet as a warning to all tribes that would cause an American trouble!"

"Let us at 'em!" a voice cried out.

"That's right!" Sublette replied. "I want no man following me who is not brave. Let the cowards remain in camp!"

"No cowards here!" another shouted.

With a wave of his war club, the Shoshone war chief ordered, "Bring your ponies!"

"Follow me, men!" Sublette echoed as he leaped back onto his horse and reined away after the Shoshone warriors.

At the far edge of the village the trappers suddenly confronted a wide crescent of the Blackfeet pressing against the lodge circle. But there was surprise, even shock, in the eyes of the enemy as they saw the numbers arrayed against them: white men and Shoshone alike, streaming through the lodges like water through a broken beaver dam.

The painted, blood-eyed enemy began to inch back toward the willow and cottonwood. Farther and farther they retreated, foot by foot, yard by yard, darting among the shadows and behind what cover they could use skillfully. After those first few minutes Bass finally saw his first real target—something more than a flitting shadow.

Dropping to his knee, Titus yanked the hammer back, set the trigger, and squeezed off his shot in one fluid motion. He thought he saw the enemy warrior spin about, clutching his side as the gunsmoke billowed up from the muzzle. Then Titus lunged forward, eyes intently watching that spot where he had seen the enemy. There, yes—the warrior was lurching off, hand plastered against his side—joining others in retreat.

Guns roared and men yelled in three tongues. At times the air was filled with arrows hissing past his ear and over his head, fired from the short bows of one side or the other. The work was agonizingly slow and dirty for the first hour until the Blackfeet backed themselves right out of the brushy cover and began a full-scale retreat.

In crazed confusion they led the trappers and Shoshone across more than four miles of rolling countryside at the upper extent of Willow Valley that afternoon. For the most part it was a game of chase, with little shooting . . . until the enemy reached the shore of a small lake. There beneath the trees and undergrowth at the lakebank they took cover, turned, and prepared for the coming assault.

As the trappers and their allies closed on the lake, it was easy to see the Blackfeet were going to sell their lives as dearly as possible. Behind the scrub brush they hid, down behind the carved, earthen banks they took this final refuge—and from there began to harass their tormentors. The battle heated up like never before.

Squatting behind a small boulder and clump of sage, Bass took a few moments to watch others crawling in on their bellies as the Blackfeet arched arrows into the air, sailing up, then falling down upon their intended targets. All the time the Shoshone cried out their grief at the five scalps taken within sight of their village—and the Blackfeet boasted that there would be more deaths before the sun set on that day.

"There's no way we can get close!" Daniel Potts shouted his frustration nearby.

Others grumbled, fired at the brushy cover, or just shouted back at the eerie war cries and chants floating up from both sides of the battlefield. For the better part of an hour it went poorly, an individual here or there making his own brave attempt to worm his way toward the brush and the lakeshore bulwarks. All were driven back by the defenders . . . until the Blackfeet themselves suddenly emerged from their shadowy cover and hurled themselves against a weak place in the trappers' line.

"Get us some help!" came one man's frantic wail.

Bass crabbed to his feet, running all bent over toward the sound of the gunfire and loudest shouting. Across the sagebrush dotting the open ground came another ten or a dozen trappers—all hurrying to the cries for help. Some of them stopped for a heartbeat, thrust their rifles against their shoulders, and fired into the wild, screaming, ghoulish charge of the Blackfeet.

Those cries of enemy warriors raised the hair on the back of Scratch's neck. Something so primitive, primordial, something that reminded him of the Arapaho warrior who, though already dying, had flung his war club at Titus. . . .

Bass dropped to his belly, yanking the buttstock under his arm, into the crook at his shoulder as the handful of warriors came screaming toward three or four trappers—one of them swinging over his head what appeared to be a long-handled war club with sharp iron spikes driven through its round head like an ancient ball of mace.

Pulling the trigger, Bass watched the bullet catch the warrior high in the chest, shoving his upper body back with its velocity as the soft lead flattened out . . . the Blackfoot's legs continuing to pump forward nonetheless—until he landed flat on his back, squirmed and kicked convulsively a few moments as Bass brought the muzzle to his mouth and blew.

From the corner of his eye he watched the warrior quit twitching as Bass dropped powder down the barrel and drove a ball home.

"Beckwith!"

Titus turned to find the one called Sublette calling. Off to his left, the mulatto fired a shot from behind some willow, then turned to shout in reply.

"Over here, Billy!"

"I see you," Sublette shouted, then pointed off toward another of the enemy dead. "See that dead nigger?"

"Yup! I do."

"What say the two of us go get that red nigger's scalp afore them friends of his drag him off!"

Beckwith's coffee-colored face creased with a wide smile, his head bobbing. "Fine notion, Billy! A real fine notion!"

The two laid aside their rifles, then crabbed onto their hands and knees. Crawling from one bit of scrub brush to the next, Sublette and Beckwith took separate paths to reach the last bit of cover closest to the warrior's body. It was there that Sublette bellied down flat on the ground and began crawling into the open.

"C'mon, Beckwith," he growled. "I cain't haul 'im in on my own!"

Plopping to his belly, Beckwith joined Sublette by crawling into view. An arrow flew over the white man's head just as he reached out for the warrior's ankle.

"Goddamn, that was close!"

Beckwith seized the other ankle and frantically began dragging the body back some two feet at a time. From the far brush at the lakeshore, the Blackfeet realized what was taking place and set up a horrible roar: howling in dismay as their comrade slowly disappeared toward the brush where the Shoshone and their white allies lay hidden.

But while Titus watched, it became clear that warrior wasn't dead. The Blackfoot began shaking his head groggily.

"Jim!" Bass shouted in alarm.

It was as if the Indian came to in the space of a heartbeat and immediately realized what was to be his fate. Twisting his torso as he was being dragged, the Blackfoot reached for tall tufts of grass, strained for a hold on the low branches on the brush—anything he could seize that would slow him down.

"Sonuvabitch ain't dead!" Sublette huffed in surprise. "Kill 'im, Beckwith!"

"With what?" the mulatto demanded as the warrior kicked out with his legs. "I left my gun back there like your'n."

"Where's your pistol?"

The warrior began to thrash even harder now.

"Ain't got it!"

"Stab 'im!" Sublette ordered. "Cut his throat!"

Like a blur a Blackfoot warrior leaped from behind some nearby cover to snap off a shot from his trade musket, the ball slapping through the brush near Beckwith—then the warrior kept on racing right for the two trappers.

Sublette growled, "Jesus and Mary!" as he began to rise to his knees, his hand slapping for knife and tomahawk at his belt.

At that moment the warrior leaped over some more low brush, balls whistling past him. As he landed flat-footed, the Blackfoot gripped his musket's barrel in both hands and swung it high over his head, bringing it down on Beckwith's back with a loud crack before the mulatto could scoot out of the way.

With a grunt of pain Beckwith fell back, losing his grip on the wounded warrior's ankle. His face drawn up in shock, the mulatto rolled and rolled again to get away, crabbing up onto his knees, then lunging forward painfully, onto his feet to retreat even more.

"Come back here, Beckwith!"

Sublette was on his knees too, pushing against the warrior, both of them with a lock on the enemy's empty trade musket. Slowly the white man rose to his feet, straining to pull the Blackfoot off balance.

"C'mere, you yellow coward!" he shrieked. "Beckwith!"

Twisting this way, then twisting another, the two struggled muscle against muscle.

"I swear, Beckwith—I'll kill you myself for this!"

Then the warrior smashed his heel down hard on top of Sublette's moccasin, causing the trapper to yelp, hop, and yank one hand off the musket. With a great wrenching the Blackfoot tore the rifle away from Sublette, then shoved, sending the trapper sprawling onto his back.

Just as the warrior raised the weapon over his head, preparing to savagely bring it down on Sublette, Beckwith flung himself back into the struggle. Flying over the low brush, the mulatto drove his head and shoulder into the warrior, sending the enemy hurtling, his musket sailing in another direction. Without delaying to find his weapon, the Blackfoot scrambled to his feet and retreated at a dead run.

Three balls nicked the bushes around the two trappers as they redoubled their efforts to drag the wounded warrior back to cover.

Crabbing over to where the pair had disappeared in the brush, Bass found Sublette and Beckwith whispering loudly with another trapper.

"You want the scalp or don'cha?" Sublette demanded.

The wounded trapper could barely lift his head up, much less argue. "You kill 'im your own self," he said weakly, clearly in a great deal of pain.

Beckwith prodded, "This is the black-hearted son of a bitch what shot you. Ain't you gonna kill him?"

"Can't you both see the man ain't got the strength to kill nothing?" Titus demanded.

For a moment Sublette and Beckwith stared down at their seriously wounded companion—but only for a moment—when the wounded Blackfoot came to again and flopped over to crawl away with only one good leg left him.

"Awright," Sublette growled harshly. "I'll kill the sumbitch for you!"

Leaping onto the Blackfoot's back, Sublette shoved his knee down on the back of the warrior's shoulder, grabbed a handful of the Indian's hair with his left hand so he could pull the neck up taut, then with the flash of his skinning knife sliced once—long and deep—across the enemy's throat. Frothy crimson spurted as much as three feet onto the grass as the Indian struggled for a few quick heartbeats; then his body went limp.

Quickly Sublette hacked off the scalp in a crude manner of one not accustomed to removing the hair of his enemies, then stood with the dripping trophy to show it to his wounded companion. His knife, hand, and forearm all dripped with bright blood, resplendent in the summer sunshine.

"Now, you—get over here," he hollered at the far line of brush. "I need some of you to drag Hinkle off and get him back to the village."

As soon as the wounded man was taken away, Sublette and the rest returned to the task at hand. Arrows sailed overhead. Lead balls smacked through the leaves and limbs. Shoshone taunted Blackfoot, and the Blackfoot cursed at their ancient enemies. The white trappers screeched above it all, knowing neither tongue but clearly understanding the age-old language of war. Hour after hour the stalemate dragged on until the sun eventually slid far beyond midsky.

Bass figured they had been fighting for the better part of six hours when one man after another began to grumble of his hunger. It took only that first one to remind the rest that they hadn't eaten since breakfast—and only those who had been up early enough to eat before the firing began, those who weren't suffering a throbbing hangover in this afternoon heat.

One after another added his voice to the complaints until Sublette agreed that his trappers could reward themselves with a temporary retreat. After telling the Shoshone warriors that they would return shortly, Sublette told the Snake that they should rub out as many of the Blackfeet as possible before the trappers would come back—because when the white men returned, there would soon be no Blackfeet to kill and count coup upon.

It wasn't a short ride back to Shoshone camp where Sublette's men began to scrounge about for something to eat. About the time the trappers found some slivers of dried meat to chew on and were gulping down water to quench their terrible thirst, the first of the Shoshone warriors appeared back in the village.

"What the hell are they doing here?" Sublette demanded.

Bass watched a group of the warriors ride up and dismount, their bronze bodies glistening. One in particular was most handsome, his carefully combed hair greased to perfection; over the crown of his head he had tied the stuffed body of a redwing hawk, the thongs knotted under his chin. He had the classic profile not seen in many of the others, with the hook high on the nose, the prominent cheekbones, and those oriental eyes filled with obsidian flints that glinted haughtily as he strode up to the white men.

Gazing after the group come to take their own refreshment, Titus said, "I s'pose we wasn't the only ones hungry, was we, Sublette?"

"Damn them," Sublette grumbled. "Now them Blackfoot gonna get away."

"You fixin' to have us go back *now*?" Fraeb asked, dragging a hand over his mouth, his beard dripping with the water he had been guzzling.

"Damn right," Sublette answered. "Let's go! All of you—now! Saddle up— we're going back to finish what we started!"

By the time the first of the trappers returned to the battleground, they found only a dozen or so Shoshone stationed among the brush to watch over their dead companions so they would not be scalped. But as the white men dismounted and began tearing through the willow and trees at the lake's edge, they were surprised to find more than thirty Blackfeet bodies had been abandoned.

"They damn well left in a hurry, didn't they?" Beckwith asked as he came up to stand with Bass and some others.

"You ever see'd Injuns leave any of their own like this afore?" asked one of the group.

"Never," another answered, incredulous.

"No, not me, never," Beckwith agreed.

"What made 'em take off so fast that they left their dead behind?" Titus asked.

With a shrug one of the trappers answered, "Yellow-bellied niggers is what Blackfoot is. Bad mother's sons when they got the jump on you. But they're yellow-bellied in a stand-up even fight of it."

In the end that night the Shoshone village was alive with celebration, wailing, and mourning. While they had killed far more of the enemy, they nonetheless had lost the scalps of the first five victims, along with the death of eleven more warriors killed in the battle. Yet those bodies and their hair had not fallen into the hands of the enemy. The drumming and singing, the keening and chanting, continued till daybreak as the Snake conducted their wake over their dead and celebrated the spoils taken from the bodies of their enemies.

Meanwhile, downstream in the trapper camps lay seven wounded men expected to survive their wounds if they were allowed to get their rest. Still, the Smith, Jackson, and Sublette men, along with Provost's outfit and the many free trappers still in the valley—all were anxious to celebrate their victory, right down to the last cup of liquor the general had hauled out from St. Louis.

For better than a day and another night the white men reveled in their defeat of the Blackfeet. Tales were told and retold of how that hated tribe first deceived the men with Lewis and Clark, then went on to take their revenge on Andrew Henry's men trapping out of their fort in the Three Forks area.

For the better part of two decades now, the specter of a monstrous enemy had steadily grown all the bigger with every Blackfoot skirmish, fight, and pony raid. But now American trappers had fought their first concerted battle with a large force of Blackfeet warriors.

Already a new crop of legends were beginning to take shape around those glowing campfires that midsummer of 1826 in the Willow Valley.

Yet the story of Blackfeet against American trapper would be a tale long, harrowing, and most bloody before it reached its conclusion.

FOURTEEN

"Mountaineers and friends!" William H. Ashley began, several days after that skirmish with the Blackfoot. "Most of you who know me must know by now that I'm not much good at this speech making."

Never a man who felt at ease speaking on his feet, even among friends, the sturdy forty-six-year-old businessman and trader had nonetheless been prompted by the emotion of this moment to gather all those who had until recently owed him their allegiance. From this day these hundred-plus men would give their fealty to the new company in the mountains: Smith, Jackson, and Sublette. So this morning before he set off for St. Louis with his 125 packs of furry treasure—a fourth more than he had reaped last season—the visionary Ashley felt compelled to call these crude, unlettered, fire-hardened men together for his final farewell not only to them, but to these Rocky Mountains.

"When I first came to the mountains, I came a poor man," he explained as the crowd slowly fell all the more quiet, respectful. "You, by your hard work, undying toils, and with your sacrifices, have made for me an independent fortune. For this, my friends, I feel myself under great obligation to you."

Across the better part of three weeks these Ashley men had camped together, sang and danced with one another, told stories of their spring hunts, and swapped outrageous lies. They had tried to outshoot, outwrestle, and outrun every other man jack among them. And they had joined in nothing short of wonderment that the general had even rolled a cannon across the plains, over South Pass, and on to rendezvous: a six-pounder! On wheels, no less!

Damn—some would say—don't you see? If wheels could rumble along the Platte River and rattle over South Pass, then the cursed wagons of settlers could not be far off! Perhaps this land was not as remote, nowhere near as forbidding as they had hoped it would be . . . not if General Ashley had dragged his cannon on its wheeled carriage all the way from St. Louis!

Yet, they figured, this institution of the rendezvous just might last long enough—if the trade goods they depended upon would continue to make it out here every summer. But as every summer must come to an end, the time had come to bid one another farewell: time for the Smith, Jackson, and Sublette men to split apart into smaller trapping brigades, while the few free trappers in attendance drifted off to the four winds—going in secret to those places where their own most private medicine told them they would find a rich bounty of beaver.

This had been only the second rendezvous in the far west, yet it was to be Ashley's last.

"Many of you have served with me personally," the general continued, "and I shall always be proud to testify to your loyalty . . . how you men have stood by me through all danger. Let no man ever question the friendly and brotherly feelings which you have ever, one and all, shown for me."

Titus Bass stood on the fringes of that group gathered in a crude crescent, the horns of which nearly touched Ashley's shoulders. Scratch was not one of them, but nonetheless he was. Somewhere a quarter of a mile off lay Bud, Billy, and Silas—those three sleeping off one last hard night of swilling down the general's liquor. Despite his own pounding hangover, for some reason Scratch realized that this morning he was likely to witness with his own eyes a man-sized chunk of history.

Out of their own heartfelt respect, many of the men had removed their hats—wide-brimmed beaver felt, or those of badger, skunk, wolf, or bear. A few men hung their heads, the better to shield their damp eyes from the appraisal of others. And a handful openly snorted back tears and dribbling noses.

"For these faithful and devoted services I wish you to accept my thanks; the gratitude that I express to you springs from my heart and will ever retain a lively hold on my feelings."

With a loud sniffle the man beside Titus whispered, "I fought the Rees on the upper Missouri for the general." He dragged the back of his sleeve under his nose. "And I'd still ride into hell and back again for the man."

Such was a commonly held sentiment among that group simply because Ashley had all but single-handedly brought them here to the Rockies himself. And it was here in these mountains that most of these double-riveted but sentimental men had discovered, for the first time in their lives, just what it truly meant to live.

"My friends! I am now about to leave you, to take up my life in St. Louis. Whenever any of you return there, your first duty must be to call at my house, to talk over the scenes of peril we have encountered, and partake of the best cheer my table can afford you."

"An' you'll always be welcome at my fire, General!" cried one of the throng. "Hear! Hear!"

Ashley held up both hands to the noisy crowd, and when they had quieted, he concluded, "I now wash my hands of the toils of the Rocky Mountains. Farewell, mountaineers and friends! May God bless you all!"

Undoubtedly he must have felt the tide of good fortune was about to carry him home after four arduous western journeys. Twice he had fought his way up the Missouri, battling the Arikara and losing more than his share of good men. And twice now he had crossed the continental divide at South Pass—the very heart of the Rockies. No more would he face the scorching summer heat of the plains, nor the terrible, bone-numbing cold of the mountain winters . . . yet no more would he ever enjoy the company of such men as these.

Slapping a hand against one cheek, there beneath an eye about ready to tear as if he were swatting at a fly, Ashley turned on his heel and took up the reins handed him by one of the thirty-man escort who would accompany him back to St. Louis with his fortune in furs loaded on more than a hundred horses and mules. Tugging his hat down on his head while the rest of the escort rose to their saddles, the general led the cavalcade away without looking back.

"Farewell, General!"

The crowd surged forward, almost as one, as if those in the lead might just drag him from his horse—yet something restrained them as more of these hard men not easily given to sentiment sang out with voices hoarse and croaking.

"God's speed, General! God's speed!"

So it was that they parted, one from another . . . again.

That quixotic booshway Davy Jackson marched his band away from rendezvous with Ashley's pack train. Somewhere west of South Pass he would bid his farewell to the general, then after trapping the country around Ham's Fork and the Green, would point his own nose north toward the rich beaver country that lay at the foot of those pilot knobs the French voyageurs called Le Trois Tetons, or the Three Breasts.

Jedediah Smith took his small band of fifteen and moved west of south toward the great and salty inland sea, obsessed with what lay across that great expanse of desert even if it took him into Mexico: even if it meant he marched all the way to the land of the Spanish Californios.

Working their way north to the Snake River, Billy Sublette would lead his brigade over to the Blackfoot River, turning east through Jackson's Hole and marching north to eventually reach the land that would soon be known as Colter's Hell. Two full decades before them, the wily trader Manuel Lisa dispatched Lewis-and-Clark veteran John Colter off from the mouth of the Bighorn to tell the Crow bands they were invited to Lisa's post to trade. Traveling on foot and alone into the teeth of a Rocky Mountain winter, Colter was the first white man to visit this strange land of sulfurous smokes, boiling cauldrons of mud, and spewing geysers that would one day bear his name.

This trip out Jim Bridger would serve as one of Sublette's lieutenants. And the stories the young trapper would soon tell of that mystical land of spewing waters and many smokes would for a generation be considered some of the biggest whoppers ever concocted by a frontiersman.

Meanwhile, the streams of the northern Rockies beckoned to Fitzpatrick once more. Despite the chances being good that he and his men might just rub up against more Blackfoot, north they headed nonetheless—hoping to trade with the Flathead for horses and skins until the beaver began to put on more fur come late autumn.

At the same time, Etienne Provost led his loose band of trappers west of north into the beaver-rich interior basin of the Snake River, where the odds were they would run across the Hudson's Bay men under Peter Skene Ogden.

"Good huntin'!" came the cry from those off in one direction.

"Yup!" called those bound away in another. "Y' best watch your topknot!"

And soon only the Shoshone village and a scattering of free trappers had Willow Valley to themselves. No more than a half-dozen small knots of hardy men tarried behind the company brigades—those of an independent streak who stubbornly refused the offers of one outfit or another to join up and ride along for the season.

"Maybeso it's better to travel in small strings," Scratch explained the common wisdom expressed by those of such persuasion. "A big outfit just hap to attract too much attention."

"Possibly so," Daniel Potts protested that last morning before Sublette's brigade pulled out, "but if'n I'm to face them gut-eating Blackfoots again, I'd ruther have me a hull passel of fellers along for the fight."

"But we don't aim to stick our noses in Blackfoot country," Bass replied.

Potts had pursed his lips as if he could see his words were winning no convert. "So be it, Titus Bass. Stay warm this winter . . . till next we ronnyvoo at the south end of Sweet Lake."

"Till ronnyvoo," Scratch repeated the word as if it had already become some spiritual incantation, shaking Daniel's hand as they pounded one another on the shoulder.

The mulatto had offered his hand next, "Could well be we could winter here again. So remember our offer stands—you come join us if you grow tired of the company you're keeping."

Bass watched Beckwith glance over to the trees where Cooper and the other two reclined against their saddles, watching the great departure of the brigades hour by hour, without much excitement of their own or interest at all.

"I got me a place I belong," Titus repeated.

His eyes filling with concern, Daniel said, "They ain't your only friends, Scratch. Anytime, you just come looking to find us—"

"It's a wonderful thing for a man to have him such good friends as you," Bass interrupted, his eyes smiling.

Understanding at last that there no longer was any sense in trying to talk Bass into joining them, Potts pursed his lips and went to the saddle in a hurry, galloping off with Beckwith to catch up with the last brigade on its way out of the valley. In less than an hour the midsummer air grew quiet but for the occasional call of birds and the incessant drone of flies or the whine of bees. No longer could Titus see the telltale smudge of dust there along the horizon. The company men were gone for another year.

All sights and sounds of that merry gathering were nothing but memories now.

What grass the stock hadn't eaten had been trampled into pathways by hooves and moccasins. Dry and flaky piles of horse droppings dotted the close-cropped pasturage of the valley floor for as far as the eye could see. The rib-bare skeletons of willow wickiups and leafy bowers built streamside now stood naked in the strong sunlight of high summer. No more were blankets and buffalo robes unfurled in the shady places where men once lounged to swap stories or merely sleep off the terrible effects of Ashley's potent liquor throughout those long, hot days of summer. Refuse and litter from repairs made to saddles, bridles, and pack harness lay discarded and scattered among what kegs and empty burlap sacking had been carried here from faraway St. Louis.

Clouds of bottle-green deerflies and black-winged horseflies buzzed in annoying clouds over every latrine hole, flitted over every campsite, and blackened every stinking gut-pile. Ants and hard-shelled beetles crawled and scritched through the trampled grass to lay claim to what refuse the robber jays weren't already picking over—wings flapping and beaks squawking when another bird landed to threaten their bloody morsel. Rings of darkened stones surrounded the countless black circles once fire pits. Butchered, bone-bare carcasses of elk and deer hung numberless like gory sacrifices from the branches of trees where the many had feasted upon the few: men cutting away a ham, or loin, or a fat steak to sizzle over the flames—each fire a gathering place where all came in turn to eat, to drink, or merely to commune with one's own kind.

In the span of less than two momentous years, a breed was born out here among these rich valleys sheltered and shadowed by the high and snowy places. A novice who was at first content to follow others up the Missouri River to the beaver country, William H. Ashley had ended up fathering a whole new strain of frontiersmen. Unlike their predecessors, those "longhunters" who had roamed the hardwoods forests back east of the Mississippi, these fledgling grandsons were only beginning to tramp across an unfathomable territory much more hostile in both geography and native inhabitants than anything ever before encountered by their eastern forebears.

Unlike their grandfathers had ever done back east, men of this new breed would live their simple existence permanently in the mountains—but without a permanent base. Such rootlessness, such unending wandering, suited this new breed just fine.

This was the dawn of a glorious era.

The mountain man had been born.

Two days after the last brigade pulled out, the morning breeze brought Titus the noise of snorting ponies being rounded up from the far meadows, driven in by pony-boys . . . the squawking orders of the women tearing buffalo-hide covers from lodgepoles, lashing travois together, and bundling every possession for the coming journey. In what seemed like a matter of minutes, the village was no more and the cavalcade was on its way north.

"Shoulda tasted y' one, Scratch."

Titus, watching the Shoshone depart, turned as Cooper and Hooks came up to stand by him. Billy had that indolent, contented look Scratch had come to recognize their winter with the Ute—the look he got when his belly was full, there was no work to be done, and his pecker was well satisfied.

Titus looked at Silas. "Tasted what?"

Cooper licked his lips. "Them Snake gals. Prime poontang—ain't they, Billy?"

As soon as Silas jabbed him in the ribs, Hooks giggled. His bloodshot-red eyes widened momentarily in remembrance. "Prime. Yessirreebob! Prime poon!"

"Hell, even Bud went off to the Snake camp and dipped his quill in some gal's inkpot. Didn't y', Tut?"

"Ever' man's got him a right, Silas," Tuttle replied smugly. "Ain't none of us had no women since winterin' with them Utes."

" 'Cept Titus Bass here his own self." Silas slung an arm around Bass's shoulders. "How come you didn't drop y' one of them bang-tail Snakes, Scratch? Still fancy that Ute widder?"

For a moment he studied the marble-eyed Cooper. Then Bass slowly unleashed himself from the long, muscular arm. "When you fixing on us to pull up pins and set off?"

A brief look of consternation crossed the tall man's face. "Say, boys—sounds to me like Scratch here got him a hard-on for one special gal."

"Yup, it do," Hooks agreed. "Yessirreebob—a hard-on for one special *Ute* gal, Silas. Must be real sweet on her."

Titus glared up at Cooper. "We going today?"

"Why so all-fired ready to trot, pilgrim?"

"There's miles to put behind us and beaver to trap when we get there."

It took a moment, but Silas finally grinned a rotten-toothed smile. "I'll be damned," he said softly. "Maybeso that's why this here greenhorn nigger gonna make a better trapper'n either of you boys."

"I ain't no greenhorn no more, Silas."

Cooper looked him down, then up again. Then the man's dark eyes slowly went to the horizon where the Shoshone were disappearing beneath a distant cloud of dust. "No—I s'pose y' ain't no more at that, Titus Bass." When his red-rimmed eyes came back to Scratch, they were filled with a begrudging admiration. "Y've made a right respectable trapper outta yourself."

It was closer to praise than anything he'd ever gotten from his pap. Titus swallowed hard, wanting his words to come out even. "Good as you, Silas?"

"Almost," Cooper conceded. "But y' ain't good as me yet. Till that day y' are, best y' hang in with us."

He finally let himself breathe as Silas stepped away, back toward the shade of the tall cottonwoods where the leaves rattled and the flies buzzed. The way it felt, that was about as good a fragment of praise as he was ever going to get, Bass figured.

"You figger we can pull out come morning, Silas?"

Cooper did not speak again until he settled on his blankets and robes, cocking an elbow beneath his head as he sank back onto his saddle. "I s'pose since there ain't no more of that goddamned Ashley's likker . . . and them Snakes has took off with all the spread-leg wenches in this here country . . . we might just as well see how the country looks up to the Bighorn."

Scratch's heart skipped a beat. "Maybeso we go all the way to . . . the Yallerstone?"

Silas grinned. "Why—don't tell me y' heard about the Yallerstone all the way back to St. Lou?"

"I did. Word was it was good beaver country!"

For the moment Cooper appeared interested. "A place where a man might winter up?"

Bass hurried into the patch of shade, kneeling near the other three. "If a man's to winter up, Silas—might's well be in country where the spring trapping is its best."

"Awright, Scratch," the strap-jawed Cooper eventually replied. "Let's us just go see for our own selves that there Bighorn country y' heard so much spoke of."

Hannah snorted downstream.

High and wheezing.

A sound he'd never before heard come from the mule.

In his chest his breath froze like a chunk of January river ice. Scratch nearly choked trying to swallow down the thumping of his heart.

Then the mule bawled.

Like he was shot out of a cheap Indian-trade fusil, Bass flung the trap onto the bank and lunged out of the stream . . . but slipped back into the icy water. Angrily flinging himself against the bank again, he dragged his weight onto the frost-slickened grass by jabbing the sharpened float-pole into the ground, then throwing a leg up and onto the slippery ground, and finally seizing hold of the branches of fiery-red willow recently kissed by autumn's cold breath.

Grunting and grumbling in his exertions, Bass made enough noise to scare half the beaver for miles around right on out of the country.

Filling one hand with the fullstock Derringer rifle leaning against that red-leafed willow, Titus bent low without missing a step, his left hand sweeping up the camp ax from the ground where it rested among the heap of long float-sticks and the rest of his square-jawed traps.

Now he heard a grunting roar. Weren't the mule. But: Hannah answered in kind—braying for all she was worth.

Shards of pinkish light exploded before him as he slashed his way through the tall brush that climbed more than two feet over his head—his frantic race causing hoarfrost and icy particles to cascade into the new day's rosy light.

Another grunt, followed by a throaty and repeated snort as that new sound faded. Then Hannah *kee-raw*ed with as close to a plaintive call for help as he'd ever heard a mule make. Not in all those years wrestling mules into harness, those hours spent behind both a plow and some mighty powerful rear haunches, his youth wasted struggling against stubborn, pigheaded animals . . . could he remember hearing a mule make a desperate plea quite like that.

His moccasins slipped and slid as he dived this way and that. Spilling in his haste, Bass crashed to the hard, frozen ground on one knee and that hand clutching the rifle. Swearing under his breath, only a puff of frost broke his lips as he sprang up and lunged forward again—with his heart high in his throat as he cleared the last of the thick willow . . . and onto the strip of open ground at the border of the shadowy timber not yet touched by that single finger of sunlight creeping down the side of the frosty bowl.

Sliding to a stop, he brought the rifle down across the left wrist that held the ax. Quickly dragging his thumb back across the frizzen and hammer to assure that it was at full-cock, Bass jerked to the left.

Hannah stood upstream, pulling hard against the long lead rope he had tied around her ears and muzzle like a halter. Yanking with all she had in her, Hannah's eyes were about as wide as his mam's fancy-dinner saucers, her powerful rear haunches bent and that rump of hers nearly swaying on the ground as her hooves dug up deep furrows in a frantic bid to free herself from danger. Again and again she flailed her head side to side, lashing herself to escape the hold of the rope, where he had left her knotted to a tree with enough line that she could leisurely crop the dead, frozen grasses there at the border of the timber.

But in the next instant he wheeled right at the sound. He saw nothing from that direction, where he was positive he'd heard the rasp of a foreign noise. The hair prickling at the back of his neck, he suddenly picked up the scent of something on the wind. Like an animal, like old Tink herself—that family dog back in Kentucky—he measured the caliber of the upwind, attempting to sort out what that musky, heavy odor was that now prickled the hair on his arms beneath the buckskin war shirt and the heavy blanket capote.

He discovered he was sweating, even as cold as it was. While he stood there in the chill half light of early morn, sniffing into the wind, Scratch sensed a huge drop of sweat gather at the nape of his neck where his long hair clung, a pendulous drop that slowly sank down the course of his backbone to land against the dark-blue wool of his breechclout, pooling there at the base of his spine. Where it froze him like January ice water.

The wind shifted. And the stench of it came to Bass, smacking him in the face. He'd never smelled anything like this before. Danger—pure and simple. Something feral, wild, beastly.

Hannah cried out, head twisting, her eyes rolling to find him. She shifted her stance, plowing up more of the loose turf made fragrant and heady by the bed of decomposing pine needles under her hooves. The instant he started her way, Bass saw a flicker of some movement in the trees beyond her. There just beyond the edge of the timber . . . it moved again. Like a chunk of black light torn off the corduroy of shadow that was the forest itself at this early hour as day splintered night into giving way to a reluctant dawn.

With his next step, and the shadow's answering grunt—he knew.

Not that Bass had ever seen one himself since coming to the mountains. Lucky, he'd always figured. But he knew nonetheless. Something instinctive, perhaps. After all, he'd seen enough black and brown bears back east in those Kentucky woods.

"D-damn," he muttered under his breath as the beast rose from its exertions.

How Bass had ever missed the elk carcass when he'd led Hannah there earlier in the dim light of false dawn, he had no idea.

But there stood that huge, hunch-backed behemoth, busy uncovering its carrion. Tearing away at the dirt, rotting pine needles, branches, and saplings it had scraped over the huge partially eaten carcass the day before. Likely an elk, Titus figured—for the size of what was left of it.

Standing rooted to the spot, Titus found himself marveling at the sheer size of that animal intent over its next meal.

Hell, out here he was no longer surprised to find everything bigger than he had ever let his imagination run. Even though Isaac Washburn had told him over and over again the tale of how the sow grizzly cuffed and mauled and chewed on old Hugh Glass up by the Grand River—never had Scratch expected the animal to turn out to be so huge, come this close, near face-to-face.

With its returning to its recent kill just moments ago—was the beast's own feral stench carried on the wind to Hannah's sensitive nose? Had she winded the deadly silver-haired creature, attempted to flee, and cried out in terror when she found herself prisoner? Is that why the monster had grunted? Was it threatened by the mule?

Up the slope far to the right came a new snort. Followed by a series of grunts slowly fading in volume.

Hannah bawled anew, high and plaintive.

Dropping to one knee, Bass reluctantly took his eye off the shadow-ribboned silvertip just long enough to squint into the patchwork of light and dark farther up the nearby hillside.

This close to it, he felt the ground tremble. Bass jerked back to the left, finding the grizzly jumping up and down on all fours beside its carrion, massive muzzle pulled back to expose the rows of huge teeth, giant forepaws tearing at the ground, wagging its massive head from side to side. It too sniffed the air, then roared again with that sound completely new and foreign to Bass. A challenge. A lure. A call to battle.

Wau-au-au-au-gh-gh-gh!

From the hillside came its answer.

Wau-au-au-au . . . gh-gh-gh!

To Bass's left the grizzly stood on its hind legs.

As it rose to full height, Scratch felt himself shrink inside. Although it was giving its full attention to the nearby hillside, nonetheless Titus felt dwarfed by the sheer immensity of the beast as it balanced on its two hindquarters, clawing at the air as if shadowboxing. Long, curved claws tore shreds of reflected sunlight: glistening, honed razors slashing at the end of each heaving swipe, rending what wisps of cold mist remained among the black timber.

They were snorting at one another nonstop now. One roar answered almost immediately by the other, and both drowning out the feeble bray of the frightened mule. The grizzly he could see whirled about on its haunches and dropped to all fours, quickly circling the elk carcass, savagely flinging dirt and pine needles back onto its kill in some feeble attempt to hide it from the approaching challenger.

Considering what to do in that instant as the forest's terror was now suddenly doubled, Bass wondered if he should dash over and release Hannah. What with the way she rolled her eyes at the grizzly, then danced back in that confining arc to roll her eyes at him—bawling with that high-pitched squeal of hers. But if he did, his instincts told him . . . he'd be left on foot.

Hannah would wheel and run, yanking the rope from his cold, bare hands, likely bowling him over in her eagerness to flee as far away from there as she could. Maybe not stopping until she made it back to camp upstream, perhaps even into the next valley, where they had trapped out just about everything with a flat-tail on it before moving here yesterday.

How he'd come to rely on her, trust her, cantankerous and contrary as a mule could be, yet coming to respect her as he never had respected such a stubborn animal while a youngster made to work with mules, together tearing long furrows in the dark, loamy soil of Boone County. But there was something entirely different about this animal.

Through the past winter and into his productive spring hunt, then as the seasons turned to summer's rendezvous and finally their moseying into the Wind River range, trapping and tramping, easing north all the more . . . Bass had come to care for the young mule, more than he had ever cared for an animal. A time or two he had even allowed himself to believe the mule cared for him too.

So it had surprised him—as suspicious as he was about mules from those long-ago days on his pap's land in Rabbit Hash—when Hannah would slip up behind him without a sound, with no warning, as he was going about some camp chore, suddenly swinging her thick muzzle into that hollow between his bony shoulder blades. Knocking him down, sprawling into the dirt that first time. Heels over head a second time. Sent skidding on his rump a third time—just starting to twist about with the faintest sound of her approach.

Always careful to pick her time and place, Hannah grew more crafty as the months rolled by. It became her own private way to play him the fool—this stunt she loved to pull on him. The mule never seemed to tire of it. Nor did she seem to take much heed of the way he scolded her, shook his finger at her as he clambered off the ground and brushed himself off, his cheeks crimson with embarrassment at the way the other three trappers gushed with laughter, snorting at how boneheaded he was to allow the mule her folly with him when he should either whack her upside of the head, or shoot her.

Each time she succeeded in sneaking up on him—he figured it was nothing more than a knot not being tight enough . . . but this time she was held fast. In that instant he decided he wouldn't free her.

Not just yet, he wouldn't—not when she'd likely bolt off and leave him stranded. Scratch wasn't about to try outrunning a grizzly. Not from all that he'd heard tell of the beast. Not from what common sense told him was purely a fool's errand. No mere, mortal man could dare outrace a behemoth like that on all fours. It made no matter that it would be an obstacle course, darting in and out among the trees, lunging over deadfall, ducking branches, and avoiding those slick, icy patches of winter's first snow still tucked way back in among the dark, sunless places. No matter that he would be on two feet and this monster on four.

Something feral, wild, and untamed within him told Titus that the surest way for a man in his predicament to throw his life away was to try fleeing. From where that spark of wildness came, he knew not. Only that it rested at the deepest marrow of him—and enough had transpired in his nearly thirty-three years that proved to him he should listen to the flicker of its voice.

Was it something in his lineage, in the breeding, in that Scottish ancestry that harkened back to all those generations among the lowlands, clan ancestors stealing down from the misty hills and out across the foggy moors to relieve the arrogant lords and the British army of so many of their horses? Was it all those centuries of Basses pilloried and tortured by fire, all those Basses hung at the end of short ropes, Basses torn apart by four stout draft horses each whipped in four different directions, all at the hands of the king's servants . . . or was it something given birth on this continent in recent generations? Some feral otherworldly sense born in the blood of his grandpap, who as a young man had fought in the wilderness against the French and their Indians, then so soon thereafter chose to make his family's stand on the Ohio River frontier against the English and their Indians, as the colonials tore themselves apart from the Tories and Loyalists and George III himself?

If that wildness was truly something passed down in the blood—then how did one explain Thaddeus? If this uncanny savvy was sunk so to the core of Titus, then why was his own pap content to carve settlement out of wilderness, to domesticate and till and build where only the untamed beasts and half-naked savages had roamed?

Was that why he was here among these great mountains and high valleys, after all? Titus had asked himself many a time.

Had he ventured far, far past the last outpost of settlement, leaping past the final vestiges of civilization, just so he could find himself as far from everything that was his father . . . if only to prove that the blood that had driven his grandpap to hack out a path through the wilderness to seek out a new home was still the blood that ran hot and thick in Titus's own veins? Was he more the grandson? Or had he come here to these far places to prove to himself, if to no one else, that he was not Thaddeus Bass's eldest son?

Wau-au-au-ghghghgh!

With the soul-shattering roar from the nearby grizzly, Bass jerked about. The stench from both creatures was unbelievably raw, primal, deadly.

Waugh-ngg-ngg-ngg-ngg!

In that moment the second grizzly burst into view on the slope above him. Every bit as big as the first, it might well weigh even more.

Now it bounced up and down on its four paws, then lumbered clumsily onto its hindquarters. With its foreclaws slashing at the air, it reared its head back, the slobbery muzzle pulled away to bare its yellowed teeth, shaking the massive skull that seemed to rest momentarily on the huge hump between its shoulders.

Crashing back onto all four legs, the second monster continued its march out of the shadows toward the first grizzly, who was pacing about his carrion territorially, putting himself between the carcass and the intruder. He clawed the ground savagely, tearing up huge clumps of the moist, partially frozen forest floor with his six-inch claws, black clods of earth spraying here, sailing there. Now and again for but a moment he would stop to growl at the interloper before returning to his bristling, defensive behavior.

At the same time the newcomer would halt after every few steps, roaring his challenge, bouncing a bit on all fours and wagging his head as he exposed his rows of teeth, jaws slobbering in anticipation of his meal. Then he continued down the gentle slope through the timber toward his opponent.

And that carcass that had lured him here from miles away.

More closely related to the hog family than anything else, the bear used its keenest sense to locate food and avoid danger. From far downstream, miles away at the mouth of another valley, the interloper had whiffed his first, faint hint of that rotting meat. And as he had turned into the wind to investigate that telltale dawn breeze, the seductive stench grew stronger and stronger. On and on he had come—until he also began to pick up the smell of one of his own kind.

Yet what truly confused him for a moment was the odor of two other creatures he could not identify . . . not with his dim eyesight as he studied the two-legged and then the frightened four-legged only briefly from this distance. But that smell of blood and sundered flesh quickly recaptured his attention each time his thoughts wandered to the other creatures. That, and the challenge raised by one of his own kind standing guard over the feast that had brought him from so, so far.

Already with the first snowfall come to these high slopes and deep valleys, the ancient clocks were ticking within these creatures as autumn aged, as winter crept farther down from the high places, a great cold racing all the faster out of the north. Something ageless and without rationale had instructed both of these boars to spend the long days of their short summer months feasting on the rich, nutritious plants of this high country. But as the temperatures began to drop, especially after that first heavy snowfall that had taken days to melt off from the exposed slopes, some new biological imperative had taken over within the beasts. As the grizzly neared its time for hibernation, it no longer was satisfied with leaves and stems and roots. Now as the weather turned cold—the grizzly needed meat.

A terrible season for these boars as they hunted the meat they craved, while at the same time the calendar within them also aroused the ancient itch to mate, to rut, to satisfy that which can be quenched only by coupling with a sow. So it was that in these last days before the deep sleep of winter, the boars roamed their valleys in search of meat and females, their temperament constantly on edge, easily irritable—more than ready for battle or the long sleep that would relieve them of their hungers and their itches.

So first the interloper had to find out if the protector was a sow.

When he reached a spot some twenty-five feet from the carcass, he raised his nose into the air again, sniffing everything he could while the protector rumbled his defiance.

No—the interloper decided: there wasn't a hint of a female here. No rich, heady aroma that heretofore told him a sow was indeed in heat and ready to accept what he needed to scratch. With a disgusted snort of disappointment he lowered his head, chin almost to the ground as he lumbered side to side, wagging that head he had drawn defensively back into the huge hump to make himself appear all the bigger.

There would be no rutting this day. But there just might be a free meal . . . if he could drive off this other boar with a few measured cuffs of his massive paws, given deadly execution by his powerful shoulders.

As soon as the interloper turned its full attention back to the protector, Scratch began his sidelong creep, slowly inching his way toward Hannah. She continued her *keer-rawwv*ing without stop, even though she kept flicking her eyes from those silver-tipped monsters to her owner, back and forth, over and over. Little chance she was relieved to see her master coming her way. He was all too slow.

While the protector backed up a few feet, he was in reality rocking back on all fours, as if cocking himself, preparing to launch his bulk right into his enemy. He crouched there, snarling, huge jaws frothing in anticipation, his body shuddering with uncontrollable passions. The same juices that prepared him to fight also readied him for coupling with a sow. And for now—the hot fire of those juices shooting through his veins and heaving muscles brought nothing but frightening confusion.

A few yards off the interloper lunged back, rising onto its hind legs, a forepaw ripping bark from a nearby pine tree. Shards of blackened bark exploded off the trunk in all directions, exposing the deep yellow wounds that would soon ooze with pitch.

Shuddering at the vicious explosion, Bass sank back to his haunches near the line of willows. Glanced at Hannah. Then swallowed hard as he turned his attention back to the two monsters. By damn, if a griz could do that sort of damage to the tough, hardened bark of an old pine tree, just think of what the beast could do against mere flesh and sinew.

Then the protector rose on his hind legs, head brought forward as far as he could out of the hump, jaws open wide, but only momentarily, until he began snapping them, clawing at the air, growling loud enough that the sound of both boars rocked back from the valley walls in a never-ending cascade of reverberation.

With a blur of silver-tipped shadow, the two bears lunged, closed, arms swinging, clawing, clutching their enemy at last. Snapping their muzzles ferociously, both tried repeatedly to sink fangs into the other—groping for an ear, biting the muzzle, sinking teeth into the tip of the nose or that thick slab of protective ridge of brow bone over an eye socket.

Then down they tumbled in a heap. Something akin to a frightened yelp burst from one of them as they flew apart, shaking their tough, thick hides . . . then wheeled quickly to relocate the adversary—charging on all fours.

When they collided again, the ground beneath Bass shook even more than it had before. As the grizzlies locked themselves together, their bodies rippled and shook with the strain of muscles tested to the maximum. Over and over one another they tumbled, smashing against the trunks of great trees and careening over saplings that snapped like kindling wood, four hind legs flailing, akimbo as each fought for balance, to seize the upper hand.

Then the protector found a soft, vulnerable target in the other boar's snout—and clamped down with his mighty jaws.

Squealing just like a scalded hog, the interloper struggled this way, then that, to free himself. But in the end he flung the protector off only by pitching his opponent over his shoulder against an old pine that shuddered with the tremendous force of the blow as the protector spilled to the ground, having released his grip on the enemy. Shaking his head in a daze, the protector sat there a moment.

Sat there too long.

The bloodied interloper was upon him that quickly, sinking his teeth into the back of the protector's neck, one front paw yanking the opponent's jaws back as he raked and raked with the long claws, biting again and again, filling his huge mouth with the neck tissue there at the rise of the great hump.

Twisting to his left, then twisting to his right, the protector tried vainly to snap at the enemy who had its teeth sunk into his neck, long claws slashing at his vulnerable throat, hindquarters raking along his back. Blood glistened the protector's coat from muzzle to rump as the boar rolled over, slamming its enemy against the tree. Still the interloper would not release his grip.

Groaning, growling, whining in pain and dismay, the huge protector flailed away at nothing more than thin air, unable to land a paw on his adversary stuck like a spring tick on his back. Meanwhile the interloper snorted each time he sank a more secure hold on the tough, thick hair and hide of the protector's neck—a grunt of impending victory. He drew his head back slightly, eyes wild, taking measure of where next to plant his powerful jaws.

Suddenly the roar of the protector became a high-pitched squeal the instant he burst free of the enemy's grasp. Free at last, he tumbled rump over head before he came up, dazed, surprised to find he had escaped. Now some ten yards or more away, he shook his whole body, licked quickly at one of the glistening wounds, then set himself for the interloper's attack.

But instead of pursuing his adversary, the interloper settled to his rear haunches, his big tongue lolling out of those slabbering jaws to slap across the bloody slashes on his own muzzle, trying to ease the torment in that most sensitive part of his anatomy. He snorted and swiped at his muzzle with a paw slicked with drying blood and his enemy's hair. Then he noticed the new scent. Turned to look. And finally discovered what it was that had lured him there from so far away.

Lumbering up the slope to the ruins of the elk carcass, the interloper sniffed it over from broken neck to the rear quarters, where the hide had been torn back and huge gashes made in the thick muscle. Then his nose nuzzled down toward the belly. With a ravenous roar he brought his muzzle out bright with gore and blood dripping, having discovered the soft innards.

At that provocation the protector leaped forward a few yards menacingly, snarling. But he was stopped in his tracks just as quickly as he had started for the interloper, which immediately raised himself halfway and growled that frightening roar of battle. It was enough to give the protector pause.

He settled back on his haunches as the interloper went back to his feast . . . then, while his adversary ate on the food just taken from him, the protector suddenly poked his nose into the air—as if catching the hint of something on the wind. A moment more and that battered snout sank slowly, his huge blood-flecked eyes narrowing as would any predator who has caught scent of his prey.

Titus watched the nostrils flare as more slobber drooled from the lower lips.

The bear raised itself to all fours and took a step from the trees when it was immediately stopped by a warning snarl from the interloper busy at its bloody feast. Instead of protesting, the defeated boar turned slightly and lumbered off at an angle away from the victor so that he would clearly present no threat to the carcass.

He had something else in mind altogether.

As the badly wounded grizzly cleared the shadows into the first spray of sunlight crowning the forest that dawn, Titus shuddered again. To watch the muscles ripple as it advanced, the way the long hairs of its coat alternately caught and hid the light with each stretch and contraction of its hide, and how the blood glistened at its torn neck, back in the dark furrows on the haunches, or gathered in frozen coagulate across the hump . . . his fingers tightened on the wrist of the rifle.

No. Bass refused to believe it.

But there was the monster, plotting a due course for Hannah.

Then the grizzly stopped, sniffed—and rose to its hind legs, measuring the breeze again. Slowly turning aside from the mule and its loud braying, as if it suddenly couldn't hear the pack animal, or at least did not care. Eventually the snout came round to point in Scratch's direction.

Titus froze where he was, squatting in the brush at the edge of the tall red-leafed willow. He was sure the beast could clearly hear his heart hammering in his chest.

After two lumbering steps forward the ungainly grizzly dropped to all fours, snorted, and turned back to its original course—the mule. For a moment he was relieved and let the air rush out of his chest in a great gust . . . until he realized the creature still wanted Hannah.

"No!"

Bass hollered before he thought, before he could catch himself. And found he was on his feet, standing, bringing the rifle to his hip, laid over that left forearm still clutching the camp ax.

As if the beast ignored him entirely, the grizzly picked up its pace. Its huge frame rocked from side to side as it rolled on down the gentle slope toward the mule. Hannah thrashed and kicked—at times she turned her rump in its direction, preparing to deliver a sharp hoof against her attacker, then other times she tried to pull away at the end of the long rope, bawling, tail whipping in the breeze.

Before he realized what he was doing, Bass found himself sprinting on a collision course for the two of them, wondering if he was going to make it in time before the angry, bloodied grizzly lunged for the helpless mule.

"You son of a bitch!" he screamed.

For some strange reason the bear skidded to a halt at that, quartered to its left as it stretched up to its hind legs, there to stand and stare at him. Then, as quickly, it lunged forward onto its front paws again . . . as if suddenly discovering Bass. Wiggling its head around—the better to see with its poor vision and to smell with that powerful nose—the grizzly no longer peered at him with eyes filled by wild aggression. Instead they appeared confused, as the massive creature poked its long snout in the air and attempted to take its own measure of this strange, noisy, two-legged creature.

But at that moment Hannah chose to let out another frightened, braying yelp.

The monster turned back to her as suddenly—drawn by the plaintive bawl of the four-legged animal. Perhaps that cry was more of something the boar understood far better than the spoken language of the two-legged mystery.

As if dismissing the man, the grizzly lumbered to its four paws and continued toward Hannah, its jaws snapping greedily as the mule's bray was choked off in a frightened peal.

Skidding to a stop less than twenty-some yards from the bear, Scratch slammed the rifle into his shoulder, peered down the barrel, and slipped the narrow front-blade sight over the slowly moving animal until he had the grizzly's chest at the center of his sight-picture and set the trigger. As the bear rocked back on its haunches, throwing one paw into the air to take a warning swipe at the mule frantically kicking at its attacker, Scratch eased back on the front trigger.

With a roar the rifle shoved itself back into his shoulder. Through the cold smudge of gun smoke he watched the boar swat at his chest with the same paw he had used to claw the air, then sniffed at his wound beginning to ooze a little blood. The grizzly licked it, snorted, then turned back to Hannah, now angrier than before.

How he wished he had time to reload the more powerful rifle as he yanked the pistol from the sash tied around his capote. His hands were shaking as he checked the powder in the pan, dragged the frizzen back down, and cocked the hammer. He knew he would have to get all the closer now to his target. Even though the pistol threw the same-size ball as his rifle, there wasn't nearly the punch, nor the powder charge.

He closed to within ten yards before the bear had reached the sidestepping mule.

"You touch her—you're goin' to hell right here!"

With a loud roar the boar stood again, swiping at the air, presenting Scratch the best shot of all. Holding right on the center of the beast's chest, Bass pulled the trigger. He felt the weapon jerk in his hand. But through the haze of smoke saw the grizzly merely settle to its rump as it rubbed its paw on its chest. Another flesh wound.

Making it even angrier than before.

Flinging the pistol aside, Bass swung the ax from left hand to right as the bear shot to its hind legs, then slowly settled a second time. It snorted at the noisy mule, then slowly began to close the distance between it and the annoying two-legged.

Clutching the ax in both hands, Scratch brought it over his head, preparing for the attack.

Run, his instincts told him.

Again, everything he had ever heard tell about the grizzly reminded him he wouldn't have a chance running. Not in an out-and-out footrace. The only prayer he had would be to leap to the side at the last instant, jump behind and to the side, and then maybe—just maybe—he could drive the ax down into the creature's skull, splitting it open like an overripe fruit.

Unconscious of anything but the beast, Scratch barely heard the snort of a horse and the warning whinny of another above Hannah's frightened bawl as the boar drew nigh—close enough for him to smell the dank, musky stench of the animal, to sense the fetid breath stinking of the rotted carrion it had been feasting upon. Hot and repulsive: every bit as much so as was the stench of death.

Lifting the ax higher in both hands, Scratch watched the bear rise slightly as it closed to within five feet . . . four feet . . . then its mighty arms came out like the jaws of a huge steel trap as the beast roared, loud enough to block out all sound—breath filled with such a stink, Bass wanted to close his eyes . . .

But he kept them open, trained on his enemy—and just as the grizzly lunged with those swinging arms and slashing razors, Scratch pitched to the left, diving right under the beast's huge front leg. Before he consciously thought what to do, before the monster even began to turn, Titus savagely hurled the ax down on the back of the bear's head, sinking it deep into the thick, tough neck muscle, feeling the bone crack and splinter at the base of the creature's skull all the way into his forearms.

As he yanked back on the ax handle, he was sure he would never budge it. Though he tried again—the ax head did not move, buried in splintered bone and sinew and muscle. Slick as the handle was with hot, sticky blood, Bass could hold on no longer as the beast shuddered, flinging the man aside.

With a cry of great pain the grizzly whirled on its two-legged tormentor just as Scratch pulled his last weapon from its scabbard on his belt. The skinning knife wasn't much—but it was all he was left with . . . and there and then he vowed he wasn't about to go down without using it all on the monster.

With a vicious swipe the grizzly split the air an inch from Titus's face. Bass jerked backward so quickly, he nearly lost his balance. Lunging, the boar was on him, arms locked around Scratch's shoulders, the first paw drawn up and back, preparing to rake as the huge jaws opened and sought to close down on the coyote-skin cap the man wore.

Then, as quickly as he thought death had him in its clutches . . . the monster freed him, flinging the two-legged tormentor away like so much river flotsam.

Bass landed on his back, stunned a moment, the breath knocked out of him—then watched in astonishment as the grizzly slowly turned its butchered head this way, then that, as the two men came up on either side of it.

From that deadly close range they both fired their pistols now, taking steely, deliberate aim. And as the muzzle smoke billowed up, he watched Tuttle and Hooks dance side to side out of the way of the bear's weakening attempts to lunge out with its immense arms . . . when an immense shadow suddenly crossed behind Bass, all but stepping over him—coming between the fallen man and the wounded grizzly.

Stopping no more than arm's length from the beast, Cooper brazenly stuffed the muzzle of his rifle right into the bear's wide, snarling mouth . . . shoved it right on to the back of the creature's throat and pulled the trigger with a jerk.

The back of the bear's head exploded, thrust backward as Cooper leaped out of the way. Both Tuttle and Hooks stepped aside as the immense beast stumbled on backward a few lumbering steps, then came crashing down on its back.

For several long moments—none of them moved. No one made a sound. Then . . .

Still holding the empty rifle pointed at the grizzly, Silas asked quietly, "It dead, Billy?"

Hooks moved cautiously forward. "T'ain't breathin', Silas."

"For balls' sake," Tuttle whispered, "he's a big'un!"

"Y' two stay back," Cooper warned. He pulled his own belt pistol, a huge smoothbore with an immense flintlock on it, and swapped his rifle to his left hand.

Only when he stood over the bear, straddling one of the beast's forelegs, did he finally look at Titus. "Y' ain't never run onto griz afore, have y', pilgrim?"

Scratch dragged a hand across his lips. "N-n-no, I ain't."

"That ax in the back of the head's a bright idee, it is," Cooper explained. "But shootin' for the heart like y' done be just a waste of time. Ol' Ephraim here can eat you and ever' last one of us in the time it takes for two dozen balls to get through his tough ol' hide, Scratch."

Gulping, Bass could only nod.

Cooper rose to full height, placed one moccasin on the bear's chest, there on the blood-slickened hide. "I s'pose I'm cursed with havin' to teach y' ever' lesson, ain't I, Titus Bass?"

"Leastways," Bass replied in a harsh whisper, "you l'arn't me 'bout bears."

"Why—lookee here," Cooper said, smiling as he swept a hand the length of the grizzly carcass, "I've done gone an' saved your worthless life again."

FIFTEEN

Ol' Scratch, they were calling him now.

"On account of you gettin' the green wore off," Billy Hooks told him one morning early that spring of 1827 as they were on their way west, making for the Three Forks country.

As if it was something learned, Bass looked over at Silas Cooper for some sort of confirmation. The big man squatted by the fire, warming his hands, late that morning after they had been out since well before first light, setting traps among the streams that watered the Yellowstone north of what would one day soon come to be known among the mountain men as Colter's Hell.

"Billy ain't tellin' y' no bald-face, Scratch," the black-bearded man agreed. There flashed one of those exceedingly rare twinkles of good humor in the marblelike eyes. "That's for sartin. Y' see'd yourself through your second winter: now, that makes a man a hivernant, or I don't know poor bull from fat cow."

"Ol' Scratch," Bud Tuttle repeated it now, grinning as he clearly took some pleasure in that coronation. "It's purely some for a man's companions to start callin' him *Ol'* this or *Ol'* that. Hell, Titus—these here bastards don't even call me Ol' Bud!"

"Plain as your own ugly mug that y' ain't earned yourself that name the way Scratch here has," Cooper sniped. "He's come to be twice the trapper y' are."

Tuttle pursed his lips and nodded. "I cain't argee with y' there, Silas. Scratch's better'n both Billy an' me—so why you call Billy Ol' Billy and y' don't call me Ol' Bud?"

Cooper slowly pulled the ramrod out of the long fullstock's barrel, doubled the small oily patch back over, and drove it back into the muzzle, shoving it all the way down to the breech as he swabbed burned, blackened, sulfurous-stinking powder out the barrel. "True enough Scratch is better'n the two of you at bringing them flat-tails to bait. But the reason I likely ain't ever gonna call you Ol' Bud is you ain't never gonna be half the mountain man Billy is. An' Scratch here," Silas said as he dragged the ramrod out of the barrel and pointed it at Bass, "why—he's already got Billy beat way up on that stick."

Instead of protesting, Hooks merely took that appraisal in stride. Looking over at Bass, Billy said, "I figger Silas got that right, Scratch. After two winters with us'ns, you already come to be near good as Cooper."

With a faint grin cracking his black beard, Cooper looked up at Bass and replied, "Near good as me, Scratch."

"You got you a long head start on me, Silas," Titus conceded, self-effacing and aware that he must never put himself in a class with their forty-five-year-old leader.

Into the fire Cooper tossed the small round patch of cloth, well-lathered with bear oil and blackened powder from the grooves of his rifle. Landing on a blazing limb, where it spat and sizzled a moment before the edges began to turn black, Silas declared, "And there h'ain't no use in you figgerin' y'll ever catch up to me neither. Makes no matter that you're a dozen years younger'n this nigger. No matter neither how good y' figger to get at trappin' or trackin' or nothin', Scratch."

"I ain't ever tried to be better'n—"

Cooper interrupted, "Because y' don't stand a whore's chance at Sunday meeting of ever outriding, outfighting, outpokin', or outkillin' me."

With a shrug Bass admitted, "Plain you be a better man'n all of us, Silas."

"Damn right I am," Cooper declared as he wiped an oily patch up and down the browned barrel of his rifle. "An' there h'ain't nothin' the three of you can ever do what can change that."

Bobbing his head, Hooks said, "You're the booshway of this here outfit, Silas Cooper! Big bull in this here lick!"

Chuckling a moment, Cooper finally said, "But don't go getting the idee that means none of y' can let up on trying to outtrap the other fellas, now. This nigger wants to have us more plew to trade than any four men rightly should."

"Ought'n make that Ashley trader's eyes shine to see all the packs we'll have to trade 'im come summer—right, Silas?" Tuttle exclaimed.

Cooper's face turned grave as he explained, "Lately I been thinkin' of just where we go come summer."

"Wh-where we go?" Serious concern crossed Billy's face as he continued sputtering, "Ain't w-we headin' down to Sweet Lake to m-meet them company boys for ronnyvoo?"

With a shrug of a shoulder and scratch at his chin, Silas replied, "Once't I got it all worked out up here in my noggin', then I figger it's time to tell y' three the way it's gonna be for summer trampin'."

"Trader's likker and all them niggers joinin' up after a long winter of it," Tuttle mused. "Ronnyvoo is what I been thinkin' on more an' more ever' day my own self, Silas."

"G'won now an' don't none of y' worry a lick 'bout it," Cooper confided with that mouthful of big yellow teeth. "When I figger out just what we're gonna do—I s'pect my idee'll damn well make sense to the hull durn lot of y'."

So it was that the three continued to let the one do their thinking for them. Where to go for the beaver, and when to move on to the next camp. Which bands to winter with and what Injuns to avoid. All the trails and passes, every inch of the routes they had traveled, moseying down one stream and wandering up the next, all across this last year and a half—how quickly Titus had learned that Billy and Bud left nearly everything requiring a decision squarely in Cooper's lap.

And that's how they had come to spend this past winter with the tall and haughty Crow, a season known among that tribe as *baalee*, "When the Ponies Grow Lean."

From that mountain valley where Titus learned all he ever cared to know about grizzlies last autumn, the white men had continued easing their way on north, down into the fertile lowlands, where many of the streams draining the high country were dammed here and there, the timbered and sheltered places converted into deep ponds where the industrious flat-tails constructed their beaver lodges. There, too late one autumn day, they had spotted the first Indian they had seen since rendezvous.

It had started off snowing earlier that morning, no more than an inch or two of fine, dry flakes. Nothing at all like the heavy, wet, icy snow that Titus had known back east. By afternoon, as the four of them saddled up once more and set out to check their traplines, the thick charcoal blanket of clouds had even begun to scatter and lift. A few shafts of brilliant light touched the valley here and there with gold, shimmering against the new, pristine snow.

"How far you figger it is till we reach this here Yallerstone country we aimin' for?" Hooks asked as the horsemen eased up out of the willows and onto the flats again, across the narrow creek from their campsite.

Cooper wagged his head, staring off. "Got no idea how much farther it be. Just that it still lays north some."

"A handful of days," Bass offered abruptly with such conviction that he even surprised himself. It took a moment before he noticed the way the other three had turned to regard him in wonder. A bit self-conscious, he added, "No more'n a week."

"That true, Silas?" Tuttle inquired, eyeing suspiciously.

"How the hell'd I know? I never come through this way!" Cooper snapped; then he glared at Bass. "So tell us just how the hell y' think y' know."

"Don't," Bass answered. "Not for certain. Just feels like it ain't all that far."

Turning back around in his saddle, Silas grumbled, "I s'pose we'll just have to see about—"

"L-lookee there, Silas!" Hooks interrupted with a sputter.

The other three looked where Billy was pointing. Off to the north on the brow of a hill sat a half-dozen horsemen, something on the order of a mile away, maybe a little more. They sat there motionless as statues, as if they had always been there on the crest of that rise.

Tuttle whispered hoarsely, "W-where'd they come from?"

"Keep moving," Cooper said, his voice gone quiet despite the great distance between the two parties.

"We just let 'em know we see 'em, eh?" Bud asked.

"I s'pose that's the make of it," Cooper agreed.

Billy dragged the greasy wool of his capote sleeve across his lower face and asked, "What you make 'em to be, Silas?"

"They ain't Blackfoot," Titus declared instead.

Flicking the younger man a glare, Cooper answered, "They ain't Black-foot—that's as plain as paint."

Tuttle asked, "How come you say not?"

"Blackfoot wouldn't let us see 'em," Silas replied.

To which Bass added, "Damn right: Blackfoot'd just sit off somewhere and watch us, maybeso wait to lay onto us somewhere up the trail."

"You figger it that way, Silas?" Hooks said, turning to Cooper for confirmation.

"I figger this young'un here might be right on that, first whack." Then for a moment Cooper studied the distant figures there against the backdrop of that lifting gray sky: loose hair and feathers, scalp locks and fringe tussled with the tease of every little gust of breeze that crossed that hilltop. "Yeah—Scratch likely be right, fellas. This here got the feel of Crow country. And I figger them Crow just lookin' us over to see what we're all about."

Bass inquired, "Ever you been to Crow country?"

"Not this far south," Cooper explained. "We come on down the Yallerstone with Henry's bunch many a year back. Got as far as the mouth of the Bighorn. But I ain't never been south from there."

Billy nodded. "Yessirreebob—this here's new country to us all!"

"What you s'pose is up now?" Tuttle asked.

They were watching as the half-dozen horsemen all turned away together and slowly disappeared over the backside of the hill.

"I figger we'll find out soon enough," Cooper answered, his words doing damned little to allay any apprehensions.

But to play things smart, Silas sent Billy and Tuttle back to camp with orders to bring in the pack animals and sideline them—just in the event those six horsemen decided to romp on through and drive off a few mules and horses for themselves.

For the rest of that afternoon Cooper and Bass never strayed from eyeshot of one another: most often Silas was the one to stay in the saddle, watching and listening, attentive to the middistance, while Titus checked each one of the group's sets, pulling out a beaver here and there if one of the wary animals had stretched his rodent luck enough. They were back at their camp to rejoin the others well before twilight as the temperature began to slide rapidly and the western sky became a burnished autumn umber—bringing with it cold enough to cause a man's thoughts to turn to buffalo robes and warming his feet by a fire.

For the next three days, as watchful as they were, not one of them saw a telltale sign of any horsemen. It was almost enough to make a man disbelieve he'd seen anything of horse-mounted warriors that winter afternoon as the sky cleared and the sun broke through.

Then came the fourth morning.

As was usually the case, Bass awoke before the others in the dark, cold stillness of predawn. Dragging the buffalo robe and blankets around him as he shifted closer to the fire ring, he punched life back into the coals, filled the coffeepot with icy water from the trickle still flowing in the nearby creekbed, then nudged the others before he moved off to the mouth of a nearby ravine where he had picketed Hannah and his horse right in camp. Being the first up most every morning just naturally saddled Titus with the responsibility of freeing up the stock from their picket pins, usually put out to graze on the downwind side of camp some distance away, taking the animals to water while the coffee heated.

After returning from the creek with Hannah and his saddle mount, tying them to a span of rope strung between two trees where he had made his bed, Titus headed off toward the copse of old timber where the rest of the stock had been picketed for the night.

He was breathless by the time he sprinted back into camp to find the others just sitting up in their blankets, rubbing grit from eyes and scratching one place or another on their dirty anatomies.

"The horses! They're gone!"

Cooper rose to one knee as the robe slipped off his shoulders, turning to stare right at the mule and horse. "Pray y' tell me what the hell those are!"

Huffing to a halt, Bass braced his hands on his knees, heaving for air at the same time he tried to explain. "Not them . . . I didn't . . . put mine down . . . with your'n."

"What're y' trying to say?"

"Rest of the stock's gone."

"Gone?" Cooper repeated. "Y' mean y' found they all just pulled up their pins an' moseyed off last night?"

"Unh-uh," Titus replied. "They didn't pull up pins and mosey off—"

Silas leaped off the ground, fists working and angry. "Goddammit! Tell me!"

"They was took!"

Squinting hard as he stood glowering down at the shorter Bass, Silas demanded, "How the hell y' so sure they was took?"

"I see'd tracks."

"Horse tracks?"

"No," Titus answered. "Mokerson tracks. Lots of 'em."

The three of them had followed Scratch to the nearby grove, where they read what story the hard, brittle grass and flaky soil had to tell them. More than a dozen of them by a reasonable count—at least ten, anyway . . . all crept into the stand of trees together, spread out, and began silently cutting the picket ropes from the pins driven securely into the hard ground. One by one the horses and mules had been led away in the direction the thieves had come on foot—until they reached a spot about a mile away, where it was plain to see the warriors had tied their own ponies.

Back and forth over the ground the four of them moved, bent at the waist, stopping to kneel from time to time, studying. But not one of them studied the ground as much as Titus Bass. The way the moccasins curved tightly down from the big toe along the tops of the other toes at a sharp angle. Except for the size of each print, and perhaps the depth of each print and the length of stride—those factors accounting for the varying height and weight of the thieves—the moccasins were all made the same: although sewn by different women, they all appeared to be cut from some very similar pattern.

"Lookee here, fellas," Bass said as he laid his own right foot down beside a clear impression of a thief's right foot.

As the others came up, Titus slowly lifted his own moccasin.

"What the hell y' got to show me?" Cooper snapped.

"Look," Bass repeated, squatting to point at the thief's print. "See how this'un's shaped like this, here an' here."

"Yeah," Hooks replied. "So?"

"See here on my print I just made," Bass instructed. "It don't look the same, does it?"

"I be go to hell and et for a tater!" Tuttle gushed, kneeling beside Bass and pointing. "It ain't the same, Silas."

Wheeling on Bass, Cooper spat, "S'pose y' go and tell me what good that's gonna do us, Scratch."

With a shrug Bass said, "No earthly good a'tall."

Fuming, Cooper declared, "Then why all the preachin', y' weasel-stoned pup?"

"Just show you something I figgered out," he said as Cooper wheeled away angry. "Figgered out . . . all on my own."

Titus stood there watching the backs of the other two join Silas Cooper's as all three stomped off for camp—on foot. The wind punched right out of his sails, and with no one wanting to share in the joy of his personal discovery, his shoulders began to sag as he followed in their wake.

For the rest of that morning the four of them worked feverishly at hiding from view and prying eyes what beaver they had taken that season, caching the packs of plews and what excess plunder they couldn't pack off now, stowing all of it here and there within the thickest clumps of willow and alder—as out of sight as they could make it. Then they covered their sign the best they knew how, dragging branches over their footprints so no tracks would point the way to their cache of beaver and camp goods.

With Hannah and that lone saddle horse swaybacked beneath all their blankets and robes, along with their cooking gear, some coffee, flour, beads, and vermilion, in addition to several extra pounds of powder and a few bars of bullet lead, the four finally set out on foot shortly after midday . . . following the backtrail of the horse thieves.

Most all day Cooper muttered under his breath until they made camp that first evening. As twilight sucked the last warmth out of the sky, Scratch took Hannah's long picket rope and tied it to the wide leather belt holding his capote around his waist when he curled up in the robes and blankets, his feet toward the fire. Billy Hooks did the same with the saddle horse. They were not about to chance losing these last two animals to whatever thieves roamed that country. That first tug, even a faint tussle on the ropes, would serve as the alarm.

By the time it was slap dark that frigid autumn evening, Silas, Scratch, and Tuttle were asleep. Each in turn would be awakened through the long night to stand his watch: to listen to the distant call of the owls on the wing, the cry of the wolves on the prowl and the yapping of the nearby coyotes; to sit alone and feed the fire while the others snored. Alone in one's thoughts of women and liquor, remembrances of old faces and young breasts and thighs. To think back as the cold nuzzled more and more firmly around a man, here in the marrow of the Rocky Mountains.

The following morning they awoke to a lowering sky. The wind that had been puffing gently out of the west quickly quartered around, picking up speed as it came out of the north. With no other choice they walked into the brutal teeth of that wind until early afternoon when the clouds on the far horizon began to clot and blacken, hurrying in to blot out the sun. Within an hour icy sleet began to pelt them, coating everything, man and animal and all their provisions alike, with a thin, crusty layer of ice.

By sundown they were exhausted, forced to stumble on foot across a slippery terrain, leading the mule and horse up and down creekbanks and coulees, forced to search for more open ground where the footing wouldn't be so treacherous—but where they knew they might be easy to spot by the horse thieves. It turned out to be the sort of day that reminded Titus just how quickly the cold could rob a man of his strength, the sort of icy cold that might even come close to stealing his resolve and will to go on.

Nearly at the end of their worn-out rawhide whangs, the four hobbled into a grove of cottonwood near the lee side of some low hills and tied off the weary animals. While two of the trappers kicked around in the snow to gather up deadfall, another brought in water from the nearby stream, and the last of them brushed snow back from the ground where they built their night fire.

"I'll take first watch," Scratch volunteered as they chewed on their dried meat and drank their scalding coffee.

"Best by a long chalk," Tuttle said, "than for a man to get hisself woke up when he's dead asleep, smack in the middle of the dark an' the cold."

Better was it to stay awake, he thought as the night deepened, and stand to first watch. But when he had turned Billy Hooks out and crawled off to his robes and blankets, Titus found he could not sleep. Instead he lay shivering beside the crackle of their small fire for the longest time—unable to escape his fear of just what might become of them out here without the rest of their animals, in the middle of a wilderness where the brownskins came and went as they pleased, taking what they wanted from a white man.

Damn well didn't seem near fair, it didn't—when he hadn't come to stay among these hills, beside this stream, after all. Only to take a few beaver and move on to new country. No more than passing through. So them Injuns had no right to have call on taking what wasn't theirs. No right at all.

Nothing like Silas Cooper, no it wasn't. The man took what Scratch grudgingly admitted was his share—but Cooper hadn't taken it for naught. No, it was his rightful share in exchange for saving Bass's life, for keeping Bass alive, for teaching Bass day in and day out. By damn, to Titus that was a fair exchange between two men.

But this stealing of a man's horses and mules. Putting that man afoot as a blue norther bore down on these high plains and uplands. And the worst part of it was that the new snow had eventually blotted out the trail the farther north they walked. Still, the four of them had a good notion the thieves were leading them north, right into the teeth of the coming weather.

That day the trappers had even agreed that they would find the thieves up yonder, in that Yellowstone country. No matter that they didn't have a trail to follow. All they would have to do was keep watch from the high ground, a ridgetop or the crest of a hill, straining their eyes against all that bright and snowy landscape—searching for some sign of a pony herd, a cluster of brown lodges nippling against the cold skyline . . . and if nothing else, maybe they'd spot some ghostly smudge of firesmoke trickling up into the autumn sky.

That's how they found the Indian camp, far, far off the next afternoon.

From a distant ridge they could make out the lighter brown of the buffalo-hide lodgeskins scalded black at the smoke flaps, each cone raising its gray offering of heat, and food, and shelter from the cold. Ponies grazed beyond the lodges on what grass they pawed free of snow. People came and went on foot among the lodges, down to the thick groves of tall cottonwoods, or to the narrow stream meandering in its crooked, rocky, springtime-wide creekbed.

"Who they look to be?" Tuttle asked anxiously as they huddled there on the ridgetop as the wind came up.

Hooks prodded, "They ain't Blackfoots, is they?"

"Blackfoot would've rubbed us out first—then took the horses," Bass reminded them, feeling exposed and vulnerable against the skyline. "Maybeso we ought'n get ourselves down off this ridge, Silas."

Cooper didn't say a thing for the longest time, studying not so much the village as he looked here and there across the valley for horsemen. Then he watched the way the men acted in camp, for it ought to be plain if they were a hostile bunch or not.

Scratch agreed when Silas explained to them as much.

"Maybeso this bunch showed us they didn't mean us no harm but for takin' our animals." Titus looked this way and that, growing more nervous what with the way they were backlit by the afternoon's light.

Cooper glared at Bass, saying, "But we come here to get them horses back. Then—maybeso I'll mean them some harm."

"Only us again' all of them?" Tuttle squeaked.

Shaking his head, Silas admitted, "Nawww—it don't have to be a fight, boys. We just wait till dark—sometime after moonset. Then we'll slip in and get what's rightfully ours."

"J-just like that?" Hooks asked. "We ain't never . . . not ever gone an' stole horses from Injuns, Silas."

"A first time for ever'thing, Billy." Having snarled the rest into the silence of their own private thoughts, Cooper gazed off into the valley for a few minutes. "Looks to be a likely place off down yonder where we can lay up and wait till it's good and dark—"

"God-*damn!*" Scratch bawled, yanking his longrifle out of the crook of his left arm.

With the sudden appearance of the horsemen, the others were doing the same—but in the span of three heartbeats they realized their four guns were little match for the two dozen or more who burst from the trees on one side, breaking over a nearby hilltop on the other.

"We gonna take what we can of 'em with us afore they cut us down, Silas?" Billy asked in a harsh whisper.

"Just hold your water," Cooper cautioned, suspicion in his voice. "Don't unnerstan' why they coming in so slow—"

"Cooper's right, Billy," Scratch confided, the short hairs at the back of his neck bristling. "Just don't let 'em get in here too close."

At times like these a man remembered the lessons in life learned the hard way—clear as rinsed crystal. And right at this moment Titus recalled the way the Chickasaws glided up silently on the black-and-silver Mississippi, then rushed Ebenezer Zane's boatmen out of the night . . . recalled how the Arapaho laid waiting in their ambush for the Ute hunting party last winter—then sprang like a cat coiled for the attack.

Bass continued, "But it do seem a mite contrary, don't it, fellas? If'n this bunch wanted our hair here and now—likely they'd come at us on the run."

As it turned out, the horsemen brought their wide-eyed ponies to a halt at a respectful distance, completely circling the trappers. Turning slowly, Bass looked each one over quickly. A handsome outfit they were, fine of form and every one decked out in their feathers and teeth, hair tied up atop their heads with stuffed birds and scalp locks fluttering from coats, robes, and shields. A few of them talked among themselves quietly, but for the most part, the ponies made the only noise, restless and restive as they snorted in the cold, pawing at the hard ground beneath the thin skiff of new snow.

"By doggee!" Hooks exclaimed only so loud. "Them ponies of their'n don't like our smell."

"Come to think of it," Tuttle agreed, "I don't think any white person with a good nose would like *your* smell, Billy."

"Hush your yaps!" Cooper snarled as one of the horsemen inched out from the others in the circle. He began to make sign with his hands. "By damn, I think we might be able to talk to these here boys after all."

Without reservation he suddenly handed his rifle back to Tuttle and quickly began to make sign.

The warrior smiled, then replied in kind, his hands fluttering before him as he nodded in the closest thing to friendliness Bass had seen since the hospitable Shoshone at last summer's rendezvous.

" 'Pears to be an agreeable sort," Bud commented.

"Don't seem so bad a bunch, after all, do they?" Hooks added.

Cocking his head around to tell them over his shoulder, Cooper said, "This here's a bunch of Crow."

"By damn, we run onto the Crow 'stead of Blackfoot!" Tuttle cheered with genuine relief.

Hooks slapped Titus on the back. "Crow got 'em some purty squaws, so the downriver talk says. Mighty purty squaws." Then he bent his head close, his lips almost touching Bass's ear. "Maybeso we can talk Cooper into winterin' up with these here Crow and their womens. Word on river says these bang-tails make the best robe-warmers!"

Bass grumbled, "Maybeso you'd better wait to see what these here bucks have in mind for us afore you up and decide you're gonna spread some Crow squaw's legs for the winter here."

With a snort Billy rocked back on his heels and said, "You grown particular of a sudden, Scratch? Gone and got picky about where you poke your wiping stick?"

"Hush, Billy!" Tuttle warned while Cooper went on talking in sign.

With some word from their leader, half of the warriors slowly turned their ponies and formed up loosely to move off down the slope toward the valley and that village nestled among the cottonwoods along the river.

"All I know is that running onto Injuns means we found us some brownskin sluts," Billy hissed with a grin on his thick lips. "An' I ain't never met me a brownskin slut what didn't kick her legs wide for Billy-boy here when I showed her a handful of my purty red beads or a little strip of ribbon!"

"Maybeso ol' Silas got lucky for y' boys again!" Cooper crowed as he turned and joyously slapped Hooks on the shoulder. "Leave it to me to find a warm lodge, and a warm honey-pot for our stingers, ever' time!"

As the remainder of the horsemen urged their ponies closer to the white men, Tuttle whispered, "What they figger to do with us, Silas?"

Cooper smiled in that long black beard of his that tossed in the rising wind, slapping both hands down on the tops of Bud's shoulders. "Ease your hammer down, son. These here Crow bucks just gave us the invite to come on down for dinner with their big chiefs."

Billy echoed, "Big chiefs?"

Taking his rifle back from Tuttle, Cooper said, "From the sign talk I just got, looks like they knowed we was coming after our horses for the last two days."

Bud asked, "An' if we didn't come after the damned horses?"

Grabbing Tuttle's elbow to urge them all down the snowy slope, Silas said, "Then they'd knowed we had us yaller stripes painted down our backs an' was no better'n women."

As the afternoon light deepened the hues of everything from clouds, to cedar, to the surface of the creek itself in that hour before the sunset, the Crow warriors escorted the white men into their noisy village. Not all that different from making their ride into the Ute village last winter, to Scratch's way of thinking. Except one thing—these Crow sure were a tall people. Men and women both seemed taller than the Shoshone, and the Ute he had come to know in Park Kyack. Too, the more he looked at not just the menfolk, but the children and the Crows' slant-eyed womankind, the more Titus felt these were as fair-skinned and handsome a people as rumors and campfire palaver had boasted they were.

Cooper turned over the two animals to a pair of young, smiling boys who appeared to take their grown-up responsibilities most seriously as they barked at the children to stay back from a wary Hannah and the restless saddle horse. And with that the trappers were shown into a warm lodge where waited at least ten men as old as Cooper himself.

That first evening of ceremonial smoking and eating boiled meat dragged on

and on as speeches were made and exploits recounted by every warrior in attendance before he began his turn at haranguing the rest. And sometime after the first
winter moon had fallen in the west, the white men were told that they would have
to wait until morning for an answer to what would be done about their stolen
horses.

When the next morning finally became afternoon, the trappers were told
they would have an answer the following day. But it wasn't until four days later
that Cooper and the others were called before the Crow council, after impatiently
cooling their heels where they were allowed to camp in a grove of cottonwood at
the edge of the village circle.

"Seems they figger they got the right to ask us to pay for the beaver we're
taking from their criks," Cooper explained what he had been told in the stillness
of that council lodge. "They took our stock to pay for that beaver they say we're
stealing."

"I don't figger they're asking for all that much," Bass said.

For a moment Silas glowered at Titus, then finally asked, "What y' think,
Billy?"

"You tell me, Silas. Think we ought'n give 'em any of our beaver?"

Cooper looked at Tuttle. "If'n we don't—these thievin' bastards said they'd
stretch us out over a fire an' let their womens do their worst to us."

"That . . . that ain't 'sactly what they said, Silas," Bass corrected.

"Oh?" Cooper demanded, smiling the best he could for the sake of the Crow
men, his marblelike eyes nonetheless glaring holes in Bass.

"From what I saw 'em sign to you," Titus explained, "they give us a choice."

Pursing his lips in seething anger, Silas crossed his arms and said, "So now y'
figger y' read sign language good enough to know what the hell these ol' bucks
said to me? S'pose y' tell us all 'bout it, y' boneheaded nigger."

Not only were the eyes of the trappers on him now, but the black-cherry
eyes of every one of the Crow elders and counselors were as well, clearly sensing
the tension among the white men.

"From what I make of it," Scratch started tentatively, then swallowed hard,
"looks to be we got us one of two ways to go at this. We can give 'em something in
trade for the beaver we been taking out'n the streams in their country, or . . ."

"Or?" Tuttle squeaked.

"Or they throw us right on out the way they found us—maybe lucky to get
our mule and horse back."

Hooks twisted to look at Cooper. "That true what Scratch said? We give
'em something to trade or they turn us out?"

Cooper nodded, his brow furrowed, anger smoldering at Bass, every bit as
plain as sun on his face.

"But they'll let us go?" Tuttle said. "Just let us ride on out—if'n we give 'em
some plunder?"

"That's the way I read the sign, boys," Silas replied.

Then Bass declared, "Looks to me like we gotta figger out just how good it might turn out to be—us trapping here in Crow country."

"What you think of us hanging back in this country, Silas?" Billy asked.

For a moment Cooper was silent; then with a smile he turned to Bass. "Let's ask Scratch what he thinks we ought'n do."

"I say we give 'em presents," Titus was quick to answer. "Never know when it might turn out good to have us friends like these up here close to Blackfoot country, don't you think?"

"Never thought of that," Tuttle mused.

"What it cost us?" Hooks asked.

"Hardly nothing. A couple of horses and a blanket here, maybe a few beads or tin cup there," Titus responded.

"That all they asking, Silas?" Hooks inquired, long ago conditioned to believe in Cooper, still doubtful of what Bass was telling them.

"By damn, Billy—if Scratch ain't picked up enough sign to know fat cow from poor bull!" Cooper exclaimed with grudging admiration. "S'pose y' go ahead on and tell us what else these ol' bucks said 'bout keeping all our plunder for theyselves."

With a jerk Tuttle twisted near fully around at that. "They gonna rob us of ever'thing?"

Cooper winked faintly, saying, "Y' wanna tell 'em, Scratch? Or y' want me to?"

"I s'pose if you're asking me to tell Billy and Bud the bad news," Bass began, then sighed. "These here Crow say we can walk on outta here just the way we walked in . . . 'cept we have to leave Hannah and the horse with the rest they took from us."

"Or?" Cooper prodded, looking all the more smug.

"Or the Crow say we can pay 'em for their beaver—which means we can keep ever'thing what's ours, and . . ."

Exasperated, Tuttle whined, "And?"

"And," Bass paused, winking at Cooper, "we been invited to stay on till spring."

The River Crow moved four times that winter, migrating each time to another traditional camping spot in another sheltered valley where wood and water were available, where the wind by and large kept large patches of the autumn-dried meadow grasses blown clear of snow. Every few weeks when the firewood became scarce and the last of the grass was cropped down, when the game grew harder to scare up and the campsites began to reek with human offal and that stench of an abundance of gut-piles, Big Hair's River Crow set off behind one warrior band or another chosen by the elders to have the honor of selecting the valley where their brown and blackened lodges would next be raised.

Not only were they a handsome people, but the Crow turned out to be less haughty and arrogant than Titus had taken them to be at first. Whereas the Ute had welcomed the white men immediately, Big Hair's band were a little slower to accept their winter visitors. But once they had warmed up to the trappers, the Crow turned out to be warm and generous hosts. As time went on, in fact, Titus discovered them not only to have a keen sense of humor—but they enjoyed playing practical jokes on one another . . . and on their guests.

"Silas!" Billy Hooks was bellowing as he came tearing out of the lodge where he had been taken by a clan elder, near naked.

To the four white men, it seemed like nothing new—just what had been the Crow's practice all winter long: one man or another would present a wife or daughter to one of the trappers for a few nights, usually no longer than a phase of the moon. This day the trappers had been seated in the afternoon sun around a fire with more than a dozen warriors, smoking, talking in sign, practicing either their pidgin English or their stunted knowledge of Crow, when a clan elder came up to lead Billy off to a nearby lodge. While Billy frequently turned and winked, rubbing his crotch a time or two in lewd anticipation, the others watched.

And when the lodge door went down and all grew quiet, the men at the fire went back to their easy chatter and midwinter socializing. Suddenly Hooks burst from the lodge completely naked but for the buckskin shirt he desperately fought to clutch around his midsection as he stumbled and fell on the slick ground, clawed his way to his feet again, and raced for the fire, screeching.

"*Dammit,* Silas!"

As Cooper and Tuttle shot to their feet, Bass instead glanced at some of the brown faces gathered at that fire ring. Strange, he thought, that the dark eyes showed no surprise at this turn of events, no alarm.

"Don't y' want that squaw they give y'?" Silas demanded as the sputtering Billy approached, shuddering like an aspen leaf in autumn. Gazing over Hooks's shoulder, Cooper and the others watched the woman emerge from the lodge, a blanket wrapped around what was clearly an otherwise naked body.

"H-her?" Billy squeaked, sliding to a stop on the slushy snow right in front of the giant trapper.

"For balls' sake, Billy! She's a looker," Tuttle agreed, nodding.

"Damn now, Billy," Cooper said, grasping Hooks's shoulder with one big hand, "if'n y' don't want the slut—I'll rut with her for a few days my own self."

As the others appraised the squaw, Bass was again glancing in turn at the faces of the Crow men. By now the eyes were crinkling, and sly grins were beginning to crack the masks of indifference. A few even held hands over their mouths to stifle laughter, and for the first time Titus noticed the women gathering here and there in knots between the lodges, having halted their work at hides or child care to whisper and watch.

Hooks shook his head, eyes as big around as conchos, as he sputtered, "B-but . . . she ain't a—"

Silas whirled Billy around and pushed him back toward the blanket-wrapped squaw. "G'won now and climb on that slut's hump, Billy boy!" he roared. "Or I'll do it for y'!"

"Silas?" Hooks pleaded, his feet locked in place, skidding across the snow as the insistent Cooper pushed him along.

"Listen—y' bonehead idjit. Y' don't poke your stinger in 'er—I sure as hell gonna do it my own self!"

"B-but, Silas . . . she don't—"

"Come to think of it," Cooper suddenly interrupted, shoving his way past Hooks as he took off in that long-legged, lumbering gait of his, headed for the woman. "She's a good-lookin' wench, ain't she? Y' done wasted your bet, Billy. Think I'll dip some honey out o' her pot first off afore y' get her all bumfoozled."

Scratch had to agree—the woman was real pleasant looking: nice featured with a gentle nose and almond-shaped eyes, her glossy hair braided, one long twist spilling over a smooth-skinned bare shoulder. But the way these Crow fellers were acting . . .

From a standing start Hooks burst into a blur, shooting past Cooper to reach the woman just a heartbeat before Silas came to an abrupt stop before them both.

"Told y', Billy: had y' your chance't. Now step 'side and let the booshway wet his whang in this'un first."

"Ain't . . . she ain't what you think, Silas!"

When Cooper gave Hooks a playful shove aside and took him another step toward the woman, Billy leaped right back, saying frantically, "Silas—you cain't . . . you ain't gonna—"

It was then Cooper took the woman by the one bare arm she had exposed, clamping the blanket to her body, and turned the squaw back toward the lodge—his eyes clearly feasting on that bare shoulder.

"Tried to tell you, Silas!"

And that's when Billy did the unthinkable. He grabbed hold of the woman's blanket and began tugging. Immediately she wheeled away from Cooper and began pulling back on the blanket. Silas lunged for them both—seizing hold of Billy's wrist.

"Leave her the hell be!" Cooper roared, shoving Hooks backward with a mighty heave. "Slut's mine now!"

But as Hooks fell, the woman's blanket came loose—and all hell came loose with it.

Billy sprawled in a heap on the snow. Cooper whirled, visibly shuddered—then stood frozen, staring openmouthed at the naked squaw. Tuttle was already on his feet, but now he too stood rooted to the spot, unable to comprehend what had just occurred.

Slowly, at first, the Crow men began to laugh—almost as one, as if on cue. Behind and all around their men, the women giggled too. Then every Crow in that camp seemed to be laughing, so hard that a mighty din it made that winter afternoon beneath the bare branches of the cottonwood.

For a moment all Cooper could do was point down at the figure naked before him, his arm trembling. Then he hobbled a halting step back, and a second, his mouth moving up and down. Lunging for Hooks, he pulled his naked friend off the ground as Billy fought to keep himself covered from all the Crow eyes.

Seething, Silas roared, "Why—y' think this is some good laugh on me, don't y', Billy?"

As Cooper shook him slowly back and forth, they both stumbled back another step. Hooks tried to explain, "I-I didn't know when she took me in!"

As Cooper and Hooks stumbled out of the way, Bass clearly saw what the Crow had been smiling about. The moment Silas moved back, Billy in tow, Titus saw it wasn't a beautiful young woman at all. Instead, it was a very pretty, thin-boned young man, vainly trying to wrench his blanket back from Billy . . . and as he did, his very apparent male appendage wagged in the cold winter air.

"She's a . . . a man!" Tuttle gushed.

"I'll kill y', Billy Hooks!" Silas vowed, nearly heaving Hooks off the ground.

"I didn't do nothing!" he shrieked.

"Cooper!" Bass hollered, starting to rise. "Cain't you see it's their joke on Billy?"

At Scratch's words Silas jerked around, still clutching Hooks in both paws. "Their . . . joke?"

"Yeah—I figure they knowed just how much Billy likes him his ruttin'," Titus said with a shrug. "I'll wager they thought they'd pull on his leg a bit."

Cooper shook Billy once. "Y' didn't know nothing 'bout this?"

"How c-could I, Silas?"

By then Bass was making sign, asking his questions of the Crow men, getting his answers amid the laughter the warriors were sharing. One hand on the scruff of Billy's neck, Cooper watched too. After a few minutes Silas burst out laughing, so hard he had to let go of Hooks and bend over at the waist.

"Say, Billy," Titus explained, "from what I can tell, looks like this here wasn't all that much a joke, after all. Seems like ever' now and then the Crow have a boy what don't wanna grow up a man."

Glancing quickly at the young man, who wrapped the blanket about himself, then whirled on his heel to head back to the lodge, Billy asked, "He d-don't wanna be a man?"

Scratch went on to attempt making sense of what to those four white men was the inexplicable, what was totally foreign to their world and time: this concept of a very powerful medicine the Crow believed those young boys possessed who did not want to learn the skills it would take to assume the role of a warrior but instead preferred to play with the girls, learning the ways of the lodge and how a woman was to care for her man. Rather than to chastise such boys for their differences and preferences, the Crow looked upon these young men as having been anointed by the Grandfather Above with some very special, and powerful, medicine.

Indeed, among these people there was no such thing as homosexuality. Quite the contrary—these rare and respected individuals actually believed themselves to be women spirits imprisoned in a man's body. The Crow revered such powerful medicine no less than they revered their clan leaders, war-society leaders, and women warriors.

Scratching at his scruffy brown beard, not in the least attempting to disguise a silly smirk, Bass chuckled and went on to explain, "Way the Crow see it, Billy—you was the sort of hoss what likes his ruttin' so much"—then for a moment Titus dug a toe at the ground, trying his best to suppress more of a giggle before he could continue—"they figgered to give you a crack at something a bit different in them ruttin' robes, Billy!"

Came to be that Bird in Ground proved to be a steadfast friend to Titus that first winter the four spent in Absaraka, home of the Crow. After being shunned by both Hooks and Cooper, days later the young man/woman offered himself as a partner to Titus. But without embarrassment or shame this time, Scratch was able to get across that while he did not hanker to set up lodge keeping with the Crow man, Titus nonetheless wanted to be a friend.

As the days deepened in the coldest heart of the winter, Bird in Ground took to riding out with Bass when the white man ventured off to set or check his traps in the surrounding countryside. Oh, at first there was some talk among the village folks—that much Scratch learned from Bird in Ground over the hours and days and finally weeks they spent together. There along the creeks and streams that fed the mighty Yellowstone, Bass and his Crow friend began to teach one another the first rudiments of one another's native tongues.

In those dark, cold hours well before sunrise, Bird in Ground would bring his pony to join Scratch at the trapper's wickiup—a crude shelter made from lodgepole saplings, willow branches, and an old, discarded, much-blackened lodge cover where Bass laid out his bed and cooked his meals when not spending a rare night coupling with a Crow woman or having supper with a family somewhere off in the village. For the most part, Scratch survived that winter, when he turned thirty-three, without the company of a full-time night woman. Not that the hungers didn't stir him at inopportune times, but for the most part there always seemed to be a woman available just when he needed one the most that season of the Cold Maker. So while the other trappers made lounging and women, talking and more women, their winter activities, it didn't take Titus long to realize he had a lot of idle time on his hands.

Just didn't seem to make all that much sense to him to let the days go by with nothing more than another notch carved on a calendar stick to show for the passage of time. But when he had told Silas, Billy, and Bud of his intention to go back to working the surrounding streams, not one of the three showed any evidence that they were all that interested in joining him in his labors, there in the heart of winter. Evidently they were much more content to wait until the first arrival of spring before any of them freed the thick rawhide tie straps from the tops of their leather trap sacks. True enough and no two ways of Sunday about it: trapping was hard enough work—made all the more miserable still in the winter when a man had to slog through thigh-deep wind-drifted snow just so he could closely examine the banks along the icy ribbons of streams or the caked shores of beaver ponds to find just where the animals traveled now that winter had frozen their domain solid.

But time was what Titus was rich in that winter. A man with a bounty of time, Bass used his wisely so that by the coming of the spring hunt he found himself already a wealthy man in fine, dark, glossy beaver plews.

Even before Silas Cooper's outfit was ready to push on west toward the fabled Three Forks country.

SIXTEEN

In taking their leave of Big Hair's River Crow, the four of them pointed their noses to the northwest, intending to strike the Yellowstone itself inside a week's time. Leaving the upper Bighorn River country, they first had to push due north past a small range of low mountains, then cross the several forks of a creek system* before they could finally begin to angle off to the west.

The chill, early-spring wind had grown strong and blustery by the time Silas Cooper's ragtag band struck the valley of the upper Yellowstone—a wind that knifed itself right into their faces and sank all the way to a man's marrow as the horses and mules plodded west, step by step, day after day. Beside the gently meandering river they made their camp each night, then marched on come morning. The four of them made quite an impressive outfit, what with all the animals they had loosely lashed together traipsing along behind the trappers—in and out and around the groves of stately old cottonwood and those mazelike copses of willow, chokecherry, and alder where the deer burst from cover, spooking the antelope into turning and bounding off across the open bottoms. Farther up on the slopes

---

* Pryor Mountains and Pryor Creek, named for Sergeant Nathaniel Pryor, part of the command who accompanied Lewis and Clark west to the Pacific Ocean

of the nearby hills the elk grazed and watched, seemingly unperturbed by the passing of so many four-leggeds.

Some of those packhorses plodded a little less lively than the others: Scratch already had them loaded with the bulging packs of thick-haired beaver he had toiled through the long winter to trap, flesh, and keep vermin free as both spring and their departure approached. Indeed, as winter had aged and the weather hinted at warming, there had already been so many packs of beaver that come the first sign of thaw, Silas needed to trade for another ten Crow ponies from Pretty Weasel and Other Medicine, both brothers of clan leader Big Hair. Now there were easily two dozen saddle mounts, packhorses, and mules among the four trappers—an enviable remuda for any outfit and, as always, a juicy, tasty temptation dangled before any horse-hungry band of thieving warriors.

Those early-spring days spent leisurely trapping from creek to creek along the Yellowstone were mild and sunny, the nights still cold and frosty. But as the season matured, the skies stayed cloudy for days at a time, raining now and again, whipping up tremendous gales often accompanied by icy hailstorms that drove the trappers to seek out the shelter of protective cottonwood groves or the overhang of riverbluff rimrock. Many were the times those sudden and capricious storms passed on by, leaving a layer of icy white piled in drifts across the ground. As the gusty torrents rumbled on to the east down the Yellowstone Valley, the four would cautiously study the receding clouds, peer hopefully at the clearing sky overhead, then urge their nervous animals out of the timber and press on upriver, all those hooves crunching every bit as loud as if they were walking on parched corn spilled across a hardwood floor.

Every day, the farther west they marched, it became clearer to Titus just how hardy and courageous the Crow people were. A huge country itself to protect, Absaraka sat squarely in the middle of enemy territory. As Bird in Ground had taken pains to instruct, to the east ruled the seven fires of the Lakota and their allies, the Cheyenne. On the south roamed the hostile Arapaho, the sometimes friendly Shoshone, as well as the Ute and the Bannock, while to the west lived the strong and amiable Flathead along with the Nez Perce. East of the great north star lived the Cree and Assiniboine. Yet a little west of north roamed the greatest threat of all—the fiercest raiders of the high plains: the Itshipite, known to white trappers as the Blackfeet.

Three powerful clans—the Blood, the Piegan, and the Gros Ventre of the prairie—who banded together to form a mighty confederation that stretched all the way east to the English holdings of the Hudson's Bay Company, then swept clear down along the northern Rockies until Blackfeet territory butted sharply against the home of the Crow.

Although outnumbered nearly four or five to one by any of its great enemies on the south, east, or north, the *Apsaalooke* held steadfast winter after winter, raid after raid, generation after generation, as few warrior clans could boast. Ever since a time beyond the count of any man then alive, the Crow had given birth to their babes, raised their children, and buried their old ones in that land. Winter after winter they had defended their home.

Although few, this proud and fearsome people, Bird in Ground had explained, was all that held back the tide of their many enemies.

"Wherever you go from Absaraka," the young man instructed gravely, "you take your life in your hands. I know of no others who would be satisfied to take only your horses."

Bass clawed at his itchy scalp as he replied in his halting Crow tongue, "These Blackfoot, they want my hair?"

Bird in Ground nodded. "You will be careful when you ride west with the others?"

"Yes," Titus had assured his friend, who helped him trap and flesh many of those prime, blanket-grade beaver that winter, "we will all be very careful when we leave the safety of Absaraka. I aim to stay as far away as possible from the Blackfoot."

For a long time the young man did not reply, as he seemed to be weighing what he wanted to say to the trapper. Finally he said gravely, "Perhaps it isn't only the Blackfoot you should be wary of."

Titus asked his new friend if he said that only because the other three made it more than plain they didn't like Bird in Ground.

"No," was the Crow's surprising answer. "I tell you this because *I* do not like *them*. And my medicine warns me that you must not trust being with them."

Trying to smile as if it were a joke, to make light of what caused him to sense a chill at the base of his spine, Bass replied, "The three—they took me in. They made me one of them. They taught me. They protected me. Why would they ever harm me?"

"I only ask that you will be careful."

Titus scoffed, "I think you are seeing ghosts."

"Seeing ghosts?" the Crow asked, his brow furrowed in confusion.

"You see something that isn't there," Titus responded. "There is no reason for my three friends to harm me."

In the end Bird in Ground gave Titus his solemn blessing, "May *Akbaatatdia*, the Grandfather Above and Maker of All Things, watch over you, my new friend."

"May the Grandfather hold you in his hand too," Bass repeated as he sensed that same sudden and overwhelming sentiment he had first experienced years before on the Ohio when he'd parted from Kingsbury's boatmen, "until we talk again, in a season yet to come."

Now as the four of them moved ever closer to the great bend of the Yellowstone, Titus had many things to think upon throughout each day as the sun tarried in the sky a little longer, a little brighter. So much had he begun to learn in his winter with Bird in Ground, all of what they talked about and struggled over during those long, cold days spent trapping, hunting, learning one another's tongue. From him Bass had learned of the tribal structure of many Apsaalooke clans; learned too of their *ammaakalatche,* or strong personal beliefs in their Maker of All Things. Bird in Ground taught Scratch that the *akbaalia,* or shamans, had the power not only to heal but to see into the future too. As the days of winter waned, Titus learned how family members related one to another within the clan through birth or marriage. And always, Bird in Ground told many, many little stories of his people's history, tales dating all the way back to the creation of the earth.

They were stories that Scratch listened to, then practiced retelling to assure Bird in Ground that every detail and facet of the tale was recited correctly. Some were stories that caused him to remember those parables taught him from the old, leather-bound family Bible laid across his mother's knees by the fire in Boone County. Tales of faraway places and people with faraway names. And now he himself had gone as far, far away from that cabin at Rabbit Hash, Kentucky, as he figured those faraway people ever were.

"I been told the beaver be as big as painter cats in the valley what's other side of that pass," Cooper stated as the last of the packhorses clattered to a halt behind them.

Billy Hooks nodded, grinning wondrously as he said, "An' a painter's a big ol' cat too, Scratch."

"I ain't never had cause to see one myself," Bass replied.

"They h'ain't a likely animal for a man to spot," Cooper assured. "Keep back out of a man's way."

"Not like a b'ar," Tuttle added. "Why, a b'ar'll just as soon mosey on down into your camp as much as a man'll come to call!"

"Best we find us a crossing," Silas instructed, bringing the others back to the task at hand, his eyes raking the gravel bed on the far bank. "I figger this here Yallerstone gonna run high an' wild with snow-melt one day real soon."

Bass pointed south up the narrow valley where the river originated before it took that big bend to the east. "What's off yonder?"

When Tuttle wagged his head, Billy confided, "I ain't ever knowed of a man been in that country what could rightly tell us."

"Devil smokes," Cooper declared as he turned his horse away toward the bank of the river. "Been told the ground shakes and spits water high as a church belfry in the air!"

Turning to wink at Bass, Hooks guffawed loudly. "I heard me such talk afore, Scratch—and ever' time I do, I figger 'em to be teched . . . right up here!" He tapped a dirty finger against one temple.

"H'ain't no flat-tails in the land of them devil smokes," Cooper flung his voice over his shoulder as he urged his horse and some of the pack animals down to the Yellowstone.*

---

* *Near present-day Livingston, Montana*

"So I'll be going where I hear there's beaver the likes you ain't never seen!"

What water flowed in the river that early spring ran nearly as cold as winter ice when they splashed their way across. As wide as were the gravelly banks, the Yellowstone was still no match for the capricious Platte. Here the riverbed was rocky, far different from the sandy, shifting bottom that had robbed Titus of half his supplies, and the Indian pony. One leg at a time, the horse beneath him carefully set each hoof down, planting it securely among the rocks before raising another leg from the strong, clear current that slowly climbed to bubble halfway up Bass's calf by the time they reached midstream.

When he turned in the saddle, Titus found Hannah picking her way across with the other pack animals, the two bundles lashed to her back swaying one way, then the other, as she shifted her weight, each hoof seeking solid ground.

Reaching the north bank, Cooper spurred his horse out with a lunge, pulling up and around on a high piece of ground where he waited for the other men and the last of their animals to leave the water before he set off to the west without a word. From that crossing the land rose abruptly into timbered hills. The four of them began to string the horses and mules out in single file as the sun continued to midsky and the trappers climbed toward the cleft* that would take them west.

That night they camped on the far side of the pass, turning the horses out for a roll and a good dusting before picketing the animals as the sky grew dark. With the cold spring sky serving as a pallet for a million stars, Bass looked east from those heights at the land of the Apsaalooke they were leaving. Then he gazed to the west, where the sun had set beyond even taller mountains.

Finally Titus asked the others at the fire busy sharpening knives or smoking their pipes, "You figger that to be Blackfoot country off yonder there?"

"Blackfoot don't come down this far south so early in the year," Silas stated with certainty.

"Where you hear that?" Billy asked.

When Cooper's eyes flared with instant anger, Hooks turned away to pick at the dirt caked under his fingernails with his skinning knife. "I s'pose you'd be the one oughtta know 'bout such things, Silas."

"Don't want none of y' forgetting that," Cooper said as he arose, beginning to work at the wooden buttons on the fly of his buckskin britches as he turned toward the shadows in the trees.

When Silas stepped out of earshot, Tuttle whispered, "You figger he knows if that's Blackfoot country or not, Scratch?"

"How the hell you 'spect me to savvy if he knows or not?" Bass grumbled. Immediately he felt sorry: if he should be angry with anyone, he should be angry with Cooper. Not with those who just followed merrily behind Silas come spring, summer, fall, and winter.

* *Bozeman Pass*

Titus wagged his head. "Maybe we'll find out for ourselves, fellas," he said in a low voice filled with resignation. "But no matter how I figger it—Silas ain't ever done nothing stupid enough to lose his hair."

"Scratch is right, Bud," Billy agreed with a bob of his head and a grin that showed off that big gap between his top two teeth.

"Yeah. S'pose you're right," Tuttle added in a whisper. "Silas ought'n know if there's Blackfeet down there."

The following day they began their descent into one of those beautiful interior valleys the northern Rockies could boast. And for the next few weeks they worked the streams that fed the Gallatin River, then eased over to trap among the streams along the Spanish Breaks that fed the Madison. As the snowline slowly retreated farther and farther up the slopes of the mountains, the four of them ranged higher and higher, finding the hunting good, and the trapping even better than they could have hoped.

"Ain't no wonder there's them what'll claim right to your face that the Blackfoot spell trouble in this here country," Cooper said at their fire one evening late that spring.

"Their kind just wanna keep it all to themselves," Tuttle replied.

Billy chimed in, "That's the gospel, it is, yessirreebob!"

"Them with Fitzpatrick was fixing to head up this way last fall," Bass said. "So maybe that country ain't all that much a secret, Silas."

With those dark, chertlike eyes betraying the falsehood of that big grin on his face, Cooper growled, "Or maybe them company trappers are the sort to figger on scaring away us what are out here on our own hook."

"If the trapping's good," Tuttle said, "I figger they'll say what it takes to scare us off."

"Fitzpatrick's brigade ain't the only ones," Titus said, wagging his head. "S'pose you fellers tell me why them Crow warned us 'bout going west, torst Blackfoot country at the Three Forks?"

"The Crow try to skeer you away, did they?" Billy asked.

Snorting with a gust of sharp laughter like iron colliding with an anvil, Cooper cried, "You damn idjit, Billy! The *Crow* didn't tell him no such a thing. That Crow feller what's soft in the head—the one trying hard to be a gal—I'll wager *he's* the one what warned Scratch. Ain't none of them warriors worth their salt gonna be so skeered to warn us away from here. Just some soft-brained manwhore what likes to wear squaw's clothes!"

Turning to Bass there beside their fire, grinning hugely with that gaptoothed smile, Hooks rolled onto his hands and knees as he asked, "What else he like to do like a squaw? Been figgerin' to ask you all along, Scratch. He let you hump him like this here?"

Tuttle and Cooper roared along with Billy as Hooks wagged his rear end provocatively, grunting and wheezing.

Vowing not to flare with anger, Titus got to his feet and started away, wagging his head, not sure where he'd go at that moment. Just anywhere but there.

"Eh, Scratch?" Silas called after him as Billy's high, mocking laughter followed Bass toward the ring of trees where they had corralled their horses. "Y' asshumped that soft-brained feller's bones, didn't y'?"

"I can tell he did, Silas!" Hooks cried out, "Bet Ol' Scratch liked asshumpin' too, boys!"

"Maybeso if'n that man-whore was soft in the ass as he was in the brain!" Cooper shouted, flinging his voice after the retreating Bass.

The three of them continued to laugh and make their catcalls as Bass swept by his bedroll, took up his pouch and rifle, and kept on moving toward the animals. Their cruelty followed him to the rope corral where Hannah was the first to smell him coming. The mule nudged a pair of horses aside and inched up to the rope as Titus came to a stop to nuzzle her.

"Care to go for a ride, girl?"

Her eyes closed halfway as he rubbed up her muzzle, then scratched his way up to her forelock.

"C'mon," he whispered to her. "I figger it's time you got used to having me sit on your back."

Bobbing her head eagerly, the mule came close to prancing smartly as he led her out of the corral and took up the extra length of her lead rope.

"Critter like you ought'n be good for more'n just packing my plews from place to place."

As he flung himself up on her broad, bare back, Hannah twisted her head around to give him as quizzical a look as he had seen an animal ever give him. Patting her on the neck, Bass gently tapped his moccasins into her ribs.

"G'won, now," he prodded, shaking the halter looped around her neck. "Let's get."

Standing like a statue for a moment more while she seemed to decide on just what to do, the mule finally set off slowly. He rode her all the way out of the timber toward the clearing at the end of the ridge where he could look both north and west at the deepening hues of twilight as the spring sun sank and the air cooled quickly. Over time the cold of the coming night helped: he came to lose the heat of his anger at the three. After a while Bass told himself they laughed for no better reason than they were plain ignorant about such things. If not outright ignorant, well—then the three were plainly cruel to call Bird in Ground a soft-brained person.

Titus had met soft-brained folk throughout his life. The first he ever saw was a flat-faced girl about his age back to Rabbit Hash. She didn't talk much, and what she said he never could understand. Her folks talked to her like folks would talk to a baby—all nonsense words and such. And while Bird in Ground didn't do any of the things men of his tribe did, the Crow man made a lot of sense when he talked. There was times, Titus had to admit, Bird in Ground made more sense than all three of them fool-headed, yabbering yahoos put together!

Hell, Scratch thought, a man's ways was just his ways . . . and if a fella turned out to do different from other men's ways—then just who could say what was right, or what was better, or just who the hell was soft-brained?

Damn, if it weren't hard at times to figger out just who had his best interests in heart. Bird in Ground, who had never said a cross word about another soul? Or them three, who didn't miss a lick when it come to whacking others down a notch or two? Hard it was to weigh them out against the other, especially because the young Crow had sure appeared to care genuinely when he'd warned Titus . . . while Silas, Billy, and Bud actually had saved his life more than once.

So confusing to think on, that it almost hurt his head to try now to sort out what he figured was likely one of the most difficult puzzles life had ever presented him. Maybe some things were just supposed to be rocks a man wasn't meant to crack—no matter how hard you hammered away at them. Some things in life just were and could defy a man's most intricate cogitation.

Like women. Nawww, not all women. Maybeso just white women. Women like Amy and Marissa, and even Abigail. No matter that she was a whore—she was still a white gal. There was just something he'd experienced with white women that made them naturally hard for a man like him to fathom, while on the other hand the Indian gals he'd rubbed up against were a lot more reasonable sort.

Seemed fair to say that most every white woman he'd had much cause to know anything about made a real tough study of herself. Rather than taking life on its own terms, white gals seemed to take such delicious relish in complicating things, enjoying how hard they made a man work at getting along with them.

Looking back now at that first woman creature he had tried to figure out in Boone County, Amy Whistler was clearly just that sort. And Marissa Guthrie too. Even the gal what had come into his life between the two of them—Abigail Thresher. Times were that riverboat bang-tail had shown signs of being a stock-and-trade woman creature with all her confusing ways and all her confusing wiles, despite the fact that she was a whore in the end . . . a woman who, for all intents and purpose, set out a'purpose to satisfy a man's baser hungers.

No two ways of Sunday about it: a white gal was just a white gal. A creature put on earth for no other purpose but to devil a man.

"Why the hell you getting yourself all bumfoozled over such a thing anyhow?" he chided himself as he stared off into the growing darkness and scratched Hannah's ears. "You're done with white gals. Done for all time."

As the sky's distant rose became purple, and in the end that purple turned a deep indigo-blue, the first stars of evening stood out all the more distinctly. Ready at last to turn back for camp, he drank deep of the chill air . . . then blinked and looked again. To be sure.

There against the darkness that was the featureless valley far beyond flickered a point of light.

Squinting his best to bring its starry point into focus, Bass wasn't sure at first what the sighting might be. Perhaps some dry timber set ablaze by a passing thunderstorm. But—that was pure balderdash: there hadn't been any lightning in many days.

Maybeso it would be Fitzpatrick's brigade of trappers, who had pushed north this spring out of the Willow Valley where they had plans to winter up all together. Then again—that was just as crazy a thought . . . because a trapping brigade of any size would have them more than one fire.

The more Titus stared down at that faraway, solitary point of light, the more it fed his imagination, and his misgivings. Perhaps a wandering war party. After all, it was late spring, wasn't it? Likely that the Blackfoot were moving about by now—no matter what Silas Cooper and any of those more experienced in such things might have to say on the matter.

"C'mon, girl," he said in a hush to the mule as he clambered onto her broad back. "We got us news to tell."

That night he led the others back to the meadow and rocky outcrop, where they all four gazed down at the faraway valley floor and that distant flicker of light.

"This far off—a man cain't tell just what made that fire," Cooper warned. "Could be a white man or a red nigger."

"Hell, we can't tell, Silas," Hooks added.

Frustrated, Bass said, "If you fellas can tell me you know of a Injun what rides off by hisself alone—I'm ready to listen."

Turning on Scratch, Cooper demanded, "Spit out what you're trying to say."

"I spent me a winter with them Utas, and 'nother winter with the Crow," Titus explained. "Not once did I see a solitary Injun from neither band of 'em go out all on his own. Did any of you?"

"Nope, I didn't," Tuttle agreed.

Silas had turned to look back at the far flicker, but Billy reluctantly said, "Not me neither, Scratch. You're right, dammit. Injuns don't travel alone—like a white man does."

"No great shakes, fellas. If'n its more'n one, cain't be all that many if they got 'em just one fire," Cooper tried to reassure them as he studied the darkness.

"But, Silas: it don't take much of a fire to keep warm twice as many as we are," Tuttle declared, his eyes filling with the first hint of dread.

"Maybe three times as many," Scratch admitted. "Them Injuns don't make big fires. And there ain't no telling how big that fire is anyway, Silas."

"How's that?" Cooper demanded.

Pointing, Bass said, "Hell—we don't even know how far off that fire is . . . so how's any of us to say just how big a fire it is?"

"We best be clearing out," Tuttle warned.

"Come morning's soon enough," Cooper stated flatly.

Billy nodded, his ready grin gone beneath the silver-pale moonshine. "Morning's soon enough, Bud."

Upon returning to their camp they nonetheless snuffed out their fire and decided upon a rotation of guards that would keep one man awake until it was light enough to pack up, load the animals, and start on their backtrail east.

"A damn shame too," Hooks grumbled as the other three settled into their blankets there in the cold darkness. "The trapping in this country was some punkins too."

"Ain't that the way it's bound to be for a man?" Tuttle moaned, rising on an elbow.

"We done ourselves good anyway," Cooper said, lying still in his blankets. "I'd care to bet there ain't four other trappers in all these here mountains what have near the plews we got in our packs already."

"Ain't that so!" Hooks exclaimed, pounding a knee and nearly toppling his cup of lukewarm coffee drained from the pot before the fire went out. "Just imagine the look gonna be on that trader's face when we come rolling into ronnyvoo come summer, boys!"

"Yeah," Tuttle cheered in the hush of their quiet voices. "We four gonna be kings of ronnyvoo!"

"Cocks of the walk, I'd wager!" Hooks continued. "Ain't nothing we cain't buy. Ain't a squaw we cain't hang with foofaraw and girlews. Why, we'll stay drunk all the time!"

"Right from the first day till the last," Bass said, joining in their imagined revelry. It felt good to shake off the fear and misgivings the way old Tink would shake water off herself after crossing a stream. "We gonna drink ourselves sick on trader's rum every day, ain't we, Silas?"

For some time Cooper didn't answer. Long enough that Billy finally prodded, "Silas? You 'sleep?"

"No. Just been thinking more on ronnyvoo . . . and what the four of us ought'n do about all these plews."

"What you mean—what we ought'n do?" Tuttle asked there in the dark as the satin-colored moon settled down on the tops of the pines to the west of their camp.

"We ain't never had near this many beaver, have we?"

Billy replied, "We ain't never had four of us afore, Silas. And Scratch here been working his ever-livin' ass off since winter."

"That's the natural truth," Tuttle added.

"So what you got on your mind?" Bass asked the question that for months now had gone unanswered as he slowly sat up and crossed his legs under the buffalo robe.

"H'ain't so sure no more we should be making for ronnyvoo with these'r furs come summer," Cooper admitted as he kicked the blankets off his legs, sat up himself, and brought a robe around his shoulders. "Not so sure we should wait till summer to sell 'em neither."

"Why not?" Hooks inquired. "Summer ain't no time for trapping beaver."

From the darkness Cooper explained, "But by then every swinging dick in these here mountains is selling his plews to the trader coming out from St. Louie."

"So if we don't sell to the trader come high summer," Scratch began with keen curiosity, "just what you got in mind for us to do?"

"Sell before the summer," Cooper stated flatly.

"Hell, Silas—Ashley and his bunch ain't gonna be back till high summer!" Tuttle argued.

"I don't figger to have nothing to do with any of 'em," Cooper admitted.

Growing more intrigued, Titus asked, "If I follow your thinking—we figger to sell our plews early, and we don't figger on waiting for no trader tromping west from St. Louie . . . then where we gonna take all this beaver we got in these here packs?"

"Down the river, boys."

"What?" Hooks asked, his voice rising. "You cain't tell me we're gonna cross that prerra?"

"No, Billy—I said *down* the river, you softheaded idjit."

"That's gonna be a bit of a ride for us," Bass declared as he thought on it. "But I s'pose it can be done."

Then Cooper admitted, "That's something else I been working over in my head too."

"Sounds to me you been doing more thinking since winter than I do in a hull year!" Hooks told Cooper.

"Ain't no doubt of that, Billy!" Tuttle cried with a snort.

Titus prodded, "So tell us what you been cogitating on about this long ride, Silas."

"No ride a'tall. Simple as that."

Billy asked, "Then how the hell you 'spect us get downriver?"

"We float."

"F-float?" Hooks said with his head bobbing. "What's a man to float in, Silas? You don't 'spect us to just ride our plews on down, do you?"

"Way I figger it, this time of year," Cooper explained, "fast as the water's rising—a man can float downriver least twice as fast as he can ride a horse following beside that same river."

The three others sat quiet for some time, clearly in their own thoughts, weighing the merits of that comparison on their own, until Scratch spoke first.

"Makes a lot of sense, it do, Silas," he admitted. "You cover twice as much ground in the same time it'd take us to tramp across it on horse."

"Maybe faster," Cooper injected.

"Maybe faster," Titus agreed with the appraisal. "You thinking of going down the Yallerstone?"

"Yup."

"But—where's that gonna put you to trade on the river?"

"Maybe nowhere," Silas answered, ". . . until we reach the mouth of the Bighorn."

Scratch asked, "What's there?"

Cooper explained, "Some winters back Missouri Fur boys built 'em a fort there, right on the Yallerstone."

Immediately Bass grew enthused, saying, "Just down the river a ways?"

"Like I said: near the mouth of the Bighorn," Cooper said. "Bud—you recollect what they called that place . . . Bentley . . . Bentling—"

Tuttle said, "Fort *Benton* what they named it, Silas."

"But wait a minute: we was in that Bighorn River country," Titus said, his suspicions tingling. "Crow country—last winter. Whyn't we ever go on down to that post for a visit?"

"Hell, Scratch," Cooper replied with a big grin, "mouth of the Bighorn was too far a piece from where we was with them Crow. Way off yonder to the northeast."

"All right," Bass conceded, working over the direction of rivers and moun-tain ranges in his mind, "if'n them Missouri Fur Company fellers still got a post there—"

"They call it Fort Benton," Tuttle reminded.

Bass nodded at the interruption, then continued, "Benton . . . then I s'pose it do make damned good sense to trade to them early—afore they start trading with the tribes in the area."

"A right handy post," Cooper stated. "Close at hand, it be."

"You been there, ain'cha?" Titus asked.

"We been there awright," Hooks declared.

"But we ain't been over to that country in some time, Silas," Tuttle re-minded.

Cooper quickly replied, "Just what the hell are y' trying to say, Bud?"

"What if they gone and closed up shop?" Tuttle asked. "What if there ain't no one there to trade our furs to?"

"I thought on that too," Cooper related. "That be the case, then I figger we gotta float on down the Yallerstone a piece."

Bass inquired, "H-how much farther you gotta float?"

"Means we gotta go all the way to the Missouri," Cooper explained. "On down to the Mandan country."

"How far you figger that is?" Titus wondered.

"A ways above the mouth of the Knife."

"That anywhere near Ree country?" Scratch asked. "I heard tell them Rees don't take to fur men passing through their land."

"Don't y' worry none—Fort Vanderburgh's north of Ree country," Silas said consolingly. "Not nowhere near them black-hearted Rees."

Billy agreed, "Ain't a one of us like going nowhere them red niggers be, Scratch."

Scratch turned back to Cooper in the dark. "Awright—so you're telling me we don't find no one there at the Bighorn, we got no other choice 'cept to float on down to Mandan country."

"That's right," Cooper said.

"Ain't that a longer trip after all, 'stead of us just heading south to ronnyvoo on horseback?"

"Longer to ronnyvoo from here," Silas declared matter-of-factly.

"And you 'member we ain't moving near as fast on horseback neither," Tuttle sized things up. "We can make more miles in a day on the river."

"Saying we do decide to make that float," Titus began after he heard the familiar snort of the mule and it prodded him into thinking, "just saying we up and decide to . . . what we gonna do with all them critters we're riding, all them packhorses?"

"That's a problem," Cooper admitted. "But I thought me on that too."

"So what you figger we gonna do with all the horses, Silas?" Billy wondered.

"We leave one of us behind."

"One . . . one of us behind." Tuttle sounded concerned. "In country like this?"

"Gonna be Crow land," Cooper reminded them.

"Sounds to me like you got this all sorted through, right down to the gnat's ass," Bass stated.

"You can lay your sights to that, Scratch," Cooper replied. "I even figgered out the best man to trust with the animals."

Tuttle was frightened when he asked, "Who—who that be, Silas?"

Cooper said, "Scratch."

Billy asked, "Leave Scratch behind on his lonesome when we take the furs downriver?"

"He's got a better head on his shoulders'n Tuttle over there—and Scratch ain't near as skeered of things as Bud," Silas explained. "And he's ever' bit as good with the critters as you, Billy. Makes sense to me that Scratch be the one to leave behind, don't you see? 'Sides, he's got him a lot more sense'n you'll ever have."

"Yep, you're right at all corners of it, Silas." Hooks applauded softly. "Bass got lots more sense'n I'll ever have. He's the man to trust with the horses, for certain on that! What you say about it, Scratch?"

"Figger a man's gotta think on something so 'portant as this be," Titus confided as he stretched his legs out and leaned back, the better to help his mind to settle on thinking.

For a long time Titus lay there in the quiet, listening to the nearby animals crop at the grass, hearing the breathing of the others become as quiet as the spring night that settled around them. Finally Bass came to the end of his consideration, sorting through it the best way he knew how.

"So you're telling me it might be a short trip of it—"

"Other side of the pass where we run onto the Yallerstone," Cooper interrupted, "the four of us'll make two rafts. I figger that's all we'll need."

"Won't take us no time to float down to the Bighorn," Billy assured. "Trader might even have him some whiskey!"

Bass said, "But if you don't find no one there, then it'll be a longer trip to the Missouri country."

"I figger we can meet up with y' afore ronnyvoo time," Cooper testified. "We'll set us a place to join back up, somewhere on down the east front of the mountains."

"Closer on to ronnyvoo?" Billy asked.

Silas said, "Where we can spend all the money we'll make on whiskey and geegaws for the squaws!"

Titus waited for their quiet, good-natured laughter to drift off. "You really do got this sorted clear out to the end, don't you, Cooper?"

"You damn well all know I been thinking on it since last winter. Long enough to know for damn certain what the hell I'm doing."

Rubbing an itch at his nose, Scratch said, "An' you figger I'm the one to stay with the critters."

"Always have figgered you to be the only one 'sides me I could trust with all them critters and the truck the rest of us cain't take with on downriver."

Gazing a moment at Hooks and Tuttle in the dark, Scratch sighed. "I s'pose if'n you boys trust me to see our horses through—"

"I trust you, Titus Bass," Cooper interrupted, smiling with deep satisfaction. "Don't you worry a bit about that, now. These here other two niggers know I'd damn well trust *you* with ever'thing I own, Scratch . . . even trust you with my own life."

Damn—but that was a lot of plew.

Titus Bass knelt there on the bank of the spring-swollen Yellowstone as he and Cooper tied off the last of the hundredweight packs in the center of their second of the two crude rafts.

"Now, don't you dawdle none," Bud reminded Scratch as Bass stood, straightened, and stretched a kink in his back.

Silas stood too, dusting his hands like a man would who'd just finished the difficult task at hand. "He's right, Scratch. Soon as you get us pushed off here, get those horses strung out in a proper train and come on downriver."

"I don't 'spect I'll run across you from here on down, will I?"

Cooper shook his head. "Likely be that we'll cover at least twice as much ground as you will, riding herd on that cavvyyard."

For a moment the four of them stared at the river in silence. How the Yellowstone had filled so that now it ran from bank to bank, flowing all the swifter, deeper too.

"She's running good, Silas," Billy declared.

The leader said, "Fast enough—and still coming up too. We'll likely make better time'n we figgered awready."

"I can almost taste some sweet rum," Billy said, rubbing a hand across his belly like a hungry child.

Bass stepped up to that grinning, fun-loving, childlike man. "You best pack some back for me, Billy Hooks."

"I will. I will most certain!"

"And we ain't gonna be paying no stiff-necked trader's prices for nothing too," Tuttle reminded. "Not no plew for a plug of burley tobacco—that's for certain sure."

"This here's gonna work out best all around," Bass assured as he stepped off the raft and onto the sloping bank where the water lapped at his moccasins. "Silas here come up with the way for us to get top dollar for them skins."

One last time he studied those packs of dark, glossy beaver pelts lashed onto the unpeeled cottonwood saplings. At each end of the craft was tied a partially dug-out cottonwood log. While the two rafts represented close to a week's work for the four men, this second of the two craft had aboard it more beaver than any of the other men had trapped since last summer . . . more beaver than Billy and Bud put together. Tied down to that second raft were the fruits of his labors for the better part of a year.

"Grab your rifles, fellas," Cooper ordered, anxious to set off.

The other two turned away as Silas flung aboard the two rafts the long poles they had cut and trimmed. While Hooks and Tuttle would man that first, Silas himself would be alone with Scratch's many bales of beaver on the second. That way Cooper had promised to personally watch over that small fortune in plew.

"You come on down and have a drink with us at the Bighorn, you hear?" Billy said, holding out his big hand to Titus. Dirt, smoke, grease, and blood were caked in the folds of every knuckle, in a pair of dark crescents beneath the nails, and at the cuticles of every finger.

Tuttle stepped up next, giving his hand to Bass. "If'n we ain't there, we had to push on."

Nodding, Scratch replied, "Means I'll have to turn south my own self, don't it?"

"If'n the Missouri Fur boys don't still have their post at the Bighorn, we'll hurry on to Mandan country," Cooper repeated as he stepped up, then dropped to the damp ground below them, took out his knife, and redrew the map he'd drawn for Titus a dozen times since crossing back over the mountains to strike the Yellowstone.

"That there's the Missoura," Billy said as Cooper scratched a long, meandering line in the damp soil where they had packed the ground underfoot for days now.

"An' here's the Yallerstone," Cooper said as he drew with the tip of his knife blade. "The Bighorn comes in here."

Titus squatted on the other side of the crude map. "From the south, yeah—I remember."

With the knife's tip at that juncture, Cooper said, "We ain't there, and there ain't no fort or traders still there—we gone on down to the Missoura."

Head bobbing, Billy added, "And Mandan country."

"That's 'bout over here," Silas said, jabbing at the ground on that Missouri River line.

Scratch nodded. "When you boys get there and trade off them plews of ours—show me again how you fix on coming back."

"Ain't along the river like we floated down," Tuttle reiterated.

"No," Cooper explained, then started dragging the knife blade from the Upper Missouri on a southwesterly beeline. "What I figger to do is buy us some horses—come cross the country, Scratch. Maybeso take us a few weeks, but you can figger on joining up down here."

"Where for sure?"

Holding the knife upright and twisting the tip into the ground, Silas explained, "I figger the best place for us to meet up is here."

"You figger that's on over that low pass, off torst the west of Turtle Rock?"*

"On over from the Sweetwater," Cooper agreed, tapping his knife even farther to the southwest. "On past that Popo Agia stream the Crow talk of."

Tapping his own index finger into that dirt map, Scratch said, "If ronnyvoo gonna be here—you figger me to meet you up here . . . somewhere east of the Uintees?"

Cooper smiled. "That's the place where we'll see y'—on down in that Green River country."

"Where General Ashley had him his first ronnyvoo back to twenty-five?" Tuttle inquired.

Glancing at Bud, Cooper answered, "On down from Henry'n Fork. There's a good park down there. A high valley, Scratch. Good grazing for all them animals. We'll meet y' there with our trade goods and our drinking money."

Billy slapped his hands together loudly. "Ready for a spree at Sweet Lake ronnyvoo!"

As Cooper stood, he said, "We won't be far from ronnyvoo there, Scratch."

"Women and whiskey—right, Titus?" Tuttle said, enthused.

"Damn shame you boys'll have a head start on me," Scratch replied, making the most of what he felt at their leave-taking.

"You just remember: ain't but one man I trust to stay behind with my

* Independence Rock, in present-day Wyoming

critters," Cooper said, gazing steadily into Bass's eyes. "Only one man I figger won't let 'em get run off by red niggers 'tween now and the time we join back up."

Titus nodded solemnly. "I won't let you down."

Silas presented his big paw as he looked down at the shorter man. "I never thought you would, Titus Bass. Not from the first days I laid eyes on you. Allays figgered you was a man to count on doin' ever'thing you could to live up to my trust in you, saving your hide the way I done more'n once."

Bass took a step back as he let go of Cooper's hand. "Time's come for me to watch out for my own hide, ain't it?"

Smiling, Cooper said, "That's for certain sure, Scratch. Keep your eye on the skyline."

Titus watched Billy and Bud wade over to the first raft with a splash, untie it, and step on board. "Yep—and you boys watch your hair!"

"Best you keep your nose in the wind, Titus Bass," Billy called out as he squatted down among the bales of beaver and took up the long rudder pole he planted down in the fork of a stout branch lashed to the back of the raft.

"I'll do that, Billy Hooks!" he called out.

Tuttle took up the long pole and pushed the first big raft away from the shore, poling toward the faster water in midchannel. "We'll have us a good, long drink together real soon, Scratch!"

"I'll count on that, Bud," he called back, raising his hand to the pair as their craft was nudged by faster water.

Cooper slipped his big hat off his head and plopped it down on top of those beaver packs Bass had worked so hard to pull out of the icy mountain streams. Taking up his long pole with one hand, Silas gathered some of his stringy, unkempt hair in the other, tugging on it as he sang out.

"Keep your hair locked on tight, Titus Bass!"

"Don't you worry none about me!" Scratch sang back in reply as he started to trot downstream along the grassy bank, watching Cooper's raft ease into the fast water now, beginning to pull away all the faster. "I'll watch my topknot!"

Then Cooper had his back turned and had his long pole reversed, putting the flat paddle end down into the water and the pole itself to rest in the Y-shaped branch they had lashed at the back of the raft. With it he would keep the craft at midriver where the spring runoff ran deepest.

Glancing downstream, Bass saw the first raft, made out the dim shape of those big bales of fur, and the pair of tiny figures on board—one of them working the crude rudder as the Yellowstone hurried them east toward that Missouri Fur Company post near the mouth of the Bighorn. Then they were swept around a gentle bend in the river and gone from sight.

He turned back to watch Cooper glide by at a fast clip, watching, watching, watching until the tall, thick-shouldered man was gone around that curve in the Yellowstone too. Then Titus stared at that spot in the river, those tall cottonwoods sixty, seventy feet or taller . . . as things grew quiet save for the nearby animals cropping at the spring grass, the cry of meadowlarks and the bothersome chatter of a nagging magpie too, the gentle breeze sneaking through the new leaves above him with a faint, reassuring rustle.

Then for a moment it got so quiet, he could almost hear his heart beat . . . except for the voice of the river running over its rocky bed, pushing itself against a boulder here and there with a foaming rush.

So quiet was it, so alone was he again, that Scratch succumbed to the temptation to fill that empty void as he watched that distant spot on the river, there between the wide banks of the Yellowstone where the three had disappeared.

"Yepper," he sighed, every bit as quietly as the breeze itself. "I'll watch my topknot."

SEVENTEEN

No one was waiting for him there at the mouth of the Bighorn.

For the better part of two weeks Scratch struggled to keep that cavvyyard together as he marched east to meet up with Silas Cooper and the other two. A lot of work for one man.

There was watering the critters two at a time every morning before he fried himself his own breakfast. And there was keeping them strung out enough on the trail that they didn't jam up so close they would bite on one another or tear at one another's tails—but not so far apart that they took on unruly notions. Good thing, he thought, these animals were used to being around one another by and large and had made of themselves a good herd. That helped each night when it came time for him to find a place to camp.

Bass stopped early enough at the end of every one of those lengthening days to water them again two by two by two while the others grazed and rolled, dusting themselves as the mosquitoes and flies came out in springtime clouds to torture man and beast alike. And when the watering was done, Titus would build himself a fire down beneath the branches of the biggest cottonwood he could find along the banks of the river. The leaves and that incessant breeze in the valley of the Yellowstone helped to disperse the smoke rising from his cookfire, as well as hold down the number of tormentors wanting a taste of his flesh, to draw some of his blood.

After broiling his antelope or venison shot along the trail, Bass would drink his coffee, light up his pipe, and enjoy the temporary warmth of the fire as the night came down and the temperature dropped. Then when the cooking gear had cooled off enough to stuff it away in one of the panniers he could sling back atop Hannah's back—closing on the time all light was just about gone from the sky, he poured out the dregs of his coffee and kicked dirt into the tiny fire.

That done, Bass mounted the saddle horse, took up Hannah's lead rope, and rode over to where the other animals grazed on the tall grass. There he clucked, whistled, and called as he pulled Hannah through their midst. And most times, without much trouble at all, the rest of the horses and mules followed. Two miles, perhaps, sometimes more, on downriver—and when he had found a likely spot for more grazing beneath the stars, a likely spot where a man could roll up in his blankets for a cold, fireless camp, then he would circle back around the small herd to let them know that here they could stop following and start eating again.

In country where the *Apsaalooke* themselves had so many enemies, it would never pay for a man to become too careless. Especially a man with so many horses.

Not that he feared the Crow. Not Big Hair's people—now that they knew him. Now that he had spent a winter among them.

Yet repeatedly Bird in Ground had warned Scratch: the Blackfoot came raiding as the spring winds grew warm. Just as the River Crow would go riding off to raid Blackfoot country. Ponies and scalps . . . and if the opportunity presented itself—the Crow would always bring back an infant or a young child. Such stolen treasures would one day grow up to be *Apsaalooke,* no longer the enemy. After all, Bird in Ground had explained, there were never enough Apsaalooke, would never be enough when it came to defending their homeland against the powerful enemies who had Absaraka surrounded.

Perhaps it was true that *Akbaatatdia* did watch over his people, the Crow, protecting them from all those who outnumbered them.

Perhaps that powerful spirit that Bird in Ground called Grandfather Above had watched over Titus Bass, as well, while he was in Absaraka. Not that Scratch had ever been one to particularly believe in the naming of spiritual forces, as others, both white and red, were wont to do. Those who believed in such things had always seemed to be the sort to turn their lives over to such spirits rather than trusting in themselves, he figured. Whether it was the white man's God, his Lord of Hosts, even the Archangel Michael and ol' Lucifer himself—or the simple, unadorned beliefs of an honest man like Bird in Ground, who explained that the Grandfather Above was present in all things, and the closest spirit the Crow had to the white man's devil could only be the playful practical joker called Old Man Coyote.

So perhaps it was that trickster who was toying with Titus Bass right now as he forded the Bighorn near its mouth, swatting his arms at clouds of mosquitoes and big green deerflies that hovered above the sweating backs of every one of the horses and mules as they splashed up through the brush on the east bank.

There simply was no fort on either side of the Bighorn River.

In angry frustration he lashed Hannah's lead rope to some willow, knowing the other animals would not wander far, then remounted and pushed the saddle horse down the bank, fording the swollen Yellowstone. Riding an arc of more than two miles from east to west along that north bank, Scratch found no fur-company buildings nor pole corrals, no sign of any white men. Only some two dozen old lodge rings and fading black fire pits on this side of the river. Sign that was likely more than a year old. That, and a lot of buffalo chips scattered among the hoof-pocked ground.

In utter, all-consuming disappointment he swam the horse back over late that afternoon, redressed into his dry clothing, then got the animals moving east once more, growing more confused and concerned for his partners.

Perhaps they hadn't made it, he began to fear. Maybe some accident had befallen them back yonder between here and the great bend of the Yellowstone. Worse still—attacked. But, no—he tried to shake off that nagging uncertainty as he pushed on east away from the Bighorn itself, resolutely.

After all, he'd come down the Yellowstone behind them. Wouldn't he have seen some sign of a fight if the other three had been jumped by a Blackfoot raiding party that chanced onto the trappers? Wouldn't he have seen one of the rafts pulled up to the bank, or if it had been set adrift, wouldn't he have seen it snagged in some of the driftwood piles the Yellowstone itself gathered every few hundred yards when running full and frothy the way it did in spring?

Wouldn't there be a chance he'd seen a body trapped in the same downriver driftwood piles?

Unless the Blackfoot dragged 'em off, he convinced himself. Half-alive. Tall and gory were the tales of how the Blackfoot loved to torture a man. . . .

And then Bass told himself that he could have missed all sign of the trio's destruction, because he had only come down the north bank of the Yellowstone until reaching the mouth of the Bighorn—and he hadn't hugged right up to the bank, at that. What with picking the easiest country to cross with all these animals, Titus hadn't always stayed in constant sight of the riverbank. Could be he'd missed something. Could be there'd been some sign on the south side of the river, and he'd passed it right on by.

But he hadn't come far from the east bank of the Bighorn—the certainty of what had befallen the others looming all the larger with every step—when he spotted the ruins squatting on a small thumb of high ground not far ahead.

After dismounting nearby and leaving the saddle horse to graze with the rest, Scratch hurried to the burned and overgrown ruins of the small log post—hopeful that he would find where the trio were to leave him their notice. At least now he knew for certain there was no Missouri Fur Company post here where the trio could trade their plews for goods and liquor. And that meant that now he knew the three would have to push on down the Yellowstone, on down the Upper

Missouri until they got close to the Knife River . . . but where was the word from them they had promised to leave him?

Perhaps an angry band of Indians had burned down the fort's cabins and stockade in some long-ago season past . . . or maybe the white traders had done it themselves when they'd abandoned the post. Maybe the Crow trade wasn't all that profitable for the company, he mulled. Not any longer, since men like Ashley had come to the mountains with skin trappers of their own to strip a piece of country bare. Maybeso the fur companies that had of a time ruled on the northern rivers no longer could survive the competition.

Stepping over the burned hulk of a cottonwood wall now collapsed into the soil where the stockade and cabin ruins were being overgrown year after year by grass and weed and the blooming purple crowns of wavyleaf thistle, Titus remembered how Cooper said the traders were operating their post not all that long ago.

"Twenty-one," Bass said to himself, scratching at his bearded cheek. "Maybe twenty-two it was."

But Silas and the rest said they had been here not long after the fort had been constructed and manned . . . just like the Spaniard Manuel Lisa had raised his own fort somewhere nearby more than ten years before that.

Back of the ruins rose a soft-sloped knoll he hurried to on foot, climbed, then carefully appraised the surrounding country. How he wished now that there was some high point of rimrock the likes he had discovered back upriver a ways, some great flat-topped promontory where a man could see for himself a good stretch of country.*

But from up here on this low knoll, and from his explorations back by the mouth of the Bighorn itself, Scratch could see no indication of another stockade. Too much time had passed since Lisa and Henry had abandoned the northern country.

"Mayhaps a dozen years or more," he reminded himself quietly, despair sinking in atop that hill.

After all those winters and summers, there simply wouldn't be much left of an abandoned stockade and some dirt-roofed cabins, a post burned down by those who sought to leave nothing behind for the brownskins. Too many seasons for the ground itself to reclaim any ruins, grass too tall for him to spot anything, anyway.

He sighed, sure there was no chance that Silas and the rest had left him some notice, some sign, some indication they had been there and were heading on downriver. For a moment there his hope had soared: if not at the Missouri Fur Company post, then likely the trio had left all important word at the earlier Bighorn post Isaac Washburn had spoken of during Lisa's day on the upper rivers.

Damn.

But in gazing west at the path of the falling sun, he realized he didn't have

---

* Pompey's Pillar, east of present-day Billings, Montana

time to mourn and brood about it now. Time he should be working on filling his belly with what was left of that antelope he'd shot two days back. And some coffee to keep him warm until he rode off to find himself a likely place for a cold camp farther downriver.

But as he descended the knoll and walked past the ruins, his belly didn't feel all that hungry. Just empty and cold—a feeling he thought for a moment was something he could remedy with a juicy steak and some strong coffee. Yet no matter how much he tried to feed his belly, what bothered him would not be satisfied until he knew what had become of the three.

Call it fear. Call it doubt. Call it what he would—Scratch figured he was smart enough to realize that until he knew for sure, then there would be plenty of room in his imagination for all sorts of possibilities.

And that scared him down to his roots.

Rising from the bank of the river with his coffee kettle among the broad-leafed cattails and slogging out of the water lapping against the shore, he told himself he did not want to believe anything but the best in people. Despite what others older and perhaps much wiser than he might believe—Titus simply wanted to give every man the sake of the doubt. Far better was it for him to fear the worst that could befall the trio than to think the worst of them. Far, far better to believe that some terrible fate had rubbed them out than to allow himself to believe that he had been taken advantage of.

Alone again . . . but Scratch would simply not allow himself to even begin to consider anything but that Lady Fate's terrible and capricious ways had robbed him of the notice they were going to leave at this post if they found it abandoned. If it had been something scrawled on a scrap of canvas with a bit of fire-pit charcoal and then hung loosely at the corner of the ruins . . . perhaps the wind might be the playful culprit. Or Old Man Coyote.

That evening as he waited for his coffee to come to a boil and he hung the thick antelope steak from a sharpened stick over the flames to drip huge drops of fragrant grease into his cookfire, Bass grappled with it until he decided there was no other way but to backtrack along the south bank of the Yellowstone. He could remember the last of the trio's campsites he had run across as he'd marched downriver. Back there on the north bank—and a hell of a distance back up the Yellowstone.

So somewhere between here and there he would likely have his answer. To find where they had pulled over to the bank, tied up their rafts, and built their night fire. If not a campsite, then he would likely find evidence of their ruin. His worst fears conjured up images of discovering one of the rafts crushed and broken against some boulders, perhaps one of their scalped and mutilated bodies tangled in the driftwood. And all those plews—a rich man's ransom in beaver—gone to the bottom of the swollen river.

That evening as the light began to fade slowly from the summer sky, Scratch ate slowly, chewing each bite deliberately but without any real enjoyment, sipping at his coffee without relish. There wasn't enough antelope or thick coffee to fill the yawning hole of his doubt, the chasm that was his fear.

After cooling the small coffee kettle so he could repack it among his camp plunder, Bass walked over to the grazing animals. Thinking he ought to try cheering himself as he threw the blanket onto the back of the saddle horse, Titus began to whistle notes of some tune that he quickly recalled as a song the boatmen sang. It helped to think back on how Ebenezer Zane's and Hames Kingsbury's crew had held together—one for all—men he could put his faith, trust, and loyalty in. Scratch's whistle became a bit merrier at the remembrance.

Then, as he bent over to retrieve the saddle and rose with it suspended across both arms, he was shoved from behind.

Dropping the saddle as if it were a hot coal, Scratch wheeled, yanking at the big pistol stuffed into the wide sash at his waist—his heart in his throat as he yanked back the hammer with the heel of his left hand.

Surprised now more than scared—he wagged his head and stuffed the pistol away, swallowing down the hard lump of instant fear that had choked him.

"D-damn, girl," he said with relief as the mule moved closer, her head bobbing up and down as if she acknowledged that term of address he often used around her. "Don't you go scaring me like that."

Quickly rubbing her muzzle, Titus turned away and went back to whistling the riverboatman's song as he bent to pick up the saddle. Again she jabbed her nose right between his shoulder blades, shoving him forward clumsily. He stumbled a couple of steps, lunging against the saddle horse that sidestepped out of his way.

"Damn you!" he growled this time. "You need to stop that, Hannah. I got work to do here."

Again he turned his back on the young mule and stepped toward the horse. Not realizing, he went back to whistling the merry tune and had just managed to throw the saddle up onto the animal's back and was bending over to reach under the horse's belly for the far half of the cinch when out of the corner of his eye he saw Hannah coming for him.

"You stay right there," he warned with a wag of his finger. "I ain't in no mood to be putting up with no pranks you done learned on your own."

Yanking up on the cinch, he twisted to keep an eye on her as his hands completed the task, and went back to whistling . . . watching her bob her head up and down as she came for him again.

"Why . . . I'll be go to hell right here," he said quietly as she moved up close enough. He scratched that forelock between her ears. "And be et for the devil's tater."

Maybe she wasn't being a devilish, cantankerous, playful sort when she came up and tried to get his attention in her own way. Perhaps he was just too dumb to notice at first. Scratch decided he'd just have to prove it to himself, here and now before they went off to find a cold camp where they would bed down.

Stepping over to the far side of the horse, he waited the few minutes until Hannah went back to her grazing. As soon as her head lowered and she began to tear off the tops of the tall stems of porcupine and bluegrass, Titus quietly moved away, taking a roundabout route as he made for the walls of the abandoned post.

Reaching the ruins, he sat down on the collapsed corner of the burned logs where the grass and weeds and the wavyleaf thistle had knotted themselves over the charred stumps, then waited a few minutes more to be sure she wasn't paying him any attention.

Then he wet his lips with the tip of his tongue and whistled. The same sort of whistle he had used to call their old hound, Tink, in from the timber at the family's farm, or back to his side when they'd been out hunting together. Not the boatman's song he had been whistling slightly out of tune—but the sort of notes a man would string together to bring an animal . . .

By gloree! She raised her big jug-head, perked up her ears, and promptly headed his way without the least hesitation.

What with the way she was coming right over, Scratch felt he should give her a reward . . . but as he stood, Bass realized he had nothing to give the mule. When she stopped before him there by the ruins, he swiftly bent and tore up a handful of the long porcupine grass and held it out in an open palm.

Hannah sniffed it, nuzzled it a moment with the end of her nose, then snorted—blowing the grass stems off his palm so she could rub her nose on his hand. As he stood there in surprise, the mule craned her neck so she could work her head back and forth beneath his hand the way she might scratch herself on a branch of convenient height. Yet . . . he saw this as something different.

She was wanting something more than just a soothing scratch. She was wanting his touch.

As Bass cooed to her, he rubbed her ears and forelocks and muzzle the way he knew she enjoyed it. At times she would rock her head over against his shoulder, lay it momentarily against his chest, then cock one of her dark, round eyes up at him—as if studying the man very, very closely. This man she was coming to know, this man she was learning to give her affection to.

"We best get moving off for the night," he finally said some time later when he again became aware of just how little light was left in that late-spring sky.

As long as the days were lasting at this time of the year, he wasn't all that sure if it might not be the first part of summer already. And now he had the prospect of losing another week or more in backtracking on his trail here to assure himself he hadn't missed any evidence that disaster or ambush had befallen the trio on their trip downriver.

After climbing atop the saddle mount, he led Hannah around and through the rest of the stock as they grazed contentedly in the bluestem, pushing aside the thistles' purple globes. It took a third trip through, with his growing a bit frustrated and slapping a rawhide braided lariat against his leg, grumbling at them all to get the herd moving. Reluctant were they to leave when it seemed they had just begun to settle in for the night.

He did not end up taking them far at all—less than a couple of miles on east of the post ruins, he noticed a spot along the bank where the bulrushes and spear-leafed cattails naturally parted wide enough to allow a man to water his stock come morning. Twisting in the saddle, Scratch looked back toward the ruins in the distance, calculating just how far he had come, then glanced at the sky, still a much paler hue in the west.

Settling himself back around, he figured that he hadn't come far enough to elude any horsemen who might be watching, needed to push on a little far-ther—when he spotted the large circle of trampled grass there among the over-hanging branches of the tall and stately cottonwoods. Near the center of the trampled grass sat a blackened circle. Several charred limbs lay within the pile of ash. No ring of rocks had they used to circle their fire, nor had they dug a pit for it. Nothing more elaborate than gathering up their kindling and starting their fire then and there with flint and steel.

Quickly yanking both feet out of the broad stirrups and kicking his right leg over the saddle horn, Scratch dropped to the grass and hurried alone to the site. He skidded to a halt at the edge of the large circle some forty feet across, studied it for a moment more—then lunged ahead to the circle of ash. Squatting there, he held a hand no more than a breath over the charred limbs. No heat.

Now he stuffed his fingertips into the ash. Still no heat. Swirling his fingers around in the fire heap, he could find no telltale warmth of a single coal still glowing deep among the ash.

His nose helped him locate the bone heap nearby where they had butchered the doe—cutting out the steaks and hams and other juicy morsels without dis-membering the carcass. They would have eaten their fill for supper, breakfasted on what had been cooked and left over the night before, then taken the rest with them when they'd pushed off.

Standing abruptly, he scooted over to that wide parting in the bulrushes and cattails. There at the bank where the foxsedge grew he saw their moccasin prints. Saw where they had scraped the ends of the crude rafts, carving scars into the muddy bank. Found the rope burns where they had lashed the two craft on up the bank, tying them off around a pair of cottonwood. Through their single night at this spot, the long ropes had brushed back and forth across the bank's vegetation as the rafts had bobbed here in the quiet eddy of the Yellowstone's current.

Back near the fire he could see where they had bedded down, those grassy places near the fire more flattened than the rest of the bluestem and porcupine grass that was barely beginning to recover. Where the trio had laid out their bedding and blankets for the night—the grass was broken, discolored, and entirely crushed.

From all the sign he could make out in the failing light as summer night surrounded him, Scratch reassured himself they had been there. At least they had come this far—and, like him, had discovered the post to be abandoned, burned, and fallen to ruins. If there had been at least the shell of a cabin left standing, then they likely would have pulled over then and there, spending the night within the shelter of the log stockade, he decided. But instead the three of them had seen no walls rising on that narrow thumb of high ground, and therefore had no reason to stop where they said they would leave him word of their passing.

He stood, anxious, looking this way and that.

So why wouldn't they leave him some sign—a scrap of old canvas with their marks on it—hanging here? If not at the post site, then why not here? Had they forgotten? he wondered. Or, as he slid closer to fearing, was it just a case of not giving a damn about what they had promised him?

And if they cared so little about the promise of leaving him a message at the mouth of the Bighorn River . . . then . . . then could the three have come to care nothing about the other promises made him?

Finally he wagged his head, steadfastly refusing again to take this as evidence of the worst. Better to keep on believing the best. Billy was a simpleminded man, but good enough at heart. And Tuttle was smarter than Hooks, so he'd remember what they'd promised Titus Bass. So it really didn't matter what he might fear at the core of him about Silas Cooper . . . because Scratch believed that come hell or high water, in the end Cooper would do exactly as he had promised: trade their furs and return for another winter season in the mountains, and another after that, and another after . . .

Scratch believed in that strongly because of what he knew he meant to Silas Cooper. There was no two ways of Sunday about it: Titus Bass was the best trapper of the four of them. And as long as Silas was getting his healthy cut of Scratch's catch, then Cooper would do everything to protect his best trapper.

Wasn't no way in hell Silas would break his bond with Bass, not by a long chalk!

Sighing, Scratch looked about again as the light faded. He decided he would sleep here and turned back to the saddle horse and Hannah. After securing them for the night near his bed, Titus stretched out and gazed up at the black dome flecked with a wide trail of dusty stars. Wondering if the three of them were looking up at much the same sky right then too.

At least they'd come this far. So chances were good they'd make it from here on down to that Mandan post just above the mouth of the Knife River. Silas, Bud, and Billy had come this far, he reminded himself . . . and that was good enough to convince Scratch that they would likely make it the rest of the way. Without accident, without attack.

Far, far better was it for him to believe in that—than to go on nursing doubt any longer. Better to hang his hope on the fact they'd been right here, ate and camped and slept right here on this ground . . . better to hope than allow any misgivings to creep in and ambush him. Always better to trust in someone than to let doubt and uncertainty nibble away at the faith he wanted to have in the three.

Best that he protect what kernel of loyalty remained than to allow something to fester inside him . . . no matter what.

No matter how long it took.

High summer was daily baking the central Rockies the way his mother had baked her double-sweetened corn bread in the Dutch oven in their river-rock fireplace, scooping hot coals onto the top of the cast-iron kettle.

In the heat he tried now to remember the fragrance of that rising bread, the surface of the cornmeal turning golden. But Titus could not remember.

Instead he rubbed his nose, finding it caked and crusted again with the dry dust of this open, unforgiving country far to the southwest of the low saddle* that took a man to the Pacific side of the great continental spine. The dust stived up with every hoof the horse set down. Dust from all those horses and mules behind him, all those hooves—and when the breeze stirred to temporarily cool the sweat glistening his skin, the breeze might just as soon blow that cloud of alkali dust in his direction.

A far, far different country, this, far different from that up on the Yellowstone in the land of the *Apsaalooke*. More weeks than he cared to think about since he'd left the mouth of the Yellowstone behind and moved south up the Bighorn. Since there was no longer a Missouri Fur Company post, all this time he had been counting on the three joining up with him far to the south.

That day after finding sign of their riverside camp, he had begun this journey south. Eager most of all to complete his side of the compact made with Silas Cooper and the others. Only way Titus knew for sure that their reunion would ever come to be was that he himself had to be there to meet up with the three when they rode in from Fort Vanderburgh on the Missouri. From there Cooper said he would bring them a little south of west. Unencumbered by all the weight of traps, baggage, camp gear, and what other truck four men required to survive one winter after another out here in the mountains, surely the three could make far better time hurrying toward their rendezvous south of Henry's Fork and the Green River country east of the Uintah.

Was no doubt in Scratch's mind that the trio could travel far faster than he had been able to since he had last seen them floating off down the Yellowstone. Considering the number of horses and mules he had to ride herd on . . . well, while he might not have as far to ride, Bass grew more certain with every day that Silas Cooper's bunch could likely cover twice the distance he could in every sunup-to-sundown ride. And that's what kept him pushing on as fast as the animals, and the rugged, broken terrain, and all the terrible storms of early summer allowed him.

The days drifted by as he scooted south along the winding path of the

---

* *South Pass in present-day Wyoming.*

Bighorn, south farther still into the Wind River country and then the high breaks of the Popo Agie, where he crossed that high saddle as a hellish hailstorm battered him and the animals early one afternoon. The icy shards hurt so much, he was driven out of the saddle, dropping to the ground and dragging a thick wool blanket with him as he huddled beneath the belly of the tail-tucked saddle mount to sit out heaven's attack on this treeless expanse of parched, high sagebrush desert. How all the horses whimpered and the mules snorted in their discomfort and pain until the bombardment moved on east and a cold rain fell. Eventually a band of blue and purple and dusty rose sky emerged along the western horizon, and the last of the storm was finally on its way over him.

Like him, the horses and mules had shuddered and shivered, and reluctantly they moved out with him once more as he urged them in motion. The wind had come up soon after and made for a damp, cold camp that night until he got his fire started. Chilled to the marrow, Scratch clutched his coffee tin close beneath his hairy chin and consoled himself with the fact that he was getting all the nearer to the country where he would await the arrival of his partners.

Partners.

It had been the first time in more than two winters with the trio that he had ever thought of them as partners. At first they had been saviors—arriving as they did just when his last horse had died of black water. Then he had come to think of them as his mentors, teaching him not only trapping but the ways of the mountains and of the brown-skinned natives who likewise called this high country home. And finally he was forced to consider Silas Cooper as his master when Cooper first exacted his tribute for saving Bass's life, for keeping him alive.

What else would he call it when he had thrown in near everything he owned, certainly everything he had worked the better part of a year to acquire, handed over that fortune of his to join with theirs in that exciting, challenging endeavor of floating their furs downriver? What else would the four of them call themselves . . . but partners?

As anxious as he was to rendezvous with them, Bass had figured he would reach the reunion site far ahead of schedule, so he had turned back a bit on the compass and headed south by east toward Park Kyack—fondly remembering that high mountain valley and the Ute band. Recalling the widow and the warmth of her blankets.

But as much as he searched the familiar ground, there was no sign of the tribe, nor much evidence of what direction they had taken. On occasions as he worked his way through the valley, Bass crossed the trail of a hunting party, perhaps a raiding party—unshod horses of one band or another haunting this high country. The one old camp he came across showed him where the Ute had likely moved out of the valley, heading north by west to hunt both the buffalo and antelope they would not find here in Park Kyack.

Staring down at the cold, blackened rings of those lodge fires, the remains of drying racks, the litter of camp life, he had grown lonely, so lonely again. It hurt every bit as much as when he watched the three float off down the river and around the far bend in the Yellowstone. The Ute had been here. But after hoping to find them . . . to find her . . . the loneliness inside made him want to disbelieve the Ute had been here at all, had crossed this ground—so close, yet no more.

Then he realized he was sore in need of seeing another human face, hearing another human voice, watching a smile emerge and eyes twinkle when they looked back at him. As much as he cherished the solitude, loved the aloneness, and savored being beholden to no one but himself . . . Titus yearned terribly. Yearned for faces and voices and laughing eyes. Hungered for the mere touch of a hand in his, perhaps the arms of a friend around his shoulders, even the mouth of a woman pressed against his as he tasted her breath and felt himself stir to readiness.

From time to time after reaching the beautiful valley, he stopped a day or so to lay his traps. But as well as he did, the pelts were poor compared to what a man could catch in winter or early spring.

"Beaver always come to bait in this here country," he spoke out loud one night at his fire, surprised to hear the sound of his own voice. "Come to bait they do: just as sure as a man'd lay down his money on a St. Louie whore's feather bed so's to get hisself a proper forking."

It was pretty country, to be sure. No wonder the Ute felt so strong about it— were prepared to defend it the way the Crow defended their Absaraka.

That was just the way he got to thinking a few weeks later after pushing up and out of Park Kyack, wondering if it weren't the same with those tribes along the Upper Missouri. Would they defend their land and the river that ran through it from a trio of white men floating down to a distant trading post? If those lone men were heading on out of that tribe's precious country, why wouldn't the warriors just let the trio pass on by? Or would they realize that the mere sight of white men meant the possibility of plunder, not to mention the presence of guns and powder to be stolen? And Bass knew, in the marrow of him, that might well prove to be enough of a temptation to spell the trio's doom.

Dropping down out of the high country again, driving that herd of horses and mules north by west, constantly keeping his eyes moving along the far skyline, watching the distant ridges, staying to the long stretches of timber that bordered every stream and creek and riverbed so that he wouldn't stand out with that cavvyyard he had stirring up a cloud of dust behind him. Then, at long last, he reached the banks of the Green as summer was growing all the hotter and the days had become their longest. For weeks upon weeks now he had counted upon laying his eyes on this river. For here was the place, and now was the time, the four would rejoin.

He waited.

The mosquitoes grew thick there in the valley of the Green as summer aged and the big bottle-green horseflies tormented the animals he was forced to move to new grass from time to time.

And he waited some more.

Scratch hunted, and watched the skyline for warriors. He rode out to the high ground northeast of where he maintained his lonely vigil and watched the skyline for Silas, Billy, and Bud.

Still he waited.

And each day he added a notch to a peeled wand of willow. So many days and notches now since he had watched the three of them float away—there were many such wands of willow stuffed down in his saddle pouch. More than he cared to count anymore. More than he cared to remind himself. Each time he did, the doubt crept back in.

He had waited long past the time Silas had calculated they would reunite.

Then he added notches he knew would put him past the time the traders' rendezvous had come and gone at the south end of the Sweet Lake. With regret, and a growing anger, Titus tried to remember the faces of the merry Daniel Potts, mulatto dandy Jim Beckwith, young and randy Jim Bridger, and even crusty old Henry Fraeb. Faces he hadn't seen in a year now, not since Willow Valley. Hard, tanned, wind-seamed faces and rough-edged voices brought easily to laughter with the tall tales he wouldn't share now for at least another year.

Unless he went, and now. Yes, perhaps some of the brigades might still be in that country close by the Sweet Lake. Wouldn't be no trick at all to find where the hundred or more had camped and traded, drank and reveled together. Wouldn't be no hard task to seeing how they had split up and moved out, what direction the brigades were headed. He might catch up, spend a few days among the company of one brigade or another. Just to have the sound of voices and laughter in his ears.

After all . . . it was plain to see that Silas and Billy and Bud had been rubbed out. Somehow he had to accept that he was on his own hook once more.

Perhaps they hadn't made it all the way down the Yellowstone and then the Missouri to that trader's post called Vanderburgh's. Then again—they might well have made it there and traded all the furs, only to be rubbed out coming across all that country where the Arikara and Pawnee and Arapaho could jump a few white men hurrying back to the mountains. Leastways, that's something Isaac Washburn had known of firsthand. The country where Scratch's three friends were to cross was the same stretch of high plains where Ol' Gut and Hugh Glass had barely escaped with their hide and their hair.

As much as he stared into the small fire he built himself for company every night, as much as he watched the water flow by in the Green every day—the feeling inside him had grown no more comfortable, no more easy to accept until he was ready to let it go. To hell with the furs. There'd always be beaver in the mountains and high valleys. Besides, he still had his traps and other truck. By God, Titus thought, he was still in the business of trapping.

So to hell with all that prime beaver he had dragged out of countless frozen streams, beaver stretched and scraped, beaver packed in hundredweight bales and finally lashed down on that crude raft that disappeared down the Yellowstone with Silas Cooper.

Only thing that mattered was that he'd lost three friends. Lost the three men who had damn well saved his life.

Down in his belly that eventual acceptance of it brought up the gorge that nearly choked him after all these years: remembering how he had lost Ebenezer Zane. A trusted friend, a mentor Titus had looked up to, a man who had taught Bass not just about the great rivers, but about life on the river—women and rum, song and friends.

Then he remembered Isaac himself. How the graying trapper had done all that he could to keep Bass from liking him there at first, but come to love him Titus had. To trust Washburn enough to plan on following him west into the unknown. Then Gut was taken from him too. Gone as suddenly.

After all these winters and summers healing over those two painful scars of loss, now he had to face the loss of three more. Silas, Billy, and Bud ripped from him.

"The Big Muddy's fair boiling with red niggers," he told himself out loud more than once as he wrestled with his inner agony. "Likely it be that the three of 'em just bought into more'n they could barter for on that river's track. Injuns got 'em up there—or Injuns got 'em coming back."

As much as a man might refuse to grapple with it, he had to accept that the three of them were gone. Dead. Rubbed out.

And the only way there was to get on with life was to get on . . . with people. Bass had to find one of those brigades. He had to be among others until this pain eased. It might take a few days. More likely it would take weeks, and Bass might just decide to throw in with Fitzpatrick's bunch for the fall hunt, joining up for as long as the winter. He could trade off what he didn't need in the way of all these horses to the company men for some coffee and sugar, anything he didn't already have enough of back there among the packs. The brigade's booshway might even have some liquor left. And rum or whiskey might just go a long way to helping numb a bit more of the pain.

Titus was sure the only way that hurting would stop and he could venture back out on his own was to do one thing. If he was to survive inside, he knew he had to scare up some faces and voices and eyes crinkling in laughter.

Knowing that the best chances for finding any of that healing lay over in that Sweet Lake country, Scratch eagerly set off before sunrise the next morning, unable to sleep after coming to his decision. All night he had brooded on it, concluding that his best chances of running onto a brigade moving out with the breakup of rendezvous lay in his striking out to the north. At least he knew there would always be one brigade moving northeast into the high mountain country to trap through the autumn. There might even be two brigades he could run across —since another was likely to march east a ways from the Sweet Lake country before pointing their noses directly north.

Chances were better than good that he would run onto one such brigade somewhere to the north—or at least come across sign of their passing, and he could hurry along their backtrail until he caught up with them. That morning he put the Green at his back and struck out east, following the meandering path of a narrow river* that he knew would eventually lead him back toward the mountains and Park Kyack. Scratch felt a new chapter opening on the book of his life. Instead of plunging back into that high country to search for the Ute, this time he would strike out to the north upon reaching the foothills.

All the better to avoid the Arapaho who came to raid the Ute for ponies and plunder. Titus knew firsthand just how that warrior tribe craved ambushing their ancient enemies.

It simply made a lot more horse sense to stay as far out of the way of those thieving Arapaho as he could.

---

* *Present-day Yampa River, known among the Rocky Mountain fur trappers as the Little Bear River*

EIGHTEEN

"Whereaway you bound, my son?"

In his dreamlike reverie Titus peered up at the old man leading a fine horse up to his evening fire. Nighttime had come early that autumn so long, long ago now . . . and with it the cold as he rode closer to the city of his dreams.

Lulled now into daydreaming once more by the late-summer heat on his back and the rocking-chair gait of the saddle horse beneath him, Scratch's wandering mind remembered that fine fall evening.

"St. Louie," he had answered the stranger.

Bass had been a sull young'un back then, with no more than nineteen summers under his belt.

"Ah," the old fellow replied as he halted, his expressionless face staring down in study at the small, cheery fire a moment, then finally regarded the youth and the rifle across the youngster's lap. "I am but a poor wayfarer. Do you mind if I share your fire and a bit of conversation this night?"

Bass tossed another limb onto the flames and shrugged. "I was just getting used to the lonesome."

At the sudden beating of several pairs of wings, his eyes fluttered open—blinking—to find himself on horseback . . . realizing he had been dreaming, remembering. How that younger man had, perhaps for the first time in his life, been truly getting used to the lonesome.

When at the age of sixteen Titus took off from home, he hadn't gone that many days before he yearned for the sound of another's voice, just the look and smell and nearness of other humans. So what with the riverboatmen and the Ohio River whore called Mincemeat, along with the others who saw him across the wide Mississippi to Able Guthrie's farm, and then with Guthrie's most desirable daughter herself . . . why, he hadn't ever been truly alone ever since the day he'd run off—just himself and the forest.

Back then he realized this aloneness would take some getting used to. Some men took to it natural. Others never would—so it was best their kind stayed back east of the river. The third sort were like himself, Bass figured: they could do with bouts of aloneness as long as there were times when a man set his sights on being with folk. Those occasions between the long stretches of aloneness before the loneliness began to creep in—the bawdy summer celebrations of rendezvous or settling into a friendly village for the winter—he had come to believe would be enough to hold the lonelies at bay.

What he would give now for to share food and fire with a friend—even a stranger as strange as Garrity Tremble.

With that steady rock of the horse as they plodded east along the Little Bear River, he let his eyes slowly droop and drifted back to remembering. . . .

Recalling how the old man turned toward a tow sack he had tied behind his well-worn saddle, explaining, "I have food to offer, young man. You decide to share your fire and your talk, I'll share supper."

Wayfarers they both had been that night. Perhaps ever after and still, they both remained wayfarers. That is, if the old man had not died in all those cycles of the seasons, those roundabout circles of his life in the intervening years. Perhaps Garrity Tremble did still ride the circuit, his only home the old saddle strapped on the back of the blooded thoroughbred. A homeless wanderer—very much as Scratch himself had come to be out here in this great wilderness. Now he rode the circle of the seasons—alone for the most part . . . yet always yearning to circle back toward those shining times when he would again look upon the faces of friends, when his ears would resonate with the sound of their familiar voices and laughter.

On that cold autumn night along the Mississippi a dozen years before, Titus had asked of the old man, "Where are you off to?"

Raising an arm that looked more like a winter-bare branch poking out of the sleeve of that huge, ill-fitting coat he wore, the stranger pointed off here, there, then off in another direction altogether. "No place special. Off to where the spirit moves me. God tells me where I am to go—as he told the wandering Israelites of Moses and Joshua of olde. Yet, truth be it, I—like you—am ultimately alone. Alas, that is God's condition yoked upon the shoulders of us all, isn't it, son? As many as we might have around us, family and acquaintances, we are still alone in this life, and God makes the only sure friend we will ever truly have."

With a snort of doubt Titus had said, "I've had me lots of friends."

From beneath the bushy eyebrows that stood out like a pair of hairy caterpillars on the pronounced and bony brow, the stranger sneered, "Yes—I can see by all these companions you have brought along with you on this journey."

"They are here!" he snapped at the sudden, harsh judgment, and tapped a finger against his chest. Then added, more quietly, "Right in here."

For a long moment the stranger regarded that, weightily, then smiled warmly as he tossed Bass three ears of the corn the preacher was donating to that night's repast. "Yes. I believe you might just be the sort who would hold a friend dear in your heart."

He always had been that sort. This matter of friends and the heart ran narrow and deep, rather than wide and shallow.

Whether it was the riverboatmen or Hysham Troost back in St. Louie, that dream reaper named Isaac Washburn, or those three who had shown up that first autumn in the Rockies to save Titus . . . friends had been just about the dearest, most precious, love he had experienced in his heart. And the remembrance of those friends was ofttimes his only protection against the lonelies. Everything else Titus could do for himself: he could hunt and trap and survive on his own. But he knew he could not last without friends, not without that sacred place his friends shared within his heart.

At those times of the most excruciating loneliness, Scratch had survived because of those warm memories.

"God has taken care of me for more years than you have been breathing, young man," Tremble had explained that cold night after they had supped. "And I trust in Him for when there are not folks to take me in and spread their board before me. At such times God will provide me the opportunity to feed myself. It was a fine feast, wasn't it, young man?"

"A good change from pig meat."

With a visible shudder the old man wagged his head. "How I have come to hate Ned."

"Ned? Why you hate him? Who's he, anyhow?"

"Not who—what. Ned is pork. Ned is pig meat. Ned is the sustenance of the devil himself! No, I haven't partaken of Ned in so long, I cannot remember." He pointed a bony finger at Titus. "And you would do well to swear off it as well. Cloven-hoofed, unclean, filthy beasts that they are."

"But if a man's hungry—"

"He's better off going hungry than biting into any Ned! God will provide for his redeemed souls . . . without any of us having to descend into the fiery depths and dine on the devil's fodder." He raised his face and arms to the sky, closed his eyes, to say, "Praise God I no longer eat such a beast."

The sudden quiet startled him, causing a crack to split his twelve-year-old reverie. As he opened his eyes and blinked in the bright summer sun, Bass tightened his grip on the wrist of the riflestock. And listened.

All quiet—except for the clatter of the many hooves coming up behind him. Glancing at the sky, he found no birds on the wing. Occasionally a breeze tussled the cottonwood leaves overhead before it fell breathlessly quiet again. Not much more than the buzz of flies that seemed to constantly hover over the sweating animals, sometimes diving beneath the brim of Scratch's hat to torment his face.

He yanked back on the reins before he realized what he had done—before it became a thought he could remember going over in his mind. Slipping quickly from the sweat-soaked saddle as the other horses and mules came up, Bass hurried toward the prints he had spotted, and knelt over them.

Unshod pony hooves. By themselves not something of concern. This was Ute country, after all. But mingled in among the hoofprints were moccasin tracks— and those sure weren't Ute moccasins.

Unconsciously, he rubbed his shoulder long ago healed from the Arapaho's war club, then realized that he was—so took that hand and laid its fingers in the moccasin tracks . . . as if to confirm that his eyes were not playing tricks on him.

They were real.

Without rising Scratch looked up, around at the brush. Then got to his feet and fo owed the tracks to the edge of the river, watched them enter the water and disappear. Two ponies and one set of moccasin prints. Maybe because one of them had to make water right then and there. Sure enough, Titus found where the warrior had stepped over to the brush and stood there. Not that the soil at the base of the brush was still damp—but he could imagine the man pulling aside his breechclout, standing patiently to finish his business, then remounting to cross the river with his companion.

"They're across now," he confided to himself. And tried to convince his thumping heart that the danger had passed with that crossing.

He'd push on, Scratch decided—not letting himself get lulled back into napping. Stay awake and watch for sign. If those two recrossed the river, they were sure to pick up sign of all these animals. Then the fat would sure as hell drop in the fire. But for now he felt safe enough to keep moving east, on toward the foothills where he planned to turn north and make a lodestone run for one of the brigades he knew would be tramping through that country right about now.

"Tell me, my astute young observer of life and the manner of mankind— have you ever thought of taking up the staff of God and preaching His word?" the old man said there beside that long-ago fire.

"Me? A preacher like you?"

"It is not easy work, let me assure you. But it is very, very satisfying."

"No, sir," Bass had replied. "I never thought on it at all. I got me my hope to make it to St. Louie. See where things sit up there. Everything on beyond is wild and open."

"Every man must find his own call. You've heard your own call, then. We'll let it rest at that," the stranger replied, apparently satisfied with Bass's answer. "Yes. The beasts and the savages of the wild. Perhaps it is you are called to see them for yourself."

"Maybeso I'll get to do that one day."

"By the grace of God, you will, my son," the preacher replied. "I trust in God. On I ride to my next flock, gathering my strength all the while, renewing my vigor in the Lord—for God will provide. Never should you doubt it, young man. The Almighty will provide."

Titus remembered gazing at the fire, the empty corn husks and naked chicken bones heaped beside the coals, thinking how a man was called upon to help himself. No one else was there to do it for him if a man did not do for himself.

"And He will provide for you, my son," the old preacher had repeated the next morning after they had arisen, saddled, and were preparing to separate.

"I don't know that I ever asked nothing of the Lord," Bass had told Tremble. "Never been much of a one to pray."

With that hard-boned and angular face of his, the preacher replied, "You yourself told me last night that for a long time you've been praying to get to St. Louie."

"Maybe you misunderstood me. I ain't never *prayed* to get to St. Louie—"

"But you've hoped, and dreamed, and done all that you could to get there."

"And I am getting there on my own."

A smile wrinkled the lined face. "You're getting there because God is answering your prayer."

Of a sudden Titus had felt most uneasy, thrown there upon strange ground. Frightened again that he might just be in the presence of something far, far bigger than himself. "I don't know nothing about that, sir."

Removing his old felt hat from his head and dipping in a little bow, Tremble said, "I certainly hope that what you pray for, Titus Bass—will not become a yoke locked about your shoulders."

Minutes later, not all that far downstream, Bass came across the tracks of a single horseman. The prints turned in front of him; then those pony's hoofprints left the bank and entered the water. Now there were three, he confided to himself, brushing the grip on the flintlock pistol he had stuffed into the sash at his waist. Reassurance. The sort he got when he squeezed down, locking his grip around the rifle laid across the tops of his thighs. And turned to glance behind him. Hannah. All the rest behind her.

Three of them on the other side of the river now. He realized he'd have to keep his eyes moving back and forth along that south bank. It wouldn't do to have himself surprised.

In bewildered silence twelve years back Titus had watched Tremble turn the big animal away and move off into the cold, frosty, autumn stillness of the forest.

Before he climbed atop Able Guthrie's old plow horse, Titus cautiously placed a hand upon one shoulder, as if to feel for any invisible weight there. Then touched the other shoulder in the same way. Still not satisfied, he shook his shoulders as if to rock loose anything perchance resting there. Then Bass decided it was all a little ghosty and superstitious of him to believe any preacher knew what he was talking about.

To think of it! Him, praying! Why, Titus knew he'd never prayed a prayer one in his entire life—leastways ever since he stopped going to church hand in hand with his mam.

A man had to provide for himself.

Just as he always had, Titus had figured.

Anything else was nothing more than superstition.

But—by damned—the hair went up on the back of his shaggy neck when after less than another mile he came upon the sign of a fourth horseman coming in from the east, turning down the bank to cross the river just as the others had. And the only way possible he thought to quell his growing fear was to talk out loud. Hardly a whisper, but still so he could be heard. Whatever it was that others believed in, that which was greater than himself—Bass spoke to it now.

"Just show me the way outta this," he whispered, his hand sweating on the reins and the lead rope strung back to Hannah.

"You know damn well I ain't ever been one for going down on my prayer-bones and taffying up to you . . . but you show me the way outta this here fix right now . . . I swear I'll be one to look for your sign and heed, no matter what."

With the back of a leather sleeve, he swiped across his sweaty face. Then added, "I vow I'll pay heed and listen too."

Hannah snorted.

Twisting around in the saddle, he watched her bob her head, jerking back on the lead rope.

He listened too.

She snorted again, her ears perked, pointing stiffly at the sky. And her glistening nostrils flared as wide as the eye sockets on a buffalo skull.

Damn, if that weren't sign enough. The mule had winded Injuns.

What with them horses coming up behind her, Bass didn't have time to stop and take account of much. Instead he tugged on Hannah's lead rope and nudged the saddle horse in the ribs with his heels, reining it off into the trees that lined the narrow river. There at the edge of the cottonwood and brushy willow, Titus kept the horse at a slow walk, his eyes moving constantly, his ears eager for any suspicious sound. Yard by yard, they covered what must have been a mile, then a second mile. How much farther would they have to cover ground at this snail's pace? he wondered.

Better to be slow, careful, and quiet? Or to jump and get the hell on out of the country—to make a race of it then and there?

He was squeezing down hard on his memory right then, trying to dredge up what it was Isaac Washburn had told him he had done coming east with Hugh Glass and two others along the Platte when they found themselves butting squarely up against an Arikara war party come down to do some raiding in the middle of Pawnee country. But all he could remember of the tale was that the two others went under—leaving Hugh and Isaac to hide for their lives in a riverbank hole.

From there they traveled by night, hid by day.

It caused him to glance up at the sun then and there. Way up high did it hang that hot summer day. A long time till sunset, longer still until it would be slap dark. If he could keep from making a sight of himself, keep all these animals from stirring up too much noise at all . . . then maybeso that old preacher's God was one to listen to a man's vow—

"Jumpin' Jehoshaphat!" he bawled as the saddle horse carried him slowly around a left-hand bend in the river.

Four of them . . . bold as brass—spread out across some twenty yards of a small, open patch of grassy ground not cluttered with trees and brush. He yanked back on the horse's rein and jerked to a halt, Hannah coming up on their tail roots.

Four horsemen all right—naked to the waist. Their brown skin glistening with sweat beneath the hot sun. Black hair tossing in the rare breeze, a feather or two stirring among them. And they were close enough for Bass to make out the dull smear of earth paint across cheeks and brows, noses and chins.

It didn't savvy to get no closer, or to try hand-talk with those red niggers—not the way they was decked out to fill their dance card at the widow-maker's ball!

Not taking his eyes off the four sitting still as statues just staring at him a moment, Bass yanked on Hannah's rope, bringing the mule alongside him. There he pulled loose the knot securing the lead rope to the next horse and flung it far aside.

Then he hurled Hannah's rope off onto her packs, slapping her on her neck and saying, "You're on your own, girl! Best you cover ground . . . now—git!"

Screeching like a scalded house cat, Bass screwed that saddle horse around in a circle about as tight as if it had been dancing two-legged atop one of Ebenezer Zane's hogshead barrels of Kentucky tobacco leaf bound south for New Orleans. As he was jabbing heels against the horse's ribs and slapping the loose end of the rein back and forth across its front flanks, Bass heard the yelps of those four behind him.

Goddamned Arapaho for sure!

Couldn't be no others, he knew. This was Ute country—certain as sun. Only raiders wore paint. And the chances were better than good that where he saw four Arapaho . . . there would be more.

Glancing over his shoulder as the horse bolted off for the open ground some distance from the river, Bass caught a glimpse of the four horsemen reaching the horses and mules. Damn, if his trick was working!

But in that instant flicker of a look through the sweat in his eyes, Bass could count only three of the four warriors slowing up, mixing in among the pack string he had just released and spooked into motion to cover his retreat.

Just where in hell that fourth horseman had gone, he could not tell in that heartbeat he gave himself before turning back and kicking hell out of the horse some more.

Hoofbeats right on his tail now—so close, it made his skin crawl, knowing that sound signaled the approach of the fourth horseman. Instead of finding a painted warrior when he turned to look over his shoulder, Bass caught a glimpse of the mule, straining with all the bottom she had to keep up with him and the saddle horse on the flat-out.

"C'mon, you girl you!" he bellowed as loud as he could, feeling his words ripped away from his lips the second they were spoken. "Get up here, Hannah! Get up! Hep, hep, girl!"

Again and again he called out, assuring her—reassuring himself that she could keep up with him despite her packs as he put more and more ground behind him, racing back downstream.

For the longest time, in and out of the brush and trees, up and down one rise after another, across shallow draws and sandy islands when he decided to ford the river itself, Bass glanced over his shoulder—finding the solitary horseman still coming. How the wind pulled at his shiny black hair feathered out behind him the way a raven's wing would glimmer in sunlit flight. His pony's bound-up tail bobbing instead of flying loose on the run. Just a glimpse . . . but it looked to be the warrior carried a bow and a handful of arrows in his right hand, that arm held out for balance most of the time, except when he swept it back and struck the pony on the rear flank—urging more and more speed from the straining animal.

From side to side Hannah bravely lunged after Titus, laboring under her two packs that bobbed and weaved, pulling her in one direction, then the other. Already he could see the first foamy flecks of lather gathering at her chest harness. Ribs heaving, nostrils slickened, muzzle gulping air as she hung as close as her remaining strength allowed.

But when he looked back at Hannah the next time, the horseman had disappeared.

Bass blinked sweat from his eyes, then clumsily dragged his sleeve across his face with the arm that clutched the rifle, bobbing up and down like a Boone County child's dancing toy. Maybeso it was a trick. He glanced at the nearby hillside, just to be sure the warrior hadn't taken another route. Then Bass twisted to the other side—and still did not find the horseman.

But it was plain Hannah had started to fade.

As much as she tried, strained, lunged into the race, she was falling farther and farther behind him. And that made Scratch afraid the fourth horseman would then be able to capture her as her strength faded. As much as she would try to stay far from the Arapaho—it would likely be a futile effort once all her bottom was gone and she could run no more.

Then she would be snared just like those other horses and mules. . . .

And that caused him his first doubt for what he had done in releasing the pack string.

Dry-mouthed, Bass no more hammered the horse with his heels. No more did he whip the rein back and forth, from side to side and flank to flank. He glanced back. Hannah was dropping behind all the farther.

He was drenched with sweat as he let the weary horse slow of its own, twisting in the saddle to watch the backtrail where he had been riding along the south side of the river, his eyes moving everywhere at once. He licked his dry lips and gulped. Thirsty as he'd ever been—or perhaps it was just the fear.

The horse fought him a minute as it slowed all the more, tired of the race and thirsty too. Then Titus brought it around and slowly halted. Hannah came up within moments and stopped, heaving, lather at her halter, foam darkening the leather straps of her pack harness.

Had they made it out?

Just he, the mule, and this saddle horse?

Maybeso it was a good ruse, you savvy son of a bitch, he congratulated himself—still watching the far side of the river from the shadows where he sat on the played-out horse. Hannah snorted in her fatigue.

But every bit as soon as he was patting himself on the back, he heard the echoes of those doubts. Very little time did he give himself for celebration.

There was a good chance he had been wrong in freeing the pack string, part of him said. After all, he had done it almost on instinct. And now—able to think more about it, maybeso even to second-guess himself and the consequences of just what he had done—that act of self-preservation might not have been the wisest of choices.

But what other choices had there been? the other side of him demanded.

Run or fight. Damn well black-and-white, cut-and-dried. Four-to-one odds, at the outside. Hell, there might have been even more of the red niggers off somewhere. Chances good of that, he told himself—justifying his wheeling about and skedaddling all by his lonesome.

An Arapaho war party of ary four warriors come to Ute country? Just four of 'em?

About as likely as one of Annie Christmas's whores showing up in a Natchez church to preach for Sunday meeting!

Nawww, he'd made the right decision. . . .

So why did it feel so wrong down in the gut of him?

Always have figgered y' to be the only one 'sides me I could trust with all them critters and the truck the rest of us cain't take with us on downriver.

That familiar, booming voice rang inside his head as surely as if Silas Cooper were right there, speaking inches from his ears.

Someone had trusted him with near everything they owned—save for their weapons they took with them on that float down to a trader's post. Near everything Silas, Billy, and Bud could tally up as their own in this life . . . and Scratch had gone and abandoned it back there: horses, truck, plunder—all of it.

What with the three of them gone off with them packs of beaver to trade high on the upper river before rendezvous, this sure as hell wasn't feeling the way a man ought to treat the fellas who had saved his life more than once.

I trust y', Titus Bass. These here other two niggers know I'd damn well trust y' with ever'thing I own, Scratch . . . even trust y' with my own life.

Goddammit.

Slamming his heels back into the reluctant horse's ribs, Bass reined around toward the river, loping past Hannah, who looked up at him almost humanly— her eyes clearly registering a very big question. If not asking what he was doing and where the hell he was going . . . then he was certain the mule was asking him just what kind of damned fool he thought he was.

"Stay or come," he muttered under his breath after she was left behind and he was urging the saddle mount back into the river crossing. "I figger you'll do only what you wanna do anyway—you cross-headed, stubborn she-critter."

He figured there was no good decision in this, no clear path to take. And that, Scratch knew, always made for a mess of things in the end, he brooded as he came up the far bank and slowed the horse to a walk—moving carefully, quietly as possible, back into what was plainly enemy country.

If he was lucky, he might just stay out of the way of that solitary warrior long enough for the horseman to give up and turn back to rejoin the other three. Then Bass could lay to until the sun began to sink. From there he'd follow their trail to the spot where the Arapaho had gathered up that cavvyyard of horses and taken off with them. Having some idea where they were headed, Titus could track them, even as it grew dark . . . perhaps even after nightfall.

One way or the other, odds were better than even that he could draw up to them by the next day. With both belt pistols, his rifle, and a pair of knives, he gave himself a chance at making a stand against the four warriors come the dark, especially if he could find them separated and making camp, gathering firewood, or just off to take a piss in the brush. No matter that it was four to one by the thinking of others, Bass figured he had to try.

He had been trusted with nearly all that the other three had in the world after all their seasons in the mountains. Wouldn't they do the same for him? Hadn't they done damn well the same when they had saved his life?

He had to try.

Whether it was coming through the Falls of the Ohio in that sleeting snowstorm with Ebenezer Zane's boatmen . . . or helping to fight off that angry band of Chickasaw along the Mississippi—Bass always chose to try. Sometimes the worth of a man wasn't so much measured in the successes or the failures he tallied . . . as it was in the simple fact that he had tried.

And when you stirred up that virtue with that solid notion of having had others put their trust in you—then there really was no decision left him. Really no choice but one. So in the end, if he were to go under before the sun fell any farther in the sky . . . by damn, he'd make him a good show of it.

Scratch drew himself up and rode on, ready to trail those horsemen and that cavvyyard until he could steal it back from the red niggers that had been dogging his life since that first winter with the Ute.

When Hannah snorted again, it near made him jump in his skin—so surprised was he that she was right behind him, loping up on the tail root of the saddle horse as if she'd gotten her second wind. Her wet nostrils flared as she snorted—rolling her eyes. And when Scratch turned back around in the saddle, there he was.

An Arapaho warrior—as big as life, brassy and bold. Slowly emerging from the timber and brush on the south bank as if he didn't really expect Bass to bolt on him.

Then Titus realized this wasn't the solitary warrior who had stayed on his tail after the other three turned back to round up the pack animals Bass had freed. That horseman had been carrying a bow and handful of arrows in his right hand.

But this one held what appeared to be a smoothbore fusil—a big-caliber flintlock trade gun. As much as he picked at it for a moment the way a man might scratch at a scab crusting over an itchy wound, Titus could not recall ever seeing many of the Ute, nor those Shoshone at rendezvous, and certainly not any of the Arapaho, carrying firearms. Only bows, lances, war clubs.

For a heartbeat longer he gazed at the fusil the warrior held in his right hand, the butt resting down on the naked top of his brown thigh, there at the top of his legging where the flesh was exposed. Then as the Arapaho began to O his mouth to holler something, Scratch sawed the reins savagely and almost brought the weary, lathered horse down on a narrow strip of sandy island in the riverbed.

Collapsing to its knees, the horse struggled to get back up as Titus heard the warning cry turn to screeching behind him. The warrior was calling the other three—perhaps more than three.

Just as the saddle mount jolted up and sidestepped on the soft sand, fighting its halter and twisting its head violently, Bass felt as if someone struck him on the back of the right shoulder with a huge stone, maybe a heavy war club—something swung with tremendous weight and velocity. So much force that he felt it picking him out of the saddle, sensed the horse being yanked out from under him as sky and sand blurred together and his dizzy head began to hail with stars.

Just before the black hood of unconsciousness slipped over him, Scratch remembered sensing the brush he tumbled into—knowing somehow that he landed on the riverbank. Then, as he sprawled on the hot, sun-seared sand, his head was no longer dizzy. His shoulder no longer cried out in pain.

Nothing more than cool, blessed black.

He felt it on the sand beneath his cheek more than heard.

The slow, methodical step and scratch of a horse's hooves on the riverbed pebbles and rocks. Click, click, clack. Click. As much as he tried to open his eyes, everything turned out to be a blur.

The sound was behind him—coming closer, closer. Down in the shallow end of that dark pool where his mind lay, Scratch realized it was the warrior. Closing his eyes into slits to play possum was easy—his mind wasn't ready to heft or tussle with anything more than lying there, listening. . . .

Then the hoof sounds ceased. Except for the breeze nuzzling the leaves overhead, there was no other sound. No other noise . . . but for the whisper of soft-soled moccasins moving across the dry streambed. Then the hiss of some sound above his head, something whirling toward his head in the space of that single heartbeat.

Then the lights exploded and even his blurred vision was gone. The cool, blessed blackness cascaded over him again.

How it hurt for him to start that climb out of the thick, oozy black of unconsciousness.

Blinking his eyes once more, he found everything blurred with a paste of sand and sweat plastered against the side of his face. He closed them again, wishing—praying—for the sweet nothingness to envelop him once again. Better, so much better, than this searing pain.

He blinked once more, forcing his one eye open into a slit. Even that made his head throb with pain. Something moved in front of him. He heard it at the same time the wet form in his vision moved in a soggy blur across the harsh light that made him wince.

Some pain in keeping the eye open forced him to close it groggily—but that pain was nothing near the excruciating nausea that threatened to overwhelm him from the back of his mind. No—more so the back of his whole being.

He felt his right arm twisted out from his body at a crude angle, his legs lying akimbo . . . slowly, inch by agonizing inch, becoming aware of the rest of his body—then suddenly the back of his head again. The pain seeped through his skull at first, then was suddenly all-consuming. The rest of his body forgotten, Bass thought his head felt as if it were one open, raw wound. As if he'd slid down a poplar tree as a boy, scraping off a generous slab of hide in the descent. Tender, pink, beginning to ooze with the first tiny bubblets of blood, a wound that began screeching out in pain louder than he could cry out with his voice . . . that's the way the head was.

He dared not open his eyes, for every time he did, it hurt the head worse. Nor could he straighten the arm, numbed, unmoving—completely unresponsive. And his legs felt as if they each weighed more than a thousand pounds, compressed there into the sand and riverbed pebbles.

Maybe they were broke. Maybe everything on him was broke.

Again he heard the pony's hooves scraping the rocks and wondered if the warrior was leaving again. Leaving him alive. Then the hooves stopped and Bass heard the scritch-scritching. A faint intrusion into the other faint sounds of that afternoon: breeze whisper, leaf rustle, sound of pony hooves and Indian breathing so close, and that scritch-scritching.

With the one eye not plastered shut with sweat and sand, Bass dared it open again. Wanting the warrior to go away, wanting the son of a bitch to take the pain and the bright, excruciating sunlight with him. Just let the shadows and the cool blackness return. Mayhaps, just to sleep. He couldn't move—so maybe it would be best if he just went back to sleep.

But as he blinked again, the blur in that eye cleared somewhat, and he made out more than the watery movement of swimming colors. Slowly he figured out what he saw were the warrior's legs . . . inches away—squatting so close, down on his haunches, for the most part turned away from Bass. Hunched over.

Titus blinked some more, trying desperately to raise his head from the hot sand stuck to the side of his face like burning grit. And in blinking a bit more, he looked across that slow rolling dance of the muscles across the warrior's bare back, looking farther to make out the movement of the warrior's bare arms as he crouched over something held in his hands. Working on it. Scraping it with his knife . . . making that scritch-scritching sound. All that Titus could hear besides the restless hooves of the Arapaho's pony, and the occasional rustle of breeze.

Scritch . . .

Then he took himself a look at what held the warrior's attention there on the sandy bank beside the river. Something dangling from his left hand where he pressed it on top of his right thigh. Dangling like . . . a scalp.

How he wanted to get a hand up to rub the hot sweat and sand out of his eye, the thick goo he blinked to clear so he could tell for sure—

Scratch's breath seized in his chest, and he wasn't sure he'd ever breathe again. It hit him as squarely and with as much force as had that blow to his back as he'd wheeled away from the warrior in the middle of the river. Like a stone war club, the realization slammed up alongside his head with its sudden, shocking power. Like a bright, meteoric light coming on inside his skull—shooting shards of hot, icy light in a thousand directions at once.

It's . . . those long brown curls . . . damn—the son of a bitch has my hair!

How Titus wanted to cry out, to reach out, to lunge from where he lay. But the very most he could do was to fight off the black cloud a little longer as he grew so very, very weary again. His head grown so damned heavy, he had no hope of holding it up. With a stifled gasp Scratch let it lie on the hot sand—sensing its prickly heat beneath his wet cheek. Gasping for air, so afraid he was about to empty his belly then and there, Bass gulped down the nausea . . . staring all the time at the warrior crouched over his gory work.

Leastways, not the whole damn thing, he told himself. It looked small—wasn't the whole thing from brow to nape.

Blinking again as the thick, warm ooze ran into the corner of his eye, Bass fought to stay awake long enough to get himself a good look at the warrior . . . the one who had done this to him. But the Arapaho was turned just so at his work. That bare brown back, the strong young shoulders. And those leggings, with the wide strip of porcupine quillwork down the outer seam—

That was what he began to study.

Concentrating through the sweat and sand and blood he repeatedly blinked to clear. That particular strip of quillwork running all the way from the top to the bottom of the legging, there at the moccasin.

His eyes locked onto the toe of the moccasin—finding it had the same central design as the legging strip, the same colors.

Maybeso like Bird in Ground's people—those colors were the bastard's own power, his private medicine in both form and color.

If he could not move, could not raise a hand . . . at least he would vow to remember those colors, that pattern, those leggings and moccasins.

As the black seeped down over his consciousness again, Scratch stared, studied, and vowed he would never forget this warrior who had scalped him.

Maybe all that was left was for the son of a bitch to come over and finish him off right where he lay. Bass figured that was next, now that the coup had been counted and the scalp taken—just a quick flash of a sharp blade across the wind-pipe . . . or the less-than-pretty river rock bashing the side of his head to jelly.

Just a matter of moments now, he told himself as the black oozed down once more.

Death would be better than this waiting. Death better than not being able to defend himself. Death was better than . . .

Then black was all there was.

As if it were coming out of a dense winter fog, Scratch heard sound. Sodden and muffled.

It hurt his head to listen. So instead of giving heed to the noises around him, Bass kept his eyes closed and willed himself back into that warm immersion in nothingness. Everything else hurt too damn much.

He was dimly aware that more time slipped past. From the blackness he came to dwell on his heartbeat. How it grew in volume to crowd out the gentle rustle of the leaves suspended just overhead in the brush. Thrum-thrum . . . thrum-thrum. So loud, it pounded at his ears with a growing ache.

Slowly the awareness of aching grew. He hurt everywhere, so it seemed. There wasn't a place Bass could not feel pain as the warm bath of that unconscious immersion gradually cooled. Then his left leg and arm began to grow cold. And he sensed the breeze stir across the flesh on the right side of his face—like sunburn.

How long had he been lying there?

For some time he remained content to stay right where he was without pushing the ache: suspended halfway between the oblivion and the total awareness he was certain he would know once he allowed himself to awaken.

Beside him the water continued to whisper. Above him the leaves churkled from time to time as the cool breeze excited them. And from somewhere farther still some birds called. He imagined them sitting on branches somewhere above him, watching him. And with the way some calls moved past him too, Bass imagined them swooping by to look at him sprawled beside the river.

That's why his leg had grown so cold. He twitched the foot. Feeling. Yes, the bottom of his left leg lay in the river. It and his left hand. Must be the way I come to rest here on the rocks, on the sand, he thought, painstakingly climbing his way out of the safe, dark pool of nonawareness.

First the leg. He struggled to drag it from the water there on the damp, sandy bench beside the river. Now for the arm. At first he flicked his fingers in the cool water—fully aware now that he had been right about the river, although his head was turned away from the water—but he had yet to attempt opening his eyes again.

Behind his lids he saw again a portrait of what he had seen the last time he'd opened them. As if it were being played out slowly—then stopped . . . slowly again—then stopped. The excruciating remembrance of that warrior scraping at . . . at his own scalp there beside Titus as he lay wounded on the bank. The Arapaho rose to his feet, stuffing the long brown-haired trophy beneath the narrow leather belt from which hung his breechclout, leggings, and the sheath for that knife as he bent over and swished the weapon in the river before plunging it home in the rawhide sheath.

That pattern of color on the leggings, across the toe of the moccasins as the warrior turned toward him, took a step his way, then lunged up the bank. And away.

Lying here now at this moment, Bass squeezed his closed eyes tightly, as if he wanted to dispel the terrible vision that remembrance brought him. Then he decided to draw both eyes into thin slits and allowed that crack of light to penetrate his thick blanket of nonawareness.

Realizing the shadows had lengthened. Branches and leaves and the trunks of the cottonwood around him—all of it had the colors of late afternoon now. Not the bright, severe colors of midday. Not that last light he remembered seeing on the warrior's moccasin.

And now his left eye pained him. Blinking to clear it, he found he could not. So matted with sand and grit, dried sweat, and the solid crust of old coagulate.

Trying his left arm, Bass found that with some struggle he could drag it out of the water, sweep it around in a wide arc, and then fold the elbow so the damp fingertips reached the eye where that side of his face lay on the sand. There was far too much there to wash off with what little dampness he had brought from the river—but it was enough that he could rub, then rub some more until the eye gradually opened without the pain of grit, opened with a blurry dance, with liquid motion.

It was late in the day.

Behind him, where he felt the sun on his back, on the bare flesh of his right cheek, and there on the back of his head—Bass knew the sun was still in the sky, but sinking low. By the length of the shadows, by the colors of the leaves and the tree bark, the texture of the sand near his face and the touch of the breeze against his sunburned flesh—he knew the sun would soon drop behind the tall cottonwoods. Very, very soon.

And then it would become dark—and he would need a fire.

His belly rumbled hungrily.

Then he moved his right leg willfully. Both of them cooperated as he tested his hips by rolling a little this way, a little that.

All that was left was to move that right arm.

God—*damn!* did that hurt.

Clamping down his teeth, he forced himself to move the arm a little more—causing his empty, rumbling stomach to lurch with the pain. He recognized it as that peculiar nausea the body produced when confronted with unbearable torture. It, too, was something he would push himself through. Like stepping through a door—that's all he had to do. Take a step: move the arm a little more.

It was so sore through the whole shoulder, the upper arm, down into the upper part of his chest . . . maybe just because he had been lying there all this time without moving it, he told himself. Convincing himself that to move it a little more, then a little more after that, all that he did would help. Every inch he managed to drag it up and toward him, every twitch of movement to dispel the numbness would eventually make this exquisite, rising pain a bit more bearable.

Then, before he realized it, Scratch had both arms beneath him, propped, pushing up, heaving against the weight of his upper body. The right arm shuddered and trembled as it drew his chest up.

Blinking quickly in the shifting of the sun's light as he came off the sand, Titus looked down, his head so damned heavy . . . looked down and saw the dark smudge blotting the sand. Then slowly turned his chin, focused his eyes on his right shoulder there near the arm. That right arm was trembling as it propped him halfway up, Bass realized.

A puddle of dried blood below him. Sand caked on the right side of his chest where more blood had soaked through the leather of his shirt.

By then the pain in the shoulder and arm was more than he could bear any longer. As his stomach lurched and he gagged with that first heave, Titus willed his legs beneath him so that he could sit up, hunch forward, and puke out what little his stomach still had in it from a predawn breakfast so, so long ago. The bile coated and burned his tongue. But he got through it.

Realizing he needed water as he spit the last of the yellow phlegm from his sand-crusted lips, Scratch slowly volved around on his left hip. Pulling himself around with his left arm—remembering that it had been in the water.

There it was. He dipped that hand back into the cool river. Soaked to the elbow he was already, seeing the dark leather as he brought the first cupped hand to his lips. Savoring the precious drops that didn't spill as he trembled. Then some more. And more after that—licking his hand each time, sucking on each finger. Every drop like the most delicious taste he had ever experienced upon his tongue—

A bird flew inches overhead, crying out. Snowflash of tail feathers. Magpie. Come to pick at me, he thought. See if there was anything rotting yet.

It made the tears come to his eyes as he ruminated on that and sucked the drops off his fingers. How the carrion birds would have picked at his eyeballs, dug away at the bloody rings of crimson blossoming out from the bullet holes, both back and front.

Looking down at the right side of his shoulder again, the tears flowed easily. Damn good thing the bullet went right on through. Some things just naturally stood out as being lucky, he figured. Other things a man had to work at to find lucky. But with this there was no question. He had stopped bleeding. The holes were too high—the Indian's round ball hadn't crashed through his lights. No lung was punctured. And as much as his shoulder hurt, he could move the arm a little.

Besides, he reminded himself, the shoulder didn't hurt near as much as his head—

It was that sudden flare of realization that rocked him to his core.

That piece of his flesh, that hunk of his long brown hair laying over the warrior's thigh, being scraped free of blood and gore before it was stuffed beneath the bastard's belt.

He took it with him and left me here—figuring me for dead.

At the same time that Bass's heart leaped with celebration that the Arapaho hadn't finished him off with a war club . . . he grew angry at the warrior, for there was no greater insult, nowhere near the coup, than to take his enemy's hair. And then Bass became angry at himself for hurting so bad. Not just the back of his skull, but his heart with the shame of it.

From somewhere in the tender, raw, agonized tendrils of his mind, he knew he had to do something about covering that head of his. Slowly, gradually, Bass brought his dampened left hand to the back of his head. Gingerly he brushed wet, cool fingertips across the sun-fevered skull at first. Strange to find it so hard, so dry. And that, his numbed mind told him, was just the danger.

Got to cover it.

Dipping his left hand in the water again, Bass brought the wet fingers to the back of his skull, again and again he tapped them gently on that bare patch of bone where his topknot had once rested. Sensing as he did so that the edges of the wound, his very flesh where the hair was matted with blood, the crust of coagulate and flesh had already dried in a hard, ragged circle.

Tears came again as he realized he had survived. And told himself he would survive.

With the left hand he dug into the sand and pushed with both legs to shove himself toward the overhang of some willow where he spotted the rocks. There, back in the cool shadows, atop some of the smooth, round-topped rocks, lay the green topknots on each one.

With his quaking fingers, he scraped off the first of the cool, damp moss— then brought it to his dry, tortured skullcap. At first the soppy material made him shiver, it was so cold on the open wound. But as he applied a second scraping of moss, then more, the pain gradually subsided. And the ragged wound was soothed.

The animal snorted—quiet hooves on the rocky bank.

The bastard had come back!

Wheeling on his hip, Bass's head swam, dizzy from such swift motion— fighting to clear his mind. Afraid. Dragging his left hand across the back of his belt, he found his scabbards empty. So fearful was he that Scratch brought both empty hands up into claws. Despite the pain it caused him in that shoulder. Those claws were all he had.

The animal snorted, and its unshod hooves clicked upon the rocks as it emerged from the brush.

He held his breath, heart thumping, ready to fight for his life now that it had been spared the first time. . . .

"H-hannah," he croaked in a hoarse whisper, the first sound his throat had made all day.

She stopped, her nostrils flaring a moment, sniffing the air and looking him over as if to be sure it was really him.

"Come . . . c'mere," he said, his voice cracking. "C'mere, girl." Bass tried to whistle, but barely got out a squeak.

Her head bobbed once, and she clattered forward on the rocks to stand over him, between her master and the sun. Shading him.

Bass was no longer alone.

NINETEEN

Just when he was feeling sorry for himself, about the sorriest he'd ever been, Hannah showed up.

That mule had a head about her, Scratch would tell himself over and over across the next few days.

As he sat there staring at her for the longest time, not able to believe at first that she was real, no one could have convinced Titus that she wouldn't eventually come back for him. Deep in his marrow, Bass knew that she had run as far as she had to until the warriors gave up their chase. Then it had merely been a case of her lying low long enough for the countryside thereabouts to clear of brownskins.

"Likely you moseyed back to stay close enough so's you could watch me," Bass murmured late that afternoon as sundown approached. "Waiting to learn if'n I was live, or dead."

His affection for her burned all the more warmly in his heart as Bass reflected on what she'd done to take care of not just her own hide, but his as well.

"And when you saw me moving there by the river," he told the mule, "you come out of hiding and made your way back to me. Just like a friend. A good . . . *good* friend."

Slowly it struck him just how little he had left in the world right about then. A year's worth of prime, seal-sleek beaver plews gone the way of dust on the wind. Now the horses and mules, saddles and camp plunder, along with the lion's share of what supplies of coffee, sugar, flour, and such he had been toting around since bidding the three farewell far up on the Yellowstone.

But at least he had Hannah, he thought as he looked up at her there on the riverbank where the mule came to a halt beside him, lowering her head so that he could reach up and rub between her ears—right there at the forelock the way she liked him to do. He had Hannah, the only friend he could imagine he had left in the world to count on.

There were others—men among Fitzpatrick's and Sublette's brigades. But they were so far away in days and distance that he told himself they could be of little help to him now—not in the shape he was in. Whereas before the attack he had planned on heading north to cut one of their trails so that he might end up with a few supplies and a whole heaping of companionship . . . now Scratch realized he just needed to get himself to anyone who could help him mend, help him heal, then reoutfit him.

Why, he might be lucky enough to find an old knife among the packs Hannah carried—besides it, he didn't have a weapon to call upon. The two pistols were gone and his belt scabbards were empty when he had finally come to beside the Little Bear River.

Again he stared at the mule in amazement. She had returned for him, steadfastly loyal. Yet he and Hannah were nonetheless alone—here in enemy country, with nothing more than one another to rely upon.

It was enough to make a good man cry . . . then he remembered the tale the old frontiersman Isaac Washburn had told him. How in his first ordeal Hugh Glass had been mauled good by that sow grizzly, then left beside his own shallow grave with nary a weapon nor a horse. But the second time Glass found himself set afoot in enemy territory along the Platte, Washburn was along to discover just how good Ol' Hugh felt despite their dire circumstances. Having his rifle, pistol, pouch, and powder—why, all that made a man feel right pert, so Hugh told Isaac.

"Damn," Bass muttered, "just look at you feeling so danged sorry for yourself. You ain't got no gun, that's for certain. But, by God—you got some fixin's there in that mule's packs . . . and I got you too, girl," he cooed to her.

The moss trickled down the back of his neck as he inched forward, reached out, and snagged her long lead rope—thankful it hadn't become tangled in rocks or brush in her getaway flight, or in her faithful return to him.

"S-steady, steady girl," he whispered.

Gradually he coaxed himself to stand beside her: dragging himself up with that rope, raising his weight with that one strong arm as he got his legs under him, rocking there on the weak, wobbly legs. Then he slowly worked at the knotted rope securing one corner of the dirty canvas covering her packs. He flipped the heavy cover back, seeing what he had been hoping for—then lay against the pack a moment. Closing his eyes, he felt as if he offered a prayer.

When he had gathered his strength again, Bass worked one-handed at the knot on the rawhide parfleche painted with earth colors in Ute designs and patterns. Pushing back the stiff flap, he reached inside, digging around carefully until his fingers found it.

Dragging out the old, much-worn rawhide belt scabbard, Titus sighed with relief. Such was his joy that his hands almost trembled as he clutched it, a mist welling in his eyes. Scratch slid the knife out. As worn and well used as it was, he had nonetheless always kept it sharp. A man could never have enough knives around camp. Now Gut's old knife would likely make a big difference.

From that parfleche he pulled a bundle of scrap buckskin, pieces of hide Fawn had tanned and smoked and used for garments sewn for him or the boy that winter in Park Kyack. As she had taught him, nothing was thrown away—least of all those odd-shaped pieces left over after making moccasins or clothing. There beside Hannah he sank to the grass and sand. Working the knot loose, he spread the scraps apart as the soggy moss continued to drip down his neck, across his chest, and onto his lap.

Then he found a rectangular scrap that, with a little cutting, might work. He left a patch in the middle about the size of three fists. On either end of that middle section he sliced two long straps. As he bent his head forward, Titus carefully centered the buckskin over the moss—squaring it so that the makeshift bandage overlapped the missing scalp lock. Now came the painful ordeal of lifting the right arm, rotating the shoulder high enough for him to accomplish the rest of this task. He bent over more . . . raised his arm a little higher, biting down fiercely, clenching his teeth against the burning agony in the bullet wound as he finally lifted the right arm far enough for his fingers to latch on to one of the straps dangling on that side of his head.

Barely able to breathe for the pain coursing through him, Titus quickly seized a strap on the left side of his cheek and knotted it crudely at his forehead.

Exhausted with enduring the torture, Scratch let the right arm drop, numbed, filled with painful arrows that radiated from the sharp torment in the shoulder. His breath came sharp and ragged . . . but at least he did not have to worry about the moss sliding off any longer while he waited for the pain to pass.

When he was prepared to endure it all over again, Bass again hunched over at the waist, making himself light-headed as he grabbed hold of those last two straps on his buckskin scrap and secured them beneath his chin—just tight enough that he could feel the knot when he swallowed, tight enough that he was sure the makeshift bandage would not slip off his head.

The wind suddenly came up, blustering down the snaking path of the riverbed—spooking him enough to jump. Startled, he lunged to his knees for the lead rope, ready to escape at any cost.

Then that gust of wind died, and he was left with Hannah, his heart hammering in his tortured head, his breath coming shallow and labored in the chest, where it tormented him to take a deep breath.

"You . . . you damned fool," he chided himself in a whisper, and sank back to the ground from his knees.

Pulling the remaining scraps of buckskin together, he retied the bundle, then shuffled on hands and knees down the bank. There beside the river he tugged on Hannah's lead rope.

"C'mon, girl," he coaxed. "Get yourself a drink while'st you can."

No telling when next we'll have us a chance at water.

She stood beside him on the grassy bank as he lay forward, held himself out over the water, and dipped his face. Drinking his fill as if it were a sweet potion, Titus drew back on the grass and sand, gulping down that last cold mouthful. Only then did the mule dip her head and lap at the river. He waited and twice told her to drink more. As if she somehow understood his prodding, Hannah returned to nuzzle more water down.

As the sun continued to fall, the wind came sinking down the ridge behind them, then blustered off toward a bend in the river—spooking him enough again to hurriedly wrap the lead rope around his left hand. When it had gone down the valley, Hannah stood over him as he crouched in her shadow.

Gazing up at the mule, he realized what they must do. "We can't stay here no longer. Gotta make ourselves tracks."

The warriors might return for no good reason at all—thinking they may well have left something on the dead man, figuring they might still find the mule carrying more of their ill-gotten plunder.

Steadying himself against her left foreleg with his good shoulder, Bass again forced his legs under him to prop himself up beside her. Pushing back that waterproofed Russian sheeting again, he dug around until he secured one of the thick wool blankets he used to roll himself within. Tugging to free it, Titus stopped suddenly—staring. Blinking his eyes. Not sure he wasn't imagining what his eyes told him he saw.

Sinking to his knees and one hand of a sudden, he sobbed as he crabbed forward around the mule, dragging the right arm. He lost sight of the object as soon as he collapsed into a crouch—afraid now that his eyes had been playing tricks on him.

Desperate, he pushed against the thick tangle of leafy brush, prodding his way in farther and farther a few inches at a time—desperate to know for sure if it was real, or a trick his head was playing on him.

With a wordless gasp he closed his eyes and raised his face to the sky for a moment. Then opened them again and reached out with that left hand, his fingertips brushing the scuffed wood of the curly maple forestock, the rawhide band. It was real. He hadn't imagined it.

Grabbing hold before the rifle could disappear with a poof of his imagination, Scratch dragged the weapon out of the brush where it had gone tumbling, pitching and cartwheeling, during his fall from the saddle horse. There it had lain, hidden in the brush while the victorious warrior stole the rest of his weapons. Hidden, just as surely as Hannah had remained out of sight until it was safe.

Collapsing back with growing relief, Titus sat, cradling the rifle in his lap, stroking that rawhide repair, treating the weapon as if it were a living creature. Suddenly fearing the lock might well be broken, he dragged the hammer back. It clicked at half-cock. Then moved on back with a crisp snap to full-cock. With a thumb he flicked the frizzen open and gazed down at the priming powder still cupped in the pan. The derringer was loaded and ready.

Bringing it off his lap in that left hand, standing it up, Bass propped himself against the rifle and rose. Now he could hobble about, using it as a crutch. Shuffling over to the mule, he pointed the muzzle down at an angle and worked the barrel beneath those ropes securing the right side of her packs. There, he figured, he could pull it out quickly if need be. With no pistols, nothing but the old skinning knife he had stuffed into the back of his belt—Titus lovingly stroked the heavy-barreled rifle. It, like the mule, were gifts granted him this day, which might well have been his last.

Steadying himself with an arm around the mule's neck, Bass hobbled beneath her head. It took a little doing, but with the sheeting finally draped back over that off side of the load, and the thick red blanket folded just so and laid over the top of the packs, Bass took up Hannah's long rawhide lead again. Looping it over her neck halfway between ears and withers, he hobbled a single step so that he could grip his left arm around her jaw.

It was an embrace she struggled against at first—perhaps not sure what he intended to do—then, as he continued to coo and pat and stroke, she settled—allowing him to hug her fiercely.

"You're all I got now, girl," he croaked, his voice breaking and his eyes filling with tears, spilling out on the blood dried and caked on his cheeks. "You gotta do for me . . . w-what I can't do for myself."

Laying the side of his face along her jaw for a moment, Bass eventually pulled himself away and hobbled back to her foreleg again. This was it—the test to see if they would be able to get themselves out of there.

Hell, he told himself—she could. That wasn't the question at all. What he was about to endure was the test of his own grit. Perhaps one of the most supreme trials he had ever confronted. And here he was alone. No one to help. No one to know. Just him, and the mule. The friend who had come back for him.

Damn near the only friend he now had in life.

"Help . . . help me," he whispered there at her ear as he reached over her withers as far as he could with his good left arm. "S-steady," he coaxed, already wincing with the pain, tears clouding his eyes.

Bass said no more. He could not. His teeth were clenched too damned tight to utter a word. But sounds came out nonetheless as he raised himself off the ground a matter of no more than inches at first, struggling to pull his weight up against the side of the shifting mule with that one lone arm.

When he tried kicking his leg for additional boost, Bass cried out suddenly . . . and hearing himself, he clamped down on his lower lip, vowing he would not make that mistake again. Instead, he could only groan, gasping for breath with every sharp jab of pain as he pulled. Pulled.

Steady . . . dear God—steady, girl, he thought as the mule sidestepped again, shifting herself with his additional weight throwing her off balance.

Then he realized he had dragged himself more than two feet off the ground, and not knowing how long he could go on hanging there with the one arm bearing it all . . . but knowing at the core of him that he would never endure another attempt. This had to be it, or they would be staying right there for the night, perhaps forever if the Arapaho returned.

Grunting, he forced that tingling right hand to seize a loop of knotted rope securing the sheeting over the packs. By rocking to his side Bass let go with his left hand and before his weak right arm failed him—he thrust out with the strong one, securing a new hold and hung there, stunned by the pain and ready to bawl.

Sure that he would weaken and cry out with the torment in that shoulder wound the next time he inhaled, instead Titus bit down on his lip, grunting as he pulled again, dragging his weight a little farther up the side of the mule. She volved her head back to look at him, see what he was doing . . . then suddenly lowered her neck.

Not waiting for Hannah to change her mind, for her to move—Bass lunged down her far side with the good hand and snatched a third hold, pulling, dragging, hauling himself on over her foreflanks until his waist lay across her withers.

As Hannah's head and neck came up, he finally gasped for breath, spitting blood from the lower lip he had just bitten hard enough that a warm ooze trickled across his tongue.

"G-good . . . g-girl," he stammered in a hoarse croak, the punctured lip already beginning to swell.

As he fought the dizziness and thumping of each heartbeat now clanging in his head with the power of a blacksmith's hammer, Titus rolled onto his left side and with the numbed right arm yanked on the thick blanket, stuffing it down beneath him. There he knew it would pad him from the mule's bony withers, here where he lay cradled between her neck and the front of Hannah's packs.

With each of those violent movements, all that stretching of the shoulder, rotating it—Bass now rested there a moment, sensing the wound on the front of his shoulder seeping. For the first time since he had regained consciousness on the riverbank, the bullet hole had torn away from the inside of his buckskin shirt where the animal hide had crusted itself against the exit wound.

And as he hung there crimped at the waist over the back of the faithful mule, Scratch began to feel a warm trickle at the back of his neck—not sure if it was the river moss still dripping . . . or more of his own blood seeping now from the entrance wound in his back.

That, or the scalping.

If he didn't bleed to death in the next few hours, he damn well might fall off because he couldn't hold on anymore. No telling how long his strength would last. And when it failed, he would just tumble off the mule's back. If that happened, Bass knew with rock-hard certainty that he would never get back on her. This was his chance. He'd been given this much by the power that watched over all things. A man had no right to expect any more than that.

This was his one chance. His to do with . . . or die. It was up to him now. Up to him and the mule.

After a moment more he tugged on the rifle one more time to be sure he could free it from the ropes; then Bass took up the long loop of rawhide rope.

"Awright, Hannah," he whispered hoarsely. "Get . . . get us outta here."

With a slight tug on the rope she started away from the riverbank with him slung over her like so much deadweight baggage. Turning slightly and taking those small steps, Hannah was careful where she placed each hoof, perhaps sensing the heavy burden placed on her. Not just the man's weight—but his call to her spirit. It was up to her now.

As Hannah turned a step at a time, firmly planting each hoof before she moved another on the uneven, sandy grass of the bank, she turned Scratch's face toward the west. Slowly, slowly she came around, turning so that he saw downriver. Through the mist of tears he got himself a long look at the sun settling beyond those tall cottonwoods.

How good this was—he suddenly thought, suddenly felt its certainty through his whole body. How damned good it was to watch this sundown.

So simple a thing to him before this day, this matter of the sun's going down.

As she brought him on around, Bass gradually turned his head and rested it against her powerful, muscular foreflank flexing with each measured step. Resting his cheek against her power when he was now weak. Gazing back at that sunset.

As she plodded forward across the uneven ground, a hoof at a time . . . he gave thanks for the loyalty of that friend carrying him away from the riverbank there at the end of that day.

Watching the sun ease down past the bushy tops of the far cottonwoods, Scratch vowed his life would not be the same hereafter. This simple matter of a sunset was the powerful radiance of what surrounded his heart with all the more warmth. Not only did he have the mule and his rifle . . . but he had been given this sunset.

The gift of another day now brought to a close.

Had things been different—had the power that watched over all things not been wanting him to see things through new and different eyes—then, Bass realized, he would not be alive to watch this sun going down behind those cotton-woods . . . splashing the river's surface with glittering light.

At the center of him he made a vow to watch each and every sunset, each and every one of those days given him from here on out. Promising to be thankful for each one he had been granted by whatever great force had spared him this day.

Surely it had to be the same, unnamed power that created the beauty of every sunset, painting each day's with a different hue as the earth slowly turned beneath that radiant, blazing horizon.

As the sun sank lower, out of sight behind the cottonwoods and Hannah carried him up the long slope from the river, Bass vowed with all his heart that he would not fail to watch them all. Given that gift of each day.

Realizing he was not just given his life this day, but given new eyes to see all those sunsets yet to come.

By the time he pushed himself over and off the mule's back late that first night, it felt like every inch of him had been scalded raw.

Scratch wasn't sure how much ground they had covered after fleeing the riverbank at sundown: he had passed out. But when he finally became aware that the mule had stopped, the moon itself was resting on the far western edge of that black dome overhead. Slowly coming awake, he realized he had been asleep, maybe more so he had passed out with fatigue, his mind and body giving up the fight against such terrible pain. And he shivered with cold. As warm as the days had been, the nights had been gradually growing colder.

Evidently, she had been standing there patiently waiting for him to awaken, unable or unwilling to take him any farther that night. The only sounds he heard as he came to were the mule's weary breathing, and the faint trickle of water seeping along its bed, somewhere out there.

As the seconds passed and his heartbeat began to hammer at his ears once more, Bass became all too painfully aware of his body. From head to toe, it felt as if he had been brutalized—not a part of him that did not cry out. While not as horrifying an ordeal as had been climbing on, this pushing himself off the mule's bare back was nothing short of excruciating torment.

Even the muscles in his good arm and the two strong legs cried out with complaint. Every part of him in agony, Bass heaved himself off his perch, drop-ping to his legs only to have them give out beneath him so he landed in a heap.

Groaning, Scratch rolled over onto his left shoulder and drew his legs up fetally—fixing to let himself cry as the pain washed over him in a diminishing flood. Sometime later, when he was prepared for what it would take, Bass told himself he had the strength to get back on his feet. Better that than lying on the cold, bare ground at the edge of this stand of trees.

First he struggled to his knees, then rose there beside Hannah, resting against her as his breath slowed until he again heard the faint trickle. With his legs stiff and unused, he gripped on to the mule and stumbled around to the far side of her to drag his rifle free. With that crutch Titus started away, following the faint sound.

The tiny freshet proved to be less than five yards away: a narrow creek fed by a high-country snowfield as yet unmelted by summer's harsh glare and heat. There he went to his knees again, and with the rifle close at hand, Bass dipped his face into the icy flow. Colder than he had imagined it would be—much colder than the river had been—he pulled back, gasping with surprise, his face and beard dripping with black pearls in the darkness.

"Come, girl," he coaxed the mule behind him. "Get you some."

When she didn't move, he tried convincing her again, but instead she only hung her head in exhaustion.

"I know," Scratch said quietly. "Me too."

Then, after he slowly dragged his tongue over his parched lips, Bass whistled the best he could.

Her ears perked and her head came up. Wide-eyed, she came over close enough for him to stroke her as he sat up beside the freshet to rub a hand down a foreleg, sensing the powerful muscle that had rescued him from destruction, carried him far from the riverbank attack.

"Drink, girl. You're gonna need it."

Gently tugging down on her lead, Titus finally got her to understand. She lapped at the water briefly, then raised her head and backed away.

"C'mere," he demanded . . . then whistled.

When she returned to his side, Scratch reached up and snatched hold of the end of the big, thick wool blanket. He wasn't about to move any farther tonight. Right here would do.

Gazing into the sky for a moment to figure where the sun would come up in the morning, he shuffled over a few yards on his knees to a soft patch of grass within a brushy crescent of tall willow. She followed him, stopped, and hung her head as he painfully, slowly, laid his body down on the double fold of blanket, slid the long rifle between his knees and arms, then brought the other half of the blanket over himself.

It took a few minutes, but much of the pain of moving eventually dissipated, and he was left with nothing but the constant, nagging throb of his wounds, and the deepening of the cold that night.

Sometime later when the sky to the east was graying, Bass awoke, his bladder full and aching. The best he could do was throw off the blanket, push himself onto his knees, then pull his breechclout aside as he made water there and then. With that exquisite relief washing over him, Titus collapsed within his thick red cocoon and quickly fell back to sleep.

There were times during that first day when he grew aware of things around him. Not coming fully awake, not really opening his eyes at all—only occasions when he was slowly brought to realizing the sun was up at one position or another in the sky. Instead of opening his eyes here in the cool of his copse of willow, Bass would smell, his nose telling him that Hannah remained close by. One time he awoke to smell the earthy scent of her dung, another time when she made a puddle of strong, pungent urine nearby.

Late that afternoon he awoke again—and for the longest time he kept his eyes closed, listening to the mule crop at the grass, tearing it off between her teeth, listened to the breeze and the birds and the winged insects droning somewhere close. With no sun on the willow grove now, he figured it to be evening and eventually opened his eyes. Rubbing the grit from them once more, Scratch sat up a little at a time, his belly as hungry as he could remember it had ever been.

For a long time his belly rumbled while he stared down at the front of his right shoulder, slowly volving it to see how much he could move it now, more than a day after the bullet wound. Sore and tender—but he could urge it this way and that more widely than before. Soon, maybe, he would have to see about patching it up, putting some sort of bandage over one or both of the holes. Carefully he tugged at the buckskin shirt with his fingers and was surprised to find that the shirt wasn't crusted to the front wound again. The hole was coagulating all on its own.

After whistling softly to Hannah, Bass pulled himself up against her, propping himself there to loosen knots on rope and rawhide. After retrieving that tight bundle of buckskin scraps, he blindly dug around in a second rawhide parfleche until his fingers felt the beaver fur. Knowing the glossy hides would do nicely, Scratch pulled out the small wrap of fur. What he saw was not just the dark sheen of the thick scraps of beaver, but tangled in it across his hand lay the blue bandanna.

Slowly sinking again with the buckskin and beaver scraps in his lap, he stared a long time at the blue silk scarf before finally bringing it to his nose. He inhaled deep and long, his eyes barely closing—conjuring up that remembrance of her through the potent power of scent.

As he rubbed the cloth gently across his bare cheek, down the bridge of his nose, over his eyelids—just to feel the caress of the fabric was enough to make him want desperately to remember the feel of her . . . that silky flesh with its tiny hairs, flesh that goose-pimpled each time it became cold in her tiny room and he flung back the blankets to look at all of her at once, to gaze upon her coffee-colored body. That big blue scarf took him back many, many miles and what seemed like a good man's lifetime—took him back to those last months in St. Louis.

To that time when he lost Isaac Washburn, and along with the old trapper—Bass lost his long-held dream. Across those seasons of despair he had nothing more to look forward to than the earthy necessities of a man's life. Spending most of his money to buy himself a drink now and then, along with the feral pleasure of a good meal upon special occasions, as well as the company of a succession of women who each one helped Titus hold at bay the numbness slowly eking in to penetrate to his very marrow.

It had been a time when, unlike before, there were no more of those raucous days ruled by whiskey-fever and whoring until he passed out. But for a time there—he no longer dreamed on the buffalo.

Across that last autumn and winter he'd imprisoned himself in St. Louis, Bass routinely had pleasured himself one evening a week with the coffee-skinned quadroon he'd grown fond of. At times they'd shared a bottle of West Indian sweet rum brought upriver on a paddle-wheel steamboat, both of them drinking and laughing until she was ready to hike up her nettlebark petticoat and climb astride him.

He smelled of the blue scarf again as he sat there in the willow. Only in his imagination did it still smell of her. So very long now had he carried it among skins and hides—on that packmare, then among Hannah's baggage.

Oh, how he believed he smelled her still on this corner or that. Remembering how he visited once a week, every payday when he could afford a bottle of that brown-sugar rum and the sweet sin of that cross-breed whore. There every week . . . at least until that Saturday night he came to call, fresh from the bathhouse and a warm meal taken in the tippling house just down the narrow avenue, ready to have that cream-colored beauty work her magic on his flesh so he could swallow down what troubled him so.

As Scratch brought the scarf from his nose and laid it across his lap, spreading it out fully, he recalled how the old woman who watched over the knocking girls informed him that his favorite no longer boarded there—having left suddenly to take up residence in a private place farther up the hill, close to where the rich and very French families dwelled in old St. Lou. Bass remembered how, as the woman had told him the news, in disappointment he had touched that blue scarf he'd always tied around his neck every one of those special Saturday nights.

No, Isaac Washburn hadn't been alone in finding a favorite trollop there in St. Louis. For Titus, his favorite became the gal with skin the color of a pale milk chocolate. A recent arrival, the quadroon had been imported upriver from New Orleans by a successful madam. Ah, how her brown skin was almost the color of that silky mud sheen to the Lower Mississippi itself.

As he hacked off two pieces of the beaver hide big enough to lay over his wounds and tied together long strips of buckskin, Titus recalled the first time he saw her sipping at her Lisbon wine. She was wearing those tall and gracefully carved ivory combs in her hair every bit as dark as a moonless midnight. At the base of her neck was wrapped a velvet choker pinned with a whalebone brooch, the ribbon clasped so tight at her throat that the brooch trembled with every one of her rising pulses. Her lips full enough to more than hint at her African ancestry, Bass found it little wonder that he came away from her so many nights bearing the tiny blue bruises and curves of teeth marks she left behind as she worked him over with her mouth, starting at the shoulder and working on down to the flat of his belly.

While he clumsily secured the scraps of beaver over the wounds with two long strands of buckskin thong, he stared at the blue scarf—squeezing hard to remember her every gliding movement, to remember the silky feel of her, to recall her potent smell.

It had been early one wintry morning after swearing she was his favorite that they heard Washburn hammering a fist on her door, announcing that he was ready to head back to the livery. Without saying a word at first, she reached up to pull down one of her scarves from a peg hammered into the wall beside her narrow, short-posted muley-bed.

"You take this," she instructed in a hoarse whisper as she settled her naked body back on the thin mattress beside him.

At that moment he didn't know what she laid across his hands in the flickering candlelight. "What's this?"

"My scarf," she said in that thick Mississippi-bottom dialect of hers, taking the fabric from him to unknot it. "Blue as the sea that rolls away from New Orleans to the home of my people."

"W-where are your people?" he had asked her over the noise of Washburn's insistent thumping on the doorway, his bellowing that he was about to come crashing in.

"I don't have no people no more," she explained, sadness filling her eyes. "But I want you always to be somebody special to me."

"I will be, always," he vowed, and let her tie the scarf around his neck before they parted in the gray of that dawn.

How he recalled wearing the scarf knotted there at his neck every time he returned to see her of those Saturday nights when he could afford the price of both a bottle of rum and to sleep till morning with someone warm beside him. Hell, even when he could not afford her and had to content himself with gazing at the whore from across the smoky room in the tippling house where she went about her business, talking and laughing with other customers, glancing at him once in a while—those eyes of hers asking why it was not he who was pushing his hand up her skirts and hungrily rubbing her legs then and there, panting to drag her back to her little room.

After struggling to get the buckskin shirt down over his head and arms once more, Bass concluded he would wear the scarf as she had intended him to. Working at the two resistant knots, he eventually freed the head bandage as the sky became greasy with twilight. Tucking the scarf under his belt, Bass slowly crabbed over to the trickling freshet, then slipped the buckskin and moss from his head.

As he set the moss scrapings aside atop a small rock, Bass grew curious—just how would the bare bone feel to his touch, how would his touch feel to the bare bone? Before he could talk himself out of it, Scratch reached up to lay his fingertips on the wound. One by one his fingers tiptoed across the exposed bone, gingerly feeling their way around the circumference of the lacerated flesh. There at the bottom of the wound he felt the thin, stiffened strip of flesh. Tugging on it gently, Scratch figured he could not pull it—that shriveled curl of skin must still be attached to some living flesh.

Drawing the worn skinning knife from its old scabbard at the back of his belt, Scratch bent forward so that he could use his right arm—the right hand grasping the long flap of skin so he could lay the blade against his skull and saw the knife through it.

Bringing the curled flesh down to stare at it, at the same time Bass also rubbed a finger along the wound where he had cut the scrap free, reassured that he hadn't stirred up any more bleeding.

A curious object it was—this long, narrow strip of his own flesh, no more than three inches in length now that it had shriveled. Attached to its entire length was some of his very own hair. As careful as the Arapaho had been in scraping the scalp itself clean before stuffing it into his belt, it appeared the warrior had made himself two cuts to free the cherished topknot, both of those cuts ending at the bottom, where they overlapped. That narrow thong of overlap had been left to dangle when the warrior had yanked off the topknot, the flesh drying, dying, shrinking into a long, twisted curl.

He knew immediately what should be done with it. After untying the narrow thong that closed the top of the small medicine pouch, Scratch stuffed the small scrap of his own scalp in among the few other objects of special significance he had been gathering since that spring parting from Fawn. Here he would keep the strip, dangling around his neck in the medicine pouch, worn beneath his shirt, next to his heart.

With the moss dampened in the trickle of water and replaced over the bare bone of his exposed skull, Titus smelled deeply of the scarf one last time. From now on the fabric would no longer even remotely carry the fragrance of the quadroon—lo, after all these many miles and bygone seasons. Remembering painfully how the whore had abandoned him and what little they had shared together.

"I'll go see her there," he recalled declaring to the madam that night she had told him the quadroon would not be back. "See her where she's working now. What's the place so I'll know it?"

"You can't see her up there," the woman tried to explain, the wounded look in her eyes showing how she tried to understand this poor man's desire for just one woman.

"She ain't coming back?"

Wagging her head, the woman explained, "Rich man bought her, took her off to the place where he's gonna keep her for himself, for now on and always. Buy her all the soft clothes she'd ever wanna wear. She told me when she left, there's a tree outside her window—where she'll sit and watch the birds sing come the end of this goddamned winter."

"H-he married her?"

The woman had laughed at that. "Sakes no! He's already got him a wife—but one likely cold as ice. Land o' Goshen, but he don't ever intend to marry the girl. Just keep her in that fancy place he bought her—just so she'll be there whenever he shows up so she can pleasure only him."

"Maybeso I can see her still. Sneak up there when he ain't around."

Again the woman wagged her head sadly. "Don't you see? She went there on her own. That means she wasn't thinking 'bout being with no one else here on out. The girl, she left everything behind. And that means she left you too. Best you forget her now."

Now, as he folded the large square of heavy silk into a triangle, Bass recalled how he had stared at the crude puncheon planks beneath his muddy boots, realizing how the quadroon's leaving was merely another piece of him chipped away, like a flake of plaster from one of those painted saints down at the cathedral on Rue d'Eglise. Then Titus had looked into the woman's eyes, vowing he would not let her leaving hurt him. Then of a sudden he had remembered Isaac's favorite.

"What about that one with the brown hair down to the middle of her back? Think she was called Jenny."

"You're two days late, son," the woman declared morosely. "A mean bastard cut her up good just last night. Up to the pauper's cemetery they buried Jenny in a shallow hole only this morning."

Swallowing, perhaps feeling a bit desperate that so much of what he took solace in was crumbling around him, Bass said, "Any other'n. Any one a'tall."

Squinting her eyes up at him, the woman rested her hands on her fleshy hips and asked, "You ain't so choosy no more?"

His eyes flicked to the left down the corridor, then right. Back to the woman. "Not choosy at all."

Here in the willow as the light quickly oozed out of the sky, Titus remembered that from that painful night on he had rutted with the fleshy ones, the pocked ones, the ones who hadn't cared to bathe in a month or more—it made little matter to him that the quality and color of whores in that city always depended upon the size of a man's purse. No, it wasn't the money that was determining his choice of solace for Bass. No good reason at all could he come up with to be particular just where he took his pleasure. And for the longest time it seemed to be that he was seeking only that particular salve of a warm and willing woman to rub into all those hidden wounds he kept covered so well.

No, he hadn't been choosy at all—until he chose to seize his dream.

When he brought the blue triangle to his head and began to knot it at the base of his skull to hold down the damp moss, Bass remembered those days when he figured it was simply too cruel to fool himself any more into believing in hope. How he had vowed never again would he cling to any dream.

Those dreary seasons passed slowly by while he choked down his despair at never hoping again, daring never again to dream—pounding out his rage on that anvil in Troost's Livery. Of every Saturday night he found himself a new whore to stab with his anger as he rutted above her. Until he had worked his way through them all and by the time a cold winter was waning, Titus started pleasuring his way back through what poor women he could still afford. As he did, Bass had grown more frightened that with each visit to their wharfside cribs, it was taking just a little more of that balm to soothe his deepest wounds. Scared they might never heal.

And when he found himself weakest, Titus had always brooded on this then faraway land—still mythical as it was to him back then. He had been weakest in those moments when the whiskey could no longer stiffen his backbone, when he found himself drained and done with the sweating torment of driving his rage into a woman and he lay beside her, gone limp and soft deep within himself as well as out.

Now with the moss protecting his skull, with the bandanna secured around his head, he knew with certainty that it hadn't been a cruel hoax his grandpap and Isaac Washburn had played on him: there was indeed a magical, mystical place where the horizon ran black with buffalo. Just as they had promised, those huge, shaggy, powerful beasts indisputably ruled their domain and were servient to none.

Like that rare breed of man who had come to test himself against these mountains. The few who indisputably ruled this wild, untamed domain.

That twilight Bass used some of the last of his strength to draw back the Russian sheeting, and desperately scrounged through what baggage was left on Hannah's back in search of something to eat. All that he found besides some green coffee beans he could suck on was a small linen sack of flour. With his blanket clutched around his shoulders, Scratch collapsed wearily to the grass, watching the sun settle far away beyond the Uintah Mountains.

He moistened the fingers on his left hand, then stuffed them into the flour. Pulling his hand out of the sack, he sucked on the fingers, repeating the movement over and over until his stomach no longer rumbled, until he could no longer tolerate the pasty, bland taste of the flour.

Bass realized he needed meat. It was the only thing that would replenish his strength—keep him from steadily becoming weaker and weaker, until he could only curl up and wait to die. He dreamed on buffalo—big, shaggy, hump-backed buffalo. All that red meat and blood up to his elbows . . . but he'd take elk or deer now, a prairie goat if he had to.

Hell, Scratch thought mournfully as he looked down at the flour sack in his lap, he'd even take a rabbit or a ground squirrel right now if he had to—close his eyes and make believe it was buffalo as he was eating it.

When he had retied the top of the sack with its strand of hemp twine, Titus keeled over onto his side, dragged the rifle between his legs, and tugged the blanket back over himself.

Twilight had faded and night had arrived the next time he awoke. After putting the flour, buckskin, and beaver scraps away among the few belongings still left him, Scratch stuffed the rifle under the loops of rope. Now he was ready for the ordeal of getting himself aboard the mule.

Again he folded the blanket over her withers in front of her packs, but this time he had something different in mind for the night's ride. Back over to the freshet, then across its narrow path he led the patient Hannah a hobbling step at a time. It was there on the far side he had seen the deadfall where he now headed.

Positioning the mule beside the big pine's trunk, Titus slowly clambered up the rotting deadfall until he stood nearly opposite her tail root. Seizing hold of the ropes at the top of her packs, he leaned against her, pulling himself onto Hannah's rear flanks. Securing a second hold farther up, Titus pulled himself a little farther onto her back. Nestled there between the two bundles that were lashed to her pack frame, he settled himself. Down between them he wouldn't be near so likely to fall off as she picked her way across uneven ground while he fell asleep.

Which was just what he wanted to do more than anything right then. With his good left arm, Bass dragged the red blanket over his head, nudging it on down over his back so that it covered his legs, flaps draping off either side of the mule's packs. Now he would be warm, here under the blanket and next to her hide, warm no matter how cold this late summer night would become as Hannah carried him into the coming darkness.

At least he would be warm here, no matter how empty his belly. Warm, though he realized how fast his strength was flagging. Were it not for that nest within the packsaddle, Bass knew he simply didn't have the strength to stay on her back. Without meat he might not be able to hold on much longer. Without meat he might never be strong enough to climb back on. Hunger was a cruel torturer.

Taking the long lead rope into hand, Scratch raised his chin to search the heavens a moment until he found what he looked for.

Gently reining Hannah around to the right, he told her, "Let's go, girl. Time to carry me some."

As he clucked to her with his tongue, Bass guided her toward that great patch of black sky there beneath the North Star. The big handle on that water dipper pointed the way he would go. In only a matter of minutes his eyes grew too heavy for him to hold them open any longer.

"Keep going, girl," he whispered to her, stroking her withers, patting her neck and mane. "Take us north."

Hannah moved out faster this evening than she had carried him that first night, perhaps sensing that now he was secured among her baggage. The ofttimes gentle, sometimes jarring rock-a-bye motion of her gait lulled him deeper and deeper as he repeated wearily, "Take us north. Find us . . . something to eat."

At times during the night he awoke, lifting his sore, pounding head, and gazing into the starry black blanket overhead. Then he might tug a little this way or that to nudge a correction to their course before he let his head collapse once more and he was asleep again in his warm nest down between those bundles lashed to the crossed arms of the worn sawbuck saddle.

The North Star beckoned the way . . . suspended far, far ahead of them in the night.

He slept again, knowing that the only way he'd ever follow that star was on the back of this mule.

TWENTY

It was cold enough that he could see his breath come in gray streamers against the murky light of predawn, curling up before his eyes, then wisping off on each gentle gust of breeze.

The land rose gently on either side of him as Hannah plodded along. Since awaking he had realized she was beginning to slow—too weary after the night's march beneath her added burden. He shifted slightly, rolling to his other hip between the sawbucks. And breathed deeply of the cold breeze that gusted against his cheeks. It was good, he told himself. With it in his face he would not be on the downwind of man or animal.

Turning his face to the right, regarding the paling sky, Scratch felt relieved that the mule had been moving him steadily north through another night. Soon enough he would have to tug on her rope, steer her off to one row of these hills or another, hoping there to find a sheltered draw where he could hoist himself off her back and crawl into the brush. Perhaps this morning he would have enough strength to yank back the thick, oiled Russian sheeting and spend the time and strength it would require of him to release the packs from their frame. But as weak as he was, how was he ever going to get the packs reloaded?

How many days now? he asked himself. Had it been two

nights? Or three? Two, he decided—which meant she had suffered for the better part of three days without having her burdens removed.

"You'll want yourself a good roll, won't you, girl?"

By damn, he knew how she must feel—knowing how he got a'times, ready to back up to a rough-barked tree where he'd strop his back up and down slowly, deliciously, giving himself one hell of a good scratching.

"Find you a good patch of grass where I can sleep and you can eat your fill."

Just the mention of food caused his stomach to roil like summer's thunderheads. That little bit of flour hadn't lasted him long at all. No better than bread for a man who was grease hungry. Lean, red meat . . . dripping juice as it was just barely seared over an open flame. Enough of it to fill not only his belly, but to satisfy his tongue and teeth and mouth with chewing on something that was a delight to just about all his senses.

Like buffalo.

He couldn't help it—thinking on the meat again the way he had last night while jabbing his moistened fingers into that flour sack. Dreaming about buffalo was about as natural a thing for a grease-hungry man to do as breathing itself.

Damn—but his imagination was even playing tricks on him! Not only was it making his mouth water and damn near drool with the fancied taste of a slab of buffalo hump ribs . . . but now his nose was getting in on the act. He could even smell 'em.

God knows Bass would recognize that tang on the wind anywhere. A herd had it a particular fragrance: musky, dank, earthy too.

So here his nose was joining in with his imagination—both of them conspiring to make him all the more miserable for meat. Why, he'd spent enough time around the herds beginning with that crossing he made of the plains to know exactly how buffalo smelled, enough time downwind from the beasts so that he wouldn't spook them as he threaded his way on through the heart of mile after blackened mile of the huge creatures that damn well blanketed the rolling hills and gentle valleys.

There simply was nothing else like that scent on the wind. Whether it was the tons of dung they dropped in their grazings and wanderings, or the sweetish-sour stench of the dusty, sweated, tick-and-flea-infested beast itself . . . there was nothing else like the smell of buffalo.

He vowed he'd have himself a talk to his imagination one day real soon. For it to make his mouth water just thinking about chomping down into a thick pink slab of tenderloin was one thing. But for his imagination to actually make him smell the creatures was something altogether too damn much to take—

And upon opening his eyes his breath clutched in his chest. Finding it hard to swallow as his heart rose with anticipation, Bass whispered, "Hannah, you brung me here a'purpose—didn't you?"

She gave no answer as he continued to stare at the widening valley ahead of them as they emerged from a neck into the great, grassy bottomland. On either side arose low hills. And from east to west, slope to slope across the bottom, the entire scene was blotted with the black coagulate of grazing buffalo.

Surely this was a dream, he told himself as the mule continued him toward the center of this hallucination. At that moment he heard the first faraway bawl of one of the beasts. Could it be that his ears were tricking him too?

Barely raising his head there beneath the red wool blanket, he stared as she carried him closer and closer to a large, slowly meandering knot of the beasts. Closing his eyes momentarily, Bass drank in their scent, deeply. Then reached out with his right arm to reassure himself the rifle was still there beneath the pack ropes. As tight and sore as was his shoulder and arm, at least it no longer caused him hot flushes of agony to move them.

How would he ever get the rifle butt pressed against that wounded shoulder? And to fear what pain shooting the weapon would cause him . . . why, he knew he'd flinch and miss his shot. Off would go his one chance at a buffalo, stampeding away into the distance.

But—was there a chance that he could fire his right-handed rifle from his left shoulder? It was about all the shot he would have at it.

His ears perked up at the same instant Hannah's stiffened. The breeze coming into their faces brought the distant sound again. That was a rifle shot. A few harrowing moments later he heard two more shots.

Clearly, more than one gun. Several. Perhaps many. The first had come from farthest away. The second seeming a bit closer. And that third round of shots closer still. A fourth shot, this one solitary, reached his ears as they pounded with the galloping race of his heart. Then, however, the dying of the rifle shot was drowned out, overwhelmed by the distant, steady hammer.

Hannah sidestepped in a lurch, as if frightened by the quaking of the ground beneath her hooves.

The hammer drew every bit closer. As it did, Bass grew more certain of it. The gunfire—that approaching thunder. Whoever was hunting these buffalo had gone and set them stampeding. Just as plain was the fact that they were coming downwind, straight for him and the mule. Blindly. Stupid beasts that they were, the buffalo would continue until they hit a river, or spilled over a cliff, or—more times than not—simply ran out of steam.

He realized he had to get the mule out of the herd's way, and now.

Already the far northern horizon at the end of the narrow valley was smudged with a thin layer of dust. They were coming, and he had to get Hannah to carry him to safety.

Lifting himself on his elbows, he grabbed for a more secure hold on the lead rope, holding it tightly there just behind her withers as he gazed off to the left. Then to the right. Finally back to the western slope once more. It seemed to offer more of a chance for escape.

"Git—git, girl!" he urged her with a croaking, little-used voice.

Tugging on the short lead, Bass managed to start her moving off at an angle.

"Hup, hup!" he ordered her, watching the dust cloud grow, seeing how those creatures near him were just beginning to turn, to listen, to pay heed to all that noisy thunder upvalley.

Stretched out along Hannah's spine, he tried to hammer her with his feet as best he could, hoping to urge more speed from the mule. Weary as she was, Hannah nonetheless gave her master all she had as the blackened knots nearby suddenly burst into a flurry of motion and sound.

Standing there grazing one moment, then raising their hairy, oversize heads to look back to the north the next moment . . . and suddenly exploding into action without delay or the slightest hesitation. Those creatures closest to him were now compelled to flee, their dull brains ordering them to join in the mindless flight.

In the space of a few seconds the beastly wall of death was coming their way beneath that long, low cloud of dust.

As Hannah reached the base of the long, gradual slope, the thunder of approaching hooves, the bawling and bellows, grew deafening. Just then it felt as if his heart stopped beating: seized with terror in his chest that refused to breathe.

When Hannah faltered on the slope, he sputtered the words, "Hup, girl!"

She heaved and with a bound lurched two more leaps, her back shudder-ing—shaking the packs and him with them. He began to slip off her hindquarters.

Gripping the tie ropes fiercely, Scratch dragged himself another half foot onto her back. Then a little more, and now he could come close to wrapping his arms down her neck. Bass clutched her, his cheek laid against her withers, crying out to her, the spill of his voice lost in the hammering of the hooves around them. Dragging himself closer to her ears, Bass gave her encouragement, calling out to her urgently, trying to will her up the slope and out of the way of the approaching mass of death.

There beneath the bottom fringe of the dusty cloud, just after the first buffalo appeared—riders emerged, bobbing figures atop their small ponies. He could see how distinct they were from the small-humped cows and their brick-red, yellowish-red, and brownish-hued calves, every last one of the beasts caught up in the single-minded rhythm of the stampede, their heads bobbing up and down in their rolling gait.

Distant riders raced beside the herd like tiny stick figures of mankind painted on hide lodges and winter-count robes.

"Hup! Hup, girl!" he shouted as Hannah faltered, a hoof slipping, her load suddenly shifting.

The thunder reached the ground below them in the next instant. Bass turned his head to look behind at those first cows and summer's young calves racing by at the head of the stampede—

Then as she stumbled sideways he was sliding off her rear haunches, fingers digging frantically for a grip on something, anything, as the mule went down on her back legs, shuddered with fatigue, then trembled when she attempted to rise beneath her burden. Arms flailing, Scratch tumbled off a flank to the ground on his belly, landing with a crash, then rolling in the tall, dusty, summer-burned grass with a groan, crying out in a yelp that was swallowed by the passing of the herd below him.

Slipping sideways on the steep slope as she regained her balance and got back to her legs, Hannah shifted, stretching the lead rope out to its limit, tugging on Scratch's belt where he had tied it.

"Dammit!" he screeched in pain as she jerked him to the side, torment shooting through him as she pitched him onto the wounded shoulder.

Spitting dust and brittle grass out of his mouth, rubbing dirt from his eyes with a grimy hand, Bass lunged to snatch hold of the lead rope that had him connected to the mule—and he yanked back.

"C'mere!"

He dared not have her drag him any farther. Feverishly working at the knot with his right hand, while he pulled back on the rope with his left for some slack, Scratch was already well past scared. Frightened, and even terrified, that she would suddenly bolt, dragging him mindlessly along the slope, even down among those thousands of slashing hooves.

But she came to him, prancing, unsure—eyes wide and nostrils flaring, wet. Lather had soaked her pack harness. As she stopped over him, Hannah shuddered, wagging her head slowly while he finished fighting the knot at his belt. When he was free, Bass wrapped the end of the rope around his left wrist and gripped it as he collapsed back in the grass. Closing his eyes still filled with grit, rubbing them savagely as he caught his breath and swallowed down the excruciating torture in his shoulder she had just spilled him on.

Closer came the pop of guns that punctuated the throbbing echo of the stampede, reverberating from one side of the valley to the other. They had guns—these Indians did. Seized with sudden resolve, Bass knew he had to get his. Had to grab the rifle and prepare to sell his life dearly if these were Arapaho.

Chances were good that was just what these buffalo hunters were. After all, he told himself as his tearing eyes watered more as he fought to rub them free of dust, he had no idea where he was west of Park Kyack . . . except that the tall range of mountains was no longer off to his right. It was somewhere back to the southeast now. Hannah must surely have covered ground for him—but just how far north she had carried him toward the guiding star, there was no way to know.

Just get his rifle . . .

Rolling onto his left elbow, Bass rose partway out of the grass, blinking his eyes, finally clearing them at last. The forms danced liquidly before him, then snapped into focus.

He froze.

At least six of them, now a seventh he could count, all on horseback as they came up the slope—seven bowstrings were taut, arrows pointed at him.

His mouth went dry as he immediately looked at their leggings, their moccasins. Jehoshaphat—but they were tall men. Yet as his eyes raced over the patterns of quill- and beadwork they wore, there was something more about their look, their dress, the way they fashioned their hair, that convinced him these weren't Arapaho.

Below them on the valley floor the bulls were passing now, thundering along behind the cows and calves—the last in the great cavalcade. Over the shoulders of some of the warriors Bass caught a glimpse of another dozen or more riders beginning to cross over from the far slope in the wake of the last retreating buffalo. They too were coming his way. And a large group of horsemen moved about on foot there on the nearby ground at the bottom of the slope, their ponies held by others who waited nearby as they gathered in a throbbing knot around something shapeless on the trampled ground.

He wondered if they were gathering around one of the fallen beasts to begin butchering it . . . then he figured they would not all cluster around one animal in such a way. Perhaps, yes—they were acting as if it was one of their own who had fallen from his pony and gotten himself trampled. Then as the dozen or so riders drew closer, his surprise turned quickly to fear. It seemed with the approach of these horsemen, the first warriors were giving him their total attention.

Maybe they were already blaming him for the stampede—believing he had caused the death of their companion.

All he had was the knife. At least to get it in his hand before too many arrows punctured his hide. Just to know he died with a weapon in his hand.

Down the slope some thirty feet the dozen riders reined up. He figured them to be the band's headmen. Lots of long hair blowing in the cool breeze of that late-summer morning. Feathers and scalp locks on their war shirts that kept them warm. A sprinkling of graying heads—the old ones, those who commanded respect and likely ruled over this hunt.

Now his back fat was in the fire.

Moving slowly so he wouldn't attract any attention, he rolled slightly to the right, onto his hip as his left hand gradually let go of Hannah's lead rope and he inched it toward the small of his back, where he hoped to seize the well-worn skinning knife and yank it from the old scabbard stuffed in his belt.

The warrior closest to his left took a sudden, crouching step forward, drawing his bowstring back even farther and shouting to the other bowmen.

Immediately raising his arm, one of the arriving dozen shouted something Scratch did not understand. Whatever it was that was said, it froze the bowmen in place. There was low muttering among the warriors as the one giving the orders, the one who had called out, stepped right up to Bass, pulling a fur cap from his head.

"Eeegod, boys! If'n it ain't a white child out here all on his lonesome!" Then he bent forward at the waist a bit to quickly study Bass. "Yep, ye are a white nigger, sure enough!"

In utter shock Scratch watched a second one, then a third, and finally more white men step up through the gaps between the warriors who held their bows on this quarry they had cornered on the hillside.

"Y-you're . . . American!" Scratch stammered with a hoarse croak. "Wh-white men!"

The speaker's eyes crinkled at their corners as his mouth drew up into a wide, friendly bow that showed a row of overly large teeth browned the color of pin acorns. The tall, stubble-faced man pulled back the cuff on his leather war shirt and studied his forearm a moment, then slapped his thigh with that fur cap, laughing as he sent a small eruption of dust puffing from his legging.

"By bloody damn—but I am that!" he exclaimed, his green eyes merry. "Rest of my outfit too."

Without turning nor taking his eyes off Bass, the stranger flung his free arm backward to indicate the others, who, although dressed every bit as Indian as did the bow-wielding warriors, were clearly white men as they stepped up for a closer inspection of the stranger. Not a one wore a beard on their severely tanned faces, all of which bore the color of well-soaped saddle leather.

With another step the first stranger came beside Bass, dropping to one knee and extending that arm he had just inspected to certify his skin color. Unable to stop the tears beginning to fill his eyes, Titus rolled onto his left hip and eagerly held out the right hand to shake.

Seizing it securely, smiling warm and genuine, the stranger announced, "Name's Hatcher, friend. Jack Hatcher."

"What strange twist of the devil's tail brings you here, Titus Bass?" Hatcher asked after he had sent some of the warriors off to the nearby coulees to locate some saplings strong enough to construct themselves a pair of travois. He had trudged back up the slope and settled there in the grass alongside Scratch with some of the other white men.

One of them, about as stocky as he was tall, handed Bass a strip of dried meat to chew on. "Take your time with this here," he warned. "Man's been without food long as you have, just take 'er easy and chew slow."

"Thankee," Bass garbled around that first hunk he tore off the strip, wanting to swallow it near whole. But he knew the sense in the man's words.

"His name's Kinkead," Hatcher announced. "Matthew Kinkead."

Bass nodded. "Moving north," he began to explain after he had finished that first strip of jerked venison and Kinkead handed him another. The rest sat nearby, as unperturbed and unhurried as they could be. "I figgered to run onto one of them trapping brigades."

"Sublette?" Hatcher asked. "That booshway's already pushed through this country, friend."

"Him or Fitzpatrick. Didn't make me no difference."

"You was with 'em?" asked a new man with about the shaggiest head of unkempt hair Titus had ever seen.

Bass spoke around his jerky. "With who?"

"Fitzpatrick or Sublette?"

"No," he answered. "I was on my own."

"My name's John Rowland," and he held out his own bony hand. "Don't think we ever caught your'n."

"Titus Bass." How good it was to talk, to look at friendly faces. To hear the sound of voices.

Hatcher's eyes fell to Bass's bloody shirt, a large, blackened stain radiating from the bullet hole in its shoulder. After a long moment his eyes came back to Bass's face, his eyes crinkling warmly. "Prob'ly wouldn't make no difference what white men ye run onto, Titus Bass. Fitzpatrick, Sublette, any of 'em. But I can tell you one thing for sartin: yer one lucky sumbitch ye run onto us when ye did. Lookit the way Titus here's wolfing down our meat, boys! How long since last ye et, friend?"

For the life of him Bass wasn't able to sort it out. The days of sleeping, the nights of riding on the mule, three . . . or more? Finally Scratch shook his head wearily.

"Longer'n he can remember I 'spect, Jack," a new voice said as the man came up the slope from the horses and knelt.

Hatcher made the introductions. "This here's Caleb Wood. Caleb, say your howdy to Titus Bass."

After they shook, Wood turned to Hatcher to explain, "We ain't found us much to make us them two travois, so I sent Rufus back with a handful of the Sho'nies to fetch us what we need from the village."

"V-village?" Bass croaked.

They all turned at Bass's question. "Snakes," Jack answered. "Camped up the country a piece. Best ye just rest for now. Solomon—fetch me the man's blanket off'n the ground there— yonder. And Elbridge, whyn't ye find something for us to put under his head. We likely got us a bit of a wait here, and Mr. Bass just ought'n have his comfort till we set off to drag him back."

"Drag? Drag me?"

"How long ye say ye been out here?" Jack inquired, his eyes flicking up and down Bass's buckskin clothing, clearly Indian made. "An' ye ain't never see'd a travois?"

"You're fixing to drag me back in one of them?"

Rowland said, "Less'n you're fit to sit a horse."

In resignation Bass shook his head, then felt his shoulders lifted as the one called Elbridge raised him, stuffing a folded saddle blanket beneath his head and shoulders as Solomon unfurled the dirty red blanket over the length of him.

Kinkead asked, "You warm enough, Titus Bass?"

"I'll do for now—thankee." But he shuddered as the wind gusted along the hillside.

"Don't tell me you're one of them fool-headed, prideful niggers, now." Hatcher turned to a knot of the others, saying, "Isaac—I seen ye pack that blanket of yer'n ahind your saddle. Fetch it up for this man's cold."

"A good man, if'n he's a little solemn," Kinkead confided.

Hatcher stood to fling his voice down the slope. "An' Isaac—get one of the boys to ride up the valley to fetch us the first hide them Sho'nies pull off."

"What you figger to use the hide for if I got this fella a blanket for to lay over 'im?" Solomon asked.

"To my way of thinking," Hatcher explained, squatting to lay a palm flat on the grassy soil beside him, "this here ground ain't all that warm a place for a ailin' man to lay hisself."

Solomon's eyes smiled as he rose to his feet and started away. "I'll make double sure our friend here gets 'nother blanket and his robe too."

Bass watched the trappers move off toward their horses not far down the slope.

Scooting closer to Bass and crossing his legs, Hatcher explained, "Like I said, we only got to wait till Rufus makes it back. So it be fine for ye get yer rest if'n ye can."

"Maybe later," Bass replied quietly. "It's about all I can do . . . just that it's damned good to run onto folks."

"I'd 'spect it would be, Titus Bass."

One by one he looked around that circle, the severely tanned faces lined by wind and weather, eyes smiling every one. For a moment he was overcome with such emotion, he could not speak. Finally, "H-how say you fellers go to callin' me by the name I was first give out here not long back?"

"Ye call me Jack . . . even Mad Jack," Hatcher replied, "then I'll damn well call ye anything ye want me to."

"Scratch."

The tall and angular Hatcher scooped up Bass's right hand again, not shaking it hard at all, more so a tight squeeze. "Pleased be to mee'cha, Scratch. Now—I've got me my ears pinned back, and I'm hankering to hear the tale of how ye come to have a hole in ye."

Rowland nodded. "Where's the rest of your plunder?"

Bass swallowed hard. "What's on the mule's all I got left me in the world."

"Red-bellies?" asked the blond-haired Solomon.

"Arapaho."

With a grunt of agreement Hatcher said, "Stands to reason, don't it? With those sons of bitches . . . well—they be just 'bout as bad as Bug's Boys."

"B-bugs?"

"Bug's Boys," Hatcher repeated. "Blackfoots."

"Much as I heard about 'em, ain't never run onto none of them."

"And you don't wanna!" Rowland cried.

"Now, g'won, Scratch," Hatcher prodded. "We got us a wait to bide our time. What say ye fill it with yer tale?"

Which is just what Titus did, beginning with the death of his last horse in the mountains and the fortuitous arrival of the trio.

"Hol' on there," Hatcher demanded. "How ye come to be all on yer lonesome, trapping by yerself in the first place?"

"Maybeso I ought'n tell you how I come out here from St. Louie."

"First whack—by damn you best start at the beginning."

So he eagerly went back to his time learning from Isaac Washburn and their plans to come out together along the Platte . . . then continued by recounting his solitary journey after Gut got himself killed in St. Louis where for a time there it seemed Scratch's dream had gone up in smoke.

Right on through it all he related the story to Hatcher and the rest, who all scooted close to sit a spell. The lot of them listened in attentively, not a one of the trappers interrupting as Bass told of his first winter with the Ute, and his first scrape with the Arapaho. Then on to his first rendezvous in Willow Valley.

"By jam, we was there!" Isaac Simms commented.

But Elbridge Gray was a little more somber in his comment, "Not much likker howsoever."

"Trader had him likker enough this summer, didn't he, Jack?" Wood asked.

"Let the man finish his story, boys," Hatcher scolded.

From rendezvous Bass recounted their fall hunt and how he had begun to bring in more beaver, bigger ones too, than the other three trappers. But he kept to himself how Silas Cooper just up and took what he believed was his rightful share of Titus's catch—not daring to tell these men how Cooper ended up beating him so badly he came close to asking to die.

"How them Crow to winter with?" Gray asked.

Simms grinned as he inquired, "Them Crow gals good in the blankets as I hear they be?"

"Hush up, now!" Jack chided them. "Mebbe Scratch here didn't get his stinger wet in none of them Crow gals. G'won—tell us how ye come to be from Crow country down south to 'Rapaho ground."

Tracing their decision to float the furs downriver and how he discovered there was no post at the mouth of the Bighorn, Bass explained his journey south into Park Kyack, looking to scare up some Ute company—and when he didn't find any of that, deciding he'd just as well head on over to the place Cooper had chosen for their reunion.

"After I waited some more, long past time for the ronnyvoo at Sweet Lake," Bass told them, "I set out, figgering I'd run across one outfit or 'nother—an' trade off some of them horses for what I needed in the way of fixin's."

In marching east toward the mountains where he had decided he would turn north, Titus told the hushed circle of attentive trappers about his coming across Injun sign, running onto the painted war party, and how he had come to be left for dead, stripped of weapons and a little less of his hair.

As soon as the words were out of his mouth, every set of eyes flicked up to stare at the blue bandanna.

"What ye done for it?" Hatcher inquired, wagging a finger at the back of his own skull. "That noggin of yer'n?"

"Put me some moss on it—soon's I was able to drag my bones down to the water."

Elbridge Gray's head bobbed in confirmation. "That's good thinking."

"Likely it was," Hatcher added. "How come it was the red bellies didn't steal yer rifle?"

"Thought they had at first," Bass said, then explained how he had found it buried in the brush where the weapon had tumbled.

"Lucky nigger you was," Isaac Simms declared.

"Best luck I ever had was that mule there," Bass admitted. "No telling for sure—but I imagine I'd been buzzard bait afore now if'n I didn't have that savvy mule to carry me away from there."

"And right into this valley filled with buffler!" Wood exclaimed.

"A white buffler at that!" Jack said.

"Lookee yonder," Gray announced, turning to point.

A band of some ten horsemen had come into sight to the north. Clearly two of the riderless horses dragged the long, crossed poles of travois strapped to their backs.

"Wh-white buffler?" Scratch repeated.

"By the by," Jack Hatcher replied, "that's what the second horse drag is for."

"See that bunch down there still?" Rowland asked.

Horses and warriors were still knotted around something on the prairie, which Bass could not make out from this distance. "I'll wager one of the warriors took a spill and got hisself trompled over?"

"Nawww, ain't had nary a man die this hunt," Hatcher began to explain. "That other travois be for a special hide . . . a white-buffler hide."

Titus whispered in wonderment, "Ain't never seen one of them."

Shrugging, Hatcher declared, "Ain't many men can claim to laying eyes on a white buffler at all, Scratch. But this here bunch of Sho'nies found 'em the critter running in the pack 'long with the others—this morning right after we started our hunt."

"Something special 'bout a white buffler?" Titus inquired. "Special enough to carry it on its own travois?"

Hatcher said, "That's right. It's big medicine, powerful doin's, Titus Bass."

"An' so be you too," Caleb Wood added.

Titus stammered in astonishment, "H-how's that?"

Turning slightly, Jack said, "Look down there. See that bunch?"

"They been there long as we been up here," Scratch agreed.

Hatcher explained, "Been busy there all morning long. Ol' medicine men and respected warriors—all of 'em been smoking and singing and praying while'st they been at cutting that hide off the critter real careful."

Bass nodded. "That hide must be something special to 'em."

"Damn right it is," Gray said.

Then Hatcher went on to say, "They'll take that white hide back on one of the travois—since it be such powerful medicine to these here Sho'nies. Why, they'll ride back into their village singing and such."

"Don't you know they're all worked up about it awready," Simms commented as Rufus Graham pointed his horse away from the ceremonial group and began making his way toward the trappers on the slope with Bass.

"They'll be singing lots of strong-heart songs for ye too," Hatcher said. "For yer healing, Titus Bass."

"For . . . for me?"

"Where ye landed here is right across the valley from where they dropped that white medicine animal," Jack said. "Don't ye see?"

Wagging his head, Bass admitted, "I don't understand."

For a moment Hatcher looked at a few of the others. Then he said, "Ye be a white man, Titus Bass. And now ye showed up with yer own powerful medicine too." Hatcher pointed to Scratch's shoulder. "That bullet wound and all—the ol' headmen down there already say ye got big medicine."

Slowly shaking his head in utter confusion, Bass found that to sort through all of this made him weak, and all the more bewildered. "Don't know what you're trying to tell me, fellas."

Hatcher grinned widely with those pin-acorn teeth of his filling fully half of his face. "Listen, the way them chiefs see it: yer the one brung that white buffalo here to bless this bunch of Sho'nies."

"Me?" he squeaked. "B-bless?"

Nodding, Jack continued. "Way they see it, besides their All Spirit taking care of 'em, yer the one they ought'n be grateful to for bringing 'em this blessing. Now they won't have no empty bellies, won't go hungry for buffler—so the old stories go."

"Stories?"

" 'Bout the white buffalo, Scratch," Kinkead said. "When such a medicine critter comes once in many generations, the Sho'nie people gonna be blessed with meat and shining times—they'll stand strong against their enemies . . . and stand strong, shoulder to shoulder, with all their people."

Knocking dust and grass from his rump as he rose, Caleb Wood said, "Matthew told you what be the honest truth, Titus Bass. Them chiefs been praying and smoking and such about you."

"But! I . . . I didn't bring no white buffalo here!" Bass protested.

Hatcher smiled, chuckling a moment before he asked, "Just how in hell ye know ye didn't?" And then he laid a hand gently on Bass's wounded shoulder. "Ye damn well been out'n yer mind for more'n the last three days, ain't ye?"

Titus answered, "I s'pose it's been that long. Yes."

Hatcher continued, "And that's how long we'uns with that village been follerin' the trail of this here herd. Face up to the bald-faced truth of it, Titus Bass: ye just dropped off your mule in one hell of a good spot!"

Shaking his head with how incredible the whole story sounded, Scratch grinned at the circle of trappers and replied, "You ain't telling me nothing I don't already know."

"And that white buffalo calf down there—Titus Bass and it are mighty big medicine to these here folks," Hatcher repeated, a look of seriousness returning to his face.

So much of it just did not make sense to him. "If'n I got all this medicine power, and you say I'm so damn special to these here Snakes, why the hell them bucks come up here on the jump and pull their bows on me?"

With a shrug Jack replied, "Mebbeso they didn't know just what ye was at first, Titus Bass."

Perhaps it wasn't merely that he was still confused, hungry, and weak, but that he was more than a little afraid, what with all that the trappers were telling him about medicine and white-buffalo hides.

Scratch looked Jack in the eye and asked, "What's that mean, Hatcher? They wasn't sure what I was at first?"

"Just look there," Hatcher said, an arm swinging in an arc to point out the nearby Shoshone warriors, who had put those bows back in their quivers.

Bass saw how the bowmen still kept a respectful distance from him, their eyes nonetheless fixed on him nearly all the time, most of those dark eyes filled with undisguised awe.

"Mean to tell ye these here bucks is likely real scared of ye—that's what it all tracks," Hatcher explained. "From the looks of things, they prob'ly still good and scared of ye too."

"Don't make them no never-mind if'n you and I both know you can't get up on your feet and fight 'em off by hand, flat on your back the way you was," Wood declared candidly.

"That's right," Hatcher added. "To them, they just figger ye be a shaman what can use yer heap-powerful medicine right where ye was."

He had gone in search of the buffalo, and found them.

Not once, but twice now. That first had been a journey that had brought him out of the old frontier of Kentucky, across the Mississippi and Missouri rivers, and to the realm of the buffalo at long, long last.

Now he had pointed Hannah north, something in him praying, something in him trusting. Gone in search of the buffalo again.

But this time Bass ended up with more than he ever could have dreamed. If it was true what Hatcher and the old men were saying, that white buffalo calf had come to him special. And in the end that sacred animal not only had just saved the Snake from their hunger, but had saved Scratch as well.

That first time he went in search, Titus found the buffalo on the Great Plains just when his doubt had been at its deepest. And now he had found them again—and the white buffalo calf had come—just when his need was at its greatest. A need not just to rescue his body from dying of hunger . . . but to save his spirit and cause it to thrive.

"That buck says he's seen ye afore," Hatcher told Bass as the trappers dragged the wounded man through the Shoshone village toward the stand of trees where the white men had erected their blanket and canvas shelters.

Bass looked again at the young warrior, trying to remember where he had first seen the face. "When I laid eyes on him back there—I had me the same feeling," Scratch admitted.

Jack explained, "And he told me where it was: over to what them Ashley boys call the Willow Valley. Summer before last winter, he said it was. He told me he saw ye at the place where all the white men sing and dance together."

"Ronnyvoo." Bass sighed with some fond remembrance.

"Yeah—ronnyvoo, all right." There was a look of immense and fond remembrance on Hatcher's face too.

The warrior walked right behind the travois where Titus lay, having taken it upon himself to follow close at hand with Hannah. Ever since the moment they had left the narrow valley where the white buffalo calf had been killed, the young Shoshone had been leading the mule behind his pony. Once the procession reached the outskirts of their village, however, all the men dismounted, leading their ponies and pack animals through the crowded camp on foot.

Once the hunters had been spotted approaching from the distance, a long gauntlet had begun to form, two long rows of old people singing their prayers, men and women chanting their praises, children shrieking and whistling in joy. Not all that long after Rufus Graham's band of hunters had returned to find the travois, word spread through the camp like a prairie fire. Just as soon as the spotters on the hill announced that they had seen the cavalcade coming, everyone had not only turned out to see for themselves that pale, curly hide of the sacred white buffalo calf, but jostled and shoved to get themselves a good look at the hairy white man with the powerful medicine who was responsible for bringing the sacred calf to the Shoshone people.

Lying there in his travois as the village folk pressed in to take a close look at him, Titus saw how Hannah danced and bobbed, straining against the young warrior who acted as her handler. She hesitated, snorted, swung her rump about each time some of the crowd got too close. Then the villagers fell back from the excited animal.

Maybe it was a good thing, after all, he thought as the Shoshone studied him in his passing, a good thing that Hannah did not particularly take to the smell of Indians. Just the way he'd heard some tell that Indian ponies didn't take all that well to the scent of a white man.

Far as he was concerned, Scratch really couldn't smell a bit of difference. But, then, he figured, critters like horses and mules were just naturally born with better noses. Still, he had been around enough Indians himself, especially the squaws for long periods of time—sleeping, eating, coupling, arguing, and embrac-ing—to say with some measured degree of certainty that neither the Ute nor the Crow smelled any different from any man Bass had bumped up against in all his wanderings.

The same should hold true for these Snake, he thought. Truth be, except for the sometime stench of the bear grease gone rancid on their hair, the Indians he had come across were a lot cleaner folk than were any white trappers out here to the mountains. Simply put, while the Indians bathed in rivers during the warm seasons and endured steam baths in sweat lodges during the winter . . . why, most ary white men he'd met out here shunned scrubbing and water as if it were poison to the skin.

Onto the framework lashed to the bottom of those two travois that Rufus Graham and the Shoshone hurried out to what the Indians were now calling "The White Buffalo Valley," the hunters took the time to lay green buffalo hides they had just skinned off the dead animals left in the wake of their successful hunt. On one of those hides would rest the white buffalo calf robe. On the other would rest the man responsible for bringing the buffalo to the Shoshone people.

As these older tribal leaders were at their work in the valley, preparing for their triumphant return with the sacred skin, more and more people showed up as news of the hunters' success spread through the village—many travois were needed to carry the butchered meat and tongues, to haul back to camp the heavy green hides that would be staked out on the ground, stretched and scraped, then tanned and smoked for lodge hides and warm bedding, protection against the winds that would howl with the coming of winter.

As soon as they turned all those horses and drags around to begin their trip north from the valley, the long cavalcade had stretched out far behind Scratch. But in front of him, leading them all, was the horse and its travois bearing the white calf hide. Ceremonially skinned by the old-man priests, the entire hide had been carefully removed, including that peeled from the skull, clear down to the nostrils, all the way back to most of the fur covering the four legs, complete with the tail.

"Small as it was," Hatcher had explained as he set off for the camp, riding beside Bass's travois, "likely the calf was born this last spring's drop. Mebbeso no more'n four months old."

"Just a babe," Wood agreed from the far side of the travois.

"But that calf being a cow makes for some strong medicine, Scratch," Hatcher continued. "Means a special power been give to these people. Power not just to feed themselves on the buffler, but power for these people to have many children—so the tribe grows strong."

Never had Titus seen such celebrating: not among the Ute nor among the Crow, even at the Boone County Longhunter Fair. At twilight, fires were lit in front of each lodge not long after hunters returned to the village. There the women and children sliced and roasted meat not just for their own family, but for any visitor who came by. There was singing, with and without the many drums that throbbed in every quarter of the village, pounding along with the hundreds of feet that hammered the earth as evening swept the day aside and presaged the night.

While the temperature continued to drop, Elbridge Gray and Isaac Simms dragged Bass's travois over to one of the closest fires where the singing was the strongest. Here by the dancing, leaping flames Bass found it was warm, the chill air convincing him that summer must surely be dying, autumn on its way. Up there in the mountains the first snows would soon be falling, and with those first cold days the elk would begin to gather and bugle—always a sound that made his heart leap and the hair stand at the back of his neck. Then, as sure as sun, the cycle would turn a little more and the snows would begin their creep on down the mountainsides as the beaver repaired their lodges and prepared for their ponds to freeze over—each and every one of the big bucktoothed rats putting on an extra layer of fat beneath their sleek, shiny fur. Under those long guard hairs would lie the downy felt that protected the animal's skin itself from the cold of water and wind. That sought-after beaver felt was highly coveted by hatters who constructed the fine waterproof "tiles," those tall, stiff top hats for gentleman types back east of the Mississippi River.

As he lay watching the joyous celebration there by the fire, the women brought him food. Not just the jerked, dried venison Hatcher's men had given him earlier, but juicy, half-cooked pink meat kissed by the sizzling flames, every last chunk of it dripping grease and juice down his lips, into his beard, and onto his buckskin shirt as he ate, and ate, and ate. And sweet, cool water too. As much as he wanted, gulping huge drafts of it to wash down the meat until he found his belly full and warm, and his eyes grown heavy.

Scratch would awaken from time to time that night and always find someone near: a Shoshone woman or two, along with at least one of Hatcher's men—folks staying their vigil by his travois to bring him more to eat, more sweet water to drink, or a trapper to help him hobble off into the shadows so he could relieve himself.

Always he would return to his blankets and sleep. No matter the singing and drums, no matter the dancing feet and the laughter in those happy voices. Bass slept. And ate. Then slept some more.

Morning slipped up quiet and cold before the sun came to chase back the chill. Slowly, through slits, he found the gray light did not assault his eyes. No more the drums and dancing. No more laughter and singing. Here in that last cold hour before dawn, the Shoshone had gone off to their lodges and shelters—this village on the move, a migratory people who had been hunting the buffalo for hides and meat to hold back the hoary beast of winter.

So still was the camp and the horseshoe of trees where the tribe had raised their lodges two days back that Bass easily heard the snore of more than one of the men bundled on the ground at the nearby fire. At least a dozen of them in all, wrapped in robes and blankets, their feet close to the coals like the spokes of a wheel. One—it looked to be Rufus Graham—lay sprawled flat on his back, wheezing like the bellow of a two-stack river steamboat, what with missing his four front teeth, both top and bottom. On either side of him lay Shoshone warriors wrapped up like woolly caterpillars in their furry buffalo robes, sleeping despite Graham's noisy serenade. Beyond, over near one of the other trappers, lay a warrior curled in a tight ball, having nothing more than a heavy saddle blanket to cover himself from shoulder to hip.

Bass sighed, closed his eyes, and went to press his cheek back against the thick fur of the stiffened green buffalo hide beneath him when he heard the quiet footsteps. Out of the murky gray of predawn shadows between the far lodges emerged a tall figure wrapped in a blanket coat, his hood pulled up so that it hid most of his face. A bundle of firewood he dropped beside the fire pit before he swept back the hood.

Scratch recognized him as the young warrior who had followed him in yesterday's procession, Hannah's handler. As he watched the warrior at the fire, Bass figured it must have been a high honor to be near the white man who'd brought the white buffalo calf, an honor to be placed in charge of the white man's mule too, Titus figured as he watched the warrior break off limbs and feed them to the glowing coals. A time or two the Shoshone bent over the coals, blew, and excited the new wood to burst into flame. When he had the fire beginning to climb, the young man rose, held his hands over the heat a moment, then turned his head.

Finding Bass watching him, the Shoshone smiled and immediately came over to the travois, picking up a small skin pouch filled with water that lay nearby. This he offered to the white man. Bass took a swallow, finding the water some of the best he could remember ever tasting. Cold and sweet. Like that he remembered in the high country. So good on his tongue and the back of his throat that again he drank until he could drink no more. Letting his head plop back onto the buffalo hide, Bass sighed and found his eyes heavy again as he rested the water skin across his belly.

In a matter of moments he opened his eyes again—the tap at his shoulder insistent.

Beside him stood the young warrior, holding on to the bail of a small cast-iron pot. Within it lay chunks of pink meat cooked last night.

Nodding his thanks, Bass gathered up a handful and brought one to his mouth. Although cold, the meat was tender, tasty. And exactly the sort of feed Titus figured he needed most to get back on his feet. Ain't nothing like buffler, Isaac Washburn had told him what now seemed like so long ago. True enough—there wasn't nothing like buffler, he'd found out for his own damn self, Bass thought as he chewed with nothing short of pure joy.

Then he suddenly realized how poor his manners had been. Around a chunk of meat Titus mumbled, "Thankee, friend."

The warrior immediately squatted there at Scratch's shoulder, patted himself on the chest and repeated the invocation, "Furrr-rend."

"Yes, you . . . friend." As he watched the warrior take a piece of meat to chew on for himself, Bass swallowed his bite and said, "Me: Titus Bass."

His brow knitting with consternation, the warrior tried repeating that. "Ti . . . Ti . . ."

"Yes. Ti—tus."

"Ti—tuzz."

"Good. Now say, Ti—tus Bass."

"Ti-tuzz Bezz."

"No," Scratch corrected. "Ba. Ba. Bass."

"Ba-azz," the Shoshone echoed, making two syllables out of the word.

"You'll make the circle," Bass replied, grinning.

"He won't know what the hell y' mean by that."

Scratch turned his head to find Hatcher propped on his elbow, then rising to a sitting position to pull his blanket over his shoulders.

"He don't know no American?"

"No, he don't savvy no American," Jack answered, inching toward the fire pit's warm glow. "But he's a right smart fella. Chief's oldest boy."

"Don't say," Bass replied, looking over the tall warrior's face again, into those eyes.

"Stick yer hand out to him."

"What? Why the hell I wanna—"

"Y' gone an' tol't him yer name," Hatcher began. "I figger y' ought'n least shake hands with him."

"Shake hands?"

"It's just 'bout that nigger's favorite thing to do," Jack explained. "He thinks its some punkins, the way white men shake hands one with t'other. G'won, stick yer goddamned paw out to him, Scratch."

A little warily, Bass held out his right hand, relieved to find that the arm and shoulder did not yelp in great pain as soon as the warrior seized the hand and began to shake it vigorously. They shook. And shook. Then shook some more.

Finally Bass looked over at Hatcher. "H-how long this fella gonna shake my hand?"

"I figger he'll shake 'bout as long as yer gonna shake with him," Jack answered. "Mebbeso, since he knows yer name, ye ought'n know his."

"All right, Jack," Titus said as he began to slip his hand from the Shoshone's grip. "You gonna tell me what be this here feller's name?"

"Titus Bass, meet your new friend," Hatcher said, rubbing his hands together over the coals. "That there Snake goes by the name Slays in the Night."

TWENTY-ONE

"Damn good thing it is too—ye starting to feel pert enough to try forking yer legs over a saddle, Scratch!" Jack Hatcher said cheerfully a few mornings later as he dragged his blanket over his back so he could hunker down near the flames he fed a few pieces of wood, then held both palms over. "Be getting time to head for the high country soon, that for sartin."

With each morning that the air became a little colder, Bass did feel a growing anxiety to be away and once more at that endeavor in the mountain valleys. Lying here so weary, beaten, and pummeled in body—still mightily hungering in spirit for those high and lonely places. "I . . . I'm looking forward to making that tramp, Jack."

"So ye figger to trap this fall, do ye?" Jack asked with a grin on his face where the stubbly beard was beginning to fill out.

"I do."

But then again Scratch realized just how little he had to his name . . . which caused a little of the starch to seep right out of him. Embarrassed, he looked away from Jack, and instead stared at the fire. "Don't have me much. What I do got, I know I'm no way near being fixed for high-country doings. After them 'Rapahos got off with nigh onto everything—ever since, I ain't had me a chance to look at what I was left in Hannah's packs."

"Stands to reason ye ain't yet looked," Hatcher commented. "Why, the way ye was hanging on to that mule for yer life. Eeegod, child—ye was just hanging on to life itself!"

With a slight wag of his head, Bass sensed the sudden sting of loss and remorse pierce him. The loss not just of place and people left back east—but the great and weighty loss of friends, the loss of furs, and now the loss of most everything he'd worked so hard to call his own. "Shit, I don't even know if I got traps, not what other truck I got in them packs—"

"Ye ain't poor, nigger!" Hatcher interrupted with a snort. "Why, ye got yerself half-a-dozen prime traps! Square-jawed they be: strong of spring and some handsome pan triggers, I might add. Some of the finest handiwork this nigger's seen. Any man got hisself traps an' truck like that gonna make it just fine. Where'd ye come on them traps?"

"Made 'em my own self."

"Don't say?" Jack commented with a little astonishment, then went back to stirring the fire with a limb. "Blacksmith?"

Bass nodded. "Was for some winters. Livery, in St. Louie."

"When we gone through your truck—I see'd ye had you a little of this and a little of that too," Jack added, turning again to eye Bass carefully. "Like I said, Scratch: a man 'thout much more in the way of mountain fixin's might have him trouble making do on his own hook—"

"I ain't no brigade trapper, Jack," Titus replied a bit testily.

"Didn't claim ye was," Hatcher explained. "But I want ye to know that with a good horse—a man what has him the fixin's you got, and that ornery mule of yer'n . . . why—he could make a damn fine go of it if'n he's planning to throw in with some others."

Bass instantly bristled. "Just tried to tell you: I ain't no brigade trapper." He locked his arms across his chest and hrrumphed as if he'd been insulted in the worst way.

Hatcher immediately roared at that, standing to turn his back to the flames and lifting his long-tailed war shirt to rub the breechclout that draped over his cold rump. "Ain't a one of us neither, Scratch! Not no bunch o' pork-eaters. No, sir—not my boys!"

Flushed with embarrassment, Scratch said, "D-didn't mean you and the rest, Jack."

"Ever' last one of 'em is cut from the same cloth you be, Titus Bass," Hatcher explained.

"I—I don't doubt it."

"So when I go saying ye might make do just fine with what fixin's ye got if ye was to go and throw in with others—I wasn't talking about ye throwing in with booshways like Sublette, or Fitzpatrick, or even li'l Davy Jackson. Why, they all good fellers, but a booshway is a booshway, and their kind is still the sort to honey-fuggle a man right outta his hard-earned plews!"

"Long as I got traps, powder, and lead," Bass explained, slowly sitting up on his travois bed there by the trappers' fire at the edge of the camp circle, "I figger to make back what I lost over the next two seasons."

When Jack stopped rubbing his rump and straightened, he peered long and hard at Bass. "There ain't really no two ways to say this to ye, Scratch. Ye figger to hunt flat-tails this fall up in that high country . . . I'm thinking ye should join up with me and the boys."

For a few moments Titus was stunned, purely astounded at the offer. When he finally found words, he said, "Jack—I ain't g-got much to put up."

"Ye got a few traps, and a damn good gun, nigger," Hatcher said with a grin, coming over to pick up the bail to the coffee kettle in one hand. "But even more important than that is what ye got in here." Jack tapped his heart. "Any man what can ride out of 'Rapaho country with a bullet hole showing daylight right through him, why—more dead'n alive and hanging on the back of a ornery mule like he was a tick stuck fast and sure to some ol' bull . . . then I figger that man can ride to the high country with me any season of the year."

How full his heart felt at that moment! "You . . . you certain about this?"

"Sartin as it's gonna snow on the high places, Scratch."

"Maybeso you should talk it over with the others."

The voice came from behind Titus. "We awready talked it over all we need to."

Twisting his head around, Scratch found Caleb Wood there. Behind him stood the others: Elbridge Gray, Solomon Fish and Joseph Little, Issac Simms and Rufus Graham, John Rowland and Matthew Kinkead.

Hatcher repeated, "We all want you to join up."

"But," Rufus grumped, "you gotta vow you stop this laying around, god-dammit. Man fixin' to light out for the high country—he ought'n be up an' around, don't you think, fellers?"

"By God—Rufus is right!" Fish roared. "Let's us get Titus forked over a horse this very morning."

The rest started toward him as Elbridge Gray turned back for a pair of saddle horses tied nearby. Lord, was Scratch ever ready when they helped steady him as he pushed himself up and off that travois. Then, slowly, the others stepped back to let Titus stand alone.

"Lookee there, Mad Jack!" Kinkead cried as Hatcher stepped up, flinging the blanket off his shoulders.

"Yer ready?" Jack asked.

Bass nodded, watching Gray lead one of the horses up to the group. "This your'n, Elbridge?"

Gray glanced at Hatcher a moment.

Jack nodded once. "Go 'head."

Then Elbridge said, "No. It ain't mine, Scratch. We'uns—well . . . we all pitched in some and traded for to get a saddle pony from these here Snakes for you."

He had trouble swallowing as the others stepped close to circle him and the horse. "I . . . I . . . I don't—"

"Ain'cha gonna climb up?" Jack proposed.

"Steady him now, boys," Rowland instructed when Bass went to stuff a left foot in the stirrup. "Help him on up there."

Fish and Simms, stocky men both, helped Titus boost himself onto that big, carved cottonwood stirrup—getting the other leg kicked over the high cantle and eased down as Rufus guided Titus's right foot into the other hand-carved stirrup.

Scratch asked, "Who's saddle this be?"

"Yer'n," Hatcher replied. "It's Injun. All we had us—but . . . from the looks of how ye sit it, gonna work out just fine for ye till we can get to ronnyvoo next summer and fix ye up with one of the trader's American saddles."

Titus shifted this way and that on the rawhide-covered wooden tree with the high pommel in front and its high, wide cantle in the back.

"Damn if it won't do, fellas," he said quietly, having a little trouble getting the words out.

"See? Told ye he'd like it," Hatcher proclaimed.

"Man got himself a rifle, a good horse, saddle, and a mule to pack along a few traps," Bass said, his eyes stinging as he looked down on the six of them gathered around his new pony, "why—that man got hisself just about all he'll ever need."

Hatcher grabbed Bass's wrist and said, "That, and a few friends along too when he points his nose for the highlands."

"Yes," Titus choked. "Man can make do anywhere, no matter what—if'n he's got him a few friends . . . f-friends like you fellas."

He could cotton to a little more riding each day—so before another eleven days had passed, Scratch felt ready to sit the saddle long enough for them to take up the trail north.

Three times in more than two weeks while he was with them, the Shoshone moved camp, following the herds south as the remains of summer faded and autumn first kissed the cottonwood along the creeks, spinning gold of the trembling aspen that dotted the timbered slopes above the valleys where the buffalo grazed. The village had been shooting and butchering and fleshing hides for many days now, every member of the tribe involved with these preparations for winter before they would turn north and make their way into a valley sheltered from the harsh winds and the deep snows. There they would find respite from the raiding Arapaho to the south, the wide-ranging Blackfoot slipping down from the north.

Whenever a harsh winter took its toll on the northern herds and times grew lean on the far northern prairie, that great confederation of Gros Ventre, Piegan, and Blood tribes were more likely to roam farther to the south in search of game and hides come spring. Never had they hesitated if their roamings took them into the land of an enemy.

So it was that for many generations the Shoshone had come to regard these as their buffalo. Each year they followed the herds migrating north in the spring, then south again before winter, a people moving before the wind. And with the first snow they would turn away from the buffalo and seek shelter in the lee of the Wind River Mountains, where they would pass the winter beneath the hides they had harvested for shelter, wrapped warm in the robes they had tanned and smoked, their bellies filled with the meat they had dried in anticipation of those lean days to come with the cold, cold time.

"They got 'em more hunting to do," Jack explained.

"Not just buffler," Caleb added. "Goats too."

Antelope skins—some of the softest of hides used in making the finest of garments. In this country below South Pass, the Shoshone could always count on encountering numerous herds of the pronghorn goats.

Scratch asked, "That why they ain't yet heading north?"

Hatcher nodded. "They got hides for to hunt. And we got beaver waiting for us up yonder."

Bass tugged one last time on the single horsehair cinch, then flipped down the big cottonwood stirrup. "Where away you figger us to go?"

"We can find flat-tails just about anywhere north," Jack replied. "Where ye take a notion to go?"

Bass shrugged and grinned. "To the high country."

"Best we go there afore winter sets in hard," Caleb Wood declared.

Elbridge Gray's head bobbed. "Easy 'nough from them foothills up north to work our way down to the Popo Agie."

"Been on that river afore my own self," Bass replied as they all turned to watch the approach of a sizable crowd on foot.

Hatcher winked and leaned close to whisper, "Be different this time, Scratch—ain't gonna be none of this here outfit getting the damn fool notion of floating your furs down to some burned-out post in Injun country."

"That was a heap of plew," Bass recalled in a hush as the procession of older men came to a stop before the trappers and the small herd of their animals, loaded and preparing to depart.

Behind the chiefs and headmen stood the ranks of young warriors. On either side of them the women formed the horns of a great crescent. And among their legs jostled the small children scooting this way and that to get themselves a good view.

Goat Horn stepped forward slowly, leading the ancient blind one whose eyes were covered with a milky covering. Over his shoulders he wore that sacred calf skin taken in the White Buffalo Valley, its forelegs tied at his neck with a thong.

"Many summers ago," Hatcher quietly translated, "our brave warrior uncle could see no more. Something cut the magic cord between his eyes and his heart."

Titus watched the old man nod, blinking his blind eyes as Goat Horn spoke.

"Ever since," Jack continued his translation, "Porcupine Brush has see'd things none of the rest of us can see with our eyes. This morning he come to me . . . come to my lodge, saying we was to go to the white men together." Then for a few moments Hatcher listened, squinting and wrinkling up his nose as if he were struggling to make out something being said in the foreign tongue.

"What's that ol' hickory stump saying?" Wood grumbled impatiently.

"Shush!" Jack hushed Caleb with an elbow. "This here ol' hickory stump of a medicine man come to say prayers to us . . . prayers *for* us."

When Goat Horn signaled, several young men stepped forward to join the wrinkled old men who stationed themselves directly behind Porcupine Brush. In their hands they clutched rattles or small handheld drums strung with feathers. At the moment the old shaman lifted his sightless eyes to the sky, they all began to play. The ancient one soon joined them, singing high and slightly off-key.

In fascination Scratch watched the old man's Adam's apple slide up and down his wrinkled, thready neck as the notes climbed, then fell. With their song over, Bass and the others believed the ceremony was over and were ready to leave—but instead Goat Horn led Porcupine Brush forward until they stopped right in front of Bass.

As the old one put out his left hand to lightly touch the white trapper's chest, he used his right hand to untie the two thongs holding the sacred calf skin around his shoulders. With the chief's assistance, the shaman got to his knees, and there at Titus's feet he spread the hide.

Rising with Goat Horn's help, the shaman called out. This time only the old men came forward, bursting into a multitude of prayers and chants, each one as discordant as the next, no two of them the same—a dozen or more different songs being sung and played on drums, rattles, and wing-bone whistles all at once. A deafening noise that had begun only when the old man had reached out, blindly seizing Scratch's two hands in his, holding them over the calf skin.

First Porcupine Brush moved one of the trapper's arms in a circular motion over the hide; then he waved the other back and forth, but always in a circle from right to left, the same direction as the sun.

When the songs ended suddenly, the singers stepped back a few feet, and everyone fell silent as Porcupine Brush once again dropped slowly to his knees. Mumbling something to Goat Horn, he held up his veiny hand.

Whispering to Bass, Hatcher said, "Says he wants the chief's knife."

"He ain't . . . ain't gonna cut me, is he?" Titus asked as the knife went into the old one's hand and Porcupine Brush bent over his work.

Locating the neck portion of the hide, the old shaman went down that edge of the hide by feel until he reached the bottom of where the skin had been pulled from the left foreleg. Although sightless, he carefully worked off a small sliver of the white calf skin.

Upon rising he immediately held out the knife, and it was taken from him by Goat Horn. Then Porcupine Brush laid the quarter-inch-wide strip of pale furry hide in one of Bass's palms and rolled up the fingers of the white man's hand to enclose it. He spoke for a moment before Hatcher translated.

"That there piece of the medicine calf is this ol' man's prayer ye can allays carry with you," Jack whispered at Scratch's ear. "Ye brung the medicine calf to the Snake people with you—and ye've helped keep 'em a strong people. The power of . . . how strong the Snakes are can go with ye now as ye leave their camp."

Titus began to ask, "H-how's that power go with me?"

But he never heard an answer as Porcupine Brush knelt to pick up the hide. As soon as he had the sacred skin in hand and was standing to return it to his shoulders, the crowd erupted into joyous singing, trilling their tongues, laughter bubbling and washing over all of them.

Suddenly Bass felt himself turned, his right arm seized. He found a grinning Slays in the Night there at his shoulder, pumping his hand as if it were a forge bellows, up and down to beat the band. Goat Horn slid in next, taking the trapper's hand from his son's and shaking Bass's arm while Slays in the Night stood there pounding Titus on the back.

"Time to saddle up, Scratch!" Hatcher called out as he and the others whirled about to take up their reins and climbed on the backs of their horses.

Hannah and some of the pack animals brayed and snorted with excitement as children shrieked, dogs howled and barked, and it seemed a thousand different hands reached out to touch Scratch from the crowd—merely to touch this white-man shaman before he left them.

"T-thank God!" Bass replied, yelling over all the noisy throats as one chief and old warrior after another shook hands with him. "I'm 'bout to get my arm yanked off here!"

"Dammit, Scratch—ye ugly dog you! Get up! Get yer arse up *now!*" Hatcher hollered inches from his ear, his thick beard brushing the side of Bass's head.

"Get away from me!"

"Eeegod—it ain't ever' day a man has his birthday!" Jack roared.

The long-maned, hairy-faced others were chattering and laughing, jigging and gaping, like a passel of slack-jawed town idiots.

"Leave me be!" Bass growled, attempting a second time to pull the buffalo robe back over his head.

"Whassamatta?" Jack jabbed a hand at Bass's nose, then pushed his own face right down close to Scratch's, plainly showing that one upper tooth that had clearly rotted, black against the tobbaco-stained others. "You better come hurraw with us—it's *your* damned birthday!"

Holding the edge of the robe right under his eyes, Titus peered at each of them in turn. The snow fell lightly on their shoulders as they stood arm in arm with one another there around their roaring fire just beyond the crescent of their half-dozen canvas shelters. Every last one of them was bleary- and red-eyed, but none so much as Hatcher, whose wild expression once more convinced Titus why some time back his friends had come to call him "Mad Jack."

"I had enough hurrawin' last night," Scratch said, his red-rimmed eyes feeling gritty. "Where'd you get that damned tonsil varnish anyhow?"

"Allays we save us some!" Caleb Wood cried out, hoisting his tin cup there beside Elbridge Gray.

"Good likker, h'ain't it?" Matthew Kinkead sang.

Bass's head felt about as heavy as an anvil as he tried to pick it up off the robes where he had collapsed sometime in the predawn darkness, not having the fortitude these other men seemed to exhibit as they kept right on drinking, sing-ing, carousing, and merrily bringing in what they calculated to be a brand spank-ing-new year.

"C'mon, now! Come doe-see-doe a jig with the hull of us!" Isaac Simms begged, hopping around so energetically that his pale, whitish-blond hair shook like a lively burst of sunlight beneath his battered and greasy felt hat. "It's your birthday, Scratch!"

As he rubbed grit from his eyes, Titus knew his head would not take any more swaying and swinging the way they had done all last night, dancing round and round, in and out among the others, thumping feet and slapping knees, singing out as loud as they could while beating on kettles with sticks to accompany Hatcher as he scratched his bow across the strings of that worn fiddle of his. Beginning as soon as the sun had set and the quarter moon was on the rise—hour after hour they kept right at it.

"We allays hurraw for the new year, y' lop-eared sumbitch," Hatcher slurred before he emptied the last dregs of his cup, then flung the cup aside. While he bent over to again retrieve his fiddle from that worn, much battered oak-colored violin case, he said, "Ye having yerself a birthday sure as hell makes a good reason for me and the boys here to keep on hurrawing right on into New Year's Day!"

"Gimme some water," Bass grumped, clutching his pounding, aching head between his hands. It seemed they all were talking too loud, stomping their feet, pounding those kettles no matter how poorly his head hurt—why, even these damned snowflakes were landing on him too hard, too cold, too damned loud.

"Get that back-strapped sumbitch a drink of water," Hatcher ordered— then suddenly caught himself. "Water, Scratch? What the hell you wanna go an' drink water for?"

Bass admitted, " 'Fraid if I drink any more of that trader's whiskey—I'm gonna puke in the fire."

Jack bent there in front of Scratch's face, the fiddle and bow swinging loose from one hand, the other hand plopped on the top of Bass's shoulder to steady himself as he rocked slowly back and forth. "Damn, nigger—ye got more grit'n most ever' man I ever knowed, Titus Bass. But ye sure as hell cain't hol't your likker wuth a Sunday preacher man!"

They all roared with that, which only made Scratch's head thump and hammer all the more.

Stumbling a little as he straightened, Jack swung his arms out as he announced to the group, "This here's the birthday of Titus S. Bass. Shhh—don't ye ever let no nigger know the S stands for Scratch."

"Here's to Scratch!" John Rowland cried, shoving some of his bushy, unkempt hair out of his eyes.

And then Hatcher was sputtering again. "Scratch be a man ever' last one of us can depend on, that's for sartin—sartin sure. A man made of pure fighting tallow."

"How the hell old are you?" Solomon Fish wondered, stuffing a hand beneath the gray wolf-hide cap of his, scratching at his blond ringlets.

"Hell if I can figger it out for you right now!" Titus snapped angrily.

"Hush your face, Solomon!" Jack ordered. "Dammit, here I am speechifying on this nigger's birthday—so ye just keep respectful of this here serious occasion and keep yer ugly yap shut!"

Beneath his sharp hatchet of a nose dotted with huge pores forever blackened with fire soot and dirt, Fish growled, "Your yap uglier'n mine, Hatcher!"

"Bet you don't know near the purty words Mad Jack here knows!" Elbridge Gray defended.

"Thank ye, child!" Hatcher roared. "Now, all of ye raise your cups to this here ugliest nigger you're bound to see out to the Shining Mountains! It's his birthday, by damned! And ain't none of us likely to see a more flea-bit, skinchewin', squar-screwin', likker-lovin' coon in near all of God's natural creations!"

With that Jack swung the fiddle up and jabbed it beneath his chin. Striking a pose, he dragged that old bow across those strings—succeeding in raising every last one of the hairs on the back of Scratch's neck and grating on Bass like a coarse file dragged across some crude cast iron. If it weren't for the sharp hammer strikes the whining notes caused in his head, he was sure Mad Jack's fiddle playing would have made him throw up what he had left in his belly from last night.

Barely cracking his eyes into slits as Mad Jack's music picked up its pace and the other liquor-crazed trappers set to stomping with one another, Titus spotted the kettle of water nearby. At the moment, he couldn't remember being thirstier. Grunting with that self-inflicted pain, he lumbered onto his knees shakily, trying desperately to shut out what noise he could from piercing his head with slivers of icy agony, just as if someone were shoving his mam's knitting needles into both his ears, jabbing them right in behind his eyeballs.

Fighting that cold, stabbing torture, Scratch peered down into the kettle, finding its surface crusted with ice. Angrily breaking the crust with his bare fist, Bass plopped over to squat in a heap, raising the kettle to his lips, where he ended up drinking less than he managed to splash in his lap—shaking so bad from a terrible concoction of numbing winter cold mixed with a brutal hangover and sprinkled generously with more of Mad Jack's wild caterwauling and fiddle playing. He drank and drank until he suddenly needed to pee.

As heavy as his head felt, as slow as his leaden legs and arms were to respond to even the little he ordered them to do—this getting himself up and moving off from the fire, to head anywhere away from the raucous merrymaking—it came as a great rush of relief to suck in a chestful of the frightfully cold air. He tramped through the snow, farther, farther still, as the sounds behind him slowly faded and his head no longer throbbed nearly as loud, nor as fitfully as it had. When he was finally able to hear the critch and crunch of his own thick winter moccasins breaking through the icy crust of the old snow, he figured he had come far enough to have himself a peaceful pee.

Yanking open the flaps to his blanket capote, tugging aside the long tradewool breechclout, he let out a sigh and for the moment found himself no longer caring about much of anything else. How very quiet the forest became out here, away from the celebration—a grating, noisome celebration he was nonetheless happy the others were there to share with him. But here it was so utterly quiet, he could hear the faint hiss of his stream as it melted the icy crust. So, so quiet he was sure he could hear the snow falling, hear when each flake tumbled against his windburned, hairy face, when each flake spun itself into his long, curly, unkempt hair or landed on the sleeves of his thick wool coat.

Through a narrow crack in the evergreen corduroy of tall trees Scratch found he could stand there in the quiet and look up at the foothills, beyond them at the east face of the Wind River Mountains extending north until their slopes totally disappeared beneath the lowering clouds bringing in this new snow. Those high mountains giving birth to the freshets that trickled down from the alpine snowfields to become the creeks and streams and eventually the rivers, all of which had been good to Hatcher's bunch that fall. Between the Popo Agie on the southeast and all those little streams that flowed off the slopes of the mountains to feed the Wind River itself, the ten of them had found a virtually untrapped haven. By the time winter began closing in for good and the high creeks were freezing over, they had moved their way northwest across a great stretch of country, just by following the base of the mountains.

Come spring and the first freeing of that icy jam holding back those winter-clogged creeks, the ten promised themselves they would again work back up the Wind's course, cross on over far upriver, then attack the streams that striped the slopes on the north side of that great horseshoe of a valley. There they were sure they would find a virgin territory in those foothills of the mountains that bordered Crow country on the east and Blackfoot territory on the west. A crossroads of war trails that land was sure to be.

Since taking their leave of the Shoshone and their grand buffalo hunt, the trappers' cooking pots had never gone empty. As the days shortened and the temperatures dropped, the game slowly moseyed down to lower elevations, called to gather with that seasonal imperative, male and female to satisfy their species' itch. Pronghorn antelope were the first to busy themselves with this annual ritual of courtship. In short order behind them the mule deer and whitetail began their dance of the seasons as bucks sparred and sought out fertile does. The renewal of life went on.

And then one cold, breathless morning Bass and the others heard that first shrill whistle gradually descending into a snorting grunt. Somewhere higher on the slopes above the stream where they were working, the dropping temperatures had once again stirred the ancient juices in the lordly elk. Just as it was in a time before any man had laid his foot down in these valleys, the young bulls sensed the same urges, were drawn by the same lure, were seduced by the same fragrance on the wind . . . yet it would not be these males most young and eager who would claim the cows. Instead it was only the deeper-throated, heavier-antlered bulls who had any chance at all to drive off all pretenders until each harem was secure from all challenge.

It was an exhausting time for these old royals. Their necks swelled up, they were in constant discomfort, and they barely had time to eat. Instead, the herd bulls worked ceaselessly night and day keeping their cows rounded up and under their watchful scrutiny. Yet—that many fertile, fragrant females were sure to cast a scent on the wind guaranteed to draw some young bulls eager enough to take themselves a shot at the reigning monarch.

Lowering their heads to dig up tufts of alpine meadow with their wide-flung antlers, each male shaking and trembling with the hormone flush of impending battle, taunting their challenger by flinging urine and semen across their own hide and that piece of ground they claimed, the bulls began their deadly dance: snorting, whistling, and finally bugling their intention not to back away from battle.

There had been days this past autumn when Scratch had finished his trap setting, done with skinning out the beaver he caught without fail, and set aside his chores of stretching and fleshing those skins in camp, days when he crept to the edge of a meadow, or sneaked off to overlook a streamside arena from above in an outcropping of granite boulders—there to watch in wonder and listen in silence to this singular song dedicated to the cycle of the seasons—the bugling challenge of a bull elk. Nowhere else on earth did he believe there could be a sound quite like this ages-old call to battle.

Overhead those late-autumn days the great longnecks strained south in wavering vees that pocked the deepening blue of the sky. Loud, raucous honking as the birds flapped on past high mountains and river valleys in their own seasonal quest.

Up these verdant slopes in the darkened timber and down among the rocky bluffs, the bears were consumed with eating their last, stuffing themselves with every bite of plant or animal, anything they could find to last them through the long, cold, deep sleep of their kind.

The leaves dried, some turned golden and others the crimson of bloody, iron arrow points—then hung there waiting until strong winds rushed down from the high glaciers, stripping tree and brush alike as the land finished off these last few pirouettes before it fell into a hush, ready to sleep on through the winter.

While their horses cropped at the last of the dried grasses and grew heavy, shaggy coats for the season on its way, the industrious beaver went about making repairs to their dams and lodges. Those ever-curious beaver who came to investigate when they encountered a strange scent on the wind as the ten made their sets and laid their traps. One by one, Bass, Hatcher, and the rest gathered in the fat, seal-sleek flat-tails, trap-set by trap-set through that autumn. Every few days they would move on to camp by a new stream—there to find more dams or lodges, to discover where the beaver felled tracts of the forest, gnawing the timbered meadows into nothing more than flooded ponds dotted with hundreds of aspen stumps.

That first morning at each camp found the ten of them fanning out in three directions to spend the day searching for any sign of man in that country—hoping not to discover sign of an enemy. Eyes along the skyline, and eyes on the backtrail. Close enough here to the Arapaho, who might raid out of the south, and close enough to the Blackfoot, who were known to come riding out of the north.

Once assured that the nearby countryside was untraveled, the ten fell into their routine of eating, sleeping, trapping, stretching, and scraping. Morning and night an autumn fire felt especially good to these men who haunted this high land as winter threatened on the horizon—a fire to hunker close to on those coldest of days, for there was always work to be done in fall camp.

If not repicketing the pack animals out to graze or riding the saddle horses to keep them exercised, there was always the nonstop scraping and stretching of the hides. If it weren't a matter of repairing a saddle or bridle or some other piece of tack, then a man might find he needed to mend a sore hoof or perhaps even the bloody wound caused when one pony nipped at another in the cavvyyard. Now was the season when the men closely inspected the back and ribs of every one of their work animals—treating the saddle sores and cinch ulcers from summer's long travels with what herbs and roots they had come to know would draw out the poisons, applying poultices that healed the flesh not only of beast but of man as well.

Yet as autumn turned inward on its shortening days and slid headlong into winter, it could become a sad time for a mountain trapper finding himself with less and less work to do now that camp was rarely moved through the deep snow, now that most of the beaver in the nearby country were already caught. In that leisure a man surely had himself more time to reflect and remember, to fondly recollect last summer's rendezvous here at a time when he must also ready himself for the long, ofttimes lonely, and idle winter . . . until spring temperatures finally freed the frozen streams, prodding the trapper back to his hard labors that would take him from valley floor on up to the high and terrible places: once more to spend his days wading up past his knees in icy water, searching out those sleek-furred rodents that were the commerce and currency of this far country.

"Who was it learn't ye to trap, Titus Bass?" Hatcher had asked him one of those glorious late-fall afternoons before Scratch wandered away from camp, just as the others had come to expect of him: off to watch the sun settling south of west.

"Ain't nobody learn't me," he had replied, then gazed down at his own hands he turned palms and backs. "Just these—seems my hands damn well learn't all on their own."

"Not them three fellas you wintered up with?" asked Caleb Wood.

For a moment he had gazed into the mesmerizing dance of the flames—thinking back on all that the three *had* taught him about survival and trust, about balancing the ledger for one's own life time and again, the way season after season Bud, Billy, and Silas had taught him just how fragile life could be out here—how important it was to have someone to trust . . . perhaps even after you realized you could not trust them completely. Especially then.

"They learn't me, sure enough," Bass finally answered, the reflection of the flames dancing across his bearded face. "But not 'bout trapping. Truth be, I was better'n all of 'em—damn near good as all of 'em put together too."

"Shit, if that ain't a bald-face!" Isaac Simms snorted in disagreement. "How you gonna be better'n three trappers?"

"Whoa, hoss!" Hatcher declared. "Just look at what this nigger's brung in already." He was pointing for the rest to regard Bass's growing packs of fur. "If'n it weren't that every last one of ye was pure punkins at laying a set—Ol' Scratch here just might have any three of ye beat at that!"

"Man does bring in the beaver, he does," Rufus Graham grudgingly admitted.

"So what's yer secret, Scratch?" inquired the rail-thin John Rowland.

With a slight shrug Titus replied, "Don't know my own self, Johnny-boy. All I know is that I hadn't been out here all that long when I come to callate that what I learn't back there across the Big Muddy wouldn't do me no good out here in this land. None of what I knowed back there was gonna hold me in good stead on the far prerra, not up in them high places. Not a damn bit of what folks learn on the other side of the river gonna do any of us a good goddamn anymore."

That autumn sunset as he had leaned his back against the trunk of a lodgepole pine and tracked the pale globe's slow descent from the sky, he brooded some more on all that he had come to know, on what he had learned across those seasons he had managed to survive since leaving St. Louis all by his lonesome, on his own hook. And in all that time Bass had come to clearly understand that if anything could come natural to a man, then he had come natural to this nomadic trapper's life. Just as the rivers came natural to Ebenezer Zane and Hames Kings-bury, how plowing at the ground came natural to his own pap and others of his kind.

When a man's clearly not cut of the right cloth for something—he best find what he is cut out for.

As the saffron orb settled its fiery ring on the tops of the distant trees, Scratch thanked whatever force was listening right then . . . thanked that power in his own way for holding Titus Bass up in the palm of its hand and thereby bringing him out of that land of the east, keeping him safe as he crossed the open danger of the plains and prairie—eventually to deliver him up before this great snowcapped altar that that same powerful force had long ago erected here, right at the foot of an endless dome of sky. Here where the temple spires scratched at the underbellies of the clouds.

Here—where there were no monuments to man, no puny steeples and church belfries—only what monuments the unseen hands and powers and forces at work all around him had created.

So once more Bass felt small . . . so very, very small in watching the sun disappear behind the trees, there beyond those granite towers of the Wind River Mountains—so far overhead no trees dared grow. In this most private, spiritual moment at the end of each day Bass had learned to expect the coming of that crushing silence at the instant twilight determined the first stars would peek through from heaven. It was the very same silence that each evening caused him to rewonder when he would come to know just what force it was that was so much greater than himself.

When would he know it with the certainty of Fawn, the Ute widow with those eyes of ageless sadness? When was he to sense in his own heart all that the old, blind Shoshone shaman sensed in his? How long, Titus wondered, would he have to go on not knowing? How long until he, like that ancient one, could touch the pale hide of a white buffalo calf and finally hear the answer reverberate within his heart?

How long would it take until he understood what the wrinkled old men had accepted—what had truly given them real peace?

Here Scratch stood in that winter forest, the boisterous singing and Hatcher's scratchy fiddle only faint wisps on the light breeze that bitter morning . . . the first of a shiny new year by Caleb Wood's careful count made on notched sticks he carried in a bundle tucked away in a saddlebag—a brand-new year for them all here in the heart of the winter, ten free men living out their days deep in the marrow of the Rocky Mountains.

Maybeso, he decided, autumn wasn't the season he could expect to discover what he wanted most to know. After all, in autumn a man was still too damned busy to allow himself enough quiet to really hear. There were beaver to be caught, distance to be covered, cold to prepare one's self for.

More likely, Scratch thought, he would come to know his answers come a winter. Perhaps . . . even this winter. A time when life itself slowed, when the spin of days wound down and like thick black-strap molasses everything barely moved ahead at such a leisurely pace that a man was allowed time to rightfully consider and plan and to give thanks for what he has been given.

From what Scratch had come to know, for most trappers winter was a time to hunker by the fire, swapping lies, carefully embellishing and embroidering their stories of coups and conquests. A time when a man did just what the Injuns did: gathered close to the fires in their lodges, doing their best to stay warm and keep their bellies filled till spring. During that long period of endless cold, there simply wasn't much reason for a man to ride his horses the way he did during the hunt for beaver or his annual trek to rendezvous—a fact that meant that come spring, a man's animals would most likely be rangy, feisty, all but back to wild mustangs again. There'd come a time just before spring trapping began when a man would have to break his pony to saddle all over. But Scratch had never been one to allow that to happen.

Here in his third winter, just as he had done for both of those before, from time to time Bass would ride his saddle pony or strap the packs on Hannah's back—to keep the animals broken in. Enough contact every few days to remind these creatures of his touch, of his smell—enough so these half-wild creatures would be reassured in the presence of a white man here in the land of so many red men.

Although . . . Scratch had to admit Hannah had been different almost from the start, right from that very first winter. Markedly different from those other mules he had known working at Troost's Livery back in St. Louis, as well as those mules brought out of the Missouri country by traders to this far country.

Thinking about Hannah and her affection always caused a spot inside him to glow not unlike his mam's bed-warming iron, no matter how cold the land became around him with winter's icy grip. Many were the times when the winds blew ferociously and the snow fell so deep that the animals had it tough pawing down to anything they could find to eat. From Silas, Billy, and Bud Scratch first learned he could feed his horse and pack animals a subsistence of cottonwood bark until the Chinook winds arrived to clear the land of snow . . . at least until the coming of the next winter storm.

Astounded at first—and convinced the three trappers were having themselves a great laugh at his expense—Bass was genuinely amazed when they showed him just how a hungry animal would take to the bark they peeled from cottonwood limbs and logs. After chopping short, firewood-sized pieces, the men would set about drawing their large skinning knives down the length of each limb to peel away the tender, soft underbark. Most times it was a cold, tedious, and laborious process, where a man was forced to kneel in the snow to accomplish his task: Scratch would lock a short length of wood between his knees as he crouched over it, then pull his knife toward him in a shaving motion, with each stroke producing a thin curl of palatable bark. Once he had enough to fill his arms, he would lay that big pile before the mule and other animals the way a man might lay out armloads of alfalfa or bluegrass.

One morning early their first winter together in the mountains Bass hadn't been peeling near fast enough to keep up with just how rapidly Hannah could make the bark disappear. Without hesitation she eased over to where he was working, snatching up the curls of bark as quickly as he produced them. When he had stood momentarily to bend and flex the kinks out of his cold, cramped muscles, to his surprise Hannah moved right up to help herself. Putting one front hoof down on the middle of a branch to hold it in place, the mule bent low and began to rake her teeth across it, peeling the bark away each time. As he watched in utter amazement, she consistently managed to pull off short lengths of bark on her own.

"You just remember that now, ol' gal," he had instructed her that first winter. "Hap' the time I don't peel fast enough for that damned hungry belly of your'n—don't you dare be shy 'bout digging in for your own self."

As he stood there this cold morning, his head pounding with hangover and finding himself a full year older, Scratch came naturally to think that Hannah was truly meant to come to him, just the way certain folks had shown up somewhere along the path his life had taken. Women. And friends. And even a mule. Times were a hand had gently touched his life, nudging it this way, or easing it there.

Mayhap it had been better in those younger days when he did not know enough to realize there was something greater than himself . . . better then than now with the nagging of this not knowing, with this wondering. Far better those days of reckless youth when nothing seemed of much import but the moment. Now, with each ring he put on every winter, Bass realized he knew less and less, so grew to sense just how precious was each day—for now he realized how those days grew less and less in number. Now he knew how each one might well be his last.

He had to know: just the way he had come to learn the alchemy of fire and iron and muscle in Troost's Livery; the way he had learned to set and bait and blind a beaver trap in those high-country streams and ponds. This was something that must not elude him: knowing what force had brought him here, then continued to watch over him, and ultimately plucked him from danger more than once already.

Likely it had to be the very same force that had guided him north as he lay all but dead across Hannah's withers. No, not just the North Star shining like some distant beacon, not only it—for he was certain something far greater than those tiny pricks of light in the night sky had steered him north to Goat Horn's band of the Shoshone, north to Jack Hatcher's bunch . . . and—dare he think it?—had guided him north right to that white buffalo calf . . . the animal that had saved his life.

TWENTY-TWO

"It true what they say 'bout that Three Forks country up yonder?" Titus asked the others at the fire one cold spring evening.

"True that it's crawling with more ways for a man t' die than most ever thought of?" Jack Hatcher asked in reply.

"Them three I was with," Bass began to explain, "they didn't want to go nowhere near Blackfeets."

"Damn them red-bellies!" Isaac Simms shouted.

"No-account worthless niggers," echoed Elbridge Gray.

Scratch asked, "I take it you fellas rubbed up again' them Blackfeets, eh?"

Jabbing his sharp knife in the air, pointing at the others in the circle at that fire, Hatcher made his point. "Every damn last one of these here coons rubbed up again' Blackfoot at least once."

"An' for most—once be more'n enough!" Caleb Wood exclaimed. "Just ask Jack hisself there."

"Ask him what?" Bass inquired.

Wood continued, "Ask him about Blackfoots—how they took his own brother."

Turning to look at Hatcher, Bass repeated, "They kill't your own brother, Jack?"

For a moment longer Hatcher sat swabbing the oiled rag on the end of his wiping stick up and down the bore of his rifle. "It be the church's truth. Jeb were with Lisa . . . long, long ago."

"The Spaniard? Manuel Lisa?"

"That's him," Jack answered Titus. "Took him one of the first outfits to the upper river."

With a knowing nod Matthew Kinkead added, "The Up-Missouri country."

Then Hatcher continued. "My brother Jeb weren't 'sactly with Lisa, howsoever. Stayed on with Henry's bunch what tramped over to the Three Forks."

"Long time back I knowed a man what was bound away to join up with Lisa out to St. Louie," Scratch announced. "It were the summer just afore I left home for good. Long ago. Gamble, I remember his name to be. Damn if he weren't a shot too: beat me good at the Longhunter Fair shoot."

"Jeb was the best there was in our country," Hatcher explained, smiling with brotherly admiration. "Damn—but there's times I do miss him sorely."

"Wait just a shake there," Bass exclaimed. "You can't be near old enough to have you a brother what went upriver with Lisa!"

"Shit!" cried Rufus Graham. "Jack Hatcher's lot older'n you think!"

"Not near so old I cain't whip your ass, Rufus!" Hatcher growled, then turned back to Titus. "Jeb was firstborn in our family. I was the babe. Ain't really all that far apart in years, I s'pose. I was old enough to carry a rifle into the woods with him the fall and winter afore he left home for to join Lisa. It purely broke my ma's heart when he left. And it broke my pa's heart when Jeb never come back."

For long minutes none of them spoke at the fire, perhaps deep in thought on what had been left behind, those who had been left behind—the price paid to seize hold of this life.

Night held back this season of the year, waiting just a bit longer each evening before it stole in to take possession of the day. Not like autumn, that other season of change: when night rushed in like a bold, brazen brigand. But for now night held off, and so did they, likely every man thinking of loved ones left behind among the settlements and places where people gathered shoulder to shoulder.

A wet, cold spring it had become—almost from the first retreat of the snow up the mountainsides. Streams swelled to overflowing with the melting runoff tumbling down to the valleys below while icy rains hammered the land until the ground could hold no more. Nearly every ravine, coulee, and dry wash frothed in its headlong rush for the sea. The beaver hunting turned poor there in the country that drained the eastern slope of the Wind River Mountains. During such spring floods the flat-tails simply did not live by the same habits. And if they did emerge from their flooded lodges at all, the beaver were much more wary, harder to bring to bait, more cautious than a long-tailed house cat trapped in a room filled with bentwood rockers.

One evening after it had been raining solid for the better part of a night and the following day, they sat by their smoky fire, broiling pieces of meat the size of their fists on sharpened sticks called *appolaz*. To his utter surprise, Bass heard that first yip-yip-yipping cry of a nearby coyote.

"Didn't think they come out in the rain," Scratch said, sniffling as he dragged his wet wool coat under his red, raw nose.

"That's medicine," Hatcher explained matter-of-factly as he poked a finger in his half-raw meat, then returned it to the flames.

"What's medicine?" Bass repeated.

"That song-dog," Graham said.

Titus scoffed, "What's the medicine in some lonely ol' coyote singing to the sun as it falls outta the sky?"

Clearing his throat, Hatcher said, "Scratch, ye damn well know I'd rather spit face-on into a strong wind than tell ye a bald-faced lie."

"You ain't ever told me no bald-face what I know of," Bass admitted.

"Then ye damn well pin ye ears back and give Mad Jack Hatcher a good listen here. Some winters back I heard tell a coyote what comes out to howl in the rain—why, that coyote really be a Injun."

"You mean a Injun coming round to scout our camp?"

"No—a *coyote*," Hatcher repeated. "A coyote what used to be a Injun."

Starting to grin, Bass was sure now he was getting his leg pulled, and good. "No matter you swore you'd tell me no bald-face . . . I can tell when a man's poking fun at me—"

"You believe what ye wanna believe, Titus Bass," Hatcher interrupted. "And ye ain't gotta believe what ye ain't ready to believe."

Solomon Fish declared, "He's telling you the straight of it, Scratch."

"You mean you ain't rousting me?" Titus asked.

Wagging his head, Hatcher replied, "No. Just telling ye the truth of it, as I knows the truth to be."

For a moment he listened to that coyote wailing off-key out there in the soggy hills. "You mean to tell me that there ain't no coyote singing out there?"

"Oh, there's a coyote all right," Caleb Wood testified. "A buffler coyote."

"What's a buffler coyote?"

Hatcher said, "Scratch, surely ye see'd how coyotes foller the herds."

Bass nodded. "Yep, them and the wolves. So that's what you call a buffler coyote, eh?"

"Yep."

Still grinning, Bass said, "So—what is it? A buffler coyote . . . or a Injun?"

Wood wagged his head like a schoolmaster who had grown frustrated explaining some fine point to one of his thickheaded young charges. "Tell 'im, Jack."

"One what sings in the rain be a coyote what was once't a Injun," Hatcher said patiently. "Kill't by a enemy while'st his medicine was still strong."

"You're trying to tell me all that howling's from a dead warrior?"

Wood nodded eagerly. "I do believe he's getting it, Jack!"

"Wait a shake here," Bass protested. "If'n his medicine's so strong, how come he gets hisself kill't?"

" 'Cause the spirits want that warrior and his powers," Hatcher replied.

"Why them spirits want the Injun for if he's been killed by a enemy?"

"Them spirits change the Injun to a coyote critter," Hatcher continued, "so's it can take some revenge for some wrong done those spirits."

Titus swallowed unconsciously, sensing a heaviness to the air about him as the coyote took up its cry once more. The rain continued to hammer the branches of the trees and the half-dozen nearby sections of canvas and Russian sheeting they had stretched over their bedding. Drops hissed into their fire pit that struggled to maintain its warmth.

"So maybe there's buffler near-abouts," Scratch finally broke the long silence. "If'n that's a buffler coyote."

"Don't mean there's buffler about at all," Jack said. He pointed with the *appolaz* in the general direction of the coyote's howl, then poked his finger at his browning meat. "All it means is that spirit critter got something the spirits want told to one of us niggers here."

"Now for sure I don't believe you."

"It be the truth," John Rowland testified.

Bass wagged his head. "That coyote wants to tell something to one of us?"

Jack tried biting into his meat, finding it still too raw, returning it to the flames. "Way I got it figgered—you was the only man here what didn't know 'bout such spirit doin's, Titus Bass."

"So I'm the one that coyote wants to talk to, eh?"

Scratch waited a moment while the others fell silent, figuring that if he was patient enough, there was sure to come some gust of laughter that would prove to him the others were having their fun at his expense. But, instead, as he looked from face to face to face, the others stared into the fire, or regarded their supper, faces grave and intent.

Finally Scratch said, "All right, you all heard that spirit critter afore. And if . . . if I'm the only one what didn't know nothing 'bout such a thing till now—what you figger such a spirit critter's got to tell me?"

Hatcher shrugged slightly and said, "I 'spect we're going to find out soon enough what all his song means."

With the first days of spring they had abandoned that country and slogged north by west, following the Wind River itself, then slowly worked their way through those mountains* they followed north as the days lengthened and the land began to bloom. Across carpets of alpine wildflowers they slipped over the passes—feasting mostly on the elk fattening themselves up as the herds migrated to higher elevations, following the season's new grasses ever higher. Overhead flew

---

* *Absaroka Range*

the undulating black vees of the white-breasted honking longnecks and their smaller canvas-backed, ring-necked, or green-crowned cousins, heading back to the north. Late each afternoon it seemed the sky would reverberate with the racket of beating wings as the flocks passed low, circled, then swooped in—beginning to congregate near every pocket of water, there to feed by the thousands and rest those hours until morning when again they would take to the sky in a deafening rush of wings.

As he watched the monstrous vees disappear to the north, slowly spearing their way across the springtime blue, the carrot-topped Caleb Wood always grumbled. "Headed to Blackfoot country—just over them peaks."

Wood's sourness always made Jack Hatcher laugh, which invariably caused the legs of that badger cap he wore to shake on either side of his face. "Damned birds make fools out of us, don't they, Caleb? Travel free an' easy while'st we watch the skyline, made to keep our eyes on our backtrail—scared for losing our hair! All while them goddamned birds go flying off to see what haps with them Britishers up north come ever' spring . . . then on the wing back here to spy on us come the autumn!"

Running his dirty hand through hair so auburn it had a copper glow to it, Rufus Graham sighed. "Up there in that Three Forks land I hear tell beaver's so thick, you just walk up and club 'em over the head, Jack."

"I got close enough to know that's the certain truth," Bass replied with a nod. "Beaver big and glossy—more of 'em on every stream than I'd ever see'd."

"A damned cursed country, that be!" Hatcher snapped. "A country I've vowed I'll never set foot in for all the grief it's caused my poor grievin' ma."

All winter Solomon Fish had been working on cultivating a beard with blond ringlets in it to match his flowing mane that reached the middle of his back. Turning to Bass, he agreed with Jack. "There be a reason why that Three Forks country crawls with beaver."

"An' their name be Blackfoots!" Hatcher snarled.

Elbridge Gray was the first out of the saddle that afternoon at the edge of a meadow where they planned to camp. With the beginnings of a potbelly starting to slip over his belt, he was constantly tugging up his leather britches. "By God, I'm a man what values his hair more'n all the beaver what's in Chouteau's warehouse!"

Proud of his considerable mane, Solomon roared, "And my hair more'n all the beaver in the hull of St. Louie!"

As the men slipped to the ground, the horses and mules began switching their tails and flicking their ears all the more. One by one the trappers began to slap at the back of a hand, swatted their neck or cheek—some tender and exposed domain of juicy flesh.

Graham quit removing his saddle, his hands on the cinch. "Dammit, Hatcher—I say we find us a better camp!"

"Skeeters bound to eat us up alive!" Gray agreed.

"Ye two just get the fire started," Jack commanded. "Smear some goober on—then haul out our sack of buffler wood."

"Why us?" Graham grumped, swatting at the insects buzzing right at the end of his nose.

"It's your night to tend fire, ain't it?" Caleb asked.

As he watched Rufus and Elbridge turn back to their packs, Bass stepped up to Hatcher, swatting at those tormentors that hovered around his face. "What's this goober?"

"Some calls it milk," Fish replied.

"Same thing," Hatcher stated. He reached for the cherrywood vial hanging on his belt, untied it, and removed the antler stopper before he brought it beneath Scratch's nose.

"That's beaver bait!" Titus exclaimed, making a face and scrunching up his nose with the awful tang.

"Damn right it is," Hatcher said, pouring a little of the thick milky-white substance into the palm of one hand. "That's the goober a man puts on where he don't want no skeeters biting at him."

In surprise Bass watched Jack, then Solomon and the others in the group, all busy themselves with smearing the potent, rancid, smelly discharge on their exposed flesh: face, neck, backs of hands—everywhere the mosquitoes might be tempted to land and begin their biting torment.

"Best ye try some skeeter medicine," Hatcher suggested. "Where's yer bait?"

"In my plunder. Hell if I'd figger to need it till we was setting traps."

Caleb asked, "Don't skeeters trouble you none?"

"Damn right they do!" Bass replied. "I just allays done my best to kill as many of 'em as I could."

"Here," Jack said, handing his bait bottle over to Titus. "Get that there smeared on ye, and quick, afore them critters ea'cha alive! We'll have us a buffler-wood fire going soon enough to take care of most o' them pesky varmits. G'won—do it, ye stupid idjit—or yer bound to be pure misery by morning."

Reluctantly Titus took the cherrywood vial from Jack, its antler stopper hanging by a narrow thong from the neck of the bottle. Trying to hold his breath, Bass poured a little of the thick goo into a palm and brought it to his cheek. Wrinkling his nose and breathing through his mouth so he would not have to smell the stench, Scratch smeared the substance over his forehead, cheeks, down his throat and the back of his neck.

"Gonna need more'n that, ain't he, Jack?" Wood suggested.

"Lather that goober on, Scratch," Hatcher declared. "Gots to be enough to drive them skeeters off!"

The nauseating repellent came from two glands that lay just beneath the skin near the hindquarters of the beaver. That castoreum was valued almost as highly as the animal's pelt itself. Milking each of the glands from trapped beaver into his bait bottle, the trapper used the thick whitish castoreum to draw even more beaver to future trap-sets. It was that scent of an unknown rival that brought the curious, jealous, or territorial-guarding beaver to its iron-jawed fate.

"Do like Jack told you," Caleb instructed as the rest of the band went about unsaddling the animals and making camp. "Smear that beaver milk on good." He started away on camp chores himself. Long in torso and short in leg, Wood was a man who swayed so much when he walked that from behind, it looked as if he hobbled.

By the time Bass finished smearing his skin good, he found he could better tolerate the stink, almost enough to stand being around himself. Jamming the antler stopper back into the bait bottle, he took it over to Hatcher. Jack squatted next to Joseph Little, who sat propped against a tree, not looking good at all.

"Thankee, Scratch." Hatcher took the bottle from Titus, opened it, and began to smear some on Little's face. "Joe here says he ain't feeling too pert. Mebbeso yer belly's all bound up."

"Ain't . . . ain't my belly," Little said, his glassy, fevered eyes half-open as Hatcher smeared goober on his mottled, grayish face.

"Gotta be what it is, Joe," Jack said. "Yer hide feels to be burning up. And yer wet as hell with fever."

"I been sweating like this near all day, Jack," Little replied with a hoarse rasp. It was clear he was scared. "What you think it be?"

"Don't have me no idee," Hatcher answered, flicking Bass a questioning look. "But I'm sure it ain't nothing to fret yerself over."

Titus shrugged slightly as he knelt beside the two. The moment he touched Little's mottled cheek, he pulled his fingers back, alarmed at the heat of the man's fever. Little's skin looked pale, almost translucent, save for the reddish splotches dotting his face and neck.

"Ever he get sick like this afore?" Bass inquired.

"N-never," Little answered for himself. "You g-get me some water? One of y'?"

Scratch got to his feet and hurried off to fetch a kettle. By the time he returned from the nearby stream, having walked through clouds of buzzing tormentors, Hatcher had Little dragged over near the fire pit where Gray and Graham had their kindling going well enough to begin work with what the mountain trapper called "buffalo wood." Each took a dried buffalo chip from the rawhide sack where the band of free trappers stored this precious commodity, breaking the chips into small pieces, which they patiently fed to the flames.

"Here, ye feed him some water, Scratch," Hatcher stated as he stood. "I'll haul over his blankets and we'll get 'im covered up."

Little protested, pulling at his own damp shirt, struggling to get the sticky buckskin off his arms, over his head, as if he were suffocating in it. He muttered feverishly, "Goddammit! Cain't y' idjits see I'm burning up! Don't want no damned blankets!"

"Brung you some water—like you asked me," Bass said, holding out a cup to Little.

With his sweat-soaked shirt still crumpled over one shoulder and at his neck, Joe snatched the cup away like a man gone four days in the desert without a drink. His shaking hands brought it to his lips, where he managed to spill more than he drank before handing it back to Bass for more. He drank and drank, cup by cup from the kettle, and while he did, Scratch noticed the tiny red mounds there beneath Little's arms every time the man raised them to gulp from the tin cup. Far more of the same small, angry welts dotted the pale flesh near his belt line.

"Jack?" Scratch tried to say without alarm.

When Hatcher had resettled beside Scratch at Little's side, Titus said, "You got any idee what them be?"

"These here red spots?" Joe asked instead, looking down at his own belly. "I got more." He tugged back his belt where the breechclout hung and the buckskin leggings were tied.

"Damn," Hatcher said under his breath. "Ye know what them is, don'cha, Joe?"

"They was t-ticks," Little replied, his eyes half-closed as he keeled over to the side wearily, propping his head on an elbow.

As Scratch dragged over another blanket and put it beneath Little's head, Jack inquired, "Ye telling us ye knowed they was ticks?"

"Yup."

"What happen't to them ticks, Joe?" Jack asked.

Slowly wagging his head, Little answered, "I got rid of 'em. All over me. But I got rid of 'em."

"How?" Hatcher demanded, his voice growing in volume and alarm. "How'd ye get rid of 'em?"

"P-pulled 'em out," Little said, quaking with a sudden tremor. He drew his legs up fetally, groaning. "Now, g'won and lemme sleep some. I'm tired and cold."

Jack pulled the blanket over Little's shoulders, then motioned Bass to follow as he got to his feet. When the two of them stopped some yards away, the others came up to join them in a hushed circle.

"Something he et?" John Rowland asked.

"Ticks."

Several of them turned and looked at the quaking figure lying huddled in the blankets beside the fire.

"He'll go under, won't he, Jack?" Caleb asked.

It took a moment before he answered; then Hatcher said, "I 'spect he will."

"Damn," Isaac replied, his eyes frightened as he pulled at his whitish beard stained with dark yellow-brown streaks.

Wood added, "With the ticks, fellers—it only be a matter of time."

"Didn't he know no better?" Gray asked, pulling off that cap he had made himself from a scrap of old wool blanket, sewn complete with two peaks on either side of it to resemble wolf ears.

"Said he pulled 'em all out," Hatcher replied.

"S'pose one of you tell me what you're talking about," Scratch finally demanded. "What you mean, he's got ticks?"

Kinkead scratched at his big red nose. "Like Hatcher said, Joe's got ticks."

Bass shook his head, then scoffed, "You can't all be so full of shit to think he's gonna die from ticks!"

Solemn Isaac Simms took off that battered felt hat of his, the brim singed in places where he had not been all that careful in using it to stir up many a dying fire. "Listen, Scratch. Joe ain't listened to all that much Hatcher tried to teach him 'bout nothing—so it's plain as paint Joe didn't learn hisself 'bout ticks."

"W-wait, dammit," Bass said. "Just how the hell does a man die from ticks?"

"He gets the fever from 'em," Hatcher explained, sadly shaking his head and the two legs on that badger cap too. "I only see'd one other like this."

"That feller go under too, Jack?" Fish asked.

"Sartin as sun."

Scratch simply could not believe his ears. "J-just from ticks?"

"From ticks," Hatcher affirmed.

"We could bleed 'im, Jack," Wood suggested.

"If'n Joe lets us, we'll bleed him," Hatcher agreed. "But Isaac the one's gonna do it. He's done it on us afore."

"Awright," Simms agreed, turning momentarily to look at the figure lying by the fire. "I'll bleed 'im if he'll let me."

Bass watched Isaac turn aside quietly with Solomon Fish and go over to where Little shivered uncontrollably in his blankets. They both knelt and began talking so low, Titus could not make out what they said. Only then did he notice the sun was easing down on the far peaks rising to the west of them.

"I'll go over see if them two need my help," Scratch declared, then turned from the group.

He stood behind Fish and Simms for a few minutes as they tried desperately to hold Little's arms still enough for Isaac to delicately prick open a vein in the sick man's wrists. But because of the growing violence of his quaking, they succeeded only in scratching Little with the tip of the knife blade.

When Hatcher came up to watch those last attempts, Bass quietly said, "You don't need me for nothing, I'll slip off for a while."

"Go right on ahead," Jack declared. "Ain't nothing more any of us can do here, I'm afeared."

Picking his way west from camp, Scratch came upon Elbridge Gray rooting among the brush along the streambank. They signaled one another with a wave, but neither one spoke a word. Already it felt as if a somber air were settling upon the valley.

Gray hunched back over his work, crawling about on his knees, working his knife into the damp soil, digging, prodding things out of the ground. At every camp Elbridge was the one to go in search of wild onions or Jerusalem artichokes among the thick undergrowth along the river bottoms, the one among them all to dig up the tipsina, a rooted tuber that grew out on the prairie.

Bass wasn't all that sure how long he walked, but when he stopped and circled back, Scratch could not see anything of their camp but the rising vale of a single wispy column of smoke emerging from the canopy of trees. That's where he decided to go no farther. Nearby ran a game trail, on the far side of which stood a nest of large boulders. Bass climbed to the top and settled, drawing his legs against him, his arms knitted around them as he stared at the last lip of the sun slipping over the far, jagged horizon.

Ticks.

A critter so small a man might think nothing more of one than to yank it out of his hide and scratch where the damned thing had burrowed its head to suck at the man's blood.

It weren't like ticks was anything new to him, neither. Hell, all his pap's animals had suffered ticks from time to time—cows, and even Tink herself. Never had he given a second thought to yanking ticks right out of the old hound's hide. Now the rest were telling him Joe Little was going to die from the ticks.

A man don't die from ticks!

Up here where a man could get froze to death or get hisself chawed up by a sow grizzly? Where a fella's pony might slip a hoof on an icy ledge or he might get hisself killed by thieving red niggers? A hundred and one things might kill a man out here for sure and certain . . . but not no ticks!

As the light began to drain from the sky, Titus brooded on it in that peculiar way he had come to dwell on all weighty matters. Scratch would cautiously reach out and barely touch a thing first before really grabbing hold of it—maybe even rub a finger or two across a subject before diving in to stir it up good. It was as if Titus Bass tested things a time or two, exactly like a man would stick his toe into the water, testing its temperature before jumping on in.

Sure enough of a time not all that long ago he had been a man with a wild feather tickling his ass, a young pup what had come to the mountains as brave and stupid as a buffler in the spring with his nose stuck high in the air. But he'd been lucky. That, or Dame Fortune had merely smiled on one more of those rare men who went out and made his own luck happen.

Luck or fate, or medicine. There was more than enough mystery to give a man pause out here.

"Mind if'n ye have some company?"

He looked down, finding Hatcher there at the foot of the boulders.

"C'mon up."

Jack scrambled up and over the nest of rocks, settling near Bass. "They're warm, ain't they?"

Scratch put his hand out to feel the boulder beneath him. For the first time he realized how the rock had absorbed the afternoon's sunlight and heat. "Damn sight warmer'n the air up here."

After a few minutes Jack turned to look over his shoulder, then asked, "Ye don't figger our fire's too big, do ye?"

Again Scratch glanced at the smoke. "You fearing Injuns, Jack Hatcher?"

"Only them what come out'n the north."

They fell quiet again, both lost in thought until Titus asked, "Joe really gonna die?"

"He might'n pull through," Hatcher replied solemnly. "But I cain't lay much stake on that. But there ain't much else we can do 'cept keep 'im at his ease. I dug out the last of the likker for 'im. With that fever—Joe was plumb going out of his head."

"You done right, Jack," Titus agreed. "Maybe help him sleep now."

"It don't feel like I done nothing right, though."

Turning slightly on the boulder, Scratch said, "This is pure crazy, Hatcher. How's a man die of ticks?"

"I ain't got me a answer for ye," he finally admitted. "Me and Caleb see'd it only once't afore."

"Seen what?"

"Man die of tick fever."

"Tick fever? A man really died of a tick bite?"

After nodding, Hatcher said, "He burns up with a fever—just like Joe's doing right now. T'weren't nothing no man could do for 'im."

"Gotta be something, Jack—like you help a body through the croup-sick or the ague."

"Joe ain't got none of that. Been bit by the ticks what kill't him. What give him the fever and kill't him."

"I know ticks. Ever since't I was a boy—"

"These out here ain't the same, Scratch," Hatcher interrupted. "Ain't the same like them back east where we both come from. Not down there on the prerra neither. These up here in the mountains . . . they can kill a man."

"Sure as Blackfoot?"

"Sure as Blackfeets . . . and that's for sartin."

Almost in a whimper Scratch asked, "W-what'd Joe do wrong that he's gotta die for it?"

"Like he tol't us his own self: he pulled them ticks outta his own hide."

"Shit, Hatcher. Man can't leave the damned things stuck in there, can he?"

Wagging his head, Jack sought to explain. "Listen, Scratch: there's a right way to set a trap, and a wrong way too. So there's a way to get them ticks off your hide 'thout things turning out the way they did for Little."

"How so?"

"Man's gotta get hisself something hot and touch them sumbitches on the ass."

"Something hot?"

"Like yer knifeblade ye heat up over the fire," Jack continued. "Just touch them ticks on the ass, and they'll come backing right on out."

"Come out'n a man's hide—just like that?"

"Ye gotta do it that way, Scratch," Hatcher explained. "Wait till they pulled themselves out, then ye grab 'em and toss 'em in the fire."

"Can't just pick 'em off."

"Joe did that," Jack said gravely.

Bass nodded. "And now he's gonna die."

" 'Cause when he pulled them ticks off him, the heads rip off then and there, and them heads stay buried there in a man's hide."

"What of it—them heads?"

"That's the wust of it, Scratch," Hatcher declared. "Them heads is what got the poison in 'em."

"So it's that poison gonna kill Joe?"

"He can't last more'n two, three days now."

"We staying here?"

Jack nodded, staring off into the distance. "We'll trap. And in the by and by let the man die in peace. Give him a decent folks' buryin'."

"Least we can do for a friend," Scratch said.

"The least I'd do for any man what rode with me," Hatcher replied as he started to rise. "C'mon. Sun's down. Time we got back and done ourselves up some supper. First light comes early—and we got traps to set."

Titus clambered down the boulders behind Jack, thinking on just how rare was this breed of man he had cast his lot with—these men with Hatcher, even Joe Little as he lay his final hours beside a fire tucked far back into the wilderness. Theirs was a special breed cut for a special place where few survived. Fire hardened on the anvil of blistering heat and soul-numbing cold. Beaten and pounded under relentless watchfulness, forged by adversity and quenched in that joy of truly relying on no man but their own kind. Theirs was truly a breed of its own.

As he settled at the fire near the blankets where Little trembled, Bass felt those first stirrings of a sense of belonging to something bigger than himself. It had taken him three seasons, but now he felt as if he was a part of the lives these men shared one with another. Among them, out here in this wilderness, there existed few rules if any—and what rules there were existed for the sake of the living. Those rules were learned, and practiced, solely for saving a man's hair and hide.

And there was a code of honor too—one that dictated that a man's friends do what was decent when it came time to bury him, to speak their last farewell and leave that old friend behind. As simple as that code was, Bass realized he had already sworn to it before taking his leave of St. Louis. He had done what was right by Isaac Washburn—then come west to live out the life the old trapper would never live again for himself.

How temporal and truly fragile life had turned out to be, Bass brooded. No matter that these were a hardy breed of men, the toughest he had ever known—tougher than any plowman, tougher still than any riverboatman—the men of this breed lived for what time was granted them, then accepted death as surely as they had come to accept life on its own terms. Each man in his own way wanting no more out of life than was due him.

They were quiet around their fire that night as the nine ate, for the most part deep in their own thoughts as they chewed on half-raw pieces of a cow elk shot that morning. While the coffee brewed, they filled themselves on lean red meat and gulped down the boiled onions Gray had scrounged from the creek-banks.

For eating, a man used his knife only, no matter how big the cut of meat. Holding one end of a reddish piece of steak between his teeth, Bass pulled the other end, then sawed his skinning knife neatly through the outstretched portion, feeding himself chunk after mouth-filling chunk. Before he poured himself some coffee, Titus chopped up a well-done piece of elk into small pieces that Little just might swallow without the trouble of chewing. These he dropped into a second tin cup set before the dying trapper, next to his cup of water.

When he had plunged his knife blade into the hot coals and left it there to set a moment, Scratch poured a cup of steaming coffee, its aroma wild and heady. Not wanting the knife to become too hot, he pulled it from the fire, wiping it quickly across the thigh of his leggings, back and forth over the buckskin until its sheen had returned, cleansed of blood and gristle so he could nest it back in its scabbard.

He was struck with a sudden thought. "Where's ronnyvoo to be this year?"

"That's right—you wasn't one to make it last summer," Caleb Wood replied.

"Got hisself jumped by the Araps," Simms reminded them.

"Then ye'll have yerself a second go-round for Sweet Lake," Hatcher announced.

Titus inquired, "Where you met up with the traders last summer?"

"The same," Fish replied.

"Ah—ronnyvoo," Mad Jack sighed as he leaned back on his saddle and blankets, one hand laid lovingly on his battered fiddle case. "Damn near what a man works for all year long, don'cha figger, Titus Bass?"

"I callate ronnyvoo is the prize what any of us gambles his hide for."

"Likker and lovin'," Caleb added. "By damn, for every man what comes to ronnyvoo, give 'im the wust of the likker and the best of the lovin'!"

Near moonrise Little began muttering and mumbling. As he lay shivering in his blankets, sweating from his rising fever, Joe rapidly slipped into a delirium. No longer did he experience any lucid moments, nor did he respond to the men who went to his side with water.

It was hard for any of them to turn away and sleep that night.

Sometime in that last hour before sunrise, the noisy muttering and thrashing quieted and Little finally fell silent. Taking his rotation at guard, Solomon Fish was the man up to hear when everything went quiet with Joe.

"Hatcher," Fish whispered loudly, and he clambered to his feet. "C'mere!"

As the others slowly sat up in their blankets, watching in silence, Jack joined Solomon at Little's side. Hatcher first held his hand just above Joe's face. Then laid his ear over the man's mouth. And finally Jack touched Little's cheek, his forehead, then the front of Joe's throat as he pulled back the blankets.

"He . . . he dead?" Caleb asked.

Instead of answering immediately, Hatcher laid his ear against Little's chest and listened for what seemed like a good piece of eternity to Bass.

When he raised his head, Jack pulled the top blanket over Joe Little's face. "Rufus, want you and Scratch start digging a hole."

"He dead awready?" Simms asked.

"Fever took him quick," Hatcher replied.

"Merciful heavens," Wood whispered, grabbing that beaver-skin cap off his head. "Damn good thing it was quick."

"No man deserves to die slow," Graham muttered as he kicked off his blankets and stretched as he got to his feet. "C'mon, Scratch. We got us a burying hole for to dig."

The two of them found a patch of ground at the distant edge of the tree line where they didn't figure they would run across too many rocks as they worked their way down into the soil with the crude, stubby-handled shovels. As they were approaching four feet, Jack showed up. The sun was just easing off the ridge to the east.

"Deep enough," Hatcher declared as he bent quickly to glance into the hole. Turning, he waved an arm in the air and brought the others—four of them carrying the body on a shoulder.

When Graham and Bass scrambled out of the hole, Hatcher ordered, "Put 'im in."

Titus could see that they had lashed Joe inside one of the huge blankets wrapped round and round with hemp rope for a secure funeral shroud.

"Any of you know some proper burying words?" Caleb asked as Hatcher stared down at the body.

These men, that blanket-wrapped body, the quiet stillness about them as the birds ceased their songs and calls—and especially the utter senselessness of Joe Little's death . . . it all brought a flood of memories back for Titus. Remembering Ebenezer Zane. Recalling how he had lived, and how the man died. How the pilot's loyal crew of boatmen buried him off the side of their Kentucky flatboat, the shroud slowly slipping beneath the muddy surface of the Mississippi River.

"Any of ye have something to say to Joe, now be the time to speak yer piece," Hatcher said quietly.

"He was a good man and a fair 'nough trapper," Caleb said after he took a step right up to the edge of the long hole.

Moving up beside Wood, Elbridge Gray added, "The sort you could allays trust to watch your backside."

"He weren't the best in the world at nothing," Simms said, "but he knew just how to be a man's friend."

"Not a better man to count on when things got tough," Fish said self-consciously.

The rest nodded.

Jack said, "Won't none of us soon forget ye, Joe Little." Then he turned to the rest of them. "Any ye niggers know any proper church words?"

For a few moments all of them stood there embarrassed and shuffle-footed in their moccasins and greasy buckskins, hands clasped in front of them, their eyes darting this way and that, or staring at the dark hole near their feet . . . none of them knowing what to say.

"Stupid for this here nigger to ask that," Hatcher admitted after a long moment. "Should've knowed better'n to 'spect any of us ever been inside a church to recollect any Sunday-meeting words to say over one of our own."

Then Caleb blurted, "Weren't no good reason for him to go the way he did."

Kinkead nodded his big head, saying, "Man figgers to be took in a Injun fight, maybeso a grizz—but to go under this a'way . . ."

"Dead is dead," Scratch muttered just as suddenly. The words surprised him as much as they surprised the others, who turned to look at him. "Don't matter how a man dies—that ain't what counts nohow. What matters most is how Joe Little lived."

Hatcher and a couple others grunted their approval. Jack studied Bass carefully there as he picked at an itchy scab on his cheek where a mosquito had landed at the edge of his beard. Then Jack said, "That's the true of it, fellas. Joe ain't here no more. He's gone."

"Ain't here no more," Wood repeated.

Jack continued. "Like Titus said, it don't matter how he died. It were how Joe lived . . . how any of us lives what makes a good goddamn."

"He were a free man," Rowland said. "Lived free and didn't cotton to working for no man."

"I don't know no better words'n that, Johnny," Hatcher declared. "Joe Little was a free man. He gone where he wanted to go. He done what he wanted to do. And he damn well lived the way he wanted to live. That's what matters most." Jack looked at Bass.

With a nod Bass added, "A man don't always get a chance to choose the way he dies, fellas . . . but a man sure as hell can choose the way he lives. I figger Joe had all he ever wanted to have, and lived the way he wanted to live."

"Let's us remember that," Hatcher reminded them. "Not how the man died. Let's remember the good days we had with our friend."

Jack knelt quickly, scooping up a double handful of loose soil and shoving it into the hole, where it landed with a muffled splatter on the thick wool blanket. "S'long, Joe."

Caleb knelt at the side of the grave and tossed in a single handful of dirt. "Keep your eye on the skyline."

One by one they came to the edge of the hole and threw in some dirt to begin this burial of their friend, each man speaking his own farewell as if it might be no more than a parting among those at the end of rendezvous. Neither one knowing when next they would see one another.

Eventually all had spoken save for Bass.

"We vow to remember," he said, repeating the grieving woman's words more than seventeen winters old, words spoken while another canvas-wrapped shroud was slipped into the waters of the Mississippi. "Those of us left behind, we vow to remember the ones what been took from us."

"Damn," Jack muttered. He dragged his forearm beneath his nose and blinked rapidly. "Promised myself I wasn't gonna do this."

Titus began, "Ain't no shame in having strong feelings for a friend—"

But he fell silent the instant Hatcher turned on his heel and stomped away.

"Goddamn—I knowed this was gonna happen," Caleb explained, wagging his head.

The others didn't even look up to watch Hatcher hurrying back to camp. Their eyes stole a glance at Titus, then went back to gazing down at the body in the hole.

"Wh-where's he going?" Bass inquired.

"To get hisself away," Simms said.

"Get away from what?"

"From you," Wood answered.

"From me?"

Caleb explained, "From what you said."

"I . . . I said something wrong?"

"No, not rightly wrong," Wood confided. "I s'pose it was bound to happen. You see, Jack ain't never took . . . he ain't never got used to losing folks. We'uns—all of us—we know Jack ain't never had him a friend what died that he wasn't all broke up about it for a long time."

"Ain't nothing wrong with that," Titus said, looking after the tall, thin man hurrying across the small meadow as the sun began to creep down the hillside toward them.

Simms declared, "Maybeso Titus here hadn't oughtta gone and said nothing 'bout having feelings for a friend. Hatcher being so techy the way he is."

"How 'bout me going to tell Jack I didn't know," Bass suggested, sensing remorse that he had offended a friend and hurt feelings. "Tell him I'm sorry for—"

They all heard the pony snort. And the forest around them go silent in the space of a heartbeat. Then came the snap of a branch somewhere behind them in the timber. Turning as one without a word, the trappers bolted off in the opposite direction as if a bolt of lightning had struck beneath their feet.

In that instant they were racing back for camp on instinct—not yet aware just what danger was riding down on them with the hammer of all those hooves.

A danger wearing death's own hideous, earth-paint masks.

TWENTY-THREE

With a wild, whooping screech, a single horseman burst out of the trees on the slope off to Hatcher's left.

Bass watched the warrior kicking his heels into the pony's ribs as he hunched forward, drawing back the rawhide string on his short bow as he swung it in an arc over the pony's bobbing head, the animal carrying him rapidly across the grassy flat that still remained between him and Hatcher.

With that war cry Jack exploded into a dead run—so tall and skinny, his movements were almost spiderlike. Grabbing free the pistol stuffed in his belt—still he kept sprinting for camp.

Voices cried out, screeching behind the rest of them. As Scratch's blood went cold, it seemed the whole forest instantly came alive with more horsemen exploding from the trees. Perhaps two dozen or more. Maybe as many as half a hundred. No matter how many—the odds were clearly stacked against these men racing for their lives. They'd been caught flat-footed, away from camp without their rifles and pouches at a moment of grief . . . having nothing more than a single load in each of their belt pistols.

Blood-chilling yelps and high, tremulous trilling made the hair bristle on the back of Scratch's neck. How he wanted to turn and look at the attackers—but dared not, knowing he had to run faster, despite the slippery grass beneath their moccasins. And in those first few seconds the eight got themselves strung out now, some on the left and some on his right.

That solitary horseman ahead of them released his arrow with a wild, demonic shriek. Jack grunted, stumbling the instant it struck him—the arrow slamming into the back of his bony hip. He was still tumbling over and over across the grass as the warrior shot past the trapper on his flying pony.

Watching that shaft sink itself deep, hearing his friend fall with no more than a grunt, seeing the long-legged Hatcher crumple to a stop—it made the gorge rise in Scratch's throat. He didn't care to run anymore. Better to turn and fight. But unlike the others, he realized he didn't have a belt pistol. The damned Arapaho had taken it—that and a good piece of his scalp.

Reaching around to the back of his belt, Titus snagged the tomahawk in his right hand, yanking the handle from the small of his back. As soon as he felt the reassurance of the weapon in his palm, he planted his left foot and rolled off it, pivoting the moment he skidded to a stop. He had the space of three hammering heartbeats before the first horseman closed on him.

The top half of the warrior's face was painted red from brow to upper cheeks, yellow hailstones splotching the lower half—in front the Blackfoot's hair was pulled up in a provocative clump tied there above his brow and those dark, menacing eyes. Back from a muscular brown shoulder swung the arm that at this distance looked as thick as a tree trunk. At the end of the arm waved a long stone club coming for the white man on a whistling arc.

Titus ducked at the last moment, feeling the handle graze the top of his skull as it passed, tearing the blue bandanna off.

But it did not matter, because Scratch was already swinging—both arms driving the tomahawk into the front of the rider's body. Belly, or chest, Titus did not know at that instant. Only that he felt the bladed weapon jar in his death-grip, sensed the hot spray of blood splattering over his hands and wrists, heard the surprised gush of air burst from the enemy as the tomahawk was yanked from Bass's hands suddenly slick with blood and gore.

Spinning on around, he watched the rider topple from side to side, staring down at the tomahawk buried in his chest—then slowly cartwheel to the right, off his pony.

Scratch's upper arm cried out for attention. An arrow whispered past, just cutting through the buckskin shirt enough to carry away a track of skin with its flight. Scooping the bandanna up from the ground and stuffing it into his belt, he yanked out the knife with the other hand, watching the mass of horsemen break apart like oil dropped on water, a few moving off for each of the white men.

"Bass!"

Over his shoulder he caught a glimpse of the blond head, saw Solomon going to his knee beside Hatcher. Beyond them at the edge of the trees two forms flitted behind trees and turned. Fish was waving Titus on as soon as he had Jack rolled over. Scratch saw Hatcher move.

One of the pistols roared in that clearing. Whirling again in a crouch, Titus watched another horseman tumble backward off the rear flanks of his pony, heels over head into the grass.

"Scratch!"

For a moment he couldn't see any of the rest and wondered where they were. Fish was struggling to hold Jack down as Hatcher thrashed on the ground, fighting Solomon to get his arm back to the arrow in his hip. Then another pistol barked from behind the tree just ahead. The horsemen were closing on them now as Bass reached Fish, throwing his weight against Hatcher as they rolled him onto his side.

"Get the—get the—"

With both hands clutching the arrow's shaft, Fish brutally snapped it off—a loud and distinct crack in the midst of the war cries and the pony hooves and the shouts of the other white men somewhere in the trees beyond them. Hatcher's back bowed up in sudden pain, and he thrashed his legs again wildly.

"You alive, Jack?"

In an instant Hatcher became still. His eyes were red, moist with pain as he stared up at Bass, grabbing for the front of Scratch's shirt. "Eeegod! If this don't hurt like hell!"

Fish turned from looking at the horsemen bearing down on them and bellowed, "Let's get him outta here!"

Grabbing for Jack's right arm, Scratch yanked the pistol from Hatcher's grip. "Gimme this!"

"Don't take it from—"

As his thumb raked back the large goosenecked hammer, finding it already at full-cock, Bass began his turn, there on his knees beside the other two. He found the closest, riding low alongside his pony's neck, a long dark tube held out from his right hand.

Closer, closer he came . . . then the puff of smoke from the tube. The dull thud of the ball furrowing the earth there between Bass and Hatcher.

Closer still as the Indian realized he had missed, jerked back, sitting up to yank brutally on the single rein, attempting to turn the pony before—

But Bass was already rising, the right arm out straight, elbow locked, sensing when to pull the trigger at the very moment the warrior sat upright, making more of a target.

The ball struck him high in the chest, there below the vee of the collarbone where he wore a brass gorget around his neck, catapulting the warrior off to the left side as his pony continued its turn to the right.

"That was purty!" Hatcher cried out, both arms lunging for Bass—to hold on, to pull himself up. "Gimme my pistol."

Slapping it back into Jack's hands, Bass took the knife from his left and slid it into its scabbard just as Fish hollered.

"Scratch!"

Hatcher and Bass both grunted as another horseman pitched off his pony right over them, arms spread wide, flying into the trappers as the pony leaped past. For that fleeting moment Titus thought how bad the Indian stank of dried meat and buffalo grease on his hair. Cold, dried sweat—days old now. Then all three of them were tumbling into Hatcher together: Jack whimpering every time Bass or Fish or the warrior rolled over that broken shaft in his hip.

But Hatcher was still all spidery arms and legs—thrashing and heaving about, attempting to throw off the Indian as Scratch struggled to secure a hold on the warrior's right arm: the hand that held a large iron knife. One of the biggest Titus had ever seen. With his right hand clutching his own knife, Bass seized hold of the warrior's hair, right up at the top of his forehead where the horseman had it bound up with a weasel skin.

They rolled off Hatcher as Fish flew in the other direction, both of them wheezing from the strain, the weight, the bare-boned knowing they were locked in something from which only one of them would emerge.

Somewhere behind him Bass heard another gun roar. Not a pistol, but the sure-enough boom of a rifle. He wondered if it was another warrior's smoothbore musket. They didn't have rifled weapons—

Suddenly the warrior twisted himself on top of Bass, his left hand shoving Scratch's head back into the forest floor. Bass felt the pine needles and dirt grind against the ring of flesh surrounding his bare skull, shooting through him with the heat of a dying star, as if his scalp were being torn from him all over again.

With his strength failing in the left arm as he held that big knife away from his face and neck, Bass surprised the warrior by letting go of the weasel-wrapped hair. In that instant the Indian glanced upward to find the white man's hand— Scratch smashed the knife handle down into the Indian's forehead. Again into the side of his eye socket . . . sensing the warrior's struggle weaken.

Again and again he pounded the hard bone handle into the side of the enemy's head, splitting open the skin over the eye, across the temple, blood coursing down over the ocher and brown face paint applied in crude lightning bolts.

The warrior's left hand came loose first, releasing Bass's hair, then shooting down to clamp around the white man's throat.

Again Titus smashed the handle into the enemy's face, feeling the cheekbone give way beneath his blow.

An instant later the warrior's right arm weakened some more, beginning to drop as the Indian's body seeped a little more of its strength.

Tightening his fingers around the knife handle, Bass brought the blade down now, striking savagely, slashing the warrior across the jaw, down the great muscles of his neck, across his windpipe.

Blood splattered over him as the warrior gasped his last, noisy breath, jerking back in black-eyed shock, yanking the empty hand from Bass's neck to his own to vainly attempt to stop the spurts of bright blood.

Then his dark eyes widened all the more in sudden surprise, slowly looking down at the white man below him as Titus drove the knife home—right into the warrior's belly . . . yanking, jerking, working it crudely from right to left, opening the cavity up, blood and gore spilling out as Bass kicked himself free of the dying man.

"Eeegod!" Hatcher gushed hoarsely. "You kill't that red-belly!"

"Him . . . or me," he gushed, hauling in snatches of breath.

"C'mon!" Fish yelled, trying his best to get himself under one of Hatcher's arms.

Bass slipped under the other, and together they raised Jack off the ground as he cried out in pain. Whirling clumsily, they dragged Hatcher toward the trees where Elbridge Gray emerged with a rifle in each hand.

"Get down!" Gray ordered.

Thinking that was a stupid thing for any man to tell him when he and Fish had Hatcher suspended between them, Bass glanced over his shoulder—finding a half-dozen horsemen coming for them at a hard gallop.

"Down!" Elbridge screamed again.

Fish was the first to obey, pitching forward, dragging Hatcher and Bass with him as Simms stepped out of the trees with a rifle in one hand, a stubby, short-barreled weapon in the other.

But Gray didn't wait on Bass to get all the way down. As soon as Scratch collapsed to his knees, Elbridge fired the shot that struck the closest warrior. His pony pitched sideways into another horse. Now Simms brought the long, heavy rifle up in his right hand, pulling the trigger as it reached the top of its arc.

Like a steam piston he let the right arm sink as he brought up that short weapon and fired it. A wide spray of orange light lit the shadows as four ponies screeched in pain and dismay, twisting and rearing, their warriors fighting for control as the animals pitched their riders off this way and that.

"Get moving!" Simms bellowed as he stuffed that strange short weapon under his right arm and pulled a pistol from his belt.

"Git on! See Hatcher gets back to camp!" Gray ordered. "We gotta make a stand there."

Just as Bass was clambering to his feet, feeling naked without a weapon, Jack suddenly had hold of the front of Scratch's bloody shirt, pulling himself up so he could peer into Titus's face. " 'Member them rocks?"

"Rocks?"

Hatcher had to be crazy with pain to be talking about rocks.

Jack struggled to hold on to Titus's shirt. Pain had turned his face into a gray, pasty mask of agony. "Where I come found you at sundown, you idjit!"

"Rocks—yeah," he said, remembering.

"Take us there—"

Bass interrupted, "We won't ever make it."

For a moment Hatcher's eyes closed slowly as if he were weakening, then opened again, a thin veil of teary pain clouding them. "We don't get to them rocks, goddammit . . . we won't none of us make it."

For an instant more Bass gazed deeply into Hatcher's red-rimmed eyes—when he realized just how right Jack was at that moment.

"Follow me!" Titus ordered as he dragged his gaze from Hatcher and raked it across Solomon Fish.

Jack croaked, "Tell . . . tell 'em—"

Bass stood, yanking the tall Hatcher up on his shoulder as Fish stood beneath the other arm to prop himself under Jack.

Titus hollered, "Jack says we drop back to the rocks!"

"No!" Wood shouted, emerging from the trees, one of his arms hanging bloody, useless, at his side. "We make our stand in camp!"

"Get your pouches!" Simms hollered, wheeling away from Caleb. "We're going to the rocks with Hatcher!"

They pushed past Wood in a rush as Caleb swore at them, but when Bass twisted his head to look over his shoulder, he found the trapper right behind them. While Fish and Bass dragged Hatcher on through the center of their camp, the rest scattered here and there to scoop up weapons and shooting pouches. Behind them the warriors were clearly working up for another rush.

"They coming again!" Jack whimpered in pain. "B-be ready!"

"We ain't gonna make it," Wood bellowed.

"C'mon!" Bass cried to those behind him now as they reached the timber on the far side of camp. "It ain't that far!"

"Too . . . too far!" Jack suddenly said.

At that moment he looked down at Hatcher. It seemed that as he watched, all the starch went right out of the man. His face turned a doughy gray, eyes sunken into his skull.

"No, goddammit!" Bass shouted at Jack, yanking Hatcher up by the collar of his buckskin shirt, shaking him for good measure. "We're gonna make it! Just like you said: we're gonna make it to the rocks!"

"L-leave me—"

"No!" Scratch shouted him down as the others reached them, their arms loaded with longrifles, belts, and sashes bristling with pistols and axes.

Gray's eyes were wide with worry as he looked at Hatcher, then turned to flick a look behind them. "How far?"

"Too far," Hatcher answered, sinking low between the two who propped him upright.

"It ain't too far!" Bass shouted. "C'mon!"

Across those last two hundred yards . . . then only a hundred, they could hear them coming. Yelping and crying out in dismay at the death of their companions—screeching louder still when they burst into the white man's camp, tearing through it looking for the white man's guns. Perhaps knowing already where the cornered quarry was headed. Rushing on out of that camp to herd the trappers as they would herd deer.

The growing noise of their coming only served to bristle the hair on the back of Scratch's neck. That, and to drive him onward with Hatcher on his shoulder. Bass was beginning to gasp for breath, his belly sickening with the effort, his head dizzying from lack of air when the boulders leaped into view ahead. Off to the right.

From there they might have a chance.

"I see 'em!" Kinkead bawled.

The forest behind them seemed to erupt with the cries of warriors as they rushed after their prey, hearing that shrill announcement from the pursued.

Simms was the first to climb up the outside shell of rocks, sliding down into the wide crevice that would take them into the center of the natural fortress. Setting his weapons aside, he reached down to pull Rowland and Kinkead in; then all three turned to helped Fish and Bass shove Hatcher up the five-foot wall of granite like a child's rag doll. With Jack propped up against the rocks, the others handed in their weapons and vaulted up themselves—just as the warriors exploded from the trees.

There were fewer of them now than there had been. But there wasn't any man counting. Hell, Bass thought, when you're jumped by that many, dropping a few from their ponies don't make all that much of a dent in the odds.

But the warriors stopped dead in their tracks, some circling left and some going right, while most of them stayed right there in the center—staring at the rock fortress. Kneeling, a few snapped off some arrows at the trappers hunkering down in the rocks. The stone tips clattered against the boulders, spun crazily in among the trappers. Noisily yelling, the Indians screeched war cries and bloody oaths.

"What're they?" Scratch asked, taking his rifle from Rowland.

"Cain't rightly say," Wood replied, wagging his head and shoving a ball down his barrel.

"Hell," Jack coughed below them at the bottom of the crevice. "We damn well know what them sumbitches are."

"Hatcher's right," Gray agreed as he slid up between Kinkead and Bass. "Blackfoots."

"Blackfeets," Bass repeated, finally slipping the blue scarf from his belt and knotting it around his head once more.

With a pained snort Jack tossed his head and growled, "Who the hell you 'specting wants hair so bad up this way—"

Twisting near fully around at the shrill cry, Bass found a warrior leaping from the rocks right above them. Simms caught the Blackfoot in his arms as they both slammed into the ground, the Indian's knife crudely raking Isaac's shoulder, opening up a bloody gash. In that next instant Gray swung the butt of his flintlock across the back of the warrior's head—driving the enemy off Simms with an audible crunch and a spray of blood. In a fury Isaac was on top of the warrior, dragging the enemy's head back to expose the neck, suddenly slashing a knife across the warrior's throat.

"Scratch!"

He whirled at Graham's cry, just as Rufus fired. A second warrior on the rocks above them jerked as the lead ball struck him, driven back a step, then crumpling to his knees. Yet as the Blackfoot clutched his bloody fingers over the wound in his side, he still managed to cock the tomahawk over his head, hurling it down into the knot of white men.

While the wounded warrior pitched backward from sight, the tomahawk spun itself against the boulder right behind Gray, then struck Elbridge a ricochet blow. Solomon leaped to Gray's side as the man slumped to the ground—a huge knot already puffing across his brow and temple, blood beginning to ooze down the side of his face.

"He's out," Fish muttered as he yanked the loaded pistol from Elbridge's hand.

"Red niggers whittling us down," Hatcher groaned in resignation.

Two more painted warriors appeared at the far side of the ring of boulders, poking their heads over only long enough to take aim, pull back the strings on their bows, and let their arrows fly. Although noisy and frightening, the two shafts clattered harmlessly into the rocky fortress.

"There!" Rowland shouted.

Where the warrior with the tomahawk had been a moment before, now three more popped into view. Two more arrows flew in among the trappers, and a Blackfoot with a musket fired his shot—the big lead ball splattering against the rock beside Jack Hatcher.

Immediately squatting beside Hatcher, Caleb Wood dusted some rock fragments off Jack, saying, "We sit in here like a bunch of nesting hens, the fox gonna get us eventual."

Hatcher's eyes flicked over the others quickly. "You coons got any idees, now's the time to be spitting 'em."

"I say we get the hell out of here," Graham suggested, his eyes raking the tops of the rocks, ready for the appearance of more warriors. He resolutely tugged down on his beaver hat with the rawhide brim scraped so thin, it was almost translucent. "Make a run for it."

"We can't: they'll catch us out there one at a time," Bass declared, wagging his head as he kept his eyes on the south rim of the rocks. "In here we got us a chance."

Hatcher drew in a quick breath of torment as he shifted his hip. "I got things figgered the same way as Scratch. Leastways in here they gotta fight to get to us. Not much of one—but we got a chance."

"The ones of us what can, we gotta climb the sides of these rocks," Bass instructed, pointing toward the skyline with the barrel of his rifle. "Up there we can keep 'em from crawling over the rocks."

"Might work," Kinkead admitted, pursing his thick lips in determination. "Let's climb."

Rufus Graham led them, scrambling up the rocks to a high position. Wood and Rowland chose to climb off in another direction. Simms and Fish, Bass and Kinkead, all spread out until the seven of them had the ring of boulders better protected, no longer sitting below, at the mercy of the enemy as the Blackfeet climbed up the rocks and fired down on their quarry. From up near the top of the boulders, the white men could now watch their enemy breaking out of the trees.

A fella didn't get him all that many chances to win big at a card game, Titus thought as his eyes raked the tree line—spotting some shadowy movement, listening to the Blackfeet hollering to one another. True enough, a man don't get a chance less'n he hangs his bare ass right out over the fire like this once't in a while.

Coming here to the mountain west all on his lonesome had been the biggest gamble he figured he'd ever made. Bigger even than leaving home at sixteen. But the bigger the gamble, the sweeter the stakes.

Off to his left two warriors skulked from the morning shadows toward the rocks, pretty much unseen for the thick brush. They scrambled to slip into a crevice that would put them between Caleb and Titus. Laying his left hand flat on the top of the boulder, then resting the forestock on the back of that hand, Bass took a quick sight target on the chest of the one who wore no leggings as he started to slip out of the brush there at the base of the crevice. Son of a bitch wore only moccasins, a breechclout, and a headdress made of a spray of turkey feathers tied to the back of his head.

It surprised him when Wood's gun echoed the blast from his own rifle. As the turkey-feather headdress twisted and slumped at the foot of the rocks, the other warrior turned on his heel and scampered back for the tree line.

Stuffing his hand back into his shooting pouch, Scratch scooped up as many of the balls as he had left and brought them out. There in his cupped hand he estimated he had fewer than two dozen shots left. Quickly glancing over the others perched near the top of the boulders nearby, Bass wondered if they were in any better shape for to make a long fight of it. He doubted that any of them would have enough shots to last until nightfall. And even then, there was a damn good chance the Blackfeet might just come to call once darkness hid their movements.

No matter that he and the rest had knocked a few off their ponies, or had shot a couple here after reaching the rocks—the warriors still had the trappers outnumbered better than four, maybe five, to one. Having to make every shot count, every last lead ball left among them now . . . that was stretching the odds even thinner.

"What other choice you got?" he asked himself in a whisper.

Little matter that none of them would likely see the sun go down on this day.

In all those years spent working and gambling beside the Ohio River, across all those seasons of drinking and whoring and playing the pasteboards in St. Louis—it had always been his way to stay in the game until the last raise of the night had been plopped down onto the table, until the last call had been made. And he'd just have to see this through to the end too.

The sun had climbed halfway to midsky with the trappers fighting off the Blackfeet that way—one or two at a time . . . here or there. Then things fell quiet. The forest became eerily silent.

Not that they couldn't hear the snort and movement of ponies yonder in the timbered shadows. But for the longest time, no warriors raced from the trees to assault the rocks.

"Maybe they're fixing to ride away," Fish suggested.

"You might be right, Solomon," Graham replied. "Niggers figger they can't get to us in here."

"I don't like the smell of it," Bass declared.

Rowland regarded Titus a moment from his nearby perch. "Me neither," he finally said.

Down below them Hatcher yelled, "Say, fellas—look who decided to wake up!"

Gray was slowly wagging his head, rubbing the huge, blood-smeared knot on the side of his brow, then inspected his fingers. "Damn, this hurts too much, boys. Must mean I'm still alive."

"You hold a gun?" Wood asked.

"Gimme minute or two more—I likely can," Gray explained.

"It's a good thing too," Scratch said. "I figger them niggers is playing some jigger-pokey to fool us."

"They ain't gonna be fool enough to rush us," Graham protested.

"Ye fellas just leave me a loaded pistol down here," Hatcher instructed, gritting his teeth. "If'n they're coming—I want me least one shot. Take least one of them niggers with me afore I go under."

Elbridge handed Jack one of his big smooth-bored horse pistols before he turned and slowly climbed up the gentle slope of the boulders to join the others. When he had reached the top, Gray asked quietly, "You figger it'll come from all sides, Scratch?"

"Don't know how to callate that."

Caleb Wood ventured his guess. "I s'pose they will come at us from all sides, Elbridge. That way they keep every last one of us all pinned down when the rush comes."

"Nawww," Simms protested. "They'll run at us from one side, figgering there ain't enough guns to shoot 'em all if'n they're quick 'nough."

"Listen!" Graham hushed them.

Even the pony noises had faded then. No birdcalls from the surrounding forest, no longer the stomping and snorting of the Blackfeet ponies. The valley fell quiet as a tomb. A dead man's tomb.

They turned their heads this way and that, looking, listening—growing more anxious with every breath.

"What's happening?" Hatcher demanded, alone down in the hollow. "Why'd ever'thing get so quiet—"

A shrill whistle blew, and all the Blackfoot war cries arose in unison, shutting off the rest of Jack's question.

"If'n that hoss don't take the circle!" Caleb growled. "They comin' in from all sides, Jack!"

Bass jammed his hand down into his pouch and scooped out more than ten of the heavy lead balls, stuffing them into his mouth where they would be ready to spit down the barrel of his rifle.

Waving his horse pistol, pain and determination painted there on his gray face, Hatcher bellowed, "I know we can take 'em, boys!"

Gray cheered the rest. "Damn sure take as many as we can afore they get us!"

Outside of a winter camp of Ute or Crow, or that Shoshone village hunting buffalo, Titus Bass hadn't seen that many warriors at one time, in one place, ever before. No two ways of Sunday about it: there were more Blackfeet racing toward the boulder fortress than Scratch had thought there could be in their war party. Either there had been more warriors back among the trees all along, or more Blackfeet had come in to join up with the first ones who ambushed the trappers.

Careful, careful, he reminded himself, holding the front blade on the closest bare, brown-skinned chest. The flintlock shoved back into his shoulder the instant before he was laying it at his side and scooping up the pistol—finding himself a second target.

On all sides the trappers were firing their guns, cutting down the first ranks of Blackfeet, then immediately pouring down a quick measure of powder before spitting a single ball from their lips into the muzzles of rifles or pistols and spilling priming powder into the pans of their weapons. The guns erupted once more, taking a fraction more of a toll on the enemy wave that drew closer and closer in those screaming, shrieking, booming, and frantic seconds of reloading.

More than four times the trappers poured powder and spat lead balls into their weapons, ramming the charges home before taking instant aim and firing on instinct. Four times only before they were forced one by one to lay aside their firearms to take up knives and tomahawks as the red wave of the warriors climbed high enough over the fallen bodies strewn across the rocks themselves.

A few were swinging their rifles about like long clubs, and all about them the air turned red with the enemy's hideous screams of blood lust, reminding Bass of that first skirmish with the Chickasaw, recalling how Ebenezer Zane's boatmen had said that a man would never forget hearing his first Chickasaw war whoop.

When the first wave spilled back, tumbling against one another, the trappers had to wait those last, long seconds for the warriors to spider their way up to the white men at the top of the rocks—about half of the trappers struggling to reload this one last time while the others rose to their knees with knife and tomahawk, crouched tensely to receive the brunt of the charge.

The Blackfeet weren't singing out the war songs now as they turned about to hurl themselves at the boulders. No songs, for this was something deadly. Five or more were scrambling toward Bass himself.

As his mouth went dry, Scratch thought of the Ute woman—how Fawn had tended to his wounds, recalling the softness of her touch at all the wounded places on his body, remembering how nothing else mattered when he lay coupled with her. His tongue went pasty when he realized he would never see her again. Never lay another trap. Not see the sun go down on this day . . . or the others to follow.

As he gazed down at all those painted warriors scrambling up the boulders to get at them, Bass realized he was staring death in the face. Such injustice this was. Not yet ready to die, for he hadn't yet learned what it meant to live. Much less had he learned what it meant to die.

The first ranks hurtled against the trappers with the grunting exertion of bare muscle pitted against muscle. Back and forth Scratch raked the tomahawk from side to side: connecting with bone and flesh, slashing at skin and sinew as warriors fell back and more leaped up behind them. From his knees he scrambled to his feet, splattered with hot blood, beginning to yell for the first time—answering their cries with his own fevered killing lust. First one, then two, and finally three bodies lay at his feet as the others surged in, lunged for him.

A warrior fell back, Bass's tomahawk still buried in his face as the Indian tumbled down the slope.

Ducking the war club that whispered overhead, Bass slapped the skinning knife into his right hand and leaped into three of them. The trio swung wildly with their own weapons—pounding at his back, slashing at the wild wolverine suddenly among them. Bass locked his arms around legs, twisting, pulling, throwing his shoulder into the bare knees he held to with death's grip. Not letting go even when two of the Blackfeet lost their balance and began to fall, Bass slid, careened, tumbled down the side of the rocks with them.

They dug fingers at his eyes, yanked savagely at his long hair, pummeled him with their fists as they all came to a stop together, one of the warriors colliding with a tree trunk so hard, the breath was knocked out of him with a gasp.

The hold on him released, Scratch leaped back, slashing, lunging to the side to slash again. Then he fell back a step in a crouch, like a crazed animal, from the warrior he had just opened up, the Blackfoot staring dumbly down at his belly as purplish intestine slithered out of the long, gaping wound.

Another warrior lunged onto his back, arm locked around Bass's neck, and they both fell as Titus rolled—momentarily staring up into the face of the Blackfoot, who drew back a tomahawk at the end of his arm as he came astride the trapper. Bass swung his arm, wildly jabbing again and again with his left fist, smashing it into the warrior's jaw—just before another face appeared above him: a second warrior seizing Scratch's left arm and forcing it down beneath all of his weight, pinning it against the ground.

The first Blackfoot with the bloodied nose and mouth once more drew back the tomahawk—then froze.

In the midst of all the noise and commotion and that deafening hammer of Bass's heart, there came the rush of a rising cacophony of shouts, war cries, and death songs spilling from the forest beyond them. Shots echoed from the tree line. Surprised, the two warriors pinning Bass to the ground jerked, looking over their shoulders at the shadowy forest behind them as if they could not believe.

Everywhere in the boulders Blackfeet hollered, screamed in dismay. In that next instant the warrior clutching the tomahawk above Bass twitched slightly, his eyes widening, then slumped across Scratch as if his strings had been cut—an arrow fluttering deep in his back as he gurgled his last breath.

Releasing Bass's arm, the remaining warrior grabbed hold of the first, turning him to the side to have himself a look, and realized—then leaped to his feet, screaming and waving his arms at the rest.

In every direction the Blackfeet were wheeling back from the rocks. Like drops of spring runoff, they came sliding down the rocks, desperately breaking into a sprint as they raced for the timber beyond the boulders.

The crescendo of screams and war cries burst from the trees an instant before the feathered, painted warriors.

Lunging up on his elbows, kicking wildly to free his legs from the body sprawled atop them, Bass struggled to slide backward as this new rush of warriors rolled toward him and the others defending the boulders. Volving onto a shoulder, he flung an arm across the grass to snag the tomahawk from the warrior, ripping a huge knife from the dead man's belt—all that he would have now to defend himself against this new wave of the enemy.

Kicking his legs free, Bass scrambled to his knees, crouching, growling—preparing to fight his last seconds, then fall under the sheer weight of their numbers.

Yet . . . the warriors exploding like blurred light from the shadows turned and hurtled right by him, then sprinted past the boulders—following the fleeing Blackfeet. They were retreating with the others.

Of a sudden one of the warriors skidded to a stop close at hand, whirled, and screamed at Titus—something he did not understand. Titus brought up the tomahawk and knife, hissing almost catlike as he prepared for the strike. Bass jerked as a second warrior seized him from behind, the painted warrior gripping the white man's bloodied shirt, exuberantly pulling him partway off the ground, locking his powerful hand around Scratch's wrist as the Indian . . . began to laugh.

Unable to free his knife hand, Bass believed he was about to be killed by a man who would laugh crazily as he slit his throat.

That . . . laugh . . . then he twisted to look carefully at the man holding him, studying the face beneath the smeared war paint—this one laughing joyously in his face. Was it really?

Slays in the Night?

And as the Shoshone warrior gazed down at him with that broad, open smile, Bass felt the first sting of tears.

By God, these were . . . Snake!

A few more guns barked and roared in the middistance as the Shoshone raced after their ancient enemies, killing all that they could, driving off the rest of the Blackfoot war party.

Slays in the Night leaned back, helping the white man get to his feet. The Shoshone warriors whirled up and around on all sides of them now—more warriors rushing out of the trees, sprinting headlong after the retreating Blackfeet. Bass found it difficult to catch his breath, to hear anything more than the loud clatter of his heart in his ears, the hammer of running feet and the screeching war cries.

Then, as that clamor of running battle began to fade, Scratch began to make out the familiar voices of the white trappers yelling above them, the rest of Hatcher's bunch realizing they had been saved, prancing and dancing there at the top of those boulders, pairs of them pounding one another on the back and whooping with joy at their miraculous deliverance.

Slays in the Night laid a hand on Bass's shoulder and looked into the white man's face. "Bass."

Titus seized hold of that hand gripping his shoulder, and barely above a whisper he croaked the only words that mattered right then: "Thank you."

His mind was a blur of questions.

Watching the other trappers ease Jack Hatcher down the granite slope of the boulders in a blanket hammock, Bass struggled to come to grips with having prepared himself to face death as bravely as he could one moment, and the next finding that he had suddenly been given another chance. Twice before that he was sure of, his fat had been pulled out of the fire. Others had happed along, or maybe he had simply blundered into them . . . but no matter that it was they or he, Scratch had no doubt that each time he had been snatched from the jaws of death.

As the white men gathered about Hatcher there at the bottom of the rocky fortress where they had prepared to sell their lives dearly, the Shoshone began to return one by one. A warrior here and a warrior there stepped out of the trees holding a bloody scalp aloft—shouting for the others to see what he had claimed from an enemy's body in the way of spoils and booty. The Snake shouted and sang, then spit on most of those Blackfoot scalps brought in across the next minutes as the trappers recounted their own fierce struggle among themselves. Now and again a warrior led in one of the enemy ponies as well, abandoned by the Blackfeet in their flight.

Wagging his head so that the tail on his long wolf-hide cap shook down his back, Solomon Fish hollered, "If this don't take the goddamned circle! These here Snakes show up just when them Blackfeets was ready to raise our hair!"

"Ain't we the lucky ones!" Simms shouted.

Hatcher just nodded his head happily. "Cain't believe it, boys! Talk 'bout yer Lady Luck smiling down on us: all the way up here—and to have Goat Horn's bunch run onto us this way!"

"I don't rightly get it," Elbridge admitted, running a bloody finger beneath the big bulb of his nose scored with tiny blue veins. "We ain't been trapping nowhere near where them Snake was heading with their village."

"Cain't you see that's why we're so damned lucky!" Caleb boasted.

"Hell if we ain't 'bout as lucky as can be!" Kinkead agreed. "They must'a been close . . . close enough to hear the guns and come running."

"Damned lucky for us they was out hunting close enough to save our hash!" Simms declared.

Soon the happy warriors, shouting with that flush of victory, had a large pile of bows and clubs, a few English muskets, many tomahawks and knives, not to mention shields, pad saddles, and other horse tack. It was clear to any of the trappers that this had been a major war party plunging south toward Shoshone and Crow country.

"Tell me, Jack," Scratch said as he knelt beside Hatcher, something not making a lot of sense to him. "I don't rightly remember what these bucks did on that buffler hunt last year . . . but I can't rightly say I ever saw these here Snake wear paint and put on their fancy war clothes when they was fixing to go on a meat hunt."

Hatcher's eyes bounced across the nearby warriors, some grave doubt beginning to cloud his face. Just as he began to open his mouth, he shut it again. Shifting himself on his elbow, he strained to listen to what the many Shoshone tongues were saying.

"I ain't for sure just yet, Scratch," Jack began, his voice strangely quiet, "but I got me the idea this wasn't no—"

As suddenly as they had appeared out of the forest, the Snake warriors around the trappers became quiet as hushed word of something was whispered among them with the speed of a prairie fire. They fell completely silent as a young man on foot led a pony and its rider into the crowded clearing at the foot of the boulders.

"Ain't . . . ain't that the old medicine man?" Titus asked in a whisper the moment he recognized the frail man atop the horse.

"Sure 'nough is," Caleb Wood replied in a whisper.

In the hush of that high-country forest the young man who was apprenticed to Porcupine Brush helped the old one off the animal's back and steadied him on his thin, birdlike legs. Then the blind man began to sing softly, shaking a buffalo-bladder rattle around and around in a circle as his apprentice helped him shuffle slowly through the gathering that parted before him. Goat Horn, the Shoshone war chief who had led his warriors there, stepped forward so he could walk on the other side of the shaman until they stopped right before Hatcher's blanket.

Between the chief and shaman a few words were quickly spoken in a whisper.

"What's he say?" Fish leaned down to ask of Jack.

Hatcher translated, "The ol' codger asked who was still alive, and Goat Horn tol't him we all was."

Porcupine Brush appeared much gratified at that answer, his wrinkled, wizened face brightening with a wide smile as his sightless eyes seemed to look left to right slowly, as if they somehow could see, perhaps as if they were in search of one white man in particular.

Mumbling something to his young apprentice, the shaman was shuffled over so that he could face Bass. Letting go of the young one's arm, Porcupine Brush's old fingers worked at the knot in the thongs holding that sacred white buffalo calf robe over his shoulders. Sliding the robe off his arms, he nonetheless clutched it in a bundle to his breast as he spoke with a soft, thready voice to the nine white men there, where they had been prepared to die.

"Wants us all to sit with him," Hatcher said, motioning them to join him on the ground.

Handing the calf robe to his apprentice, the old man sat a few feet from Hatcher and Bass. On the ground in front of the shaman the young man spread the beautiful curly hide of the sacred buffalo calf. When the shaman was told all the white men were sitting before him around the calf skin, he raised his face to the sky above and began to sing his prayers. Through every chorus of his difficult song, the shaman rubbed his gnarled hands back and forth across the white hide, at times stuffing those swollen knuckles of his fingers deep into the thick fur.

Putting his lips up behind Hatcher's ear, Graham asked, "What all's he saying?"

Shaking his head a minute as if struggling to understand, Jack tried to explain. "All he was doing was just praying a bit ago . . . but, but now he's saying . . . he wants to tell us that—that he knowed we was in trouble."

"He kn-knowed?" Wood echoed.

Hatcher nodded, his eyes half closing in disbelief. "Says something 'bout his spirit helper four days ago."

Gray roared happily, scratching at his ample belly, "Whatever it was—I'm sure as hell glad the ol' codger's spirit helper was up to talkin' that day!"

"Hush!" Jack ordered. "Says . . . wait: ol' man here says he was told we was in a fix days ago."

A sense of something grand and very holy enveloped Titus Bass at that very moment. As certain as he had ever been about anything in his life, Scratch suddenly felt a great power there about them. At long, long last he stood in the presence of that great and unexplained mystery. Perhaps it was even the force that guided the way of all things.

"Sure," Hatcher continued. "Makes sense these here Snakes knowed we was in a fix long afore this morning, don't it? How the hell else was they gonna get to us in time?"

Simms turned to ask, "You don't figger they was out hunting, Jack?"

"No—the ol' feller says they come straight here, ready for war. And they knew right where we was s'posed to be," Hatcher replied, his voice going softer as he peered down at the calf robe, sounding a little less sure of himself now as they stood upon this strange ground. "I don't have me no idea how in heaven . . . but the old'un says they knowed we was about to be rubbed out by their enemies—the Blackfeets."

"How he know all this?" Wood inquired.

Graham asked too, "Yeah—how this here ol' man know about us days ago when we ain't even made it here yet?"

From out of the very air around them, Bass understood. Without the slightest hesitation he quietly said, "I s'pose his spirit helper told him."

The rest turned toward Scratch—staring, unbelieving, and about ready to scoff until Hatcher asked a question of the shaman in the Shoshone tongue. The old man smiled, his blind eyes pooling with tears as he answered.

Then Jack turned to look up at Titus Bass with great wonder, even stunned amazement, on his face as Scratch leaned across the hide, taking one of the old hands in both of his.

"Tell 'im it's me, Jack—the one what's got hold of his hand," Titus said.

When Hatcher explained, tears spilled from the shaman's blind, milky eyes onto his wrinkled cheeks.

"The old'un says he knowed about Scratch here—Porcupine Brush calls Titus the white man's buffler shaman—that he knowed when Scratch needed their help," Hatcher explained, wagging his head slowly. When he brought his eyes up to look at Titus, Jack said, "Since't he was the one what the All Powers chose to bring the medicine calf to the Snakes—"

Gray interrupted, "Hold on there—you're telling us that something tol't him about Scratch and the B-blackfeets coming to jump us?"

"Yup," Hatcher solemnly answered Gray's question. "Porcupine Brush says behind his blind eyes he saw all what was to happen to Titus Bass. Says he was told 'bout this four days ago."

Isaac Simms asked, "Just who in hell told the ol' man 'bout all of this?"

"Not *who* tol't him, Isaac. But *what* tol't him," Jack said as he reached out and laid his hand atop Scratch's. "Porcupine Brush knew all 'bout it . . . 'cause he was tol't by Titus Bass's white medicine calf hide."